EVERYTHING THE LIGHT TOUCHES

PRAISE FOR *EVERYTHING THE LIGHT TOUCHES*

"A novel like none other: Janice Pariat brings vividly to life a conception of plants as beings endowed with a powerful inner vitality."

—AMITAV GHOSH, author of *Gun Island*

"A novel of great charm, curiosity and adventure—a passionate call for shaking up the certainties of science and history so as to heed the intuitions and instincts that perhaps only fiction can give voice to."

—ANJUM HASAN, author of *A Day in the Life: Stories*

"Janice Pariat traverses the inherent dignity of life in all its forms and the conflict between doing and being that is alive in all of us. Timely and timeless—a masterpiece and an absolute thrill to read."

—AVNI DOSHI, author of *Girl in White Cotton* (aka *Burnt Sugar*)

"What a feast of a novel! *Everything the Light Touches* thrilled my seeker's heart. It served as a potent reminder of the value of empathy, deep listening, and ways of seeing that expand our field of perception. Janice Pariat is a prodigiously talented storyteller whose writing effortlessly crosses borders."

—JINI REDDY, author of *Wanderland: A Search for Magic in the Landscape*

"Ingenious in its nested structure, treading lightly across centuries and species, *Everything the Light Touches* tackles every subject from the humble leaf to the mighty empire—then proceeds to ask, with Pariat's characteristic wit, if we perhaps haven't got that last bit backwards. An elegant, passionate book (which doubles as a warning) about the impossibility of understanding a single thing about our world without first acknowledging the wonder and mystery inherent in all that surrounds us."

—MADHURI VIJAY, author of *The Far Field*

"Capacious and wise, *Everything the Light Touches* is a magnificent reminder that the natural world does not lie outside of ourselves, and that when we break trust with the earth, we break our own spirits into scattered fragments. Janice Pariat finds a new language of connection, wonder, and loss, for the songs of the earth from Lapland and Goethe's Europe to the Lower Himalayas and remote villages in India's Northeast, her stories dancing between centuries in this generous and intricate work."

—NILANJANA S. ROY, author of *The Wildings*

"*Everything the Light Touches* weaves the timelessness of nature and the urgency of human emotions into an elegiac tale that is evocative, intelligent and deeply thought-provoking. A seminal work by a novelist and a poet at the height of her powers."

—PRANAY LAL, author of *Indica: A Deep Natural History of the Indian Subcontinent*

"Wise, funny, touching, wide-ranging, deep-delving, whip-smart, graceful. Written by a novelist with the eye of a poet, and a poet with the narrative powers of a novelist—a novel that needed to be written, that tells true things, is entirely its own being."

—ROBERT MACFARLANE, author of *Underland: A Deep Time Journey*

"A dynamic river is certainly better than a static pond. Because still water stagnates, causes stagnation. It is moving water that carries life; it is motion that personifies life. Janice Pariat's *Everything the Light Touches* is about motion. As we read the novel, we too travel, meet other travellers. It is a book about the contradictions precipitated by time, space and circumstances. A novel that touched me deeply as a whole as well as with its ease of storytelling."

—S. HAREESH, author of *Moustache*

"Written with a curiosity that jumps across geographies, time, discourses and disciplines, *Everything the Light Touches* is a gift to those who question the forms and preoccupations of the modern novel."

—SHUBHANGI SWARUP, author of *Latitudes of Longing*

"*Everything the Light Touches* by Janice Pariat is a gorgeous novel about four characters on four different journeys, each in a different time, but linked by their passion for botany and the diverse ways they try to understand the natural world. It is warm, tender, precise, full of charm and humour, but also hugely ambitious and lit by wonderful flashes of gorgeous prose."

—WILLIAM DALRYMPLE, author of *The Anarchy: The Relentless Rise of the East India Company*

"With language that glows intensely, words that are layered and yet cascade like music, no praise for *Everything the Light Touches* by Janice Pariat may be high enough ... This is a book that will glow like a rare emerald on any bookshelf in the world and still be relevant."

—*DECCAN HERALD*

"This is a broad, expansive work, and it is richly served by the author's luminous prose ... In binding together philosophical questions of narrators searching for themselves through various centuries, the book is an exploration of the often opposing world views of science and art, but also how we must live through life's largest questions through time and patience and long meanders ... An important contribution on seeing the world with depth and breadth."

—*FRONTLINE*

"An epic story of travellers and discoverers set across continents and centuries ... As the reader journeys through this atmospheric and accomplished novel, they discover that the natural world around us is loud enough for those willing to listen, and Pariat has found the language for it."

—*THE GUARDIAN*

"A near-magical space ... a magnificent wish-fulfilling tree hiding many secrets ... Janice Pariat is a weaver bird of stories, [her] particular skill is to occupy each different nest that she weaves not as an interloper but as its original inhabitant."

—*THE HINDU*

"By historicizing what is arguably the most pressing contemporary concern, Pariat's novel becomes one of ideas ... A reader will have no need to speculate about the necessity of reading the book under review as soon as they start on the first page."

—*HINDUSTAN TIMES*

"Wildly ambitious ... Shows us the complicated history of exploration, journeys as driven alternatively by curiosity and lostness, the ever-evolving nature of science, and the lengths the human race will go to acquire meaning and knowledge."

—*OPEN*

"An extraordinary story of trave lers spanning continents and centuries ... vast, strange, and ambitious."

—*SCROLL.IN*

"*Everything the Light Touches* embodies the very best of eco-fiction ... The book tries to get to the root of the inequalities and discriminations that have led to the present devastation by historicizing what is often mistaken as a contemporary concern."

—*THE TELEGRAPH*

"Pariat's landscapes, deftly woven with layered detail, reflect a melancholy that has become synonymous with the Anthropocene: the sadness with which we view all natural things of beauty. Her language is gentle, her prose elegant–but her words pierce through to the deepest places of the heart."

—*VOGUE INDIA*

EVERYTHING THE LIGHT TOUCHES

A Novel

JANICE PARIAT

FOURTH ESTATE · *New Delhi*

First published in India in hardback by Fourth Estate 2022
An imprint of HarperCollins *Publishers*

HarperCollins Publishers India, Cyber City, Building 10-A, Gurugram, Haryana-122002, India

www.harpercollins.co.in

This edition published by Fourth Estate 2023

P-ISBN: 978-93-5699-531-4
E-ISBN: 978-93-5629-143-0

Printed and bound at
MicroPrints India, New Delhi

MIX
Paper
FSC FSC® C218906

This product is made of FSC®-certified and other controlled material.

HarperCollins Publishers, Macken House, 39/40 Mayor Street Upper, Dublin 1, D01 C9W8, Ireland

For those who told me stories

The first step in wisdom is to know the things themselves; this notion consists in having a true idea of the objects; objects are distinguished and known by classifying them methodically and giving them appropriate names. Therefore, classification and name-giving will be the foundation of our science.

—Linnaeus, *Systema Naturae*

All is leaf.

—Goethe, *The Metamorphosis of Plants*

CONTENTS

Let us wait, let us listen.

We tell this story often, and in the telling it is different every time, but that, you see, is the nature of stories. There is always a tree, always a tiger, always a small bird that knows the secrets of the forest and helps humankind. The rest is smoke that never curls the same way twice.

We tell this story around a hearth. Come, gather by the fire.

What will it be tonight?

A tale of moral caution, say the elders. Of reaching too far, too high.

But the children plead for something lighter, where giants turn into mountains and their baskets into boulders.

No, say the lovers, tell us about the man who played the flute amidst the branches, so sweet, so clear, and won the heart of the queen.

Tonight, we tell the tale of creation. The one in which a tree is a golden ladder linking earth to sky.

Why? ask the children. Why?

So that the first tribes of our celestial people could wander freely, working their fields below until the evening, climbing up to rest in the house of God at night.

Listen, now, to how the tree, the tallest-in-the-world tree, was felled; how seven tribes were rendered earthbound; how its branches smacked the lands of the south, laying them flat and rich with the mulch of foliage, how the trunk crashed and carved our hills. Look how they bear the mark through all the ages still.

Listen, listen, for a story told once may not be told again.

SHAI

In truth, there have been nobler reasons to make a journey.

Someone once stumbled out of Africa and populated the world. Pilgrims trudged for miles to pay obeisance to their gods. People fled war and hunger. They sought knowledge and new worlds, carving shipping routes for their queens and countries. People have travelled to visit the sick and the dying. For love, for adventure. To fulfil their dearest, most precious dreams. To see the Pyramids or the Galápagos. They've saved and scrimped and quit their jobs and headed out in triumph. While I—well, for me it's a somewhat different matter. I'm travelling out of Delhi, this mad, magnificent city at the edge of a desert, to go back to where I came from—the wettest place on earth.

About all this, the lady at the counter is blissfully unconcerned. Her shiny gold name tag says Monika, and Monika cares only about whether the passenger before her has stowed a power bank in their checked-in luggage.

"No."

"And a coconut, ma'am?" Monika's face is inscrutable, masked by a variegated coastal shelf of makeup.

I decide I will answer her now and google this later. "No."

Whatever next? But it looks like I'm done. My suitcase is tugged away on the conveyor belt in spasmodic bursts; I'm handed my boarding pass, a quick smile. Gate 42B.

"Have a good flight, ma'am."

By the time I'm through security and spat out the other end, I know all about the coconut, its high oil content and how its meat is potentially combustible. Even though, so far, there hasn't been a single incident of fire on an aircraft resulting from a flaming nut. At least not of the palm-tree kind.

In the bit of the airport that looks like a mall, I stroll past beige chinos and pots of body butter, bags as big as bears, women in jewelled saris selling ayurvedic cosmetics. Above, a board is lit up with inspirational quotes, something by Rumi, *What you seek is seeking you.* Good. I knew it was meant to be—coffee and me.

Upstairs, the queues are long at Starbucks, but I join one nonetheless. Everyone is peering into their phones; I peer into mine, too. Two texts. A TED Talk link from my father—"Tomatoes talk, birch trees learn—do plants have dignity?"—which I save for later, and a message from "Joseph Bangalore."

In Delhi this weekend. Catch up?

By catch up he means sex. Quick, good, a couple of rounds at night, and once in the morning before he heads off to save the world. I jest. He's a pharmaceutical sales rep, not someone I might have met through friends or colleagues, but that's the magic of Tinder. Match. Chat. Date. Regret. Though I see Joseph Bangalore infrequently enough for this last to not have set in—yet. Pity I must tell him I'm not in town.

When you back, babes?

I hate it when he calls me that.

Gate 42B is tucked away in a godforsaken corner; down a long corridor, past potted palms, vending machines, and a bald bronze boy perpetually working his surya namaskar. Above me, the airport rises like the inside of a high-ceilinged shell; below, a carpet the distinct shade of diarrhea. When I get there, it's crowded already, passengers, luggage, kids, spilling higgledy-piggledy off the seats on to the floor.

Since when is Tuesday morning a busy time to travel?

I stand some distance away, sipping my coffee. Pretty awful, but still half-decent compared with what's available where I'm going: Hello, Nescafé.

Last time waiting to catch a flight like this, I met an old classmate from school; she seemed delighted to see me while I stood there desperately trying to fish for her name, *Nandita, Namrata, Namita,* and then—like a magician performing a favourite trick—she drew a child out from behind her. A child! Of three or four.

I still borrow earrings when I'm invited for a wedding, and she has a daughter.

No such intrusion now, thankfully, but it returns, my disquiet.

Not because I want children—I don't, or at least I don't think I do—but because of something else. Perhaps this is why I'm leaving. Not because of my schoolmate, still nameless, but something else, also unnameable. Not love. Not the weather. Not to prove myself right, or wrong. But because something—I don't know what exactly—has been lost.

Across from me, on a silent news screen, a fire rages through the forests of, I think, South America. The president of somewhere insists it's not. "The media is lying," read the subtitles under his pink, belligerent face. He's saying something about how it's a fallacy that the Amazon is the heritage of humankind, when my phone rings.

"Hi, Mei."

"You're coming home?"

"Yes."

"Are you sick?"

"No."

"You've been fired?"

"No."

"Then?"

"What? I need a reason?"

"Of course not. I'm only asking because you usually come around Christmas."

This is true. I shrug. "It's the air, Mei. Four seventy-seven AQI and counting." About this, I'm not lying. Delhi hovers a very close second to Bishkek in the World Air Quality Index list. Bishkek—this, too, I have googled—is the capital of Kyrgyzstan.

"Had something to eat?"

I'm thirty-two and my mother still asks me this.

"Yes," I lie.

There's a pause before she asks, "What about the award ceremony, Shai?"

"It's not *my* award."

"Yes, but you should be there, after everything Nah Nah Pat's done for you. She's—"

"Family," I complete. "Yes, I know." Nah Nah Pat is my mother's cousin, and she heads a Christian evangelical development agency that I once worked for in the invigoratingly titled role of "assistant social transformer."

Mei stays silent.

I sigh. "I'll call and apologize . . ."

"Yes. And go see her as soon as you're back."

It's time for a swift change of subject.

"Mei, do you think plants have dignity?"

She says she doesn't know; she hasn't watched the damn video yet.

"Also," she adds, "your father's gone off again . . ."

"He has?"

She snorts, lightly. "Yes. On another one of his crusades."

I ask, because I must, "Where to, this time?"

"Not far. But he's becoming impossible."

Before she launches into the million reasons why, I cut her off, not so gently—"Mei, we're boarding, I'll see you soon." We're not. The stewards stand desultorily by the still-unopened gate. A daughter nobler than I would have said it's a good thing, then, that I'll be home, but for the moment, I want to selfishly, quietly, sip my foul brew in peace.

Why are you coming back, Shai? I wish I could have told Mei that sometimes you must make the journey to find out.

We land in a place that falls off the map.

So far east in this vast country that it feels not of this country anymore. I emerge from Guwahati airport into ferocious heat and dust, and a wake of clamouring cabdrivers. I'm looking for Mohun, a guy from home who's meant to pick me up. We always hire him, though I'm not entirely sure why. He's busy on the phone for most of the three-hour drive up winding mountain roads, and he chews alarming amounts of betel nut, intermittently opening his door, while we're moving, to eject a stream of red liquid onto the tarmac. All along, we leave a trail of little crime scenes.

Thankfully, now, he finds me. Ale, he says in Khasi, even though he is Nepali, and whisks my suitcase out of my hand. I follow him dutifully across the parking lot, to a shiny white Santro. The good thing about Mohun is he doesn't feel the need for conversation, apart from near-monosyllabic questions—AC? Tea? Toilet?—and so I watch as Assam passes by outside the window. After a traffic-clogged section at Beltola, we drive through long quiet stretches, fields edged by graceful palms, ponds choked prettily with hyacinth, and then we hit the truck-heavy highway—also the border between the plains and the hills. Booze shops line the Meghalaya side on the right, where alcohol taxes are lower; on the Assam side, busy markets spill with colourful produce backdropped by cement factories belching white smoke. All this is familiar. All this, I have known all my life. Etched into all the journeys I have made to and fro, from elsewhere to home and back to elsewhere again, an oddly reversed ordering, I know, but home, for me, has always been a place not to live in but to leave.

After we cross Jorabat, a grimy, sprung-out-of-nowhere town, we begin to climb, and I roll down the window because this is when the air turns fresher and the dust lightens. Soon we're in the mountains, and the way down turns long and steep, the road curling like a ribbon. I find it peculiar, how vast, majestic landscapes like these feel unwaveringly timeless. As though they've always been this way, permanent and perennial. But fifty million years ago, all this was underwater; a shallow sea extended from these hills across to Rajasthan. Everything, in its own time, changes.

Though now, too, we could be submerged—I've arrived after the end of the monsoon, and the forested slopes shimmer in shades of green I find difficult to describe to people back in the city. Light and luminescent as the first leaves on our planet. Dark and deep, the colour of ancient emerald pools. Perhaps because they are drummed from the earth by what we call 'lap bah—rain so heavy and long-lasting that it's the mightiest rain of all.

Soon we stop at a makeshift restaurant, with baskets of early oranges, pickle-bottle armies, and swaying banners of silvery Lay's. I want nothing more than water, and wait while Mohun eats a quick lunch.

When we resume our journey, it's late afternoon and the air has turned cool. It will cut to the bone when night falls, but I will be home before then, before the shadows grow long and the sun begins to slide behind the hills.

✧ ✧ ✧

We live a little out of Shillong, at the top of a hill, up a steep slope.

Mohun puts the car into first gear; in second, we would stall and roll all the way back. I'm bracing myself. Always this strange feeling upon arrival—of not being sure why I'm here, or whether I should be here at all. Pine trees tower over us, their shadows falling slenderly across the windshield. Soon, Mohun rounds the last corner, and there, to the right, flanked by bamboo thickets, stands the green gate through which we must enter, and we come to a halt on a porch with a garage housing an ancient Fiat that's driven only when I'm around. When Oiñ, my nanny, still lived with us, she'd be standing outside to greet me. Today, my mum steps out alone, and it takes me a moment to realize that this pepper-haired lady is her. It's been less than a year since I've seen her—in which secret hours did she age?

When I hug her, though, she smells familiar, of wool and naphthalene and hand cream, and at this moment . . . cinnamon. "You," she says, cupping my face like she would a candle flame. I look at her, smiling. Mohun is duly paid, my suitcase extracted from the car, and we stream inside.

We live in a big house, far bigger than required for two people who don't speak to each other much. And emptier, now that Oiñ has moved back to her village and my mum's parents have died. This does mean sections of the house feel unused—because they are—and my room stays undisturbed. Visit to visit, outgrown yet intimate, palimpsest of every room it has been over the years. Papered with posters of boy bands, Greenpeace, and tennis stars; an old collection of postcards, "Cities Around the World"—Rome, London, Stockholm, Paris, New York—which I thought bestowed on my walls a certain sophistication.

For now, we head to the kitchen. Mei has baked a cake, and the warmth of it lingers in the air. "Your favourite," she says, placing a slice before me. I also accept her offer of tea. I watch as she busies herself with the electric kettle, the teapot, the cups, not attempting to help her because I know she will refuse and brush me aside. *You've had a long journey.* My mother looks thinner, as though her bones have lightened, but her cheeks are flushed with warmth. It's strange how she can seem robust and frail all at once.

"How long are you staying?" she inquires. Pleased as she is to see me, Mei is never too keen for me to be here long. Here, where once there was always trouble—or the possibility of it. After Independence, when the people of these hills found themselves swallowed up by Assam, with nothing much in common with the plainspeople apart from newly drawn national borders, they fought for their own state. Meghalaya. A Sanskrit name given to a place that spoke no Sanskrit. The Home of the Clouds. After that, a drive to chase out dkhars, outsiders—the Nepalis, the Assamese, the Bangladeshis, the Bengalis—every decade bringing with it fresh waves of unrest. My mother wished none of this for me—the curfews and violent disturbances, the clashes between our local "militants" and the army and Central Reserve Police Force, of which there always seemed to be an endless reserve to bring here, she said. So, when I was old enough to be sent away, I was. To boarding school, to university, for employment. Always elsewhere. Mei considers our hometown a dead-end place, where nothing ever happens except militancy, and no one makes much of themselves. Except, well, I'm not sure I'm making much of myself elsewhere either.

"So?" she asks again. "How long?"

I give her a reply I haven't before: "I don't know."

"What do you mean?" She sits across from me. "And work?"

"I'll have to find something else."

"Again?"

"I've been there three years, Mei! And besides"—I take a deep breath—"they're shutting down." Little hope remains these days for a publishing house specializing in travel guides—we've been replaced by apps and Google Maps, our boss told us. And while the rest of my colleagues scrambled around looking for new jobs, I didn't. I bought a plane ticket. I'm here. This, though, is not something I share with Mei.

"Well," she says finally, "that's a pity."

I sip my tea, but I sip it too quick. It's hot, and I scald my tongue.

"Careful," she says, frowning.

"Grace sends her love." I hope this will placate her. My flatmate is a bona fide parent charmer; Mei has only ever spoken to her on the phone, but even this is sufficient for Grace to work her magic.

"Oh, how is she?"

Grace is doing well, I tell her, working as a counsellor at the reputed Bluebells School. My friend is the daughter my mum could be proud of; me, I think, not so much.

The cake, soft and warm and studded with walnuts, goes down heavy.

I sip the tea gingerly and ask about Papa. She cradles her cup in her hands, steam rising gently in front of her face. "Why don't you go see for yourself?"

"Okay, then," I say, "I will."

"You can take him his tea."

When I walk out later, flask in hand, the hills have begun to darken. No more than an hour of daylight remains. Delhi feels far away. Always this, when I arrive home. This sudden downsizing of the world. In some ways, I feel resized myself, smaller somehow, more compact.

I walk up the winding colony road; ours is one of the last few neighbourhoods with old houses still standing intact, low-roofed, limewashed, fronted by neatly trimmed hedges, with names like Hacienda and Little Cloud. Much of Shillong has been given over to manic construction, an inglorious clutter of unplanned cement structures—mostly illegal, of course, in an earthquake zone such as this. Every so often, the town is rattled by tremors, or a series of small rumbles. Warnings of what's to come, my mother likes to say, sounding as though she might even be wishing it upon us.

My father has no such views. In fact, it's difficult to discern whether he has views on anything at all apart from things that grow in the garden. And trees. Especially when they might be felled. And "plant bias"—our human tendency to underappreciate or ignore the flora around us—according to him, our species's greatest, gravest crime.

He has always been this way, for as long as I can remember. Growing plants and saving them, from frost and aphids and too much rain. He's not as tall as my mum, and built smaller, stouter, less lean, with the air of always being elsewhere. Though now he is very much present—and immobile.

"Hello, Papa."

"Oh, hello." He smiles benignly, as though I've never been away a day, and that my visiting him under these present circumstances is perfectly normal.

I've reached the edge of the colony, from where a pine forest extends over the hills. It's protected, which means it's meant to stay unthreatened by housing or commercial developments, but something has driven my father out here to strap himself to a tree. I have visions of gated colonies like the ones in Gurgaon, Western Heights, or Maple Crescent. Or worse, a swanky mall or humongous cathedral.

Instead, he tells me, someone has decided to build a wall.

"What exactly it would be keeping out or in, I'm not sure," he adds, "but it means cutting down trees to make way for it."

"How many?"

"At least a dozen."

The way my father says it, one would think the Amazon's burning.

"All they need to do is build the wall about a foot thinner," he continues, gesturing, "and it will miss them completely."

"Yes, it will," I say placing the flask beside him. He's sitting up against the widest of the potentially doomed pines. "How long have you been here, Papa?"

"Three days. We're taking shifts," he adds quickly, seeing the look on my face. According to Mei, he slinks in and out of the house like a thief, to eat, to change, to sleep.

"Who's we?" I look around. There's no one else here.

Kong Nuramon, apparently, the woman who lives opposite and runs her own nursery. Every day of the year, something or other blooms wildly in her makeshift greenhouse, in the rows and rows of pots along the wall, on her veranda, all along the steps up to her front door. She's the colony flower lady.

"And?"

Bah Kyn comes over sometimes. My father's closest friend, who lives across town; given the distance, though, I don't see how he could be a reliable earth warrior.

"So, what's happening now?"

"Well, we're not sure yet," he admits unhappily. "Kong Nuramon says the wood has already been sold, a lakh, a lakh and a half for each tree. Which is why officials are reluctant to do anything. But Bah Kyn's been trying to get in touch with someone he knows in the Forest Department who might be able to help."

"That's good." I pause before asking, "Must you be here all the time, then?"

"Just in case."

He's sipping his tea now. Mum also sent him some cake. I sit down with him. It looks like we're having a picnic. The scent of pine rising around us, damp, mulchy, sour. My father looks older, too, grey at the hairline where all was once coal black. Why are you doing this, Papa, I want to ask, but I'm afraid he'll give me an answer I won't comprehend. I sit with him quietly. He's never been one to ask many questions, so usually, I make the effort. "I watched the video you sent this morning," I tell him.

His face brightens. "Fascinating, isn't it?" I nod. This prompts him to chatter—about plant communication, their immense aromatic vocabulary, their capacity for memory.

"Birch trees can remember a past event for up to four years," he says in delight.

Yes, I joke, it's possible they have a better memory than I do.

He beams. "The lady in the video says that, too."

It's growing dark now, quite suddenly as it does in the hills, and here in the forest all light has seeped away.

"Papa," I begin, "why don't I request Kong Nuramon to keep watch for any . . . activity here during the night, and you can come home for now?"

I expect him to put up a fight, or just flat-out refuse, but to my surprise, he agrees.

Later, as we walk home together, a thought swoops into my head like a bat: *All the trees in the world remember.*

Tonight, I'm tired. I lie in bed listening to strange silence—in Delhi, always the sound of cars, of flights overhead, the night guard thumping his walking stick on the road every hour. My window here, next to my single bed, looks out into the pine forest, the edge of which my father is trying to protect. From here rises the chirrup of crickets, and from near the stream, a bright chorus of frogs. In the distance, a dog howls, joined by another and then more. I'm almost asleep, when suddenly there's a sharp rap on my window.

Must be the wind, the branch of a tree, something, I think drowsily. But there it is again, a series of strikes, like pellets or hard rain. I sit up, draw back the curtain, and wrench the window open. Below my first-floor window, a face grins up at me, bright and shiny, full as the moon.

"What are you doing here?" I hiss.

The moon says something in a half whisper.

"Wait," I add. I pull on a sweater, socks, and scamper downstairs.

My parents' room, like mine, is on the upper floor but on the far side of the house. They won't hear a thing. Still, I tiptoe into the pantry and gently unlock the back door.

Standing outside is my friend Kima. "Hello," he says.

I give him a quick hug as he steps in. We know the routine. I carefully shut the door, and we head back upstairs, but to the TV room, through the attached bathroom, and out into a small balcony from where we climb up to the roof, to a platform where the water tanks sit like squat black monsters. We have been coming here almost a decade. It might be my favourite place in the world, although I would never confess that to this fool. We sit at the edge, the lights of Shillong before us, sprinkled like jewels along the slopes.

"Heard you were back," he says.

"Yes, but for like three hours now. How did you find out?"

He shrugs. "Small town."

"Or I'm just insanely famous."

"I'll let you take your pick."

Actually, he'd seen me in Mohun's cab, taking the turn off the main road heading for Lum Kynjai, where my parents live. Kima roars around on a silver-streaked Yamaha. I met him while dating his friend Dajied—they played basketball together—and while the romance didn't last, the friendship did. Kima lights a cigarette, a short, stubby Gold Flake, and offers me one even though he knows I don't smoke anymore. He also offers me kwai—bits of quartered betel nut and tobacco leaf flecked with lime. I decline; I've never told him this, but kwai makes me nauseated and dizzy. He will laugh, I know, and call me a bourgeois softie.

"How's the teaching going?"

He exhales, his face plumed in smoke. "Going along." This, I've realized, is Kima's answer to mostly everything. "And how're you?" he asks.

"Okay, I guess." And this is usually mine.

"How're your folks?"

I tell him about my father: how, at sixty-two, he's strapped himself to a tree.

"He's still there?"

"I managed to get him home tonight."

He chuckles. "Your mum must be so mad."

"So mad, her blood pressure has spiked," I tell him. He commiserates. He has a sick mother beset with diabetes; he rarely talks about her, but I know she was a hawker in the streets of Shillong, providing for a child the father never stayed around long enough to see born. He's told me he did his PhD in literature to make her proud. Compared with Kima, my mostly directionless existence seems abysmally meagre.

"How long you here?"

"I don't know."

"Oh? And work and stuff?"

I tell him.

"That's shitty. When you get back, you'll have to look for another job?"

"I don't know."

Kima stubs his cigarette out and chuckles. "What *do* you know, Shai?"

He means it in jest, I'm certain, but something like a fish bone catches in my throat. I try to laugh it off, declaring that I'm going through a cosmic dark age.

"The fuck's that?"

"Well, the night sky didn't always used to look like this, you know." We glance up, the stars bright and clear and glittery. "At one point, for a hundred million years after the Big Bang, there were no stars, no galaxies, only fog. The universe was devoid of light."

He looks at me. "Still watching Discovery Science?"

I nod. "Especially since I lost my job."

"And then what happened?"

"I now know a *lot* more about the cosmos?"

"No idiot, I mean after the cosmic dark ages."

I shrug. "I guess we're still finding out."

✧ ✧ ✧

Usually, I return to Shillong for brief spells, like quick spring showers.

I rush around, do some local shopping—turmeric, pepper, smoked meat—and visit people, mostly family, an elderly grand-uncle, a cousin who might be in town, a kindly aunt who'll ask when I'm planning to settle down and have babies. I just about have time to notice how things are different, more cars, more houses, how things are the same, the hills, the light. My parents and I will go for a meal on my last evening here, somewhere nice, which always turns out to be a restaurant in a heritage building on the next hill from ours. Because it's close and convenient.

And then I leave.

This time, though, it is different. I have no plans. To shop or to see anybody.

And it is strange. I'm oddly restless, like when you pose for a photograph and don't quite know what to do with your hands and feet.

I am unhabituated here, I realize, in all senses of the word.

What should I do? Should I . . . leave? For Delhi? For elsewhere?

I tell myself I just need, for a while, to breathe.

So I stand in the sun, outside in the garden, where I'm left in the quietness with my own thoughts. I watch the chrysanthemums coming into bloom. The guavas ripening. A small jewel snake slithering into the bamboo grove. The sparrows rising and swooping. The grass growing. The poinsettia changing from green to gold.

I also find odd jobs to do around the house—cleaning out drawers, rearranging bookshelves. I look through a box of old letters, my old diaries. What strange archaeology am I indulging in? I ask Grace over the phone. "Shai, you're looking for yourself." And we both laugh—though I do wonder, am I not really? Am I not asking the same question the first creature who could did looking up at the sky: Who am I?

Some afternoons, I abandon my father and the pines to walk farther into the forest. I haven't done this in many years, and I walk along, passing the occasional kid on a bicycle, or a runner, feeling like a stranger. I wish I could say I find peace here—or joyous communion—but apart from some sort of measured contentment, I don't. Perhaps the city has dulled my heart, my senses. Perhaps because, unlike my father, I can't name anything I see. Is that why the forest doesn't speak to me? Because for me it's all surface? The tall, ungainly pines, the ferns like swords and ostrich feathers. I am walking through a landscape, pleasing and peaceful, but what does any of it mean? I feel deeply unknowing of the world.

It doesn't help that at home, a sliver of tension sharpens. My mother, I can tell, is a little disquieted—*why are you not making plans to leave?*—even though she hasn't said anything to me yet.

So I begin to stay out of the house more.

Luckily, it's that time of the year when the weather is briefly stilled between monsoon wet and biting cold. I venture into town. Along the main road, towards Wah Umkhrah—once a stream in which the British fished for trout, now the biggest drain this side of Shillong, clogged with colourful plastic. I pass newly built churches, old houses sitting small and incongruous, a line of little shops. A bakery, a Chinese restaurant. Above, signboards advertising homes in New Shillong, faster Internet, a hot-air balloon festival—"See the city from the sky." On the streets, faces pass by, sometimes in a blur, peering into phones, sometimes I catch chatter and laughter.

In a town small enough to always bump into an acquaintance, I know no one, and no one knows me. I glide about like a ghost.

✧ ✧ ✧

A fortnight after my flight from Delhi, I'm outside, behind the kitchen, chatting with Kong Rit, our daily help. She's telling me about a man from her village who went missing and was found a few days later, "lying on a rock like a dried fish in the sun."

"Where did he go?"

"Ngam tip," she says. Nobody knows. "Some say he met a 'suid tynjang . . . you know?"

I do—mischievous spirits who lead travellers astray, apparently.

"But some think he was with his mistress and some drama happened." She giggles, and I'm expecting to hear more about this when we're interrupted by the landline phone, ringing loud and prehistoric. Mei answers—"Hello, hello," I hear her shout, as though she's speaking to someone on the moon. She's not on the call for long.

"News from Oiñ," she says. "She's coming to Shillong . . . for a checkup."

Oh, it'll be wonderful to see her, I say, it's been so long—and here, I feel a little stab of guilt for not having taken the trouble to keep in touch more. "What kind of checkup?" Mei shrugs. The line dropped, and when she tried calling back, she couldn't get through.

How old would Oiñ be now? I wonder. I find it difficult to calculate. Perhaps seventy? She was slight, wiry, strong, and only in her last year with us did she succumb to a little weight, on her face, her tummy. I'd tease her, and she'd say it was my fault, for growing up and not needing her to run around anymore.

When we first met, the story goes, I stopped crying instantly. Me, a swaddled, snotty, cranky four-month-old, and Oiñ, at our doorstep, recommended to Mei by a friend, holding out her arms, drawing me from my exhausted mother. In the twenty or more years she was with us, she drove Mei a little crazy, being similarly stubborn, but a few things saved her from dismissal—she had no "bad habits," didn't steal, smoke bidis, drink secretly, or chew foul-smelling khaini. What also made it impossible for Mei to let Oiñ go was her complete and absolute love for me. I was bathed, fed, held, and entertained—and I adored her, too. So much so that at night, if I had nightmares, or a storm thundered outside, it was Oiñ's bed I would clamber into, not my parents'. "Khun, thiah suk," she'd say. Sleep peaceful, child.

It'll be good, I tell myself, to see her again.

When I visit my father that afternoon, tea and cake in hand, I discover he's turned into a minor celebrity. A reporter from the local paper has appeared on the scene—to write a story on the "Treeman of Shillong." Papa's friend Bah Kyn is also here, and he reminds me as always of an affable penguin. Small, round, with a bit of a wobble in his walk. He, too, has the same distracted air as my father, except his preoccupations are entirely nonbotanical. "Here," he says, handing me a flyer.

"What's this, Bah Kyn?"

"My dream come true," he replies mysteriously.

After Papa's interview, the journalist snaps a photo of him—looking slightly dazed—with his enormous DSLR and departs. As does Bah Kyn, though Kong Nuramon joins us for cake and tea. I'm beginning to enjoy this little ritual—there's no cause I wouldn't get behind if it involved protest picnics in the forest. Especially on evenings such as these, when the sky promises it will always stay blue, and the sun shines warm and benevolent.

"This could really help us," says our flower lady, "if the reporter doesn't mess it up." She's a little worried because in a recent story about a curfew in town, he wrote buses were still seen "flying" on the roads. Our laughter rises like birds through the trees.

"What was the curfew for?" I ask.

Kong Nuramon makes a face. "The usual. Demands for an Inner Line Permit. To keep out dkhars."

Then, as though to swerve away from all this, she tells my father how much she enjoyed the video he'd shared on their colony gardeners' group, the one about the wood wide web . . .

"The what?" I'm sure I've misheard.

"The wood wide web," she repeats, and then gestures to the forest. "See this? These trees stand singularly, one by one, but underground they're all connected by fine-fine threads . . . What are they called again?"

"Hyphae," says my father. "Sent out by fungi through the soil, from root to root."

Beneath our feet exists another world, I learn, a network of infinite biological pathways, through which trees share resources, information, nutrients. Some regard it as a competitive system, regulated through self-interest, sanction, and reward. Others believe trees care for one another, and act as guardians, sharing resources, with the healthy supporting the weak. A free market versus a socialist's dream.

I say that's quite something, but Papa is hesitant to agree. "I think," he begins, slowly, "forests are more complicated than we can ever imagine. They're beyond these two stories . . . We have no language yet with which to begin to speak of trees."

We sit in silence, the pines and us, listening to the breeze.

That night, I'm in bed reading, when a text comes in, and—surprise—it's from Dajied. *Hey, how's you? Heard you're in town.* (Thank you, Kima.) We're in touch rarely, if at all. There was a time when we were, let's say, quite in tune about my comings and goings—we waited breathlessly to meet—but not anymore. Still, I spend too long trying to decide on a suitable reply to this most succinct of questions, and finally send what I'd typed out initially: *Good, thanks. Yes, I am.*

Almost immediately: *For how long?*

A while, I respond vaguely, expecting him to suggest we catch up, but my phone stays silent.

He's a strange one. Always has been. All right, no, that's not true. He was awkward around Mei, but then, she never really liked him and didn't try to hide it—local boy, unconverted to Christianity, and his family not from the same class, living in a crowded, noisy part of town, where everyone's backyards intertwined, and no one had gardens.

She'd tell me I deserved someone better. And maybe I believed her then, I don't know. Perhaps it was just easier to, especially at the end. Otherwise, being with him had felt . . . abundant.

But I don't wish to think of Dajied now. I've done too much of that already—when we were together, when we were apart. I put my phone away and slip under the covers.

But sleep, as is often the case, will not come.

I'm thinking of him and our last parting. Maybe someday, we'll collide again, as we're fated to, two stray galaxies meeting in four and a half billion years.

I admit this is a bit dramatic. But it is difficult for me to make sense of it any other way. To love, to lose, and what then? Do paths not cross for a reason even if the trajectory of the story is so vast, we cannot fathom it in our lifetimes?

Else, all of it to what purpose?

Papa may have been right, that there's no language to speak of trees—but I find there's no language also to speak of so much else.

✧ ✧ ✧

Sooner rather than later, I know, my mum will ask whether I've found a job. And I'll tell her about the date seed in Israel that germinated after being preserved for two thousand years—"Mei, things take time."

I suspect she won't find this amusing.

Perhaps I should look for something. Here. That Teach First English school Mei retired from a few years ago is still running. Or maybe I could drop by the Ri Khasi Press, across town in Umsohsun—though it publishes mainly local literature, and my Khasi, once fluent, is now less so.

To be honest, something—an inner voice, Grace, the two are often the same thing—tells me not to take a leap.

Back in Delhi, every evening, I'd stop off at our neighbourhood park on my way back from work, to walk along a path that wound all around its edges. Me and many other residents, some walking their dogs, others just themselves, round and round we went, until one evening, something—like a stepped-on twig—snapped. *What am I doing? Is this*, I thought, as I rounded another curve to take me back exactly to where I began, *all of my life?*

Finally, or at least for now, I have quit all this—the jostling commute, the "trying to make it in a big city." What's the point if all I do is rush into something else I'm unsure about?

"You have no inner compass, Shai," Grace once told me. And I was struck by this image. Of my heart as a big whirring instrument whose needles spun wildly—unsure of where north was. How do I find my north? If you ask my father, he'll say follow the bend of the thuja tree, that's the direction in which they lean. Sadly, this is of little help to me. Migrating birds, it's been discovered, find their way by sensing the earth's magnetic field. They see directions as lighter or darker shades in their vision; for them north is a colour. I am deeply amazed and envious.

Grace would also say I've lost my own sense of direction because I've always been told what to do—by Mei, mostly. "Steer your own ship, Shai." Yes, all right, but where to, where to? I have no clue.

For the moment, I align myself only to follow the sun. I wait for Oiñ, and at the end of each day, wonder only what the next will hold. What will happen will happen, and sometimes just being open to that means a new path might unfurl before you.

✧ ✧ ✧

Today, adventure.

I'm speeding along—well, as fast as our Fiat can go—across town. I've hit Mizo Colony, where Kima lives, the locality, I often tease him, with the greatest number of churches per household in the world.

What to do? he says dolefully, we really liked the missionaries.

Beyond here, a part of town I rarely visit, Assam Market, Assam Rifles, the neat, clean slopes of the cantonment grounds.

On the dashboard, Bah Kyn's flyer flutters.

"Welcome to the Ever-Living Museum," it says, "where the heartbeat of Culture and Heritage lingers on." Below, a list of attractions, a motley mix of ethnographic objects. I'm not surprised. My father's friend is an old-fashioned collector of everything. Scavenging the khrums—the basements—of people's houses for objects, unused and forgotten, and persuading the family to "donate" them to him for safekeeping. From our house, too, he's retrieved a khiew dek, a heavy pot for cooking meat, and an old mohkhiew, a garden hoe. Admittedly, I haven't displayed much interest in his eccentric quirk before—and not much more in "learning about the rich Culture of Meghalaya"—but well . . . there's a first time for everything.

I'm driving through a shaded forest, up a winding road that eventually leads to Sweet Falls, a popular canoodling spot for local couples, or so I hear. I turn off much before that, though, at a green signboard announcing my arrival at the museum. It looks like someone's home, with a sloping garden, and an orchard at the back. I buy a ticket from a young lad at the reception—a table and chair placed in the garage near the gate—and head inside. I'm the only visitor in this large space built on two levels with wide windows all along one wall. In the middle, a fibreglass tree "grows" along a pillar, spreading its branches at impossible ninety-degree angles across the ceiling and down the opposite wall.

Is this what he means by Ever-Living?

Before me stands the first, and largest, exhibit—a life-size model of a "traditional Khasi hut." Thatched roof, thatched walls. I peer in through the door. Inside, a rympei, a wood-fire hearth, around which lies a careful scattering of knives, mulas, betel-nut baskets, rugs. In the corner, a tiny bed. It's quaint, but I find the emptiness strangely unsettling—what sudden unnamed tragedy befell the inhabitants and forced them to leave?

Next, I wander past the shelves along the walls: preserved fungi from the Khasi Hills, an ancient Petromax kerosene lantern, a hat made of leaves. I'm not sure what to make of it all.

When I'm at the "Items Used for Rituals" section, someone else enters—a young woman, strikingly pretty. She's tall and slender, with tight curls cropped fashionably close to her head—effortlessly stylish, too, in jeans, UGGs, an oversized sweater. I find myself wishing I'd taken the trouble to throw on more than just some track pants and a sweatshirt. And that I'd combed my hair.

I watch her in the glass. She, too, is looking wonderingly at the fantastical tree.

I pretend to be interested in a flat wooden object on which, the plaque informs me, "the egg ceremony is performed," when Bah Kyn walks in. He's pleased to see me, wobbling over with an arm outstretched.

"Welcome, welcome," he says. "Oh, I see you're looking at the pliang shat khan."

"Yes," I say, "I am."

"Do you know how the egg ceremony is performed?"

I have little clue. "Not in detail, no."

"I had it done for myself, you know, to find out if my illnesses were natural or"—he lowers his voice—"caused by the evil eye."

I'm not sure where to look.

"The priest chants into the egg," Bah Kyn continues, "invoking the gods to reveal the answers, and then he smashes it on this"—he gestures towards the wooden slab. "If the eggshells lie mostly upturned, the illness is natural . . . if not, it's the evil eye."

I'm almost afraid to ask, but I must. "What was it for you?"

"Thankfully, natural. What no one wants to see is bits of shell lying in a line."

"Why?"

"That's the road to a funeral pyre."

We move along, with him pointing out the star attractions: a blanket made with bark from the Garo Hills, a pair of looped feathers from a racket-tailed drongo. Then we come to the kyrwoh, a plaited cane—like an outsized bangle or an elvish crown—once used in these hills, I'm told, to send messages between villages and their chiefs.

"How?" I ask, confused.

It's very clever, Bah Kyn explains. Depending on the width of the weave, the kyrwoh conveyed the urgency of the call. One finger meant come immediately, three, more leisurely, or five, a hand, take your time.

"Like a medieval text message?" I say, quite delighted, but he appears unimpressed by my analogy.

Next we head to a tiny adjacent building at the end of the garden. The natural history section, with shells from the Bay of Bengal, plant fossils, bits of glittery quartz. We stop at a large circular stone—once an exercise weight for young Garo men. Bah Kyn says he found it abandoned in a forest, and only after he asked the stone for permission to move it, to "sumar," or look after, did it turn light as a feather, and he was able to carry it away with him and bring it back here. I blink, not quite sure what to make of the story—who would believe it was true?

After we're done, we step outside into the garden, filled with lady's slipper orchids and flowers that look like small stars. The sun is high and strong today, the light sharp and clear and autumn gold. I look around, but it seems the stylish visitor has already left.

"Enjoyed?" asks Bah Kyn.

"Very much."

I don't tell him that wandering around his museum left me feeling a little like I do on my walks in the forest. Everything distant, lying behind glass.

✧ ✧ ✧

I've been in Shillong almost a month, when finally, I feel my heart begin to lift to the sky. Something shifts, recovers. "Maybe it's the water," I tell Grace in jest; it comes from the forest spring, after all, and tastes fresh and sweet. She thinks I'm on the upswing in a cycle of lows and highs. Perhaps. Or maybe something's *really* lifted. As they say here, how long can the fog hug the ground? Embrace it, I tell myself. Good things will happen.

Already we've had some happy news—the local TV station would like to interview Papa, and all is abuzz. Kong Nuramon has been quick to capitalize on the publicity—she's started a petition for colony members to sign, and who wouldn't want in at this point, including those initially indifferent to the plight of the pines. This will be moved to Bah Kyn's contact at the Forest Department, which now, Papa says, cannot afford to "look bad." The trees might be saved after all.

And then, this evening, a gig to look forward to with Kima.

I told him at first that I didn't want to go, but he can be persuasive. *You're hardly around, Shai... come on, everyone will be there.* So I relented, also in the small, secret hope that *everyone* would include Dajied—it would be nice to see him again, and didn't he text me the other day perhaps for this very reason? So we could, you know, meet and catch up?

When I head out on an afternoon walk, the world seems eager, expectant—the pines reaching for the sky, the cherry trees in early blossom, the swifts in swooping flight. Who knows what the day will hold? In all honesty, this is the most amount of anticipation I've felt in months, and isn't it true, that to anticipate is to feel alive?

Before I realize it, I've walked all the way to Ward's Lake.

Even if the sky's a bit overcast, and already a mild 'lap ñiup-ñiup is falling, my spirits aren't dampened. Around me lie the openness of water, the sweep of slopes edged with flower beds and weeping willows. I can see ducks, blooming lotuses nestled in green. I do what I often used to as a child with Oiñ—buy a packet of popcorn from a woman selling snacks at the gate, stand at the bridge across the middle, and feed the fish. They're not massive but many; hundreds roiling around in the muddy water like one giant slippery thousand-finned monster.

Didn't she once tell me a story about an ugly fish who turned out to be a beautiful river nymph? Possibly. Oiñ told me many stories. Usually, in the kitchen, while she fed me spoonfuls of rice. Likai, the woman who turned into a waterfall; Pahsyntiew, the goddess lured out of a cave by wildflowers; Manik Raitong, the lowly flute player loved by a queen. Long and convoluted, they varied wildly from telling to telling—depending on her mood, characters would either fall in love or off a cliff.

My favourite was the legend of the Diengiei. About a giant tree atop a mountain that grew so large it hid the rays of the sun and covered the earth in shadow. And when the woodcutters tried to fell it, miraculously, every night, it was healed. How did it begin, then? There was a tiger, I know, and a small bird . . . When Oiñ gets here, I tell myself, chucking the last of the popcorn into the water, I shall pester her to tell me the story again.

A few hours later, I'm shivering on the back of Kima's Yamaha.

We're headed to the rooftop bar of a hotel in Laitumkhrah, a shiny new place, all fake wood, glass lifts, and a 1970s brown-orange colour scheme. Not long ago, there wasn't anything like this in Shillong, and people drove out in their cars and drank at scenic viewpoints. If you didn't have a car, well, you found a spot on the road in a nice, quiet colony, or an empty parking lot. All this, I know from Kima and Dajied.

Guests have gathered on the rooftop—and the members of the band. "Nine," I exclaim. "They're all farmers," says Kima. "Farmers by day, passionate musicians by night. Or at least," he adds, "that's what the posters say."

He knows many more people here than I do, but I recognize a few: Jeff, the Ashkenazi Jew whose grandparents fled Germany, arrived in Calcutta, and eventually ended up in Shillong; Apdor, who disappeared to the UK for a degree, and returned with a girlfriend named Gemma; Valte with a mohawk who loves the Beatles. I head to the bar, order myself an overpriced beer, and by the time I'm back, the band is introducing themselves. Ngi, ngi dei Khlieh Asem. From villages in the East Khasi Hills.

The lead singer is a cheerful, balding man in a blue shirt, fluttering about like a sparrow. They begin with a hymn, a song of devotion that sounds like nothing you might hear in church. *Jisu ba ieid, Jisu ba jem, nga ieid nga ieid ia me.*

I move to the edge of the terrace. Kima is lost in the crowd, nowhere to be seen. Then I hear someone call out. It's Dajied, walking towards me in a long black coat. He looks the same, though leaner, and still with that air of a lone wolf about him. His hair slicked back, his stubble light and fuzzy. Only briefly do our eyes meet, before he says, "Hey, how's you?"

"Good, thanks."

We first met at a wedding, a grand, dull affair, where I was bored enough to sneak off to the back, behind the canopy, and ask a couple of guys, strangers, for a cigarette. Sure, said Kima, holding out a Gold Flake, and Dajied lit it for me. I also discovered they'd carried Coke spiked with rum, so I stuck with them for the rest of the evening. I was finishing with university in Delhi, and Dajied had just started, though not because he was much younger. "First, my parents forced me to do engineering in Chennai," he explained, "so I made sure I flunked so badly they had no choice but to take me out . . ." He was a film student at a college in Shillong then, allegedly the best in the region. By the end of the night we'd kissed; by the end of the week he was slipping in through the back door and into my bed. We called them our "expeditions," and they continued all through my summer break, between finishing university and beginning an internship at my aunt's organization, and off and on through the years after, each time I returned home.

Until, one winter, we stopped. For many reasons. It was complicated. But we've never talked about it since. Not once. And obviously, I'm not about to bring up anything now.

"Read about your dad in the papers."

"He's quite the celebrity."

Dajied chuckles and leans over the parapet. This comes as a surprise, but I realize he's nervous, too. Somehow, that makes me feel better. We don't speak for a bit, listening to the music.

"Good, no?"

I nod. "They sound . . ."

"Like they come from the Deep South?"

I'm taken aback. "Of India?"

He laughs. "No. America. Bluegrass."

Ah, right. "How's work?" I ask.

He's a documentary filmmaker, perched between aspiring and established, and even I can appreciate the precariousness of this. At the moment, he's helping out on a nature programme, he says, sponsored by the Arts and Culture Department. He's been filming in the Sung Valley, between the Khasi and Jaintia Hills, for a documentary.

"About?"

"Jah Khei."

"What's that?"

"You haven't heard of it? It's a flower that blooms only once in twelve years, which means, goddammit, we couldn't afford to miss it this time."

"And did you?"

"What?"

"Find it?"

"We did, yes. We looked for it for days, and then suddenly there it was, all over the hillsides." He gestures widely and smiles, and suddenly I would like to step up close and lean into him. I want to be held. He has always felt solid and strong and steady.

And right now, I am air.

"You?" he asks. "How are you, Shailin?"

I'd forgotten how it felt to hear him say my name.

"I'm good," I say, blinking.

"You came with Kima?"

I nod. "And you?" My voice catches in my throat. "You're here on your own?"

He shifts; I don't quite catch the look on his face. "Yes . . . my girlfriend couldn't make it this evening."

I swallow my beer, the cold, damp air, everything unsaid, and the music, unheard, spirals up into the night.

I'm poking around the kitchen later, trying to scramble together a late dinner, when Mei comes in and tells me she's had news about Oiñ. I'm feeling slow and sluggardly, but my heart lifts.

"She's here?"

"Not coming."

"To Shillong?"

"Where else?"

"I mean . . . but why?"

Mei shrugs. "No idea."

"But . . . her checkup?"

"I don't know . . . The line was so bad I could barely make out this much."

Something in my chest drops.

"Well," I say, "maybe she recovered, and didn't need to come anymore."

Mei is about to step out, but not before saying, "I hope so."

I stop buttering my toast. "What do you mean?"

"Just that . . . I hope you're right."

It's a long, out-of-time night. I lie in bed, looking at a square bit of inky sky from my window. I'd wanted to see Oiñ; her coming had given my being here a gentle sense of purpose, and even lent my journey home, I thought, a grander design.

I doze. I wake. I sip some water.

I'm a white dwarf, I tell myself. A dead star. Exhausted of everything life-giving, heavy not just with the weight of the past, but also the sense that nothing lies beyond, no further evolution. I'm lost and hollow. What to stand in the sun for now? Nothing, I tell myself gloomily. Even Oiñ won't be coming. Nothing, then, to relive or look forward to.

I don't know how the hours slip past, how light is restored to the sky, blazing briefly at the edge of night, and then lifting into morning. Suddenly, birdsong. And the crowing of roosters.

I might as well get up.

I do not move.

Eventually, though, a shower—a long, hard scrub of soap and loofah, and water slapping against my skin. I feel more alive, more decisive. I find my mother; she's in the TV room, reading the papers.

"We should make sure, don't you think?"

"What?" She peers at me above her spectacles.

"Oiñ. You said earlier that you hoped she's all right. We should make sure . . ."

She sighs. "I tried calling yesterday . . . all day. It's impossible to get through."

"Then maybe we should visit her."

"I can't travel," she says, shaking her head, "not with my blood pressure fluctuating like this. And your father, he'll be camped you-know-where for days on end . . ."

"Then I'll go," I say.

Mei stays quiet.

"I'll go to see her," I repeat.

"How? Not on your own."

"Why not?"

She narrows her eyes. "Do you even know where she lives?" This is met with silence, so she continues. "Mawmalang is at least a day's journey from here . . . and there might not even be any proper roads."

But by now I'm determined. I fish out my phone and open up Google Maps. There, I see it, at the edge of Meghalaya. Where my parents and I have never been. Not even close. Even on the map, the space around the name looks empty—and to the south, only the fat meandering blue of a river that flows into Bangladesh. From here, by road, six hours. I could take the bus. Yes, I say, that's what I'll do. I'll go see her, and, if it's okay with them, I'll stay a night or two.

"When will you leave?" my mother's face is drawn tight.

"As soon as I can."

I can see this doesn't please her. It means I'm not heading back to Delhi just yet. I brace myself for a flood of questions, for reproval, but they don't come. Instead, she says quietly, "All right."

✧ ✧ ✧

Even at six in the morning, Shillong's MTC bus stand is all hawkers and hollers, callouts and conductors. The vehicles rattle and roar in front of a sooty grey building just off Khyndai Lad, a junction where nine roads meet—some call it the heart of town—and in the air hangs an unholy blend of smoke, exhaust fumes, urine. Kima, who offered to drop me off, stands over my seat, grinning. "Bougie urbanite makes trip into rural Meghalaya, also known to her as the great big unknown." I tell him to fuck off before his sorry arse ends up with me in the South West Khasi Hills. Where, incidentally, I point out, he, too, has never set foot. "True," he admits, "but remember, I have a working-class soul." I ignore him and try to push my rucksack under the seat in front of me; it won't fit, so I resign myself to using it as a tall footrest.

"You'll be okay, no?" Kima asks before he steps off.

"Yes," I say. *I hope.*

When we shudder to a start and move off, I do wish he—someone—was coming along. Kima is annoyingly right: I've rarely stepped out of Shillong to travel anywhere around here on my own or with my parents. Hard to believe, I know. We weren't the kind to go on many family holidays—my father hated to leave the garden, my mother the house, so we've travelled little together, in the state and outside. Me on a bus now is some kind of rupture, and Mei senses it and is unsettled, and admittedly, so am I. But I'm trying to set that aside as I'm taken away from all that's familiar. What's more important, I tell myself, is I'm going to see Oiñ, and I'm hoping she's well, and alive.

This early in the day we leave the city easily behind us, climbing to Upper Shillong, past the Air Force grounds, and turning to take the Mawkyrwat road, which leads us to open countryside and a smattering of small towns. Soon, some traffic, shop shutters lifting, and kids in uniform walking to school. In the bus, along with me, a father and his two boys, a group of women wrapped in shawls, an elderly couple sitting side by side. I wonder if any of them are heading to Mawmalang. Highly unlikely, I soon realize; the road is long, littered with many stops, and the bus rapidly fills and empties. With morning well upon us, we wheeze into Mawkyrwat—here almost everyone disembarks, except for the father and his sons, and plenty more get on.

I step out to stretch my legs, feeling somewhat anomalous in my squeaky clean Keds and light denims. No one is unfriendly, though I do get a few curious looks, and when I ask in Khasi for tea and jingbam, this is met with surprise from the lady in the stall.

"Phi dei Khasi?" she asks.

"Hooid," I say. "Yes, I'm Khasi."

The road, though already potholed, starts deteriorating rapidly beyond Mawkyrwat.

Despite the bumps, in front of me the two boys have fallen asleep—one on the seat, the other on his father's lap. The father chats with a man in a cap across the aisle. They're discussing plans for a main road, joining Shillong and Nongstoiñ with the far reaches of the South West Khasi Hills.

"It can mean only one thing, ymdei?"

The man in the cap is noncommittal. "Perhaps."

The father continues, "Yes, it's hard to know about these things."

I wonder what they mean, but they fall silent, so I stare out the window. We're high up, looking over an unfolding valley with forested slopes, silvered through by a faraway winding river. We could be at the very end of the world, except I can see clusters of houses, small villages, for whom this is all life, the centre of everything. I'm troubled, though, by a persistent question: *Phi dei Khasi?* I have never really known what this means . . . Is it to speak a certain language? To be born in a certain place? To live somewhere many years? Many of these markers have shifted constantly for me. Not for someone like Dajied. Or even Kima, who's from Mizoram but has made Shillong his home. Have you thought about leaving? I've asked him. Plenty of times, he's said. "But I can't leave my mother . . . and honestly, I don't really want to be anywhere else." How unfamiliar, this kind of certainty! About place, and people, and belonging. Isn't life so much messier and more complicated than that? Who knows . . . Right now, I tell myself, I'll just enjoy the view.

As we near the Domiasiat area, the tar road ceases to exist. In fact, it's more a riverbed, all boulders and deep pits, and our bus is the lone vehicle rafting on these rapids of mud and stone. I am captivated, though, by what lies beyond on either side—wide, wide country, with black knobbly boulders jutting out like knuckles from the earth. Where had I read this? That everything you see for the first time you see for the last time, because either the view changes, or you do. During the rains, I imagine these green peaks lost in lyoh khyndew, low-lying "mud" clouds, but now there is bright clarity to the landscape, the grass cleanly yellow, the hills outlined sharply against the winter sky. What's odd is that we pass row upon row of compact housing structures lying abandoned and empty—a camp without inmates. What were they meant for? Rather, whom? The buildings rise like ghostly spectres against the scrubby landscape.

Soon we will be upon the river, I hear. Ranikor. The two gentlemen talk of how they've fished there often in the past, usually with the roots of kharu—I've learned from Papa that this is a sedative plant—for carp, silver and common, and for something rarer called the golden mahseer. Not so many to be found now, they declare. "And have you seen," asks the man with a cap, "Ranikor's waters have turned green?" But the father is distracted, his young sons have woken up and demand his attention. He distributes Parle-G biscuits and water, and the tenderness of his gestures leaves me moved.

The journey begins to seem endless. Copses, hills, goats and cattle, laundry fluttering in the breeze, stubbly harvested paddy fields. Where am I? There is nothing here to orient me—despite the unvarying landscape, all is new and unfamiliar. We pass village after village with unknown names, Diwain, Sohsyniang, Myriem, Dennar, Nongdiloin. How much longer? I cannot tell. My phone lost reception several centuries ago. And by now my legs, my back, are beginning to cramp and ache. Finally, though, we arrive at Wahkaji. A dusty, tin-shack settlement with a desolate frontier air about it. This is where we're asked to disembark–I'm informed the bus will go no farther.

"Balei?" I ask. Why?

The driver shrugs. "You see for yourself," he says, "if there's any road."

"But I need to reach Mawmalang," I insist, panic rising in my chest.

"You'll have to walk," says someone behind me. It's the man with the cap. He speaks softly, a cloth bag dangles from his right shoulder.

"How far it is?" I ask. "How long will it take me?"

"More than a few miles," he says. "And it will take you as long as you choose to walk–slowly or fast."

That's wonderfully unhelpful, but I hold my tongue and say only that I wonder if the way is easy enough to find and follow. For a moment he is silent, as though sizing up my capacity to survive on my own. I'm certain to disappoint.

"You're travelling alone?"

I hesitate, though I have no choice but to admit that I am.

He stands undecided. Finally, he beckons, "Come. I'm going there myself," and I, rucksack strapped to my back, scurry after him.

"Phi kyrteng aiu, Bah?" I ask.

His name he says is Karmel, Bah Karmel. He doesn't ask for mine.

For a while, we walk along a mud track. I stumble on the loose stones, but he doesn't slow down. My Keds aren't shiny and clean anymore. We pass a few people–a woman with a khoh strapped to her back, leaning forward against the weight, while two kids prance around her. We tramp past another seemingly abandoned construction, smaller this time, with fewer buildings.

"What is this?" I ask.

"The primary health care centre . . . built by UCIL."

I nod, pretending to be familiar with the abbreviation.

"Is it operational?"

He makes no reply but gives me a look: *What do you think?*

Soon the mud track ends and we are at the edge of a sloping forest.

"Nangne," he says.

"What?" I exclaim, suddenly realizing he means "this way." The bus driver hadn't been fibbing; there are no roads to Mawmalang.

I must stand there looking particularly pathetic, for the gentleman says it's all right, it's not too far. In my head, only one question rings out: *Is it safe?* But I have no choice, I must keep the faith and follow. He's wearing open slippers, but the undergrowth doesn't seem to bother him, even though I'm whipped and snagged by brambles and slip repeatedly on the mossy stones.

We tramp through in silence, until he asks, "Why have you come all this way?"

"To see Kong Stian Kharwar," I reply. "She lives in Mawmalang."

"I know her."

I'm surprised, though I shouldn't be. If everyone knows one another in Shillong, surely, more so here. "She was my nanny," I explain, "for many years, and I heard she might not be well." I hesitate before continuing, "Would you know how she is? We can't get through on the phone . . ."

He shakes his head, saying he's sorry to hear that, but he's been away a few months now, and he's had no news from Mawmalang.

My heart sinks. Soon, I suppose, I'll find out.

We come to a stream trickling through the undergrowth, and I stop and bend low, thinking I'll cleanse my hands and face; it will be refreshing.

"I wouldn't do that if I were you," he says quickly.

"Oh, why?"

He gives me a strange look and walks on. I follow hurriedly, wondering if I have offended him in some way. Intermittently, we pass big cement tanks—water reserves?—almost at ground level, and I also notice manhole covers littering the forest floor. Animal traps, perhaps, or some kind of hefty storage space.

The late afternoon is beginning to wane around us. I want to ask how much longer, but this might seem like a complaint. The rucksack straps dig into my shoulders, my shoes are beginning to bite, and my jeans are uncomfortably thick and stiff for this trek. And maybe because I'm tired, I'm soothed little by the jungle around me—the palm leaves and torrents of poinsettias serve only to obscure the way, the sounds of frogs and crickets are reminders that evening is approaching.

Soon, though, the forest thins and we step onto a road of mud and stone. To our right, the view begins to open—a grassy meadow, and beyond that, more hills. In the distance stands a cluster of houses made of tin and wood; variations on the hut I saw in Bah Kyn's beloved Ever-Living Museum. It is somewhat unreal. Then a wandering stream, a stone bridge. Ridiculously idyllic.

Bah Karmel stops. "We're here. And Kong Stian's house is that way"—he points to the right. I turn to him to say thank you, but he's already off, going around the other side of the village. Khublei, I call, and he waves his hand in brief acknowledgement. Strange man.

I hitch up my rucksack, heavy as lead now, and walk towards the houses.

✧ ✧ ✧

The road is empty. On a patch of grass on the side, someone has laid out clothes to dry. Then a neat stack of chopped wood. A basket of potatoes. I round a corner hoping to find someone I can ask for directions, but there's no one in sight. It's quiet, my footsteps crunch through the air. In the distance, I hear what, at first, I think is a bird call. Or perhaps a massive swarm of bees. But as I near the houses, it's unmistakable. It's the sound of weeping. A chorus of long grieving sobs. My heart is in my mouth. I stumble on something, stones, a clump of mud; I stand at the small window of the house from where the crying rises, and peer inside. I can see the backs of people, women, hunched over, wrapped in black shawls—but nothing more. I'm cold, my limbs frozen. I force myself to walk around to the front.

Suddenly, I know there's someone behind me, even though they haven't made a sound. When I turn, I see a girl, no more than ten, slight and skinny, holding a cat.

They carry the same look in their eyes—wide, wary, mistrustful.

"Kumno?" I greet feebly.

They both stare back.

"Mano ba lah khlad?" I ask. Who has died?

I hope she understands me; the Shillong Khasi I speak, and the dialect here might—will probably—vary. She stays mute. I stand there, unable to say anything, as though all my words have fallen away from me.

Then the creature and the girl turn, startled, hearing something I can't, and scamper off like wild creatures.

Meanwhile, the funeral procession has begun. They are moving outside now. I am a terrible intruder in this space and in their grief. I should wait elsewhere for this to finish, but I can't bring myself to until I know who has died.

The women in their black shawls move in cohesion; the coffin, a paltry thing, is heaved onto the backs of four men, and they begin their descent down to the road that, I assume, leads to the burial ground.

People have started noticing me now. There are stares and whispers. I should leave. Head back and wait by the edge of the forest. Just then, though, a hand clutches my arm. A woman, and I look into a face that could have been Oiñ's when she first came to us.

"Dei ma phi?" the woman says. "It's you, it's really you?" I have no idea who she means, but I nod. "I told Kong Thei you'd come," she whispers in delight.

"Who?" I ask.

"My sister. Come, I'll take you to Meirad."

I allow myself to be led; I figure it's easier than trying to ask her questions amid all this. She chatters away—and mostly, I follow her, though she uses certain unfamiliar words and turns of phrase. I think she's telling me about the mobile network in this part of the world. We don't walk too far, only across a road, a short slope, and then we stop before a house that stands slightly separate from the rest, and on higher ground. It's very dusty, the mud dry and loose. I make to take off my shoes at the door, but she stops me.

"Em phi," she says. "There's no need for that."

"Actually, there is, Mem," says a voice from inside.

A woman emerges from behind the front door, and I can tell they're sisters.

Next to me, Mem frowns.

"It's okay," I say, hastily slipping off my sneakers. I stand there in my socks, my back aching from the weight of the rucksack. "May I put this down?" I ask.

Mem rushes to help. Of course, of course. "Niiii map mo . . ." she apologizes.

"It's okay," I say, and slip it off gratefully, placing it on the steps.

The sister, who I assume is Kong Thei, watches. Her eyes sharp and narrow. Her hair tied neatly up into a bun, her jaiñkyrshah spotless. Her feet bare.

Come, I'm summoned by Mem, and I follow.

"Kumno?" I greet Kong Thei as I pass, but this elicits no more than a nod.

We walk into the front room, littered with mulas and one long seat with a worn cushion pushed up against the wall. Beyond that, the house is in shadow, some walls planked with wood, others papered with woven shylliah. The other rooms lead off from this one in the centre; we duck into a doorway on the left.

There, by the window, is Oiñ.

Before I can call out to her, Mem says, "Peit, Meirad, lah wan mano."

Oiñ turns away from the window towards us. She's so frail, my heart aches.

"I expected you earlier," she says.

At once, I begin to apologize, saying I had to walk from Wahkaji, that there was no road, no bus . . .

"I meant at least five years earlier."

This silences me. But when I look at her, she's smiling, and suddenly looking more like her old self again. She gestures for me to come closer, and I do, giving her a hug—in my arms she's a bird. I sit close, at the edge of the bed. She looks across the room and asks Mem to bring us some tea.

The woman who'd led me here scurries out.

"That's my grand-niece," says Oiñ.

I say yes, I'd figured that out.

"She looks after me very well."

"I'm glad." The words catch in my throat, and not only because I'm speaking Khasi. I tell her how Mem found me at the funeral. Before I can stop myself, I'm saying, "I was so afraid it was . . ."

"Me?" There's that brusque wickedness in Oiñ's voice again. She chuckles. "I'm not going anywhere. Though at the rate people die here, who knows?"

"How did Mem know it was me?" I ask.

"She's seen your pictures, of course."

"My pictures?"

"Silly child," she chides me. She digs into the space behind her pillow and draws out a book—no, a photo album, one of those old plastic ones I haven't seen in years. I flip through it. It's all me. I'm so touched I want to hurl it out the window.

"There's your pretty face," says Oiñ, stabbing a knobbly finger at a photograph. I couldn't be more than two, in pigtails, and I'm scowling into the camera. Then me and some puppy I'm about to, it looks like, strangle. Me and Oiñ on a sunny grassy patch in the garden—you can barely see my face, I'm wearing such a large floppy hat, but Oiñ is smiling and she's so young I can hardly recognize her.

"I don't still look like this, Oiñ," I protest.

"Oho, here." She flips the album to the end, and there's me and her from just before she left us. I'm wearing a sparkly hairband, a purple T-shirt and jeans, and I have my arm around her as though I will never let her go.

Just then, a young girl enters, carrying a tray of tea things, and behind her, Mem. "This is my elder daughter," she says. Banri, who smiles at me shyly.

"Mem has two more little ones, twins," adds Oiñ, "but they're with their father."

Banri has brought a cup over for me, and a plate heaped with 'pu-syep. It's delicious, freshly steamed, and the ground red rice is delicately sweet. In my hunger, I finish three slices—and only notice afterwards how everyone else has shared or not eaten any at all. I must be more careful.

"Where's Thei?" asks Oiñ.

Banri and her mother share a quick glance. "Ngim tip," they both say in unison.

"She should be here . . . has she said hello?"

"I met her," I add, "when I came in."

"Yes, but did she give you a welcome?"

"No one has to," I say quickly. "Except if Mei visits. She'd expect a grand parade."

Oiñ chortles. "How is that old thing?" Mei wouldn't be pleased.

"She sends her love," I say.

"She let you come like this, on your own?"

I nod.

Oiñ looks pleased. "Finally, she's accepted that you've grown up."

"When do we ever accept our children have grown up?" chirps Mem.

Oiñ frowns. "I did. My kids learned very early on that I wouldn't always be there to spoon-feed them and change their dirty nappies."

"Because you," I plant a kiss on her head, "are wisest."

She scoffs but looks terrifically pleased.

An hour later, Oiñ is dozing, and I'm also ready to sleep, anywhere, on any surface, cushioned or not. It's late evening, and all this while, we've been talking—they wanted news, about me, my parents, about Delhi and Shillong, and now they wish to know how I found my way to the village through the forest. I tell them about Bah Karmel.

"Really? Bah Karmel Lyngdoh?" Mem sounds surprised. "He brought you?"

"Yes, he did, why?"

She hesitates. "Just that he was away for a few months. We weren't sure when he was returning, or whether he'd be coming back at all."

I am happy to bring out the presents—though for Oiñ these are largely practical—jars of Horlicks, liver tonic, strips of multivitamins.

"Where's my pork chow from Wok?" she demands in jest, noodles from a Chinese restaurant in Shillong, her favourite.

For the others, socks and mufflers, old sweaters, chocolates for the kids.

And then, just like that, my fate is decided. I'd stay not just one night, but a few days—a week, they insist. "You are most welcome to," says Mem when she senses my hesitation. "Silly child," adds Oiñ, "you can't leave now."

Banri will vacate her small room for me, and though I protest, saying I wish to inconvenience no one, it is settled. They will not hear of anything else. You are our guest, they say, and that is it.

Later, when I'm lying on the bedding on the floor, thinking I ought to let Mei know I've arrived safely, I fall almost instantly asleep.

During the night, I wake only once to the murmur of voices, the sisters talking, one voice slightly raised—*How can she just show up like this? Who does she think she is? How long will she stay?*—and the other intoning soothingly, *Ym lei lei. Let it be. She's come a long way. It will be all right.*

✧ ✧ ✧

When I awaken, I'm in a cave.

A sightless underland, ancient and quiet, untouched by sun or sky.

I sit up, and stay still. The room is in an awkward corner of the house, so there are no windows except for a slit near the ceiling letting in pale milky light. Slowly, I pick things out around me—schoolbooks in a pile, a small tin trunk, probably holding clothes, a pair of black bow shoes in the corner. Banri's small belongings. One of the things Mei had asked me before I left was *how will you manage*—and all I feel as I sit here is *this is more than enough.*

The toilet is around the back of the house, a compact double-doored structure, with a bathing area on one side, complete with bucket and stool, and a squatting loo on the other. The loo is scrupulously clean, and I take care to splash into all corners when I'm done. There's no water coming through the tap, though, and I don't quite know how to refill the bucket. I stand on the step outside, helpless, and thankfully Banri comes along—"I'll do it," she says, and I refuse so vehemently that eventually she tells me there's a large tank nearby from where to draw water. Whoever uses the loo, she explains, fills the bucket for the next person. I can do that, I think, and resolve not to forget.

At our midday meal, I meet the household. The twins, three-year-old toddlers with snotty noses and small, pointy faces like pixies, hiding behind their father, Bah Kitdor, a shy, soft-spoken man who looks like he'd like to hide behind something himself. He can barely meet my eye.

"Nga trei kam dieng," he tells me when I ask him what he does. He's a carpenter.

"What are you making these days?" I ask, hoping this will set him a little at ease.

"Ki jingsiang ja," he says, ladles, and points to the one that's serving us each a mound of rice. For some reason I am delighted by this; that it was carved by him. I hold it in my hand, light and curved and smooth, and remark on the neatness of the work.

"Khublei," he says, looking pleased.

Oiñ, I've been informed, is feeling brighter today. She ate an egg with her morning tea. "It's because you've come," says Mem. "She's so happy."

"And we've started her on new medication," adds Kong Thei.

I clear my throat.

The syrwa, a stew of mustard leaves and bits of fish, is light and flavourful, but the pudina chutney trails fire in my mouth.

"What exactly is ailing her?"

"Old age," says Mem.

"We don't know," says her sister at the same time.

"Has she not been diagnosed?" I ask, and then catch the look on Kong Thei's face. Maybe she's right. I wasn't around all this while, and now I show up out of nowhere and ask intrusive questions.

Mem says no, and this is why they'd tried to convince Oiñ to get a checkup done in Shillong; she agreed, reluctantly, at first, and then later she flat-out refused.

"Is there anything else we can do?" I add quickly.

The sisters glance at each other; the twins are chirping at the door, wishing to be let out, and Bah Kit excuses himself and obliges. At the other end of the table, Banri is quietly clearing up their plates.

The nearest health clinic used to be in Wahkaji, I'm told, the place where the bus route ended.

"I passed it," I say. "It looked abandoned."

"It is now," says Mem. "Not too long ago, a doctor used to visit once in a while. Still," she adds, "Kong Thei managed to meet a doctor last week, ymdei?"

Her sister nods.

"Where did you go?" I ask.

"Mawkyrwat."

"But that's so far," I blurt out, and am almost about to add, *and the road is terrible*, but I stop. In Kong Thei's eyes, I see a flash of something—anger, I think, that says, well, we have very little choice.

At the end of lunch, there's a loud banging. It's coming from Oiñ's room, and we all rush over.

She's sitting up in bed, walking stick in hand, and she's thumping it on the floor. "Well, that got your attention."

"What do you need, Meirad?" asks Kong Thei.

"Company."

"Your daughter's here," says Mem, nudging me forward, and I scurry over and sit on a mula by the bed. First, I'm asked a string of questions—Did I sleep all right? Have I called my mother? Did I eat? Am I comfortable? "I know this is not the comfort you're used to . . ." she begins to say.

"I'm fine," I insist. "I'm very comfortable."

"Don't lie."

I laugh. "But I *am*!"

She eyes me suspiciously. "If you say so . . . I've asked Thei to kill one of our chickens, we'll make your favourite." This I won't refuse—I loved Oiñ's chicken curry, whenever she cooked it in our house.

Then she lies back, tired from the effort of sitting up and talking. I begin to fuss. Would she like some water? Something to eat? Would she like to rest?

"No, I'm fine . . . apart from my legs. They just don't listen to me anymore. Slowly, slowly, they went."

"They're here, Oiñ," I say, pressing them from over the blanket.

She sighs. "Here, but not here."

It was so gradual a deterioration, she hardly noticed it at first. "Old age," she spits. "I wasn't old until I got here. I'm luckier than that Kong Tharina, though. She went much faster, and with a lot more pain."

"What happened to her?"

She shrugs. "Lah kem ksuid." Caught by a spirit, but I think it means epilepsy. "Her son also died, you know," she continues, "a few years ago. Only forty-five, and suddenly, from nowhere, throat cancer."

I try to say something commiserative, that life is so unpredictable, and she snorts in contempt. "You ask them," she says, "if it's so simple."

"Who?"

"The people in the village." She closes her eyes. Her hair, silver as the moon, frames her face in wisps.

"Shall I leave you to rest?" I ask again.

"No. When I'm in my grave, that's all I'll be doing. Now tell me what you have been up to all these years . . ."

And so I do. I tell her that after I finished university, I interned with my aunt one summer, ended up working there several years, and since then I've been doing a few things. A city magazine, a lifestyle magazine, a publishing house.

"Hmm . . ." says Oiñ. "Phi biang em?"

I hesitate. She's asked not if I'm happy, or if everything is all right, but whether I am enough. And this is difficult to answer.

"Of course," I say.

"You don't want to get married?"

"Batno?" I ask in return. "Who should I marry?"

She grunts. "Why you asking me?" Then she takes my hand. "You go to church?"

"No."

"You should."

We glance at each other and guffaw. She, who never attended mass all her life.

Then I tell her about other things. The flat I share with Grace, the colony park, the evening walks, the scorching Delhi summer, the rains that are brief and fleeting and so unlike here. How Grace loves baking, and we subsist mostly on cake . . . At some point, I don't know if Oiñ is listening anymore, I think she is asleep, but I keep speaking, on and on, into the quiet afternoon air.

✧ ✧ ✧

In the week I'm here, my fitting in is clumsy.

As though I'm suffering from some strange sort of jet lag. I'm out of time, fumbling around, unused to the rhythms of the household, which rises early, when the light is barely breaking over the hills, and sleeps not long after sunset. I scramble to bathe and brush and clean, trying not to be late for meals—lunch, for instance, is eaten here at eleven. Dinner at half-past five.

Then, whenever I stand at the kitchen door, asking, "How can I help?" Kong Thei ignores me, and her sister sings out, "Nothing, nothing," from the corner where she's cooking, and I'm left at a loose end. I sit with Oiñ, and we chat, but I notice she tires easily, so I keep my visits to her room frequent but short.

There isn't much else to do. I'm hesitant to walk around the village, awkward as I feel about the way I look, the way I dress, my halting Khasi. But it's hard to keep the village out. People drop in, to chat, to borrow potatoes, children to play with the twins in the front yard, tumbling in and out of the house, and people are curious to see me. I'm shown off by Mem in the front room. "Isn't she something? She came to visit us all the way from the city," she'll say, while I stand there embarrassed by the attention. Small generous gifts are pressed into my palms—plump oranges, a bunch of radishes, rice cakes sweetened with jaggery. Everyone's faces and names are a blur; I catch them for a moment, thinking I'll have little opportunity to get to know them all. And though I tell myself I ought not to generalize like this, I'm struck by their gentleness and their generosity, the sing-song cadences of their speech, so new to my ear.

When evening comes, everywhere the smell of wood fires rises, and while I imagine there are rooms behind some doors here that hold unhappiness, it feels pervasively peaceful.

When I do venture out for a stroll, I weave through uneven mud paths, sleeping dogs, grazing goats, and chillies laid out to dry. It doesn't take me long to make my way across the village; there aren't more than thirty houses, but I take my time, passing elderly men smoking pipes, shawls wrapped around their heads like turbans, and women winnowing rice, sweeping, splicing kwai. At the other end is Mawmalang's only shop.

The owner, Bah Albert, greets me warmly enough, though with a touch of wariness in his voice. He looks to be in his late forties, and he perches on his stool like a king surrounded by flour and spices, crates of fizzy drinks, and stacks of tobacco leaf.

The first thing he asks me is whether I'm a journalist.

"Me? No . . ." *Does this place make the news?*

"Hmmm . . ." He frowns. "They say a journalist is coming next week."

"Okay," I say. "Coming here to speak to you?"

"Yes, to the people."

"What about?"

He looks surprised. "The mining, of course."

Another customer approaches, so I buy sweets for the twins and a tube of Boroline for Oiñ, and leave. What did he mean? The coal mines aren't around here, of that I'm certain—they pockmark the Jaintia Hills at the eastern edge of the state. This region produces vast amounts of charcoal, but that isn't mined, it's made by burning trees. What then? Only now a glimmering remembrance comes back to me, from a while ago, of news, on the radio, in the local papers, caught in snippets when I was in and out of Shillong, of another kind of mining—for uranium.

Of course, I kick myself, I'm in uranium country.

It had died down by now, as far as I knew, the "uranium issue"—although my knowledge on the subject, I'm ashamed to say, is patchy at best. There had been a tussle for years, between the central government, I think, and NGOs and environmentalists in Meghalaya, as well as the people living here. To mine or not to mine. Curfews and bandhs were called, and protests were strong and furious. But who had won? I'm really not sure . . .

The only place to catch a phone signal, I learn, is at the top of a hillock behind Mem's house. If you're lucky.

Banri takes me there, after watching me desperately try to make a call.

"Come," she says, and I follow. She leads me outside, past the vegetable garden, the smelly pigsty, a cluster of chickens and their fluffy chicks, and through a small squeaky gate. Banri has a quiet, determined air that somehow reminds me of Grace. Her hair is always neatly tied, hanging down her back in a long braid, her dress faded but clean and darned.

"Are you on school holiday?" I ask.

"Yes," she replies.

"For how long?"

"Forever."

"You're done?" I'm surprised because she looks no older than fifteen.

She isn't. But she finished at the government secondary school in Wahkaji, and the higher secondary school at Nongstoiñ is too far. There are no schools in Mawmalang.

"Oh," I utter foolishly, but whatever I say would feel inadequate.

We've begun our ascent; a short, sharp climb, and we don't speak again until we reach the top.

"Oiñ insisted I finish, you know," she tells me shyly. "Even though it meant I had to stay with a relative in Wahkaji, and it was not very convenient. I think my aunt and Mei would've taken me out of school earlier otherwise."

"I'm glad," I say, but this, too, sounds feeble.

"See?" She gestures to my phone.

One bar. But it allows me to make contact with Mei, Kima, and to receive a text from Dajied—*Nice seeing you the other night.* It sounds like he wants to be friends, I suppose. Should I reply? Should I not? What do I say?

You too, I type, and hit send but the message delivery fails.

Mei isn't entirely pleased about my extended stay. Only when I tell her they said I've come all this way, how can you leave in a day, does she fall quiet. Papa has only just realized I'm gone. *You went where?*

Afterwards, I sit looking at the village below. It's tiny, smaller than a small neighbourhood block back in Delhi, lying low and close to the earth. As the sun sets, everything before me turns into white gold, the chirrup of the ñiang-kongwieng pierces the evening silence, louder than

I've ever heard elsewhere, birds settle to roost in the trees behind me. I'm struck by a rare sense of immensity.

When I tramp back down, through the small, squeaky gate, past the roosting chickens, the pigsty, and the watered vegetable garden, I find the family waiting for me to begin their evening meal, and I gratefully take my place at the table.

✧ ✧ ✧

The day before I leave, I want to bake a cake. Somehow, Grace has managed to text me the simplest recipe—PLAIN CAKE—with instructions for how this can be made in a pressure cooker. A pressure cooker has been duly procured from Bah Albert, and I'm at his shop buying ingredients. I'd like to replenish supplies for Mem, too—rice, oil, flour. I also overheard Kong Thei saying they were running low on soap, the lumpy brown stuff that brought back memories of my grandmother at the sink, washing dishes.

"Shini, moida, pylleng," lists Bah Albert. There's milk at home, and we will have to do without vanilla essence.

"Khublei mo," I say, handing him the money.

"Phin leit noh, ne?"

I tell him I'm leaving tomorrow. Bah Kit and Banri will accompany me through the forest to Wahkaji, from where I'll catch a bus back to Shillong. My mother is relieved, my father, too, though he's happier that they've finally managed to save the trees. The new wall, it has been mandated, will be slimmer. A victory for the Treeman of Shillong.

Bah Albert is interested in knowing where it is that I live in town.

"Near Laitumkhrah."

He nods. He also has been considering leaving the village and moving to Shillong. "Things were bad," he says, "now they're a bit better, but who knows when they'll be bad again. They always return, those diggers."

"Are they allowed to?" I ask.

Not anymore. "But who waits for permission?" Then he shrugs and adds, "Leit suk." Travel in peace.

All afternoon, I slave over the cake. I hardly ever bake, but this simply must be perfect. I want to offer some tangible proof of my gratitude—for Oiñ, for the others. I don't know why it must be cake, but I can think of nothing else. Interested parties drop in to check on the proceedings. It's not going well. I think the mixture is too runny. I can't even get in touch with Grace unless I run up the hillock and back, so I pour it into a pan, place it in the cooker, and seal it off with a prayer.

An hour later all is revealed, and it is a minor triumph.

When we gather for tea and cake in Oiñ's room, we do so with an air of festivity—she's sitting up and orchestrating the proceedings with a wave of her walking stick, the twins run around in squeaky excitement, Banri and her mother are smiling widely, Bah Kit looks the most comfortable I've seen him since I arrived, and even Kong Thei appears more relaxed, possibly because I'm leaving. The cake is a little chewy—Grace will tell me I overmixed the batter—but still surprisingly palatable, fragrant with bay leaf in lieu of vanilla essence. Everyone sits around Oiñ's bed, munching, and there's plenty to go around.

My heart is fit to burst.

Later, when the room has emptied, I sit by Oiñ. We don't speak much, except for her telling me she wishes I wasn't leaving. I'll come back, I promise, and I mean it, but she looks at me as though to say there will be no next time. I have no words. I hold her hand, gnarled and lined like the slim root of a tree. She closes her eyes, and I make my way to Banri's room, heart heavy, to pack, to sleep.

I'm awakened, like the first night, by the sound of women talking.

This time, though, there is little attempt to hush up and not disturb me. I'm groggy; is it time to leave? It feels deep and dark, not yet light. The voices are urgent, even fearful, and when I catch what they're saying, I, too, scramble off the bedding, up from the floor.

The sisters are hurrying in and out of the sickroom. Oiñ has suddenly taken poorly—maybe from all the excitement of the evening. She called for Kong Thei, saying she was feeling light-headed and having difficulty breathing. There's little we can do, apart from mixing a spoon of ORS in some warm water and getting her to sip it. We also heap blankets and pillows under her feet, so they're placed higher than her heart. Her old, strong heart that has held me all my life. For a stretch of time, Oiñ's breathing drops so low and light it's barely there. Kong Thei holds her hand out before her nose to check.

"It won't be long now, I think," she says.

I don't even realize I'm crying, tears streaming down my face of their own accord.

You cannot leave, I say silently, *you cannot leave. I just got here. Stay and I'll stay, stay and I'll stay.*

We wait a long time, watching her every breath, holding our own, waiting for her next one, and finally, after what seems like forever, the bad spell passes—her breath is ragged but slightly stronger, some warmth returns to her hands, her face. But not before pale silver light is spilling across the sky. We have been up all night. The sisters sit silent at the foot of the bed, and I to the side; we're a solemn biblical painting.

"I think she's resting now," ventures Kong Thei. Her voice is strained at the edges.

Her sister nods, tiredness pulling around her eyes, and then she looks at me.

"You will have to leave soon, Shai."

"No," I say. "If it's okay with you—both—I'd like to stay."

✧ ✧ ✧

Sometimes, on my fleeting visits to Shillong, I'd go for a walk, pass one of many churches, and despite telling myself, *Don't waste your time*, I'd enter.

Something there is about an empty church.

The hush. The light. The stoic saints. I'd feel seven again. At the pew with my grandparents. Singing the opening hymn, making the sign of the cross. Bowing, at the end, to everyone around me: *Peace be with you*. Perhaps this is what is meant by the comfort of ritual. The act of standing, sitting, and kneeling. Of always knowing what to do next or uttering the right response at the right time.

So unlike life.

Where we hurtle through our days, asking frequently, frantically, of ourselves and the universe: *Is this right?*

"How do we know, Grace?" I've often asked her.

And she'd shrug, and say exactly what I expected her to: "You can't for sure."

It's okay, I've begun to tell myself. If I can live with far greater ambiguities—Why did flowers emerge? How did life begin on earth?—I can take a leap and hope to land on some sort of ground that will hold me.

And so, since I've decided to be here, the first thing I do is begin waking up early.

Okay, earlier.

And wash. And breakfast on atta—thick, white parathas—and tea. And even though when I stand at the kitchen door asking how I can help, Kong Thei still ignores me, and her sister sings out, "Nothing, nothing," from the corner, I now head outside instead and help Banri in the kper, the vegetable garden.

The patch hugs one side of the house and extends all the way to the back, hemmed by an unruly bed of yams, with their large, umbrella leaves, and a row of fruit trees—mandarin and plum, myrtle berry and lime are pointed out to me. I hoped she'd be welcoming of my offer, and she is, except, I confess, I know nothing and have little idea where to begin.

Banri is gracious enough to say I'll learn. It's forty-eight hours before the full moon, she explains, a good time for sowing, so that is what we do. Now is the time to plant leafy vegetables, rows of mustard, tyrso, which will be cooked in warming stews through the winter, pungent and sharp on the tongue. It'll be easy, I assume—and I begin my sowing, scattering the seeds in neat lines in the soil until Banri stops me. "You have to dig a little deep, deep, and space out the seeds so they don't crowd each other. Now, cover them with just enough soil so water doesn't run it all off and expose them to the sky, or then they will die." She shows me, and I learn slowly, and through the mornings we bend and dig and sow and press the mud. We harvest phan Garo, spindly and red, and fat, fat radishes and winter potatoes.

I smell of earth and earthworm, and my nails are rimmed dirt black. Everything begins to ache: my thighs, my arms, and muscles in my bum I never knew I possessed. By eleven I am starving.

After lunch, I climb the hillock.

Up there, I'm mostly alone, though sometimes the girl I saw on my first day here scurries through the bushes with her cat. They don't approach, though I often see them staring from a distance. Here, I try reconnecting to a world that, after a few days, seems fast receding—my decision to stay weighs less heavy on me than it does on my mother.

When I tell her my plans have changed, I detect in her voice for the first time a trace of panic. She switches tactics. She is soft and soothing. *Of course* she understands, and how relieved she is to hear Oiñ had pulled through. It will be good to stay with her for a few days, a week at the most? We'll see, I say, and hang up, and realize that my hands are shaking. Grace, too, has asked when I'll be back, and I say not this month; Kima is puzzled, wondering if I'm doing a domestic version of a firangi finding herself. My father is unperturbed, and strangely, we have more than usual to talk about. You must unearth the seedlings and replant them, he urges about the mustard, pull them apart into clumps, and sow them a few inches away from each other. This is what replanting does—allows them to grow faster, healthier, to yield more leaves.

Then, it's time to head back down—for quick tea and more atta, which must sustain us through the afternoon, and then I help feed the livestock, scatter grain for the chickens, and empty the vegetable peels and rice water into basins for the pigs. Banri and I then water the kper—I have bought a new can from Bah Albert's shop and gifted it to her, and I walk around with the old one that drips diligently all over my feet. When I ask for another at the shop, he says they're out of stock, but perhaps I could check in a few weeks. Nothing here arrives fast.

Except day's end.

Even on winter afternoons, the mist rolls in, low and stealthy, enfolding the world in white. The sun is suddenly gone, the air turns sharply cold—dait thah, ice that bites.

We eat our evening meal early, and it is simple. Rice, red and heavy, dal and vegetables, both bright turmeric yellow, sometimes a boiled egg, rarely a piece of fish each, fried to a crisp in mustard oil, salt, and chilli. Then I sit with Oiñ.

She has recovered, but only to a shadow of herself.

She has some good days, when she's wicked and funny and bosses people around, and some that are not. Then she seems to slump into the past. Did I know she had a missing son? "No," I say gently. He left home, she tells me, when he was old enough to, and never kept in touch. Did I know, for quite a few years, she lived in Assam? "No," I say, "how come?" "I looked after the children of tea planters." And she talks about them—Sonny and Pinkie. And I listen with jealousy. Wasn't I the first and last? I want to ask. But obviously not. And this comes as a shock. That I wasn't the only one she loved.

Some days are the worst of all—the walking stick lies unthumped, she doesn't sit upright, and she sleeps for longer. When she's awake and I'm with her, I usually do most of the talking. I tell her about the tyrso seedlings and how they're just beginning to show through the soil, and how Banri couldn't stop laughing when she saw me with my nose to the ground, peering at them in joy. Tomorrow, I tell Oiñ, we are planting peas, and when you are well, we will eat them straight from the pod, like we used to when I was little, and we roamed my grandmother's garden and stole them fresh off their stalks.

What also arrives fast here is strange deaths.

I sit with Oiñ while the rest of the household attends the funeral of a Bah Borlin, who'd suffered a muscular disease that went undiagnosed. Even when they took him all the way to Shillong. And another soon after, a baby who was stillborn. This, it seems, happens frequently. There's talk of ksuid lum, ksuid wah, and ksuid suiñ, malicious spirits of the hills and water and air, but Oiñ says it's been like this ever since those people came, almost twenty years ago . . .

"The ones who dig?" I ask cautiously.

Oiñ nods, then turns, closing her eyes, and so for a few moments, I watch to make sure that she's breathing.

Most disconcerted by my staying are the sisters. The twins are happy enough to have me around—I play catch with them in the afternoon, running about outside. Sometimes I pretend to fall, and moan and groan, and this sets them off into hysterics. Bah Kit has come around to being comfortable enough to say hello without looking like he'd prefer to vanish. Mem, though, has scolded me because she says she doesn't expect me to work. You're our guest, she protests, and I tell her she can't call me Oiñ's daughter and not consider me part of the family. This seems to mollify her, but not Kong Thei, who, I think, would prefer me out of the way, out of the house, and ideally out of the village. She says nothing about my being here, but I sense she is less than pleased. I get a nod from her every now and then, not much else. I try to not let this unsettle me, silently resolving to earn my place in the household for however long.

But it isn't easy. I keep messing up.

I leave the chicken coop door open one evening after their feed, and a fox or a cat carries off one of our fattest birds. This is a terrible loss. I also overwater a patch of radishes, and root rot sets in and they all wither. Worse, I forget to fill the loo bucket once or twice, or maybe even three times, and it always so happens that Kong Thei uses it right after. Banri has to run and fill another bucket and pass it to her behind the door. I apologize, of course, but the older sister meets my words coldly, unforgivingly.

I'm still not considered capable enough to be given any work inside the house, the kitchen, to cook—about which I'm quite relieved. I offer to clean, and once I'm allowed hesitantly by Mem to scrub the dishes and dry them in the sun, but I see them being washed again later by Kong Thei. "Didn't I do them properly?" I ask anxiously, and Mem tells me not to mind, that her sister just likes doing certain things herself.

I decide then to solely designate the outdoors as my responsibility, along with Banri, if she'll have me.

"If you help me with the kper, I'll have more free time."

"Yes," I say smiling. "And what will you do with it?"

"I will study," she says shyly.

Sometimes, in the evening, when Oiñ falls asleep earlier than usual, I sit on the front steps with Mem. We chat about this and that—her worry about having to send the twins away to school in Wahkaji. Banri, she's also a little concerned about, she's too quiet, that girl. "I'm glad she talks to you," and she gives my arm a squeeze.

"Did Kong Thei never marry?" I ask when we're comfortable enough in our acquaintance.

"My sister . . ." she begins and pauses, "hasn't had the easiest time. Our parents died when we were very young, and she looked after me, and our two brothers . . . both dead now. And even when she fell in love and was meant to be married to this man . . . he left her."

I mumble, "I'm sorry to hear that."

"She's very protective of us," adds Mem. "Of me."

This much I know. She doesn't say any more; this story makes me a little sad.

Sometimes I sit on the steps alone, with the household behind me resting in early slumber. Often the chatter at dinner is playful, the twins entertaining us with little songs, Bah Kit telling us funny stories. Sometimes we turn to uranium talk—who knows if the mines are closed, they reply to my query, who knows when the diggers will return, or if they have already.

"Our fight," says Bah Kit quietly, "has been long. We are tired."

I sit under a clear sky, thinking how six and a half billion years ago, supernovae out there sent it into space—the uranium found beneath this ground, present from the very early formation of the planet. Then I'm ashamed that I've known this and not the story of this land's resistance.

I learn about it by talking to Bah Albert, and Bah Syiem, the village headman, a stocky farmer with wise eyes and a woolen hat drawn over his head. Such a long history. Explorations began here all the way back in the 1950s, and uranium was discovered in 1984. For years, they dug into these hills, taking samples, making minute calculations.

"Did you know," I ask, "what they were looking for?"

They shake their heads. No, and even now we have no name for it save the one they gave us: *yellowcake*. Why would we name what we didn't need? To the people from the government, though, it mattered. So much so that they returned, with bigger smiles and bigger promises. "In the interest of the nation. Always they say that."

It is late afternoon, the light is softening, and a white mist rises from the slopes.

They look around, saying, "Our nation is this—the hills we see around us, the rivers we know as well as our loved ones, the trees we call by name. And what happens if it's in the interest of the nation—but not in ours?"

To this, there is no answer.

I listen as they recount how, for years, this land was mined, with machines like monsters opening up the earth, bringing to the surface what ought not to touch air.

We put up with them for a while, they say. With their boozing and teasing and loud outsider ways.

"Then we noticed our birds were dying. Our cows and dogs going mad, our bay trees wilting, our fishes floating. Then our people started bleeding."

Still, it took time for the resistance to grow. Simply because there was confusion. No harm would come if the mining was done in a safe way, they were assured. "And so . . . why not? Us, poor and forgotten—left to languish. Perhaps all the terrible things that had happened, all the disease and the dying, was the work of evil spirits. The digging would bring us hope, and wealth, and light."

Now it's evening; the crickets have set up their chorus, the tap-tap-tap of the 'niang kynjah, the endless rise and fall of the ñiang-kongwieng.

"What made you change your mind?" I ask.

They say something I do not expect. A documentary.

Buddha Weeps in Jadugoda. Dubbed into Khasi. About a place they'd never heard of, but whose people, too, lived in a land of forests, and played music like them.

We learned that they thought the uranium in their land a curse. That radioactive waste is hard to contain. It runs like water, sits like stone, and rises in the air as dust. And even if it's "safely" stored, in our hills the rain can break through rock, the winds rattle our sturdiest pines, and earthquakes carve the ground into canyons. We learned that this thing kills slowly.

All people here, a woman said in the documentary, die young.

So a few years ago, we gathered like a storm in summer, they tell me, led in our march by Kong Spelity, a woman of rare and ferocious fire—vowing to protect our land.

You know, they whisper, it's difficult to trust even the people from Shillong, the big city, those businessmen and politicians with big cars and big houses. Who tell us, *Maybe we can dig for yellowcake ourselves?* We find we must protect our land not just from the centre—but even from our own people.

Still—they shrug—permissions were finally revoked for exploration, for surveying, and though they left, we suspect they return in secret.

"Like rodents," spits Bah Albert, "digging in the dirt."

Only once, recently, did they take matters into their own hands.

I wait, and hold my breath.

They were collecting soil—a scientist and three officials—and we found them, and we waved our khukris and raised our voices and pummelled them until they fled.

Leave it in the ground, we said. Leave it in the ground.

The other person with whom I enjoy having long conversations in the village is Bah Kit, who I discover, once he opens up, is quite the historian.

It began one day when I asked if I could drop by his workshop—a small shack some way down the road from the house—and he looked tremendously pleased and nervous. "Maybe you can make something for me," I said, and he almost choked on his tea.

What could I possibly need?

"Many things," I told him, "I'm sure."

It becomes a ritual—after lunch, Banri accompanies me, and we sit outside the workshop in the afternoon sun, eating oranges, the smell of wood shavings in the air. He's been making more ladles—they're in great demand, apparently—and also some simple stools and tables. It is calming, to sit and watch him work, and as he shapes, saws, and carves the wood under his hands, he answers questions, he talks.

He tells me when the villages in these areas were founded—some ancient, their origins lost in the distant past, some as recent as the 1960s. That he grew up in a village not far from here, but met Mem at a wedding, and had to move, as was the custom, to his wife's home. "I come from Jakrem," he tells me, "the village with the hot sulphur springs." The waters so warm and mineral-rich they could cure almost anything—at least that's what they believed, that it came from deep underground and carried with it all the powers of the earth.

"It also made for the best rice beer," he chuckles.

He knows the landscape well, and speaks of natural sights I've never seen—and I'm ashamed to say, have never heard of. Synrangbah Cave, he says, with bats as big as eagles; the secret hollow behind Dongnob Falls, where in winter, the sun turns the stone into gold; Tynrong Manbasa, the timekeeper's rock, which casts a shadow by which farmers know when to head home for the evening. And near his own village, Lum Symper, protected, it was believed, by a powerful mountain deity. He shudders. "My father told me he's seen what happens to people who trespass in the forests . . . their heads get twisted around." He mimics this with his own hands and we squeal.

Banri has also outgrown her shyness and asks many questions.

About my life in Shillong, in Delhi. She cannot believe most of the things I tell her about the city. That you place an order, for food, groceries, laundry services, and people show up at your door. Like magic, she declares. That a taxi can be called from your phone, that invisible money is transferred just like that to the driver.

It sounds—it is—a different world.

We have started also to go for extended walks around the village—up and down hilly tracks, through forests rich with mulch and mushrooms, to a waterfall or two, silvery and small in this dry season. I like exploring the area, mapping the place with my steps and breath. Banri also takes me to the sacred grove, the place that must remain untouched—with not a twig or leaf removed.

"What happens if you do? Bad things?"

She says she doesn't know anyone who's dared to disobey.

At the edge of the grove is the stream that later joins the Ranikor River, whose waters are so blue, she says, it looks like the sky has been inverted. "Though when I was small," she adds, "I remember people saying fish were found dead by the thousands. Belly up and floating."

She shows me the paths to Nongtynniaw, Domiasiat, and Mawthabah, nearby villages—"We can go there someday, if you like"—and farther away lie Nongjri and Nongkulang. "That's where babies are born like monsters," she says sadly.

"What do you mean?" I ask, startled.

"It's what I've heard."

I then ask her about a track that runs alongside the stream and disappears into the undergrowth. "Where does this go?" Her eyes widen, and she whispers something I don't catch.

"Where?" I ask.

"The abandoned village," she repeats.

"Abandoned by whom?"

"The Nongïaid."

"Who?"

"The ones who walk. Nomads." There's no word for nomads in Khasi, so she says "ki briew ki bym shong shi jaka." The people who do not stay in one place.

How mysterious. I'm intrigued.

"They all deserted it, that's what Papa told me," Banri continues. "And even the ones who stayed didn't survive."

"But why?" I ask. "Why did they leave?"

She shakes her head. "I don't think anyone knows . . ."

However much I try to convince her, though, she is unwilling to take me to this place. "People says its haunted. No birds sing there, and no animals will graze on the grass. And even on a hot summer's day"—she shudders—"it's cold."

"How far is it?"

"Far enough. And even if it wasn't"—she looks at me pointedly—"you shouldn't go there alone."

I try on a few more occasions to persuade her—we can visit in the morning, at the brightest hour of day, we'll take a quick look and turn back—and then I give up.

"Maybe we can go together with some other people," she finally offers.

And until this can somehow be arranged, I must be content with that.

✧ ✧ ✧

Today, Mawmalang has some visitors.

They arrive around lunchtime. A dozen young men, who move about freely, greeting people, and clustering at Bah Albert's shop for kwai and soft drinks. They seem well known to everyone in the village.

"Who are they?" I ask Banri.

We've snuck out to lorni, to nose about the proceedings.

"KSU," she whispers back.

"Oh, really?" Whatever I was expecting, it wasn't the Khasi Students' Union. In fact, all this while, I've associated the KSU with why Mei sent me away from home. However noble or justified their causes might have been, according to her, they were the ones fighting the state, creating trouble.

"People say they've done a lot of good here," Banri tells me. The uranium miners were driven away mainly because of them. They rallied people together, screened documentaries, held protest gatherings.

One of the young men, Shemphang, the leader, I assume, stands up to greet us and thank us all for gathering. He says they're here to update us on some recent developments.

A murmur rises from the crowd, like the low buzzing of bees.

"Several years ago, the central government claimed to withdraw their exploratory digs . . . They even closed the Uranium Corporation of India office in Shillong, but—"

"They keep coming back like flies," shouts someone from the crowd.

Shemphang nods, waits a moment. "Sadly, it appears so. About a month ago, a package was apprehended in Moreh, at the Indo-Myanmar border. It had an inscription marking it as an explosive. It also carried a voltage charge number, and two tags . . . UCIL and AMD North Eastern Region Headquarters, Shillong."

A gasp ripples through the gathering, connected by a single troubling thought. That this could mean the extraction and smuggling of uranium are still being carried out. Illegally, and perhaps with the involvement of UCIL and AMD.

What did the package contain? we ask.

"Nobody knows." It disappeared, of course. Without a trace. Gone, like it never existed.

I look around, at the fear written on people's faces. *How can this happen on our land?*

But it is hard to keep track. Who comes, who goes. In the shadows, and in the dark of night. How vast and secret these hills, and how much can be hidden from view.

Shemphang asks us to be vigilant, to keep watch. "If there is any mining activity going on, if you see or hear anything, we'll put a stop to it."

The crowd buzzes, this time in anger.

He raises his hand to quiet us, and we obey.

"We are here," he promises. "We will make sure this doesn't continue."

It's reassuring, but not reassuring enough. Around me, people murmur, *How will they make sure? They don't live here.*

"The second thing," he continues, "is that there is a proposal for a highway to be built between Shillong and Wahkaji, and a road down to Mawmalang."

At this, whisperings begin again. *It's true. The rumours are true.*

"Except," he adds, "the proposal is from the Uranium Corporation of India."

It comes back to me, the conversation I'd overheard on the bus.

"You see why we must resist this plan. We cannot allow UCIL, the organization that's looking to extract the uranium, to build the road that will be used to transport it away."

At this point, someone interrupts him: "But don't they say they will only build the road . . . and not carry out any mining?" To my surprise, it's Bah Karmel. He's standing close by, I hadn't noticed; from here, I can hear the faint quiver in his voice.

Shemphang shrugs. "Yes, it's what they've said, sure, but that's like the spider telling the fly, come into my web, I promise I won't eat you."

Amid the snickers, Bah Karmel persists. His hands are clenched tightly by his side. "I beg your pardon, but it isn't the same thing. The road will allow us access to healthcare, to schools, to jobs . . . The road will save us, and many of our loved ones."

The murmuring continues, in disapproval, in agreement.

Banri whispers into my ear, "She died, you know, his wife."

My heart stills. "What happened?"

"She was bleeding. They couldn't get her to a hospital in time. He left Mawmalang, for months . . . He was distraught with grief."

The long afternoon is reduced to this—the clenched fists, the quiver in his voice, the look in Bah Karmel's eyes. Here. And when he helped me through the forest.

That evening, after the KSU are gone, the village gathers in Bah Syiem's house. Next to him, I'm told, are his mother, the matriarch of our village, and Bah Sumar, the nong kñia, the storyteller, the bearer of the word. The mood in the room is sombre, though restlessness fizzles in corners where young men sit with their khukris.

The village has gathered because it is troubled. The news today has largely not been welcome. I look around for Bah Karmel, but he is not here. Cups of tea are being handed out to bolster our spirits, black and strong and sweet.

"What can we say?" the headman begins. "We live in a small corner of the world and own nothing, and yet people want to take away our land."

The fire burns fiercely at the hearth, fed with sticks and coal.

"We know people in the city have money . . . But what will we do with riches? Riches may run out at some point, but not land. Our land has always been there for us, our ancestors tilled it, and we take care of it for our children. Without our land, we are lost."

All of us are turned towards him in silence, our eyes lit by the flames.

Sometimes, I admit, I struggle a little to follow; my Khasi has improved over my weeks here, but Bah Syiem speaks a strong and sweet dialect. I'm certain, though, that he's saying something about us being a people with an intangible past, that we have only our spoken word—ka ktien—and, here he looks around, our collective memory to rely on. In some ways, he says, we don't have a past. "Perhaps that is why our existence is mainly expressed through land"—he places a hand on the floor, on the hard-baked earth. "The more they try to take it away, the more we will fight. Not because we are its owners, but because we are its caretakers."

Bah Syiem sips his tea. He sighs. "We can do nothing for now. We wait and watch, and see what rumours the wind brings us, and what we can learn from the birds who know the secrets of the forest. For tonight, perhaps Bah Sumar"—he gestures to the person next to him—"can lift our spirits with a song."

The nong kñia—so old, he looks like the earth itself, the colour of it, its creased texture—unfolds and sits up, longer, straighter. He is holding a stringed instrument, a duitara, and he plucks at it, and says, yes, yes, of course, he would be happy to, and he begins to tune his instrument, and speak, and he slips, almost without us noticing, into narration—not singing, not speaking, but something in between.

"To ïa ap, to ïa sngap," he begins. Let us wait, let us listen. "What story shall we tell tonight?"

"This is a trick," whispers Banri into my ear. "He always pretends to ask, but he's decided already."

"Tonight, we shall tell the tale of creation, our khanatang, sanctified and true. In the beginning, when there was nothing but emptiness, God created Mei Ramew, the guardian mother spirit of the earth, and her husband, Basa. They lived happily but alone, and soon began to long for the company of children. Please, they prayed, to our god U Blei, bless us with a child or two so our line may continue, and after many such pleas, God granted them their wish five times over. The sun, their first daughter, their only son, the moon, then water, wind, and fire, who all grew up into beings of great accomplishment, and shaped the earth with grace and beauty, and gave life to mountains and flowers and trees. But do you know?" says the nong kñia, plucking, singing. "Something was missing."

Someone who would tend and sow and harvest, who would walk the earth looking after the birds and the beasts. None of them could do this, the sun and the moon were busy roaming the skies, water could not travel freely, wind and fire ran too fast, too wild. Please, prayed Mei Ramew and Basa to our god U Blei, send us someone who will not only be heir to all this bounty, but also be steward of the world.

"And who did U Blei send?" the nong kñia asks.

"Kyllang and Symper," the children shout in reply.

Two powerful spirits of the mountains, brothers, who once stood next to each other on the road to Mawnai. But as it turns out, they were kept too busy quarrelling, squabbling between themselves, to see to the welfare of other living things. And so, our god sent the tiger, ferocious and grand, but the tiger was a despot, a terrifying overlord who began a rule of tyranny and fear.

Eventually, it was decided that none but the sixteen clans living in heaven could be fitting caretakers of the earth, and for them U Blei created a golden ladder on Lum Sohpetbneng, the mountain at the centre of the sky, linking the kingdom of God and the kingdom of man, and for many years, there was great happiness and contentment.

"But men," the nong kñia sang, "men in their terrible greed and selfishness angered our god, as they swerved away from the path of goodness and truth. So he planted a tree, a special, divine tree. As evidence of his displeasure, and to mark the end of the years of joy and light, he planted the Diengiei, the tree of gloom and shadow, the tree of all trees, which grew so huge that its branches covered the sun, and all the world fell into darkness."

The instrument twangs into the night as his voice rises and falls with the music.

We sit and listen carefully. Banri leans against me, I lean against Mem, and for a long while, we do not move, for everything is entangled.

✧ ✧ ✧

"You did what?"

I'm trying to speak to Kima, and it's not going well. The cellular fault lines are worse than ever today, and I've spent all my time on the hillock yelling, *Can you hear me?*

I wanted to tell him about my evening at the headman's house. About the nong kñia.

"He sang you all a song? What kind of song?"

"Ka khanatang . . . a sacred story . . ."

"A what?"

"Never mind," I shout back. It is impossible.

"Have you participated in some profound ritual that's changed you forever, Shai?"

Why does the line clear only when he's teasing?

"Nothing like that," I say stiffly.

He chuckles. "I'm glad you're having a good time, but when are you coming back?"

"Maybe I never will," I say, only half in jest.

He laughs. "Don't be silly. You don't belong there."

I say nothing, sending only silence down the line.

"Anyway, good you called," he continues. "I wanted to tell you—"

I'll never know. The line drops, and when I try to call him back, it doesn't go through. I sit there a moment, though, thinking about his words. *You don't belong there.* How strange he should say that. And how strange that I'm unsettled, but not because I've been telling myself with any compulsion that I do. In my time here, I haven't felt the need—or indeed had a moment—to think it over. It isn't what people expect, I suppose . . . that you move from a city to the countryside, and slip right in . . . After all, I imagine them wondering, isn't there an awful lot to miss? But what have I missed? Truthfully, not much. Not the TV, nor my Netflix subscription. Cafés, maybe, and coffee, but definitely not crowded bars and parties at people's houses, at which I was always, always awkward.

And couldn't the question be *what have you gained?* Because to live in a city is also to live without so much . . . Silence, and darkness, and slowness. All these things that allow you to be with yourself . . .

Maybe Kima's right, though—I shouldn't pretend my time here is something it's not, like some foolish romantic. But what is it, and what is it not? And how does one tell?

I'm still a little perturbed as I tramp back down to the house.

In the backyard, I check in on the chickens scratching around, the smelly pigs snuffling in the mud, and the kper, where the tyrso is leafy, and the beans and peas are beginning to show their soft white flowers. It is here that I begin to feel calmer, at the sight of silently growing things, pushing into the soil and out into the world. Next we'll be planting some turmeric—the queen, Banri tells me, of edible roots. I will probably never be one of these people, like my father, or Kong Nuramon, who remembers botanical names, or can identify plants at a glance. But lately, I have come to find something else—some peace in this cycle of sowing and harvest, this replenishment. Here, a sense of the seasons.

Back in Delhi, I'd tell Grace that I was a bit like Uranus.

"What?" She'd blink at me.

Uranus, the planet with the unfortunate name. Unlike the other planets in our solar system, I'd explain, spinning quietly in the same plane as their orbit, magnetic fields running primly perpendicular, Uranus tumbled around on its side, its orientation changing in all sorts of directions. Often, I felt the same.

Except here.

And thinking about it now, perhaps it hasn't really happened overnight—the slipping in—but what has helped is being occupied, almost straightaway, in learning to tend and grow, prune and harvest. In this, I've found something I hadn't anywhere before—purpose. Which sounds grand and exalted, I know, but truly, I've realized, it is merely to sleep well at night and to wake up knowing you are needed—by someone, a plant, a pet, a person, the world, yourself.

Of course, I am also among people who have allowed me to feel this way—though my decision to stay on was initially met with some puzzlement. Phin leit noh lano sha sor? When are you leaving for the city?

they'd ask. And then, after a while, they stopped. Bah Albert treats me as one of his regulars at the shop, Bah Syiem tips his hat when we cross. I've grown acquainted with a few others—Kong Dabari with her hearty, cackly laugh; Bah Shaiñ, who insists that he once could shapeshift into a tiger; Kong Midalis, who makes the softest rice cakes in the village. They are curious about me, but not too wary, perhaps because I already have a household here to call my own. I am, in some way, already family.

And so, somehow, something feels . . . aligned. Yes, that's it. That's the word. As though I've found my orbit. This is a galaxy to which I am attached and gravitationally bound—all of us moving in synchronicity. And I think I feel it more strongly after last night, at the headman's house, where we were listening, listening. I don't know how to explain it, what it means to gather together and listen to a story. How in this simplest of acts all of us are participants, listeners, tellers, all responsible for bringing a story into existence and keeping it alive.

When I step into the house, there's no one in the kitchen, stirring the pots on the fire, crushing pepper in the mortar, rushing around to ready lunch. Instead, farther inside, I find a small commotion has broken out. Everyone has gathered noisily in Oiñ's room.

"What's happened?" I ask.

Oiñ, they tell me, is insisting on stepping outdoors.

Mem is trying to soothe her—"Let's see if we can take you out tomorrow."

"What is she talking about?" exclaims her sister, hiding none of her exasperation. "She hasn't even been able to stand for months and months."

This is true, but perhaps that is why, I offer.

Kong Thei snaps at me. "Yes, you know everything."

I am silenced, but Oiñ is not. "Nga kwah ban ïuh ki kjat ha ka khyndew," she says. And when none of us make a move, she grows more agitated. What do you mean? we ask. You want to *walk*? "No." Her head trembles, as do her limbs. "I want to stamp my feet upon the earth."

Somehow, we manage to gather her and lift her out of the bed, through the front room, and then down the steps with difficulty—Bah

Kit has to help—and finally, we place her down, supporting her on either side.

"Bare feet, bare feet," she insists.

So I bend down and slip off her socks.

She places her toes on the grass, squealing like a child, and all of us gathered around her can't help smiling. The tension that was brewing inside dissipates.

"Oh," cries Oiñ, closing her eyes, turning her face to the winter sun.

The sky is blue, the dust has settled after a brief shower this morning, and something—the brightness of the world—beckons us all out.

Kong Thei and Banri support her as she takes a turn on the grass. The twins shriek and prance about in delight. Bah Kit tries to make sure they don't bump into Oiñ. Mem and I stand aside, watching, smiling.

"You know," she tells me, "our elders say we must make it a habit to walk barefoot outside every day . . . that our feet must touch the ground often . . . They believe that the earth has special powers running through it, and doing this strengthens us and keeps us healthy and strong and upright." Then she laughs. "All this is silly, you think, I'm sure."

I say I don't think that at all.

"But we have forgotten, haven't we?" she adds.

I nod.

"We pave the earth and cover our feet, and we forget to place them on the ground."

From across the lawn, Oiñ grins at us. "You, too," she commands, pointing, and so we oblige. We fling off our slippers, pull off our socks, and step on the mud.

It's sun-warmed and scratchy and uneven. Different from the soil in the kper which I tread on, moist and soft and mulchy. This is hard, resilient. With its own life underneath. I remember the conversation with my father and Kong Nuramon, about the network that webs the deep, dark soil. And here, something else also runs through it—what we're trying to protect, what could power the earth and destroy it, and scatter us, this circle of imperfect steadiness.

We are so immersed in keeping Oiñ standing, and supported, and in stamping our feet on the grass, that I don't notice two figures approaching. They walk down the road, hesitant, unsure where to go, and they have heard us and probably wish to ask for directions. Or perhaps they know their way and are merely passing by. It is impossible to say. We are laughing, and Oiñ looks as though she has never spent a day of her life unwell.

The two visitors stand aside, with rucksacks hanging heavy on their backs, almost embarrassed, wishing not to intrude upon our odd gathering—except one of them, the young man, is looking at me, in recognition. Their gaze remains on us, and I lift my head, and turn towards them . . . I stop laughing, moving, breathing. It cannot be, and yet it is.

My voice comes from elsewhere, from someone else, as I blurt out, "What the

EVELYN

Evelyn Adelia Alexander is borne away from England in a blaze of gaily-streamered glory. Around her, the crowd cheers and waves, goodbye they call, farewell to all, and handkerchiefs flutter like a flock of small white birds. The band has been playing with unwavering gusto—so far "Auld Lang Syne" and "Where Is Now the Merry Party?"—and she fears for the trumpeter, who, she is certain, has not taken a breath since they left. Now, as they steam out of Tilbury, they have struck up "Soldiers of the King," a lively tune to inspire good humour among the passengers—for more than a few faces are saddened, she notices, at the sight of those left behind.

They are on board the SS *Maloja*, and since she knows very little about ships, all she can say with any accuracy is that it is very new and very big. Indeed, it is the single largest ship she has seen in her life. A sleek and shiny beast, gleaming like a thing of wonder conjured from the future—and it must be so with electricity installed throughout, wireless telegraphy, and even, she has heard, modern and elaborate anti-rodent protection. She tries not to betray any of her astonishment, as though to all this she is an old hand, but she has failed already. It is written clearly all over her face, and truly, she is alight with excitement—*I am on my way; I am on my way!*

She can hardly believe it.

Is this her journey's beginning or its end? Where will it take her? To what will it bring her back? What might she learn? What will she see anew?

Stop, she tells herself, enjoy this moment, be present, observe.

The long, empty lines of Tilbury's coastal fort gliding past, Gravesend's cast-iron piers falling away on the opposite bank, docks and warehouses giving way to flat, wet marsh, seagulls wheeling above her in a winter grey sky, and the river glinting thickly, leading them out into the North Sea. She stands on the deck lost, somewhere between waking and dreaming, which she might well be given their frightfully early start to make the boat train from St. Pancras this morning. How very quiet her mother and father were on the way, as was Florence, *dear Florence*, with only Patrick making an attempt at conversation, though he, too, soon gave up and resigned himself to silence.

The crowd around her begins to disperse soon after they have passed Dover, its coastline as undulating as the waves, and the cliffs sheer and white and gleaming. These, too, seem to arouse strong sentiment in the passengers—*When, oh when shall we see home again?*—but not so much in Evie, whose thoughts lie ahead, tumbling, stumbling into the future, wondering what it might reveal. Three weeks on board! This is terribly quick, she knows—it once took months and months before the Suez Canal opened—but even then, it feels decidedly extended. If only there were a way to get there faster so that her adventure could truly begin.

Only when the straits have opened up, and the water lies wide and blue around them, does she realize she is one of the last few stragglers still out on deck. She also notices that she seems to have lost her chaperone, Mrs. Ward, a large, fussy woman who, one would think, would be difficult to misplace. *Must I find her?* Perhaps given this is their first hour on board, she must. Though before she heads inside, where she knows there will be company and chatter and the busyness of settling in, she lingers for a moment at the railing, with the wind, light and playful, the smell of the sea rising up strong and salty, and before her, the ribbon of coastline fast, fast receding.

They are three to a cabin: Evie, Bessie, Mrs. Ward's blonde-haired, blue-eyed niece, and slender, serious Victoria Baker—both of whom are about seventeen.

Mrs. Ward, who is elsewhere, in plush accommodation, at first makes a fuss about being away from "her girls." "What if you should need me?" she frets. "We won't," they chorus so emphatically that their chaperone looks wounded. "What we mean," Evie adds quickly, "is that we would not wish to trouble you, but we are so awfully glad you are here." Beside her, Bessie nods vigorously. Mollified, Mrs. Ward sweeps off and swiftly forgets about them.

Back in their cabin, Evie unpacks her belongings. This will be home for a few weeks, and while it may not be the most cheerful of living quarters, Evie does not like to complain. Bessie, though, feels no such reluctance.

No windows, no heating, and only *one* lamp overhead? How will they dress?

Evie thinks it best not to inform her at this moment that the bath cubicles down the passageway are shared.

"Why isn't there a porthole, even?" Bessie continues. "For some light and fresh air."

Victoria replies, already sounding like she is at the end of her patience, "Because if it were left open, water might sluice in on us while we are sleeping and that would be dangerous."

Evie asks if Victoria has made this journey before.

She has, for she was born in India, she tells them, and had lived on a tea plantation in the Nilgiris until she was ten, when she was sent away to school in England. "Now I'm returning to be with my family and to get married."

"Oh! As are we," says Bessie, brightening. "To be married, I mean. Our families are in England." There is nothing more Bessie likes to discuss, Evie has discovered, than marriage plans, despite having no suitor yet in sight.

"Isn't that right, Evie?" She looks across at her, her eyes as blue, Evie imagines, as the sea outside their windowless cabin.

Evie laughs, nervous. "Yes, we are part of the fishing fleet!"

Her fellow passengers look visibly displeased. "I do not feel entirely comfortable with that term," says Victoria primly. "Nor me," adds Bessie, and she turns to shove her trunk beneath her berth. Evie is glad, though, that her silly comment has put an end to the marriage talk for the moment.

By the time she is done unpacking, Evie is alone, and she sits on her berth in the quiet. Was it just this morning they had arrived at Tilbury? All abustle with ships being loaded and fired up, the smell of coal and damp pungent in the air, the *Maloja* towering above the P&O dock, black smoke billowing from her funnels. Amidst the swirl of passengers and porters, there was Papa, solemn yet kindly, Mama, her face set tighter than usual, and Florence, by now crying small, quiet tears. Evie had stood among them feeling like a wretched Judas, betrayer of Christ and all that was good in the world.

"You will write to us often, won't you, Evie?" her sister had blurted out. "Don't be lazy and vanish off into the wilds of India without a word."

"No. Unless," she jested, "I am eaten by a tiger."

No one laughed.

Thankfully, Patrick returned just then with the news that her belongings were safely stowed, and her cabin luggage sent up. "You will please give Charlotte my love," he continued. Of course! She was also carrying letters for his sister in Calcutta, and presents—lavender soap, silk stockings, sweets for the children. Florence clasped at his arm; they had been married two years now, and soon hoped, Evie suspected, for a happy expansion to the family. Florence is the least suspicious of her story about making a trip to the colonies to look for a match—she had found marital happiness, and it seemed only true and right that Evie, and all the world, would wish to as well. Her father, as was his nature, went along with things, although her mother, despite apprehensions about Evie, now twenty-three, ending up an old maid, had not been easy to convince. Surely she could find someone in England? This was not a discussion to pick up at Tilbury, however, and soon enough, Mrs. Ward arrived with Bessie, hellos were exchanged, then farewells, and shortly after they were pressing through the crowd, stepping straight up the gangplank. From the deck, her family's upturned faces looked small and faraway already, and Evie's heart—if only for a moment—was tugged back to them, onto land.

It is dark now in the cabin, and their single lamp sheds no more than a feeble yellow glow. Evie, though, is undimmed. She might have a moment where she feels she has not arrived yet, wholly, on the ship, that she is still travelling from the place she has left behind—a quick whiff of London air, the feel of it crisp and wintry against her skin, a sudden vision of trees shedding their golden leaves, and fat chimneys hotly smoking, but just as swiftly, she has shaken it off.

I am leaving England! I have left! I'm off to—

Evie is unburdened by superstitions, save one, that saying out loud the thing she seeks will render it unattainable. So she decides that until she has stepped on Indian shores, she shall not name it, regardless of how strongly she may be tempted to along the way.

What will it be like?

She reminds herself again that questions like these are futile. *One needs to be there!* She has seen many Daniell prints and glossy Bourne & Shepherd photographs of landscapes, temple scenes, train stations, fakirs, and is unconvinced about pictures being able to truly capture places; instead, they feel distinctly more . . . removed somehow. Besides, she has a feeling it will be different, where she wishes to visit, and in some ways, she is glad it yet remains a mystery, unglimpsed and concealed.

✧ ✧ ✧

How oddly easy it is to begin to feel as though all of this is quite normal, ordinary even, to be aboard a ship, floating along on a journey. Since this is her first time, Evie had not really known what to expect—*would it be an entirely different world?* Perhaps not. There's a distinct holiday feel in the air, but even on a ship people settle into doing everyday things . . . reading, writing letters, strolling, taking tea.

What does take a bit of getting used to, though, is being *at* sea, and the thing Evie finds more disorienting than the roll and slope of a big wave is the deck moving persistently beneath her feet. She does not like to think of it too often: the world suddenly turned watery and fathomless. Thankfully, it is easy enough to distract oneself on the upper deck, with its variety of organized entertainment, a slew of deck games at which, it turns out, Bessie is ace. She wins the egg-and-spoon race, and is quite an expert at quoits, throwing the metal hoops skilfully over the hob. Evie is happy enough to be an occasional participant. She is well aware her expertise lies not in sport. Instead, she wanders to the quieter edges, recruits an empty deckchair, and lounges. *This* is nice. Dutifully, she has carried with her Roxburgh's *Flora Indica*, although she finds it is so . . . learned that she can barely go two pages without seeking diversion.

"It's all nonsense," Grandma Grace would have said. "Go get some mud on your hands."

Advice ill-suited for while at sea, sadly.

All this unwavering blue around her, endless and immense, and unlike anything she had imagined, even though she has pretended to be on a ship, as a child, every so often—in the nursery, Florence serving tea to her dolls, Evie atop a chair, or swinging from the curtains—"Land ahoy!" This was usually followed by a brisk chiding, and exasperated instructions from Mama to be "more like her sister." She has failed in this regard. One could blame it on a diet of Nesbit books, and unruly days spent with Grandma Grace. Florence and she are fated to be night and day, storm and spring.

Not a half hour passes before she fishes out Frank Kingdon-Ward's *On the Road to Tibet.* She cannot resist—he is a new author, recently published, and recently acquired by her local bookshop. For the last few years, Evie has harboured a great passion for travel memoirs, particularly those with a botanical bent. She has read them all: George Forrest's account of his journey on the Upper Salween, both volumes of Marianne North's *Recollections of a Happy Life*, J. E. Smith's translation of Linnaeus's *Tour of Lapland*, Reginald Farrer's *In Old Ceylon*, Mary Kingsley's *Travels in West Africa*. They thrill her—the setting out, the promise of newness, the tricks picked up along the way, the wealth of new flora, all that adventure. This one is particularly promising, she is pleased to discover. *As the sun rose*, Kingdon-Ward writes from the mouth of the Han River, *we sailed out into the wide, free world* . . . At this, a delicious affinity overcomes her, and she looks out to sea, and smiles, small and secret.

On the ship, the passengers are prescribed a daily routine. Rising at seven, prayers at eight, breakfast at eight thirty, luncheon at one, and dinner at seven thirty—all of which Evie considers happily missable except the meals. The second-class dining saloon is cavernous, supplied by natural light through portholes, and set with long rectangular tables at which diners sit on mahogany swivel chairs bolted to the floor. She shares her table with Bessie, an elderly bearded gentleman by the name of Professor Bower, Mrs. Ward, and a chatty young girl in a pastel taffeta dress who, Evie is soon informed, is off to stay with a cousin married to someone stationed in Ceylon.

"I have missed going out for August Week," she adds woefully over carrot soup.

Evie clears her throat. "What is August Week?"

She almost drops her spoon. "Don't you know? It is the biggest social week of the year there! Hundreds of dances and picnics. It is the perfect time to find—"

"A husband," Evie finishes for her.

"You *do* know about it, then," she says happily.

When they are done with soup, the head waiter beats a gong, and the stewards appear in a rush, pounce on the empty plates, and just as swiftly, serve the fish.

"Why are you going to India?" she asks Evie.

"To look for treasure."

"What kind of treasure?"

"I am not sure yet."

The girl's pretty face is drawn in puzzlement. "How do you mean?"

"Sometimes," says Evie, digging into her haddock, "you don't know until you find it."

There are many things to learn from Kingdon-Ward's travels in Tibet, about mules and rhododendrons, Lamaism and hunting sheep on high precipices, but also this: that the weather in the mountains is as changeable as at sea. For two days, it is glorious, the sky and water united in their benevolence, though seasoned sailors on board murmur about how things will change once they approach the Bay of Biscay.

On the afternoon the storm breaks, Evie is invited to join her chaperone at the Veranda Café. *Must she?* Perhaps because it is the first of such summons, she must. Mrs. Ward is lunching with a group of ladies at the café beneath a trellised canopy of fake flowers. She makes the introductions and does not think it indecorous to furnish them with details of Evie's husband hunt.

"So, if you happen to know of anyone . . ." she ends coyly.

One of the ladies, Mrs. Hopkins, she believes, turns and chuckles. "Well, my nephew, if you will have him. My sister's boy. He is joining us at Marseille. Still unmarried, to his mother's disappointment . . . he is too busy collecting plants."

Evie catches her breath. She wants to ask for his name, but it will be misconstrued as interest on her part, which it is, but not for the reasons they would assume.

"Evie," asks her chaperone, "didn't you study plants at Cambridge?"

Before she can reply, one of the women turns to her. "Oh, you have been to university?" She sounds not so much surprised as disapproving.

For propriety's sake, Evie acknowledges this unfortunate shortcoming on her part.

"What did you study?" asks Mrs. Hopkins, sounding genuinely curious.

"Natural sciences . . . at Newnham College."

She can see this does not impress most of the gathering.

Mrs. Ward laughs. "Well, don't go around publicizing it, that is all I can say."

Evie excuses herself early from the lunch party to walk the deck.

The sky, like her mood, has darkened, and white frills rim the waves, rough and choppy, under the wind. For a fleeting moment, she allows herself the pleasure of picturing the Veranda Café swept away by a storm. If she were home, a temper like this would solicit cups of tea and kind words from Florence, while in Cambridge, Agnes, her friend and mentor, her science sister, would offer neither. She had no time. "If you're looking to leap overboard," Evie imagines her saying, "please get on with it."

She misses Florence, but Agnes even more.

If there is one person she would have liked to accompany her on this trip, it was Agnes, but Agnes would have hated it. Being away from her study, her at-home laboratory, her garden. All the world is here, she would have said, why leave?

When the storm breaks, ice-cold rain pins Evie in place. It begins to fall harder, in thick sheets, the sea morphs into undulating slopes, the ship heaves, and beyond, clouds fall low, obscuring all the world in white. By the time she rushes in, her hair is wet, her jacket soaked, and her annoyance dissipated.

In moments like these, one can feel only briskly, dizzily alive.

✧ ✧ ✧

Her first year at university, Evie stood outside a lecture hall, undecided between tears and fury, when a woman stopped to ask what the matter was. She was tall, and had strong features, a large nose, dark eyes, and raven-black hair, though most striking of all, she held a large bouquet of pink lilies.

Evie told her she had been thrown out of the classroom.

"Did you have permission to attend?" Women students were required to ask for the approval of certain professors to sit in on their classes. She did, but the professor did not seem to think this also allowed her to ask questions.

"You asked a question?"

Evie nodded. She expected an outpouring of sympathy, admiration even, but instead, the woman looked as though she would have liked to call her an idiot.

"What makes you think a professor from whom you need permission to attend his class will put up with anything less than you pretending you're not even present?"

"But–" she began.

"Nobody really wants us here–women, I mean–but since we are, how do we best get our work done?"

Evie opened her mouth, then shut it.

"Whose class was this?"

"Professor Bateson. Delivering a lecture on plant cytology."

"You have an interest in botany?" the lady asked, her tone softening.

"Yes, but after today–"

"You will spend your life wallowing in the unfairness of it all?"

"No," she said, slightly offended.

"Good. I'm headed to Balfour. Come with me."

On the way, the lady introduced herself as Agnes Arber. She had studied at Newnham too, she said, and on her marriage, had recently moved back here from University College London with a grant to undertake her own research. Evie was in awe–it was not easy for a woman to be offered these kinds of opportunities. Their footsteps echoed through the quiet Cambridge afternoon, and soon they arrived at Balfour, an abandoned chapel in Downing Place, converted in 1884 into a laboratory for women. This, because the university did not allow its female students to attend practical sessions with men.

"See," said Agnes, as they stepped inside. "This is how we get our work done. By keeping out of everyone's way."

It was a large, high-ceilinged space, with light streaming in from arched windows, cabinets and workbenches running along the walls, and more workspaces down the centre. They were greeted by a clutter of pipettes, test tubes, and pinned notes requesting students to "kindly wash any glassware after use."

Agnes placed the lilies on the counter, next to a pile of glass slides. "Now, why don't you help me prepare these?"

"For what?" stuttered Evie.

"A Christmas wreath. What do you think? For the microscope, of course. Consider this a catch-up class for the cytology lesson you just missed."

✧ ✧ ✧

The storm off Biscay is short and gusty, a temperamental rage that swells and surges, and just as quickly fades. Evie grows restive, though, lying in her berth, listening to wild wind and water, wondering if they are going to sink. She had always fancied herself a brave one, right from when she was a little girl running at the waves on their holidays to Brighton while Florence held back, shrinking behind their mama, but she realizes now that all she has known so far are safe and familiar dangers, and that every peril on this journey will be new.

She is first to head outside after the storm, with both Bessie and Victoria still pale and precarious in the cabin, united in their resentment of Evie's seemingly miraculous immunity to seasickness—she even managed *meals*, apples, eggs, heaps of buttered toast.

On the upper deck, the wind remains brisk and the sky overcast, but passengers are out and about, a group is setting up quoits, she can hear someone suggest a game of tug of war somewhere the band is playing something cheerful. If nothing else, there is a sense in the air that one must make the best of things.

She greets a few familiar faces, then sits and sips a horse's neck, a concoction of brandy and ginger ale that is being liberally handed around on doctor's orders to help settle the stomach. It is delicious, warm and sweet, and quickly helps restore her spirits. Soon she brings out a notebook in which she has been filling out details of her journey—hastily. She is not one for pouring thoughts and feelings and minute details of her life into ink and paper. This leads her to suspect she will never write a travel memoir—though first she needs to travel so much more. Oh, that she were a man and could throw on a pair of trousers and a jaunty hat, and be off to see the world!

On the first page of her journal, a question beckons: *How will I get to where I need to be?* And underneath, a scribbled answer that sounds almost reproving: *One thing at a time, Evie.* What she means by this is arriving in Bombay alive and well to begin with, then taking the train across to Calcutta with Mrs. Ward and Bessie, staying with Charlotte and her husband in the city, and once there, finding a way to meet a Mr. George Mackay Muttlebury at the Agricultural and Horticultural Office, armed with little more than her wits and a letter of introduction from Agnes.

"We haven't met, but we have corresponded a few times, and maybe he can help. But what if he can't, Evie?"

Then—well, she does not have the faintest idea. She will work out a plan. This is what she calls the spirit of adventure and Agnes calls stupidity.

For certain, blame must be placed for this on Grandma Grace—she had not inherited her dogged obstinacy from anyone else. Mama would claim Grandma Grace had nurtured it too, from Evie's childhood.

"Stop filling her head with all these fancies," she would say crossly. "The other day, she insisted on staying up all night to watch the toadstools."

Grandma Grace would try to stifle a chuckle.

"Why?" her mother would query irritably. "Why would she want to do that?"

"I might have mentioned that some had grown in my back garden . . . overnight."

She is certain Grandma Grace would think this journey worthy, because for her every journey was—whether right outside the door to the bottom of the garden, or to the woods behind her house, or farther away, to the river, down by the coast, to the sea. And what excitement if they found the first bluebell, or a rare fern, or a patch of wild strawberries!

"To strive, to seek, to find, dear Evie," her grandma would sing, "and never to yield."

"Never to yield to what?" she would ask.

A smile, an arched brow. "A life bereft of wonder."

Now, after bringing her travel journal up to date—*Storm*—Evie stashes it away.

What time would it be back in England? It looks like that hour in the evening when Mama will be preparing supper, Papa and Patrick making their way home from Mandall & Alexander, and Florence readying tomorrow's lessons for the primary school where she teaches. In Cambridge, Agnes will be outside, humming, watering her garden.

All this feels far away; the past, she realizes, as much as the future, can be veiled.

Evie is soon summoned back by the sky, though, and how extraordinary it appears at the moment. Somewhere there has been a break in the clouds, and the palest of pink-gold has spilled across in a watercolour wash—a too-lovely sunset. She watches the light collecting over the horizon, dipping low, and sinking into the sea.

✧ ✧ ✧

Today, Marseille! A confluence at which all the world meets—yet tragically, tantalizingly out of reach, as all passengers are not allowed to step off the ship.

But *why*? Evie has asked the steward at the door.

Not enough time, miss.

So she must be content with gazing from afar, leaning over to catch the sounds and smells wafting up from the busy dock. The *Maloja* has stopped to restock on coal and pick up passengers who, to avoid the wrath that is Biscay, and who could afford it, took the overland train from Calais.

"A lot of grand people," says Bessie, including, she points out helpfully, a Lord and Lady Bute, the Duke and Duchess of Hamilton, and even a young Maharaja, distinguished by an elaborate silk umbrella held over his person. "Probably off to Delhi," she adds, "for the coronation."

Evie is vastly uninterested in grand people. Not for them has she sat, as a child, with the atlas of the world open at her feet, reading out names slowly, tracing a finger across distances, over land and sea, to see how far she could reach—São Paulo, Nanjing, Moscow. Only for this—the thrill of a new place.

For her, the ships docked as far as she can see, the bustling row of warehouses from which porters come and go lugging their wares, the sudden oddly inviting odour of water meeting land. She notices there is not a plant in sight, so built up is this part of the old city. To the north stands a lighthouse; to the south, the imposing abbey of St. Victor; and in the distance, next to many stylish shops and hotels, the grandest of buildings, a cathedral—all this filtered through the haze of fine coal dust that, she has heard, can sometimes grow so thick it settles on the soup served onboard.

Thankfully, there is no such condimental disaster at lunch. Her minestrone is clean and uncoated, but something else comes to pass that Evie had hoped would not. The gentleman seated next to Mrs. Ward,

Professor Bower, turns his attention to her. He has discovered she is a botanist, and so, he declares, is he.

"At Cambridge in '74," he informs her.

"How old does that make him?" hisses Bessie into her ear. *"Two hundred?"*

Evie tries not to choke on her soup.

Professor Bower, bulbous and heavily bearded, enjoys the sound of his own voice. "At the time, Cambridge was not an inspiring field for a beginner in the sciences, especially botany." Evie has a feeling she will soon learn why, in spite of no prompting on her part. "Collecting, classifying, and recording, that was the order of the day, while everything else was neglected, if taught at all."

Eat faster, mumbles Bessie, *eat faster*.

He drones on. "I did, finally, find myself supplied with some laboratory work in my third year, but it was not until just before graduation. During eight weeks of a hot summer in Wurzburg, I learned laboratory methods directly from Professor Julius von Sachs."

Evie is, grudgingly, impressed—to be tutored by the monumental German botanist himself!

The stewards remove the soup plates and replace them with chunky beef stew.

"He taught me the Hofmeisterian methods of the time. These were, of course, pre-microtome days," he adds fondly. "Our slide preparations were made by hand."

Bessie's right, Evie thinks, he *is* two hundred.

"How did you do that?" she asks, genuinely interested—though at a price, for under the table she receives a well-aimed kick.

Bower puffs up at her query. "Well, we sectioned fresh ovules between finger and thumb, and I remember obtaining fine hand sections of *Althaea* pollen grains by embedding them in gum arabic, dried on the end of a cork."

The second course is nearly over; the end of their meal is nigh.

"Dessert!" exclaims Bessie, as bowls of wobbling trifle are set on the table.

"Now things must be different." He glances at Evie. "Very different."

Not different enough, she wants to say.

"The focus finally shifted to physiological botany in the late '70s, didn't it?"

She nods. "This is true."

"For so long, Britain was only interested in the dead," he continues, happily applying himself to the pudding. "Too busy with industrialization and the railways, in consolidating her empire, with the result that, botanically, she was counting her assets not in a rational study of the structure, development, or physiology of the plants, but in plucking, pressing, cataloguing and describing them in their dead, adult state. Now, of course, we have thankfully seen a change . . ."

Rude as it might be to insert herself into the monologue, Evie cannot help it. "Pardon me, professor, but perhaps in some ways *nothing* has changed . . ."

He is visibly taken aback. Next to him, Mrs. Ward looks distinctly displeased. This is no way to address a distinguished gentleman. Evie feels as though she is back in university, speaking when she ought not to in class.

To her surprise, he clears his throat and asks if she would care to elaborate.

So she does. "There has been a shift to physiological botany, yes, but the methods of studying plants and their living processes are rooted within a history, as you said, of an interest in the dead." The table has fallen into a small silence, but she might as well finish now. She takes a deep breath. "The concern, I think, ought to be as much *what* is taught as *how* it is taught."

The professor raises his eyebrows. "And what are these alternative methods of teaching about which you feel so passionately, Miss Alexander?"

"I am interested in the way Goethe studied botany."

"Goethe? Well . . . admirable fellow, and quite the writer, but not a scientist, surely?"

"Oh, but he was!"

"A dilettante, then, an amateur."

Evie had expected him to say this, and takes pleasure in the fact that he does—he has affirmed all the prejudice she can now be fully justified in feeling towards him.

"The thing is, professor, to acknowledge Goethe as a scientist means taking seriously a radically different way of doing science."

He blinks, slowly, incredulously. "How do you mean?"

"It means to look at the phenomenon of colour and not reduce it to numbers, to look at a plant and not see it merely as a collection of parts . . . To do this entails a moving away from traditional scientific methods of inquiry that seek comprehension via boundaries, linearity, uniformity, all of which emphasize distinction and separation. Goethe called for something more intuitive, a state of mind that is simultaneous, nonlinear, concerned with relationships rather than discrete elements. The question is," she adds with a flourish, "is this something of which we are capable?"

"And are you, Miss Alexander?" He sounds amused, and worse, patronizing.

She flushes. "Well, professor, I try."

They eat the rest of their trifle in silence.

Later, back out on the open sea, Evie wanders into the reading room. It is a cool, quiet, and airy place, with plenty of comfortable armchairs, and a generous selection of newspapers and periodicals lying scattered on the tables.

She sits in a corner with Kingdon-Ward, though her mind is elsewhere. The number of people she has met like Professor Bower! Teachers in school and university, a scientist she apprenticed under at Reigate one summer, the dour gentleman who interviewed her for a place at Newnham.

"Why would you like to specialize in botany?" he had asked, and she had her answer ready, one she had rehearsed repeatedly, trying to get it just right. *For as long as I can remember, I have had questions about the natural world.* She confessed to storing boxes of seeds and piles of pressed leaves under her bed, that she would take walks and stop to look at unfamiliar flora, that she was intrigued by certain plants and their habitats and had thought about their nature—why were lady's mantle leaves waxy? If butterflies loved cottage pinks, why didn't animals?—and, she had added with excitement, why did people find flowers beautiful?

The professor had laid down his pen and fixed her with a sad, disappointed smile. "Miss Alexander, I must tell you, this is not science. These are not at all the things with which botanists concern themselves." Evie had sat there with no rejoinder, paralysed, embarrassed at her error, certain she had failed to gain admittance. And truly, she had been given a place at the college only because a woman sitting there quietly all this while had intervened, saying, perhaps they ought to give Evie a chance? Since she had won a scholarship, she must show some promise?

Well, thinks Evie brightly, *look how that turned out!*

She has just opened her book when voices float across from the other side of the reading room. It is Mrs. Hopkins speaking with a gentleman of about thirty, darkly tanned, with thick cropped hair and a generous moustache. She supposes this is the plant-hunting nephew.

"You cannot imagine, Gerald, the state your mother was in . . . after she heard you had fallen off a cliff—"

"But saved by a bush, Aunt Aida."

Mrs. Hopkins expresses little gratitude towards the heroic shrub.

"And besides," he continues, lighting a cigarette, unperturbed, "no alternative route, really, to the blue poppy. I promise you, as I promised Mother, I do not take unnecessary risks."

"Yes, you keep saying that. But the last time you went days without food, and the time before, were you not almost impaled by a bamboo spike?"

I know his type so well, thinks Evie. She has been reading about them for a while now. The bold male adventurer, travelling the world, risking life and limb to gather botanical knowledge for God and gold and country. She is intrigued by him, of course, and excited, too, that a real plant hunter is on board, but she cannot deny that there is some envy and resentment to be reckoned with on her part—if only because women could never enjoy such sponsorship or receive imprimatur, the kind offered to men by professional institutions or commercial nurseries.

She peers back into her book—*Caves*, Kingdon-Ward declares, *always seem to me overrated places of amusement* . . . Aunt and nephew continue to converse, though, and she finds it difficult to concentrate.

There he goes, telling her about a recent meeting of great importance in Marseille, apparently, with a certain Dr. Heckel, who wished to consult him about the new botanical garden planned for the city. "Critical work, Aunt Aida," he adds.

Braggart, mutters Evie, and she heads back out to the deck to look for a friendly steward serving up some of that horse's neck concoction.

✧ ✧ ✧

What makes it so distressing is that botany had been their own for so long.

The roots of which lay in herbalism, Agnes had told her, our oldest system of healing, and not in the many fanciful associations between plants and women in myth and literature.

"Who would tend to medicinal home gardens? Who would care for sick children and administer herbal remedies?"

Botany had been their own for so long, but no longer.

Many heated discussions were had about this in her years at Newnham, usually in someone's room, after dinner, over cocoa and biscuits and a healthy helping of rebellion, the last inspired largely by the whirl of suffragette news around them. Women disrupting speeches at political meetings, unfurling "Votes for Women" banners in public places, being jailed, going on hunger strike, and recently, even sending themselves by Royal Mail to the prime minister's residence to try to obtain a meeting with him. (Alas, Downing Street didn't accept the parcel.)

Even in their quiet college, this spirit burned.

"Blame it on John Lindley," someone would say. "Dead and gone now, but in his time he was on a quest to *defeminize botany*." "Who is Lindley?" the younger girls would ask, and someone else would doff an invisible hat, puff out her chest, and march across the room, announcing, "Botany teacher, writer, institutional powerhouse, and first-class prig." The room would erupt into laughter.

Botany was also once seen, the older girls would explain, as an extension of flower arrangement and floral painting, as something merely for women to busy themselves with for entertainment and improvement. But when new disciplinary boundaries were being established in academia, people like Lindley thought it imperative to separate what they considered "polite" botany from "real" botany, since nothing scientific and modern could possibly involve women.

At this point, a voice would pipe up: "But ought there not to be a 'botany for ladies'? Would this separation hinder our intellectual development?" Then many voices would rise at once. "Yes, but that is not the point!" "The accomplishments of women, even if 'polite' and informal, must not be dismissed!" "Why can't there be room for both!"

Evie came to realize only later that the matter was more complicated than one in which men, as they always tended to do, were sidelining women in the field. It was also a question of how botanical knowledge was sought, gathered, processed, gleaned—and whose methods were considered sound and "scientific."

Certainly not Grandma Grace, who gained little regard from her own daughter, or her neighbours, for "tramping around" gardens and forests, not for exercise or improvement, which would have rendered the activity somewhat respectable, but unforgivably, for clear, unadulterated joy. Friends often gave her books—Robert Tyas's *The Sentiment of Flowers*, Hibberd's *Familiar Garden Flowers*, Kate Greenaway's *The Language of Flowers*—but they were placed on the shelf and rarely glanced at again. "How do you know so much about plants?" Evie had once asked her. "They tell me," she replied. And she had believed her, for Grandma Grace spent hours outside, in a hat and scarf, with a basket in hand, and she talked about her plants as though they were intimate confidants. "My sweet peas are feeling poorly today," or "The pumpkin requests to be moved somewhere less shaded." Evie would grow to realize that this was not what her mother called "airy-fairy" talk; rather, it sprang from knowledge gained through the rigour of experience—nothing less than what was upheld in a laboratory. Day after day, year after year, over a lifetime, until she died, getting to know plants intimately—how much shade, how much sunshine, when to water, when not to, when to prune, when to leave well alone. It was a deep knowing, one gained from touching the earth every day—*being in touch*—and attuning herself to the lives of growing things. It was intuition, clear, precise, and hard-won, too.

Evie learned an awful lot sitting in on those fiery conversations at Newnham, but only later, elsewhere with a different group of discussants, did she come to see that knowledge itself was hierarchical, and that Grandma Grace's knowledge about plants and the way she herself had been learning all her life was not recognized as valid or important.

✧ ✧ ✧

As they sail across the Mediterranean, the mood on the ship turns decidedly festive, with games and competitions running through the day—tie-and-cigarette races for the ladies, to test who could tie a tie or light a cigarette fastest, things no "lady" would normally do, and a spot of deck cricket or spar fighting for the gentlemen. After dinner, still no respite. Dances are organized, usually by the lords in first class—reels by the Scottish, step dances by the Irish, both always vying to outdo each other.

One evening, while the pipers are gaily piping, Evie wanders off until she finds a quiet corner of the deck. Overhead are wonderful stars, while around her, the sea is lit by flashes of silvery blue phosphorescence, trailing in ribbons of light. She is not often sentimental, but it might be nice to share this moment with someone, Florence or Agnes, perhaps even a betrothed. In this regard, she fears, she may bring perpetual disappointment to her parents. Poor Papa, who has worked so hard to build up his firm and introduce her to worthy apprentices in the hope that there might be a blossoming of love, just as with Patrick and Florence. Mama, solid, steady, practical—everything she believed her own mother, Grandma Grace, not to be—is more straightforward: "Remember, Evie, women have two ages: marriageable or not." But has Evie been tempted by the thought? *Not really.* And has she met anyone with whom she would like to spend her life? *Good heavens, no!* For a while, she was certain that if she did it would be someone who would be to her what Edward was to Agnes, for theirs was a marriage of mutual respect—for each other, and each other's work. When she apprenticed with Agnes last year at her small in-house laboratory, she would often overhear them in the study, discussing their research. Edward, a palaeobotanist, was now involved in geological studies, while Agnes was writing her first book, a history of herbals. Now she was beginning to think this lovely, calm steadiness was not meant for her. She might be bored in a week and—was one even allowed to say it?—divorced in another. Yet what could possibly sustain constant newness and excitement? Life dictated that this was a sad impossibility.

At this moment, someone steps up behind her, glancing over her shoulder. A tall, auburn-haired woman.

Evie turns, startled.

The woman places a cigarette to her lips and lights it. She would have won that competition easily. "Where am I?" she asks.

"The second-class deck." Evie expects her to be surprised, aghast even; it is clear she has wandered over from first by mistake.

"Oh, thank God. He will never follow me here." She does not offer further explanation. "It is madness up there," she says instead. "One ball after another. Everyone already discussing what they will be wearing at the end-of-voyage fancy dress. Can you believe it? And we have only just boarded! Although I must admit I also already know, so I am quite the hypocrite."

Evie smiles. "And what will you go as?"

"A peasant." She drags on her cigarette like a sailor, long and deep. "An Irish peasant," she clarifies.

"Why Irish?"

She lifts an eyebrow. "English parents, but I grew up in Ireland."

Ireland! Why, she's only known London, says Evie, and the spires of Cambridge.

"And soon enough, India," adds her new companion. "Where will you be?" She's standing alongside her now, leaning out to sea, smoke trailing from her cigarette.

"Calcutta, mostly. And you?"

"Delhi . . ."

"For the Durbar, of course."

"Yes, then a little travelling around, about which I am far more excited . . ."

"Why is that?"

She laughs. "I think because somewhere deep within my Irish soul the fires of Republicanism have been stoked." Evie makes no attempt to hide her surprise. "But it is a paradox really," she continues, "believing in the inherited English social and political order, all this, my life as I have always known it . . . And yet also in the natural rights of the Irish."

Evie is silent for a moment. "And what of the Indians?"

She shrugs, flicks the cigarette ash overboard. "I am sure we're doing good, but at the same time I wonder why we are not moving towards the granting of greater self-government . . ."

At this, there is silence, and the sound of water lapping against the sides of the ship. Then the woman asks, "And why will you be in India?"

Evie suspects the woman thinks she will say she is looking for a husband, or joining one there, or travelling back with him now at the end of his leave.

"I'm searching for a plant."

The young woman arches one perfectly shaped eyebrow. "Are you a . . . what do they call them? A plant collector?"

"In a way, I suppose, yes. I am a botanist."

"And what kind of plant are you looking for?"

Evie smiles, a little nervous. "I'm afraid I can't say."

"You can't? But why? Is it some sort of secret mission? How thrilling!"

It is hardly that exciting, she admits, only that—and this sounds silly—she is afraid. "That if I say it out loud, I will never find it."

The woman flicks her cigarette away. "Then clearly only one thing remains."

"Which is?"

She smiles. "For me to wish you luck."

✧ ✧ ✧

Evie had not yet turned nine when she was sent away from home.

Only for a while, she was told, long enough for Florence to convalesce from a bout of scarlet fever. Everyone feared for her sister, eleven years old, always a little delicate, racked as she was by a raspy cough and high fever—it was deemed safer for Evie to stay away. "Besides, she is a handful," she overheard her mother say, "and we really can't manage with her around."

So off she went to Grandma Grace, who lived alone in forested Richmond—Grandpa Henry having succumbed years ago to inexplicable illness—and for the first three days, she could not stop crying. It was all her fault; of that, she was certain. She had troubled everyone so much that Florence had fallen ill, and now Mama and Papa wanted to be rid of her. She had always known she was less loved.

Her grandmother tried to convince her otherwise—*Don't be silly, child!*—failing which, she tried another tactic—distraction—and in the only way she knew how. By taking her into the garden, to be "more in the world," as she called it. There, they propped up the sweet peas, plucked peaches, trimmed the hedgerow. She indulged Evie's many questions—Why are trees straight? Does honey come from honeysuckle? What's inside an acorn? Why are flowers beautiful?—and allotted to her a patch in which to grow vegetables, carrots and radish and lettuce. Evie overwatered and underwatered, sowed too deep, too shallow, but once in a while, harvested perfect produce with great pride and joy.

For weeks, they roamed far and wide, through the woods, over the hills, by the river, and sometimes they even made short trips to the coast. Grandma Grace had friends there, women who collected strange rocks with impressions of long-ago fish and other sea creatures. On their explorations, if they found dandelions in a field, or a four-leaf clover, she would be asked to make a wish—*Quick, quick!*—and she would close her eyes tight—*Please let Florence be well. Please let Mama and Papa love me*—and then she would either blow the puffball or collect the clover to press into the pages of a book. "You know, you mustn't tell anyone what you wished for, Evie," Grandma Grace would instruct her, "else your wish might not come true."

After many months, Evie returned home, though she would always visit Grandma Grace for holidays and long weekends, and Easter and Christmas, and for no reason at all—this was where she had found happiness.

And how were things at home? Well, Florence had recovered, and Mama and Papa seemed pleased enough to see her—though she could not help but feel that some sacred familial circle had been drawn in the time she was away, and that she would always somehow fall outside of it.

✧ ✧ ✧

It is her first evening in the East.

They near Port Said just as dusk falls, and suddenly, as if borne in one afternoon over some invisible hemisphere, Evie is in a different world.

They drop anchor opposite the Custom House, a white building with emerald-green domes and rows of graceful arched windows, and as they begin to disembark, the town lights up, casting its shimmering reflection on the water. Everyone agrees, even Mrs. Ward, that they have not seen anything quite so beautiful.

Despite her wobbly sea legs, Evie has a thoroughly enjoyable time, strolling up Commerce Street, bustling with shops, cafés, and vendors poking their wares under her nose—strange fruit, pottery, carved replica sphinxes and other knick-knacks. They stop at Simon Artz, rising in ornamented splendour, stocked with topis, parasols, and fly whisks, and anything else one might need for the tropics.

By the time they return to the *Maloja*, the officers have changed into white uniforms and double awnings have been erected over the decks. They watch the ship's coaling. Piled-up baskets from the barges hoisted up by Arabs, small yet strong and agile. "They look like monkeys," giggles Bessie. Evie says nothing, watching them hard at work in the warm evening, set against a soft black-and-green sea.

Early the next morning, they depart, and sail cleanly through the Suez Canal. Evie does not expect the scale of it: an endless waterway flanked by miles of flat desert, banks studded with towering palm trees. They pass barge after barge crowded with Arabs, small waterside settlements shaded by date palm and eucalyptus. On the shore's edge rumble camels with riders in bright garments, while at intervals, Bedouins with muskets appear in robes of black and white, or men of the Egyptian Camel Corps in their khaki coats. At one point, the canal opens out into Great Bitter Lake, so wide it briefly feels like being back at sea again, then it narrows, and the sandy banks continue.

She is certain that this is one of those moments when she is "more in the world."

How could she describe it? Usually, she feels it by the sea or atop a high hill, or walking through a forest, and now here, sailing through the canal—it is being minutely, wholly, heartfully present in a way that all walls and barriers, of mind and stone, are dissolved. When no obstructions seem to lie between the world and her, and her and the world, just plain air, and in this moment, with the sun, the stars, the moon, and the whole unknowable universe beyond, a feeling of unbridled oneness.

Beyond Suez, heat. Heat as she has never experienced before. The kind of heat that makes it difficult to hold any other thought in her head.

Everyone on the ship changes into white linen, white muslin, and sun helmets—*But does it help?* Evie lounges on the deck, subsisting on iced lemons. Beside her, Bessie is in a faint, wondering whether they might be allowed to sleep out here at night rather than in their airless cabin. Victoria is convinced this will give them malaria, caused by an early morning vapour off the shores of the Red Sea. Evie would like to protest—Ronald Ross won the Nobel Prize for scotching this idea, didn't he almost die experimenting on all those mosquitoes?—but it is much easier to stay silent, and shut her eyes against the heavy air and doze.

A few days later, they steam into Aden. Evie can see why polite London circles refer to it as the Abomination of Desolation, and this is one of its more generous sobriquets.

In contrast to gay Marseille and bustling Port Said, it is a sombre place, surrounded by mountains black as soot, the harbour itself lying in the crater of a dormant volcano. On land, there is not a tree in sight, nor plant, nor leaf; only dry, greyish sand dotted with sharp rocks.

Still, she has four hours before the ship departs, and she wants to make the most of it. She heads out alone, as everyone else has declined her invitation to see the ancient tombs—or, a few miles away, the Aden gardens. "In this wasteland?" cried Bessie, and she refused to disembark. She walks down Main Pass Road to Crater, and passes the market, suddenly finding herself amidst a mix of people from around the globe: Arabs, Negroes, Greeks, Levantines, and others whose origins are unrecognizable to her eye.

Just then, a strange covered carriage draws up next to her.

Inside are Mrs. Hopkins and her nephew. "We're off to see the gardens," she says. "Would you like to come with us?"

Would she! Thrilled, Evie climbs in, and they are off at breakneck speed. Introductions are made—Mr. Gerald Finlay, the nephew, who she fears may have caught her staring rudely at his moustache, and his friend Mr. Edwin Dossett, who is what they call a "fixer"—someone who, apart from arranging expeditionary requirements, also ships plants across the seas. Like her, they are on their way to Calcutta, from where they will catch a steamer to the foothills of the Himalayas.

"Why there?" she asks.

Mr. Dossett smiles. "Orchids." There is something about him she dislikes instantly—a quality she can only describe as acquisitiveness.

"I had mentioned, hadn't I, Gerald, that Miss Alexander studied botany at Cambridge?"

"You did, Aunt Aida. Impressive." He tips his hat in her direction.

They rattle on, the road sharp and rocky, passing camels, and a landscape of sandhills with dense palm thickets and low maritime scrub. The gentlemen discuss the latest improvements in Wardian cases, including crossed battens to hold the plants in place on rough crossings, and ventilation holes covered with perforated zinc to keep out rodents. Most excitingly, some of the newest ones can hold up to fifty samples!

"No plant left behind," says Mr. Dossett, and Evie must try very hard not to make a face.

"Not collecting anything from around here, Gerald?" asks Mrs. Hopkins.

"Not if I want to return alive, no." Apparently horned vipers infest the area—"very venomous."

The gardens they're headed to are at the oasis of Sheikh Othman, a town bordering the colony and protectorate of Aden. When they arrive, it could be a mirage before them—a sudden scar of green, spread over forty acres, with lush, well-irrigated millet fields, tall date palms raising their plumed tops, banana plantations, and rows and rows of pawpaw trees.

Inside, they're greeted by roses and bright flowering bougainvillea, sweet-smelling jasmine, shiny dark green mango trees, and elegant cannas. Evie strolls beneath the cool shade, revelling in the tropical richness around her—dizzy as though she's drunk too much wine. At the huge screw pine trees, she stops, as does Mr. Finlay.

In great excitement, she points at the aerial roots, sent down from the dense spreading clumps, forming new stilt-like stems. "Aren't these marvellous?"

Mr. Finlay smiles. "Quite a treat for a botanist."

She hesitates, then says, "Yes, it is." The spindle-like structures are enormous, seeming to prop up the entire tree. "Though most botanists," she adds, "would ask: Are they root or trunk or branches?"

He furrows his brow. "But not you?"

"I try not to." He appears interested, which is rare for a man, so she continues. "It is not something we think about much, I suppose, but plant form is often forced into categories . . . and this becomes more obvious when structures like these are encountered . . . ones that don't quite fit. Yet even then the question is asked: Does it belong to this or that category? Is it essentially this or that?"

They walk around the screw pine, taking in the breadth of the tree.

"Wouldn't that be what is . . . usually done, though?" asks Mr. Finlay.

"Oh yes," says Evie. "Aristotle, Linnaeus, Troll, the most influential botanists in the world were all essentialists . . . And as a result, we also have this." She gestures around them.

"The botanical garden?" He sounds surprised.

She nods. "It is beautiful—but look how the plants are organized. In ways that distinctly demonstrate systematic botany . . . according to classification, nomenclature. Why, you might call it a colossal project to fix and categorize the natural world."

He glances at her, smiling. *Is he intrigued?* she wonders. *Or does he think her crazy?*

"And so, what is it that you ask, Miss Alexander?"

She shakes her head. "Nothing."

"Nothing?" He laughs. "Well then, that would be the same as me. I ask no questions either. I simply collect."

No, it is not the same at all, Evie would like to tell him. She prefers to ask *nothing* because she is striving to move away from a way of seeing that is quick to judge, and sort, and categorize—based usually on preconceptions. But the day is short, the garden is large, and there is much to see—so she smiles and says, "Yes, of course."

✧ ✧ ✧

One summer, Evie was apprenticed to Ethel Sargant—a scientist, and mentor to Agnes.

"Shall I write and make introductions?" Agnes had asked, and soon afterwards, Evie found herself at the Jodrell Laboratory in Reigate, a cheerless place two hours out of London. Worse, it was hardly a happy communion. Miss Sargant was in her fifties, brilliant, strict, demanding, and while her teaching methods were agreeable to Agnes, a patient, dogged worker, they did not suit Evie, who in Miss Sargant's eyes managed to do little right—"That is not how to microtome a carrot, Miss Alexander"—and made observations she thought very silly.

"It's astonishing, isn't it? That a seed once sown knows which way is up."

"It is called geotaxis."

"Yes, I know the term, Miss Sargant, but—"

"It has to do with gravitational fields; plants orient themselves accordingly."

Once, while examining the experiments for studying seedling structures, Evie stopped at a pea shoot. "I wonder if we have a word for it in English?"

"For what?"

"The force that pushes a leaf up through the soil towards the sky."

"No, we do not. And it is not a leaf, it is a hypocotyl."

Day after day it went on like this, she was chided, corrected, sometimes derided, oftentimes dismissed.

Two months later, back at the university, Agnes asked how it had gone, her summer apprenticeship.

"Oh, quite well."

Agnes threw her a long look.

"All right, it was awful."

Agnes sighed. "I know, Ethel can be demanding . . ."

Yes, but Evie thought she ought to be fair to Miss Sargant. "It didn't help that I couldn't really manage . . ."

They were strolling through the botanical gardens; it was early autumn, and the world around them was turning amber gold.

"Do you have any plans for after you finish?" asked Agnes. If she didn't, she had a small offer to make. "I have set aside some grant money for an assistant, and I thought I'd ask if you might be keen to take it up."

"Me?" Evie hesitated. "I mean it is kind of you, but I'm not . . ."

"You are not what?"

"I don't think I would make a very good botanist."

"Why do you say that?"

They were walking past the West Tropical House, where the *Medinilla crassata,* which bloomed in the warm, humid Philippines, had burst into its chandelier blossoms thinking it was still summer.

"It's something I have come to suspect since the first term."

Agnes frowned. "But you enjoyed your classes, did you not? You grew interested in leaf structures, photosynthesis?"

Evie fell silent. Where should she begin? That she felt as if she had been wrenched from the forests of her childhood into university. That from lying in fields of strawberries—*how silly this sounded*—she was now dissecting the fruit in a laboratory. Not that she did not savour the pleasure of precision or had not learned to honour the chain of evidence and logic—but all she felt she had been trained to do was . . . separate. *Learn how each part of a plant works.* "Once you have removed one part of the plant, try to identify it, and place it on the corresponding plate—stem, petal, leaf, pistil, stamen, and other. Put it in the section that is labelled with the right name." And how much more to measure? Oxygen pressure during photosynthesis, CO_2 production during glycolysis. And how many more times to prove that light is essential for photosynthesis? *A thousand quod erat demonstrandums.* Agreed, the more she performed the experiments, the better she got at them, and she had studied all the textbooks she needed to—Pfeffer, Sachs, Strasburger—collected and classified every plant in Cambridgeshire, microtomed every angiosperm she could lay her hands on from here to London, memorized the concentrations of essential plant nutrients and hundreds and hundreds of botanical names . . . Yet something was missing. And what this was, she had attempted to articulate to herself and failed.

Instead, Evie wished to gesture towards a bed of spiral aloe before them, radiant in their geometric swirls, and say: *I want to know what is at the heart of this, and I think it cannot be seen under a microscope.* But nothing came to her, and she faltered.

"Lately—I feel that I study, but I'm not learning anything about the world."

Agnes nodded. "I can understand that."

It was nice of her to say so, but Evie still felt she had failed her. "I am not a good scientist . . ." she began again.

"I think you're not a *particular* kind of scientist," Agnes interrupted, "which does not make you a bad one."

Evie had not thought of it that way before. Or even known that there might be . . . different kinds of scientists.

"What should I do?"

"Many things, but first," said Agnes, "we feed the swans."

With that, they walked down the path leading to the stream where the lilies grew.

✧ ✧ ✧

On their last day on board, Evie sits out on the deck for a long while.

The sky and the sea are darkening rapidly, and the clouds are edged with the last of the sunset's silvery glow. Her things are packed, ready to be offloaded, the letter for Mr. Muttlebury tucked safely into her bag. A strong wind springs up, tugging at her skirt, her hair, though no warning has been issued about rough weather.

Onward, onward, she thinks. *The wind is blowing me towards my wishes.*

Evie caught her first glimpse of India when she was ten. When she and Grandma Grace took a bus to Kew Gardens to see the work of Marianne North, and she wandered through the gallery, a large wood-panelled room hung with paintings from floor to ceiling, and then came to one—of gardens laid out in Agra around a white building with a great dome—and squealed, "Grandma, this looks like an onion!"

Even afterwards, she was a regular visitor at the gallery. Here was Australia, there Ceylon, Chile, Japan, Java, and she did not stand there only with an extravagant longing to trot around the globe, she was also enamoured of the plants. She felt about them the way some people feel about books—that there were exasperatingly too many to encounter in a lifetime. When might she see the flaming crimson mahoe of Jamaica, for instance? The trumpet trees of Brazil? When the plant collectors bring them to Kew, her sister would say pragmatically, and she had to be satisfied with that.

Over the last year, she had visited the gallery to inspect the India paintings more closely and discovered that Miss North had travelled through the subcontinent far more widely than she had imagined—she had painted in the north, in Simla, Delhi, and Agra, to the west in Rajputana and Bombay, in the south all the way to Cochin and Tanjore, and even—how exciting—the far east, beyond Benares to Calcutta, Darjeeling, and Sikkim, though no farther.

And here she is now, in a clanking train, chugging towards the east, looking out at a landscape that could have come from one of those paintings.

How am I here? It seemed to have all happened so fast. She was awakened that morning by a strange stillness, and it took her a moment to realize that the *Maloja* had docked in Bombay. From the deck, she could see small sailboats and large steamers on a smooth oily sea, and beyond that, in the pale grey-blue light of early morning, misty hills and banks of gold-tipped clouds. Later, they descended into the hubbub on the quay, festooned with madly fluttering decorations—for the impending arrival of the king—and crowded with hawkers and journalists. They drove into town in a low hooded carriage, the narrow streets crammed with animals and people, clanging bells and music, spicy cooking smells and radiant colours. Bessie nearly screamed for joy as they passed a water carrier with bare brown shapely limbs and turbaned head who she was certain looked straight out of a picture book. Slowly, the musky scented twilight subdued the bright patterns of the day and the setting sun threw long shadows across the streets. Only a short while ago, Evie had been in foggy London . . . unbelievable, impossible even, that she had arrived in India at last.

The train journey has not been the nightmare Bessie and Mrs. Ward make it out to be, but it certainly feels . . . constrained. They share a three-berth compartment, with no connecting corridors between the carriages, so there is little they can do to escape one another's company. For four days and three nights, they speed across a thousand dusty miles, across changing landscapes and temperatures. Evie takes all the outside in—grey monkeys with white chests and long tails darting about in the trees, parakeets flying at sunset, carts drawn by great horned bullocks, peasants farming, washing their clothes along riverbanks. Small stations come at regular intervals—Manmad Junction, Akola, Badnera, Nagpur, Raipur, Rourkela—and at each stop there are oranges to be bought, or small bags of nougat and tangerines. Once, when Evie steps out, she is surrounded by a swarm of small boys in brilliant turbans, bargaining, begging, or performing conjuring tricks.

All of this is new and beautiful, though somewhere along the way she begins to feel it is also strangely superficial to be so wholly removed from the rhythms of the outside world, to speak to no one from here, to know little or nothing about the places they pass through. Then she tells herself to be patient—she is on a train!—and that it will be different once she arrives in Calcutta.

They rattle through the fertile United Provinces, with fields of green crops, mimosa trees, and mango plantations. Villages are frequent, huts hung with pumpkin vines, or sometimes a small town with whitewashed houses and a temple, or a mosque with a minaret. When they enter Bengal, the Grand Trunk Road runs alongside the railway track, carrying its traffic of horse-drawn vehicles and the occasional motorcar or lorry.

Then, finally, they chuff into Howrah Junction—which, even at five thirty in the morning, hums with activity.

As Evie tries pushing her way through, hands pluck at her for alms, and boxes of sweets, fruits, and flowers are pressed to her face. Mrs. Ward and Bessie are changing for the train to Serampore, and Evie had said her goodbyes earlier. To her surprise, Bessie had flung her arms around her, tearfully, "I shall miss you so!"

Evie feels lost, too, stepping off the train alone, and just when she thinks she will be wandering the platform forever, a tall, fierce-looking Indian stops her. "Miss Alexander?" She nods. "Mr. and Mrs. Hall, waiting," he says, and gestures outside, and then with an authoritative declamation—"Be off with you!"—he clears the crowd around them.

She hopes Calcutta will not be the end of way for her like it was for Miss North.

Though there is much to like about the city, too. It has the same busy air as London, docks lively and dirty, markets bustling, and the river palpably central to people's lives—or so it appears, for she has only just arrived and does not wish to make hasty observations. She has passed many grand buildings already, the Great Eastern Hotel facing the Maidan, and another whose construction is still under way, an immense memorial to Queen Victoria—beneath the scaffolding, she can glimpse the shape of turrets, and possibly a gigantic dome.

It strikes her then: *This is the capital of the empire!*

So much around her also feels bewilderingly new, and the pretense she had attempted to put up at the beginning of the journey, of being unperturbed, has melted away—that is also, possibly, because of the heat. "This is the beginning of the cold season," she has been told, while around her brightens a day as warm as any in a London summer. She realizes she ought to have brought more cotton, and infinitely less flannel.

Charlotte, her husband, Victor, and their two children live off the Strand, close to the Hooghly River and the Calcutta Port Trust headquarters, where Victor works as assistant to the chief commissioner. They have servants, a pretty garden, and have been assigned one of the better government quarters. "Though the damp still rises through the walls during the monsoon," Charlotte tells her cheerfully, "and sometimes our living room floods. But we are very quick at removing furniture and carpets now."

She comes to learn swiftly that the household runs with clockwork precision—meals are laid out and partaken of on time, all surfaces—wood, silver, glass—gleam despite the perpetual onslaught of dust, the children, Sam and Eleanor, four and two, are entertained, bathed, fed, and put to bed at appropriate hours by the ayah. What also amazes her is that their cook conjures miraculous "home" dishes—one does not expect pea soup, beef rissoles, and caramel custard for one's first meal in India, but apparently "Babarchi has learned to cook everything English." His greatest triumph? A giant honey-glazed ham for Christmas, complete with paper frill on the knuckle. Occasionally, Charlotte says, he has been known to spice a baked fish pie with cardamom and brighten the chicken roast with turmeric, but apart from these culinary misadventures, the Hall household operates smoothly under Charlotte's firm, watchful eye.

The quest to find Evie a husband is met with similar efficiency.

A few days after her arrival, they are in Evie's room, sitting at the edge of the bed—Charlotte, like Patrick, has light eyes, but hers are a stormier blue. She also exudes a certain spirited energy Evie had not expected. She is just done doling out handy hints—all silks in the teak trunk, please, else termites will ravage them overnight; if you are stepping out in the evenings, be wary of mosquitoes, and *always* shake out your shoes before slipping them on, in case a frog has climbed in, or worse, a scorpion. Next she chalks out their winter itinerary. "You've arrived at the beginning of the season," she says. "Which is good." Upcoming events in the social calendar include races, polo matches, cricket week, paperchases, and an array of garden parties, cocktails, dinners, and picnics, both by day and by moonlight. Then there's Christmas, of course, and a whole slew of activities arranged around it at the clubs.

At this rate, thinks Evie, *she will be married off by the end of the month.*

"Did you not meet someone nice on the ship?" Charlotte asks. She was a fishing fleet girl too—she had travelled out with her mother, and on the way she met Victor, an officer returning from leave, and they were married in Bombay in six weeks. "Almost as soon as we docked," she says, laughing. This would be no surprise for two people passionately in love, except Evie finds it hard to imagine Victor being swept away by his emotions, or even swayed by them in the least. He is older than Charlotte by ten years or more, with a serious way about him that Evie finds almost comical.

"Also, is there anything in particular you'd like to do here?" asks Charlotte.

"Well . . ."

"Yes?"

"I'd like to see the botanical gardens."

Charlotte looks surprised and then she laughs. "I'd expected the races or a visit to the Marble Palace . . . I'm not sure how much of a chance you'll have to meet eligible men all the way out in Seebpore, but I'm sure a trip can be arranged."

Her guest is thrilled. "Wonderful," she says. "Thank you."

Charlotte stands up, making to leave, but stops. "I also wanted to ask . . ." she begins, and then hesitates. Evie waits for her to continue, wondering what this is about. "It's what you want, isn't it? Coming out here, getting married? I know it's what we must do, but these days women have a little more time."

For a moment, Evie holds her breath. She is sorely tempted to be as candid, to tell her the truth, but if she does, would it not make its way back to London? Could she trust Charlotte? And more important, was it fair to burden her with the truth?

"Well?" asks her hostess.

Evie manages to nod, somewhat convincingly, even if she's unable to bring herself to actually say, *Yes, yes, this is what I want.*

✧ ✧ ✧

Evie's association with the Goethean Science Society began towards the end of her final year at university. She saw an announcement pinned to the noticeboard outside Balfour, calling for a meeting, and beneath that, a quote: *The many in the One.*

How odd, she thought. Not long after their walk in the botanical garden, Agnes had lent her some books, which she had only glanced at briefly, but among them lay a pamphlet—a translation of a volume by Goethe titled *The Metamorphosis of Plants.*

Evie wound her way to Queens' College that winter evening out of curiosity. What did she know about Goethe? Not much except that he was a German novelist and poet, author of *The Sorrows of Young Werther*, which she remembered reading in school and dismissing for its annoyingly lovelorn protagonist. Was it not extremely popular in its time? An eighteenth-century bestseller! A key text of the Sturm and Drang movement, she remembers her English teacher saying. A harbinger of Romanticism, she had called it. He'd written a few plays, too, if she was not mistaken. Why on earth, then, was there a Goethean *Science* Society? It all seemed very peculiar.

At Queens', in room CC43, she found three others waiting.

"Hello," she said, "have we started, or are we waiting for the rest?"

A skinny, straight-haired youth with spectacles, told her, "Well, this is it."

"For today, you mean?"

The girl spoke this time. "What my brother Phineas means is we are all there is." Evie recognized her as a student at Girton; she had seen her before at Balfour.

"Oh, I see." Evie had stumbled upon the tiniest society in the university.

The last of the three, a stockier student who introduced himself as Oliver-please-call-me-Ollie, made her feel more welcome. "We are . . . err . . . a small group, but passionate." She was offered a cup of tea and a biscuit.

"How did you hear about us?" She told them. "And what is your academic background?" Natural sciences with an emphasis on botany. "We are botanists too," said Ollie, indicating himself and the girl, whose name was Luella though they called her Lulu. "Phineas is a mathematician." Phineas bowed, and added solemnly, "Despite Goethe's critiques of the overuse of mathematics, his ideas on morphology may be connected with it, especially in D'Arcy Thompson's work, where he extends it into a science of form by applying physical methods to biological subjects. Of course, we'll know more on the subject when his book is published, which should be soon now."

Evie said she couldn't wait.

Ollie cleared his throat. "For Lulu and me, well, we were beginning to feel a deep sense of alienation from the natural world, after engaging extensively with scholarship that condoned strictly mathematical interpretations of nature . . . we felt they had lost their connection to the senses entirely." He paused. "Might that be what you began to feel, too?"

Evie nodded slowly.

Lulu narrowed her eyes. "Why are you here?"

She decided to be honest but before she was done, she was being admonished. "You have no clue what this society is about?" Lulu was aghast.

"No, but–"

"I don't think you understand. We are not here to waste time. We read, we discuss, we aim to revise contemporary scientific practices."

Phineas muttered that this was why they never had any new members, while Ollie tried to placate everybody all around. "There, there, Lulu, everyone has their own journey into Goethean thought . . ."

Lulu said Evie should try meeting them when she was farther along her journey rather than when she hadn't even begun.

"And now I probably won't," said Evie. "I came here inspired by the one principle that guides the beginnings of all pursuits, scientific or otherwise. Curiosity. And you have squashed it."

She was halfway down the hall before Ollie caught up with her, apologizing on behalf of the society. "Please stay," he said.

And because she was intrigued, she did. She was given another cup of tea, but no biscuit, and the meeting reconvened.

"Thank you," began Evie, "for bearing with my ignorance, and I apologize for being ill-prepared, but I assure you I am eager to learn." She looked at the others. "What is Goethean science?"

First, there was a moment of silence, and then, she was given an answer she didn't quite expect: "Life."

She shook her head, bewildered. "What?"

In that, the botanists explained, it was a way of learning that didn't wrench one away from nature in all her vitality and aliveness.

"Nature is ever shaping new forms," added Ollie, "that's what Goethe said. What is has never yet been; what has been comes not again. Everything is new and yet nothing but the old."

Evie wasn't sure what to make of it—*what exactly did they mean?*—but she knew she was drawn to this, the idea of nature as infinitely changing, infinitely alive.

They told her that in trying to understand Goethe, she first needed to understand what came before him, his scientific inheritance. What made him break away from it? It was hardly difficult to see how the Age of Enlightenment played a part, its obsession with order, control, with the classification of the natural world, its rule of reason, of "pure" rational thought, its eventual crystallization into Cartesian science, bound by the empirical and analytical. However, in Germany a rebellious wildness had begun to grow—Romanticism!—and it was within this spirit of defiance and questioning and freedom that Goethe's science was born.

"He was an outsider to science, really," Ollie continued. "A scientist with a poet's eye and a poet's sensibility. Who had heard of such a thing? But he recognized and actualized a new way of seeing . . ."

"And what might this be?" asked Evie breathlessly.

"Of seeing in wholeness. He wished to understand nature by experiencing it as a living organism whose ever-changing, ever-growing dynamic the observer—us, you, me—is a part of, and in this way to train one's mind to be as flexible as nature herself."

Evie was quiet for a moment before she asked, “Did anyone take him seriously?”

“Oh, no,” the three replied. “Hardly anyone does even now.”

“Then why do you?”

Ollie said simply, “Everything we missed over the course of studying for our degrees–intuition, inspiration, imagination–we found here in abundance.”

✧ ✧ ✧

After ten days in Calcutta, she is finally en route to the Agricultural and Horticultural Office in Alipore, where Mr. George Mackay Muttlebury is a senior council member.

She is accompanied by Bahadurjee, the fierce-looking Indian who had picked her up at Howrah Junction. They drive along the Hooghly for the most part, the banks particularly noisome in this warm spell, although the odour lightens as they manoeuvre away from the river, past the half-constructed Victoria Memorial, Alipore Zoo, and a maidan where children are playing in the dust. She is curious about her chaperone—although she has not yet had a chance to strike up a conversation with him. Charlotte and Victor treat him fondly—but with a carefully maintained distance. He is from Punjab, he tells her, for many years employed by an English family, who were finally posted to Calcutta before returning to England.

"They wanted to take me, miss . . ."

"Oh, and did you not go?"

He shudders. "Too cold." Then he adds, "People should be where the temperatures suit them." She agrees, adding with a laugh, "That would mean all British people here need to relocate back to their rainy little island."

He nods sombrely, as if to say *eventually that will happen.*

The Agricultural and Horticultural Office is well protected by high gates and hedges, and a pebble track runs to the office building ensconced within well-trimmed lawns and rows of blooming hibiscus shrubs. It doesn't feel at all like being in a city.

Inside, she first encounters the secretary, a young man in owlish spectacles, a bureaucratic pedant, she discovers, who makes her fill out form after form.

"But all I need is for you to hand over this letter."

"And I will, Miss Alexander . . . as soon as this is filled out."

When that is done, she is kept waiting in a dusty lounge before being summoned.

Behind the desk sits a smiling man with a neat moustache, neatly parted hair, and noticeably pointed ears. "I'm given to understand you were Mrs. Arber's assistant?" He gestures to the letter. She confirms this, saying she apprenticed under Mrs. Arber for a year in Cambridge. "Wonderful." He had made her acquaintance when she wrote to the institute asking for information on the Indian holy basil, tulsi, a medicinal plant native to the subcontinent. They have corresponded a few times.

Evie knows all this, but she listens politely, waiting until he is done.

"Now, what can I do for you, Miss Alexander? Mrs. Arber's letter indicates that you are interested in undertaking botanical excursions while here in India."

She says this is indeed the case.

"Not a problem," says Mr. Muttlebury airily. Well! She had not thought it would be this easy. "What would you like to see? The botanical gardens?"

She says that is already being arranged by her hosts.

"What about the Sundarbans?" he offers next.

Their conversation is punctured by the arrival of tea, after which she mentions that she is also happy to venture farther afield: "I would like to make productive use of my time here, and I am lucky Mrs. Arber is acquainted with someone like you . . ."

The flattery seems to work, as flattery tends to; the tips of Mr. Muttlebury's ears turn pink.

She directs her gaze to the map of British India hanging on the wall, and gestures with her white-gloved hand. "Look how much there is to explore. I am sure you have seen it all."

Mr. Muttlebury protests, saying that would simply be impossible, but yes, he adds modestly, he has travelled in the east a fair bit, to the farthest parts of Burma and the jungles of Assam.

"Oh, Assam," gushes Evie, "how marvellous!"

"Yes, it was. Until we were ambushed by leeches." She exclaims, hand to chest, wondering if her dramatic interlude is too much. Clearly not, for

Mr. Muttlebury puffs up and continues, "Quite the biggest I have seen." He holds his hands apart to indicate an impossible length.

She hopes never to encounter such terrifying creatures, she says, although she is *fascinated* by the hills of Assam, especially, she lets drop casually, the places where Hooker roamed.

"Ah, orchid country."

"Yes, I have a passion for drawing them," she says, lying lightly. If there are any expeditions to the area that she could join, she would be so grateful if he could inform her.

He has been won over. "Immediately, and at once, Miss Alexander!"

After she is ushered out, she decides to take a quick walk around the garden. "No, don't worry," she tells Bahadurjee when he makes to accompany her. "I will be back shortly."

She strolls down the winding path that opens out onto a lawn, while to her left sits a squat greenhouse, filled with potted plants in bloom, blazing golden, maroon, and white chrysanthemums. Evie continues down a path snaking around the grass; the place is sun-drenched and quiet, and not until she crosses an arched bridge does she meet anyone else: a gardener taking a nap.

She walks on and enters the next greenhouse—brimming with orchids. One is shaped like a slipper; another is of purest white with a hint of magenta at the tip of its innermost petal. Each of them a symbol of high social status and wealth back home, so rare were orchids there and difficult to grow. Orchid mania had not died down entirely even now—they still fetched high prices at auctions in London, which, of course, explained Mr. Dossett's continued interest in collecting them.

From the greenhouse, Evie wanders out into a nearby rose garden, also in bloom—damasks and albas, Kashmiris and miniatures. A distance away, the gardener is back at work, the gentle swish of his khukri slicing through the grass. She prefers it here, outside: the air is scented, and the roses rise plump and petalled from their bushes, lifted towards the sky.

✧ ✧ ✧

The next day, all is not well at the Hall residence.

Victor is subdued at lunch, and he conveys the news that all arrangements have been made for Evie's visit to the botanical garden as though telling her that someone is dying.

"Is everything all right?" she inquires.

"We'll see."

Evie does not pursue the matter—she is thrilled about her trip, and thinking about how she ought to prepare her inks and sketchbooks and flower press. Finally, she will get to see the ancient banyan, which she has heard is so vast it is its own forest. She can hardly wait.

To occupy herself, she stays outside for most of the day, sketching the bougainvillea in the garden. The children play around her, chasing butterflies and bumblebees.

"What are you doing, Evie?" Sam asks breathlessly, his sister standing behind him.

Evie shows them the drawing, which she thinks is coming out rather nicely.

"Flowers!" he yelps.

The colourful blossoms are not flowers but bracts, which surround the true white flower sitting tiny and unnoticed at the centre. But perhaps four is a little too young for lessons on botanical morphology.

By the time she returns to the house, it is late afternoon and tea is laid out in the veranda.

"There has been a bit of news," says Charlotte. "Victor's office has had a telegram."

Oh, no. Evie hopes, selfishly, that whatever it is, it will not interfere with her plans.

"There was an announcement at the Durbar yesterday . . . The capital is being moved to Delhi."

For a moment, it fails to make sense.

"Can they do that?" asks Evie. "I mean, what happens to Calcutta?"

"We don't quite know. It is a shock . . . Poor Victor, he can hardly believe it. It was a betrayal, he was saying, and done in such secrecy, too. No one knew about it—not even the king." Charlotte stirs her tea, absently. "I suppose if we are not the capital any longer, we will be reduced to nothing more than a marginal provincial town."

In the days to come, it is all anyone discusses, at the gymkhanas and the clubs, at lunches and dinners, the shift of the imperial capital, and what it will mean for Calcutta.

Evie hears often that it is a tremendous loss, of power and prestige, "a stab in the back" according to one belligerent officer, "utterly shocking" for many ladies. More than a few officers are now considering a transfer. If the centre of power shifts, so will they. Except that Delhi is yet ill-equipped to accommodate the British. They have heard it will take twenty years or more to complete laying out a "New Delhi" to the south of the old Mughal city. A few approve of the decision—it makes little sense for Britain to govern from Calcutta, located on the eastern extremity of its Indian possessions. Still others lament, "This city will never recover."

"What might the Indians think?" Evie would like to ask, even though she suspects this is not what anyone else considers an important question.

Nevertheless, she is kept occupied. Many outstation gentlemen are present at these social occasions, whose time is limited and cannot be spent bemoaning Lord Hardinge's drastic decision—they are on leave and in Calcutta expressly to find a wife. So far, Evie has been introduced to an eager young physician from Patna, a few fun-loving tea planters from Darjeeling, a handsome railway engineer currently posted in Burma. And she smiles and says, *How do you do, how do you do,* then spends the rest of the evening trying to avoid them.

✧ ✧ ✧

The morning doesn't start out as blue skied as she hoped it would be, but by the time she and Bahadurjee set off for Chandpal Ghat, a brisk breeze picks up and the clouds begin to clear.

In her step is a happy lightness. They catch the steamer from near the Port Trust Office and sail down the Hooghly, past Howrah, making a few stops along the way, first at Tuckta Ghat, then Kidderpore, and Shalimar, an ugly place with a pretty name. On the steamer are several other passengers, including a thin Indian man, dressed in a traditional dhoti and turban, who bursts into song.

"What is he singing about?" she asks Bahadurjee, who answers suspiciously quickly, "The greatness of the British."

As they speed along, the river churning behind them, she turns to him again.

"Bahadurjee, what do you think? Of the British changing capitals like this?"

Before he can reply, the singing man chuckles. "They should move it farther west . . ."

"Oh? To Bombay, you think?"

"No, no, farther."

She's puzzled. Isn't Bombay on the coast?

"All the way back," he adds, "to London."

They finally arrive at the landing stage for the botanical gardens, which leads to a long, elegant avenue of royal palms. Walking between them feels processional, as though they are here in attendance on matters of state. Bahadurjee, less fond of outdoor activity, appears none too impressed.

They are a short walk away from the famous banyan tree, the largest in all of India, he tells her, but it is a long time getting there because Evie stops to examine every single plant that catches her eye. Among the exotics she finds a nutmeg, and a pretty tree, like a myrtle, with a delicate peach-like blossom, planted in a sheltered situation and carefully matted around with moss.

Finally, they approach the banyan which from a distance looks like a grove of trees. "This is just *one* tree?" she confirms with Bahadurjee. "Yes, miss, just one."

She has never seen anything like it, not even in Kew Gardens with its ancient black walnut and splendid Lucombe oak. She walks around the grove; the main trunk is lost somewhere in the depths of the overhanging roots. Just as she is about to step inside, though, someone calls her name. She turns to see Mrs. Hopkins, accompanied by an elderly lady and her plant-collector nephew, whom Evie can barely recognize without his moustache.

"Evelyn, dear, how wonderful to see you!" She returns the greeting less warmly, saying this is a surprise. "Well, we are all plant lovers here, so it is not too shocking," counters Mrs. Hopkins, smiling. They have been in Bombay all this while and have only just arrived in Calcutta. "It is much nicer weather here."

A few more pleasantries are exchanged before talk swerves to the shifting of the imperial capital. "It might have to do with growing anti-British sentiment here." Mrs. Hopkins drops her voice as though to even say this is treachery.

Evie, straight-faced, says she has not heard anything of the kind.

"No, they wouldn't proclaim it, would they?" Gerald, she adds, can hardly wait to get away from all this and make for the wilds.

Tempted as Evie is to exclaim *me, too,* she must feign polite interest. "When will you be off, Mr. Finlay?" She is suddenly aware that the ladies' eyes are on them.

"Directly after the New Year. My aunt insists I stay for the season and spend some time with humans rather than plants for a change."

The older ladies laugh, and he smiles, looking boyish.

As she feared, they invite her to join their party and share their luncheon—ham sandwiches, lemonade plenty to spare. "Oh, but I would not wish to intrude."

Mrs. Hopkins is quick to reassure her this is not the case. Evie cannot think of a reason not to join them, apart from not wishing to—and this she cannot voice, so she accepts. What flusters her though, is that Mrs. Hopkins strolls ahead with her neighbour, leaving her to walk with Mr. Finlay.

"I apologize if we have intruded on your day, Miss Alexander. My aunt can sometimes be quite . . . insistent." She says it is all right, that the promise of ham sandwiches is hard to resist. "But I must warn you, we will be stopping every so often to allow me to make pressings." Pressings? He is happy to stop and uproot entire plants if that is what she would prefer. She smiles, her mood lightening. He is definitely improved without his glinty-eyed friend, Mr. Dossett, and also without his moustache.

They are deep inside the grove now, and sunlight filters through in dappled patterns. It is an eerie place, bare-branched and leafless. From the branches rising above them drop hundreds of spindle-like structures, crutches that seem to prop up the entire forest.

"I remember what you said at Aden," begins Mr. Finlay. "And believe me, I am not standing here asking whether these are trunks or branches or roots." She laughs, pleased—saying she hadn't imagined he would remember at all.

"How could I not," he says, looking at her, and somewhere in her stomach she feels a flutter.

They continue to stroll through the strange forest, and out the other side, into a sudden sweep of openness. "You may know already," begins Mr. Finlay, "that these gardens were designed . . . or rather redesigned in the 1840s by William Griffith . . ."

"I did not!" *I have read his travel memoir*, she wants to add but does not wish to interrupt.

"He took over from a superintendent of an older generation, Nathaniel Wallich . . . let's just say they did not see eye to eye over many things. On taking control of the garden, Griffith described its neglected state in an official report, saying it was a mess."

They walk along again, away from the banyan, to catch up with the older ladies.

"I assume what you are suggesting is that Griffith's objections stemmed from more than personal animosity?"

Mr. Finlay nods. "You are quite right. I think the informal layout of his predecessor's garden was offensive to his conception of ordered rational science. So what he proposed was radical reorganization . . . and here we have it, what you called a colossal attempt to fix the natural world."

He remembers everything, she thinks warmly.

"Admittedly a more picturesque arrangement than what Griffith had planned," he continues, "and following a geographical planting plan, but still, as orderly as ever."

"You are well informed on the subject, Mr. Finlay."

"And you are surprised?"

She nods, smiling.

He feigns offense. "Miss Alexander, I may be a lowly scavenger of plants, but I am rather interested in the history of my profession."

"Yes," she says, teasing. "That is quite unusual."

He laughs, heartily now, and looks at her as though to say something, but changes his mind. Up ahead, the older ladies have stopped and are waiting. They head to a bench overlooking a still lake, one of many dotting the gardens, its surface glistening with algae and yellowed leaves.

✧ ✧ ✧

After Evie stumbled into her first GSS meeting, she attended the next, and all the ones after—more enthusiastically, it must be said, than any of her classes. So much fresh learning! And a realization, from which there was no coming back, that the history of science was untidy, except it had been pruned and neatened—to exclude scientists who did not contribute to conventionally accepted narratives.

Goethe did not feature in any of the textbooks she had studied—his story, as with so many others, was written out, erased, uncelebrated. His way of seeing remained dismissed, much like the work of the women botanists they discussed at Newnham, deemed to be forever engaged in—and judged for—their "domestic" botany.

She came to these meetings with many questions, but first, what was Goethe's way of seeing, exactly? What did it mean to see in wholeness?

To not reduce a phenomenon to its parts, she was told promptly, as is the rather reductive way of conventional science.

"Have you noticed the quote on our poster?"

Evie nodded. *The many in the One.*

"It is exactly that."

By Goethe's late Enlightenment age, he inhabited a world stricken by separation. Everything in the natural world had its place—with humans, *naturally*, placed on top, scrutinizing, demystifying, and harnessing the power of all aspects of the natural world. To do this most effectively, all kingdoms—plants, animals, minerals—were named, systematically categorized, and fixed.

"By Linnaeus, mainly," added Phineas.

"'God creates; I organize,' he said," added Lulu. "Pompous man."

Ollie nodded in all seriousness. "It was the grand scientific mission of the time. To impose order on chaos, so everything could be made knowable. Then Goethe came along discounting it all, asking, *Is this the only way?* He was post-Linnaean, you see, hoping to identify some sort of *natural* taxonomy, if indeed there even was such a thing."

Linnaeus's obsession with classification supported a way of seeing the natural world, and everything in it, as made up of separate entities working together to produce what we, from a distance, then observed. "Open a textbook on botany," said Ollie, "and look at how the language on the page directs you to see . . . the internal and the external, the constituent parts of a cell, the parts of a flower that seemingly exist with little connection to each other . . . drawings separate and divide too, each part labelled and numbered, emphasizing boundaries, walls, studying the workings of a plant in isolation . . ."

These textbooks don't magically, benignly, come into being—they are written to prop up a particular scientific view. "All of this"—Lulu gestured around them, by which Evie took to mean the university—"upholds it too."

For someone like Linnaeus, the belief was that the sum of the parts made up the whole. "Take all of these parts, throw them together, and voilà! You have a plant! A human! A planet!" Similar, Ollie supposed, to a machine. But did she see how this held the whole subservient to the parts? At its heart lay this irrevocable inequality.

"And Goethe?" asked Evie, holding her breath.

For him, unity. Alles eins—aus! Not a mechanistic reduction of living, breathing beings. Each part, even in its minuteness, contained the whole. The leaf is stem which is flower which is seed which is the entire plant, and on and on it goes in an unending cycle of life. In this way, the parts and the whole are equal. Calling for connection at the deepest level—one denied by the other, more conventional Linnaean view.

There is diversity, yet a unity in this multiplicity.

The many in the One.

So many revelations for Evie in a musty room in Queens', huddled over a cup of tea.

She pored over Goethe's scientific writings—first, the essay "The Experiment as Mediator of Subject and Object." "It's a whole new way of seeing," she enthused to the others, and even though written more than a hundred and twenty years ago, still remarkably prescient. In Goethe's age of empiricism, focused on the testable by observation and experiment, how vividly aware he was of science as a human activity, easily open to the flaws and biases to which they were susceptible. "Die Natur," his essay that read more as an ode—*Nature is the only real artist*—championed a "good science" that took her back into the world, that reinstated imagination at the heart of the subject, as well as wonder. Both of which by Goethe's time, served little purpose in the practise of science. Instead, dependence on the quantitative method—one that gave primacy to qualities that could be expressed mathematically in a direct way—had grown.

"Number, magnitude, position, extension," explained Phineas. "While in contrast, qualities that couldn't were made *secondary*. Colour, taste, sound. Demoted to being no more than subjective experience, would you believe, or illusions of the senses, and not part of nature. In fact, secondary qualities were seen as unable to exist on their own, and were understood only when explained in relation to primary ones. As though primary qualities were always there *behind* them, hidden by appearances."

"Newton, for example!" exclaimed Ollie. "He replaced the phenomenon of colour with a set of numbers." But where he "split" colourless light and calculated angles of refraction, Goethe saw something else—he refuted the notion that colour was determined solely by light and the colour spectrum, arguing instead that it is shaped by perception as well as light *and* darkness. He saw darkness as an active ingredient of the spectrum, one that made colour perceptible rather than being mere absence of light.

"Colour as 'light's suffering and joy,'" murmured Lulu.

With Goethe, all focus, all attention was on the phenomenon itself, which he believed could be accessed through observation—or what became Evie's favourite term, *anschauung*. A word with no equivalent in English, but which could be interpreted as intuitive knowledge gained through careful patient contemplation, a "gentle" empiricism or "thinking with the mind's eye."

"We tend to treat observation as a matter of opening our eyes in front of the phenomenon," said Ollie. "As if it were something that happens to us when visual information flows in through the senses and is registered in the consciousness. Here is a flower"—he gestured before him—"look how it functions."

But observing in Goethe's way required one to be more than usually alive to seeing.

"And not just gaining a visual impression," he added.

Goethe spoke of it as seeing with *a certain purity of mind*, although one should not assume that he was recommending a naïve or precritical view. He accepted the essential role of the mind's activity in rendering experience meaningful.

"Just that," said Phineas, "despite recognizing the many failings of our ways of knowing, Goethe believed that a knowledge utterly in tune with the nature of things in the world was possible."

"How so?" asked Evie. "I mean, is there some sort of . . . method to this?"

Stages is what they preferred to call them, or modes of perception, which for a beginner could be distinguished quite sharply, though the aim was to experience these processes in a seamless flow.

"In preparation, it is important to first acknowledge who we are," began Ollie. "Our daily likes and dislikes, our personal history, and the impressions that ordinary encounters with the natural world create in ourselves as observers." This is also when the observer chooses what to study, perhaps when one is struck by something; Goethe called it "being spoken to" by the thing.

"What, then?"

"The first stage, 'exact sense perception.'"

Evie blinked.

"A detailed observation of the 'bare facts' of the phenomenon that are available to our ordinary senses. Seeing what is present with as little personal judgement and evaluation as possible. All our theories and feelings about a thing must be held back in order to 'let the phenomena speak for themselves.'"

The stage after was "exact sensorial fantasy." To perceive the time-life of the phenomenon, that is, to see it as a phenomenon *in* time, not as an objective frozen present as prompted by the first stage, but as a thing with a history.

"The growth of a leaf or the blossoming of a flower," explained Ollie. "Observing it undergoing this process in your imagination, and seeing minutely how it changes, how it exists as a sequence of forms."

Then a move towards "seeing in beholding," or an attempt to still or quieten active perception to allow the thing to express itself through the observer.

"To make space for it to be articulated in its own way," added Lulu, though she looked doubtful that Evie was following any of this.

Ollie nodded. "Yes, and this is usually expressed in emotional language, poetry, painting, or other art forms."

If the first stage used perception to see form, the second imagination to perceive its mutability, the third inspiration to reveal the gesture, the final process—"being one with the object"—called for intuition to combine and move beyond the previous stages.

"In terms of a Goethean methodology," added Phineas, "each of the stages is dependent upon those which precede it."

Evie nodded slowly. "Is that why each stage is more difficult to explain outside of the context of having experienced the previous ones?"

"Exactly!" they chorused.

But "being one with the object" was meant to allow for an appreciation of the content or meaning of the form as well as the form itself. The outer appearance and inner content combined by conceptualization.

All this brought a bewildering newness for Evie, and she was not entirely certain she had understood it all, it seemed abstract at the moment, and theoretical, but she felt great excitement and also great relief—that she was not dull, or worse, stupid, that she had not chosen to study the "wrong" subject. In short, there was little the matter with her, the problem lay in the way science was being taught. At this realization, something in her lightened. An understanding of plants depended as much on a scientist's personal sympathy with nature as on her systematic study of it! Grandma Grace, it struck her, was a "Goethean scientist" long before she was aware the term existed. What better way to honour her memory than to resolve to practise good science, to be a wiser botanist, and, like her grandmother, to be more in the world.

✧ ✧ ✧

Finally, letters arrive from Mama and Florence. They await with the morning post at breakfast, and Evie retreats to the garden to read them.

Her mother sounds much the same as she does in person—brisk, sensible, cheerful enough. Papa is hard at work, as usual, she writes, though recently recovered from a bad cold, while she has been busy with charity work at the church now that it is coming up to Christmas. Collecting old clothes, as she usually does, and food rations for the poor.

In other news, she is sure Evie would like to know that the winter hellebores have flowered early—they might not last through to January, but they are rescuing the garden from winter dreariness.

What about you, dear Evelyn? she asks finally. *I hope so far you are finding it fruitful being in India? I look forward to your news.*

Evie has the grace to blush. No news! At least not the kind that her mother expects. She will need to compose a reply carefully, or not write at all, laying the blame on the dreadfully unreliable Indian post.

The letter from Florence, though, carries a joyous announcement.

She and Patrick are expecting a baby in the new year. *I cannot begin to say how glad it makes me to share this with you. Soon there will be three of us, a proper family, and you an aunt, and Sam and Eleanor will have a cousin to play with.* Evie clasps the pages to her heart. A baby! She is happy for them—she knows it is what they dearly wanted. If she were back in London, they would have celebrated, of course. Presents for Florence, perhaps even that rarest of treats—tea at Brown's with crimped sandwiches, dainty pastries, and pillowy scones. But here all this seems like another life, another world, distant and unfamiliar.

She places the letter away. How strange to receive this news in Calcutta from where everything before seems to have fast receded.

After this, Evie finds herself restless and impatient.

The problem is that there is no news on any front. She has tired of keeping up the "husband hunt" for Charlotte, Victor dispenses gloom all day from his armchair, and above all, she has been in Calcutta almost a month, and there is still not a plan in sight. It does not seem likely that Mr. Muttlebury has found her an expedition. *What must I do?* Be reckless and marry a plant hunter? She considers it, not entirely in jest; how convenient this arrangement would be for purposes of travel. The problem is she is acquainted with only one, who might grow back a frightful moustache and who will soon be off to the remote Himalayas—and there will be no opportunity to ensnare him before that, surely.

Someone less determined might be tempted to consider this a lovely holiday and board a ship back to Tilbury—it would be easy, and her family would be pleased at her return. But *no*, there is little chance that she would come all this way and give up, despite the looming possibility of failing, and the fact that a long journey yet remains if she does embark on an expedition. Who could she blame for this mess and madness? Agnes? Herself? She sighs.

It isn't that simple. It takes many winds to sail a ship, plant a seed, shape a mountain.

Another week passes, and she begins to lose hope. She spends her afternoons outside, sometimes with the children, sometimes on her own. She is done with Kingdon-Ward and has abandoned Roxburgh. Her journal lies unfilled. *Maybe now there will be nothing more than empty pages.*

More than ever, she needs the vitality of someone like Grandma Grace, but Grandma Grace is gone. Two years ago, she suffered from a sudden illness, so quick there seemed to be no chance for recovery. After the funeral, tired from weeping, Evie had walked through the forest behind the house, where they had walked together many times before. How would it ever again be possible to search for joy and adventure? And yet the trees around her seemed to whisper, always to strive, to seek, to find, and never to yield to a life without wonder.

For the first time, though, since she set out to catch the boat train from St. Pancras, she is brought down low. Otherwise, it had never seemed impossible. All she had to do was get here! To Calcutta! And something, anything, would work out, a miracle would take place, a hidden path newly revealed.

Today, instead of the bench where ladies perch, she squats inelegantly on the grass. She does not care. She only wants to feel the earth beneath her, the spikiness of the blades, the faintest of damp in the mud. There, closest to the earth, she begins to feel better. Miss Sargant was right when she said geotaxis determined the motion of a seed, but she did not mention phototaxis, how after the plant has grown, the stalks and leaves override the gravitational impulse and grow towards the light.

I am here, Evie tells herself. She needs to be still and orient herself to the world. And the world, as Grandma Grace would say, would orient itself around her.

Hope springs anew in the form of Mr. Muttlebury, who drops by, unexpectedly, a few days later, before luncheon. He apologizes profusely for the imposition and for the delay, saying he had been unwell, and hence unable to call on her earlier. "I won't take up much of your time." His voice still carries the jagged edge of his illness, like a vocal battle scar, and the tip of his nose is red and raw. They drink tea, and he keeps it brief and to the point.

He knows of no expeditions to Assam that would be suitable for a young lady such as herself. Her heart begins to droop in disappointment when he adds that, however, he is acquainted with the Wheelers—Charles and Margaret—who have been recently transferred upcountry. "They are leaving Calcutta in mid January," he tells her, "if I am not mistaken." It is a bit last-minute, he knows, considering it is already late December, but it had slipped his mind all this while. Regardless, he is happy to make introductions, and the parties could perhaps work out something suitable to them both.

This sounds promising. She is delighted, she says, and greatly appreciates his help. Their meeting ends with him assuring her that he will be in touch soon, and he exits blowing his nose into a large white handkerchief.

Sure enough, she receives a note from Mr. Muttlebury the next day. The Wheelers are away at the seaside in Puri but will be back just after Christmas. He will set up a meeting as soon as they return.

For now, there are club dos to attend—in fact, at breakfast, Charlotte insists they all go out for a spot of fun and dancing, especially after all the gloom. "And really, you should be meeting more people," she adds, looking at Evie.

Evie nibbles guiltily on her buttered toast.

For Charlotte's sake, she makes an effort, donning her best evening dress, pinning up her hair, and even dusting a light bit of rouge onto her lips and cheeks. "Oh, you look lovely," says Charlotte when she emerges. "Let's see how many hearts you win tonight." None, she hopes.

Despite the mood across the city, the Calcutta Club is decorated gaily for the Winter Ball—streamers everywhere, and a glistening Christmas tree stands tall in the ballroom. Bessie had once told her that, given the scarcity of European women in India, one may look about as attractive as an umbrella stand and still be propositioned.

She was right.

Evie does not remember garnering this much male attention ever, although she can tell they find her less appealing as soon as she mentions she's a scientist. "You have a degree?" Yes, she lies; two, she says, if she desires a quicker exit. All this seems a world away from the one where she and Agnes worked late in her makeshift laboratory, excited over their small discoveries, from her meetings with the GSS, from her quiet life at home in London. She sips her wine slowly and feels very much a stranger here.

The band strikes up another cheerful tune, and she makes her way outside, weaving past the dancers, through the lawns, all the way to the back, where it is shadowy and quieter. She takes a deep breath. She is certain no one will miss her. The air has a gentle nip to it, and the thicket behind her is dotted with dancing fireflies. Next to her, a hydrangea rises in full, gorgeous bloom, with its pale flowers glowing silver. It takes her a moment to realize there is someone else on the other side of the shrub.

It is Mr. Finlay, standing, smoking.

"Miss Alexander," he says. "I assume you, too, are fleeing the two hundred and fifty-seventh rendition of 'Boiled Beef and Carrots.'"

"I am indeed, among other things."

"Oh? What might these be? Persistent suitors?"

"I have managed to stave them all off."

"Did you now? And may I ask how?"

"I tell them I have been to university."

"And it is effective?"

"Like garlic to a vampire."

"I believe you," he says, laughing.

Perhaps it is the moonlight, the fireflies, or even the silvery hydrangea, but she is glad for his company. When she asks after his aunt, he says she has not been well and isn't at the club this evening. "Though she insisted I go, so I am here."

"With the plants," adds Evie.

"With the plants, and you."

In the shadows, she smiles. "Well," she says, "I am not sure I belong here, either."

"Where?" he asks.

"In the city, with its social circles and social obligations. In some ways, it feels like being back in England." She laughs. "Why, I have met more Indians at Cambridge than I have in my time in India! I mean, it is frightfully strange, isn't it?"

He nods. "Which is why I enjoy it most when I'm travelling. You're only with the locals, and at their mercy, really, and away from all *this* . . ."

She says she sees what he means—this is a little England within which everyone here moves. Before she can help it, she blurts out, "And it's not even what I came here for."

"No?" He looks at her curiously. What did she come here for, then?

An expedition, preferably, through forest and mountain.

"I see." Anywhere in particular?

Yes—it is a relief to tell him, perhaps because she has not spoken of it in so long—near to where he is going, she says, the hills of Assam. "I'm looking for a plant which I think might be found only in that area, close to if not at the wettest place on earth. I have done some research but I'm being driven mostly by a hunch. You must think this silly . . . everyone thinks this silly . . ." she adds.

Actually, no, he says, he understands all too well. "My whole career is built on hunches." For a while, he does not speak. The moon is hidden behind a cloud. The fireflies dance even brighter before them.

She is certain he is going to ask her what plant exactly she is looking for, and braces herself to deny him—but he does not. Instead, he lights another cigarette and says, "Miss Alexander, I have no qualifications, at least not in the conventional sense . . . I am no botanist, or geographer, or horticulturist . . . But the essential qualifications for this work are not university degrees but a deep, one might say an insatiable appetite for the hunt. Whatever it is you are seeking, the more impossible, the better."

✧ ✧ ✧

The Wheelers live close to Dalhousie Square, in a white double-storeyed house that's smaller than the Halls' bungalow but with a larger, less formal garden. The house is set away from the road, at the end of a grassy, mud-holed tract where cows graze languidly.

At the gate, a small dog appears, barking and wagging its tail. "Dustbin, Dustbin," the servant calls, bowing to her and leashing him up. *What funny names people choose for their pets*, thinks Evie.

In the garden are some unusual potted plants, a miniature cherry blossom, a trailing epiphyte with long red flowers. The servant, now tangled with Dustbin the dog, ushers her into the living room filled with teak furniture and mandala paintings on the wall. He takes her out to the back garden, dotted with wicker chairs, where Mrs. Wheeler is reading.

"I'm so glad you could make it."

She is older than Evie had imagined—perhaps forty-five—but tall and striking, with a youthful smile. Against her dusty pink day dress, her eyes shine leafy green.

"I hope Dustin wasn't a bother?" she inquires.

"Dustin?"

"Our dog. He likes to be the first to greet people at the gate." Evie assures her he has welcomed her warmly.

They sit in the garden; Evie is plied with lemonade and fresh fruit.

Mrs. Wheeler is a relative newcomer in Calcutta, having lived with her husband, a principal chief conservator in the Forest Department, in Burma for many years. "We have been here eighteen months, and I still don't feel quite settled," she tells Evie. "And now we are leaving again." They were on what is called a "mercy posting," meant as respite for being in off-the-map places for a long time, but she misses Rangoon, she says, and even more, the mountains—Arakan Yoma, the Shan Hills, and Bago Yoma. "I accompanied Charles on many of his official inspection tours, some to the most remote areas imaginable. He would survey the timber and I would survey the plants."

Evie is thrilled to hear this. Did she collect them, too?

Mrs. Wheeler smiles at her excitement. "I did indeed."

Charles, her husband, joins them for lunch before he heads back to work; a neat, heavily moustached gentleman with a long face and intelligent eyes. Pipe in hand, he smells faintly like Evie's father.

Over bread and pea soup she is glad the conversation does not veer towards the usual topics of the day. Rather than lamenting the shift of the imperial capital, they talk of other things. They tell her about U Dhammaloka, the "Irish Buddhist," challenging Christianity and British rule in Burma on religious grounds.

"He is the first Westerner to be ordained a monk, they say," adds Mr. Wheeler, "and wildly popular with the natives for his anti-missionary, anti-colonial stance. At some point, though, the Burmese people won't need a foreigner to lead them in their fight for independence."

Evie has never heard anyone else be this candid about these matters, but the Wheeler household seems to be concerned with different issues, and she likes that. Out there, endless club lunches. In here, it feels as if there is a bigger world.

"I imagine you both saw a fair bit of Burma?"

They did, they tell her, and it was exciting exploration.

"And Mrs. Wheeler mentioned she collected plants . . ."

"Like a fiend," her husband answers. "She even discovered a new species on Natmataung, though she did not name it after me."

"No dear, *Rhododendron charlesianum* didn't quite have the right ring to it."

They laugh, and Evie feels pleased—she is comfortable in their company.

Finally, Mr. Wheeler brings it up. "We hear you would like to come with us to Assam."

Evie stops slicing at the chicken. "Very much, if that's all right."

"Why, if I may ask? It is not where most visitors wish to go."

"I haven't made this journey for reasons most visitors do," says Evie truthfully. "I am interested in the plants that grow in the wettest place on earth."

Mrs. Wheeler adds that Evie is a scientist, with a specialization in botany.

"Oh, marvellous," says Mr. Wheeler. "You must show her your herbarium, Margaret."

No more is said on the subject for now, and Evie wonders if this was a test and if she had passed.

After lunch, Mrs. Wheeler leads her upstairs, to a wing of the house separated from the rest by a long corridor.

When they step inside a room, Evie expects to be amazed—but it is simple and unadorned, with a desk by the window, chairs, and a large chest of drawers pushed against a wall. *Hadn't Mr. Wheeler mentioned a herbarium?* The only floral arrangement here is a jar of magnolia sprigs.

"These are lovely," she says.

Back in Burma, Mrs. Wheeler tells her, they place them in front of the Buddha statues, and they last longer than a year.

"So . . . this is your herbarium?"

Mrs. Wheeler laughs a small laugh. "Well, Charles likes to call it that, but to be honest, it was impossible to dry plants given the weather in Burma. The humidity ruined everything. So I have no herbarium specimens, but . . ." Mrs. Wheeler hesitates. "I painted."

"Please," says Evie, "I'd love to see."

Mrs. Wheeler walks across to the chest of drawers, from where she lifts a stack of long folders. She pauses before she brings them over. "I haven't had these out in a while . . ." The folders lie thick and heavy in Evie's hands—*Margaret Rosamund Wheeler, Burma*—and when she opens one, she gasps.

There on the page, a fluted *Aeschynanthus*, drawn in crimson taken from a sunset, its leaves freshly green as though it has just rained. Then, a golden cluster of plumeria edged in pink, a white-and-butter-yellow orchid, branches of swirling cherry blossom. They are different from Marianne

North's oil paintings in their delicacy. The colours are lighter, the details infinitely finer. Evie holds the binder up and exclaims in delight—"How beautiful they are!" They ought to be on display, she adds.

Mrs. Wheeler seems pleased, and, perhaps sensing genuine joy and interest, she begins to tell Evie how it became an obsession, collecting plants she had never seen before, finding the ones with a "soul"—for else you cannot paint them. "I would bring them back to my garden and try to keep them alive . . . at least long enough to sketch them. Sometimes I sent the plants to England, thinking they might be better equipped to study them there than I was in Burma, with barely any equipment, indulging in my . . . domestic botany."

Evie looks up. Mrs. Wheeler seems a little uneasy. "I must be honest," she begins. "I envy you your Cambridge studies. It legitimizes what you do in a way my work will never be." Evie finds she has no words at first. She is taken back to Newnham, to their heated evening discussions. *For so long botany had been our own . . .*

"What you say is true," she begins, "and it is appalling, how the work of women is dismissed. First, men do not permit us to pursue scholarship, then they punish us for it."

"But," says Mrs. Wheeler, "you have been able to study the subject . . ."

"And that has not always been a good thing."

Her hostess frowns, asking what she means.

Evie begins to tell her—about her early days in gardens and forests with her grandmother, how this was the spirit with which she had wished to study botany, with curiosity and playfulness and a compassionate regard for plants as living, growing, ever-changing beings. "My studies served to take me away from this," she says, "so I don't know if it is a thing to envy."

Mrs. Wheeler's face softens. She says she hadn't thought of it that way. "What did you do then?" she asks.

Only recently, admits Evie, has she found a way back to the gardens and forests of her childhood.

And how?

Evie smiles. "With a little help from here and there."

JOHANN

On the morning of September 3, 1786, so early the mist hasn't lifted off the Töpel, and the sky shows no tender glimpse of dawn, a figure steps out of the Three Moors Hotel.

He is alone, encumbered by little more than a portmanteau and a knapsack. He walks quickly through the empty market square, and then hurries down a side street, his footsteps echoing in the quiet. He doesn't look back once, and not until he reaches the post house does he stop, place his portmanteau beside him, and adjust the knapsack slung across his back. At this hour, in the small town of Karlsbad, he is the only one there, waiting. His presence goes unmarked by the slumbering inhabitants behind their shuttered windows; around him are empty balconies, darkened buildings, and beyond them a river unseen. It already feels like winter. And if the inclemency of the past few weeks, months even, is anything to go by, tomorrow, too, it will rain. From somewhere, a breeze lifts, brushes past him coldly, and vanishes.

In a few minutes, a post-chaise draws up in a great and noisy clatter. The man climbs in, joining three other drowsy passengers, pays his fare, and when asked what name he is known by, answers gruffly, "Möller. Johann Philipp Möller."

The driver inquires because it is needed for the records, but he casts a second glance at him, noticing the passenger's soft cloud-grey travelling coat, with its long shoulder cape, topped by a warm velvet collar. Not many of his kind grace this humble coach. Strange, too, that he is alone, without any servants, and with so little luggage. Well, never mind all that. None of his business.

He makes to shut the door, when the traveller speaks. "How long to Egra?"

"Nine hours at most."

At that he sits back, seemingly satisfied.

"We're ready to leave, sir."

"Yes," the traveller repeats. "We're ready to leave."

The chaise makes its swift way southwest, in the darkness, along the fringes of Kaiserwald, the forest looming beside them, prehistoric and immense. By half-past eight, they arrive at Zevoda, the day foggy but beautifully calm. The other passengers are awake now—two portly gentlemen, one with a flourishing moustache, and a young man apprenticed to a bookkeeper in Munich—talking about the weather, how they hope that, after so wretched a summer, they should enjoy a fine, dry autumn.

"Look at the sky," exclaims the traveller in the grey coat. "The upper clouds are streaky and fleecy, while the lower ones are heavy." He smiles. "This appears to be a good sign, don't you think?" The others, not wishing to admit how little, to them, this observation portends, amiably agree.

Farther on they travel, descending into the valley. The landscape now alight and green, undulating before their eyes. At noon, they arrive at Egra, lying at the foot of the Fichtel Mountains, under a warm and shining sun. Here they stop for lunch. And although the friendly gentlemen invite him to join them inside the rest house, the traveller declines, and eats his midday meal alone beneath a bright sky.

At two, they continue southward. The passengers doze, despite the rutted road, lulled by goulash and beer, though the man in the grey coat keeps his gaze vigilantly turned outside. He is drinking in the air, the scenery, as though seeing everything for the first, and last, time.

Later, after entering Bavaria, they come at once upon Waldsassen, lying in a cauldron-like hollow in beautiful meadowland, enclosed on all sides by fertile heights. They marvel at the basilica—they do not stop, but take in the view of its baroque towers, rising splendidly on either side of the narrow arched doorway.

"Is it true?" the young apprentice asks. "About the skeletons."

"What?" says the moustached gentleman. "That they line the walls of the church?"

The young man nods, looking uneasy.

"The Holy Bodies, they're called," adds his companion. "Christian martyrs, exhumed not long ago from the catacombs of Rome."

"But is it true," the apprentice insists, "that they're dressed like royalty? In velvet and silks and jewels?"

The gentlemen confirm this is so.

He shudders. "Is it not macabre?"

The traveller in the grey coat, silent all this while, chuckles. "Perhaps. But if I were them, I'd be greatly displeased." The other passengers stare at him, befuddled. He continues, "To be happily buried in Rome, the capital of all the world, and then rudely awakened and installed . . . here. Despite being bejewelled for all eternity—what a fall!"

His fellow passengers appear unconvinced. Is Rome truly *that* wondrous?

"Yes," he insists. "Yes, it must be so."

"And have you been to Rome?" they inquire.

"No," he admits, "not yet. But soon," he adds, "God willing, soon."

Well, when he gets there, the others declare, he must write up a report, for God willing or not, they are not planning a journey to the capital of the world anytime at all.

"I shall," he promises, and they fall into companionable silence.

From Waldsassen begins an excellent road of firm granite, and this, coupled with the gradual descent from the plain, allows them to doze more comfortably—and travel on with welcome rapidity.

They speed onward and are at Tischengreut by five. Here the two gentlemen opt to stay the night. The apprentice and the passenger in the grey coat continue. They are in Weyda by half-past eight, one in the morning at Wernberg, half-past two at Schwarzenfeld, half-past four at

Schwandorf, and finally, half-past ten at Regensburg, having covered one hundred and thirteen miles in thirty-nine hours.

They have made good time.

At Regensburg, the traveller in the grey coat books himself into the White Lamb, a pleasant three-storeyed corner building overlooking the Danube.

"Just you, Herr Möller?" asks the innkeeper.

He, too, steals a quick glance at the expensive clothing.

Him alone, he is informed.

"This way."

He assigns a lad to help with the scant luggage, up to the third floor, as requested by the guest, for the views. Regensburg is beautifully situated. Outside the window, the medieval town shines in the midday light, with churches upon churches, and monasteries at every turn. Across the river, the suburb of Stadtamhof stands neatly clean and pretty.

It isn't long before the traveller reemerges onto the streets. He heads away from the noisy market square, bustling with shipping men and vendors, and walks towards the river, the Danube flowing great and wide before him.

There he greets an old woman selling fruit.

"Any grapes or figs?"

"Not yet," she answers, "you'll have to head farther south for that."

"I shall, ma'am, I shall."

He buys a few pfennigs' worth of pears instead, and sits on the bank, eating them, like a schoolboy, for all to see. Afterwards, he walks through town, stopping at churches and towers, frequently making notes. He drops by the College of the Jesuits, where the pupils are acting in the annual play. He doesn't stay long; the performance is tragic, unintentionally so.

That evening, he eats an early meal and retires to his room. At the table, he opens up a notebook, and writes: *From now, the taste of pears will always be the taste of freedom. How long it has been! Perhaps not since I was a student, and Herder and I roamed around the villages of Strasbourg collecting folk tales and folk songs, have I enjoyed such delicious liberty. Alas, too long. Some may cry coward, but I stole out of Karlsbad in secret; they would not have let me go otherwise. They could tell I wanted to get away, and they had in some degree acquired a right to detain me. However, I wasn't going to be stopped; finally it was time.*

The next day, he steps out into a morning that is cool but promises warmth.

Since the post-chaise to Munich leaves at noon, he ambles through town, stops for a coffee at Café Prinzess. Here he scribbles quickly: *It is impossible to express how happy I am, dear one, and what I'm learning every day. Everything speaks to me and shows me its nature.* He concludes his morning ramble at Montag's bookshop, selecting Kant's *Metaphysical Foundations of Natural Science*, a new edition of Linnaeus's *Mantissa Plantarum Altera*, and finally, for some light reading, Raspe's *The Surprising Adventures of Baron Munchausen*. At the counter, he waits to pay, while the chatty bookseller tallies up the purchases and makes small talk.

"Where did you say you were from again?"

"Karlsbad."

The bookseller stops, places his hands on the counter. "Sir, I used to work at Hofmann's in Jena . . . and I could swear I saw you in there."

"That would be remarkable!" the traveller exclaims and makes to pick up his purchases, but the bookseller is undeterred.

"I'm quite certain . . . you are Herr von Goethe, are you not? Author of *The Sorrows of Young Werther*! It is an honour, sir."

At this, the traveller looks him in the eye. He smiles. "You do *me* great honour, but I'm afraid you are much mistaken. Now, how much do I owe you for these? I have an appointment to attend shortly."

The bookseller hesitates, then apologizes. "Of course, sir, pardon me."

He hands the traveller his change, and watches as he leaves—the bell tinkling gently as the door shuts behind him.

The traveller has not lied. He does indeed have an appointment—a visit to the Schäfferianum Museum. He clutches the books to his chest like a shield, and hurries, keeping his gaze low to the ground.

The museum is located at the residence of Pastor Schäffer, dean of the Protestant parish in Regensburg, also an avid mycologist, entomologist, botanist, and inventor, most recently, of a contraption that washes clothes, while saving on fuel, lye, and water. It is a thing of wonder!

The museum houses the pastor's rich and extensive personal natural history collection—a cabinet of curiosities that spans shelf after shelf, floor to ceiling. Only here, while gazing at specimens of native Bavarian fungi and freshwater molluscs, several varieties of greenish quartz, the illustrated life history of the apollo butterfly, and detailed drawings on the anatomy of the water flea, does the traveller begin to relax.

When he meets Pastor Schäffer, large of nose and regal of forehead, he introduces himself as an admirer, adding how he looks forward to perusing his latest publication, a three-volume series on insects found in and around Regensburg. The traveller was familiar already with Pastor Schäffer's earlier botanical work *A Self-Taught Botanist on Expedition: Illustrated with Woodcuts and Drawings*, and his richly illustrated four-volume study on fungi.

They chat awhile about the pastor's current undertakings and then the traveller inquires, with barely concealed excitement, about the correspondence the pastor had maintained with the great Linnaeus, "the biggest influence in my life."

"Is that so?" remarks the pastor, and confirms that they did indeed exchange letters regularly until Linnaeus's death a mere eight years ago. How supportive the Swedish philosopher had been! Linnaeus helped the pastor identify insects for his publications, and expedited his membership of the Royal Society of Sciences at Uppsala.

The benefits were mutual, I'm sure, the traveller says generously.

The pastor makes to object, but admits that Linnaeus had indeed specifically requested his insect illustrations for a new edition of *Systema Naturae*.

"What an honour!" the traveller declares with a flourish.

They part on friendly terms, the pastor gratified by the interest and attention shown him. "The pleasure was all mine, Herr Möller," he replies to the thanks he receives for his time.

And the traveller departs with heart uplifted not just by his visit to the museum, but by the thought of all that still lies ahead.

The post-chaise fills up, packed with passengers for the big city, and makes haste, driving straight through Abbach, beyond which the Danube breaks against dramatic limestone cliffs as far as Saale, where they arrive at three o'clock. They travel on through the evening and night. As morning seeps across the sky, they arrive in Munich.

Despite the long journey, the traveller isn't inclined to rest. He heads out from his lodgings and spends the day seeing the sights. From a fruit seller, he buys figs—but they are not yet summer ripe. He lunches at Augustine Brau, where all of Munich seem to be, such is the crowd, and then walks across to the Frauenkirche. He climbs the tower from where a young woman had leaped to her death the previous year, over love gone wrong. She was called, he'd heard, the female Werther. From up there, he hopes to catch a glimpse of the mountains of the Tyrol. But they elude him, swathed as they are in thick mist.

Later that evening, in his room at the Royal Inn, he sits at a desk, writing. *I saw people in town who might recognize me—but I enjoy going among them like this, unnoticed and anonymous. Tomorrow it's straight on to Innsbruck! I'm leaving out a lot along the way but this is in order to carry through the one idea that has almost grown too old in my soul.*

For a long while, he stands at the window watching the last of the day's sunshine catching the cathedral's towers. Then he walks back to the table and adds: *Farewell, dearest one. I think of you all the time.*

He doesn't glimpse the mountains the next morning either, early, when he leaves. The sky is clear but clouds have settled unmoving on the peaks. For a while the chaise travels along the Isar, up above it on alluvial hills of gravel, the work of old high waters. He watches the mist on the river and water meadows dissipate as the day brightens. The other two passengers, husband and wife, complain of the heat, while he looks unperturbed, even quietly delighted. When they stop to rest, he skips about, plucking at plants, sniffing at flowers, exclaiming over stones, pocketing some, tossing others aside.

Quickly, they pass through Benedicktbeuern, nestled in its fertile plain with a broad and high mountain ridge behind it.

"Look!" exclaims the traveller in rising excitement, "they are emerging from the clouds!"

The couple peer at the sky, expecting something biblical, like angels or locusts. "What is?" he is asked.

"The mountains!"

He whips off his hat and waves it energetically out the window.

"What are you doing?" the other two inquire politely.

"I'm saluting them."

By half-past four, they are at the Walchensee, where they stop briefly, for the views and a rest. Before them, the lake fills the valley, still as glass, the water so clear they can see the stones beneath. It is exceptionally quiet. Only the sound of the wind in the tall rushes, and the crunch of footsteps as the traveller walks around, deliberately, casting his eyes to the ground. He plucks several flowers, a sprig of thistle, a single gentian.

"It's always near water that I find the new plants first," he mutters. "I wonder why that is . . ."

The other passengers don't query his actions; perhaps, they whisper to one another, he's a medicine man. When he's done, he stands by them, gazing across the lake.

"Do you know," he says, "the name of this lake comes from a word in High German?"

"Which is?" the man asks.

"*Welsche* or even *Walche*. It means 'strangers.'"

"Strangers?" His wife looks puzzled.

"This is what all Roman and Romanized peoples of the Alps south of Bavaria were called by the locals," the traveller explains. "Beyond this," he turns to face the path they'll be taking, climbing up and through the mountains, "it is a new world."

On the rocky road south, they soon come across two travellers, walking, a harpist and a young girl of no more than eleven. The man hails them to a stop.

"Please, good people," he says. "My daughter is weary from many hours of walking. Would you be so kind as to give her a lift a little way?"

Space is made for the girl, and their sparse luggage. The father will walk on and meet her up ahead at an appointed spot. She sits next to the man in the grey coat, perched like a bird, with brown locks and a high delicate forehead.

"Thank you," she says, "though it isn't true."

"What isn't true?" he asks her.

"That I'm weary. I told father so. I can walk for days and days and never tire."

"Maybe you *have* walked that long already, and your father is concerned."

"Only from Munich this time. Not far."

"Almost fifty miles, child!"

She looks at him, her chin lifted, her dark brown eyes defiant. "That's nothing, I tell you." She rattles off the names of places they have visited, all on foot—Württemberg, Frankfurt, Hamburg, Waldeck, Berlin, and even, she ends grandly, "Einsiedeln. To see the shrine of our lady."

"And how was that?"

"Crowded."

"Who did you go with?"

"My mother. We walked all the way together. My mother likes to travel."

"And you?"

"Yes," she said simply.

"What do you like about it?"

She looks at him, and with no hesitation says, "My mother tells me if you don't travel you grow old."

He laughs, heartily, and then laughs again.

"But it's true!"

"Yes," he says quickly, "I agree. Except I don't think I've been to as many places as you."

She considers this for a moment before declaring, "You still have time."

"I'm relieved to hear that."

Outside, the landscape is slowly opening up into a wider valley, the road relieved of the tight press of trees.

"And what have you been to Munich for? Another pilgrimage?"

She shakes her head. She was there, she says, to play the harp for the elector.

"That's very impressive!"

The smile she gives the traveller is suddenly sweet and childish. "He enjoyed it greatly, he said, and has given my father many letters of recommendation." They travel together, performing, from one princely personage to another; so far twenty-one in all. This was how they earned a living. In Munich, they were paid more handsomely than usual, and she was permitted to buy something special for herself.

"What did you get?"

In reply, she reaches for a hatbox near her feet, one she's placed closest. She holds it on her lap, carefully. Inside is a new bonnet—pale green, her favourite colour, she says, edged with snowy ruffles and a white-ribboned bow.

"Oh, that's pretty!" exclaims the lady opposite.

The girl looks pleased, "Thank you. I chose it myself."

After she puts it away, she asks the traveller where he is going.

"South," he replies. "Far south. Farther south than I've ever been."

"Why?"

There's a long pause before he replies. "Because I am tired of the cold."

"Oh!" she says, and is immediately distracted. "What's that?" She points out the window. It's a tree. "It's different," she declares.

He smiles, pleased. "It is. How so?"

She furrows her brow and purses her lips. "Well, the other ones are straight and tall and thin . . . and pointed at the top. This one . . ."

"This one?"

"It's spread out." She stretches her arms to either side. "The leaves are bigger."

"Well done. That's because it's a plane tree. The first one I've seen on this journey. Do you know what that means?"

She shakes her head, her eyes large.

"It's getting warmer."

"Yes. I know," she says seriously. "My harp told me so."

"Your harp?" At this point, the couple sitting opposite, who have been mostly dozing, also smile.

She nods her head vigorously. "It tells me about the weather . . . it's like a . . . a . . ."

"A barometer?"

But she hasn't heard the word before.

"Never mind, it doesn't matter. How does your harp tell you about the weather?"

"The strings," she replies. "If the strings go sharp it means fair weather."

The traveller says he is pleased to accept that as a good omen.

Soon they arrive at the village where she is meant to be dropped off. He helps her out, and hands her the hatbox. She will wait at an inn for her father to arrive shortly. Her name, she says, is Greta.

"And you?" she asks.

"Johann," he replies.

She waves him goodbye, and he climbs back into the chaise.

By half-past seven, they are in Mittenwald, where they will rest the night. The day, though, is still bright and warm. As the traveller steps out, the coachman, who's been whistling a merry tune, attending to the horses, says cheerfully, "Good fortune to you, Herr Möller. Today was the first beautiful day this whole summer."

The traveller smiles. "And from now, I trust it will go on."

They leave Mittenwald early next morning. The traveller trains his gaze on the landscape—the nearest slopes dark and covered in spruce, then grey limestone cliffs, and high white peaks against the clear blue of the sky. At every angle the view changes, and for fear of missing something, he keeps himself from dozing.

When they near Inzing the sun is strong and hot. The traveller takes off his overcoat, his long-sleeved jerkin, and puts them away. On they go, towards Innsbruck, lying in a splendid position, in a broad rich valley between high rock walls and mountains. The traveller has a choice: he may stay the night here, or catch another post-chaise onward. It's only noon, there's much to occupy him here—but he chooses to move on.

The way up gets more and more beautiful. Small settlements, painted white, lie between fields and hedges on high, sloping ground. Water plunges large and roaring down a ravine. Soon he sees the first larches, and near Schönberg, the first pines. He collects a bundle of needles, some pine cones.

It begins to grow dark, the details of the view are lost, while the mountains grow larger and more splendid, and everything shifts like a deep mysterious picture. At half-past seven, they arrive in Brenner, at the foot of the pass that marks the border between Austria and Italy. This, he decides, is where he will rest.

The next day he rises early; there's much to do.

He sorts his books and papers—choosing what to take and what to discard. He inspects his botanical samples, carefully pressed in a folder.

I've acquired a great deal for my creation, he writes, *but nothing yet wholly new or unexpected. Also I have been dreaming of the model I've been talking about for so long, which might be the only way to give you a clear picture of the thoughts I carry around with me all the time.*

At noon, he lunches lightly and quickly, downstairs, and heads back to his room. When he's almost finished, he leaves aside his packing and stands at the window. The view is dominated by mountains, circling the hamlet, opening up to the sky. He feels himself in a more expansive mood than he has been so far along this journey. Ten days ago, he turned thirty-eight, which is perhaps neither too young nor too old, but how time seems to have spun away from him. Life has been . . . unexpected, with work, with love. So much accomplished, some would say, yet he feels so much remains undone. And—this is not a question he often asks himself—what if he were unequal to the task? Only this journey could make him grow into greater maturity, he is certain, for there are parts of himself he can discover nowhere else but in Italy.

He turns back to the table to write: *Up here I look back once more in your direction. From here some streams flow towards Germany, some towards Italy, and these I hope to follow soon. How strange to think that twice already I've stood at a similar point—St. Gotthard Pass in Switzerland, June 1775 and September 1779—rested, and not got across. I shall not believe it either till I'm down there. What other people find commonplace and easy, life makes tough for me. Farewell! Think of me at this crucial moment of my life.*

Afterwards, with daylight still stretching long and empty before him, he strolls out, sketchbook in hand. He perches on a nearby rocky slope, with an aim to draw the hostelry. An hour later, he heads back inside, in a mood less pleasant. The drawing has not turned out to his satisfaction. *The shapes*, he thinks, *are all wrong*. He's no good.

At the doorway, he meets the innkeeper.

"I hope you've found everything to your satisfaction here, Herr Möller?"

"Yes, thank you."

"And you wish to leave tomorrow morning?"

"At the earliest."

"That's easily arranged. In fact, if you wish, it could be arranged sooner."

Oh, says the traveller, how soon?

"Now."

The innkeeper explains that there is the small matter of him requiring the horses the next morning for another errand—so if Herr Möller is willing, they can drop him to Sterzing and be back by dawn. It works out well, if he doesn't mind him saying so, for both parties. The traveller, after only a moment's hesitation, agrees.

Later that evening, as the sun slips behind the mountains, he climbs into a post-chaise and heads for Italy.

✧ ✧ ✧

On the afternoon of October 29, 1786, in a top-floor room of a modest yet well-appointed hotel near Piazza Navona, the traveller stands by a window—outside is Rome. What a thrill, what a thrill! He can hardly believe it. And as much as he'd like to announce this across the rooftops, he desists, and opts to smile, widely, to himself.

He has spent five weeks in Italy, but has only just arrived the previous night in the first city of the world. The dreams of his youth have come to fruition; the first engravings he remembers—his father hung views of Rome in the hall—he sees now in reality. Everything is just as he imagined. And when he leaves here, he is certain he shall wish he were arriving instead. But no thoughts of departure! So much discovery lies ahead! And this morning, a messenger was dispatched with a note, and the traveller is awaiting the arrival of its recipient imminently.

He feels bolstered, not only by being here, but for how much he has already accomplished. Over the last few weeks, he has come to know and love Venice, the city of water—astounding, the view from the top of St. Mark's tower, his glimpse of the sea for the first time in his life, how it pounded high against the beach, how he followed its retreat over the lovely threshing floor it left behind. So many places are not just names now—Trento, Verona, Vicenza, Padua. How much better to see something once than to hear about it a thousand times. The sight of blue grapes in the valley around Bolzano. The gigantic cypress in the Giusti Garden. The unforgettable Lago Garda. Palladio's Renaissance buildings in the big northern cities. And where was it that the crickets sang at sunset? How easily days faded around the edges like a dream . . .

Two things, though, remain most firmly imprinted in his mind.

First, the thrill of hearing in Roveredo, for the first time on his journey, a mix of German and Italian. How happy he was that the beloved language was now going to be the language of everyday use. There, he also bought a new set of clothes and a pair of walking boots, all in the local style, suitably light and less conspicuous. From then on, the traveller blended in, almost a local.

The other, Padua's botanical garden, with its central, subdivided compartments surrounded by a great circular wall intended to symbolize the world. He has sketched them all—the old chestnut tree, the gigantic plane tree hollowed out by lightning, and inside the greenhouse, the ginkgo with its twin-lobed leaves, a blooming magnolia, and a tall palm planted in 1585—before which he stood in awe, then collected leaves, from the small and simple to the largest fans with spiny stalks.

Although the way here from Venice felt interminable.

If it weren't for his daily notes, he would remember little of this part of his journey. Cento and its pointed poplars, Bologna, where he ascended the Asinelli tower, and Lugano, from where he wrote, *I am at a miserable inn in the company of a worthy papal officer and an Englishman with his so-called sister.* In some places, the hostelries were so awful, there was little chance of even spreading out a page. Florence was a blur of an afternoon. He breezed through the Boboli Gardens, the cathedral, the baptistry, and rushed onward. He did notice the olive trees, though, around the city, wild and wonderful. On some evenings, he was outright cold and miserable, trying to warm himself in vain. *Still three days to go, I feel as if I'll never arrive.*

But arrive he did.

And here he is, in this small room with a bright fire. He moves away from the window towards its warmth; he's not cold, but he'd like to sit, he might be a little tired. Where is Tischbein? Surely he must have received his note by now? In his understanding, the neighbourhood where the artist resides, near Villa Borghese, is not far. But he could be wrong. He wonders what he will be like—they have been in correspondence for a few years—in fact, thanks to his recommendation, Tischbein is on a grant that allows him to live in Rome—but they have never met. With all the time he's spent here, three summers or more, the traveller hopes to find in Tischbein a guide—perhaps a friend.

Not long after, there's a knock on the door. The innkeeper is back, and with him Tischbein. He rises and walks across, both swiftly and with careful measure, glad, curious, smiling.

Tischbein smiles back.

The traveller takes his hand. “Hello,” he says, “I am Goethe.”

“Yes, I know. I mean, it is a great honour.”

Goethe is silent, but still smiling.

“How was your journey?”

“Long, but worth every minute.” At this, he glances out the window. The sky is sharply, pristinely blue, the clouds so white they hurt the eye.

“Rome has been waiting for you,” declares Tischbein.

Goethe laughs, then says, “It is I who have been waiting for Rome.”

“Well, you are now here, and we are very glad for it.”

“It is a change most welcome,” says Goethe. “Up north, the winter is beginning to freeze us over already. I don’t remember the last time I saw the sun in late October. And this year, we’ve also had a wretched summer. Wet and dismal and dull.”

“I have to say I don’t miss it!”

“You will make me call you rude names already!”

They both laugh, and something shifts between them; they like each other, they will be friends. In real life, not just over letters—and anyway, what can one tell over letters, really? Nothing like meeting face to face and being in the same city.

“Now,” begins Tischbein, “before I hear all about your adventures, there is a small matter that begs immediate clarification.”

“And what might that be?”

“Your accommodation.”

It is settled before the discussion can even properly begin. “You simply must stay with us,” Tischbein insists, when Goethe says his intention is to spend a month or more in Rome. It is no inconvenience. They are few occupants in a house with a bedroom to spare. He will have space to himself to work, to write. Goethe acquiesces: he will move into 18 Via del Corso the next day.

The setup there is quite perfect, he finds. Smaller, of course, than anywhere else he’s lived in the last decade, back in Weimar. His beloved garden house within Park an der Ilm he has had all to himself, and the house in the centre of town, a gift from the duke that he recently moved into, is spacious enough to accommodate several families. The shared apartment on Via del Corso is far from tidy, and the facilities basic, but he walks into it with a lightness he hasn't felt in years. Perhaps it's the golden Roman sun, streaming deliciously through the unshuttered windows. Or the sudden sense that time here lies luxuriously before him to do with what he will.

When Tischbein asks how he occupied himself in Weimar, he replies, "I'm a busy civil servant."

"Are you saying this with gratitude or resentment?"

"Both."

And it's true. That was his job, his principal reason for being kept in Weimar, with no lack in material comfort, but his being a writer, a scientist, an artist, seemed to serve as a necessary though glamourous addendum.

Then there was Charlotte. And the entire impossibility of her.

Sometimes what else is there to do besides leave?

He didn't know what to expect after he sneaked out of Karlsbad—so undramatic an exit, he'd thought. Why hadn't he needed to chase after the carriage, take a flying leap on to it like a runaway thief? No matter. Perhaps, they were over, the days of such high-spirited shenanigans—carousing with the duke through the streets at dawn, naked swimming in the Ilm, endless flirtations at court parties. At his age, sneaking away without telling a soul was thrilling enough. And even then, some guilt, but what would he have told his friends anyway? That it was time. He had to go. He was off, searching for something, and he hoped, here in Italy, it would all be revealed. They would have laughed, detained him, or worse, teased him. As they had, a few evenings before he left—*Faust, Iphigenia, Tasso*, they taunted, calling out names of his works in progress, lying for years incomplete.

Goethe is given a room twice removed from the long hall—small but airy, overlooking the busy side street. It has clean, bare walls, and a timbered ceiling set with painted floral decoration in blue and red. He will like waking up here, he's certain. Perhaps, he dares to think, even with someone by his side.

First, though, the unpacking. He sets out the rock samples he's collected—limestone from the Apennines, travertine found near Terni—and alongside, he arranges his botanical collection—seeds, drawings, pressings, with pride of place given to a branch from a cypress in the Giusti Garden and the palm leaves from Padua. Then he drags a desk to the window through which he can see, in the distance, a clump of umbrella pines. It's not a view he's accustomed to. Around his garden house, he could see green fields, patches of forest, the river, and from his study in the town house, the garden, brimming seasonally with vegetables and flowers. It pleases him, though, to call this his own. Even though, of course, he is sharing the place. Friedrich Bury, a shy, quiet student, is in the room next to his own, and Georg Schütz, a young landscape painter, occupies a tiny corner next to Tischbein's large spacious studio. Schütz is from Frankfurt, and everyone calls him "Il Barone."

"Why?" asks Goethe.

Tischbein laughs. "Just like that."

This is their artists' colony. And he, of course, is most welcome. They are honoured to have him stay.

Domestic affairs at 18 Via del Corso, he finds out, are well in order. The house is kept by a seventy-two-year-old coachman, his wife cooks their meals, and there is a manservant, a maid, and a cat, a fat grey cloud called Callisto.

Arrangements are such that the maid comes in to clean and tidy every day, and the landlady provides them, in the evening, with lit lanterns. She will cook what they like, and fetch groceries for them from the market.

"What do you wish to eat, signor?" she asks Goethe.

"Anything," he replies happily.

There is also no dearth of options for dining out. This is Rome! The occupants eat out often at a variety of trattoria around town. "We'll take you to them all," declares Tischbein. "And show you everything!"

Later that day, Goethe sits at the table to write some letters. The sounds of the street carry up to him, loudly, easily. Back in Weimar even the bark of a dog in the distance served as a disturbance, but he must get used to this, he supposes—the daily hubbub of a bustling metropolis. The plan, among many, after all, is to catch up on his writing. Rework *Iphigenia.* Complete *Faust.* Perhaps even begin something new altogether.

Not a thought he could have easily entertained otherwise—between overseeing the silver mines, the roads and army and forestry, running the theatre, and most exhausting, navigating the tangled web that was life at court, he just about manages to compose a little poetry now and then.

Why are you in Weimar? his university friends had asked at first, the ones with whom he'd shared visions of a new humanism, a better world. Where should he begin? And would they, or anyone else, understand?

For now, he needs to send news back to the people he's abandoned. First to his employer, the duke. *Forgive my secretiveness and the virtually subterranean journey here.* To his other friends he's more light-hearted, boisterous: *Now I'm here and at peace with myself and, it seems, at peace for the whole of my life. For it can well be called the start of a new life when you see with your own eyes the whole thing of which you knew so thoroughly the separate parts.* To his mother, joyful. *I shall come back a new man and live to my own and my friends' greater pleasure.* To Charlotte, solicitous. *I hope they have arrived, my notes and drawings from Venice. I want to go on writing a diary here for you. You are never far from my thoughts, dear one.*

Before Tischbein takes him everywhere, he escorts him eight minutes down the road to what he deems the most important locale in Rome.

"The Colosseum?"

No.

"The Vatican?"

Not at all. Caffè Greco. Rome's artists' bar.

"Oh? Is it old?"

Twenty years or more. But more important, serving the cheapest wine in the city. They come here almost every evening, Tischbein tells him; it's where they all meet before usually heading back to Via del Corso for more drinking and art talk. "More drinking *than* talk," adds Schütz. It's a grand place, running the length of the building, a large high-ceilinged room topped by a bright chandelier, a long corridor stuffed with drinking tables, and more booths to the side where one may sit and dine at leisure.

"Signor Gigi," calls Tischbein when they're all seated, "tonight, your best."

"And tomorrow?" answers a smiling, portly man behind the counter, towel flung over one plump shoulder.

"Tomorrow, Signor Gigi, we might all be dead. Which is why every night, we drink your best."

And so they do. Carafe after carafe of fragrant Frascati. They are joined by Hofrat Reiffenstein, a white-haired, shrewd-eyed diplomat, oldest of them all. The talk around the table mostly concerns their visitor's time in Rome.

"Where should I start?" asks Goethe. What must he see first? Will the wonders of ancient Rome spontaneously unfold themselves before his eyes?

The others blink. "No," they say, "probably not."

"I'll tell you what," ventures Reiffenstein. "Don't start with the Vatican paintings."

Might he know why?

"If you don't mind my saying . . . one must earn it." He gestures with his hand. "One doesn't just walk into the Raphael rooms or Michelangelo's Sistine Chapel . . . First one undergoes a rigorous training of the eye, and then the pathway opens to appreciate the masters."

As the evening wears on, the Greco grows more raucous. Other patrons greet Tischbein and his friends, some raise glasses at them from across the room. Before they're joined by these acquaintances, Goethe makes an urgent plea. He'd like to remain anonymous. Not just for this evening, but for the months to come when he's in Rome.

"But why?" asks Schütz. "I mean, you're here now. What's the need?"

He'd like to lead a completely private existence, Goethe explains, so he may concentrate on art and architecture and any other personal pursuits without being feted as a literary celebrity. Or condemned, as an imperial baron and privy councilor, to an expensive and time-wasting round of visits and receptions.

For this reason, to everyone else, he is Johann Möller.

"Johann Möller?" repeats Reiffenstein.

"If this is your wish, that's enough for me," says Tischbein.

Reiffenstein looks across over the rim of his glass. "How will you meet the people you wish to meet? The ones who require letters of introduction . . ."

Goethe shrugs. "I'll find a way. Or I shall not visit them. I presume there's more than enough to keep me otherwise occupied in Rome."

"To Möller!" says Tischbein, raising his glass.

"To Möller!" they all echo, except Reiffenstein.

"You are unhappy with this?" Goethe looks amused.

Reiffenstein bows politely. "I will drink only to you."

And with that they empty their glasses.

Over the next few weeks, Tischbein is true to his word. Every day it's a new assemblage of sights to discover. And they walk everywhere.

"It's the best way," Tischbein insists, "to get to know the city."

Goethe is pleased with this, for, he tells his new friends, here in Rome, as he's been doing recently in his life, he wishes to practise seeing and reading things as they are, slowly, to faithfully let his eye be single, and to continue his complete renunciation of all fixed views. This is the only way to learn the truths of things.

They heartily commend his efforts, but when Schütz asks later what their guest meant by "let his eye be single," they confess they're not entirely sure.

"Perhaps he means focused, undistracted?" offers Bury.

Reiffenstein thinks it might be in reference to a passage in the Bible. "Wasn't it Matthew? 'If thine eye be single, you are filled with light.'"

The others aren't fully convinced—"Yes, but what does it mean? And what does it have to do with being a tourist?" Next time, they could just ask.

"The problem," says Schütz, sighing, "is that I think he expects us to know."

They are impressed, though, by their visitor's energy. The days are no longer summer hot, but rainless and still genially warm, and he is out from the early hours until late. Nothing is uninteresting to him—churches and villas, ruins and palaces, gardens and statues, cottages and stables, triumphal arches and columns, fountains and markets. He says delightedly that everything speaks to him and shows him its nature.

In the evenings, they usually come upon the Colosseum, when it is already twilight. Looking at it, all else seems diminished. The edifice is so vast that one cannot hold the image of it in one's soul: "In memory," says Goethe, "we think it smaller, and then return to it again to find it every time greater than before." He bemoans, though, that Rome has no proper botanical garden, unlike Padua, and how this might slow down his botanical studies.

Botanical studies? His friends ask in puzzlement. But you're a famed author, a renowned poet and playwright, an artist! What's this about botanical studies?

In these past few years, he admits, botany has grown to be a cherished, all-consuming pursuit. Busily, quietly, he has been occupying himself with nature. It's true that, until he moved to Weimar a decade ago, he was largely uninterested in plants. He'd lived in cities, Frankfurt, Leipzig, and perhaps his time in Alsace brought him close to the warm, wide Rhenish countryside. But only in Weimar, in the small town, thrust with the sudden responsibility of taking care of the royal parks, was he required to turn his attention to living things.

"Before that," he says, chuckling, "I might have also been too busy falling in and out of love." He had little choice then but to observe and learn. It helped that he was surrounded by wooded countryside, and that his garden house stood in the ducal park. "It was here I began to notice—truly notice—the living world around me. I planted a garden with beehives and linden trees, and tended to them through the seasons. I grew interested in the humble kitchen garden . . . It is extraordinary," he adds with a smile, "how munificent the earth is, how bounteous." He fed himself, the servants, sometimes even giving his friends fresh treats—tender artichokes, baby potatoes. At the front, he planted flowers—his favourite were rows and rows of red poppies—and every morning in spring, the view from his window changed, with buds coming into flower, flowers wilting, and others rising, shining, their faces open to the sun.

"In all this time, I've come to a realization . . ."

"Which is?" they ask.

"That my scientific work will be more important than the bulk of my poetry."

At this, his friends are amused, though unconvinced. They could easily accept a scientist who wrote poetry, perhaps even a poet who wrote about science, but a poet who is also a scientist? Unlikely. Still, they humour him, and tell him there's an impressive botanical garden in Palermo, spread over thirty acres by the sea.

Is that so? He'd quite like to see it . . .

"You've just arrived," they tease, "and yet you already speak like you are thinking of leaving! Perhaps it isn't so steadfast, this love you declare for our city."

His protestations are incandescent—he speaks of far in the future, naturally, for now his heart is in Rome and only Rome.

✧ ✧ ✧

“I have decided to give you a new name, Herr Möller, if you shall have it.”

They are at Reiffenstein’s villa in Frascati, just outside Rome, where they have been invited to stay for a few days. It’s early evening, the landlady has placed the bronzed lamp with its three wicks on the round table, and wished them “felicissima notte.”

Now is the time they gather for their daily art session, a practice for which credit must be given to Philipp Hackert, an artist who lived here not long before but who recently moved to Naples. Now the practice is continued diligently by the diplomat.

“And what might that be?”

“Baron gegen Rondanini über . . . the baron who lives opposite the Rondanini Palace.”

The party burst out laughing. The palace stands exactly where the title suggests. Across from 18 Via del Corso.

“And what about you?” he asks Reiffenstein. “What are you called?”

All the members of their German community have jocular sobriquets. Tischbein is the “twisted-nose phlegmatic.” Hackert is “God’s son, the redeemer of free lunches.”

Reiffenstein laughs. “Tell him.”

“God the Father Almighty,” everyone choruses.

“Exactly. And God the Father Almighty says let us begin.”

They busy themselves presenting the day’s sketches. Bury and Schütz with landscapes, Tischbein a horse grazing, and Goethe a field of maize. During the session, merits are discussed, opinions shared as to whether the objects might have been drawn more favourably, whether their true characters have been caught, and whether all requirements of a general nature that may justly be looked for in a sketch have been fulfilled. “In other words, am I any good at this?” asks Goethe.

In reply comes a raucous clamour: “Not yet.”

That night, Tischbein and his guest go for a walk. The village lies on the side of a hill, or rather of a mountain; and the prospect is unbounded. Rome spreads before them, and beyond it on their left is the sea. Under moonlight, all is dark and silver.

"If I may ask," begins Tischbein, "why Weimar?"

Goethe laughs a small laugh and says he isn't the only one who's wondered.

"I mean," continues Tischbein, "why leave Frankfurt? Or Strasbourg? Or any other centre of culture, with *Young Werther* to your name?"

"Because of that," says Goethe. "I think I shall spend the rest of my life fleeing that book." It is a creation, he adds, like the pelican, who feeds his offspring with the blood of his own heart. For the public, nothing he ever writes will match up to what he first wrote. No success can again be as great or as far-reaching. He and Werther are bound inextricably and forever. "Weimar offered a respite. To lead in some ways the unromantic life—I did what Werther would never have done." Before long, he'd lost sympathy with the Sturm und Drang friends of his youth, who saw nothing revolutionary in being an administrator. "But," he says simply, "it gives me a steady salary, and allows me to put into practise many things and not just to write about them." Every place, he adds, gives and takes away.

They are walking along the edges of the garden, venturing not too far out into the open darkness. "And Rome?" asks Tischbein. "What does Rome give you?"

Goethe smiles. "I can only promise you this, that any answer will fall short." Sometimes a place is more than just a place. It becomes the thing that shines like a beacon, where all your dreams and aspirations are fulfilled. It is that way with him and Rome. Does he see? The beginning and end of all his journeys, the completion of his life's education. Yet for so long it remained a dot in the distance, receding with the years, ever out of reach. Mired as he was in a web of work and life at court, which kept him from writing, from travel. From all this and more, Rome became also an escape.

"And in this web, is there a lady?"

Goethe doesn't hesitate before answering, "Yes and no."

"You mean there used to be and now there isn't?"

His friend shakes his head. "From the very beginning, it has been both."

"And when was the beginning?"

This time, he does give pause. "Ten years."

"My dear Goethe, time enough surely for no to turn into yes, or vice versa . . ."

Time enough, he concurs, for that and a million other things.

They have stopped at a bench, and are resting. The night is quiet around them.

"Her name," Goethe begins simply, "is Charlotte von Stein."

They met in the winter of 1776, when he first moved to Weimar at the invitation of Karl August, who had just come of age and been crowned sovereign duke of Saxe-Weimar. "I didn't quite know what I was doing there to begin with, but there I was. And so was Charlotte." Older than him by seven years, long married to a country squire, and mother of many children—four of whom had died in infancy. "When I first saw her, I remember thinking she was wounded, that she had composed herself to suffer in order to survive."

"And had she?"

Goethe nodded. "I think so . . . or at least until we met, and became inseparable." It was sunshine and shadow, light and dark, a crown of gold and briar. Charlotte was descended from courtiers and born and brought up among them, the embodiment of court values. "It was as though I'd left for Weimar *just* to find her," he declares.

For years, she groomed him for court and courtly life. "There never was a day in this decade that I didn't see her, or write to her, or think of her." He made himself available to her every whim, her every fancy—constricting his life, slowly, to wrap his company around hers only. He belonged to her wholly, and yet not at all. She offered him not simply a welcome distraction from administrative duties but essential support. He'd drop by every day, for supper at the Stein household. He tutored her children and was especially close to her son Fritz. She had a favourite spot by the river, and in his garden. He even inscribed a verse for her in stone to commemorate her seat.

"I am like the English poet Spenser, writing poetry to the unattainable."

"So it remained a . . . shall we say . . . strictly spiritual communion?" asks Tischbein.

Goethe nods, purses his lips. "Always."

Tischbein mutters that he understands now why Goethe needed to escape.

From the start, the "friendship" was public knowledge, and Frau von Stein had no desire to be thought an adulteress.

"And the . . . husband?"

"A complaisant type. A bore. It would be more fun conversing with a doorknob."

"Yes, I'm sure, but did he not mind this intense friendship?"

Goethe shrugged. "I think he was thankful, and probably thought it good for his wife to have someone to talk to about things that went, frankly, over his head."

They've reached the edge of the garden, where a stream flows, the water so clear it's almost invisible in the moonlight.

"Sometimes," says Tischbein, "we are involved in something because we know it has no future." At this Goethe is quiet. "When we are certain something has no future," his companion continues, "it is safe."

"Until . . ." adds Goethe.

"Until?"

"Until safe also begins to mean death." From somewhere in the trees, an owl hoots gently. "I'm hoping this journey . . ."

"Will revive what's dead?"

Goethe shakes his head. "Will make way for something that's alive."

✧ ✧ ✧

They return to Rome a day later, just before a storm that brings rain in torrents amidst thunder and lightning. Then, when the weather clears, it's as though the storm never happened; it's bright and warm again, day after day.

Slowly, Goethe falls into a routine—the first few hours of the morning are spent revising *Iphigenia*, then he's free to visit the sights, systematically following Winckelmann's *History of the Art of Antiquity*, with Tischbein ushering him from place to place. The Pyramid of Cestius, with its brick-faced concrete covered with white marble slabs; the grand Hippodrome of Caracalla, designed for ten thousand spectators; the Palace of the Caesars on the Palatine Hill with its fabulously painted walls; and also, of course, the Vatican.

Here, for a while, they walk about St. Peter's Square, enjoying the spacious views, eating grapes purchased in the neighbourhood. They enter the Sistine Chapel—*I could only see and wonder.* After they look at the paintings over and over, they leave the sacred building and walk into St. Peter's Square, receiving from the heavens the loveliest late afternoon light. They sit on the ground, finishing the last of the grapes.

"Tischbein," says Goethe, "I have a request."

"Anything."

"Take me to a garden."

Of these there are many, scattered in and around the edges of the city.

Their first expedition takes them to Monte Mario, the highest hill in Rome, lying northwest, beyond the Vatican. He has heard about its wild richness, and hires a carriage to drive them to the foot of the hill, and then they walk up slowly. In delight, Goethe stops at cork oaks and Aleppo pines, at bay trees, scrunching and sniffing their leaves. It's too early for them to be in bloom, he guesses; their small yellow-white flowers will emerge later with warmer weather. Even in the undergrowth, the hairy garlic are yet unadorned with white-flowered umbels. Only bear's breeches carpet the ground with their thick, vivid green leaves.

They also head to Villa Pamphili, whose grounds are much visited for amusement. Around the villa, they wander through the secret garden enclosure on its south side, the formal parterre with low, clipped hedges that slopes all the way down to the woodlands at the bottom. A large, flat meadow, unfolding before the formal borders of the villa's garden, is enclosed by long evergreen oaks and lofty pines, and sown with daisies that turn their heads to the sun.

Here Goethe throws himself on all fours, nose close to the ground. "This is what I'm unable to see up north!" The working of a vigorous, unceasing vegetation, unbroken by severe cold. Plant life that's constantly flourishing because the conditions are perfectly suitable. "There are no buds!" he yelps. Growth is so intense, so rapid, there is little time for this organ of in-betweenness. The strawberry is in bloom at this season, for the second time, while its last fruits are still ripening. The orange trees growing in pots farther up at the balustrades are also in flower, and at the same time bearing both partially and fully ripened fruit.

Occasionally, Goethe plays what Tischbein thinks is a botanical game. He strips a plant of its leaves and carefully lays them on the ground.

"What's so special about this?" asks Tischbein, bending over to look.

"Nothing and everything."

It is common groundsel, or as it's called here, old man in spring. Goethe has arranged the leaves, pinnately lobed like a feather, covered in fine hair, in progression, as they grow on the stem, small to large, and then diminishing again. "Tell me what you see."

Tischbein shakes his head. "A bunch of leaves."

"For now, that is enough."

Towards the end of November, under a too-warm sun, they visit Villa Madama, also on Monte Mario, a structure incomplete but still fine and elegant, with a monumental flight of steps and a terraced garden with views of the Tiber.

They walk among the chestnut trees and firs of the top terrace, and stop to look down over the plant beds, where spring flowers are being planted—cyclamens, crocuses, anemones.

"I hadn't imagined," says Tischbein, "that your interest in botany ran this deep."

It didn't always, admits Goethe. "It began as uncertain reflection, and I still consider my botanical studies uneven and incomplete . . . but it's true that I've been constantly and passionately pursuing them. This is not generally known; still less has it been accorded any attention."

His friend throws him a quick glance. "Why so?"

"What can I say, Tischbein? Every man to his field."

The painter sees little wrong in this but he doesn't say so.

"The world is full of fools," continues Goethe. "One must be either this or that . . . poet or scientist . . . not both, and not anything more. We must spend our lives inculcating one interest, specializing in one art . . ."

Tischbein hesitates. "Some would say that is the way to true knowledge."

Goethe snorts. "True knowledge! This division lies only in our minds, Tischbein. Not in the world. The world continues to be exactly as it is."

Around them, a brutto wind whips up, the southerly sirocco, strongest at noon, often bringing with it quick, short showers.

"I don't know which is a consequence of which," says Goethe quietly. "Perhaps they bolster each other . . . this obsession with specialization and the direction that science has recently taken." When his companion remains silent, he presses on. "Everything is dead. The plants we study, the animals, the rocks beneath our feet, the clouds above us." He shrugs. "Static. Natura naturata. Nature already created." But how can this be, he gestures around them, when everything is alive. Natura naturans.

"Natura naturans?" asks Tischbein.

Yes, he says, nature *naturing*, becoming. "I've grown suspicious of the kind of scientific thinking that doesn't acknowledge this." Why, botany may be the study of plant *life*, but plants are treated as inanimate, immutable machines! Back in Weimar, he has friends with great knowledge and experience—Dr. Heinrich, a local apothecary who keeps an immense garden of medicinal herbs; Gottlieb Dietrich, part of a family who, for generations, had collected plants and made herbaria. They were tied by their interest in Linnaean botany. They'd head out on excursions together, collecting, identifying, naming, carrying Linnaeus's *Termini Botanici*, his *Fundamenta Botanica* and *Philosophia Botanica*.

Tischbein admits he hasn't read any of these.

"No matter," says Goethe cheerfully. "They are about one thing and one thing only: classifying and organizing the natural world, and I will admit in their own way they were useful to me—inspiring me to begin to see, to sharpen my eye, and they were enjoyable too . . . Indeed, some of Linnaeus's lists I thought read quite like poetry! I was a staunch devotee at the time. Analysing in minute detail, counting, counting . . . two stamens, three stamens, four . . . naming, labelling, systematically arranging. But to do this is to take away life, Tischbein. Everything is dead," he repeats. "I discovered that this method lies beyond my nature. What is necessary for comprehensive and intensive systematic work is an aptitude of a special order, which I do not possess. I've had to find my own way . . . and I think my journey truly began when I started asking why. Why this particular way, and not any other? Was there anything *natural* about what was considered natural classification? And more important, was that the only way to learn about plants?" He looks out at the garden, soon to brim over with life. "About this I've been thinking more than ever since I've been in Italy."

✧ ✧ ✧

At this time, a young writer, Karl Philipp Moritz, also arrives in town, and is a welcome addition to their circle. Goethe is particularly pleased; he enjoys the company of the painters, but here is someone with whom literary discussions may be had.

They begin to meet frequently on walks through the city—talking about *Iphigenia*, and a new semi-autobiographical novel that Moritz has begun to work on. The young writer was born into poverty, and hasn't led an easy life, with scant schooling and an assemblage of odd jobs. Goethe finds him deeply perceptive, though, with a sensitive face carved by quiet introspection. Their favourite path lies along the river—with the oaks drooping over the water, shimmering in shades of yellow and green. They stroll here, talking of books and travel and poetry, and one evening, when the sun is sliding low over the horizon, Moritz says, "I haven't had many occasions to declare so . . . but being here, aren't we lucky above all else?"

A small hesitation on Goethe's part before he agrees makes Moritz ask if he feels differently.

"It is nothing," says Goethe.

"But it isn't." Moritz is seven years younger, but endowed with wisdom and sharp observation.

They've come to a stop at Ponte Fabricio, and stand on either side of the Quattro Capi. Goethe looks out at the river. "I'm not certain I can explain it. You know how along a journey a traveller's biggest fear . . ."

"Is not to arrive?"

"Is to arrive and find your enjoyment not measuring up to expectations."

Moritz turns towards him, the late afternoon sun falling on his face, on the stone, on the water. "Rome isn't quite what you expected?"

"It's too simple to say so, and untrue."

Moritz stays silent, waiting for him to continue.

"I could hardly confess this to Tischbein; it would hurt him so," he says, hesitating, "but the ruins, the monuments, all this stone, they seem to me lifeless . . . I am trying hard to listen, to hear their voices, but they remain silent."

They walk away from the river now. Down a crowded main road, stopping to allow a laden cart to pass, and then a carriage.

"Perhaps," Moritz offers, "enjoyment of a place comes slowly, and one must pass through uncertainty, even disappointment, before appreciating a destination with any depth."

Goethe nods, yes, there might be something to what he's saying. For now, he's happier in the company of green, growing things. Even in their quietness they speak to him, as they stand there doing what they must, in their gloriously complex, gloriously simple way.

✧ ✧ ✧

For many weeks now, the talk in town has centred around an eruption at Vesuvius, and it sets almost all the visitors here in motion. It seems as if all the treasures of Rome have disappeared: every stranger, without exception, has broken off the current of his contemplations and is hurrying to Naples.

Goethe, too, is keen—what if he were to continue his journey farther south? How tempting it is to stay on in Rome. Yet how tempting it is to leave.

"To wash my soul clean of the image of so many mournful ruins," he tells Tischbein at the Greco one evening.

"Your flight to Rome will then be a journey to Italy," says the young artist.

"Yes," Goethe responds thoughtfully, "it will indeed."

On their way back to Via del Corso later, Goethe and Tischbein walk awhile in silence.

It is always beautiful in Rome at this hour, and tonight there's a moon out, the wintry air is sharp and clear, and the buildings edged in silver. It is an hour that coaxes out talk on matters of the heart, and Goethe admits that something has been on his mind.

"All this while," he says, "I've been telling myself it's too early to be concerned, but I haven't heard—"

"From Charlotte?" finishes Tischbein.

Goethe nods. "We're well into December now. It takes sixteen days for letters to get there, maybe a little more back, but that's enough time for her to have received my letters, even from Rome, and to reply. But nothing."

Tischbein stays quiet, and then asks, "When you left Karlsbad, and you told no one, did that include her?"

"Yes." If there had been enough light, Tischbein would have seen the look on his face, one of deep and anguished sorrow. "I had no choice," he continues unhappily.

"No?" asks his friend.

"The way we were, our days, our lives so intricately enmeshed . . ." Goethe shakes his head. "It would have been impossible. I know she'd have talked me out of it. She has before, and she would have again. What wish do you speak of to spend our lives together, Johann, she would have said, if this is what you do . . . leave me alone for all this time. I'm certain she feels betrayed but what could I do? There was no other way."

For a moment, Tischbein is quiet. "Perhaps then she hasn't forgiven you—yet."

"Perhaps she never will."

"I'm certain that isn't true, but—"

"But?"

"You do know this already."

Goethe nods. "That all will not be as it was."

They've rounded the last corner and are almost home. Beyond, at the end of their road, Piazza del Popolo lies strangely quiet and empty.

"And maybe," adds Tischbein, "*that* is something to be desired."

Later, in bed, Goethe lies awake for a long time. He recounts all the little gifts that were shared between him and Charlotte over the years—the first asparagus from the garden, a framed landscape he'd painted, some pheasant from the hunt, soft milchbrötchen from the bakery, and books that were bought for each other and read together. Could she not find it in her heart now to gift him her forgiveness?

✧ ✧ ✧

With the arrival of Moritz, Goethe has new company on his botanical walks. Tischbein is pleased, perhaps even secretly relieved, and Goethe, too, for in matters concerning botany he finds the young writer a more interested and perceptive companion.

All through December, they keep up their botanical expeditions with walks out of the city. How few here are the signs of winter: the gardens planted with evergreens; snow nowhere to be seen except on the most distant hills to the north. The citrus trees against the garden walls are now, one after another, covered with protective reeds; but the oranges are allowed to stand in the open. Many hundreds of the finest fruits may be seen hanging on a single tree, which is not, as in Germany, dwarfed and planted in a bucket, but standing in the earth, free and joyous. The oranges are even now very good, but it is thought they will be still finer.

They head out often to the villas on Monte Mario, and after a few such expeditions, Moritz asks, "I notice you return always to the same plants—the laurel tree, this strawberry tree. That shrub . . . viburnum, I think. Why so?"

They're sitting on the lawn; Moritz has a book in hand, Goethe is sketching.

"You could say," he says, looking up at his young friend, "I'm attempting to hold a conversation with them."

"What about?"

"Whatever they wish to tell me," replies Goethe. He's trying, he says, to keep what the analytical mind does at bay; its keenness to address, to swiftly determine causal relations—"which can be useful only some of the time"—and in this haste approaches a living plant as an object. *What is it? How does it work?* These questions are asked immediately, and the answers themselves are usually classificatory in nature.

He holds out his drawing of the viburnum. "A plant *is* language. Yet all we wish to do is make it speak our own."

Later, they stroll through the circular court of Villa Madama, around which the formal gardens are arranged. On this fine day, many people have gathered outdoors. They dodge a mayhem of children laughing and running. Then Goethe comes to a stop at a row of bay laurels and gazes into their lush, unresting leafiness.

"Are you," asks Moritz, "conversing with them?"

"Not yet," Goethe replies in all seriousness. "I'm thinking: aren't they each a thing of wonder—all growing things in the world!" He turns to his companion. "Back in my garden house in Weimar, in my study, I placed a potted Bavarian gentian on my table near the window. Every day, I worked and I watched it, but only after a few weeks was it noticeable, how it turned, leaves and stem, towards the light. So I'd alter its position, turn the pot around . . . And a few weeks later, I'd see again that it had changed its orientation." Goethe looks up at the bay laurels, squinting in the sunlight. "During my botanical studies, Moritz, I've come to be suspicious of the notion held by some of our greatest scientists—yes, even beloved Linnaeus—that the world is out there, separate from us. In this way, sadly, we are perfecting what I've come to call *object thinking*."

Moritz asks him what he means.

"I fear it is the primary emphasis of our culture . . . or it will grow to be, undoubtedly." He looks around them—taking in the stretch of garden, the line of trees, in the distance the unruly woods. "Object thinking turns all this, our sensuously rich world of living nature, into generalizations, categorizations, abstractions . . . seeing it as no more than a complex mechanistic system composed of physical entities interacting on the basis of impersonal laws. In fact, it takes this notion for granted. Absurd!"

Goethe plucks a bay leaf, then crumples it and holds it up to his nose.

Moritz does the same.

"No doubt this kind of perspective gives us the ability to control and manipulate nature to a great degree. But as a consequence, it causes us to lose our close and immediate experience of the palpable world. In our minds, we are dealing with *things out there*"—he gestures to the sky—"a world of externality in which we share little or no involvement. We are not participants in the science we practise, the observations we make. I shudder to think of the consequences of this."

Moritz nods, still holding his leaf.

Goethe points at it. "How does this smell to you?"

Moritz sniffs it again. "Oddly enough, of my mother's tomato sauce . . ."

"To me, a stuffy university hall in Leipzig filled with graduates wearing laurel wreaths." He smiles, his eyes shining. "We have rich facilities with which to absorb the world—the gift of our eyes and noses and ears—and yet often we sacrifice all these at the altar of our so-called intellectual mind." He taps his forehead. Then he steps closer to the laurel tree. The leaves press into his shoulders, his chest. "I think one way to overcome object thinking is to approach a living being as the subject that it is . . . this calls for careful looking, thinking with the mind's eye, Moritz . . . Anschauung . . . And then, asking one and only one question of any importance."

"Which is?"

"What do you have to teach me?"

The laurel towers above his head, its leaves waving in the breeze.

"Do you see why, Moritz?"

His friend hesitates. "Because this invites dialogue?"

"Yes!" says Goethe, pleased. "A way by which we strive to stay close to what is being studied, to learn what the plant has to tell us, rather than to impose on it what we already believe."

Moritz leans closer to the bush. "How does one do this?"

In Goethe's voice, a tremor of excitement. "If we wish to behold nature in a living way, we must follow her example and make ourselves as mobile and flexible as nature herself." With this, he detaches himself from the laurel and makes to walk away. Moritz follows.

"We must aspire, my friend," Goethe continues, "to think like a plant." By this he does not mean they need to learn how to purify air using the action of the sun. He laughs, pleased with his joke. "Rather, we learn from plants a way of *living thinking* . . . With my gentian, it struck me how, even in its apparent stillness, it was a dynamically sensitive being, forming and changing itself through dialogue with whatever conditions it met in the world . . . air, moisture, light . . ."

They clatter down the monumental stairs, and take the path that leads to the wooded slopes of Monte Mario.

"To be inspired by plants, Moritz, is to learn to drop fixed ideas, to enter into an open-ended dialogue with the world." Goethe gazes up at the canopy, raising his arms in a gesture of embrace. "And maybe then, all will be revealed."

✧ ✧ ✧

Amidst all this, the writing.

Goethe isn't one of those for whom the day is not long enough to do everything. Botanical exploration, sightseeing, dining out—there is time for all this and more, including the revision of *Iphigenia*. In fact, he is making good progress. The scene at the end, with the two sisters, Electra and Iphigenia, at the altar, reunited just at the point of tragedy, he thinks is especially effective—indeed, if he has succeeded in working it out well, he will have furnished a scene unequalled for grandeur or pathos by any that has yet been produced on stage. He hopes to soon send the manuscript off to Herder, to Goschen, his publisher in Leipzig, and his friends in Weimar.

But midway through the month, his peace is disrupted by a letter.

He finally receives word from Charlotte. It is cold in tone—something he'd expected, but he wasn't quite prepared for the switch from the intimate "du" to the formal, brisk "Sie." This is the sharpest stab to his heart, and for a moment he feels a flash of hot anger towards her.

I gave you everything, he begins to scribble, *a simple and complete sharing of my life. You have needed my affirmation and I gave it to you—but you desire that it never stop or be diverted elsewhere. I gave up more and more for your sake, living at last in almost complete isolation. I have affirmed your identity by making you the only person who mattered to me. I have done my all to prove this to you, with all the richness and deprivation it brought me: how small my circle of friends, how I lack the consolations of a home and children, and a long . . .* Here he stops and tears up the page. The anger is gone, and what's left is a childish sullenness.

Just when things seemed to be settling, he writes, *your letter has broken it all off for me.*

His gloom is further deepened by a mishap that takes place before Christmas. In fact, it plunges all their little domestic circle into sad affliction. They spend a day by the sea at Fiumicino, and have a wonderful time—but in the evening, poor Moritz, as he is riding home, breaks his arm, his horse having slipped on the smooth Roman pavement near the Pantheon. He is carried back on a chair to his rooms in Via del Babuino, and there, after a surgeon sets his arm, he remains.

Over the following days, Goethe drops by to see him, bringing little gifts, pastries or fruit or a book or a delightful story. Like the one about Callisto, the cat, who was found, in great excitement by their old landlady, in Goethe's room, "saying its prayers."

"What!" Moritz is incredulous.

The cat had sprung up on a table, placed her forefeet on the breast of a cast of the bust of Jupiter, and, stretching her body to its fullest length, was licking his sacred beard. Probably for the grease that had transferred from the mould to the sculpture.

"But I left the good woman to her astonishment," says Goethe. "She was saying how she's long observed that the animal has as much sense as a Christian, but this was really a great miracle."

"Amen."

Moritz is up and about only in early January. On the day his arm is out of its cast, he is summoned to Via del Corso for a viewing. "A viewing of what?" he asks.

Outside Goethe's room stands a colossal head of Juno.

It is a plaster copy, he's told, of the original in Villa Ludovisi. It stands five feet high on a plinth. Goethe is tremendously proud of his outsized acquisition.

"She is my first Roman love," he declares.

"Hopefully not the last," teases Tischbein.

To celebrate Juno's arrival, and Moritz's recovered health, they head to the Greco for drinks and supper. It is a cool, crisp evening, with the sky turning a deep silvery blue. Against it, the umbrella pines in the Borghese Gardens stand like dark guardians.

After a carafe or two, Tischbein sidles over to Goethe's side. "I had something to ask of you," he says. "I'm thinking . . . of painting your portrait."

"Ah, this is why I've noticed you closely scrutinizing me."

Tischbein nods. "It is true."

"And how do you wish me to pose?"

"I have a few ideas."

"Go on."

"As a traveller."

Goethe smiles.

"It will be life-size, you'll be wrapped in a cloak, sitting on an architectural fragment, an obelisk perhaps, and looking towards the ruins of the Campagna di Roma in the background."

"Well . . ."

"I've almost finished the sketch already!"

"What?"

"And stretched the canvas."

Goethe drains his glass. "Then I happily have no choice."

"No, you don't. And if you find yourself a lovely maiden soon enough, we could paint her by your side."

"Alas, that is not to be fated, my friend."

"It doesn't seem fated with the one in the north either, and I say this for . . ."

"My own good, I know. But," he lowers his voice, "there's not much choice."

"My dear Goethe, are you saying Italian women aren't beautiful enough for you?"

"Don't be absurd." He glances at the others, but they're thankfully engaged in their own discussion. "But I can't be with women with whom services . . . come at a monetary price."

"Prostitutes, you mean?" Tischbein grins, making no attempt to lower his voice.

Goethe glares at him. "Yes, that's what I mean."

His friend leans in. "Why?"

Goethe shrugs. "I don't wish to catch anything."

"That is a fair point."

"And other unattached women . . ."

"For whom services come free."

"But they don't. Marriage is expected in return."

"That's Catholicism. And you, dear Goethe, are not Catholic."

"Indeed not."

Tischbein raises his glass. "Then we must find you someone married and willing."

By now, the rest of the party is interested in their conversation.

"Married and willing?" asks Schütz. "What for?"

"To lift the curse of Goethe's second pillow."

Most of January is fine and dry, though with a cold north wind that blows through the streets. Soon the rewriting of *Iphigenia* is complete—*i.e., it lies before me on the table in two tolerably concordant copies*—and swiftly it is parcelled off to Germany.

The new year brings to Goethe a sense of rejuvenation, a sloughing away of the old. He writes to Charlotte hoping for some sort of reconciliation. *I'm much improved; I've already given up many ideas I was attached to that made me and others unhappy, and I feel much freer. But do now help me too, and meet me halfway with your love . . .*

But the trickier letter to write is one to his friends in which he wishes to convey his decision with regard to his stay in Italy. He'd informed them that his purpose was to leave Rome immediately after Easter, and return home. *Recently, however, friendly voices have reached me to the effect that I ought not to be in a hurry, but to wait till I can return home with still richer gains. From the duke, too, I have received a very kind and considerate letter, in which he excuses me from my duties for an indefinite period, and sets me quite at ease with respect to my absence. My mind, therefore, turns to the vast field which I must otherwise have left untrodden. I intend to stay here till Carnival; and, in the first week of Lent, shall set off for Naples, taking Tischbein with me, both because it will be a treat for him, and because, in his society, all my enjoyments are more than doubled. I purpose to return here before Easter, for the sake of the solemnities of Passion Week. But there Sicily lies—there below.*

After this is dispatched, he is filled with a sense of something comfortably, wonderfully extended, if not endless.

✧ ✧ ✧

Despite the cold, there is still abundant flora to be enjoyed this far south.

Goethe and Moritz spend many mornings strolling through the woodlands of Villa Pamphili. Today they have stopped to press leaves and gather bay buds, and Goethe's pockets are bulging with pebbles and pine cones. In his hand, a bouquet of hairy garlic, its white umbels prettily drooping. Now they are close to the crumbling grotto at the edge of the lawn, from where a series of unfinished sculpted figures emerge from the semicircular rockwork.

"Look," exclaims Goethe, "like plants, they are always becoming!"

When Moritz asks what he means by this, Goethe hands him the hairy garlic.

"Allow me to show you."

He leads them to a grassy clump at the end of the portico, and gestures to the ground. When they're seated, he fishes out his sketchbook and rifles through the pages. Around them, tiny bees hover about the flourishing groundsel, soon to bloom.

"Here," says Goethe, holding out a page. "I drew this last spring, over thirteen weeks . . . whenever I could get away from work . . ." A poppy plant, sketched in hasty but sufficient detail.

"We begin here, three weeks from sowing." Goethe points. "A rosette of small foliage leaves has emerged from a very short shoot."

Moritz peers into the page. "Yes," he declares attentively, "this is so."

At five weeks, he can see, it has grown markedly. The plant has produced more leaves, larger, too, retaining the rosette form in which leaf after leaf grows out of the shoot, with small spaces between.

"Viewed from the top," Goethe gestures, "it forms a spiral. Isn't that beautiful?"

After this, new leaves develop, and in the middle of the rosette, the younger leaves are more upright, and they also have a different shape, being more deeply lobed. The lower, older leaves spread outward, some lying close to the ground.

"They are turning yellow . . ." says Moritz, frowning. "They will soon decay."

Between the seventh and ninth week, the shoot elongates greatly upward. The space between the leaves increases, and the oldest basal leaves die away.

At nine weeks, "Flower buds are visible at the ends of the drooping stalks," finishes Moritz. He is following intently.

Yes, and soon after, Goethe continues, the first buds open, the green sepals that encase the red petals fall away, and the scarlet flowers unfold to form the chalice of the blossom.

They both gaze at the pretty flower.

They're short-lived, continues Goethe, and fall off within a few days, but new flowers open over the course of several weeks. While the plant flowers, the lower part thins out—"Can you see?"—as more of the leaves turn yellow and die.

"Nothing much remains at thirteen weeks," remarks Moritz. It's a skeleton, with no flowers, few leaves, and the fruit capsules, which carry the seeds.

"Yes, but when it looks the most dead, in truth it carries abundant life," says Goethe, smiling widely.

He now holds the page out at arm's length, so they can look at the sketch in its entirety. "Can we build a picture of the plant's life cycle from this?"

Moritz furrows his brow.

"It's a continuous process," urges Goethe. It develops for as long as it lives. And although it's a poppy plant as a whole, it is never whole at any moment. Everything is sequence after sequence.

"It is always *becoming*..." says Moritz.

"Precisely. Throughout its form, it is always incomplete and changing. When something new develops, something that seemed essential before drops away. In growing," adds Goethe, "it is always dying."

A moment's silence between them is filled with birdsong, a sudden breeze, the distant shouts of children.

"What we may also observe," he continues, "is that while a plant as a whole undergoes transformation, so do its parts." He examines the ground they are sitting on, finds some groundsel, and does what he did once with Tischbein—he plucks and arranges the leaves in progression, small to larger, and then diminishing again.

"Tell me... what do you see?"

Moritz sits up on his haunches, fingers them gently. "They're all from one plant," he says, "but they're not the same leaf. In that, they are a variety."

Goethe looks pleased. "Exactly, my friend! In herbaceous wildflowers, especially in annuals like these, there is a marked and yet easily overlooked transformation within the foliage leaves."

Moritz says he is amazed, that he has never noticed this previously.

"This diversity, you must know, is not what the analytical mind concerns itself with primarily. It prefers uniformity. In the case of these leaves, it would focus on what is common to them—that they are instances of leaf—and overlook their individual differences."

Goethe touches one leaf, and then another.

"It is impossible to pinpoint what the foliage leaf looks like in a plant... there are too many varieties. This is what I realized through a practice of handling plants closely, and for that at least, I'm grateful to Linnaeus."

He gestures to his leafy arrangement. "*Leaf* is not something still and static and clearly circumscribed . . . it is dynamic, alive, it is always changing."

Moritz nods, saying he can see this now.

"This is a fine example, don't you think, of how we tend to overlook what is there to be seen, and how, when we do look carefully, wakefully, we see what reveals itself is rich diversity."

"It also gives us context, does it not?" Moritz muses. "Each foliage leaf points both to the leaves that came before and to the ones that are to come. It has history behind it, and it is developing into the future. To single out just one part is not understandable of itself . . . it doesn't tell the complete story."

Goethe smiles at him, agreeing. He then gathers the leaves and tosses them in the air; they fall around them in disarray.

✧ ✧ ✧

By the middle of February, Tischbein's portrait of Goethe is taking shape.

There have been many sittings—to pass the time, Goethe would recite from *Iphigenia*, occasionally Bury and Schütz would attend, bringing with them a bottle of wine, and it would turn into a picnic. But Tischbein is diligent, and the painting begins already to stand out from the white of the canvas. The sky is a delicate light grey, with the hills and ruins slowly coming into being. The figure at the centre is mere outline at the moment. Goethe is told he will be gazing out through the landscape, his eyes resting on far infinity.

"Will I have a hat?"

"Most certainly." A fashionable grey one, large and wide-brimmed.

After one particularly long sitting, Goethe heads out with Schütz and Bury for a walk.

It's late, the moon is full and high. The buildings are swallowed up by great masses of light and shade, and appear no more than grand and general outlines. Peculiarly beautiful, at this time, is the Colosseum, to which they make their way. At night, it is always closed. As the trio stop at the gate to contemplate the scene through the iron grilles, the moon shines brightly above. In such a light they'd also like to see the Pantheon, the Capitoline Hill, the portico of St. Peter's, and the streets and squares.

Here the sun and moon, as well as the mind, must do what is quite different from elsewhere—here, where vast yet elegant masses present themselves to their rays.

At the end of the month, it's Carnival time in Rome, and famous and anticipated as it is, Goethe isn't in the mood for revelry. Since he's decided to extend his stay, and travel to Naples and Sicily, he's filled with the restlessness of impending departure.

But Carnival goes on regardless. The horse races in the evening, the all-round mayhem. Everyone has leave to be as mad and foolish as they like, and everything, Goethe is informed by his young housemates, except stabbing and fisticuffs, is permissible.

Worse, when he tries to work in the evening, the noise is maddening. It begins after sunset, when all semblance of order vanishes. People in fancy dress and masks throng the streets—here a young man disguised as a woman of the lower classes, there a Pulcinella running around with a large horn dangling between his thighs.

What helps is that, lately, he's been socializing with some new acquaintances. Reiffenstein has introduced him to Angelica Kauffman and her husband, Antonio Zucchi. Both artists, they live nearby, in Via Sistina, where they occupy the top two floors of a large house amidst a substantial collection of paintings. It is a respite from the storm. Goethe has heard of Angelica—of her charm, her beauty, her astonishing talent. And also the rumours that have followed her to Rome from England, where she had lived for fifteen years away from her Swiss homeland. How she was married to an imposter who duped her; the whisperings of her many affairs, with the painter Joshua Reynolds, with the physician and scientist Jean-Paul Marat. But all this seems of no consequence when he walks through their door and is greeted warmly. She is older than he expected, close to Charlotte in age, with lustrous dark hair and bright, questioning eyes.

"Welcome, Herr Möller," she teases, holding out her hand.

"Is there a pseudonym for you that I should be aware of?"

"Too many to remember."

They both laugh, and he has a feeling they'll be good friends.

From then on, he is a frequent visitor to their home in the evenings, and even though he'd never admit it, it is a welcome change from his spartan quarters at Via del Corso. Here all is luxury, all richness bathed in warm light, with plates of fruit at his elbow, and superior wine in his glass, a fire always ablaze in the hearth, and lively, sophisticated conversation to be had. They speak of travel, and literature, and discuss her work as a history painter.

It is an unusual designation for a woman—one she is all too well aware of, and the reason she adamantly identifies as one. "It is the highest form of art, lucrative, more important than portraiture—and hence the domain of men? I should think not."

Goethe enjoys her company immensely. She's been given the Italian sobriquet "La Madonna" by the party, and he cannot think of a more spirited, more engaging blessed lady.

In the daytime now, spring is in the air. The weather is fine, with the days sensibly lengthening.

Moritz and Goethe take walks together daily, admiring the laurels and boxwood that are in blossom, as are the almond trees. The daisies, too, are pushing out of the ground as thick as ants; the crocus and the pheasant's eye are less plentiful, but rich and ornamental.

Early one morning, Goethe is delighted with a strange sight: he sees in the distance a leafless tree, its slender trunk covered over with the loveliest pink flowers. On closer examination, he finds it's the plant known in the hothouses of Germany as the Judas tree, and to botanists as *Cercis siliquastrum*. Later, he examines it with Moritz. "See . . . its blossoms . . . butterfly-like, or papilionaceous . . . are produced directly from the stem. They'd been lopped last winter . . . but now, out of their bark these well-shaped and deeply tinted flowers are bursting by the thousand."

"There might be a lesson there," adds Moritz, "for life."

As his departure for Naples nears, Goethe grows increasingly concerned for his young friend, who seems to have become ever more quiet and withdrawn. He is sorry to be going away and leaving Moritz alone. He does well in Goethe's company; but when left to himself, he immediately shuts himself up to the world. Goethe tries to draw him out; he encourages him to write to Herder, to forge a new and nourishing connection; he invites him along on his visits to the galleries to see art and the opera.

He also takes him to the sea at Fiumicino, but this appears to further deepen his melancholy. Only their long excursions to Villa Mellini, he is relieved to note, seem to cheer him up. Along the way, they are shaded by tall cypress and poplar trees, and they pass rich strips of vineyards. The roadside is carpeted by bitter dock weed, and clumps of hairy garlic in bloom. Often they stop to sketch, and picnic on fruit and cheese in the pleasant warmth of the sun.

Moritz says he has been thinking about how the notion of "plant as process" reminds him of the word *bildung* . . . that it, too, refers to something finished yet also always in the process of becoming.

"Yes, that is so," says Goethe, pleased.

There is yet more that he's thinking about, he adds. "I feel I'm close but not quite there, and perhaps journeying farther south, where it will be warmer, and with a wider variety of plants to observe . . . perhaps that will lead to greater clarity."

At the mention of this, Moritz looks away.

"And," Goethe adds quickly, "I will be back. Like a plant, in going, I return."

✧ ✧ ✧

A few days before departing for Naples, a small reading of *Iphigenia* is arranged. Angelica and Reiffenstein will be in the audience. Signor Zucchi, too, has solicited an invitation, in accordance with the express wish of his wife.

It is arranged at Via Sistina, with the German party invited, and they all gather in the evening. Goethe is nervous—*Iphigenia* is, after all, new, even if reworked, but it is received warmly. Iphigenia, lamenting her fate as an outsider in a foreign land, trying to find her way home through treacherous waters.

At the end, everyone stands, applauds. Angelica embraces Goethe, and promises him a drawing of one of the scenes. "Johann, you must keep it in remembrance of me," she instructs. After this, the wine flows freely, as does the conversation.

At the height of the evening, Goethe finds a moment to stand apart. Just as he is about to leave Rome, he's beginning to feel tenderly attached to these people. It's a source of mingled pleasure and regret to know that they are sorry to part with him. But what joys, what lessons the more southern land will impart, he wonders, and what new revelations will arise from them!

He spends his last day packing, and just as he is placing away his sketches there's a knock on the door; he's received a letter. From Charlotte. He falls upon it in delight, and reads it with love—she is as well as she can be, Fritz has recovered from a sudden fever, spring seems to be delayed in Weimar. He is happy to notice the cherished "du" make an occasional appearance—it is as though she is swaying between her love for him and her anger, but in uncertainty lies hope!

Until he comes to the part in which she requests, in a tone polite yet firm, that he burn all her correspondence immediately. He puts it away, not reaching the end. Then he picks it up again, to see if she changes her mind. But she repeats her request before signing off with a distant "best wishes."

He tries to finish packing, but he cannot; he's too distracted. He rummages in his bag for her letters; she hasn't written many to him in Italy, but he suspects she wishes for him to burn the Weimar ones, too.

"Are you done?" Tischbein pokes his head around the door. He's leaving with Goethe tomorrow and hasn't begun packing. He sees the look on Goethe's face and asks, "Has something happened?"

Goethe tells him haltingly, the words sticking in his throat.

His friend looks perturbed. "Do you not think it's merely a request?"

"No. I mean it is, but it's also symbolic, I'm sure of it . . ."

"Symbolic of what?"

"That something . . ." He breaks off to look out the window at twilight settling into Rome. "That something has come to an end."

Tischbein sits next to him on the bed. "I'm inclined to think that's not altogether the worst thing."

Goethe nods, slowly. Perhaps not, but in this manner? And all for him deciding to do what he'd wished to all his life? What punishment was this? What cruelty?

He looks at her letters in his hand. "Is the fire lit today?"

"Yes, and miraculously it isn't dead yet."

They walk into the anteroom. The flames flare as they curl around the paper, and then nothing remains but ash.

"Tonight," says Tischbein, "we head out to drink and dine." Goethe begins to say he doesn't feel up to it, but he's cut off and reprimanded. "Finish your packing—we leave in an hour."

This evening, somewhere new.

Osteria alla Campana, on Vicolo della Campana, a little farther away from their usual Greco, but closer to the river. It's a family-run place, a large, simple rectangular room with several arched doorways leading to a pantry and a kitchen. The party huddle around a table—Moritz looks more withdrawn than usual, and the others express voluble sadness at their friend's impending departure.

"But you will be back in Rome, will you not?" inquires Reiffenstein.

"Yes," replies Goethe, glancing at Moritz. "I'll halt here on my return to Germany."

"Stay back, stay back," the younger artists demand. "Don't return ever."

A middle-aged man with a tremendous moustache sidles up to the table. "What may I get you gentlemen tonight?" For a treat, they order the Falernian wine, and stuffato, a stew of mixed vegetables, macaroni, and a platter of animelle fritte, lamb sweetbreads rolled in flour, dipped in beaten egg and deep fried. It is one of Goethe's favourite dishes.

The carafes empty rapidly, and the food vanishes amidst the chatter. They keep drinking steadily; the Falernian, dark as amber, is strong and fruity. The place has filled up, and it's warm inside. The party asks for another carafe, and this time it is delivered by a young woman, no more than twenty-five, with a lovely oval face, and dark hair that spills out from under her bonnet. Everyone at the table is busy—they're deciding on a sobriquet for Signor Zucchi—but she catches Goethe's eye, and, rather than blushing, looking down, or away, she smiles. A tiny glimmer of amusement that lifts the corner of her mouth. He catches himself holding his breath, smiling back. And in a moment, after she's deposited the carafe on the table, she's gone.

He finds himself thinking of her as they walk back to Via del Corso. She hadn't revisited their table; also, they'd decided to bring their evening to a sensibly early close. Something about her drew him, and their encounter, if one could even call it that, was too brief for him to consider why with any depth—but there was a directness, an openness in her gaze that he liked.

"Are you feeling better?" asks Tischbein at the door to the apartment.

"Yes. Much." And he's telling the truth.

In his room, in the silence and lateness of the night, he catches himself thinking, as one might do on the eve of a journey, of departures of many kinds. Of every earlier separation. How many times he has done this, the packing and unpacking of his life. *Man*, he thinks, *is always making far too great and too many preparations.*

In his room, he can make out the outlines of the bust of Jupiter, a cast of Medusa. Watching him. Outside his door, Juno keeps colossal and patient guard. They—Tischbein and himself, that is—are leaving all this behind, they must soon turn their backs upon it all, and more, even upon this well-furnished museum. Parting from everything as though they are not.

He's overcome by tiredness now, and closes his eyes. He thinks of Charlotte; her fine, light profile, her laughter, the way she bends over a book, a picture, and these images transform themselves, as though in a dream, into something else. Like her letters to ash. He jolts himself awake, tearing himself back from the brink of a nightmare, and turns to his side. The empty second pillow mocks him, but he falls asleep thinking how lovely the girl's dark hair would look spread out against its whiteness.

CARL

TRAVELLING TO LAPLAND

Be sure to leave, as I did, on the day when you turn twenty-five. But first be appointed by the Royal Academy of Sciences for the purpose of investigating, in this country, the three kingdoms of Nature. Seize the four hundred daler. Promise to report faithfully on your travels, and to be useful. Leave at eleven o'clock, on the twenty-third of May, in the year 1732.

Choose the season when nature wears her most delightful aspect, with all of creation glowing with light and life. When the winter corn is half a foot in height, and the barley is just shooting out its blade. When the birch and elm have begun to put forth their leaves. The starting point must be to marvel at all things, even the most commonplace.

In a leather bag, half an ell in length, furnished on one side with hooks and eyes, so that it may be opened and shut at pleasure, pack the following items: light coat of Westgothland linsey-woolsey cloth; leather breeches; round wig, green leather cap, one shirt, two pairs of false sleeves; two half shirts, and a pair of half boots.

Inkstand, pen case, microscope, and spying glass; a gauze cap for protection occasionally from gnats; a comb; a journal and parcel of paper for drying plants, both in folio. Pocketbook containing travel papers, and a recommendation from the Academy. A small fowling piece, as well as an octangular stick, graduated for purpose of measuring.

Set out from Uppsala.
Through the old northern gates, past the burnt palace, and three large sepulchral mounds.
For a quarter of a Swedish mile, walk by fertile cornfields bounded by hills.
Head towards the spacious forests.

ALONG THE WAY

Find your steps attended to by the lark.
At least until Okstad, where the red wing will then welcome your approach.

Enjoy the weather.
The breeze that springs up from the west. Watch the clouds rising in that quarter.

Pluck *Byssus flos* aqua.
From ditches by the wayside, particularly in places sheltered from the wind.

Watch animals grazing.
Mares with their colts. Geese accompanied by their young.
(Best, as I found out, not to approach either.)

Make a description,
if you observe a plant in bloom and it has not already been scientifically described.

Stop, near Läby, at a landmark of curious construction—
four flattish upright stones placed in a square with a fifth in their centre.

Wonder.

LADY OF THE SNOWS

North of Elf-
Carleby, for the first time
I behold, what at least I had never before met
within our northern regions, *Anemone vernalis*. The leaves
of which, furnished with long footstalks, had two pairs of leaflets besides
the terminal one, every one of them cut halfway into four, six, or eight seg-
ments. The calyx, if I may be allowed so to call it, was placed about the
middle of the stalk, and was cut into numerous very narrow divisions
smooth within, hairy without. Petals six, oblong; the outermost
excessively hairy and purplish; the innermost more
purple and less hairy; all of them white on
the inside, with purple veins. Sta-
mens numerous and very
short. Pistils coher-
ing in a cylind-
rical form,
longer than
the stamens,
and about
half as long
as the petals.
To examine
at length, check
my folio, for
I have
placed a
specimen,
plucked and
pressed,
within
its pages.

LINNAEA BOREALIS

The road from hence lies across a marsh called by the people "the walls of Troy," a quarter of a mile in extent, destitute of large trees. A quantity of large stones lies by the roadside, dug up in order to mend the highway. They look like a mass of ruins, and have been there a while, clothed in Bauhin's *Campanula serpyllifolia*.

When you pick a favourite flower, as you must, pick this,
with its trailing roots, verdant leaves and pink blossoms,
perfectly symmetrical.

It was not I who later named this *Campanula* after myself—it is taken that the name of a plant must display no connection to the one who names it. But I dream—and urge Gronovius, fellow botanist, to do this favour for me. This plant of Lapland, insignificant, disregarded, lowly, flowering briefly—name it after poor Linnaeus, who resembles it.

HOW TO BE A TRUE BOTANIST

This much is clear—
have a real understanding of botany,
and know how to name all plants
with intelligible names.

Then, be either of two things:
collectors or methodizers. The first,
concerned primarily with the number
of species of plants.

The second with the arrangement
of plants and nomenclature.
(The amateurs of botany
are those who have produced various

works about botany, though they do
not properly pertain to botanical science:
anatomists, gardeners, physicians,
and miscellaneous, within which fall

economists, biologists, theologians, poets.)
Without fail, studiously seek out
the natural method—of classification.
For this is the beginning and the end

of what is needed in botany. Remember,
nature does not make leaps. All plants exhibit
their contiguities on either side,
like territories on a geographical map.

UNCOMMON

When I arrive at Hamränge post house during the night,
I find a place by the fire, listen to the people here talk much
of an extraordinary kind of tree, growing near the road, which
many persons have visited, but none could find out what it was.

Some say it is an apple tree that has been cursed
by a beggarwoman, who one day having gathered an apple
from it, and being on that account seized by the proprietor
of the tree, declared that the tree should never anymore bear fruit.

The next morning, I rise with the sun in order to examine
this wonderful tree, which is pointed out to me from a distance.
It proves nothing more than a common elm. Hence however, I learn
that elm is not a common tree in this part of the country. That is all.

RED HERRING

At last, to your immense satisfaction, find yourself at the Liusnan River. From this part of the forest to the sea, the distance is three miles. Here and there in the woods lie blood-red stones, or rather stones that appear to be partially stained with blood. Pick one up. On rubbing it, find the colour merely external, and perfectly distinct from the stone itself.

It is, in fact, *Byssus jolithus*.

In this way, work always to uncover the tricks of nature.

DAY OF REST

Arrive at Fjähl on Ascension Day, spend it here, partly on account
of the holiday, partly to rest your weary limbs and recruit your strength.
Take a walk about the neighbourhood; amuse yourself with the beauties
of Flora, which are here but in their earliest spring. Commit them to writing.
And as a true botanist, accept the natural genera, set forth the separate
species, be not satisfied with just any nomenclature but find true names.
Carefully examine the smallest parts of the plants and be illuminated.
Be ever and forever systematic with names and arrangements, else all is hell.

Find that aquatic violet with a white flower. It always grows near water.

Head back before the evening; it will rain very hard.

BRUNAESBERGET

For Linnaeus

As you approach Brunaesberget, turn left,
find a cave formed by nature in the mountain,
resembling a dwelling, made all out of stone.
The front is open, narrower, lower than within,
which is so lofty you cannot reach the roof.
The entrance is concealed, guarded on the outside
by two large trees, a fir and a birch, while the descent
lies hard and steep. On the floor, you find rocks,
burnt stumps, and the neighbouring people inform
you that, for two years, a man—sage or criminal?
—concealed himself in this cavern. You linger awhile
for moss on stone, for fungus textured like sponge,
and something else entirely undiscoverable.
Everywhere near the road, glittering in the sun,
lies spar full of talc or fine Muscovy glass. Stones
are piled on stones. Are you outside or in? You cannot
be certain. Not everything the light touches can be seen.

THE HEART OF THE FOREST

In the heart of the Angermannian forests, trees with deciduous leaves, *Befula alba* and the hoary-leaved *Betula alnus* var. *incana*, abound equally with *Pinus sylvestris* and *P. abies*, while among the humble shrubs the *Erica* and the *Vaccinium myrtillus* alternately predominate. The woods also abound with matted branches of the birch, I know not from what cause. Take note. And if time will allow it, make a detailed sketch.

The end of travel must be to depict nature more accurately than anyone else.

LAMENT

Weep, for no flowers are to be seen here,
not even *Oxalis acetosella*, my only consolation.

Before you reach Sormjole, you are accosted
by two male reindeer. No good omen, this, some say.

Sure enough, you mount a mare that nearly throws you.

Towards evening you reach Röbäck, where you pass the night
shivering. It is cold and the wind blows hard from the northeast.

HOW TO TAME THE WILD

Baron Grundell, governor of the province, a picture of mildness, receives you in the kindest manner. At home, he has two *Loxia curvirostra* in a cage, which feed on the cones of the spruce fir with great dexterity. Baron Grundell tells you how he often had *Emberiza nivalis*, northernmost bird in winter, and *E. hortulanus*, captured alive, which last, he sold in France for the value of a ducat.

He shows you the skins of blue and black foxes, and also of a variety called *korssraf*, which is yellow and greyish black. He tells you he has lately sent the king a live *jarf*, a wolverine with brown fur and golden stripes, and once he had another of that species so much domesticated that when he would turn it into the water at first cutting of the ice, it would not leave him, nor would it feed on any kind of fish alive.

LAMENT II

When you leave Umeå, the weather is rainy, and continues to be so the whole day. The road grows more and more narrow, so that your horse goes stumbling along, among stones, at the hazard of your life. Your path is so narrow and intricate, along so many byways, that nothing human could have followed your track. In this dreary wilderness, you begin to feel

very

solitary

and to long for a companion. The mere exercise of a trotting horse on a good road, to set the heart and spirits at liberty, would be preferable to this slow and tedious mode of travelling, which you are doomed to experience. The few inhabitants you meet have a foreign accent. Through this day's journey, nothing occurs to your observation worth notice.

EVENING AT LYCKSELE

At eight in the evening, I arrive at the hospitable dwelling of Mr. Oladron,
the curate of Lycksele, who, as well as his wife, receive me with kindness.
They first advise me to stay with them until the next fast day, to rest, get acquainted.

At dinner, I regale them with all my observations so far, dwelling on the details.

MORNING AT LYCKSELE

I find my hosts have changed their opinion, saying they're apprehensive
of my journey being impeded by floods if I delay. They advise me to make
haste, make haste, and show much concern for me to be quickly on my way.

THE ACT OF LEAVING

Notice on both sides of the river several summer huts of the Laplanders,
in which they reside, for a short time together, during that season. It is said

a Laplander never remains more than a week in one spot, not only because
of seeking fresh pasture for his reindeer, but because he cannot bear to stay

long in a place. He drives the whole herd together, young and old, into the river,
more than eight gunshots wide, and they all swim easily to the opposite shore,

happy to be on a perpetual pilgrimage, their homes brief and convenient, and yet,
and yet, surely the point of a journey is that it comes to an end, and we are at rest.

In this way the world and everything in it is kept in its rightful place.

LOVING YOUR COLONIST

The Finnish colonists who reside among the Laplanders are beloved by them, so it seems, and treated with great kindness. These good people willingly point out to the foreigners where they may fix their abode so as to have access to moist meadows affording good hay, which they themselves do not want, their herds of reindeer preferring the driest pastures.

It is simple.

They expect only that, in return, the colonists should supply them with milk and flour.

CHURCH GOING

The Laplanders
all find church
festivals, or days
of public thanksgiving,
in the spring of the year, burthensome and oppressive, as they are obliged
to pass the river at the hazard of their lives. At this season, the water is neither
sufficiently frozen to bear them, nor open enough to be navigated; so, they are under
the necessity of wading
frequently up to their
arms, and are half
dead with cold and
fatigue by the time
they get to church.
They must undergo
this hardship or be
fined ten silver dollars
and do penance for
three or more Sundays.

BAPTISM

When you meet with a new plant,
never observed before, do not touch it
immediately. Observe how the flowers
are not yet in bloom but appear within
a few days of coming to perfection. Now
open a few, finding them papilionaceous.
The tip of the standard, as well as of the
keel, has a purplish hue. The whole habit
of the plant shows it to be an *Astragalus*.
For the present time, call it *Liquiritia minor.*

Nomina si nescis, perit cognitio rerum.
Only after it is named is a thing known.

GUTTA SERENA

The people bring you a peasant's daughter,
a year and a half old, deprived of sight,
though she clearly enjoys being in the light
near the window. But first, some water

to cleanse her face, her eyes, and check
whether her complaint may be cataract
although the fact of the matter is that
her eyes are well formed, free of specks

or clouds. "Was she born in this state?"
you ask the mother. "Was there gradual loss?"
The mother says she's convinced, of course,
when she was with child, all night, all day

she tended to her mother, supposedly dying,
who recovered her illness, but recovered blind,
and try as they might they could not find
a reason for her blindness. She'd be lying

if she didn't think this was the cause. You fear
for such misfortune you know of no remedy,
except perhaps the child's cradle should be
placed with the feet towards the window. Clear-

ly, this is so she might gradually acquire
a habit of turning her eyes in pursuit of light.
Blindness passes on blindness, just as sight
is earned by repeated efforts to be purer, higher.

SESTINA FOR THE LOST

For Linnaeus

When you're in town, make a visit to the church
in old Luleå, half a mile distant. Proceed by sea,
for there are no horses to procure in the whole place.
On the way, you'll pass "old man's beard," strange
grass, known here as Lapland hair. Also, deep
in the wet soil, shellfish crackle, while above

flies swarm, numerous as atoms, and above
them the northern sun, falling on the church—
built from fieldstone that doesn't lie deep
but on the earth's surface, washed by seas.
This one is old, constructed after strange
peace was negotiated with the Russians, placed

here to secure the state, and what a place
for a house of God, amid fields emptied
of harvest, and four hundred wood-built houses strangely
silent. Go ahead, step inside the church—
it isn't quite the place to sweep you in a sea
of emotion, but doesn't mean you don't feel, deep

in the quiet. You think these roots run deep
but nothing has always been in this place—
no matter how eternal, God, Christ, the sea,
something else was there before, below, above.
A thing uncontained by wall and altar, a church
of wind and water, tall trees to whom strange

gifts were offered. Here, old statues of strange
martyrs, in whose heads are cavities deep,
holding water, so that priests in the church
can make them weep at pleasure. Go on, place
your hand on the book teaching mercy from above
and not between us sinners. Look up, you can see

the two pedestals with images upon each. See
how their hands are contrived to lift upon strangers
when they enter, folding in adoration from above.
Here, all is neatness. The lined pews tell of a deep-
seated need for order; everything in its rightful place—
we may fritter away on the fringes, so long as the church
is at the centre. And above. While all around a sea of chaos,
the fieldstone church plays anchor; no place for our strange
loyalties to deep wilderness, calling to replace churches with trees.

TRUFFLES

Found: *Lycoperdon tuber* between Heden and Swartla. Good lunch.

THE ASS AND THE LYRE

After much trouble and fatigue, I reach Jockmock, where stands the principal church of this northern district, and where its pastor resides. Mr. Maiming, who is schoolmaster, and Mr. Hogling, the curate, torment me with their consummate and most pertinacious ignorance.

The learned curate begins his conversation with remarks on the clouds in this country, setting forth how they strike the mountains as they pass, carrying away stones, trees, and cattle. I venture to suggest that such accidents are rather to be attributed to the force

of the wind, for clouds cannot of themselves lift, or carry away, anything. He laughs at me, saying, surely I've never seen any clouds. For my part, it seems to me that he cannot have ever been anywhere but in the clouds. I reply that whenever the weather is foggy

I walk in clouds, and when the fog is condensed, and no longer supported in the air, it immediately rains beneath my feet. At all such reasoning, being above his comprehension, he only laughs with a sardonic smile. Still less is he satisfied with my explanation of how

watery bubbles may be lifted up into the air, as he tells me clouds are solid bodies. On my denying this, he reinforces his assertion with a text of scripture, silencing me by authority, and then laughing at my ignorance. He next condescends to inform me that

after rain, a phlegm is always to be found on the mountains where the clouds have touched them. Upon my replying that this phlegm is a vegetable called *Nostoc*, I am, like St. Paul, judged to be mad, and that too much learning has turned my brain. This philosopher,

who is as fully persuaded of his own complete knowledge of nature as Sturmius was of being able to fly by means of hollow globes, is pleased to be facetious at my expense. At length, he graciously advises me to pay some regard to the opinions of people skilled in

these abstruse matters, and not, at my return home, to expose myself by publishing such absurd and preposterous opinions as I have now advanced. The other, the pedagogue, laments that people should bestow so much attention upon temporal vanities, and consequently, alas, neglect their spiritual good; and he remarks that many a man has been ruined by too great an application to study. Both these wise men concur in one thing. They cannot conceal their wonder that the Royal Academy should expressly have appointed

a mere student for the purposes for which I have been sent, without considering there are already as competent men resident in the country, who would have undertaken the business and completed it assiduously, and with much more thought.

My head hurts.

TRACES OF FIRE

Opposite Parkajaure, the first lake you reach after leaving the place where you slept, rises the lofty peaked mountain of Tornberget, upon whose summit the Laplanders used, in ancient times, to offer sacrifice for the health of their herds of reindeer. These have stopped but the mountain still shows traces of fire.

KNOWING TIME

Midnight is *kaskia*
The remainder of night before dawn, *pojela kaskia*
Dawn, *theleeteilyja*
Sunrise, *peivi morotak*
Two or three hours after sunrise, *areiteet*
Hour of milking reindeer, *arrapeivi*
Noon, *koskapeivi*
Late afternoon, *eketis peivi*
Sunset, *peiveliti*
Night, *iä*

For months, the Laplanders have no names, but the middle of summer is *Gaskakis*, the middle of October, *Talvi*. And reindeer-fawn week, *Ornjk*, for that time of the year when in a fawn two years old the horns begin to bud.

HOW TO HUNT A BEAR

Do not miss.

NEW WORLD

When I ascend Wallavari, I scarcely know whether I am in Asia or Africa,
the soil, the situation, and every one of the plants being strange to me.

Snowy mountains on every side, and I walk in snow, as if it is severest winter.
All the rare plants I previously met with are here in miniature, and new ones
in such profusion, I am overcome with astonishment. Silky *Alchemilla* with
fingered leaves, three-toothed *Jussiaea*, *Dillenia* of woody stem and purple
flower, *Bannisteria*, large and ovate, *Saxifraga* with hairy leaves and creeping
stem, yellow-bearded *Pinguicula*, blunt *Ranunculus* with triangular plaited
flowers, flat-podded *Hesperis*, humble *Salix villosa*, upright *Veronica serpyllifolia*.

I look upon all that I have named and see that it is good.

KNOWING

I can't help wondering how Laplanders know
which of the herd they have already milked
from the rest, as they turn each loose as soon
as they are done with it. No marks are made
that I can glimpse, no visible garnish. So I ask,
and I'm answered that every one of them has an
appropriate name, which the owners know perfectly.

This seems to me truly astonishing, as form, colour
are so much alike in all, and the latter varies in each
individual every month. Their size, too, changes—
depending on how many summers the animal has
seen. To be able to distinguish one from another
among such multitudes, like ants on an anthill,
is beyond my

comprehension.

BOOK

Today, I show a Laplander some drawings in my journal.
He is alarmed at the sight; takes off his cap, makes a bow,
and remains with his head inclined and his hand clapped to his
breast, mumbling some words to himself, and trembling
as if he is going to faint away. I'm told he's afraid I am a conjuror,
the book a magical drum to which the Laplander resorts in times
of trouble with as much confidence as a devotee to the shrine of a saint.

CONVERSION

First take away their drums and idols.
Commission a person to check, procure
information of any Laplander who's kept
such things concealed. Then request
to have them brought forth. If the owner
refuses, and having long used entreaties
to no purpose, lay hold of the Laplanders'
arm, slip up the sleeve of his jacket,
and so contrive at length as to open a vein.

The Laplander, near fainting, entreats you to spare
his life, promising to bring the drum, the idols
required; upon which the arm is bound immediately.
This ploy has been frequently pursued with success.

LIVING LIGHTLY

The mountain Laplanders, or those who live
in the Alps, build no huts, only tents of sticks
and beams and walmal cloth. When they lie
down, they fix a hook through the coverlet
to let in the stars. Their furniture consists
of kettles and pots, made sometimes of brass,
sometimes of copper; rarely stone, on account
of the weight. They own nothing they cannot carry.

SIGNS

The peasants who reside near the cliffs or rising ground judge by the crows the approach of bad weather; for these birds seek the marshy country before it comes on.

They say they have been reading such signs for years.

HOW TO FIND NORTH

Consult, as Laplanders do, natural objects by way of compass as you travel.
Large pine trees bear more copious branches on their southern side than towards the north. Anthills, too, the south sides of which bear grass, the northern whortle berries. The bark of aspen trees is rough on the north side, and smooth on the opposite. Old, withered pines are clothed, on the north with the black usnea, or filamentous *Lichen jubatus*.

By such marks are you able to find your way through pathless forests.

Have we any guides so certain?

WHITE WATER

The lakes in this part of the country do not afford you so many plants as farther south. Their bottoms are clear, and destitute of vegetation. Their shores are no less barren. No *Nymphae*, no water docks, grow about their borders, but the surface of the water is covered with *Ranunculus* bearing round as well as capillary leaves, and whitening the whole surface with its blossoms. The lake appears covered in snow. Though it is not so.

FOREST FIRE

Winter is kinder than fire.
Several days ago, the forests
were struck by lightning, and
the flames, fuelled by drought,
raged with great violence.
In many places, the devastation
extended several miles' distance.
The forest was in deep sable,
a spectacle more abhorrent than
white snow, for ice, though it
destroys the herbage, leaves
roots in safety, which fire does not.

BLANKET

On a heath very near the Sangis River, notice some earth of a red colour. The dry part of the forest, which had been burned down, produced *Lichen rangiferinus* in such abundance that the whole face of the ground was covered with it. This is how you discover that, despite it all, things still grow.

HARBOUR

Arrive at the town of Nykarleby, where every single street is laid with timber
like a bridge, which gives it a handsome appearance. The harbour of this place is near the river, a quarter of a mile from the town. On the shore, lie vast piles of wood destined to be conveyed to Uppsala for fuel.

You, too, are ready to be home.

JOURNEY'S END

Before you arrive at Uppsala, at one o'clock in the afternoon, take stock.
If you have travelled as you ought to, committed to writing all you have
observed and found useful, here is your reward: natural knowledge
of plants, animals, and minerals, influence in the system of the world,
and usefulness to the human race. Else, no point in journeying anywhere.

JOHANN

In early June 1787, on a day bright and summer warm, Goethe passes through the Porta del Popolo into Rome. This time couldn't be more different from the last. His mind isn't on the capital of the world, the eternal city, the city most sacred.

He is thinking of Vesuvius. And the lava stream that's issued forth from the summit, coursing its way to the sea.

An incommensurable tragedy to miss this experience! But the volcano erupted after he'd said his farewells in Naples, and though he'd stayed on a day or two, hoping to witness this rare geological marvel, the lava stream was slowing—it might take weeks to touch water, he was told.

So he departed, and here he is, one hundred and forty miles away from the volcano, en route to 18 Via del Corso.

Schütz and Bury are overjoyed to see him. They hover around, wishing to know all about his adventures in Naples, down to Sicily, and back again. They want to see his sketches, his watercolours. They want to know if the sea looks different in the south, if the fruits are sweeter, the women more beautiful, more compliant, the wine stronger, the towns more ancient, and the sunsets more maddeningly glorious.

Goethe laughs. "The answer to all of this is yes. Except the women—I wouldn't know."

"The second pillow still remains cursed, then?"

Alas, he sighs, yes.

Just then, Tischbein enters the room, and even though their reunion is amiable enough, there's a distinct coolness in their exchange. "How was Sicily?" he asks politely.

"Good."

"Good?" interjects Schütz. "You wrote to us saying it's a dream . . . that one hasn't seen Italy without seeing Sicily . . ."

Goethe begs their forgiveness; he is weary. He'll retire now and be with them later. Schütz and Bury steal a quick glance. They know little of what transpired between the two friends in Naples, but their guess is that whatever it was came in the way of Tischbein accompanying Goethe farther south. He returned from Naples while Goethe was in Sicily. For now, they do not speak of it and graciously excuse Goethe, saying of course he must rest.

This time, unlike the last, it is a strange settling in, because as the plan stands, Goethe is meant to leave Rome in time to be in Germany by early autumn, before the Alps become impassable for the winter. Should he bother to unpack?

He remembers thinking, a month earlier, while waiting for the ship back to Naples in Messina, the last city he visited in Sicily, that this was it. There was no turning away from it now. He had begun his journey back north, back to Weimar. When he arrived in Naples, this felt even more real. Count Fries, a Viennese visitor, handed him post he'd collected for him from Rome. Several letters from Fritz Stein, two from Charlotte, and three from the duke. Weimar, which had seemed so far away during his two months in the deep south, was now pressing upon his attention again. In his letters back home, he had to sound definite about his achievements—*this was a tour of the homeland of classical culture on which I have hastened from peak to peak*—even though his mind was still a whirl from all he'd seen on the island. Journeys don't end when you disembark from the boat or step out of the carriage, he had wanted to write. It takes time to comprehend their purpose, and this is ruined when it is drawn into a narrative too quickly, too soon. *I have seen much, and that is all I have to say*, he began in one letter, then crumpled it up and started another.

More important, he'd needed to be clear about his intentions. So he outlined in detail his plans to be in Germany in early autumn. The greatest care he took, though, was over his reply to the duke, working on the letter for several days before he finally gathered the courage to request a complete revision of his official commitments as a civil servant and to be relieved of all administrative work in Weimar. It wasn't easy, but perhaps because he'd embarked on this adventure, ridden a mule through mountain rain, scaled Vesuvius three times and looked into the depths of a volcano, or because the bottle of Nero d'Avola he was drinking was a particularly strong vintage—he signed, sealed, and dispatched the letter.

He hoped to have a reply waiting for him in Rome.

There is no reply awaiting him in Rome. Only days that grow ever warmer.

In the long afternoons, his living quarters are stifling, despite closing the shutters to keep the sunlight out. He despairs, but sets out to complete at least the botanical work with which he's tasked himself. From the market square, he buys terracotta pots, fills them with soil and sand, and plants the prickly pear cactus seeds he brought from Sicily—after lightly scratching the seed coat and soaking them in water. Hopefully, in this heat, they will germinate before he sets off north. He's telling the others how that's all his room is good for at the moment, as a tropical hothouse, when Tischbein makes a surprising offer.

"You can have my studio," he says.

The party is at Caffè Greco, taking refuge from the summer, drinking locally brewed German beer, which is surprisingly good. They're joined by their artist friend Hackert, here from Naples to help move the renowned Farnese art collection back to the Neapolitan royal family.

"And where will *you* be?" everyone asks Tischbein.

"I'll be leaving for Naples."

There are cries of confusion around the table, though Goethe is silent.

"When?" they ask in chorus.

"Early July."

"So it worked out," says Goethe. "Congratulations."

Tischbein thanks him and then turns to the others. "You are now looking at the new director of the Accademia di Belle Arti di Napoli."

The uproar at this is even more boisterous, and many congratulatory rounds of beer are consumed.

Afterwards, Goethe is asked what he thought of the city at the foot of Vesuvius.

He answers quietly. "Rome is where you study. Naples is where you live." When he first arrived in Naples, he says, he thought that here was where one casts aside all memories, even of Rome. As compared with the free, open situation of Naples, the capital of the world, on the Tiber flats, was like a wretchedly placed monastery.

Most of the party protests. "Surely not, sir!"

"You asked." He shrugs. "I'm being honest."

Later, when they leave, Goethe finds that Moritz has fallen in step with him. His young friend has stuck close to his side ever since he has returned. On his suggestion, they take a short walk, although daylight is failing and Rome's streets are dangerously unlit.

"Did you really prefer Naples to Rome?"

"If I said I did, it would make me the freest, most fun-loving, pleasure-seeking German I've known. To live in Naples is to have no thought for tomorrow, it is to be perfectly content in the here and now, to be comfortable with happy frivolity."

"You couldn't bear it, could you?"

"By the end, no."

They manoeuvre their way around a pile of bricks and what looks suspiciously like horse dung.

"Did Tischbein pushing for the Accademia job have anything to do with it?"

"With what?"

"The two of you falling out."

"Somewhat."

Moritz doesn't press him further, but Goethe continues. "I think we found ourselves at odds with our separate agendas. He with official work, and me with my exploration. It's a waste of time to scale the heights of Vesuvius when attending aristocratic lunch parties would be rather more fruitful to furthering your career."

"I would have climbed Vesuvius with you."

Goethe smiles. "I know."

He doesn't mention the argument that had broken out between them, how it spiralled out of control and ended with Tischbein saying unspeakable things. Compounded perhaps by the frustrations of travelling together, they were fired, all the accusatory arrows—Tischbein was foolhardy, Goethe too cautious; Tischbein was tardy, Goethe gave constant counsel. He doesn't remember how they'd come to him and relationships, and Charlotte, but they had. He was called a coward, involved with her only because it helped him avoid the fixity of marriage. "For you only the charm of endlessly *becoming*," Tischbein had spat, "whatever that means!" And along with this, the illusion that he has freedom. By this time, Goethe had been too livid to speak.

Later, Tischbein had approached him, abashed and profusely apologetic, and Goethe had said it was quite all right—but something remained unhealed between them.

It takes a moment for him now to realize that Moritz has asked him a question. He has asked what his most treasured experience has been, that he's carried with him from the south. Goethe is silent a long while, and Moritz expects him to protest, saying that there are far too many and he cannot choose, but he doesn't. He finally replies: "Light."

On one of his last evenings in Naples, he says, he left the theatre by the harbour and walked out along the Molo in the warm air. “At a single glance, I saw the full moon, the moonlight edging the clouds, the moonlight in the sea and on the edges of the nearest waves, the lamps of the lighthouse, the fires of Vesuvius, its reflection in the water, and the lights on the ships.” Southern Italy became then what he thinks it will always remain to him—a memory of light.

To get away from the heat, his stuffy room, and Tischbein, Goethe accepts an invitation from Hackert to spend a fortnight sketching at Tivoli and in the Alban Hills, about nineteen miles from Rome.

He had first met Hackert while in Naples, in the artist’s comfortable living quarters in the royal palace at Caserta, where he instructed the princesses in painting. Goethe had shown him some of his work, and been the recipient of Hackert’s blunt judgement: “You’ve got talent, but you’re incompetent.” His advice? Study for eighteen months if he wanted to produce something that would give pleasure to himself and to others. From then on, Goethe’s painterly ambitions had quietly dwindled, relegating art to a “pastime.”

But he is more than happy to go sketching with Hackert now in a place so picturesque. They wander amidst woods and waterfalls and classical ruins, with Hackert bestowing upon Goethe the attentions of an instructor. There are, he declares, only three forms of leaf that the painter needs to know: the chestnut, the poplar, and the oak, and all other foliage could be constructed from these elements.

“Oh, I’ve been thinking about . . . how should I say it? . . . templates, too.”

“In painting?”

“No, in botany.”

Hackert blinks, his face blank as a brick wall.

Goethe wonders for a moment whether he ought to take the trouble to share with him some of the botanical ideas he’s been harbouring over the last few months, shaped by his travels south, and decides against it. Something tells him Hackert might not be a sympathetic audience.

"Never mind," he says. "Show me how to draw foliage."

When he returns to Rome, later in June, a letter awaits him from the duke.

He rushes out of his room after reading it. "I can stay," he announces, except there's no one in the anteroom apart from Tischbein, who looks up inquiringly from his book. Goethe hesitates. "I just received a letter from the duke. He's in Prussia, taking up the rank of major general in the army, and he doesn't see the need for my return until he himself is back in Weimar early next year."

"That's wonderful. And as I said, you're welcome to take my room."

Goethe nods and makes to leave, but he has more to share—in fact, *this* bit of news is even more exciting than the first. He stops at the door.

"What is it?" asks Tischbein.

In his previous correspondence with the duke he'd requested a revision of his official administrative commitments in Weimar. To this, the letter indicates, his employer is not entirely averse. The duke is happy to consider retaining him even in the rather indefinite role being proposed.

"Finally," says Tischbein, "you can be there as an artist."

Despite all that has unfolded, unravelled, between them in Naples, Goethe must admit, even if grudgingly, that Tischbein, his first host in Italy, his earliest friend in Rome, would understand best why this was so important to him.

With this unexpected windfall of time stretching before him, Goethe settles more comfortably into life in the city.

He decides to start reworking, and hopefully finish, *Egmont*, a play he'd abandoned five years ago. By early July, he is able to move into Tischbein's vacated studio, larger and cooler than his own room. Here he shuts himself up, sleeps long hours, emerging at dawn to walk through Piazza del Popolo to the fountain of Acqua Acetos, where he takes the mineral waters in Bernini's pump rooms. By eight, he returns to the studio, works on his play, inspects the seeds in the pots installed on the window ledge.

This is his first summer, he feels, never having known temperatures like these before in his life. Something is quickened, yes, but something is quietened also. It is a muted time, as though a veil has fallen on the world. Perhaps because of this, he retreats into a strange despondency.

I keep to myself as much as possible, he writes to Charlotte. *The artists wish to take me along with them wherever they go—which is kind and generous of them—but I usually decline and keep to my solitude.* He writes to her faithfully still, filling her in on all the details of his life, but something feels irrevocably changed since he burned her letters. Something else was relinquished to the fire. He'd been convinced that she'd understand, that eventually she'd forgive him his truancy—and why shouldn't she? Did he not have every right in the world to do what he did?—but all her letters are now briefer, less affectionate, studded consistently with the formal "Sie." Only briefly does she break once to say *du hast mich allein gelassen*. You left me alone.

Yes, he did, he thinks, bristling defensively, *and there was no other way.*

Occasionally, he visits Angelica; she, too, has begun a portrait of him, although it is composed in close up, and in a more formal style than the one Tischbein painted of him in the Campagna. On some evenings, he bathes in the Tiber, not freely—some would say wildly—as he did in the Ilm, but by using a respectable, well-appointed bathing machine out in the water. Sometimes he goes out to watch a comic opera, or simply for a cool walk, to the Colosseum at twilight, or to the top of Trajan's Column to watch the sun setting over the city . . .

He meets Moritz for some hours almost every day—and even though they haven't been able to resume their botanical excursions because of the heat, Goethe is keen to share with him details of the flora he'd seen on his southern travels.

When he and Tischbein headed out of Rome, almost immediately the vegetation was unfamiliar, he reports—prickly pears pushing their large fleshy leaves amid the grey-green of dwarf myrtles, the yellowish green of the pomegranate, and the pale silvery green of the olive. In the meadows, the narcissus and the *Adonis* were in flower. As they travelled farther, they were greeted by orange trees hanging over walls flanking the road, loaded with so much fruit "I could scarcely believe my eyes!" In Sicily, he was welcomed with fresh green mulberry trees, evergreen oleanders, and hedges of citron. In the open gardens, large beds of ranunculi and anemones bloomed. The roads were lined with wild bushes and tangled shrubs brilliant with flowers: the lentisk, a mass of yellow blossoms with not a single green leaf to be seen, the white thorn, cluster on cluster; the aloes rising high, promising to flower; rich tapestries of amaranthine clover and little roses; hyacinths with unopened bells; asphodels and other wild flowers. Flowering thistles swarmed with countless butterflies; wild fennel stood high, dry and withered, of last year's growth, but still so rich that one might almost take it to be an old nursery ground.

Goethe pauses to take a breath, and then laughs. "Pardon me, I get carried away."

"Please," says Moritz. "There is nothing to forgive."

This evening, they have walked to the top of Janiculum Hill, and are standing beside the Fontana dell'Acqua Paola, before its three arches. From under the middle arch, the water falls into a pool so blue that it looks as though it is pouring into the sky. They turn, and before them lies the city, glowing in the evening sun. On the distant hill opposite, across the river, stands the elegant white form of Villa Medici.

"It sounds wonderful," says Moritz, "a world undreamt of by us in our more northerly homelands . . ."

"It's true, Sicily is extraordinary to the eyes . . ."

"What I'm curious about is whether all of this revealed something?"

Goethe nods. "Many things I think . . . Isn't that why we embark on journeys? Not only to see new things but to see things in new ways." He is about to continue when a shout is raised from behind them. "Look who it is! The baron who lives opposite the Rondanini Palace." Hackert and Reiffenstein, also out to take the evening air, are striding up to join them. Their presence brings to a close any further botanical talk, for now a fervent discussion breaks out instead over where to wine and dine this evening.

Soon it also becomes an unspoken understanding that Goethe is to lunch with Angelica every Sunday. In the morning, her carriage draws up for him outside 18 Via del Corso, and they drive to one gallery then another, to look at paintings.

In her company, Goethe meets Jacob More, "More of Rome," a Scottish landscape painter who visited the city in 1773 and never left.

"I can paint," he tells them, "nowhere else."

"Is that true?" asks Angelica.

"Well, the wine here is so much better."

One Sunday, they visit the Barberini Palace, with its rows of windows and graceful arches. He usually finds it a pleasure to accompany her, with her sharp, trained eye, and her immense knowledge, but that afternoon is scorching and the rooms are warm and airless. As they move from one painting to another, he falls slowly silent.

"Are you well?" she asks. He's mopping his forehead and leaning against the wall.

"I'm afraid this northerner is suffering from the summer a little."

"Oh, it must be unbearable for you, Johann . . . you must get out, to the country."

He informs her he has an invitation from Reiffenstein to be in Frascati in September.

"And the month after, we'll be at Castel Gandolfo," she adds. "You simply must join us."

Feeling more cheerful at the prospect of getting away, he turns to the painting he had been in no mood to admire a moment ago. Raphael's portrait of his mistress, "La Fornarina." Angelica guides his eye over the details of the night landscape, the way the woman is carried forward to the viewer by the contrast between light and dark.

Goethe exclaims, in delight, "It is incredible how much you know!"

She waves him off, smiling. "I've been painting since I was ten; if I didn't, it would be embarrassing, shameful, even." Her first accomplished self-portrait was completed when she was thirteen, at the same time she was painting portraits of bishops and nobles.

"And yet, alas, you have failed with mine, Angelica."

"Are you saying I have not managed to pull it off, the portrait of you?"

"Exactly. He bears no resemblance to me whatsoever. He's far too handsome."

"Then, my dear Johann, we would have fooled the world forever."

Now that Tischbein has left, and is firmly ensconced in Naples, Bury and Schütz appoint themselves custodians of Goethe's social life.

They have many friends in the German community in Rome, musicians, composers, painters, singers, and there is no dearth of events they wish him to attend. They manage, finally, to get him to come to a dance being held in the garden behind their house.

"This is the only reason I'm agreeing," says Goethe. "So that if I faint while waltzing like a fool in this heat, you can carry me up to my room with no trouble."

It's a young, carefree gathering. A quartet plays lively tunes in a corner, the wine flows freely, and a generous number of ladies are in attendance, willing to dance. Goethe whirls around with one and then another, and is pleasantly surprised: he's having a jolly time. The women tease and flirt, saying that the northerner needs to thaw, that they must show him an unforgettable time. One in particular, Catarina, is tipsily audacious. They dance three dances in a row, and at the end she leans closely over, and whispers into his ear—*Upstairs?* But he doesn't continue this flirtation, or any of the others. Ten years ago something might have happened but that kind of fire, he thinks, is now cold.

Later, quietly, before the festivities come to an end, he slips away. Instead of heading back to the house, he goes for a short walk. It is one of those silver-stained nights. Sometimes, when there's a cool breeze, groups of people gather in the streets playing music, singing until the small hours. Tonight, he can hear a duet, somewhere in the distance, beautiful as anything one hears at the opera or in a concert. Usually, this lifts him up, but at the moment he's filled with sadness, certain he's doomed always to be on his own and on the outside of things.

Perhaps Tischbein was right, he begins to think, that he is not brave enough to make a commitment—and then he stops himself. No, that way leads to lies, a madman's delusional ramblings, to insanity.

✧ ✧ ✧

August, he discovers, is the warmest month, and so he stays quietly home all day.

The hours stretch before him longer than ever. He works and occasionally he takes a break to examine the prickly pear. All this while he'd anxiously waited for the seeds to germinate, sometimes checking the pots three times a day. Had he covered them too thickly with soil? Cactus seeds have small amounts of stored energy, and are unable to break through to the surface if planted too deep. For weeks the soil remained undisturbed, but in mid July, tender tips of green broke through, and swelled into small, fleshy shoots. He'd sat there chuckling to himself. Who would think a plant with such an ungainly form would begin life with such elegance?

Now he's chosen to sketch the one that's most robust—and he draws it every day; watching the cactus grow and take shape. First, no more than a globule, like a fingernail, with an indentation on the top that becomes more pronounced as it enlarges, and pushes up two succulent leaves, the twinned cotyledons that lengthen blade-like and tapering, edged all around by a reddish green. At the centre, a dome dotted with glochidia, hairlike spines, begins to appear, fine and soft and white. It is fascinating; a phenomenon he hasn't had a chance to observe previously. Slowly the dome elongates, and the surface between the glochidia grows. He can see now that they are arranged in clusters, usually of five.

How marvellous!

There is nothing more enlivening than being entangled in this manner with another living being. It never ceases to surprise him, that however jaded he might be—of life, of court, of poetry, even—the presence of a plant, in the woods, on a windowsill, renews him endlessly.

It is something he had also felt with the little potted gentian in his study in Weimar—a gift from Charlotte, he might add—how his thinking becomes enlivened by a plant's living presence, as it flows in wholeness from seed to leaf to flower and back to seed.

With the gentian, he'd also begun to practise seeing. Not the usual hasty cast-a-glance-this-way-and-that of the analytically inclined eye, but a seeing that called for a long, careful looking.

He is still trying to work out what exactly it entails, but he strongly suspects that this mode of perception will draw on instinct, imagination, inspiration, what he holds close and feels are insufficiently employed—often dismissed—within the scientific practices emerging today. At first, for certain, a preparation—a "first meeting" with the phenomenon. The most useful characteristic at this stage being a childlike receptivity, an openness, a willingness to wonder. "Simply, what piques your curiosity?" he'd explained to Moritz. "Is it not obvious that we are drawn to certain phenomena on account of who we are? Why is this rarely, if ever, acknowledged?"

Then, perhaps a need to stand back and approach the subject with nothing to aid us but our ordinary senses. To attempt to observe with as little judgement and evaluation as possible. "Hold back your theories! Let the phenomena speak for themselves!"

For this, he's found drawing to be a useful tool—where one's attention may be closely brought to previously unnoticed details or patterns. *See* a particular prickly pear, rather than employ a *seeing-prickly-pear* mode of perception.

"What else can we do?" Moritz had urged. "To help us to see anew?"

"I recommend throwing away the names of things," Goethe declared. This would allow for new descriptions outside of learned classifications. "If I could, Moritz, I would place a restriction on the use of nomenclature—at least to begin with. Find other words to describe the part you're looking at . . . New words give us new eyes . . . words that work not to fix but to encourage exploration."

It was also important to use all your senses. Smell the plants. Touch them! Use the non-visual to engage with the phenomenon.

"And then?" his young friend inquired.

"I'm not entirely sure yet."

"No?"

Goethe shakes his head. "But I have found it useful to imagine the observed phenomenon in my mind." At this point, he mainly employs a retreat into silence, because to verbalize, he'd begun to feel, was to taint, even to distract from a sensory experience before one had come to understand it. For months now, he's been trying to reinvest attention in the sensory experience. No more thinking, he vowed. Plunge instead into seeing. For hours he would do this—produce imaginatively, for instance, a leaf that filled a developmental gap between those that were evident in a plant. This helped shed light on the process of growth as opposed to recording only the plant's form. He experienced the leaf sequence as if he were living in the changing forms of the leaf rather than seeing the individual static representation. This helped him attune himself to seeing movement and to seeing things in transition.

As he'd told Moritz, "I am trying to see all at once." To see all at once is the only way to truly understand something that is alive.

There are more stages to work through, he is certain, but for now he turns back to the prickly pear, sitting young and green and gleaming before him—filled with potential. Of course, there's no hope of planting and growing these in the north—unless he owned a hothouse. He toys with the idea of requesting one of the duke, and then decides against it. He's just been relieved of all administrative duties and still draws a salary; he ought not to push his luck.

When Goethe tires of being in the studio, he heads outside—it does not rain at all these days, the sky is always cloudless, and at noon the heat ferocious. *My greatest consolation during this heat wave*, he writes to his friends in Weimar, *is my conviction that you, too, must be having a fine summer in Germany.*

He escapes the worst of it by seeking out spots in the city where he can work. Some palazzo or the other, with high ceilings and fortuitous cross-ventilation. Ideal, though, is the Sistine Chapel, which stays dimly lit and cool. A generous tip to the custodian allows him in through the back door next to the altar, and he settles down wherever he likes. Sometimes he smuggles in bread and cheese, some fruit, and after a meal snatches a nap on the papal throne.

Despite the season's slowness, *Egmont* is almost done—he has completed the fourth act, and soon he hopes to announce that he has finished the play. It is a miracle, this effusive productivity. What is it about Italy that calls forth this uninterrupted creative flow?

Perhaps because not a day goes by that doesn't add to his knowledge—of art and improving his skill—here, if one is willing and receptive, one can easily fill oneself to the brim like an open bottle plunged underwater. That must be it. To learn is to create; to create, learn. Always to walk both paths, and not just one.

How much more at ease he feels, how little he can recognize the weary person he was a year ago. It is only here, in this plenitude, that he has really come to know himself—and the city. To acquire an intimate knowledge of Rome, its atmosphere, and to feel natural and at home, one must do what he has been able to—live here and walk about the city day after day. He feels he'll never tire of it, that he could easily do this all his life.

The greatest of his delights still remain his daily walks with Moritz.

The young writer tells him what he has thought for himself during the day, and what he has read in other authors—"You are filling up gaps in my knowledge, Moritz!" As they walk, they look at buildings, landscapes, monuments, and when they come home in the evening and sit chatting and joking, Goethe draws up some view or the other that struck him particularly, to share with friends or keep as a memento.

This evening, a pleasant tramontana is blowing from the north, and the air is perfectly fresh. Moritz is telling him about his novel—that he is still working on it, but it will, by his own admission, take a while. The writing, over the summer, has slowed. In fact, the only progress he's made of late is to come up with a title.

"Well, more than I did in ten years at Weimar," says Goethe. "What is it, if I may ask?"

"I thought . . . *Anton Reiser.*"

They are sitting by the lake at Villa Borghese. Across from them, on a small island, a temple to Asclepius is almost reaching completion.

"It's the name of the character," Moritz goes on to explain, "but it also hints at the theme. *Anton* from Saint Anthony the hermit and *Reiser* being a wanderer."

"I like it."

"Yes?"

Goethe nods. "It's clever . . . simple yet hinting at something deeper."

They speak more about the novel, and Moritz's other new idea—to study the works of antiquity with the intention of writing something unstuffy and accessible for the young, average reader, but around them, rapidly, the crowd grows stronger, drawn outside by the salubrious weather.

The friends move away from the lake, from the noisy picnickers and beggars and hawkers, and into the gardens, where it is quieter, and cooler in the shade. Goethe walks ahead and sits under a great old Turkish oak. He has turned pensive, and Moritz senses this—he is used to his friend's changeable temperament—and stays quiet; waiting for him to share his thoughts.

Sure enough, he begins: "Do you know, in the corner of my studio, next to Tischbein's portrait, are my most precious items . . . they have been in my possession for the last ten months or so."

"Tischbein's painting is *less* precious?"

"Let's say it is treasured for reasons other than botany."

Moritz grins. "What are these items you speak of?"

What he has collected from the botanical garden in Padua.

"I've told you," he says, "I saw many wondrous things there, vegetation new and unfamiliar, plants growing outside that survive only in hothouses in Germany." Of all the plants, though, the one that struck him most was what Linnaeus calls *Chamaerops humilis*, the fan palm. "I couldn't take my eyes off it. I stood there, gazing, unthinking . . . seeing it in a new way."

Moritz asks him what he means.

"I collected its leaves, not because they are rare or unusual but because in that moment, something stirred in me. An idea!" Goethe breaks off, suddenly too enlivened to sit still. He rises, paces about, then sits down again. "What if all of its lateral outgrowths were simply variations of a single structure—the leaf?"

Moritz shakes his head. He doesn't follow.

Goethe plucks a flower from a nearby pink. He holds it up. "Once this dianthus was a seed. It fell to the ground, germinated, and its cotyledons appeared . . . Are you familiar with that term?"

"The seed leaves?"

"Yes . . . which may be fleshy and quite unleaflike, but if you look carefully, you can see the veins . . . which makes them *modified* leaves. The formations that follow on the stem"—here he points to the leaves on the pink—"are commonly known as foliage leaves, mistaken for the only *true* leaves." Then he gestures to the flower. "In an ordinary perfect flower, like this, one with all its parts present, we first see a group of green *leaflike* sepals, here united in a tube." He turns the pink upside down. There! Observe!

Moritz nods vigorously.

"Then come the corolla," continues Goethe, "in this case, five petals, pink in colour, they usually lack green pigment, but can be understood as a transformation of the foliage or stem leaf." He pulls off the petals. "Next are the ten stamens, arranged as a tight outer circle, and whose ends, the anthers, bear pollen. Might they not also be variations of the petal? Can you see?"

He holds it out for Moritz, who peers into it, furrowing his brow.

"Last in the series of modifications are the pistils, the most transformed of the fundamental leaf in the centre of the flower . . ." He points. "These become the fruit, and that brings us back to the seed, which carries within itself the seed leaf. Do you see what this means?"

He stands up and paces again, the bedraggled remains of the pink dangling from his hand.

"For Linnaeus, the flowering plant is described as if it were an external assemblage of different parts—leaves, sepals, petals, stamens—separate and independent of one another. There is little hint of any necessary relationship between them. This is the analytical plant, Moritz, the plant as it appears to the intellectual mind." He holds the pink up in the air. "Of course, Linnaeus did this for a reason . . . He produced his system for organizing plants into species and genera, on the basis of comparing these parts of the plant as they occur in different specimens. But"—he hands the flower to Moritz—"what if there's another dimension to the plant, an intensive, previously unimagined depth, in which these different organs are intimately related. That they are really all fundamentally one and the same organ. A plant simply as continuity of form."

"And what would this mean?"

"In place of classification, metamorphosis."

In the distance rises the sound of chatter, laughter, music; here, a light rustle, a breeze. "What you're saying . . ." Moritz stops and sits up. "What I *think* you're saying is that all these so-called parts may be grouped under one concept?"

"Yes." Goethe looks up at the canopy, the Turkish oak that embowers them generously. "All is leaf."

The sun has long set, and the dark is gathering in the east, but they don't yet make to leave.

"For so long," says Goethe, "I've wondered: might there be an alternative to how I was learning botany. Was there no other way apart from obsessive differentiation, reduction, analysis? And I was led to this . . . this revelation . . . that one fundamental ideal structure lies at the heart of all plant life. In this way nothing is to be divided, Moritz. Where classification separates and fixes and deadens, metamorphosis allows for life. And perhaps this way of thinking has larger repercussions, too . . . Inspiration for a scientific method that unifies, and acknowledges the marvellous simultaneity, and interconnectedness of living phenomenon, rather than forcing upon it a mechanistic sequentiality that doesn't exist except in our heads. The natural world is no machine, Moritz," he adds, smiling. "It is alive."

For a long while, they are quiet. The park spreads before them, cool and empty in the late evening light. Soon it will be too dark for them to find their way back into the city, so they brush themselves off, head towards Villa Medici, and onto the road that will take them to Via del Corso.

Behind them, only the wind moves through the trees.

✧ ✧ ✧

In early October, Goethe journeys to Castel Gandolfo, fifteen miles southeast of Rome. When he arrives there, his first thought is that it is close to paradise. The village is perched on a rocky outcrop overlooking the waters of Lago Albano, clear, calm, and almost as blue as the waters around Sicily.

He's here at John Jenkins's invitation, or rather on an invitation that Angelica has obtained for him from the affluent English antiquarian. Jenkins has lived for many years in Rome, and established himself as cicerone of choice to visiting British tourists. "There's nothing he can't arrange," Schütz had told him. "I heard he once managed for his guests an invitation from the Pope for tea." When Goethe meets him, he finds this not too difficult to believe. Sharp-nosed, sharp-eyed, and with a crop of wavy light brown hair, Jenkins reminds him of a shrewd monkey. Luckily, given the size of his house, there isn't much chance for them to meet too often, and Goethe hopes it stays that way.

It's a merry party at the mansion, though none of his artist friends are there. Thankfully, Angelica is staying nearby, and he will have her for company. After a few days at Castel Gandolfo, he realizes that this autumn resort is remarkably similar to a spa town, like the one he visits annually at Karlsbad—persons who have never met before are brought by chance into close contact, while meals, walks and excursions, and conversation encourage rapid intimacy. But here the diversion of discussing in detail about taking the cure and one's ailments is absent—small talk on other less exhilarating matters must be made. Goethe rises early, and slips away, spending the morning on his own, walking, sketching, bracing himself for the rest of the day when he is expected to be sociable. Meals are taken together, the salons are the scene of gay parties, and comedy plays are performed for their entertainment in the evenings.

"It's impossible not to fall in love here," declares Angelica.

They are strolling down one of the many covered walks in the garden.

It is overhung with a scented variety of rambling rose, and the sun falls soft and dappled on the path.

"If by love you mean rushed affection formed through enforced proximity in an, admittedly, bucolic setting, then yes."

"Oh, hush, Johann. As the English say, don't be a bore."

"My dear Angelica, you know my heart belongs only to you."

"Nonsense."

"Well then, to art."

She makes a face. "Far worse."

The path leads them along the edge of the garden. Here the beds are planted with autumn crocuses that are just beginning to bloom.

"Not that I don't think art is the highest and noblest of all callings, and that one shouldn't be utterly devoted to it." She turns to him. "But there are some things even art can't give you."

"Like what?"

"I don't know—companionship."

He laughs, and she swats his arm. "It's true, I tell you."

"My dear Angelica, I appreciate your concern for this lonely northerner, but I just don't feel . . . that way inclined for now."

"And that, my dear, is exactly the moment that love will find you."

The evening after their conversation, when he's thought about what she said—if only to give himself the pleasure of dismissing it—Goethe is on his way to his room to change for dinner when he meets, suddenly, neighbours from Rome, a lady and her daughter. So far, they've only ever exchanged polite greetings, but here they are now brought together like old acquaintances.

"How splendid," the mother declares. "We've often wondered when our paths might properly cross."

The daughter, Livia, dark-haired and pale complexioned, has a somewhat more reserved manner, but she is charming when spoken to, her Roman dialect distinct and dignified. They are joined by her friend Maddalena, a young woman from Milan who is holidaying with them. She, Goethe notices, is a study in contrast to Livia, with her light blonde hair and blue eyes—blue as the waters of Lago Albano. When they speak of Germany, of Weimar, it is she who asks him questions—about the duke, the weather, the theatre, the food. She isn't so much forward as eager to know about things.

He crosses paths with the women often after this, and is always pleased to see them, though the mother less so. She's pleasant, but he feels that she watches him closely, and is hoping for him to take an interest in her daughter.

On a series of windy days, when the party stays mostly indoors, he plays cards with the young women, and enjoys himself very much. They play a game similar to lotto, where players form betting alliances—he first pools his stake with Livia, and then, as the game proceeds, with Maddalena. When it ends, the mother, who's been a bystander all this while, says pointedly, "You need to choose, you know, Signor Goethe. It isn't *comme il faut* to shift allegiances like this."

"I apologize, madame," he says, trying to stifle a smile at her French. "In my country it is customary to be polite and attentive to all the ladies."

Early next morning, he slips away on his own again, and takes a walk through the garden. There's a light mist on the water, and a haze still rises from the grass. Everything is damp with dew. It's marvellous to be out here before anyone is up.

Is he getting old? Does he solely desire his own company now, and that of only a few others? No, it isn't that, though perhaps everything that takes him away from writing he begrudges—and no writing will happen in this sociable place.

It is nice to have the garden to himself.

But soon he realizes someone else is also there—walking behind the rose bushes, shockingly unchaperoned.

"Oh! It's you!" Maddalena sounds pleased, he thinks—or perhaps she's just relieved. "What are you doing here?"

"I could ask the same of you," he says.

"Breathing," she replies, and smiles, and suddenly the sun is out. "What are you looking at?"

He shows her. An aloe plant from India—and it doesn't look happy to be here. "It will probably never bloom," he says, "and in Sicily I was too early to see any flower. Most exasperating."

"You have travelled to Sicily?" Her voice is tinged with envy. "Have you seen Etna?"

He admits he has, although he's afraid he only managed to climb Vesuvius.

"You climbed Vesuvius?" Her mouth falls opens, her eyes widen.

"Three times."

He likes her curiosity, and her capacity for amazement. It is refreshing. And maybe she thinks admiringly of him, too. Of course it's too soon to tell. Since they cannot walk back to the house together, they stand for a while by the drooping aloe.

"It's not proper to complain," she says, "but I haven't always been allowed to study as much as I wanted." She gazes out, beyond the waters of Lago Albano. "We aren't taught to write, for fear we might write love letters. We wouldn't even be taught to read if we didn't have to read our prayer books." She looks back at him. "How many languages do you know?"

Four, he says, five, though not all equally fluently.

She laughs, but doesn't sound mirthful. "Nobody would dream of teaching us foreign languages. I would give anything to know English . . . I often hear Mr. Jenkins, Signora Angelica, Signor Zucchi, and others talking to one another in English, and I listen with envy . . . I see all those yard-long English newspapers lying on the table, full of news from all over the world, and don't know what they are saying . . ."

Before he can stop himself, he's saying, "It's a shame . . . especially since English is so easy to learn . . . Why don't we have a try later?"

"Could we?" Her eyes glint like blue diamonds.

His heart hammers in his ears. "Yes, of course."

The lesson takes place that evening. Goethe picks up one of the English papers from the dining table, glances through it quickly, and chooses an article for his pupil.

First, he translates all the nouns, and tests her to see whether she remembers what they mean. She is quick and clever, grasping them easily. Next they tackle causative, qualifying, motivating words, with him pointing them out to her in as entertaining a fashion as he can, showing her how they bring the whole to life. At the end, without any prompting, she reads an entire passage aloud quite as easily as if it had been printed in Italian, accompanying her reading with the most graceful gestures. He notices she furrows her brow when she's stuck on a word. It is endearing.

He is, very quickly, losing his heart.

Around them, visitors increase in number; Angelica has also arrived at the long common table. His pupil is standing on the other side, and while the others are taking their seats for dinner, without a moment's hesitation, Maddalena walks around and sits next to him. Angelica looks surprised; she can see at a glance that something has happened. Goethe, outwardly, manages to control himself fairly well, though he, too, is struck by her boldness—she sits there enraptured by him, by the foreign language she has just learned, and like someone blinded by a sudden long-wished-for vision who does not know how to readjust herself to these normal surroundings.

Things progress well, though, over the next few days; they snatch moments together whenever they can, in the company of Livia or Angelica. The former seems oblivious of any goings on; the other seems pleased. They walk the gardens together, stop to admire the lake, play endless card games, steal glances through the evening's entertainment.

Her English lessons, too, continue, and she improves, swiftly.

"You," she tells him, breathlessly, "are a new world."

And then and there, he wishes to take her into his arms—*And you are simply too bright, too beautiful to bear.* Now he cannot, will not, hold back. Goethe feels something in his chest loosening, as though a binding is being undone. He permits it, that rush of excitement, the dizzying happiness of early attraction. Should he write her a poem, pick her some wildflowers, or—Does he dare? Is it too soon?—offer to make a sketch of her?

He can barely sleep, the nights too long before he can see her again the next morning, and then the day is too hastily gone. In him rises rapidly the anticipation of new affection. In her it appears to blossom, too. Doesn't she look up at him with nothing less than adoration? He warms at the thought.

One evening, he goes looking for his young friends, his new beloved, when he chances upon the older ladies sitting in the pavilion. "Come join us," they insist, and he has little choice as space is made at the window with the best view.

It isn't long before he realizes that they are discussing that inexhaustible subject: a trousseau—what would be needed, the number and quality of the wedding presents, the essential items the family will be giving. The conversation then turns to the happy couple—the merits of the bridegroom, whose shortcomings, which were no secret, would certainly be corrected by the intelligence, grace, and amiability of his bride. Uninterested though he is, Goethe asks discreetly who the bride might be. They're all surprised and then remember he isn't a friend of the family.

"It's Maddalena," says Livia's mother archly.

"Oh," he says, "I see."

After this, he manages to disengage himself from the company and goes for a long walk. All the way out of the grounds, down through the small cobbled village to the lake, and then a path that runs along the bank. All passion is extinguished beside the cool, clear water. He returns very late, and the next morning takes off again, after leaving word that he won't be back for dinner. He tramps up hills and through forests, grieving, at first, for a love lost, a love still tender, snatched away too soon—and then for something else.

After so long, he'd felt the way he'd done in his youth, when love was an arrow, strong-feathered, with freshly sharpened points that pierced to the marrow and quickly inflamed the blood. And losing this meant, in some way, also losing a part of himself.

But am I not old enough to know better? he chides himself. To pull myself together without fuss or fury? How terrible, though, to be unwittingly taught so cruel a lesson.

The rest of his days at the mansion, he avoids the company of the three women—and when he does encounter them is polite and unfussy in his exchanges with Maddalena.

"Will we not have another lesson?" she asks him, her eyes wide in disappointment.

"Perhaps later," he says. *In another lifetime.*

On his return to Rome, he finds it has rained and the city is fresh and newly green.

But the pile of letters awaiting him deepens his gloom. Mostly from his friends in Weimar who are impatient now with his absence. *Too long, dear Goethe, too long! Will you ever return?* And one which announces that, inspired by his accounts, they would also like to follow him, travel around Italy, visit Rome. The duke's mother, Duchess Amalia, expresses that a special wish has long been alive in her heart to make this journey—and she, along with her entourage, would like to begin serious preparations to cross the Alps.

He sits at his table unmoving, suddenly feeling as though the walls around him are pressing close. He attempts a reply, and discards one letter and then another; the right words refuse to come to him.

He stands at the window, looking out at the crowded street, ringing with the cries of beggars, the rumble of carts, and stamp of pedestrians. He feels a sudden flash of anger. He's worked hard to make Rome his own—and they cannot take it away from him. Perhaps he ought to leave before they arrive. He has a premonition that it won't go well otherwise. His way of looking at things would not be theirs. Or at least not at first.

It has taken him a whole year to adjust, to rid himself of . . . northerner views . . . and become more a person of the south. To finally breathe more freely here.

Later he allows himself to hope that they won't embark on the journey at all. How often people make plans, on the spur of the moment, after too much wine, which dissipate like ghosts as soon as morning arrives. He hopes it is so for them.

✧ ✧ ✧

November heralds the arrival of a new addition to their artist colony—Philipp Christoph Kayser, a German composer and musician who lives in Zurich. A sharp-nosed, birdlike, fussy little man, he has long been acquainted with Goethe, and it is on his suggestion and sponsorship that Kayser is in Rome.

He moves into Goethe's old room in Via del Corso. The others welcome him, saying they are now complete, their *trois*—painting, literature, music. "Who could ask for anything more?"

After a piano has been procured for Kayser, and a place found for it—with some difficulty, for either there is too little or too much light, or the acoustics uneven—the composer and Goethe begin work on setting the songs in *Egmont* to music. The project keeps Goethe intensely busy, and more focused than he has been for a while. He stops drawing almost completely, halts all other literary works in progress, and delays his weekly correspondence. This last, also, because he doesn't feel motivated to reply—not to Tischbein, asking for news, nor to the duke, who thinks he is wasting his time not "tasting" all the women in Italy. In his head, a flash of blue eyes, light brown hair, the smell of roses, and he places the letters aside.

For now, he devotes himself to their domestic academy. Here, away from the court and its courtly duties, is a small paradise. "It is," he tells Moritz, "what I imagine as an ideal Germany."

The weather turns dry and autumnal. On clear days there is a brilliance and, at the same time, a subtly graded harmony of which one can hardly conceive up in the north. Goethe acquires a set of watercolours by a minor artist to send to his friends in Weimar. They fall short of capturing the colours in the landscape—brilliant and earthy now, merging into a haze in the distance, softened by the atmosphere—but he thinks he himself can do no better.

When the promise of fine days continues, Goethe sets out on a short walking tour with Bury and Kayser. They arrive at Frascati, and from there walk to Monte Cavo via Rocca di Papa. They manage to get to Ariccia and Genzano, back to Albano and Castel Gandolfo, from where they return to the city. Along the way, he misses Moritz, his botanical companion—especially when he finds some trees, apart from the evergreens, that are still in leaf, including the chestnuts, though their leaves have turned yellow. He even comes upon a plane tree, and remembers Greta, his young companion on the coach journey from Munich to Mittelwald. It all seems so long ago, the flight across the Alps. And here he is, poised again between past and future, north and south, with his time in Italy running out.

On his return to Rome, he shares with Moritz his plans for a *Harmonia Plantarum*. It came to him on the walking expedition, he explains, the idea of publishing a new system of botany that would supplement Linnaeus's *Genera Plantarum*. Instead of dividing and counting, this would offer "a harmony of plants," he says. "A botanical survey that goes beyond taxonomy to morphology, beyond the classification of species in separate compartments to their continuity as a single process of formation."

Regarding the development of this *Harmonia Plantarum*, various strategies could be adopted, just as in any other harmonic work. But what might be best for this? What schema should they adopt? Perhaps none! Perhaps they ought to throw out all the old uniform methods of investigation! After all, what could be more detrimental to a project such as this?

"It will be like nothing anyone has set eyes upon before," says Moritz happily.

Some afternoons, while they are in the company of the others, talk on botany also comes up, though it tends to be more general and wide-ranging. Once, they are lounging in the gardens of Villa Pamphili, the weather cool and golden, a cloud of pigeons wheeling above them in shimmering grey unison. The topic under discussion—for everyone is in a silly mood—is what everyone wishes to be in the afterlife. A horse for Bury, a cat for Schütz; Hackert says himself, and rather than this being disqualified, the others echo in chorus, "But *why*?"

Hackert is not amused.

Moritz says he would like to be a dragonfly.

Then they realize that Goethe hasn't yet given them a reply. He is lying on his back, hat over his eyes. "An oak tree," he replies. A good choice, they concur—to be sure, it's the closest to immortality, living so many hundreds of years.

"If conditions permit," adds Goethe.

For certain. Although, on second thoughts, might it not be tiresome to be stuck in one place all of one's life?

"If by stuck you mean that you cannot physically move, then I suppose yes," says Goethe. Else it would seem to him that plants live an ideally rich life, dynamic and ever-transforming, resilient and connected, reaching out into the world, not just towards the sky but into the earth and being in touch with air and wind and sunshine and soil.

Here he plucks at the grass and throws it up like confetti.

"They show us the necessity of inculcating an awareness of being sensitive to context . . . indeed, if not so, they wouldn't survive, would they? And the result? No two plants are the same," he adds, "even within the same species, if their environments differ slightly even fifty yards apart."

Surely not, his friends protest. It cannot be!

"Have you not noticed? What you all suffer from is a penchant to generalize," says Goethe.

At this, there is further profuse objection, but he shakes his head. "It is true. What do you see when you look at a field? A forest? Foliage, in general? A hazy impression of green? But to take the time to look, to observe closely, would allow for a revelation of great and exhilarating diversity."

All right, they concede, perhaps this is true. But what he said about plants of the same species differing drastically in growth yards from each other . . . this sounds difficult to believe.

Wait, says Goethe, sitting up. He is happy to conduct an experiment for them. He rises, instructing them not to train their eye on him, nor to follow, and he disappears into the woodland. He's gone longer than they expected. What is he doing, they wonder.

"God knows," says Schütz. "To this day, I understand little the things he does." Remember when he told them he wished to let his eye be single?

"Hush," says Moritz, "I'm certain he will return with plants."

Sure enough, when he emerges, he's holding one in each hand. "Behold," he says triumphantly, "the lowly but lovely *Lactuca muralis* . . . wall lettuce." He holds them out. "What do you observe?"

His friends blink up at him. At first glance, the one in his right hand is taller, with a more complex web of roots, while the other is smaller and more sparse.

"And to what might the differences between them be related?"

A chorus pipes up in reply, a flurry of unintelligible voices.

Goethe sits down before them and requests silence. "The urge to know is strong, but I want us to restrain that urge, and take time to observe the plants. Why do we always wish to explain something before we have even considered it with care?" He glances at the wall lettuce. "What can we learn from these?"

The group offer up their observations: the one in his right hand, Iphigenia, let's call her, has more profusely branching roots and her foliage leaves are short-stalked and strongly divided. The other, Orestes, has a few long main roots and long-stalked leaves with larger, wider blades.

"The leaves are also oriented differently," adds Moritz.

Goethe smiles and nods at him.

"The leaves on Iphigenia are perpendicular to the stem and curve downward, in the other the leaf stalk grows noticeably up and out from the main stem. I suppose you could say it's wider."

"Good," says Goethe. "I can tell you now that we're dealing here with an environmental difference . . . One of the plants was growing in half-shade and the other in full sunlight. But which is which?"

There is a moment's pause as the young artists examine them closely. Now, admittedly, they're intrigued.

"This one is the shade plant," says Bury, gesturing towards Iphigenia. "It's taller because it's reaching for light, and its roots need to spread out and branch and find nutrients to compensate for the lack of sunlight."

"No," interjects Schütz, "it's exactly the opposite. Iphigenia is growing in full sunlight, can't you tell? It has plenty of light and so it can spread out and form more roots. The smaller one has been growing in the shade—it branches less because of less light, and its leaves are broader to catch more light."

Moritz agrees. "Although," he adds, after a moment's hesitation, "Orestes looks more harmonious somehow . . . and well proportioned. An expression of more light, wouldn't you say?"

Bury furrows his brow. "You mean Iphigenia is more straggly?"

The arguments and counterarguments continue—while Goethe sits aside, in quiet amusement.

"Well?" they say finally, turning to him. "Which is which?"

"To begin with," he says, "as you can see, both perspectives have their merits. This is a fruitful exercise in speculation, is it not? How easily we may come up with convincing explanations that are in and of themselves coherent. Coherent explanations, such as the ones you have provided, may contradict each other and may have little to do with reality. The only way to solve the dilemma is through the phenomena themselves. We must go back and inquire which plants grew in which conditions."

He rises once again, and the group follows him into the woodland, all the way to the crumbling grotto. Iphigenia, he explains, was growing in a clump before it, in full sunshine. Orestes towards the back, behind the rockwork, where the ground is cooler and in the shade. “Here the plant stays simpler and ramifies less boldly into the environment,” says Goethe, “while light calls forth greater differentiation.”

In this way, he lectures them gently: learn to look, with patience, with rigour, withhold judgement, and go back always to context: this is where life—of plants and people, he adds with a smile—is differentiated.

✧ ✧ ✧

This year, Christ is born amidst thunder and lightning—a massive storm that dissuades the party from attending mass at various churches as they did last year. In fact, this Christmas for Goethe is a solitary affair; he spends it in a lower quarter of Rome, not too far from the river, in a monastery complex with three chapels built on a site called Tre Fontane. According to legend, it's the spot at which St. Paul was martyred, three fountains springing up where his decapitated head bounced on the ground.

Inside one of the chapels, large and unadorned—and the reason he is here—are paintings of Christ and his Apostles, life-size, one to a pillar, endowed by Raphael with their distinctive attributes and character. Goethe is filled with them, even when he returns to the city: John noble and beautiful, Thomas grave and sad, Christ walking towards him, his hand raised in blessing. Something of their melancholy stays with him as the year draws to a close, and even when the new one opens.

His walks with Moritz, also, fail to cheer him.

One dank winter day, the friends find themselves in a square in front of San Pietro in Montorio. They've attempted a stroll despite the overcast weather, and although there hasn't been any rain, the wind is sharp and unwelcome. They had intended to continue to the Baths of Caracalla, but they decide to cut their rambling short and head home. Back at Via del Corso, Kayser is improvising at the piano, Schütz and Hackert are quarrelling over the merits of Sulzer's ideas on art, while Bury listlessly dangles a string for Callisto the cat, who bats at it with a lazy paw. Moritz and Goethe join the subdued party, sinking low into their armchairs.

The mood remains glum—until Reiffenstein enters, exclaiming that he thought he'd lost his way and had walked into a crypt by accident. He hustles them up and out the door—tonight they dine at Osteria alla Campana, he announces, and when he's met with cries that everyone, at the moment, is deeply impoverished, declares generously that it is his treat for the New Year.

Their spirits rise on the way, and then even higher after a carafe or two.

A group of Schütz and Bury's artist friends are also at the Campana that evening, and so they all merge into a larger, merrier, more raucous party.

Goethe is trying to throw it off, the sinking feeling that's been plaguing him lately, that Easter, when his time here will end, is fast approaching. He looks around him, the faces that he has come to know and love, the friends who have formed a warm circle around him. Maybe it's the wine, or the melancholy, but he feels a disconsolate sense of loss—close to the grief of losing someone beloved.

He tries to draw himself back into the evening—someone is telling a funny story about scholarly friends who take the ferry from near the Vatican, and on the way are locked in an intense argument. If they disembark at Ripetta they will have to separate, and the argument will be left unresolved. So they all decide to do the crossing a second time, but by now they've really got going and even this extension is insufficient. "Just keep going up and down," they tell the ferryman, who has no objection since he's earning a *baiocco* for each passenger and crossing. He complies with their wishes in complete silence until his little son asks in puzzlement, "What are they doing this for?" And he replies laconically, "Don't know. They're all mad."

The table erupts in laughter, and even Goethe chuckles. He looks up and glimpses the young woman with the dark hair who had smiled at him the last time he was here. Since this is a family-run trattoria, she's clearly part of the family. The middle-aged man with the magnificent-moustache, who manages the place, looks too young to be her father. And, he hopes, too old to be her husband. After they order food, Goethe finds himself looking to see if she will serve them. And she does. She sets the plates down, one in front of Goethe, and they glance at each other. There's a small brown mole to the right of her upper lip, and suddenly he wants to kiss her. It's a strange feeling, strong as it is instinctive. Goethe, who prides himself on forming attachments over intellectual compatibility, conversations about favourite books, for instance, has rarely felt anything as explicitly carnal. At least not since the early, heady days with Charlotte. A feeling that he vanquished like sin when she came to realize it and was upset—though surely it couldn't have come as a surprise as she'd claimed? We're wedded, she'd said, in the higher realm of mind and spirit. All right, he'd replied, and there it had remained.

"Faustina!" someone shouts from the kitchen.

She turns, and answers, "Coming, Uncle!"

Goethe tucks happily into his plate of macaroni.

There isn't any opportunity for more elaborate interaction, apart from quick, secret glances and small smiles. The trattoria is busy tonight, their table large and rowdy, and she's constantly being summoned by her uncle or, he presumes, her mother. He watches as she skips lightly between tables and customers—petite and quick, and efficient, and her face only grows in loveliness to him. She is adorable! Perhaps it's the warmth inside the osteria, or the wine, but he wishes he could somehow, impetuously, make her acquaintance. But he can't and she couldn't possibly do the same.

The next time she's at their table, clearing the empty plates, she accidentally knocks over a glass of wine. "Oh! Mi dispiace," she exclaims. As she mops it up, she dips her fingers in the spilled liquid and traces lines on the table, doing this so quickly that none of the party notices except for the intended recipient.

At first, Goethe can't quite make out what it is. An upside-down "V" and before that a mark. It isn't intelligible. Until he realizes they aren't letters, they're numbers. IV. Four. Four what, though? He looks back at her, in confusion, but she's gone, hurrying to the kitchen. He studies it a while until a thought, through the haze of the Falernian, slowly dawns upon him. Could it be a proposal . . . for them to meet . . . at this appointed hour?

He's walked in Rome at night many times, but this is the latest he's been out.

At 3:50 a.m. the streets are eerily silent, beggars' bodies slumped on the sides of the roads emptied of carts and carriages. It's dark, darker than he thought it would be. And the smell of horse dung and garbage is strong, rising up to his nose in sickly sweetness.

He must be mad. He'd thought himself mad in Naples, living, for a while, a life untethered to anything—art, responsibilities, intellect—but this is a different kind of madness. He's stumbling around in the dark at this godforsaken hour, following an invitation written in wine.

He hadn't seen the mysterious Faustina again before they left the trattoria; most of their party was more than lightly inebriated, and it was a task getting everyone to leave. Bury and Schütz insisted on building a fire at home, despite pleas from Goethe that it was late. Then they consigned all their "bad" art to the flames. "You too, you too," they insisted. "Is there a poem you just can't rhyme? A libretto that's failing? A play that won't resolve itself? Burn them all!" To keep them quiet, Goethe complied—throwing in blank paper, though his housemates were too drunk to notice. Finally, at three, they collapsed. One in his bed, the other beside it.

If all went well, Goethe's night had only just begun. So he slipped out quietly, although he doubted if even the apocalypse would awaken them, and made his way back to the river, and then down once again to Vicolo della Campana.

Only now, when he nears the osteria, does he think this might be lunacy. What if she'd done it in jest? Or worse, unintentionally. Maybe he'd imagined it all.

The January night is cold, but Goethe finds himself perspiring, his hands clammy, his heart racing. Also, how would he know where to go? The osteria would be closed, and the family sleeping. Where did they live? Above the restaurant? He realizes he hasn't really thought this one through. If his flight to Italy was the most impulsive thing he'd done in his life, this is even more so. Eventually, he decides he'll walk past the osteria twice. If there is no indication that someone—Faustina—is waiting for him, he'll leave and just treat this as a late-night saunter. Even if he does meet her, though . . . what then? He tries not to think of her mouth, that delicate mole.

As expected, Osteria alla Campana is tightly shuttered, and no one, not even the friendly neighbourhood drunks seem to be about. He walks down the street once. Above the osteria, the row of windows remains darkened. The door locked. He turns to walk back, convinced he's the biggest fool to have been born. "This is where lust leads you," he chides himself.

Just then, a wooden gate, quite hidden, next to the osteria is unlatched and opened a sliver. A single word is uttered. "Come."

And he follows. If he's robbed, killed, so be it. The gate leads to a narrow side alley, lined with doors. The smell of oil and garlic hangs in the air. Cats scrounging through garbage scatter at their feet. He follows a slight, darkly cloaked figure. They don't speak until they've climbed up some stairs to a room, large enough, with one shuttered window, and simple furniture—a table, a bed, a chair. No curtains of silk, no embroidered mattresses here. The door that opens, he assumes, into the rest of the house is locked and bolted.

She pushes back the hood of her cloak. They look at each other and laugh.

"You're mad!"

"No, *you* are!"

"I thought you wouldn't come."

"I thought maybe I'd imagined it all."

"That I was being so forward?" She raises an eyebrow.

"That you would wish to be so forward with *me*."

She moves closer. Her eyes catch the light, they're the colour of the darkest bark of trees.

"What's your name?"

"Johann."

She furrows her brow, and remains quiet.

"And you are Faustina."

"So I am." She moves to discard her cloak, and then sits on the edge of the bed.

"Usually, I sleep here with Ettore."

"Who is Ettore?" Husband, he's thinking, alarm bells sounding in his head.

Faustina smiles. "He's my son. Tonight I make him sleep with his nonna." She gestures to the locked door.

"Your son," Goethe repeats before he can stop himself.

"He's three years old and very clever."

"Just like his mother, then."

"Far cleverer than me!" she declares.

And the father? But since she doesn't mention him, perhaps it is inappropriate to ask. It would be too much, too soon. In fact, all this is too much and slightly surreal.

He sits next to her on the bed. She doesn't move. Her mouth, her mole, her neck are all temptingly close. He doesn't know how to proceed, what it is that he should do? Perhaps she senses this, for she leans forward a little, and they kiss.

By the time he leaves for Via del Corso, it is past dawn. The streets are being swept, the stray dogs are awake, and the early-morning carts and coaches carrying bread and fish and other fresh produce are on the move.

He feels more inebriated than any wine has ever made him. And more alive. She is magnificent! And he wants to shout it out to all the world.

Back home, the artists haven't stirred. The fire, though, has died. He tiptoes into his room, falling asleep with the memory of looking down at her, her dark hair spread out on the pillow.

✧ ✧ ✧

Over the next few weeks, the preparations for Carnival reach peak frenzy.

Last year, he'd avoided it all, being in a strange mood, feeling that Rome had somehow let him down. Complaining about the noise filtering up to his room while he tried to work, about the masked revellers and horses clogging up the roads. This time, though, the revelry allows freer licence for him to meet Faustina, and for this reason he's out and about amidst the celebrations.

Something in him also feels lifted, lighter. And he finds he enjoys the spectacle rather than resenting it. This Carnival, the fancy dress trend seems to be for stable-boy costumes, though the usual traditional characters are also present—peasant girls, women from Frascati, fishermen, Neapolitan boatmen, and the Greeks. Once, on his way to the osteria, a figure wrapped in a sheet hops out at him from the shadows, hoping to be taken for a ghost.

At first, with Faustina, it is a series of simple assignations. He drinks and dines at the osteria in the evening, and watches to see whether she traces out a time on the table. Will they meet? Won't they? It is a deliciously tentative suspense. And in the midst of the Carnival, this subterfuge and secrecy seems also somehow appropriate. He arrives at the designated time, she opens the gate for him, and he leaves at dawn. The only thing that changes is that he now awakens at noon, where once he was an early riser.

"Up late working," he tells Bury and Schütz, standing, looking worried, at the foot of his bed.

Moritz, too, has no inkling that he's embarking on these adventures, even though he asks more than a few times why his friend seems a little distracted.

"Oh, just thinking about something I'm working on."

He shares the news only with the duke: *I can now report on some agreeable promenades . . . You are perfectly correct, that such moderate motion refreshes the spirits and puts the body into a delightful equilibrium.*

Perhaps, he catches himself thinking, *this will all be over after Carnival.*

That their trysts, like the revelry, will be discontinued. But even after Ash Wednesday, her instructions appear on the table. In fact, he notices, they begin to summon him at an earlier hour. *Good*, he thinks, *I'll finally get some sleep*.

Turns out, he's still there until dawn.

This is because, after they make love, they've started talking. Blessedly, she knows nothing of Werther and his sorrows. And rather than answering questions about himself, which is what tends to happen once it is known who he is, he is able to demonstrate his deep interest in her. Her life in Rome, which he considers the capital of the world, and she simply calls home. All she's known here, she says, is the osteria, occasional trips to the sea, and her son. The father had died no more than six months after his birth.

"He wasn't a bad man," she says, "just drunk most of the time."

"Why did you marry him?"

She doesn't reply immediately. "It was time. I was nearly twenty. He was . . . well, the best thing I can say about him is that he was kind."

She turns to him. Her cheeks are reddened, her dark luxuriant hair tangled. She smells of sweat, and faintly of the osteria. They kiss long and deep, and he feels his heart fill with both happiness and sorrow. Soon it will be Easter, and by then he will have more than a city to leave.

He begins to bring paper and pen to her room. He sketches her, naked on the bed.

"My hair is not falling over my breasts," she complains, looking at a finished picture. "Why have you drawn it so?"

"For modesty?"

She makes a face. "*Modesty* is a man's word. Draw me as I am. Only then are you a true artist."

And so, blushing furiously, he does.

He brings some of his work to show her. His sketches of Rome. He wants, he realizes, her approval. Why it should matter so much, he has no idea. Except that she is seeing with the eye of the everyday, the unelevated, and he feels there is some instinctive truth in this that all of art history—and his many admirers—cannot muster.

"What is this, Johann?" she asks, holding up a sketch.

"Why, it's the Colosseum. Isn't it obvious? Surely I'm not as unskilled as all that . . ."

"Oh, I know it's the Colosseum, but where are the beggars who live near this wall? And the homeless family who burn a fire here every night?"

"They weren't there?"

"They're always there," she says impatiently. She sifts through the rest of the drawings. "Everything looks so . . ."

"Ugly? No. That's not what you were going to say."

She looks at him. Her eyes narrow, displeased. "I was going to say, everything looks so perfect. Too perfect. Unreal."

"But these are mementos . . . you know, to show my friends in Weimar, when I return."

At this, she falls silent, and so does he.

"Then why are you showing them to me?"

"Because . . ."

"So you can gather my untrained opinions and make fun of me with them."

"No," he says desperately. *"No."*

"Then why?"

"Because you see Rome with the kind of clarity I envy."

She softens. She places her hand on his face. "It makes me sad to think of you leaving," she says with a directness and simplicity he's come to adore.

And because love is about seeing yourself as you are seen by the beloved, he asks, "Why will it make you sad?" She lies back on the bed, looking up at the ceiling. "Because," she says simply, "my days are full of you in places where I didn't know they were empty." They hold each other, deep and tight, until long past dawn.

By now, the others have guessed that something is up—even if they're not sure what. When he tells them "the curse of the second pillow has lifted," it is met with resounding cheers and many congratulations. To Angelica, he says nothing. Moritz, when informed, is subdued. Until Goethe assures him that he and Faustina only meet at night, and that his days are as free and unencumbered as they always were. They still have time for their evening walks, to talk of literature, and art, and botany.

Recently, they have started favouring a new garden—the one at Villa Mattei, on the summit of the Caelian Hill. Not only is it beautifully laid out, but works of art from the family's collection are also displayed on the lawns. Here they wander, admiring the obelisk in the villa's theatre or resting at the fountains overlooked by Poseidon and his giant spear.

They also begin their own small botanical projects—ones that require, as Goethe calls it, for gentle empiricism, to watch and observe carefully and faithfully. "Have no wish to explain the plant . . . I would say merely observe, but so closely that you become identical with it."

Moritz says he will try.

They walk around the garden, looking to see what draws them—the boxwood, the juniper trees, or the dangling pendent trusses of wisteria. What will each reveal?

The problem, of course, is that gentle empiricism requires time, and Goethe doesn't know how much of that he has.

One evening, after a day out like this, he finds a letter waiting from the duke.

The letter is warm and filled with personal and political news, and it also asks Goethe to stay on in Italy to await the arrival of the dowager duchess later in the year.

He rushes out of the house, unable to contain his unbounded joy. All these streets, and houses, and beggars, and antique ruins will be his for a while longer. Then he returns, and begins composing a reply almost immediately—he will be ready, of course, to leave as planned after Easter, but he could devote all these extra months to paving the way for the dowager's arrival by presenting himself to the French and imperial ambassadors, to royalty. He would prepare the ground in Naples, Florence, wherever else she might wish to visit. His earlier misgivings are forgotten in the happiness of being able to stay on.

When he meets Faustina later that night, he kisses her and lifts her up in an embrace.

"To what do I owe this jubilation?"

When he tells her, she covers her face with her hands.

"I thought this would make you happy," he says in alarm. "Faustina, tell me, what's the matter?"

When he prises her hands apart, he finds that she is laughing. He clasps her and they fall onto the bed, feverishly taking off each other's clothes, and they do not part from each other for hours.

✧ ✧ ✧

Perhaps it is the expectation that he will remain here for many months to come that acts as catalyst, but suddenly Rome is in spring.

Everywhere laurel, viburnum and box peaches, almonds, and lemons come into bloom, and the gardens are bursting with anemones, hyacinths, and primroses. He and Moritz can now properly resume their botanical excursions. The pots of prickly pear are doing well in his room, and he's also added to his collection. Seeds from a pine cone that are giving out promising shoots. Some date palms that he's grown from stones. With Moritz he gathers more, violets, yellow-flowering celandine, fennel, ground elder, and even a sapling of mulberry.

"I've been thinking about your shade-and-light experiment," Moritz tells him, one afternoon as they are wandering through the wilderness just beyond the Borghese Gardens—out of the city limits, and untended. "For the first time, I realized the diversity and differentiation in plants of the same species depend on where one finds them."

"Much like people, don't you think?" Goethe is in a playful mood.

"Do you reckon, then, that plants of *different* species respond to differing environmental conditions in a similar way?"

"Good question. And yes, remarkably, at least from what I've observed, this is so."

They stop at two pines that have grown in strange ways, leaning against each other.

"It's a duality, isn't it?" Goethe continues. "The plant has the ability to integrate itself into the environment in such a way that it reflects in all its parts its relation to that particular environment."

"And this, too, is like people."

They also continue their discussions on the *Harmonia Plantarum*, and even begin tentatively laying out illustrations for the compendium. This might be Goethe's first scientific publication, and in the face of Moritz's visible excitement, and his own, he tries to discard his misgivings—rare as it is for him to have any over his work—about how a text like this from his pen might be received. At worst ridicule, at best indifference.

And why so? Because, as he'd once told Tischbein, the public demands that every man remain in his own field. Sadly, this was how the world seemed to be proceeding, narrow and constrained, knowledge splintered and sorted until it lay broken and bereft of all life, all resonance. It would soon be a punishable offense to be interested in everything. To seek knowledge regardless of where it originated, and to love it precisely for its vast, exuberant interconnectedness.

About all this Moritz is unperturbed.

"I think," he says, surveying their work, "that this will change the world."

On some days, Goethe goes plant collecting with Faustina and her son, even though with the child present it turns into playtime. He is a cheerful boy, dark-eyed and dark-haired like his mother, and can be kept happily occupied by gelato and strawberries.

Sometimes it's just him and Faustina who walk through the city together. It is unlike strolling around with anyone else. Here, Faustina remembers, they would get their milk and cheese—from a dairy next to the Pantheon. He laughs in delight.

"What's so funny?" she asks in puzzlement.

"For you the Pantheon is a landmark for the dairy, and not the other way around."

At the Colosseum, she distributes alms, just as her family has done for years. Which is how she knows the beggars who live there. They come to greet her, thankful for the gifts. For her, the Roman Forum, which she barely glances at, is the place to find the freshest peaches, from a lady she fondly calls Nonna. In Piazza Navona, at the Fontana del Nettuno end, is an alleyway of blacksmiths, from where she buys the strongest pots and pans for her uncle's kitchen.

This is when, for Goethe, Rome truly comes alive. The stone finally speaks.

When they lie in bed later, he strokes her, as he likes to, gently tapping along the length of her spine. Her woolen dress, alongside his clothes, lies crumpled on the floor.

"I'd like to thank you," he says.

"For what?" She turns to lie against him, her head resting on the curve of his arm.

"For your Rome."

She smiles sleepily. It's late, and it has been a long, busy evening at the osteria.

"Rome, though you are a whole world," he says, "a world without love would be no world." She lifts her head, smiling. He leans over, kisses her. "And if there were no love, Rome would not even be Rome."

She snuggles closer into him. "You should be a poet."

While Goethe awaits the duke's response to his letter—which he's quite certain will be positive, and allow him to play courtier for the dowager later in the year—he keeps himself busy. His nights are mostly well occupied, but the hours in a day are long.

He reads Herder's new book, *Ideas for a Philosophy of Human History,* and enjoys it enormously. "The end is magnificent!" He continues to work on *Faust*, a play he began fifteen years ago—and an unwieldy beast. The more he writes, the further it seems from completion. Perhaps, he considers in jest, I shall have to sell my soul to the devil to finish it.

What keeps him buoyed are reactions from Weimar on *Egmont*, which have been mostly favourable—"bold," "seamless," "profoundly moving," and only one tentative "some scenes too long." Charlotte, though, has not expressed much enthusiasm for the play. *I suspect*, he writes to her, *you have been more pained than pleased by it. But it is difficult for a work on this scale to be in perfect tune throughout. I think no one but the artist really knows how difficult art is.*

One Sunday in early March, he misses mass at the Sistine Chapel for a gallery outing with Angelica. Today they visit the collection at the Accademia di San Luca, and pause before a painting by Guercino, in which a bearded St. Luke gestures to a portrait of the Virgin while a surly angel looks on.

Angelica turns to him and asks, "Well?"

"It's an unusual piece, is it not? It makes me think of the Christian tradition of image making, and their desire to have the subject connect . . ."

"Not the painting," she interrupts. "Have you had a think, my dear? The nobleman's physician's daughter I wanted to introduce you to . . ."

Lately, she has been trying to present him to her "friends"—eligible young women, he's noticed, from good families—but he hasn't followed up on any of her offers. What Angelica is asking now is would he court this young lady? It would be . . . easy. Respectable. To be swiftly engaged, and for them to travel back to Weimar together to be married.

But his mind is drawn to a room without curtains, where a simple woolen dress lies slipped off on the floor.

"If you'd like to . . ." she begins.

"No," he says quickly. "I'm grateful to you—but at this moment I find I am preoccupied."

For his next meeting with Faustina, he takes her a gift. A shawl of fine merino.

"Oh, Johann," she says, holding it to her cheek, "there must be nothing softer than this."

He's pleased to see her happy.

"What's the occasion?" she asks.

"Nothing. Just this." He plants a kiss on her forehead.

From now on, he always brings her presents. Boxes of fruit, dates, walnuts, a dress or two, tickets to the opera for her and her mother, when they are collected in an elegant coach.

"What am I now? Your kept woman?" she teases.

"Rather, I'm your kept man."

Tonight, they lie in bed sharing a glass of wine; she's smuggled a bottle from the osteria downstairs. The night is warm, the window stays open, and a sweet breeze blows in, carrying the sounds and smells of the city.

"What is your life like in the north?" This is the first time Faustina has ventured to ask a question of such intimacy. He sits up a little, his arm around her, her head on his chest.

"It is cold."

She turns her head to look up at him. "That's it?"

He laughs. "I suppose it is lively in its own way." He tells her he is employed at a small court, but makes out that he works at its very periphery, overseeing this and that. Still, her eyes are wide—at first he thinks in wonder, but rather she is surprised.

"I wouldn't have placed you as an administrator . . ."

He leans on her heavily, he likes the feel of her bare skin against his. "Where would you place me, then?"

"Right here," she says, pulling him on top.

They kiss for a long time; his mouth travels to her mole, her ear, down her neck.

When they part, he looks at her. "I have never . . ." he begins, and stops.

"What?" she says, her dark eyes shining.

How should he put this into words?

"For me," he begins again, "life has never felt so . . . complete. As here in Rome, with you."

She nuzzles into his shoulder. "For me, too."

When he returns home the next morning, the post has arrived. Here are the landscape sketches he'd commissioned on his journey through Sicily, also a new edition of Mengs's writings, letters from Weimar—one from the duke.

He has returned from his Prussian expedition, and after discussions with his mother, Anna Amalia, can confirm that Goethe's administrative responsibilities, as requested, will be withdrawn. He will have no specific duties, though opportunities for these would certainly appear in due course. He can devote himself to whatever he considers important—including, the duke hopes, as in the past, the improvement of Weimar's parks. He is also to receive a salary increase of two hundred marks a year.

Reading this, Goethe's heart is racing, his palms begin to sweat. The news, so far, is good. What then, about Italy?

Both the duke and the dowager agree that there are better things for Goethe to occupy himself with than act as her courtier. He need not feel that for this reason he must tarry in Italy. The letter doesn't instruct him to return. Or order him to leave Rome at the earliest. Rather, it's a hint for him to journey back, and it is enough. It cannot be ignored.

The end, when it comes, is quick.

Goethe lays the letter aside.

In due course, all the others here will need to be informed. For now, though, he will shut himself up in his studio, look out the window, and mourn.

He stays in all day, and the next. Afterwards, he writes a response to the duke: *To your kind and heartfelt letter I reply at once with a joyful: "I come!"*

✧ ✧ ✧

The last month is hectic with the busyness of departure.

And he finds that as soon as he has made up his mind to leave, he loses all interest in everything. He is oddly disconnected—from the city, his friends, and most of all, Faustina. For days, he cannot bring himself to see her, to tell her. Finally, he visits Osteria alla Campana, and sits at a table with an untouched plate of fritti before him, and an unsipped glass of wine. He can tell she is furious.

"Two o'clock," she whispers angrily, as she pretends to fill his glass.

It is the longest of nights.

"Where have you been?" she spits at him as soon as he enters the room.

When he tells her, slowly, falteringly, she flings the shawl at him, the one he gave her, and then she cries. He cannot bear it; he stands there, unable to move, closer or away, and finally, he leaves.

For days afterwards, he doesn't return.

I am in Rome but I am not in Rome, he writes in his journal. *I can't do anything anymore.*

He would rather have left immediately after he received the duke's letter than be here in this strange in-between time—in the flesh, but not in spirit. But there are loose ends to tie up, and so much packing to be done. He looks around helplessly at his studio. He'd had no conception, until now, of how much stuff he'd managed to accumulate. What was he thinking? That he'd be here forever?

He can take a few items—the smaller busts, several Jupiters, the Medusa Rondanini, a Hercules Ajax, and Mercury. He must leave behind the bas-reliefs, casts of terracotta works, casts taken from an Egyptian obelisk, and other heavy fragments. The giant Juno head he gives to Angelica. The plants he has been growing he begins to distribute. The pine seedlings for Angelica's garden. The date palms, or at least the ones not sacrificed to observe the stages of their peculiar growth, he gives to a friend who plants them at the edge of his lawn at his house on Via Sistina. To Bury and Schütz, he hands over the prickly pear cacti, for these are the only plants, they admit, they'll be able to keep alive.

The days go by and I can hardly bring myself even to look at anything.

The celandine remains in his room until eventually he carries it with him to Osteria della Campana. It's late afternoon, but he doesn't care anymore if he is seen. The family are at siesta. When he knocks at Faustina's door, he can see she hasn't been resting.

They don't speak when he enters.

He places the pot on the table, by the window.

"You know . . . celandine comes from the Greek word *chelidon,* which means 'swallow,'" he says, "because it comes into flower when the swallows arrive and fades at their departure."

She looks at him without saying a word.

"And if that's not enough . . . I grew it myself."

She still stays silent.

He looks down, at the floor on which so many times their clothes and shoes have been discarded.

"Of all your gifts," she finally says, "this is the least useful."

He murmurs that that is true. He stands there, thinking he should leave. That there is little hope for reconciliation. For a last warm, familiar touch.

"But I like it most," she adds suddenly, "because it is alive." She presses its small yellow blossoms, its leaves like feathers. "And it hasn't faded. So maybe the swallows aren't gone yet, after all."

The last garden that he visits with Moritz is at Villa Albani, lying just outside the city walls. The villa houses a vast collection of antiquities and Roman sculpture, but they aren't heading inside. This spring day, they are in the garden, where the almond trees are now in leaf, the peach is beginning to shed its blossoms, and the lemon flowers are bursting open in the top branches.

Moritz had no words when he was told Goethe would be leaving, that his date of departure was set for April 24. "But that's so soon" was all he had to say.

Today he is in a similarly reticent mood. Goethe, too, despite the beautiful surroundings, is subdued. If only he were heading south, not north. Oh, to be back again in Sicily, where all around him lay such richness!

"You know," he begins to tell Moritz, "at one point while I was there, I found myself on a wild, though possibly futile, quest."

Moritz glances at him. "A quest for what?"

"The rarest thing."

"Oh?"

"At first, I wasn't sure what it would look like . . . but surely if it did exist, and I was certain it did, then there could be no other place in the world than Sicily."

Moritz frowns. "Why didn't you mention this to me before?"

Goethe stays silent. "In honesty, because for a while now I've been thinking that it cannot be found."

"You mean . . . you've given up?"

He sighs. "If I were ten years younger, I would travel more, search more, go to the farthest places, to America, to India, to look and look again."

"Look for what?"

They have arrived at the edge of the garden, where terraced beds cut into the hill.

"I was walking by the sea in Naples," he begins. "It seems so long ago now . . . but there, a certain notion came to me. I wondered if this concept . . . of one fundamental structure, of all being leaf . . . could also be true in a higher sense?"

Moritz nods, listening intently.

"If within the part of the plant we're accustomed to call *leaf* lies . . . a shape-shifter, if you like . . . which can hide or reveal itself in all vegetal forms. I wondered, could it not exist as an Urpflanze?"

"Do you mean . . ." Moritz hesitates. "An archetypal plant?"

Goethe looks at him, unable to put into words how much he will miss his company.

"Yes, that is what I mean." He'd spent much time strolling through the public gardens in Palermo, amidst groves of lemon and orange trees, and thousands of plants he'd never seen before, dazzled by the lushness, the green. "The more I tried to find how these many and diverse forms differed, I always found them more alike than unalike . . . no matter how distinct the shapes of leaves, and flowers, it was not difficult to imagine them related, morphing from one to another in a flow, shape to shape . . . And their similarity kept calling to mind this idea of the Urpflanze."

Moritz is quiet a moment. "And is that what you were looking for?"

"I was." The archetypal plant that carried within it all plants of the past, present, and future. "It sounds ridiculous, perhaps, but I've had visions of it . . ." he adds. "Would the Urpflanze be the strangest creature in the world? Who knows? But wouldn't it make it possible to go on forever imagining plants and know that their existence is logical; that is to say, if they do not actually exist, they could, for they're not shadowy phantoms of some vain overactive imagination, but possess an inner necessity and truth."

They have walked over to a peach tree, whose blossoms are falling to the ground with every shift of the breeze. Here, like in the north, it might be snowing.

After a long silence Moritz speaks again, hesitant. "What would it look like? I mean, how would you know what to look for?"

Goethe shrugs. "Something simple? Small? Unassuming? Or perhaps at the other extreme, a magnificently complex shape from which all other shapes could be derived . . . I am not certain." He looks up at the sky through the branches. "But if I found it, I think I would know."

"How?"

"I have no reasoned answer," he confesses. "Only a feeling that I would."

Before them the peach blossoms shimmer.

"What would it mean to find it?"

Goethe looks at him, smiles. "Perhaps we'll know when we do? I've said before, we must fight the urge to explain and understand prematurely, to come to something with preconceived notions of what it might reveal to us."

"Then this is not something to give up on . . ."

"Maybe not." Goethe pauses, looking out over a garden falling slowly into evening. "Maybe you're right. But I'm journeying back north now, and I feel certain that that is not where the Urpflanze will be found."

Why not, asks Moritz. Surely the Urpflanze might be found anywhere?

"Possibly," his friend concedes. "But I sense it might thrive in abundance in a place where conditions for growth are optimal, a place of greater floral diversity."

"There will be another chance, then, to come south, in the future, another journey . . ."

"Perhaps," says Goethe, but his heart, and his spirit, tell him there will not.

✧ ✧ ✧

For the last three nights before he leaves Rome, the moon is full, shining in a clear sky, diffusing its light over the immense city.

At the end of each day, spent packing and sorting his belongings, he takes a walk, once with Bury and Schütz, once with Moritz, and the last on his own. Earlier that day, he'd visited Angelica, who wept as they said goodbye. "Will we meet again?" "Of course, my friend," he'd replied. It was comforting to say so, even if they both knew it might never happen. That night, he wanders along the Corso—perhaps for the last time—and walks up to the Capitoline, which rises like an enchanted palace in a desert. *Faustina would hate that description,* he thinks, and laughs, and is filled with sadness. He passes the statue of Marcus Aurelius, and comes to the triumphal arch of Septimus Severus, which casts a large and darker shadow. Along Via Sacra, a main street that's usually bustling, he's alone, and the world, the ruins along the road, seem ghostlike and alien to him. Finally, he reaches the Colosseum, which that night fills him not with magic, as it usually does, but with a strange fear.

He stands there, thinking of another poet, Ovid, who was exiled and forced to leave Rome on a black melancholic night like this, lit up by the moon. *Cum repeto noctem. When I recall the night.* He cannot get him out of his head—with his homesickness and memories of Rome, his sadness and misery on the distant shores of the Black Sea, how he felt he'd abandoned so much of what he treasured.

Goethe, too, had no choice, and soon he, too, would be gone.

He pushes himself to look through the gate into the interior of the ruin. All is still, no voices, no barking dogs. He makes haste and returns home, his soul agitated, his mood no less than elegiac.

Early on April 24, a day blue and burnished by the sun, his friends gather around him as he installs himself in the coach.

Kayser is leaving with him, too, but the musician doesn't seem to feel the same sorrow. Moritz, in a change from his usual self, cannot stop talking. He makes witty remarks and silly jokes. Bury weeps openly. Schütz turns his face away. Goethe settles in, and then Kayser. The postilion blows his horn. Arms reach out, and hold, and wave.

For a moment, everything is frozen, as though everyone, including fate, has changed their minds.

Then the coach begins to move, rumbling down Via del Corso, scattering people and dogs. It gathers pace slowly, across the wide expanse of the piazza, and passes quickly, too quickly, through the Porta del Popolo, down Via Flaminia, and over the old Milvio, bearing Goethe out of Rome.

EVELYN

All day, the steamer has headed south, past Diamond Harbour, and the sacred Sagar Island, before emerging into the Bay of Bengal.

Now, it skirts up along the coastline, flanked on one side by open water, and on the other by a thick press of mangrove forests, the swampy islands of the Sundarbans. Evie likes it best when they pass close to the banks, when the dark, leafy forest seems to take over, and the quiet is broken only occasionally by paddles tossing up the fruits of the nipa palm with a hollow thud. From the deck she can see the mangroves' spiky pneumatophores and the tiny red hermit crabs burrowing into the mud. Everyone on board hopes to spot a tiger. *How predictable*, she thinks. Why, one may be as enamoured of the chattering macaques and shy chital, dipping their heads at the water's edge, their large eyes liquid and wary. Mrs. Wheeler feels the same. "Isn't this wonderful!" she'll exclaim, and Evie agrees. Apart from the mosquitoes, it truly is.

She suspects the Wheelers were happy to leave Calcutta; they seem more at ease here, in the middle of nowhere, than in their city bungalow. It probably had not been difficult to persuade Mr. Wheeler to relinquish a comfortable posting and head back to the wild. Although it had taken a little more to convince Charlotte that it was a good idea for Evie to accompany them. *You want to go where?*

The steamer is a much humbler vessel than the *Maloja*—it is hardly as big, hardly as shiny—and carrying about a hundred passengers; twenty in first class who are mostly British, including themselves, and a handful of Indians. Mr. Wheeler tells her that on the deck below are Bengali businessmen and Marwari traders, while the crowded space at the back is taken up by tribals from eastern and central India.

"Where are they going?" she asks.

"Being *taken*, you mean," he corrects her. They are indentured labour on their way to the tea estates of Upper Assam.

"Oh," she says, suddenly silenced. She remembers the fun-loving tea planters she met at the clubs in Calcutta, and finds it difficult to reconcile their youthful frivolity with any role that demanded of them the management of other people.

Soon the forests are left behind, the boat enters the mouth of the Meghna and heads north, swerving between the islands off the coast, which are topped by morning mist and edged by armies of palmyra. Some are nameless and uninhabited, while others Mr. Wheeler points to and names—Char Nizam, Hatiya, Bhola.

"Look," he says, "they are gradually being eroded by the sea; one day nothing of them will remain." He says this not with despondency but crisp pragmatism: *this is how it is.* The world moves to its own rhythm and reasons. How lucky she is to have him as a guide, and personal cicerone.

He smokes a briar pipe just like her father, but is unlike him in every other way. There is something of the modern in Mr. Wheeler, his gaze is turned towards a larger world, while Papa, *dear Papa,* stands with his feet planted firmly in the past. The Wheelers are as unconventional as her family is not, content in their roles as intrepid co-adventurers, and Evie is pleased to have been accepted as a minor participant in their travels. Even if nothing comes of her trip, at least she would have had an adventure—especially since she is no Marianne North, and this might be all the world she sees.

Along the river, the landscape changes, the waterway rising on either side into forested slopes, where sometimes a bullock cart and farmer gently trundle, children run alongside waving, or cattle stand and graze peacefully. Evie watches it all with wonder, even the loading of goods onto the steamer, sacks of paddy and mustard seed, clay-fired pots and woven mats and baskets. She is mostly up in the saloon, a roofed deck perched on top of the first-class cabins, from where the view is best, and the breeze coolest. Around her lounge a few women, and many men uniformly dressed in linen suits and straw boaters.

Mr. Finlay would have made this steamer journey, similarly attired, she thinks, earlier in the month. She remembers their last meeting—at the shadowy back of the Calcutta Club, beside the fireflies and the shimmering hydrangea—and a warmth rises up her cheeks.

✧ ✧ ✧

Eight days after they leave Calcutta, they reach the point at which the Brahmaputra flows into the Ganges.

The steamer chugs on, heading farther north, where the riverine plains are now covered in lush forest, and the distant low hills are softened by a smoky haze. Sometimes Evie catches a glimpse of river dolphins, grey bottlenoses taking graceful leaps into the air. Once, to her excitement, they pass a herd of elephants on the bank, bathing. Often it is just her, a flight of wood ducks, and the river. It feels abundant, as though the world is offering itself to her, and yet also oddly limiting, her journey confined only to this slim, prescribed course.

Eventually, they draw into Gauhati, a small port town with busy bazaars and a modest European quarter, standing at the foot of the Shillong plateau. Farther upstream, the river dominates the landscape, Mr. Wheeler tells her, flowing through a wide valley pointing northeast into the very corner of the empire, where India meets Tibet and Burma. Where they have docked, the banks are a muddy, squelchy mess, and the mosquitoes have multiplied, but they have arrived just as the sun is setting, turning the Brahmaputra into liquid gold.

All along the roads are tall graceful betel nut palms, and the surrounding hills lie green and thickly forested. They are staying at a boarding house for the night, where the geckoes are the biggest Evie has seen in her life, and the crickets the loudest. They are not in Calcutta any longer, she realizes with a jolt. This is remote in all the ways the world can be—in all the ways she has yet to know. It is frightening, and delicious!

Tomorrow they set off for Shillong, the capital of Assam, most thrillingly in a hired motorcar christened Maharani. “A service only recently started,” according to Mr. Wheeler, and since it is winter, and dry, he thinks the journey should not take them more than half a day.

Perhaps it is the newness of the place, but Evie finds it difficult to fall asleep.

How far I've come from Tilbury! From home. Even Calcutta! Charlotte had been understandably bewildered at first—*Why?* And surely they ought to seek her mother's advice? Except that by the time they would hear from her, the Wheelers would have long ago left.

Evie had sat herself next to her hostess. "I do not know if you remember, Charlotte, but when I had just arrived you asked me whether I was ready to be married, whether it was what I wanted. And I am telling you now what I should have told you then: I am not, and it isn't."

She had expected this to be met with some annoyance, but Charlotte was triumphant. "I knew it!" Besides, it was quite obvious, she had added, especially when Evie had been far more excited about the botanical gardens than the Winter Ball. But why Assam? Really, as far as she had heard, it was wild, hardly civilized at all, and, worse, filled with leeches. Stay here, or travel to Orissa, she had urged, or if she wanted to venture farther, head to Delhi and Agra. See the Taj Mahal!

Her guest insisted she wished to go east. Charlotte sighed. "I don't think you should do it, Evie." Evie had remained silent, thinking that nothing in the world was going to stop her.

Back in London, they would have probably received her letter by now, informing them of her decision. She is certain her family will meet the news with some dismay, though perhaps not outright surprise. They have been resigned for a while now to Evie doing what they think she ought not to. Tramping around the woods with Grandma Grace, for instance, or turning down chances to meet potential suitors, and more recently, working as Agnes's research assistant.

This had thrown Mama into a great panic. Evie had obtained the equivalent only of a low second in the final tripos—convincing her mother that she ought to have studied the classics and become a governess, instead of scampering about in a makeshift laboratory in someone's house. "I just don't know what to do with you, Evie." Florence, too, had taken her side. "Mama wants you to be happy, Evie."

But Evie *was* happy—helping Agnes in the laboratory, learning to practise Goethean botany. When she tried to explain what this was to Florence, her sister frowned. "Oh, Evie, it all sounds very academic." But it was not, Evie insisted. "It is like being in the garden with Grandma Grace." She hoped saying this might allow Florence to see how much it meant to her, but her sister shrugged, and said, "Then why go to university?"

Then, as now, lying in a strange bed in a darkened room, listening to the crickets, she felt a little alone.

✧ ✧ ✧

Maharani refuses to start this morning, despite the persistent coaxing of their Anglo-Indian driver, Mr. Pokes, and the many attempts at cranking the engine by his young helper. Eventually, they concede defeat. It will have to be a pony trap—which must now be procured at short and urgent notice, a pace evidently unfamiliar to the sleepy little riverside town.

It is well past lunch by the time they leave Gauhati.

The Wheelers stay calm through it all, although when they are finally trundling out of town Evie overhears Mr. Wheeler tell his wife that he had been a little concerned, "for night falls quickly in these parts."

At first, they travel through low grassy hills, passing thatched huts and little else, before emerging onto a flatter road that continues for a long while. "Aren't we meant to be heading up?" asks Evie in some bewilderment. "We will." And they do, but so gradually that she does not notice until the air is suddenly fresher, and nips at her skin. Soon they are trailing up a slope with mountains spilling all around them.

Evie longs to take a closer look at the forests, a mix of temperate and subtropical growth, with pine, banana plants, bamboo, and even in winter, all a deep lustrous green, but because of their delayed start they are barely able to make any stops.

As evening approaches, the cold is palpable, stinging Evie's face, reaching under the blanket spread over her knees. This feels a world away even from Gauhati, more desolate, perhaps because they are hemmed in by hills, and followed only by the melancholic drone of crickets, the sound of the wind, and a large yellow moon.

An hour from Shillong, they cross a bridge over a river roaring far below, which Mr. Wheeler said he had read was called Umïam—Crying Water. The road climbs steadily from there; on either side, the forest is now dark and thick and indistinguishable.

They enter the town to find that it wears a deserted look, the narrow sloping roads lined by rows of houses with low roofs and shuttered windows. Shillong seems to have retired and emptied for the day.

✧ ✧ ✧

Evie awakens in a room filled with light, but not the kind she has seen anywhere else before, not in London, nor Calcutta. It is clear as birdsong, sharp as the edge of a knife.

They are accommodated in Mrs. Dyer's boarding house in an area atop a hill in the European Quarter—La Chaumière it is called, after a crop of bungalows with straw roofs that dot the slopes. The neighbourhood overlooks Government House, which is set on the next hill, amid gardens that Evie hopes she can soon visit. The boarding house is also a tidy bungalow with wooden floors, limewashed walls, and a cavernous fireplace that is lit in the evenings. In employment here are a cook, and a maid, a local girl named Deng, younger than Evie—although it is hard to gauge. She has a smooth, unlined face, but eyes that appear much older.

Evie breakfasts with the others in the garden, where sweet peas are growing all in a row, and marigolds are already in golden bloom. Maybe it is the cold, but she is ravenous, and porridge with milk and honey is welcome as it has never been in Calcutta.

Afterwards, Mr. Wheeler makes for the Forest Department office, while Evie, who is eager to explore, is happy to accompany his wife for a stroll about town. They are driven to a lake at the heart of the European Quarter. One long curve is dotted with bungalows, peeking through the pine trees, reserved for high-ranking government officers, while on the other stands the red-roofed Shillong Club. Good for a spot of lawn tennis, she is informed. Beyond the club, they come upon a busy commercial junction, rows of shops selling shoes, clothes, stationery. There is a chemist, and many tailors. Mr. Wheeler had mentioned that commerce in these parts was driven not by locals but by migrant mercantile communities such as the Bengalis and Marwaris. Around the market are the main government buildings, the Assam Legislative Council, the Secretariat, all built in white-walled, tin-roofed neatness, while nearby stands a half-timbered church with a tall steeple.

"Where do the natives live?" asks Evie.

In villages around the European Quarter, she is told. "Laban, I think one is called," adds Mrs. Wheeler, "and I cannot for the life of me remember the others."

They head back down to the lake and stroll along the pathway running along its edges, the slopes dotted with willow trees and flower beds. This seems to be a popular spot with the Europeans—many of whom are out taking the air. For a moment, Evie is convinced she has seen Mr. Finlay far ahead. Don't be idiotic, she tells herself. It is merely someone who *looks* like him. He is plant hunting somewhere in the Lower Himalayas, thrashing about through hill and forest, and she is certain that not for a moment does he spare a thought for her.

In the evening, after an early supper, they sit by the fire, stoked by Deng to a bright hearty blaze. They feast on oranges, small, juicy, the sweetest they have ever tasted, and then Mr. Wheeler brings out a bottle of port. Glasses are arranged for all—and the wine goes down in strong and welcome warmth.

"My tour will begin soon," he reports. And will cover the areas in and around Cherrapunjee district, a two-hour journey south from Shillong. It is understood that Mrs. Wheeler will accompany him, as will Evie.

What will she discover in the wettest place on earth?

She can hardly wait to find out, but there is one thing she would like to do before they depart. "Is there someone I could speak to? About local flora?" she ventures. Someone who's a native naturalist, perhaps.

"Hmmm," says Mr. Wheeler. It is best for him to ask around at the office. One of his colleagues should know. "Is there something in particular you would like to inquire about?"

She shakes her head, and lies. "Not really, no."

✧ ✧ ✧

Since she became a member of the Goethean Science Society, Evie had not missed a single meeting, and even Lulu grudgingly had to admit that she was not there to waste her time, or anyone else's.

One evening, they gathered to discuss *The Metamorphosis of Plants,* which Goethe had written a few years after his trip to Italy.

"What I do not understand is why he left Karlsbad in secret," began Phineas. He held a copy of Goethe's *Italian Journey* in his hand, which he considered a companion text to *Metamorphosis*. Evie thought it was because he was fed up. "I mean, was he not overseeing the building of roads and mines in Weimar?" She was certain it was an escape, and that if he had not undertaken the journey, *Metamorphosis* would have remained unwritten, and his botanical insights ungained. "I wouldn't be so sure," countered Lulu. To any destination lay a number of different routes . . . Though they all agreed that Italy yielded to him flora, both wild and cultivated, rich to a degree unseen in his northern homeland. That all this had set in motion a train of ideas which was to dominate his conception of the plant world for the rest of his life.

Yes, said Lulu. Now, please could they focus on *Metamorphosis*? It was a concise text in which Goethe had attempted to tell the story of botanical forms *in* process. "The doctrine of formation is the doctrine of transformation," Lulu read out. "Genius."

They had many questions: What did Goethe mean by "eyes of the mind"? What exactly was "intensification" and "polarity"? And most important, why metamorphosis? A term long applied to the transformation of caterpillars into butterflies and tadpoles into frogs.

"Perhaps by extending this concept to the development of plants," ventured Ollie, "he was suggesting the presence of some kind of universal process working throughout nature. *Everything* alive is in a state of always becoming."

Sadly, the original book had fared badly, and been roundly ignored by botanists and the public alike. "It took eighteen years for the first references to it to begin appearing in botanical texts and other writings," said Lulu. It mostly sank into obscurity, translated into English in 1863 and more recently revived by Rudolf Steiner, the Austrian philosopher, in the 1880s and '90s. Still, the text could hardly be considered "well known."

"Didn't he mean to also write a *Harmonia Plantarum*?" asked Evie, looking through her notes. Yes, but they supposed he never got around to completing it. All they had inherited was *Metamorphosis*, which was revolutionary, though not without its flaws, they realized.

"He had nothing to say on roots," said Ollie ruefully. "It is as if they did not exist!"

Goethe also treated the volume as largely a complete and finished work. "Perhaps because of his nature as an artist," added Lulu. "It ought to have been seen as a scientific treatise in progress, one that could be expanded, rewritten, and corrected."

"He copied Linnaeus, too, did he not?" added Phineas. "In format, I mean. Writing in numbered paragraphs." Ollie nodded. All the major scientific texts Goethe had read by the Swedish botanist were written in this manner of lists, and he thought he should, too, but that was where the similarities ended.

"He steeped himself for years in the works of Linnaeus, and respected him, but his own botanical work represented a radical departure from Linnaeus's approach. He found it artificial and mechanical, this practice of naming, and enumerating plants."

"And worse, he found it inadequate," added Evie. "How was it possible to accommodate the immense variability of plant life within this static, set terminology?"

They also all agreed that the text's moment of greatest illumination lay in how the line "All is leaf" became an expression of the principle of wholeness, that the whole is reflected or disclosed in the part.

"Do you remember, Evie?" they reminded her. "No subservience between one and the other; they are both equally important, each to each."

✧ ✧ ✧

Grandma Grace would call this a claggy day; the sky clotted like cream and carrying with it the imminent threat of rain. It is remarkably changeable, the weather here, Evie has noticed. Wilfully windy one moment, sunny the next, and then, without warning, grey and overcast—although thankfully with none of the heat and humidity of the plains.

She and Mrs. Wheeler head out for lunch at the Shillong Club, and then they walk to the Secretariat building up the road. The receptionist is expecting them, so they are led straight through, down a corridor leading off into many rooms with files arranged on desks like miniature mountain ranges. They stop at a locked and bolted door. As the receptionist opens it for them, they glance at each other, smiling.

They are here to visit the Assam Forest Herbarium; waiting for them inside are thousands of carefully filed herbarium sheets.

Afterwards, they discuss the herbarium at length on their stroll around the lake—*How exciting! I had no idea! This treasure, all the way here in this remote town!* Was it not akin to leafing through pages of history? Every sample perfectly preserved, capturing the very second a plant was picked and pressed. They discovered that some dated back to the 1870s when Gustav Mann, a German botanist, and one-time gardener at Kew, started the herbarium during his tenure here as conservator of forests. They had not the time to look through the whole collection, but what they had managed to see delighted them.

Evie is astonished by the number of bamboo species in the region. There are dozens in these hills and surrounding plains, including the gigantic *Dendrocalmus hamiltonii*, used by the natives for making huts and basketry, the ethereal thin-stemmed *Melocanna bambusoides*, the long narrow-leaved *Microstegium ciliatum* . . . "Which looked like something out of a Japanese picture, didn't you think?"

Mrs. Wheeler agreed. "That *Pseudostachyum polymorphum* from Sylhet, too . . . so ordinary yet so beautiful . . . I would like to paint it."

"You must!" exclaims Evie.

Her companion laughs and agrees.

They have stopped at the Japanese-style bridge that arches across Ward's Lake. The sky reflects silvery grey on the water. Ducks glide along, as well as a few swans. Since their first afternoon together in Mrs. Wheeler's "herbarium" in Calcutta, they have talked about little else besides botany. Sharing observations over swampy palm vegetation in the Sundarbans, riverine reeds along the Brahmaputra, and the moss and ferns they have noticed growing here in abundance. Mr. and Mrs. Wheeler—could she say this?—were the parents she had always dreamed about. They were deeply interested in her, in the world, seeing their place in it as wanderers and explorers, rather than settlers. She could not imagine Mama and Papa anywhere else, apart from their home in Primrose Hill, with their daily routines and set little rituals. Everything, from waking to rest, dictated by the clock.

A wind lightly whips up the water. Below them, more ducks and swans drift by. Evie can see they are heading for a tiny island on the far side of the lake—it seems to be a preferred gathering point for these feathered creatures.

"Did I mention?" begins Mrs. Wheeler, "that Charles has found someone for you to speak to." A local woman, Kong Bathsheba, who lives in a house in the woods. Evie says that this sounds more promising than she had dared hope for, and they laugh.

The sky is darker now, and the wind stronger. A light drizzle begins to fall as they head off, walking briskly down the bridge. There will be a blazing fire and hot tea waiting for them at the boarding house, and Evie is thinking of this when she comes to an abrupt stop.

In front of them stand Mr. Finlay and Mr. Dossett.

Then, before she knows it, they are smiling and wishing them good evening, and Mr. Finlay is apologizing for the intrusion—"But we could hardly pass by without saying hello."

Evie is lost for words for what feels like an eternity, and then she hurries to make introductions. She meets Mr. Finlay's eye, and asks about his expedition. "I hope it went well?"

"Not too badly," he says. Earlier this month, from Gauhati they had headed to the Garo Hills, where they collected a sizable number of orchid specimens.

"Which ones?" inquires Mrs. Wheeler.

"The small fragrant *Acampe*," Mr. Dossett replies, "and the multiflowered *Aerides* with its waterfall of blossoms." They are hoping to travel in the Khasia Hills now.

"How is Mrs. Hopkins?" asks Evie. Mr. Finlay says his aunt is well, and still in Calcutta.

"I am glad you found a way out of the city," he adds.

"Yes." She smiles. "I did." She can see Mrs. Wheeler glance at them with curiosity; there will be questions later, which she will do her best to avoid.

"What do you hope to find in the Khasia Hills, Mr. Finlay?" asks Mrs. Wheeler.

"I am content with anything new," he replies.

"Ah, something as yet undiscovered . . ."

He bows his head. "*New* is a comparative term for me, though . . . I think a collector, well, a true collector, derives just as much joy from finding a plant new to him, whether it has already been discovered or not. And any new plant introduced into England surely has already been seen and remarked upon by the people of its native land."

Mrs. Wheeler smiles. "Very true, very wise."

✧ ✧ ✧

Only once was the GSS invited by the Cambridge Scientific Society to give a talk.

What an honour! What recognition! This was a chance not only to disseminate their ideas but also—and this was truly exciting—to attract new members. There was so much to say, and so much that could be discussed—but who would speak? After some deliberation, it was decided that Ollie would deliver the lecture, even though Lulu was the clearer-headed, more commanding speaker—things were changing but not so drastically that a woman could address a room full of men.

The talk took place on a summer evening and, thankfully, a respectable number of people showed up. Lulu, Phineas, and Evie made their way to the back of the room; Ollie, up front, looked as though he wished he were anywhere but here, shuffling through his notes, mopping his forehead with a large handkerchief. Finally, everyone took their places, and Ollie stepped up to the podium.

"All is leaf," he began, "and through this simplicity the greatest diversity becomes possible." He paused as though expecting someone to stop him. "I begin with this because it is the key to understanding Goethe's way of seeing. The leaf he refers to must be understood in the universal sense as an omnipotential form and not as a particular foliage leaf."

He slowly gained momentum, and stood taller, his voice less shaky. He started to explain Goethe's idea of plant metamorphosis—that organs which could be quite different in outer appearance were recognized as being manifestations of the same form.

Evie looked around; a handful of Girton girls sat in one corner, a cluster of male undergraduates were crowded up in front, and from them she feared there might be mischief later. For now, they sat quiet; a red-haired chap had stuck his legs up on the empty chair in front of him. Evie turned her attention back to Ollie.

"It is an extraordinary experience to look at a flowering plant and see it in Goethe's way," he was saying. "Seeing the plant intuitively is to experience it 'coming into being' instead of analysing the plant as it appears in its supposed finished state. Where Linnaeus was concerned with taming plants, Goethe was concerned with making the plant visible. Where Linnaeus imposed an organization on the plant so that each specimen had a place in a system, Goethe allowed the plant to speak for itself."

It was after this that the trouble began.

Ollie had just started speaking on the Urpflanze. "Goethe's notion of the fundamental unity of the plant extended to the plant kingdom as a whole. He came to believe that there must be an Urpflanze, whose metamorphic variations are what we see as all the many different plants today. Goethe thought this might even exist as some kind of simple primitive plant out of which other plants would develop in time, and which he could encounter if he searched diligently enough. In fact, he did so on his journey through Sicily."

The students at the front were openly smirking now. Someone whispered that Goethe might have been a little too fond of his drink.

Ollie continued, oblivious. "He soon came to realize, of course, that the Urpflanze could not be *found* in this tangible, physical way, but the idea of it offered him, and us, a certain mode of perception . . ."

Before he could sweep to a finish, Ollie was interrupted by the red-haired youth. "Are you saying the archetypal plant is the lowest common denominator of all plants?"

At first, Ollie handled this with aplomb. "It is quite commonly supposed that Goethe started with finished plants as visible to him in the environment, and that by comparing them externally with one another he abstracted what was common to them to produce a generalization. And that in this way, he found unity in multiplicity but—"

He was not allowed to finish. "So did he do that, then? Gather several sets of different plants, produce a generalization for each. Then a generalization of these generalizations until he reached the ultimate generalization, the archetypal plant?"

Only the speaker did not realize that he was being mocked. He stumbled, and faltered, and Evie could hear Lulu, next to her, catch a sharp breath. Phineas, on her other side, was as quiet as a tomb. The Girton girls were stifling their laughter.

In the next instant, Lulu was standing, saying, "This is how the analytical mind tries to find unity, in this static, inflexible way. What you speak of is the mechanical unity of a pile of bricks, not the organic unity of life. *You* might be required to resort to this"—Lulu looked directly at the redhead—"but not Goethe, whose mind worked differently, and, might I add, in a superior way."

There were hoots at this, and someone booed. Lulu was trembling, but she continued. "The archetype is one plant that is all *possible* plants. It is not a blueprint for plants, a general plant, or a common factor in all plants. It has the quality of diversity within unity, it is the many within the one." Her voice grew stronger, sharper now, more like her own. "Goethe saw the plant as one single organ, and he saw the entire plant kingdom as one single plant. As plant organs are fragments, containing the whole, for the archetypal organ the many plants are the fragments, containing the whole, of the archetypal plant. Do you understand?" *You lout,* Evie imagined she wanted to add. "The Urpflanze is inherently dynamic and infinitely flexible—and as Ollie mentioned, though you may not have been listening, or capable of comprehending, the idea of it offers us new, exciting, and necessary perspective in our practise and philosophy of science. I hope at least *that* much is clear."

There was a long silence.

At the next meeting, they were joined by no new members, but they still considered the talk a triumph.

✧ ✧ ✧

Evie is on her way to meet Kong Bathsheba.

The previous evening Mr. Wheeler had returned from work and told them over dinner that he had dispatched a peon to her with a message, and her reply when it did arrive was cryptic: "So be it."

"So be it?" Evie laughed, almost spilling her soup.

"Kong Bathsheba has a reputation for being somewhat enigmatic in her responses," explained Mr. Wheeler.

His wife turned to him. "How does the Forest Department come to be on such good terms with her?"

He cleared his throat. She has helped them on a number of occasions. "A forest fire once, that she forewarned them of, I believe, and then another time she helped detect a fungus ravaging the local pines."

"Is she a native woman?" asked Evie, more curious than ever about her now.

Mr. Wheeler nodded. "She worked as a tea lady in our offices for some years, so she speaks English well enough."

It was all arranged. Kong Bathsheba sent instructions for Evie to be dropped off at the edge of the forest, from where she would be guided to the house. So here she is, following a small man, sized like a boy in his teens, with a face that looks at least thirty.

Mrs. Wheeler had wanted to accompany her but was kept away by a prior engagement. "She will be perfectly safe," Mr. Wheeler had said, so she let Evie go on her own.

Evie is glad for this outing. The forest smells of mud and wet decay, and, somewhere not far off, she can hear running water. Her guide walks steadily, silently before her. The pine needles are slippery underfoot, and sunlight lies in patches on the ground. She would like to stop and pick up pine cones, inspect the dark velvety moss growing on the slopes and on fallen trees, but she dare not for fear of being left behind. They continue climbing, the forest unvarying around them. The town seems far away, and when they reach a clearing, she can see it lie below them.

Soon the pines give way to a wealth of fruit trees—peach, plum, guava, and pear, though only the oranges are in bright golden fruit. The edges of a garden appear, built in terraced levels, with towering *Rhaphidophora* scaling the trees and rows of plump succulents edging the beds. Kong Bathsheba's house comes into view, and it is easy to imagine this as a tiny cottage somewhere in England, built with stone and wood. She thinks of Grandma Grace, and how she would have liked this place.

Her guide has melted away, leaving her to walk up on her own. Kong Bathsheba is standing at the door, wearing a woolen skirt and sweater, and, as local women here do, a chequered cloth tied over one shoulder. She is a slight woman, but knotted and strong, like a resilient olive tree. Her hair is up in a bun, and her face moon-shaped and unlined, though she is older, Evie feels, than her aspect betrays.

She gestures for her to follow, and Evie steps inside a house that is frugal and well tended. Almost as soon as they are seated, her guide, now bearer, appears with a tray—kettle, teacups—and places it on a table next to them. She does not ask how Evie likes her tea, but when it is served, it is perfect: no milk, a little sugar, strong and gingery, and with a faint hint of wood fire.

"Thank you for this, and for seeing me," she blurts out.

The lady smiles.

Oh dear, thinks Evie, she hopes Mr. Wheeler was not misled into thinking she understands more English than she actually does. Then Kong Bathsheba speaks, and her voice is soft and grainy, the texture of dry sand.

"I will tell you not to go and it will make no difference."

Evie pauses; her cup travels back down to the saucer. "Go where?"

"Where you must."

This is a little annoying. "Nothing has been decided," she informs her.

"Everything has been decided," says Kong Bathsheba cheerfully, sipping her tea.

"Well, then I am not sure why you agreed to see me."

"I was curious." Again, she smiles that strange smile, "Go on, you are free to ask me anything."

This takes Evie a little by surprise. In truth, she has many questions.

For no pressing reason, she begins with "I hear you have often helped the Forest Department?"

Kong Bathsheba shrugs. "A few times. It was nothing. It is a forest department that knows very little about our forests."

At this their eyes meet, hers are as dark as wet earth. Evie says, "I, too, know very little about your forests, but I would like to learn." The woman does not say a word; Evie hopes this means she is permitted to continue. "It might be that I am misinformed, but I seek something . . . that I think may only be found here."

"There are many of those things."

"Yes, of course, but this is . . . different, I think." Evie leans over, as though her words must reach her in secret. "Have you heard of something called the . . . Diengiei?"

Will she be understood? Has she pronounced it right?

To her surprise, Kong Bathsheba bursts out laughing.

She is loud and unrestrained and makes Evie terribly uncomfortable. *Please stop*, she wants to plead, *just give me an answer.*

Instead, the lady wipes her eyes, rises, and says, "Come."

She walks to the back of the room, through a door, and Evie tentatively follows to find herself in the kitchen, a small, sparse space, immaculately clean. Kong Bathsheba seats herself at the hearth, where a fire glows. A calico cat lies curled up on the floor. She gestures to a stool—mula, as they call them here—and busies herself stirring the pots. Above the hearth, strips of meat sway slowly, deep red and streaked with fat. Evie sits, not knowing whether she ought to wait for an answer or repeat her question. Something tells her to stay quiet. *Wait and see.*

Next to her, the cat lifts its head, sniffs the air, and sits up, watching with interest as the food is stirred. Kong Bathsheba places some rice and gravy into a small bowl and sets it aside. She sees Evie eye it questioningly and says, "This is for Ka Mei Ramew."

"The cat?"

Kong Bathsheba chuckles, and prods the creature, who does not budge. "She would like to think so, I'm sure, but Ka Mei Ramew is our name for Mother Earth."

"Oh . . . and you keep out food for her?"

She nods. "Always. In . . . gratitude."

The cat starts meowing, so Kong Bathsheba picks up a small piece of fish, fried to a bright yellow in a pan, and throws it to the floor. In an instant it is gone; the cat licks her paws and strolls out of the back door.

"She is a miaw-wa now," says Kong Bathsheba.

"What's that?"

"A cat who once used to stay home and then turned wild." She adds with a grin, "I know people like that, too." She pours out more tea, for herself, for Evie.

"Kong Bathsheba . . ." Evie begins again, hesitating. "I have another question for you."

The lady nods.

"Who are the Nongïaid?"

This time, she does not laugh. "They are the ones who walk . . . nomads."

"Around here?" She had read about one such tribe in Kingdon-Ward's book on Tibet, the Drokpa, the "people of the solitudes," who herded livestock on high-altitude pastures. "So they are a tribe without a home?"

Kong Bathsheba scrutinizes her for a moment. "Or a tribe whose home is in many places." She sips her tea. "I do not understand you people and why you always . . . define things through lack. These are people with no alphabet. This is a place with no books. This is a place with no paintings. These are people without Christ. These are people with no home."

Evie sits there, feeling chided—perhaps deservedly so—although before she can apologize, Kong Bathsheba continues, "But it is not as if they are easily accepted around here either. People also call them bam neh shnong—the ones who cannot stay—and it is said . . . not in a good way. So they are secretive, moving around like cats in the shadows. They are difficult to trace." She looks at Evie directly when she says this.

Evie tries to sound unperturbed. "What do they have to do with the Diengiei . . . ?"

There is a trace of pity in her eyes. "They are the only ones who would be able to tell you, I am afraid. What it is. Where it is. Maybe. What I mean is they *could* tell you, but the question is, would they?"

The tea has turned lukewarm in Evie's hand. The light is fading outside. They sit for a moment in silence; Evie has a feeling that she will not be getting anything more out of her.

"It is getting late," says Kong Bathsheba, and with that, she rises and calls for someone from the back door. A little girl appears, bright and alert. With no explanation of who she is, Kong Bathsheba says, "She will take you back."

Evie follows the girl into the garden; she is barefoot and steps lightly, her dress looks much too thin to be keeping her warm, but she is flushed as though she has spent all day outdoors. Evie can see dry grass tangled in her long hair. *She is a wild child, like me, like I used to be*, she catches herself thinking.

It is early evening, and shadows fall long in the forest now, in strange geometric arrangements. The girl says not a word, gliding down the path like a sprite. *That is probably what she is*, thinks Evie, and at that moment, the girl turns, glancing back—her eyes like the cat's, sharp and wild and wary.

That evening, at dinner, the Wheelers discuss their impending departure for Cherrapunjee. It is good weather to travel—warm and dry during the day, though the nights will be even colder there than in Shillong. Evie is also informed that Deng will be coming along as a maid for the ladies.

She nods, saying little, still absorbed by her strange meeting with Kong Bathsheba. It has lent her little or no greater clarity. She is here in Assam. *So near, so far.* How should she proceed? Ought she to go back to the cottage in the forest? See her again? She has a feeling this would not be fruitful or welcome. Just then, she realizes, Mr. Wheeler has addressed her.

"Your friends are headed there, too," he repeats.

She blinks. "My friends?"

"Yes, dear," says Mrs. Wheeler, "the gentlemen we met at the lake the other evening."

The couple ran into them at the club earlier, and found that they were bound for the orchid-laden forests of Mawsmai and would be staying in the same village in Cherrapunjee as the Wheelers. "There is only one boarding house there," adds Mr. Wheeler, "so I daresay we will be seeing a lot of them."

Evie sips her chicken soup; it is hot and wholesome but goes down mostly unsavoured. Everything is decided, Kong Bathsheba had told her—and if this is true, then this, too, has been preordained, that she is to meet Mr. Finlay time and time again. Does this displease her? Not entirely. *Stop it, Evie!* She tells herself all this is of little importance as long as she is able to seek freely what she is here to find.

✧ ✧ ✧

A summer ago, when she came across the Diengiei, her thoughts were occupied not with India but Japan. Evie had just read *The Garden of Asia*, an account of Reginald Farrer's plant-hunting adventures on the archipelago, and was filled with longing. Oh, to see the islands of Goto! To glide into the harbour of Nagasaki! How tragic to be stuck instead on this cold little island far from all kinds of excitement and adventure!

"Might you have any other books on that part of the world?" she had asked the librarian, and was directed to William Griffith's *Journals of Travels in Assam, Burma, Bootan, Affghanistan and the Neighbouring Countries*. Well, close enough, she supposed.

She had very little idea about the region, so she opened up an atlas, and set off with Griffith, doctor, naturalist, and—as she found out later—archnemesis to Nathaniel Wallich of the botanical gardens in Calcutta. Up the Padma River in Bengal she went, following his trek to the "distant elevated land" that he called the Kassiya Hills. He stayed at Moflong, which Griffith, curmudgeonly as ever, described as a bleak exposed village; the many days of continuous rain did not help. He was warming himself at the hearth of one of the small village homes when he heard of the Diengiei, or as his translator told him, what the natives called the "first tree." "I do not know what they mean," he noted grumpily, "and I was so tired by the fire it could all have been a ridiculous dream."

The first tree! How mystical that sounded. Something Grandma Grace would have loved to hear about, and she would have hastened to tell her, but Grandma Grace was gone, and Evie had no one else to share this with, so she set it aside. Until several weeks later, she came across the mention of something similar in a book by J. W. Masters, the less than succinctly titled *A Memoir of Some of the Natural Productions of the Angami Naga Hills, and Other Parts of Upper Assam*. She almost missed it—there, buried in the list of plants, between Umbelliferae and Berberideae, was the ancient Araliaceae, which his local guide compared with the "first plant, found in the Khassiya Hills."

She was by then a regular at GSS meetings, and it stayed with her. *The first plant!* What would Goethe have made of that?

Although it was not until she browsed Joseph Dalton Hooker's *Himalayan Journals* that her curiosity was piqued—*What could it be? And why has nobody ever seen it?* His travels through the "Khasia mountains" in 1850, took him, like Griffith, up the Soormah River and into Cherrapunjee. He was amazed by the sweetness of the oranges, the immense variety of palms, and the "living bridges" built across gorges and rivers by intertwining, over decades, the roots of fig and Indian rubber trees. "These bridges are used by the people from the villages," his local guide told him, "but also by the Nongïaid, the nomads, the ones who walk . . . so the Diengiei may be carried where they wish, or where they deem safest." What was this Diengiei? Hooker had inquired. What the locals called the first tree. The tree that held all trees.

At this, Evie had shut the book. Then she opened it again, and read and reread the lines until they had burned themselves into her memory. Even when she put it away, it stayed with her. What could it be? *The tree that held all trees.*

"I would like to search for it," she announced at the next GSS meeting.

Around her, chuckles break out in amusement. "In search of what now, Evie?" The trumpet tree of Brazil? Or was it the Tāne Mahuta in New Zealand?

"I would like to see those, too, but this is different," she insisted.

Lulu had not yet arrived to declare they had no time to waste, and Ollie and Phineas were always more indulgent of her, so she told them with great and uncontained excitement about the first plant—at this, their interest was pricked.

"The first plant?"

She nodded. That is what it says wherever she has found mention of it . . .

"How many mentions?" asked Phineas.

She paused. They raised their eyebrows. "All right, just a few, but look at this . . ." She held out a book, *Journey East: Mapping Calcutta and Beyond* by James W. W. Wallace. "He was surveyor and cartographer to the commissioner of Assam in the late 1870s, and spent several years in the Khasia and Jaintia Hills." She pointed to a page. "*Natives here seem to believe there is a Diengiei, the one plant, though what it is exactly is difficult to discern for they seem reticent when questioned about it. It might be medicinal, for their use and knowledge of herbs is formidable.*"

She looked up, triumphant. The others appeared impressed, though perhaps not as much as she had hoped.

"The one plant . . . that is not quite the same, though, is it?" Phineas pointed out.

"No," she admitted, "but perhaps the terms are used interchangeably . . ."

"It is possible," Ollie agreed. But what did she think it meant?

"That's what I want to find out," she declared.

A small silence followed. "And you will travel all the way there?" they asked.

Evie was miffed. "Luckily, Goethe did not have friends like you when he set off searching for the Urpflanze." He did, they told her, and they reminded him repeatedly that the Urpflanze was an *idea*, that it was Platonic in nature, an ideal form. Yet he still searched for it, Evie was quick to point out, and once wrote to Charlotte von Stein saying "it was no dream or fancy."

True, but what she was seeking, did it not sound like a figment of folklore? Aren't folkloric traditions everywhere beset with motifs like these, the first tree, the first animal, the first human? And isn't there an abundance of sacred trees scattered around the world?

She stayed silent, which they took to be defeat, or at best a quiet relenting.

"Right," began Ollie, "shall we get on with Goethe's colour theory?"

"Yes," said Phineas, and they began to discuss how Goethe had conducted Newton's prism experiments, but not under special controlled conditions, and how it was then that he found something quite different . . .

It did not take them long to notice that Evie was in a sulk. They glanced at each other.

"All right, Evie, why this, then?" What made her certain that the Diengiei existed?

Evie snorted. "I'm not *certain* . . . How can I be? But there is something to the name, don't you think? The first tree, the first plant . . ."

Ollie nodded. "There is, there is . . ."

"I wonder what it looks like," mused Phineas.

She shrugged. "It's no good sitting here resorting to conjecture forever, is it?"

Might she also remind them that this was the wettest place on earth. A place that received more than a thousand inches of rain a year! What flora might that support? Gigantic ferns, perhaps, ancient forests . . . True, true . . . they concurred. It would make for fascinating study.

"Anyway," she continued, "I haven't read other accounts in which something similar is mentioned . . . which I know doesn't mean those accounts don't exist . . . but this is what I have come across so far, and I don't think it's insignificant."

She left the meeting later, still discontented.

She wished Phineas and Ollie had been more encouraging; from Lulu, she had not expected much support, and did not receive any. "The *what*?" she had asked, incredulously, and then told Evie not to be absurd, and to go if she wished to but not to bring this up again during their meetings. "I am leaving it out of the minutes," she added primly.

Evie tramped along, simmering with annoyance. *How much I miss Grandma Grace.* Now more than ever, her chest hurt with a deep and inconsolable ache. With her gone, it truly felt like the end of all adventures.

"Nonsense," she could hear her say. "Follow where you will."

Yes! Perhaps she would. But how? How would she make it all the way there?

By the time she had returned to her room, a plan had begun to form. She could take a voyage under some pretense, secure an invitation to India, to Calcutta, which in her atlas did not look all that far from Assam. Here it was again, stubborn wilfulness, making her more determined than ever. But it was simple, was it not? If no one believed her, then she had no choice but to go see for herself.

✧ ✧ ✧

Early this morning, they head out of Shillong in a pony trap, moving through a landscape of rolling grassy downs dotted with rice fields, pine woods, and low hills. The district of Cherrapunjee lies to the south, close to the edge of the plateau, from where views of the plains, vast and shimmery, can be enjoyed.

The British administration had originally set up its official headquarters in the village of Saitsohpen, Mr. Wheeler tells her, before they shifted to Shillong in the 1860s. The evidence of their presence still remains—schools, churches, a sanatorium, even an abandoned tea estate. He will be touring all the smaller villages in the vicinity, especially the ones to the south, perched at the very lip of the plateau. These were surrounded by timber gold—sal and teak forests untouched for centuries—and all this a convenient few miles from the waterways of Bengal by which the wood could be easily transported, to Calcutta, to Dacca, to the world. Evie learns from him that attention has fallen on these forests because years of laissez-faire timber practices in Burma have depleted supplies alarmingly. Forest rules, such as those requiring licence holders to plant five trees for every one extracted, were flagrantly ignored. Burma had not run out of forests yet, but now, especially with rising nationalist sentiments, it was important to harness "viable alternative sources." Though where there are forest resources, he adds, there is usually always trouble.

They journey at good speed, slowing down only when a riding party travels ahead of them. Soon enough, it turns off the main road and up a dirt track.

There are many such riding trails weaving around the outskirts of town, Mrs. Wheeler tells her, should she be so inclined. Evie says that sounds nice. Her mind, however, is on other things, and she asks Mr. Wheeler, "What kind of trouble?"

"The usual." Conflict had first arisen between private businessmen and natives, over wages, commissions, land, and then when the state intervened and took over, the conflict shifted, pitting the Forest Department against the locals. "They practise jhum cultivation, slash and burn, which is very destructive, and which the state is keen to ban, and of course we are trying to preserve the forests by creating reserved areas. It is for their own good, really, but they cannot see it yet." Mr. Wheeler is a stern critic of private enterprise, that she can tell, but when he says, "Thanks to Lord Dalhousie we have a more modern system of forest management, in which state rights enjoy precedence over all other rights," she finds herself thinking of the young woman on the deck of the *Maloja*, her Republican soul, and talk about a greater push for self-government.

Once they approach Cherrapunjee, the landscape changes, with the slopes suddenly giving way to deep and dramatic gorges. To her immense surprise, the hills are barren and treeless, and the winter-yellow grass is only now turning lightly green.

"Aren't we in the wettest place on earth?" she ventures to ask.

"Yes," the Wheelers confirm. "Is it not what you were expecting?"

Admittedly, no. She had imagined the wettest place in the world to be lush and tropical. "All the topsoil has been washed away," she is told. "Nothing grows." Except in the folds of the mountains, where thickets of forest burst forth in sudden profusion, and in the deep valleys carved by roaring rivers. Along the sheer cliff faces, several waterfalls throw themselves off the edge of the plateau—apparently during the monsoon they are thunderous, though even now they froth all the way down into faraway emerald pools.

They arrive shortly at Saitsohpen to find what Griffith would probably have described as another "bleak exposed village," and she is not entirely entranced either. The houses are constructed in stone, and the roofs sit very low, she presumes to keep the rain out, but it lends them a closed, melancholic air. The newest and largest construction is a stone church, whose cross sits crooked atop the humble steeple.

Their boarding house, if such it may be called, stands next to a school run by a group of Welsh Baptist missionaries—and they arrive just as the children stream out, higgledy-piggledy, socks pooled around their ankles, all attired in some semblance of a blue-and-grey uniform. The lodging arrangements are simple: the Wheelers and she are each to a room. She is in a corner "bedroom," which she suspects was until recently used for storage and whose harvested contents have been hastily emptied; the smell of sack and grain hangs heavy in the air.

Deng helps to set out her things, without saying a word.

"Are your lodgings comfortable?" asks Evie. "Your room is all right?"

"Yes," although she looks surprised at being asked.

"Thank you for coming along with us."

Something in her face softens. "It's my job, memsahib."

That afternoon, Evie ventures out for a walk into the village, on her own, unchaperoned. The Wheelers are resting, Deng is nowhere to be seen, and who else could she ask?

What joy! Here she is, in a small corner of the world, far from Calcutta, and London, free to do as she pleases. You *always* do as you please, her family would have interjected, but Evie cannot find the words to describe the delicious thrill of stepping out alone in a new—*so much to be discovered*—place.

Beyond the boarding house compound with its patchy grass and garden, the village houses stand compact and clean, each swept and neat, reminding her somehow of the tidiness of Kong Bathsheba's kitchen. She assumes that almost everyone is out working in their fields, for it is very quiet, apart from old men dozing in the sun, or old ladies eating oranges or minding toddlers. A dog bounds up to her, wagging his tail, chickens scatter, squawking loudly, and she is beginning to feel as though everything is quite strangely bucolic, when a young man exits a gate behind her, and begins to follow. She hastens her step, but he is quick, and falls alongside her, saying, "Excuse me, excuse me, memsahib."

She stops, and with as much haughtiness as she can muster, says, "Yes?"

He can't be more than eighteen, with neatly combed and parted hair, wearing a white long-sleeved shirt, and waistcoat. He reminds Evie of an altar boy. "I am sorry to trouble you, memsahib, but my grandfather would like to say hello." He gestures back, down the path. "He is the headman of the village, and considers it his duty to know who comes and goes." Then he adds, as if it explains everything, "He is very old."

Evie is relieved; *it is only this*. She walks back with him to a limewashed house whose patch of yard up front is hemmed by a scraggly hedge. The boy's grandfather is sitting on a mula, sunning his back. He wears a large turban, and has twined a thick shawl around his shoulders. When Evie enters, he bows lightly, and gestures to a seat next to him. His grandson remains obediently standing. The grandfather speaks in his own tongue, his voice low but authoritative; when he stops, his grandson translates.

"My grandfather says he is sorry he could not stand up to welcome you, but in winter his knees will not allow him."

Evie smiles. "Please tell him I understand, and that I am happy to meet him."

"He is pleased to meet you, too."

The old man issues what sounds like instructions, and the boy picks up a small basket and offers it to her—inside are spliced betel nut and green tobacco leaf.

"He says he knows bilati people do not usually eat kwai, but he would like to offer it to you anyway . . ."

Evie hesitates, he is right, she has never tried the stuff before, but would it be offensive to refuse? More important, should she care? She steals a quick glance at him; he is undoubtedly the oldest person she has ever met, his face lined as growth rings on a tree. He has been through many seasons, and he would know many things. She dips her hand into the basket.

An hour later, Evie is lying in bed, her head spinning. It is worse when she closes her eyes, so she stares instead at the cracked ceiling swirling above her. She has tried drinking lots of water; it has not helped. *This is it . . . this is how I will die.*

At that moment, there is a knock on the door, and even though Evie is expecting the Angel of Death, it is Deng, here to ask if memsahib would like to take some tea with the others in the garden.

She declines politely. "I am feeling a little unwell."

When Deng asks if there is anything she can do, Evie explains about the kwai, and how it perhaps does not quite agree with her. Without a word, Deng leaves the room, and returns with a cup.

"Oh, I could not possibly drink anything . . ." Evie begins to protest.

"Not drink. Eat." It is filled with sugar. A few spoonfuls later, Evie is sitting up, less pale, less nauseated, and then they look at each other and laugh.

"I thought I was going to *die*!"

"If you do not mind me saying so, memsahib, you looked like it, too."

"*How* do you eat this stuff?"

Deng grins, the first proper smile Evie has seen on her face. "Years of practise."

Later, in the light of a feeble, fluttering candle, Evie enters her conversation with the headman into her notebook. He told her he had been headman for more than thirty years, that he had opened his eyes in the morning to his village, and the surrounding mountains, every day of his life. That the white men arrived long ago, maybe when he was ten years old, and he was amazed that they had stayed.

"Why is he surprised?" she had asked.

"Because for months on end here, we get slap bam briew," the boy explained. "Rain so strong and long-lasting it does not stop until it has taken lives."

He was pleasant enough until she asked about the Nongïaid. Then his aged face clouded over. Beasts, he called them, the ones who would not stay, and for no good reason, too, merely to roam like animals in the wild. "If they are passing through, they will steal livestock, crops." He would be happy if the white man wiped them off the face of the earth. "They are good at that," he had added.

The kwai was already beginning to take effect, her head felt a little woozy, but Evie pressed on. "What about the Diengiei?" But she is not sure he understood for he frowned, saying, "They stole that, too."

The boy walked her back to the boarding house. His name was Aaron, he said, he lived with his parents in Shillong, and he was here to visit his grandfather. He studied at St. Anthony's, which was how he spoke English. "Don't mind what my grandfather tells you. He follows the old ways, and those won't be around for much longer."

A small wave of nausea had hit by then, but Evie managed to ask, "Why not?"

It is simple, he explained, Christianity had come to them now; and they could finally make progress. His people were in the light.

✧ ✧ ✧

The second party arrives the next day by noon. It is made up of Mr. Finlay, Mr. Dossett, and an American lepidopterist, Dr. Herman Swimmer—a tall, bearlike, bespectacled man whom Evie somehow cannot imagine frolicking around catching butterflies. The boarding house is now full to capacity, and at lunch they form a large gathering out on the little lawn.

Evie must admit she still feels ambivalent towards the fixer, although he has greeted her as politely and effusively as he has done in the past. Somehow that is precisely what disquiets her; something about him—his voice? his smile?—strikes her as fake. As Grandma Grace would have said, "I trust him about as far as I could throw him."

With Mr. Finlay, she is thrilled and shy and trying to be nonchalant all at once—*What is wrong with you?* Perhaps because there is no denying it now, she *is* pleased to see him, and the thought that they might have some time to spend together here, in this beautiful wilderness, is filling her with more joy than she imagined.

You had just better not allow him to get in the way of things.

After the meal, Mr. Wheeler heads off to work, while it is decided that the others will take a walk to the nearest sacred grove. They follow the local guide, Bah Khrawbor, a small, wiry, talkative man, who, as befits the hill folk, skips lightly over mud and stone. The rest of the party trudges inelegantly through the undergrowth.

Each village looks after its own sacred grove, he tells them, and though each might call them by different names, Law Kyntang, Law Niam, Diengkaiñ, Khlaw Blai, they all serve the same purpose. "Do you know what that is?"

They make their guesses: spirit dwellings, preservation, a link between earth and heaven, ancestor worship.

He shakes his head and looks at them pityingly. "They are playgrounds for the gods." Then he repeats what Evie has heard from Mrs. Wheeler about the sacred forests in Burma, that to lift anything out of the grove—a leaf, a twig, a stone—is to risk incurring the wrath of the gods. "One time, two outsiders collected firewood from here, and they went mad," he tells them cheerfully. "They ran out naked, leaving all their clothes behind."

Evie spies Mr. Dossett dropping the flower he had plucked.

People are allowed to drink the water here only if they are thirsty, to pick and eat the fruit only if they are hungry, and hunt the birds and animals, if and only if they are truly starving. "You must be in need," adds Bah Khrawbor, "and everything must be consumed within the forest."

Soon they come to a row of low stone benches, roughly hewn. "This is the place for remembering," he says, the point at which, before proceeding to the altar deeper inside the forest, people could rest and confirm they had not left anything behind that would be required for the rituals. "From beyond here, it is forbidden to turn back. Not even to turn your head."

At this spot, everyone's attention is also caught by the *Armillaria mellea*, a small cream-coloured growth, like finely dissected coral, sprouting from the mulchy soil by the path. The group crowds around, and Evie steps aside, only to find herself next to Mr. Finlay.

Perhaps because they are in this ancient forest, the evergreen trees rising high above them, the air fresh with the smell of young leaf and old, she feels emboldened to give him a smile, and say, "This is unexpected, Mr. Finlay?"

"It is, indeed." He purses his lips, and after a moment, adds, "Though I hope . . . not entirely unwelcome?"

Her smile widens. "No, not at all."

This seems to make him happy. He looks towards the party, still enamoured of the fungus. "I must confess I do not usually travel in a group. Plant hunting is not like big-game hunting. Usually it is me on my own for months on end, but"—he steals a glance at her—"well, this is . . . a very pleasant change."

She takes a deep breath to steady her heart.

"How long will you be here, Mr. Finlay?"

His smiles, and bows his head. "If I may, as long as you are."

Only on the way back does she have a chance to speak with their guide.

They walked up to the altar—although Evie was surprised to find not just one but five, arranged in separate circles in a clearing. "Every ninety years, a new one is built," Bah Khrawbor explained, at which to offer a sacrifice, usually a bull.

Evie stood there in silence. It did not feel like being inside a church, but something about the place inspired a quiet reverence. The deep greenness of the leaves, the smell of vegetation and cool damp rising, the moss thick and dewy—all bearing witness to centuries of gratitude and hope.

To walk all the way through the grove would take a whole day, so they turned back.

She waits until Bah Khrawbor finishes telling her how she should return in March when the rhododendrons are in bloom, and the forest transformed. "Mr. Khrawbor, you are very knowledgeable," she begins, a compliment that he receives with neither protest nor reticence. "Maybe you know something about the Nongïaid?"

His answer comes all too quickly. "I do not know about this, memsahib."

"No . . . ?"

He shakes his head, looking straight up the path before them.

She is a little taken aback, but presses him again. "I have read some books which mention the Diengiei . . . I am sure you know about *that*?"

He laughs, reverting to his smooth guide self. "What do I know about things in books, memsahib? I, who have hardly spent a year in school, and whose teachers told my parents I would come to nothing."

"That can't be true," she protests. "Besides, you speak English very well."

"That is because of Father Jones and the Sisters, and Jesus," he adds for good measure, and even lightly folds his hands.

She has lost him now for certain, and there is nothing she can do to steer him back.

After dinner that night, the party gathers at the fire.

The mood is jovial and chatty, prompted in no small part by the wine consumed during the course of the meal. Mr. Wheeler is pointing out how the fireplace has been constructed with great skill—that it is cavernous, yet the back wall is perfectly angled to throw out heat and prevent smoke from belching in. Dr. Swimmer, in his gruff American way, remarks how it would have been nice had the geniuses built a few more hearths around the house, that his room is colder than anything he has ever experienced in his life.

"It is like spending a freezing night under the stars."

Mr. Finlay turns to him. "Believe me, *nothing* quite compares to that . . ."

The lepidopterist chuckles. "You have probably had a few of those?"

Indeed he has.

"Oh, do tell," everyone urges.

Evie watches him, but his expression is hard to read; he must be used to such questions.

Most recently in Burma, he begins, while on the trek to Fort Hertz, when he strayed from the caravan in search of a pheasant. "For about an hour, I wandered from one patch of forest to another, and after skirting several hilltops I returned to the open valley, picking up what I thought was the correct trail." But it was not; he had his bearings all wrong, reading the rivers as flowing westward where they flowed east. He plunged knee-deep into icy torrents and tramped through bamboo forests fifteen to twenty feet high and so thick that he had to force the stems apart. Then dusk started closing in rapidly and he stopped for the night at the edge of a forest. It began to rain. His mackintosh had been ripped to shreds while he was buffeting his way through the thickets, but he covered his head with what remained, kept his gun and cartridge handy in case of wolves, and lay down to rest, curling up like a cat. He had no matches, nor could he, in any case, have lit a fire on such a wet night.

"But what about food, Mr. Finlay?" interjects Mrs. Wheeler.

"I had none, ma'am." So he made do with sorrel, rhododendrons, any other young leaves he could find, and—at this, the ladies gasped—an unfortunate finch. He made it back the next day, retracing his steps, splashing through mud and snow, beset by extraordinary hallucinations, and finally stumbling into Wei-hsi town late in the evening. Never again, he adds, would he be hunting for pheasants.

"It is difficult to convey the relationship, or rather the lack of relationship between distance and time in northern Burma," he continues. "There is no other country like it in the world." Evie can see the Wheelers nod in agreement—she has been listening mesmerized, and more than a little envious. She has read about similar escapades—*But this is real!* "Elsewhere there is jungle as thick," Mr. Finlay is saying, "there are mountains as high, climates as humid and extreme, but the combination of all three is unique."

For the rest of the evening, he is pestered with questions.

"What must one *always* carry?"

Jam, for it makes everything more palatable, and whisky, for it is antiseptic, and well, it is whisky. And if travelling in Tibet, he adds, then brick tea, for it is immediately useful, and the Tibetans in the mountain villages prefer it to silver.

"What is to be most feared in the jungles, Mr. Finlay?"

Unlike what most people believe, the deadliest are not tigers and vipers, he says, but battalions of leeches, blister flies, ticks, mosquitoes, sandflies and horseflies, all avid bloodsuckers whose bites cause fevers, festering sores, and a crazing irritation.

"When have you been most frightened?"

Evie asks this, and he looks directly at her as he replies. "Crossing a suspension bridge, dangling in midair, swaying from side to side. I can scramble up any narrow pathway, thin as a ribbon, sheer against a mountainside, but those bridges scare me the most."

✧ ✧ ✧

Is it a dream or a memory of walking through a forest with Grandma Grace?

She was nine, and something caught her attention, a beetle, a colourful toadstool, and when she straightened up she was alone. She was not immediately frightened; she was certain Grandma Grace would be ahead, tall, handsome, smiling, with her hat and scarf and basket, the sun behind her lighting her up like a painting.

Evie walked on, but Grandma Grace was gone.

She stumbled forward, calling out, but the woods were silent around her, undisturbed, except for the thud of her small footsteps and her heart. Soon it was a path no longer, but rough undergrowth, the trees growing taller and closer. She was crying, but not too loudly, in case someone other than her grandmother would hear her—wolves, bears, or other monsters.

When she started slowing down, exhausted, she suddenly came to a stream, and on the other side, standing as though she had always been waiting, was Grandma Grace.

"Come," she called across the water, gesturing to her granddaughter, and Evie stood on a stone on the opposite bank and hesitated. "Don't be afraid, darling," she said, her arms open and waiting, so Evie leaped across.

But this is when she wakes, or the memory ends. Does she make it? Does she not? She does not remember, she does not know.

✧ ✧ ✧

Every morning, Evie awakens to the strains of "Nearer, My God, to Thee" sung stridently, and decidedly off-key. Young, high-pitched voices float in from the school grounds, where the children gather for assembly. Through the window, she has seen a tall, thin lady in a blue-and-white habit standing before them—she must be the headmistress—while others in similar attire cluster behind her. The lyrics are undecipherable until the last line in each verse, sung with renewed gusto: *Nearer, myyyyy Goddddd, tooooo theeeeeeee.*

Today they are especially reverberant, and it is impossible to fall back to sleep, or indeed to remain in her room, so she washes and dresses and heads to the small front garden.

The day is chilly though bright, and the yellowed slopes around contrast starkly with the clear blue sky. On the next hill stand the church and cemetery, white crosses shining, while the rest of the township huddles around companionably.

She must admit her arrival here has been less eventful that she had imagined.

What did she expect? Well, definitely not to spend this past week strolling around sacred groves, or picnicking at Kutmadan—though it is a particularly captivating spot, at the very edge of a slope, with endless views of the green gorges.

They have been exploring, gathering bits of bubbly basalt from the open grassy slopes, visiting nearby villages famed for their weaving, and once or twice she has ventured out riding with Mrs. Wheeler. They have also hiked to waterfalls—one in particular with unusual rock formations, called Daiñthlen, once the lair of a monstrous serpent, Bah Khrawbor informed them. "He was slaughtered here," he said cheerfully, "and they say the implements the people used are scattered in these pools." And strange pools they were, too, hollowed into flat rock, deep and crystalline blue. On another occasion, they hired a pony trap to take them to Laittyra, to a gigantic boulder shaped like a conical khoh that the natives believe belonged to Ramhah—an evil giant who was killed, and his basket turned to stone.

This is all very well and interesting, but not at all what Evie is seeking.

She has wandered into the village several times more, but it feels futile. Just as Kong Bathsheba said, the key lies in finding the ones who walk, the Nongïaid—*but how?*

For now, she decides to try and find some breakfast.

The kitchen is built at the back, separate from the boarding house, and she must walk all the way through it to get there. It is dark inside, the windows barely letting in any light, and she bumps against a table, then a chair, and must bend low to step into a corridor.

A murmur of voices rises from one of the rooms, and she pauses outside the door only because she hears her name. It is Mr. Dossett, and he is wondering out loud why she is here.

Mr. Finlay does not reply right away. "We all have our reasons."

"Yes, but what are hers? I heard her talking to the guide the other day, in the forest, asking him questions . . . Do you know about this, do you know about that? What is she looking for?"

"It might be none of our business."

There is a moment's silence before Mr. Dossett's voice pipes up again. "What if she is looking for something valuable . . ." She catches her breath; she can picture his face, that sly, acquisitive smile. "Isn't she sweet on you? You should try to find out, Finlay."

His friend mumbles. "I don't know about *that* . . ."

She does not wait to hear any more.

At the kitchen door, she meets Bah Khrawbor on his way out. He bows, avoids her eye, and walks away hurriedly. Inside sits Deng, looking surprised, and another woman trying to revive the fire at the hearth. She realizes only now that it probably is not customary for guests, European guests in particular, to show up here like this.

"Memsahib, can I help you?"

"No, I mean yes, I have come to see if I can find some breakfast."

She is told it will be served in half an hour.

"All right, then may I get a cup of tea?" And with that, she strides in and perches on a mula. Deng almost falls off hers, and the other lady stops blowing at the embers.

"I can bring it to you, memsahib, to your room, wherever you want."

"Right here is fine," she says, and it is true, she does not feel like being in the main house. "If that is all right?" she adds.

Deng's expression is as inscrutable as ever, but she nods, and busies herself.

"Thank you," says Evie gratefully.

The cup of tea she is handed is golden red and smoky, just like at Kong Bathsheba's, and she finds she has grown to prefer this to the usual with milk and sugar. Deng and the other woman make no conversation, either with Evie or with each other. They work swiftly, silently, and rather than being awkward she finds this calming. Outside the door, a brood of yellow chicks chirp around the mother hen, and a cat watches them lazily from atop a wall.

Later, at breakfast, Mr. Wheeler tells them that there has been a bit of trouble in one of the villages to the south, a small place called Umwai.

It is calmer now, he says, the private businessmen, against whom the villagers had been rebelling, have been driven out, and since it is important not to alienate the natives any further, they have been told that despite their assault on two forest officers, their only punishment is to hand over partial jurisdiction of the forest to the government. "As we did in Burma," he adds. "It makes for a smoother transition, especially if we elicit their help in protecting the forests from fire and other threats."

"But don't the villagers do that already?" asks Evie. From the time she has spent here, it would appear so. "The sacred groves have been standing for hundreds of years without our intervention. Is it necessary to do this? Why must we take their forests and turn them into reserves?"

She is afraid she might have gone too far; there is silence at the table, and everyone has stopped their chattering to look over at her. She had not meant to sound this hostile—at least not towards Mr. Wheeler, but it is done now.

If Mr. Wheeler is annoyed he does not show it. Calmly, he butters his toast and sips his tea. "Yes, they have, but we find there is no strategy on their part to make any money from them. It's a waste. Added to that is the threat from unmonitored shifting cultivation. We are here to ensure a balance between conservancy, which is a priority for us, and sustainable profit. We are here to help. One day, when the empire is gone—and it will go, if you ask me—we will leave this model behind for them to follow."

Evie stays quiet. At the other end of the table, Mr. Dossett leans over to speak to Mr. Finlay, and she would very much like to fling her omelette at the fixer.

✧ ✧ ✧

Before they left Shillong, letters had arrived.

A breathless two-page update from Bessie: *Where is Assam? Does this mean you will be gone the entire season? Mrs. Ward thinks it a great pity. I do, too! There have been such splendid balls* . . . and on and on it prattled, disclosing details that served only to make Evie glad to be away. The other was from Charlotte—also enclosing a letter from Agnes that had arrived after she had departed from Calcutta. It was full of Cambridge news. The GSS meetings continue, as do classes and practical sessions at Balfour, and experiments in her at-home laboratory. At the time Agnes was writing, the botanical garden was golden, in the throes of late autumn. She was well, as was Edward, and they were hard at work on their books. *And you?* she had asked, which made Evie suddenly, stupidly weepy. *Have you found it? Was Muttlebury of any help? Or shall I burn the holy basil he sent me?* The last letter was from her sister, not brief and curt as she had feared it might be, but mystified. *Why are you there? I speak on behalf of Mama and Papa when I say we worry, and wish you would come home.* She had sat there, letter in hand, and then told herself that it was too late for regrets now, over what she ought to have shared with them, and how she could have done this differently. She was here, and that is what mattered.

She had decided, then, that it was best to put the letters away. She fishes them out now, and spends a quiet morning, out in the garden, writing.

First to Charlotte, to convey that all is well, then to Bessie—*have fun on my behalf*—and to Florence, sending love and reassurance.

You will be happy to know I am safe and having a wonderful time. I am seeing the world—or at least parts of it not many can claim to, and I am travelling with companions who have many exciting experiences to share. Florence, I can confess at least this to you—that my focus never has been on finding someone to marry but on living an adventure to its fullest. I am sorry for this deception on my part, I am certain you will be hurt but there it is.

She knows she ought to add that once her travels are over she will return home, that she cannot wait to be an aunt, that she will seek a teaching job, perhaps at her old school, the North London Collegiate—

but all this brings to her a sense of the end of things, and she has no wish to think of that until she absolutely must.

Last of all, she writes a letter to Agnes. *Touch not the holy basil! I am happy to report that Muttlebury has proven useful. Where I am now, Agnes, you would think it a dream. The ferns, and mosses, and fungi growing in the folds of the hills . . . I am yet to explore more, but I can see this is a flora befitting the wettest place on earth. As for my quest, there is little to say except the search continues. Oh, I do miss you, and the sparganium. Does it still thrive well in a bucket in your kitchen? Give it my love. And to you even more.*

✧ ✧ ✧

Today, Evie joins the others on an excursion to see the living bridges, the ones that fascinated Hooker more than half a century ago. She wonders if they have grown in magnificence.

They leave Cherrapunjee for a village called Tyrna, from where they begin their descent to the "riat," or valley, with Bah Khrawbor as their guide. The dirt track is steep, at times precipitous, as the ladies had been warned it would be—in fact, perhaps they ought to stay behind? *Stay behind?* Mrs. Wheeler said she would have none of it, and neither would Evie. They pass a few villagers on the way, and Evie looks at them in open curiosity—they are wrapped tightly in their shawls, and carrying vegetables in conical baskets on their backs. Around her, the scenery is splendid, the folds of the mountains pleated in light and shadow, the plants growing lusher and greener as they descend. Areca palms wave over her head and plume in abundance, young bamboo culms stand sentry-like, and bright red and yellow poinsettia blossoms overhang the path.

She has carried her flower press along, and manages to find some fern specimens along the way—delicate maidenhair, finely dissected *Asplenium*, and leathery *Polypodium* with its graceful arching leaves. The day is bright and warm, the sky a marvellous blue, and while she collects leaves, she feels a rare sense of contentment.

Bah Khrawbor leads the way, and he is followed by Dr. Swimmer, the Wheelers, and Mr. Dossett, which leaves Mr. Finlay to accompany her. She wonders if he will do as his companion instructed, and ask her questions about the plant she is seeking. But for as long as they walk together, he does not, which pleases her. They talk of other things, the garden they visited in Aden, the banyan tree in Calcutta, vast as a forest and ancient. How pleasurable, this easy spontaneity. It is now she notices the slant of his jaw, his well-shaped mouth, the strength of his arms as he helps her over a stream or rocky crevice. Evie does not really need help—but she does not mind that he offers, and is happy to accept.

When they finally reach level ground, they pass through a small village, Nongriat—the ones who live in the valley—where peppercorns and cinnamon are spread out to dry in the sun; the air is heady with their fragrance. Dogs bark, and women with children on their hips watch warily. The huts are compact and clean, and Evie notices that each has its own patch of kitchen garden growing chillies and potatoes and mustard leaves. She can hear the river before she sees it, a gentle roar that in the monsoon, Bah Khrawbor says, turns thunderous. Knobbly gigantic boulders line the banks, and she scrambles atop one and stares in amazement.

The water is iridescent below, and strung above it are two airborne bridges, one over the other, woven from the aerial roots of the fig trees growing on either side. Evie has never seen anything like it. She climbs up to the lower bridge and steps on it, tentative at first, but she realizes soon enough that her weight, along with that of the others, can easily be supported. The roots are trunks beneath her feet, knotted and gnarled, covered in moss, and raised at the sides like balustrades.

Bah Khrawbor tells them these are alternatives to wooden bridges, which are more easily damaged or washed away during the monsoon. Evie remembers Hooker's account, of how these bridges were also made for the Nongïaid, so they could carry the Diengiei where they wished, or deemed it safe. *It is pointless to ask Bah Khrawbor again*, she thinks; he would surely still claim ignorance.

"How long before a bridge like this can be used?" asks Mrs. Wheeler.

"At least fifteen years."

Evie is moved to silence, struck by how many decades it takes to create this, how much foresight is required, and patience. She sits on a boulder, away from the others, feeling that this place, with its deep pools and waterfalls, its glinting sunlight and butterflies, is where magic could happen.

They arrive back in Saitsohpen early that evening, and Evie is in her room, freshly bathed, and tired.

The trek up the gorge was back-breaking, but she has not had a more enjoyable day in a long time. All through her body runs a pleasant ache. It will not be so pleasant tomorrow, she has been warned, and

Bah Khrawbor has handed her a bottle of what he calls "dawai" to massage onto her aching limbs. "Medicine," he replied mysteriously upon inquiry. The container holds a deep red salve that smells strongly of raw herbs and shoe polish.

She is examining it in her tiny bedroom, by the light of a candle, when Deng knocks and enters. She is here to turn down the bed as usual, slip a hot-water bottle under the covers, and take away the day's laundry—tasks that she does with swift and silent efficiency. Usually, she asks if there is anything else Evie requires, Evie says no, thank you, Deng, and that is where their interaction ends. This evening though, Deng lingers, and Evie can feel her flutter uncertainly like a bird behind her. She turns around. Deng's eyes hold the candle flame at their centre. She is still deciding whether or not to speak.

"What is it, Deng?" whispers Evie.

"You asked Bah Khrawbor about . . . the Nongïaid."

Evie cannot hide her surprise; this she was not expecting. "I did."

Deng looks down at her hands, holding the laundry. "Why?"

Now Evie is a little confused. "I read about them in some books . . ."

"But why?" Deng is looking at her directly. This is a threat, a dare, and Evie is certain that if she lies now Deng will exit the room.

"Because they are the only ones who know about the Diengiei."

For a long moment, Deng does not say a word, then she sinks silently onto the mula. "My mother was one of them."

Evie catches her breath. "She was?"

Deng nods. "When she was very young, she was . . . caught."

"By whom?"

"The missionaries."

"I'm sorry," Evie blurts out.

Deng furrows her brow as though unsure of what to do with this apology. "They put her in a school for orphans, even though her own mother and father were living."

"But did she manage to . . . go back?"

Deng looks at her with pity. "Once you leave the Nongïaid, whether through your own choice or not, you cannot *go back*."

"But why?"

"It is just the way it is . . . the way it has always been."

Evie has come to realize that many things here are explained in this manner. She holds her breath when she asks, "Where is your mother now?" and immediately regrets it, for Deng says the words that are already written on her face.

"My mother died."

"I'm sorry, Deng."

"It was a relief for her, and for us."

Evie does not ask why, instead she gently inquires, "Have you ever met with anyone . . . from your mother's side of the family?"

She nods. "We have cousins, who come to see us sometimes, when they are . . . in the area. The older people do not like it, but somehow they manage to arrange it."

At this, Evie pauses. There is a ringing in her ears, in her chest a rapid thudding. "If it is all right with you, may I meet them?"

Deng looks up at her; she does not seem surprised. "I can leave them a message, but I cannot promise they will reply, or wish to meet with you."

Early next morning, Evie flies into the kitchen. Deng is not there. The other woman, their cook, Thei, without a word begins to prepare her a cup of tea.

"Oh, thank you," says Evie, "but I am looking for Deng."

"Deng?"

"Yes?"

Thei points in the direction of the back garden, where their living quarters stand—tiny shacks of wood and stone.

"Thank you," says Evie, and rushes off.

In one of the rooms, she finds Deng, sitting, weaving.

"Memsahib," she says, startled. Definitely no guest, European or otherwise, has ever set foot in here. She makes to stand, placing what look like thin ribbons of neatly plaited bamboo on the floor.

"No, no, please . . ." says Evie. "I only wished to know whether you had managed to send a message?" She tries not to sound too excited, too pressing.

Deng gives her a small smile. "I am making it right now."

Evie's eyes widen. "What do you mean?"

She learns that when Deng said she would leave a message for her cousins, she did not mean via telegram, or letter, or anything that takes the form of text at all. Deng is weaving what she calls a "kyrwoh," which she will pass on to a messenger. To Evie, the kyrwoh looks like a pretty Celtic band, to wear around the waist or neck, but in the old days, Deng tells her, kings used them to send messages to their people, from village to village, that there was a war coming, or a drought, a feast, or a funeral, or as in this case, that the recipient was being summoned. It is not used as widely as before, but for Deng and her cousins, it is convenient.

"It is all in here?" Evie holds it in her hand, lightly, amazed.

Deng nods, "Not everything that can be read is written on paper, memsahib."

She has woven the kyrwoh to a width that conveys to the recipients that they ought to come when they can—in between "emergency" and "take your time" so as not to alarm them.

"But how will the messenger know where to find them?"

"He does not. He just knows where to leave it for them to find."

"But . . . they could be anywhere?"

"Yes, but they check this spot often. It is how they get their news of the world."

All right, says Evie, and now what?

"And now, memsahib, we wait."

✧ ✧ ✧

Waiting does not come easily to Evie.

How long, how long? she wonders. Sometimes they reply quickly, Deng tells her, within a week, and at other times . . .

At other times?

Well, it might take a few months.

Evie decides it is best, then, to keep herself occupied. She takes walks with Mr. Finlay—around the sanatorium where British officers are sent to recover from the illnesses of the plains, the grounds of the abandoned tea estate—where they exhume a funny assortment of artifacts, spoons and forks and old bottles—and all across the open hills surrounding the monument to David Scott, erected in 1832 and already blackened with age.

They have long talks, too. Mr. Finlay was born and grew up in Manchester, and studied Natural Sciences at Edinburgh, he tells her, but before he could finish, in his second year, his father fell ill and died, leaving his family impoverished. "So I left."

Something about the way he says it makes Evie glance at him—but there is no trace of regret or self-pity on his features. It is as it is.

"What did you do then?"

"I had to work." With the help of a university friend of his father's, he was offered a post in Shanghai, as a schoolmaster.

"A schoolmaster!" exclaims Evie, saying she simply cannot imagine him . . . indoors?

He laughs, admitting that that was why he did not last—before the year was out he was accompanying plant hunters such as Fritz Anderson on expeditions across China. "I went up the Yangtze River to the border of Tibet."

Wide-eyed, Evie asks what it is that he discovered there.

"Not much . . . apart from a love for exploration." At that, they both smile at each other. "And you?" he asks simply. "How did you come to love the natural world?"

She tells him about Agnes, and Grandma Grace, even her friends at the GSS, who helped her, she says, to see things anew. She does not add that they also think she is a bit crazy, coming all the way here on a wild quest.

"I remember you told me in Calcutta," says Mr. Finlay, "that you were seeking something, a plant, on little more than a hunch . . ." *Wouldn't you—or rather Mr. Dossett—like to know!* But before she can tell him that she would prefer not to divulge any details for her own reasons, he adds, "I am a plant hunter, so I cannot deny I am curious, but if there is one thing Anderson taught me it is—to each his own quest."

"What do you mean?" she asks.

He looks at her a long moment. "Just that if you had wanted to, you would have told me."

She nods. "I would have."

"Sometimes," he continues, "talking about something dissipates the energy you collect around it, the energy required to find it, to accomplish the mission."

Yes, she says, yes, exactly. To open up a wish to too many lightens it, makes it frivolous. How impossibly lucky, she tells herself, that she has met the one person who understands.

Enjoyable as they are, their walks must be put on hold, for they go away suddenly, the fixer and Mr. Finlay, on an impromptu plant-hunting expedition—"I wish you could come too," he tells her, and so does she, but that is impossible.

She is determined, though, not to be left behind in a lost and forlorn state. She resumes riding, and visiting waterfalls and other scenic spots. She accompanies the Wheelers on a day trip to Umwai, and treks to a viewpoint just beyond the village, at the edge of the forested plateau, from where the drop into the plains of Sylhet is high and sheer. Mr. Wheeler says that during the monsoon all this transforms into a shimmering watery basin—every year, rain from the wettest place on earth floods Bengal. Standing there, the plains spreading endlessly before her, she is taken back to a morning on the *Maloja*, gliding down the Suez Canal—*Here, too, I am more in the world.*

On most days, Evie walks out on her own.

She does so early in the morning, while the sun is still strong and bright, before the winter fog she is now used to creeps cold and silent over the golden hills in the afternoon. Deng packs her a snack of oranges, fruit buns, and rice cakes.

"You'll go alone, memsahib?"

"Yes," she says, "but I have company . . ."

Deng looks bewildered. "Who?"

The best kind. All the green and silently growing things around her.

She begins by exploring the sacred grove from edge to edge, finding streams, grassy clearings, a small mossy cave. It is peaceful, enchanting even, but she does little else apart from sketch, and read, and nap with the winter sun on her back—not so much for fear of upsetting the gods but the locals. Soon enough, she begins to venture farther, beyond Saitsohpen village, scrambling down the slopes to reach the forests in the folds of the hills. Here she can collect leaves and flowers, seeds and samples. As Hooker had written in his journals, it is true that the extraordinary diversity of species here is not so much attributable to the elevation, but to the variety of exposures and habitats, the pools and lakes, the tropical jungles, both in deep, hot, and wet valleys and on drier slopes, the rocks, the tablelands and stony soils, the moor-like uplands—*It is a dream!*

Sometimes, in this quietness, while examining a curled fern frond, or a closed jasmine bud, she is reminded of Goethe and his words. *Each of Nature's works has an essence of its own,* he had written, *each of her phenomena a special characterization: and yet their diversity is in unity.*

During this time, the unexpected happens.

In this out-of-the-way part of the world, tramping through forests as she had done with Grandma Grace so long ago, and so far away, she finds she is closest to being as happy as she was in her childhood or, dare she say it, even more. Perhaps it is because of this that she finds her "seeing" improves. They had talked about it often in their GSS meetings, the seeing that Goethe called for, and although Ollie and the others had explained it to her carefully, she felt she knew of it only theoretically rather than through experience. "But what does it mean?" she would ask. "To see feelingly?"

She finds herself drawn especially to ferns. An initial glance around brings to her attention a general foliage, but on closer inspection, a great and extraordinary diversity is revealed. The majestic, and fantastic, flying spider-monkey tree fern with its swirling leaves and rough, shaggy trunks; the delicate maidenhair creeper, its leaflets edged with odd little teeth; the lovely, leafy oakleaf fern, with basal rosettes sticking up like feathers; and the splendid winglike *Dipteris wallichii* so admired by Hooker. Closer to the ground, tiger's whiskers with their straight, upright stems, standing like miniature pine trees. Behind the veil of ferns a blanket of haircap moss, growing close against the slope, and which looks, from above like stars; on a fallen log, a layer of turf moss, soft and slippery like velvet.

This green! I have never known this green before, she writes in her journal. What must it be like in the rains? The rains of the wettest place on earth. How she longs to stay, to find out.

And then—this is the part she has always struggled with most—she tries to retreat into *exact sensorial experience*, as Goethe spoke of it. Think the phenomenon! She was afraid that this lay quite beyond her and always would, and although even here it is not as exact and undistracted as it ought to be—*Maybe I don't have the patience necessary for this?*—she imagines in a way she has not before, in closer and more striking detail. Perhaps it is because of the quiet, of her aloneness, the light, the air, even the quality of plants that she finds thrillingly new and unfamiliar. The fern fronds unfolding—alive, in transition, rather than frozen in static form.

On occasion, she invites Mrs. Wheeler to join her—come, she will say, let's go and examine the pandanus, or see whether the sapphire berries are ripe for collecting—but the days when she is alone, she finds more inspiring. She discovers a flattish boulder perched precariously at the end of a slope—to get to which she must jump over a small gorge, between hill and stone. Then she sits at the edge with her feet dangling over nothingness, the valley falling away steeply below her. She does not think it an exaggeration to say that this might be the spot where she is most in the world.

If she could infuse one thing into her scientific training, it is this feeling, intangible, inexplicable as it may be, because from it flowed all else, inspiration, no doubt, but also respect—and reverence—for the *aliveness* of life, and its infinite and unfathomable interconnectedness. What a science that would be! What a way of knowing! *Because to isolate is to deaden, isn't it?* she thinks. To take away from . . . circumstance. But to see in Goethe's way, to vividly perceive the metamorphosis of a leaf, the coming into bloom of a flower, is no longer to see the thing in an objective frozen present, but as a thing—a subject—with history. She realizes this here, that history can be drawn from a phenomenon by imagining it in time, and in this way also draw closer the temporal and physical relationships within all living things.

"All of us," she murmurs, sitting aloft the boulder, the wind in her face, "every living thing carries history."

The days pass by in a quiet, steady routine. She takes her morning tea in the kitchen, sometimes with a freshly steamed rice cake drizzled with honey, enjoying the smell of wood, the warmth radiating from the fire. Deng tells her that this was where the elders would recite stories, around the hearth, and she can see why—it is in so many ways a place of sustenance. They have also spoken about her mother.

"She drank herself to death on kiad." Evie knew the word, a term for a local rice brew in these hills. "She had her children . . . all five of us, but we could never be enough for everything she had lost." In her voice was a sadness, but also a trace of relief, as though this was the first time these words were seeing air.

Evie was almost afraid to ask, but she did. "What about your father?"

Deng shrugged. "He was sometimes there, most of the time he was not." And then she paused, glanced at her, and said almost shyly, "But you must be wondering how I speak English . . ."

"And such good English, too!"

"The missionaries, the ones who took away my mother, they helped us out, gave me an education, and work to earn a living. And now I don't know . . ."

"Don't know what?" asked Evie.

"Whether to hate them or to be grateful."

✧ ✧ ✧

On the day they receive word from the Nongïaid, Mr. Dossett and Mr. Finlay return from their expedition to Mawsmai.

Evie is out in the garden, sketching, when Mr. Finlay joins her. "Do you come bearing marvellous tales of discovery?" she teases. He laughs.

He is clearly pleased to see her—and she is pleased to see this, and him, too.

"Well, Dossett is convinced we have found a new species of orchid."

How exciting! "Though I remember you saying this matters little to you."

"It is true," he says, adding that he is flattered at her recollection. "I care to find a new orchid only if I may be permitted to name it after you."

"Oh! *Aerides evelynae* certainly does have a ring to it . . ."

They smile at each other, and maybe it is because of the time they have spent apart, all the days they have not met, that Evie feels certain that in their exchange lies something indiscreet—a longing, a hope. He leans closer across the table. His eyes are as dark as peat, his skin tawny from his expedition. She hopes for one of them to say something—anything—that acknowledges this pull between them, but she senses him faltering.

"I have not seen you sketch before," he says, "you have a good hand."

"Why, thank you, Mr. Finlay. It has been said that every drawing conveys a view."

"Yes?" He looks amused.

She nods, and asks if he draws, too.

"Couldn't, even if my life depended on it, alas, but I have been trying to write . . ."

"Write what, Mr. Finlay?"

"A travel memoir," he replies a little shyly.

"Oh, I love travel memoirs," she blurts out. "I've read so many!"

He looks gratified. Maybe, if she had the time, and the inclination, she could take a look . . . someday?

"I would be delighted."

They sit there, quiet for a moment, the air punctured only by the buzzing of bees, and the lunch gong from the school.

"Mr. Finlay," she begins, "how long have you known Mr. Dossett?"

"Too long," he says without hesitation. "Why do you ask?"

Evie shrugs. "No reason, really. I merely wondered . . ."

Mr. Finlay throws her a quick glance. "We are not *friends* . . . if that's what you are wondering. He is a rascal, but a very resourceful one." Which is what makes him a good fixer, of course. He knows how to find the best coolies and guides, where to hire the strongest mules, and can even, he adds, stump up a bit of cash when you need it—which all plant hunters do, more often than not. "He is being paid a hefty sum by Dr. Swimmer to be here," he continues, "and since I am here, too, Dossett thinks we ought to go hunting for . . ."

"Orchids," she finishes for him.

He laughs. "You don't much like him, do you?"

Evie shrugs. How is she to explain that he makes her uncomfortable, like he is watching her when he thinks she is not looking? Or that he inflames her with his remarks about the "sly natives" or their ugliness and stupidity. To Mr. Finlay she says simply that she prefers it when he is not around.

"I am sure he will be off plant hunting again soon"—he gives her a small smile—"though I am happy to stay where I am for now . . ."

Good, says Evie, for she would die of jealousy if he went off again on another trip so soon. It isn't fair!

"One day, Miss Alexander, you will travel the world."

She looks at him, grey eyes meeting his own, steady and strong. "Oh? And how are you so certain?"

He reaches across, turns her hand over gently, and runs a finger down her palm. He smiles. "It is written in your stars."

She is heading to her room afterwards, when Deng rushes up to her. "I received a reply," she says, breathless. Evie glances about them; there is no one around. She motions for Deng to follow her inside. Once she closes the door she turns around.

"And?"

"They will meet us."

Evie drops into a chair. "When?"

"Tomorrow morning." Then she adds apologetically, "The messenger fell sick, otherwise we would have heard sooner."

Evie says it is all right, that she is just glad they received the message.

"Where do we meet them?"

"Usually in a tea shop, but the headman of this village . . ."

"Does not feel too kindly towards them?"

Deng nods. "Which is why they have asked us to come to the lawkyntang. At the remembering stones." They will be meeting her mother's youngest sister's daughter, and her brother.

"When did you last see them?" asks Evie.

"Almost a year ago," she replies. "It is getting harder for them to set up camp near Shillong . . . people do not like it, they chase them away . . ."

"Where do they go? What do they do?"

Deng shrugs. "They have no choice. They have to keep even more on the move."

All through the evening, Evie can hardly keep still, and least of all make conversation at dinner—or eat, despite the fact that Thei in the kitchen has miraculously managed to "roast" a whole chicken, and has not steamed the vegetables until they are pulp.

To her joy, Mr. Dossett excuses himself after dessert—"bit of work to be done"—and leaves the dining room. A bottle of port is fetched to celebrate the plant hunter's return, and when they gather around the fire, Mr. Finlay is pestered for tales of their recent travels. This is a relief—lately conversations have been more lepidopterously inclined than she would like. Evie knows all about how difficult it has been for Dr. Swimmer to "relax" his specimens in this cold; how they turn brittle and splinter at the prick of a pin. This evening, Mr. Finlay regales them with funny stories from their latest trip, including one about his encounter with the fever nettle, a plant that causes severe itching on contact with the skin.

"As if you are on fire!" he explains. "And you cannot put it out!"

Evie and the others laugh; she is feeling benevolent towards the world, prompted by the port and the warmth, and the thought of tomorrow. She listens intently, holding closely her happiness and excitement.

Later, when she is off to bed, she bumps into Mr. Finlay outside; he had stepped out to smoke.

"Your travel memoir will be superb." She can barely make his face out in the dark, but she can tell that he is pleased, and smiling. "You are a wonderful storyteller."

"And you, Miss Alexander, are . . . wonderful."

She looks at him, their breath changing to white mist.

"I am glad you're back."

"Are you?"

She nods.

He steps closer, bringing with him the smell of smoke and leather. "Miss Alexander," he says, and in his voice she detects the faintest tremble.

"Please, call me Evie . . ."

"Evie, would you allow me . . ."

They are standing close to each other, closer than ever before. The air is suddenly warm between them. She thinks he is leaning in towards her when a door, a window, somewhere, in the wind clangs shut. They are startled apart. Then they quietly laugh.

"Well," she says, "I must go . . ."

He takes her hand and presses it to his lips.

"Yes, of course," he says, "goodnight, sweet Evie."

✧ ✧ ✧

Long before breakfast, when no one is up or about yet, Evie is awake and dressed and ready. Ought she to take her notebook? *Yes.* Her sketchbook, too? *Why not?* And for good measure, a pebble from the river at Nongriat.

When Deng knocks, she is at the door in an instant. "Memsahib, let us go." She follows, pulling her shawl tight around her, for it is cold, the sun is pale, and last night's mist still clings to the hills. They are almost out of the boarding house compound when they bump into Mr. Dossett.

"Good morning, Miss Alexander."

She returns his greeting with a distinct lack of warmth.

"Where are you off to so early?"

"I suppose one may ask where are you back from so late?"

He grins, although in his eyes something flashes, anger, contempt; but Evie bristles, too, from nervousness, and a strange feeling of having been found out.

"Deng is showing me . . . the village," she says, and then is annoyed she succumbed to offering him an explanation, one that sounds flimsy even to her ears.

"Well, I must not keep you from your exploring." He steps aside gallantly, sweeping his hat low.

Only when they enter the forest does she begin to recover her composure. It is colder here, and quieter, too, except for the chirruping of birds.

"Will they be there, Deng?" she asks, suddenly tentative.

"If they have said so, they will, memsahib."

It takes them a little more than twenty minutes to arrive at the remembering stones, but the clearing is empty. With the sun hidden, the light around them is milky pale, falling thinly on the leaves and undergrowth. Evie looks at Deng, eyebrows raised, but her companion seems unperturbed. "We wait." She proceeds to sit on a stone, and Evie follows. The forest stays silent, with no echoing sound of footsteps or voices.

No one's coming. No one's coming. She tries to distract herself with the fan-shaped oyster mushrooms growing like stairs up a nearby tree. *No one's coming.*

It isn't long though before Deng turns and exclaims. Two figures stand behind them, silent as cats, clad in cloaks of dark grey wool pulled over their heads and tied under their chins. The boy, who is smaller, stands a little way behind the girl, even though her own slight frame barely gives him cover. Deng rushes over, and for a moment Evie thinks the girl will not drop her walking stick, nor the boy his bow, but they do, and they embrace, uttering exclamations in their own tongue.

Evie stands aside, feeling like an intruder, and when they finally turn to face her, she offers a nervous hello. Deng makes the introductions. The girl is Phyrnai, the boy Ïada. They are quite visibly siblings, both with the same high slant of cheek and eye, the same small rounded nose. Their hair is long, unruly, and windswept.

The girl nods. "Kumno?" The boy says nothing, his eyes curious yet cautious.

"Thank you for meeting me," says Evie.

She expects Deng to translate for her, but the girl nods again. "We were not far."

They seat themselves around one of the larger remembering stones, except for Ïada, who paces noiselessly at the edges of the clearing. From under her cloak, from a cloth bag on her back, Phyrnai extracts bunches of fruit—wild oranges from the Garo Hills, where they spent the winter. Some for their cousin, and some for Evie, too.

"Oh, this is so kind." Evie is mortified she has not brought anything in return, even though Phyrnai waves her apologies away.

She sits in silence as the cousins converse, their language sharp yet musical. In her time here, she has familiarized herself with some Khasi words, but this is dialect, she thinks, and they do not use the few words she knows—except *Diengiei*, at which there is a pause, and Phyrnai glances over at her. Even her brother turns, his hand moving along the length of his bow. Perhaps they are not pleased at her snooping around like this, but she supposes the worst they could do is send her away with nothing more than wild oranges.

Finally, Phyrnai turns to her, and asks haltingly, "How do you know about the Diengiei?"

Evie was expecting this, and has tried to prepare a clear, simple response. She leaves out Goethe and his Urpflanze, and how the Diengiei had caught her attention because she had been introduced already to his ideas, and plunges straight into how she had read about it in some books. "I like learning about other places," she says, "other people, other kinds of plants . . . The world is very big, and full of mystery, don't you think?" They stay silent, so she continues. "I read about the Diengiei, and I was curious . . . It sounds like it is something very special that can be found only here . . ." It is also called by many names, isn't it? she adds. And there is confusion, isn't there, over what it might be?

The cousins converse again briefly between themselves.

"It is what the other ones said, too," Deng tells her.

"The other ones?"

"Yes, the bilati men who came before you."

Evie blinks. She is more than a little surprised.

"You thought you were the only one?"

Truthfully, she had. "When were they here?"

"Long time ago, before I was born," says Phyrnai—which Evie would not number at more than twenty years.

She itches to ask what happened to them, but feels it might not be the appropriate moment. What matters right now is her winning their trust, and she has a feeling that all these questions are a test.

"Why do you want to find it?"

This, too, she had expected, though she has a less straightforward answer. *A love of adventure!* She avoids using the word *scientist*, saying instead that it intrigued her. There is a notion, she tells them, that somewhere there could exist the original plant, the one from which all others arise. "Not that I think that is what the Diengiei is," she adds quickly, "but I have not read about anything else like it . . . And I wondered whether it was real, and why not many had seen it . . ."

Deng shakes her head. "What Phyrnai means is what will you do if you find it?"

"Oh, nothing."

There is a moment's silence, the boy has stopped pacing, even the birds seem to be quiet. Then the two young women laugh, loud and unrestrained. It reminds her of Kong Bathsheba.

"But I mean it," she insists.

Look around you, she is told. Do white people come to our lands to do nothing?

Evie has no answer.

They converse again in low tones, and she is certain they are speculating on how best to refuse her. When Deng finally addresses her it is to say that her cousin thinks it better that they part ways amicably. "I know you must be disappointed, I am sorry," she adds, and sounds it, too. They make to pack up and leave, and Evie stands there, holding the oranges, cold and numb. *This is it.* This is how her adventure ends. At the remembering stones with nothing to remember.

Ïada approaches them now, perhaps to bid his cousin goodbye. The Nongïaid drape their cloaks over their shoulders, tying them neatly under their chins; in a moment they will have melted back into the forest, and be gone, like leaves blown by the wind.

"Please," says Evie, suddenly, and they stop to look at her. "Please," she repeats, "though please is . . . is . . . perhaps nothing would be enough, really . . . but I ask that you consider, if only for a moment, how what might seem one morning's conversation is the smallest part of a long, long journey." She pauses helplessly. "A journey that has made little sense to anyone else, my friends, my family, and honestly, sometimes even to myself, but . . ." She takes a deep breath. "If there was a way . . . the tiniest chance even . . . that I could do this on my own, I would, because I've travelled so far, with much hope and little else . . ."

The others stay quiet—the boy is impatient, Deng gazes at the ground, while Phyrnai looks at her strangely, silently. Evie continues, confused, unsure what it is she wishes to say.

"My grandmother would tell us . . . be more in the world . . . and no one seemed to understand that . . . Not my sister, or my parents, maybe not even my friend Agnes . . . and it is hard to explain, but I think this is my way of trying to find out what she meant, not by being shut inside a classroom or a library, but being in this forest with you. I know this is an enormous favour to ask . . . and I wish . . ." She is mortified to feel the sharp, hot prick of tears. "I wish I had some way to convince you . . . but I don't . . . except to say, please, I would be grateful for your help."

The forest is quiet again, with no wind, no rustling leaves, but beyond its edges someone calls in the village, a dog barks. The world rolls on.

Phyrnai turns to Deng, her voice low and urgent. Evie does not believe she has been her convincing best—*what on earth was I saying?*—and she stands aside drooping, out of steam. They speak for what seems like ages; Ïada has lost interest and disappeared into the undergrowth. The sun is much higher now, although hardly stronger; it will be a cold overcast day.

"All right," says Deng. Evie nods, assuming she means it is time to head back to the boarding house, and turns to make her way out of the forest. "All right, they will take you," repeats Deng.

This does not register at first, and Evie stares at them in disbelief.

"We must walk, two or three days," says Phyrnai, her face calm, watchful, steadily holding her gaze. They will leave early tomorrow morning, before daybreak, for this is not a Nongïaid-friendly village, and they must swiftly move on.

Evie opens her mouth to request more time—How would she explain this to the Wheelers? To Mr. Finlay? How would she make preparations so quickly?—but she is relying on someone else's goodwill, and that being the case, there is little room for negotiation.

She decides simply to say yes, she will be ready.

✧ ✧ ✧

In her first few weeks at Newnham, Evie was expected, as a new girl, to return the calls she had received "at home" from the others at the college. Most faces faded into a blur, except for a Miss Philippa Bowen, whom she remembered in particular.

The girls Evie had visited so far had been busy at their needlework, writing letters, or reading. Miss Bowen was arranging rocks. Where others displayed pictures of family and pets in their rooms, she had rock samples spilling out of boxes onto her desk, some on the floor. All this overseen by Fergus, Sidgwick Hall's resident cat—a furry black creature with green eyes, seated on the windowsill in a patch of sunlight.

Miss Bowen had grown up in Lyme Regis, on the Dorset coast, she said, and spent most of her time tramping around on the beach. "Look what I found this summer." An unassuming peach-brown limestone slab, but when Evie turned it over she gasped. It was hollow, filled with . . . "Calcite crystals." Rosette-shaped, and radiating from a central boss, glinting in the light. "Isn't it a wonder?"

Evie nodded, hardly able to speak. She was shown other specimens—rocks with ripple marks formed by waves on shallow water, some with mud cracks the colour of silver, dreikanter rocks sandblasted by the wind.

"In your room is a million years' worth of time," said Evie.

"Yes, you are right." Miss Bowen looked around her. "And all the world, too . . . For who knows where these have formed, and where they have been washed away to and from."

The stones lay silent, but not quite—like plants they, too, revealed wordlessly.

Miss Bowen stepped up to the window. She stroked Fergus, who pushed his nose up against her palm. "Did you know," she began, "one of the rarest stones in the world is the grandidierite, found only in Madagascar . . . It is said that if you hold it up to the light, it is not one, not two, but three colours . . . I would love to see it, wouldn't you?"

Evie agreed.

"It is crazy, isn't it? For someone who has never left the south of England, and who may never leave this island, to long to travel to Madagascar . . ."

"Is it?" said Evie. "I would not wish . . . for this to be all the world I see."

Miss Bowen turned to her. "Then what must we do?"

In that instant, Fergus leaped gracefully out the window, and was gone.

They decided that this was exactly how one ought to set out on an adventure.

✧ ✧ ✧

When they leave, dawn has not yet broken, though the sky is lightening in the east. The mountains stand bare and dark, patiently waiting to be transformed into slopes of grassy yellow.

The previous night, Deng gave her a cloak, similar to the ones worn by her cousins. "It is a jaiñ kup, you will need it," she said. Evie already possessed a travelling paletot, but she takes it along, not wishing to hurt Deng's feelings. Apart from this, she carries very little—a change of clothes, her sketchbook, her plant press, and for some reason, the last letters she had received from her mother, Agnes, and Florence.

They are joined by Phyrnai and Ïada at the edge of the village, and their party walks in silence. The cricket chorus has ceased, and cockerels crow across the valley as the sun rises. Evie has bid the Wheelers farewell—I wish to go on a trip, she told them, trying to sound casual. She did not think they would attempt to dissuade her from the plan—but it was sudden and unexpected and she was not sure how they would react. She would be gone for a few days, she went on to explain, accompanied by Deng, who was taking her to see her uncle's village. This last was a fabrication, but Deng and her cousin had supplied her with very little to go on. It gives her a chance to see the area more extensively, she added for good measure, before they return to Shillong, and for her, eventually to Calcutta.

Mr. Wheeler turned to his wife—"Well, what do you think?"—and she looked at Evie a moment, and said, "I think no matter what I say Evie will go anyway."

Evie made no attempt to deny this.

"I'm happy about one thing," said Mrs. Wheeler,

"Which is?"

"That you are not turning into a pukka memsahib."

Evie is thinking of this, smiling to herself, when Phyrnai calls out in warning. They are walking on a road with a sharp drop to the right, and a small landslide has narrowed their path to a precarious ribbon. They clamber over mud and stone but make it through safely.

The valley is flooded with light now, and the sheer cliff face shines warm and gold. Phyrnai points to something. "Do you see those rocks?" Halfway up the cliff three boulders jut out, balancing miraculously one on top of another.

"Yes," says Evie.

"They say when those fall Sohra will vanish."

Sohra, she has learned, is what the locals call Cherrapunjee. Why do bilati people keep naming places that already have names? Deng had asked her.

"And how will they fall?" she asks.

The cousins glance at each other. "We do not know . . . Maybe when an earthquake will come again, like the one that opened the ground to the centre of the earth." Mr. Wheeler had told her about it, the Assam earthquake of 1897, whose ructions were felt in distant Calcutta, and which made the Brahmaputra rise more than seven feet. "Every fifty years, it comes," adds Deng matter-of-factly, as they begin to descend.

They will be walking a path that trails through the valley. Insects chirp, and there is birdsong in the air; around them the leaves catch the sunlight and shimmer. It is difficult to imagine this as a site of terrifying destruction.

Just before mid morning they stop to rest—like birds, the siblings eat oranges and nuts, while Evie and Deng slather slices of bread with jam. *Mr. Finlay was right*, thinks Evie, *jam will turn out to be the most useful item they have carried.*

They walk through the afternoon with the sun high above them, shortening their shadows and those of the trees to stubs.

The undergrowth here is more lush than on the barren hilltops, and early rhododendron flowers punctuate the view with sudden scarlet and white. They fall naturally into a travelling order: the boy skips nimbly first, followed by Phyrnai, and Evie finds herself usually beside or in front of Deng. She wishes the girl ahead would pay her more attention, but she seems to have undertaken the expedition as a duty to be fulfilled rather than a generous favour. She shows no interest in her, with no questions except the ones asked yesterday in the sacred grove. Evie has many, but restrains herself, as she suspects they will not be welcome.

Whether it is deliberate or not, they pass no villages on the way. Perhaps the Nongïaid feel this is safer. Evie also wonders whether there are wild animals about. Had she not heard Mr. Wheeler speak of Himalayan black bears and clouded leopards? It might be wiser to not inquire. What she does ask is where they will be spending the night, and she is told, "You'll see."

By early evening, she is weary, her feet are beginning to ache, and she is relieved when Phyrnai signals for them to stop. It is not a special spot in any way, though there is a stream close by, and the ground seems comfortably level and dry.

Phyrnai and Ïada set about busily gathering wood, while Deng collects water. Evie sits on a small tree stump—*How can she help?* She is not even sure how to make such an offer. Out in the wild, is she still a guest? Are they not the ones doing her a favour . . . ?

She is thinking this through, when a cry—of someone in pain—rises from the direction of the stream. *Deng!* Evie rushes over. Deng lies fallen at the edge of the shallow water, clutching her leg. She must have slipped; even before Evie gets up close, she can see the swollen ankle, already turning an ugly purple.

"Deng," she calls, and just then the cousins also arrive.

Evie stands aside, for they seem to know exactly what to do. Ïada disappears into the undergrowth, reappearing in a few minutes with what looks like a sheaf of leaves. Thynriat, they call it, as they crush the leaves quickly, and pat the paste onto her ankle. Over this, Phyrnai gently ties strips of cloth torn from Deng's jaiñkyrshah. Deng looks pale but manages to totter to her feet. It is clear, though, that she will not be able to walk any great distance.

"I am sorry, memsahib," she says, almost in tears, and Evie says she must not be, that they must hurry back so she can see a doctor.

"Oh, I don't know . . ." she begins.

"Deng, we must have that ankle attended to . . ."

The cousins converse, though Phyrnai seems to be the one taking charge, talking briskly, firmly. Finally, Deng nods, and looks up at Evie. "You will carry on." Evie makes to protest, *this is absurd*, but Deng continues. "We are close to a family friend's village. Phyrnai will take me there, and they will look after me. You may wait here with Ïada, and tomorrow you can continue."

Evie does not know what to make of this, she is flustered and stung by worry, but also secretly, guiltily relieved—"Why don't I come along?" she offers, but she is told that it will be quicker if their luggage is left behind, guarded by her and the boy.

"We must go before it gets dark," says Phyrnai.

Evie says a brief goodbye, *please take care*, and they are off, descending into the valley. Ïada shoots her a glance, looks as if he does not want to hang around, and bounds off into the forest.

Wonderful, thinks Evie. *Now I sit and wait for a leopard to show up.*

There is no leopard, and not a soul either as dusk gathers and the crickets set up their persistent grinding. A forest is a very dark place, Evie realizes. It also feels like hours and hours have passed, but Ïada has not returned and neither has Phyrnai. What if this was all a ploy to be rid of her?

Alone in the shadows, this seems a distinct possibility.

One word though forms itself in her mind through the cold and disquiet. *Fire.* Why has she not yet lit a fire? Probably because she does not know how. She picks up the wood the siblings had gathered, collects some dry grass and leaves, and sets up a small bonfire as best she can. She is certain there will be matches in one of the bags, and fishes around for them. *Don't waste any*, she chides herself as she strikes one and then another, and nothing catches. Carefully, with the next match she lights the tinder in several places; it begins to smoulder. Gently she blows, and a flame flickers and she has never been happier—*As though it is the first fire, what a wonder this sight!*

In the half hour it has taken her to get this going, night has fallen, and she is hungry. Should she call for the boy? Why hasn't he returned? She eats more bread, but worries about how little is left. Don't be absurd, she tells herself, if nothing else, she can find a village tomorrow, buy some rice and eggs. But tonight, well, she would have to survive. She bunches the bags together and lies down. What must the Wheelers be doing? And Mr. Finlay? She flushes at the thought of him.

The night before, she had met him again after dinner, outside, smoking.

"Evie . . ." he said as she approached, "I have been waiting . . ." *Hours, days, all his life!*

"I have some news," she began. "About the plant I've been looking for."

He blew out smoke, and nodded.

"I met Deng's . . . friends . . . who said they will take me, and show me." She expected him to ask many questions—Who are these friends? Are they trustworthy? Will she be safe? How long will she be gone? And really, would she just tell him now about this plant?

Instead, he grinned widely. "This is superb news."

"It is?"

He looked at her inquiringly.

"I mean, yes, of course, it is . . . I have been wondering about it for so long, and I planned all of this . . . to be here, somehow . . . and now . . ."

"And now?"

She stayed silent, unwilling to admit it.

"And now you are getting what's called plant-hunter's feet."

She couldn't help laughing. "What?"

"The itch to travel, along with trepidation over what is to come . . ."

She nodded.

He dropped his cigarette and stubbed it out with his foot.

"When are you leaving?"

"Tomorrow."

This time, he laughed. "You don't waste a moment, do you, Evie? Good on you . . ." Every day, he continued, you wake up and the world lies before you, waiting to be explored, but tomorrow—and this is the best part—that's exactly what you are going to do. He smiled at her, in the dark she could see his eyes shining. "Evie, there's nothing like the call of adventure." She was about to say that this was true, when he added, "But I ask only one promise of you . . ."

She held her breath. "What?"

"That when you are back, and you have found it, we will celebrate, and you will tell me all about it."

In a flush of joy, and gratitude, she stepped up and kissed him, right then and there. For a moment he was taken aback, but his mouth softened against hers quickly, and their kisses grew deeper, more urgent. When they parted, they were breathless.

"Evie," he whispered, "come back soon."

Now, on her own by a feeble fire, she is not so sure why she left in the first place. *Come on* . . . she tells herself again. *You are finally on your way!* It is not long, though, before tiredness overcomes her, and despite everything, she dozes off.

When she opens her eyes, she sees two figures sitting across from her. The siblings have returned, and she almost cries out in relief. She sits up, and Phyrnai nods to her; she is stirring a pot over the fire, which is now well tended and ablaze.

"How is Deng?" asks Evie.

"She will be well."

Phyrnai hands Evie a small wooden bowl, holding soup, or a clear stew, with ginger and pungent mustard leaves. *Delicious.* Nothing has ever tasted as wholesome in her life. They eat in silence, quick and hungry.

"I learned your language from Deng, you know," says Phyrnai suddenly. "She taught me. My father, he is the rangbah, our people's elder, he will be angry if he knows this, but I think we need to learn English . . ."

"Why?" asks Evie quietly.

"Because we do not know what will happen now the bilati are here."

Evie is silent a while before saying, "Thank you for telling me."

"I am telling you only because you did not ask."

After eating, Ïada lays his jaiñ kup on the ground and pulls it over himself—it serves both as mattress and blanket. Evie understands why Deng, *poor Deng*, had insisted she take one along. Soon the boy emits little snores. Phyrnai stares into the fire, looking thoughtful, staying quiet.

Evie sighs. A lonely journey lies ahead.

✧ ✧ ✧

When she wakes, it is long into daylight, and around her the remains of last night's meal and camp are gone, except for a mound of soft ash where the fire had burned. Phyrnai and Ïada have been patiently waiting.

She is mortified, and apologizes profusely, then hurries to wash at the stream. Her muscles ache, much like the day after her trip to the root bridges, but she readies herself, uncomplaining, and they set off and make steady progress. They are climbing today, up an open and unforested trail, edged by long grass arching in the breeze. It is all quite uneventful until Evie slips while crossing a stream. Her feet are soaked, as are the edges of her dress.

"Are you all right?" asks Phyrnai.

"Yes, I'm fine, thank you." And that is as far as the conversation goes. Fortunately, the sun is strong in the sky and dries her off quickly.

On the way, the landscape varies little, though sometimes they are on higher ground from where the views of the valleys are breathtaking. When she pauses to admire the sight, the other two also stop and wait.

"It is so beautiful," she cannot help saying out loud once, and she thinks she sees Phyrnai break into a smile.

That evening, they stop for the night in a cave, or rather a hollow in a hillside that is shielded by thick undergrowth. This time, Evie helps gather wood and dry leaves; she walks to a stream—quite a distance away—to collect water. She waits hungrily as the stew warms, bolstered with mushrooms foraged along the way. From somewhere, Ïada has managed to find eggs, so those are thrown in, too. It is a feast. She helps with the clearing away; the cleaning will be done in the morning. Then she spreads her jaiñ kup on the floor and gathers it around her just as she saw the boy do, and falls fast asleep.

At some point, she wakes. It is still dark. It is silent. *What woke her?* She has no idea, except something in the air feels tense and alert. Ïada is sleeping, but when she sits up, she sees Phyrnai crouching, watching at the mouth of the hollow. She rises and moves towards her as quietly as she can. For a long while, they are both silent until Phyrnai says, "Someone is here."

"I—how do you know?"

Phyrnai does not reply. She inches forward, then stops. Evie can hear it too now, footsteps, a definite rustling of leaves and undergrowth. It paces once, twice, and then fades.

"Is it an animal?" Evie whispers. Phyrnai shakes her head. This time Evie does not question how she knows.

"Someone is following us," she says.

"But . . . why?"

Even in the dark, the girl's eyes glitter as she looks at Evie. "You tell me."

The implication of this dawns on her at once. "No one else knows," she promises. "I have not told anyone about the Diengiei."

"Is that true?"

Evie swears solemnly that it is.

Phyrnai nods. "I will make sure we lose them tomorrow."

They remain at the entrance listening, but the footsteps do not return. The crickets wail wildly, and a light wind brushes through the trees, scattering the view of the half-moon hanging overhead, but all is otherwise silent.

Evie moves back to her corner of the cave. Ïada, even if he hasn't been sleeping through it all, has not budged. She wraps herself in the jaiñ kup; the ground is hard and she is wide awake. She senses it might be the same with Phyrnai. Many questions crowd her head, but the one she falls asleep to is *Who did those footsteps belong to?*

✧ ✧ ✧

The next day Evie and her companions trudge along the river winding through the valley.

"Do you think we are still being followed?" she asks.

"No. I made sure of it," Phyrnai tells her firmly, and she feels a little reassured.

It is a crisp, fresh morning, and this also helps banish from her thoughts the strange events of the previous night. Ïada is also a happy distraction, bounding up and down the boulders like a squirrel, showing off, making them laugh. "He's a dear!" exclaims Evie, and Phyrnai beams. After this, she begins to walk alongside her, and Evie hopes this means she is more amenable to conversation.

When they stop to examine some alarmingly fresh leopard tracks on the muddy path, she asks, "Are the Nongïaid afraid of wild animals?"

"Not the ones inside the forest." Walking along, she continues, "Maybe you do not know this but the wild is kind."

It is not what Evie expects to hear. "Why do you say that?"

"Because it takes only what it needs."

Later, as they pause a moment to watch the river flow past, she inquires why it is that they move from place to place.

Phyrnai frowns slightly, as though it ought to be obvious. "There is somewhere for every season. The Bhoi plains in winter, the forests around Shillong Peak in summer, the hills around Mawkyrwat at harvest times. And during the rains," she shrugs, "there is nowhere to hide."

"Have you always been moving?"

At this, Phyrnai looks at her bewildered. "Haven't we all always been moving? Until someone decided staying in one place was better . . ." They tramp on in silence; the track is slippery from the mud. "People are made to move," she continues. "Even when they stay in one place, look how they grow their food . . . A few years here, then there . . . They clear the land with fire, then move on, allowing the land to rest."

Evie hesitates, saying she has heard this is destructive.

"To let the land rest? And fire . . . it also brings out new growth." She points to the trees and shrubs around them. "We do what everyone has always done, move with the seasons of the earth. Some have stopped. I do not understand why." She looks at Evie. "To be still is to be without life."

For lunch, they feast on a jungle fowl that Ïada has hunted.

Like Kong Bathsheba, they set aside a small portion of their meal. "For Ka Mei Ramew," remarks Evie, and the siblings look at her in surprise.

The bird is succulent and filling, and they rest a while after their meal beneath an overhanging hibiscus shrub, enjoying the cool, quiet afternoon. They pluck at the flowers, showing Evie how to suck on them for nectar. Tired from all his scampering, Ïada falls lightly asleep, clutching his bow to his chest.

"Does he carry this with him all the time?" asks Evie.

"On the day of his naming ceremony, a Khasi boy is given three arrows . . . to protect himself, to protect his clan, and to protect his kingdom. My brother is very serious about his duty," she says with a smile.

As they pack up to leave, putting away the bowls and cooking utensils, Evie asks where the rest of their belongings are—have they left them behind with the other Nongïaid? Phyrnai tells her that this is all they have, that they own only as much as they can carry.

This afternoon, the light is particularly golden, and falls flickering through the trees. *I am here*, thinks Evie in a rush of happiness, remembering the morning when the *Maloja* docked in Bombay. *I am here*—with the bush warblers swooping in the sky, with the water rushing in the distance, with the wind in the trees.

Before evening falls, they stop at a ledge that they have spent an hour climbing to. "Is this where we are spending the night?" asks Evie warily; it is precarious, the ground dropping sharply away on almost all sides.

"No, here we watch the sunset."

And so that is what they do. The outline of the mountains has softened in the fading light, and the sky has turned a silvery orange. Evie thinks she might bring out her sketchbook, but something about the way the brother and sister sit, gazing at the horizon, makes her decide against it. It is enough to carry this moment as a memory.

In the glow of the fire that night, Evie writes up her notes.

Phyrnai watches her for a while, before saying, "You know, there is an old story we tell about a book . . ."

"Oh?" says Evie. "I thought . . ." *The people of these hills had no script.*

Phyrnai looks at her inquiringly.

"Please," she says hastily, "I would love to hear it."

The story is about a Khasi, a foreigner, and a book of wisdom . . . she begins. From the other side of the fire, Ïada interrupts; it sounds like he is teasing his sister. Phyrnai ignores him. "He says I am a bad storyteller."

"Oh, I'm sure that's not true."

She grins. "You will find out."

A long, long time ago, when the world was young, a Khasi and a foreigner were summoned by God . . . U Blei . . . to a mountain, the name of which is now lost. They did as they were told and travelled there, and stayed for three days and three nights, and in this time U Blei set down the laws of life in two books and gave them one each. Phyrnai deepens her voice. "Now return to your people," U Blei tells them. Ïada dissolves into giggles. His sister glares at him but continues. "On their way back, a river they had crossed earlier had risen and become very deep because of the rain. They had no choice, they would have to swim, but they did not have anything with which to protect their books. Do you know what the foreigner did?"

"What?" echoes Evie.

"With his long hair he tied the book on top of his head and he swam across. The Khasi, who had short hair, put the book in his mouth. Like this . . ." She mimics biting something between her teeth. "But the river was very strong . . . and he was so afraid he might drown that he swallowed the book in fright. He returned to his people empty-handed but he said that he would teach them everything . . . whatever he could remember. So they called a great durbar of all the Khasis, and with his help they decided on . . . how do you say . . . the guidelines . . . the rules on how to lead a good life. Since that day, Khasis have passed traditions down like this . . ."

"Through the spoken word?" finishes Evie.

Phyrnai nods. "We call it ka ktien. Wisdom from our ancestors who attended the great durbar after the sacred book was lost."

"But without books, how do you remember?"

Phyrnai glances at the journal. "This is not the only way. You think if it is not in a book, it is light, that it can be lost in the wind, but to not have books means . . ." She struggles to find the words. "It means we remember more carefully." From the ground, she picks up a pebble, sharp and glistening. "Our word for memory is kynmaw," she adds. "To carry like a stone. You see? For us memory is a stone we carry. We do not take remembering lightly . . ."

For a long moment, Evie is silent. She thinks she somewhat understands but she is also unable to grasp this completely. Questions whirl about in her head. She supposes it is possible to pass on values and a moral code through the spoken word, but what about something more complex . . . like the law? In her father's office, she remembers reams and reams of papers, constantly referred to, filed away, signed, sealed, exchanged, notarized.

"I mean," she persists, "things like contracts . . . are they not required to be written?"

"We give someone our word, we keep it. It is a matter of honour," says Phyrnai simply.

"But if you break a written contract, you can be held accountable in court, you can be punished, and justice can be served . . . What happens if one breaks the spoken word?"

Phyrnai shrugs. "You must live with yourself."

Around them the forest has been robbed of all distinction by the night—the trees are only shadow. Ïada has fallen asleep. The fire is burning low.

"Also," adds Phyrnai, lowering her voice, "we have mantras."

"Mantras?"

She nods. "To make people pale and sick, and some to give them bad dreams."

What does she mean? wonders Evie. *Magic spells?*

Phyrnai chuckles. "My favourite is one that makes a mula stick to your backside when you stand up." Evie laughs along with her, agreeing that it is indeed an excellent curse.

When all is dark and silent, and the fire has died down almost completely, Phyrnai speaks up again. "You know why my brother says I am not a good storyteller? Because for us, telling a story is like leading someone through a forest . . . It is richer the more time you spend in there, the more you walk around and stop to look at the trees and the flowers and the leaves. He says I walk too straight through my story." She grins. "Too quick. That I am too much in a hurry."

✧ ✧ ✧

On the last day of their journey, Evie and the siblings walk through the outskirts of some small villages. Children run behind them squealing "memsahib, memsahib," men throw curious glances their way, while the women keep their eyes to the ground, the baskets on their backs laden with winter vegetables, bound for the market.

"Do you not buy anything with money?" asks Evie.

Phyrnai shakes her head. "If we take something, we leave something in return. Sometimes people do not find what we leave behind, and they call us thieves." They walk in silence for a while before she adds, "I cannot say we have never stolen. Sometimes the winters are very long, and oranges are good but they are not meat, but we try to take only as much as we need, never any more."

By early afternoon they reach the edge of a forest, and the path before them lies hidden in the undergrowth. The grove is thick, and they must walk carefully in single file. Every so often, Phyrnai breaks off a branch to mark their path, possibly so it will be easier for them to find their way back.

When they stop for a short rest, by a stream running shallow and clear, Evie asks a question she has long wished to. "What should I expect? You know, when I see the Diengiei . . . Is it a tree or something else?"

Phyrnai cups some water in her hands and splashes her face. "Do you know the story about the Diengiei?"

No, she admits she doesn't.

"There are many stories about it, actually. Some say it is the tree that U Blei planted to punish man and his infinite greed, that it grew and grew and covered the sky until the sun couldn't shine through. Others believe it was a golden tree, like a ladder, linking earth to sky, man to God and the whole universe, but that again, as punishment for man's evil ways, it was cut down and the link was broken, but that because the Diengiei was planted by U Blei, it survived, and was saved . . . by my ancestors."

"Oh," says Evie, drawing breath.

"That we, the lowly but swift of foot, protected the Diengiei from those who wished to find it and use it for their own advantage. But we ourselves do not know exactly how it came to be this way . . ."

"But that is what you continue to do? To protect it?"

She nods.

Evie presses on. "Why is it called the tree that holds all trees?"

Phyrnai looks over at her. "Because it does."

When they resume walking, the sun has shifted, and the trees seem to crowd closer around them. A hornbill perches high above, watching, and Evie feels as though there are many invisible eyes on her. She grows increasingly uneasy; all she can hear is the thud of her own heart. Everything seems constricted—to this path, this moment. She shudders, hoping it will not be long before they get there.

Overhead, grey clouds have gathered in thick, voluminous company.

"It looks like rain," she remarks.

"It will not rain," says Phyrnai, "but it will get cold."

This is true. As they set out deeper into the forest, the temperature falls, and despite the distinct warmth of spring in the air lately, the afternoon carries a deep chill. They pass tall evergreens and Khasi pines, and here and there, orchids droop from branches. Evie would normally be tempted to stop, but not now, even though she does pause a moment beneath a blue vanda that is glowing in the light. When they rest again, she hears a sudden sharp crack, a twig breaking, like a gunshot in the quiet.

"What's that?"

"What's what?" asks Phyrnai. Then she says, come on, they must be off.

Where are they leading me? For a brief moment she wonders if this is some sort of terrifying trap. But to what end? She is not worth any sort of ransom. She has nothing of any value on her person. She begins to wish, though, that Deng were with her, or Mr. Finlay; that she were not with strangers.

Soon they begin to climb a gradual slope. Evie barely registers it all—the fallen tree balanced oddly against its neighbour, the frenzy of ferns beneath her feet.

"Is it here? Are we close?" she asks.

Phyrnai glances ahead. "Almost."

At the top, they come to a clearing with a stone altar, similar to the one at the sacred grove in Saitsohpen village; this one is damp and heavily mossed over.

It has been a while since the last sacrifice.

"Look," says Phyrnai, pointing. Evie glances up. There, on the branch of a towering pine, grows a cascading symphony of a plant. A glorious orchid in pristine, immaculate white.

"What is it?" she whispers.

"What you seek."

Phyrnai and Ïada are watching her; she can feel the press of their gaze as she takes in the sight. She wants to say it is beautiful, but the words fail in her chest and on her tongue.

She steps closer, and the orchid seems to shimmer, its leaves rich and dark and abundant. It is unlike anything she has seen before, and surely the world hasn't either. A cloud orchid, but more resplendent, with white flowers growing all along the stems, in hundreds and thousands of blossoms, bursting, glowing forth.

Just then, a sudden stamp of footsteps rises behind her, and at first she thinks it is her companions, but they move always noiselessly. It is some other person, or perhaps there are more than one. She hears an unexpectedly familiar voice—Bah Khrawbor, speaking in Khasi to the siblings. They remain mute, watching him, standing rooted to the spot. Ïada is a little way behind his sister, his hand tightly on his bow. Then someone else follows the guide—Mr. Dossett, whom Evie somehow is not too surprised to see.

"Good afternoon, Miss Alexander," he says. "Just look what you have led us to."

The siblings stare, and something in her snaps to realization. "I did not know," she tells them. "I did not know they were following us."

Phyrnai gazes back in disbelief.

"You must believe me." They think she works with him, with the fixer, that she has led him here intentionally. Panic flutters in her chest, but what can she say that would make a difference now? "Why are you following me?" she asks, trying to keep her voice steady.

Mr. Dossett cocks his head. "Why not? I have always wondered what mischief you were up to. When Mrs. Wheeler told us you would be leaving, I thought . . . hmmm, I'd like to see where she is headed. Mr. Finlay thought it a good idea, too."

"You're lying," she spits at him.

He smiles. "I am. He has no clue. Mooning about, awaiting your return."

His gaze rises to the orchid, his eyes gleam, the corners of his mouth turn up in delight. "This is even more priceless than I had imagined."

The next thing Evie knows, he is giving instructions—while he uproots this specimen, Bah Khrawbor is to destroy all the others of the same species that he comes across around here. "We cannot have anyone else finding this," he adds briskly.

"No," Evie blurts out, "you can't do that!"

"Pardon me, miss, I don't know about you, but this is what we came for." He steps up, holding a small, sharp knife in his hand. "If you like, we can name it after you."

In her anger, she splutters. "The people here . . . they hold this sacred . . . you can't be so ignorant!"

He laughs. Evie's blood is in her ears, the world is roaring. She is enraged, but more distressed now by what he is about to do. *Will no one help?* She looks around wildly; Bah Khrawbor is hacking away at anything that is growing before him. The siblings have moved farther away, almost disappearing into the trees.

Mr. Dossett lifts his hand. The knife glints, catching the light.

Evie does not know what it is that throws her forward. "No," she shouts, pushing him aside. "Stop it," he says in irritation. "Move away." But Evie does not listen. She lunges at him again, but this time he swipes at her with the knife, she dodges, holding out her hands, and the blade slices cleanly across her palm. The pain is astonishingly sharp, but it does not stop her from pummelling him with her fists, blood splattering onto his coat and his shirt. He recovers just enough to lift the knife again—

she can see his face, contorted in anger, the blade drawing closer—*He will kill me*—but before he can take another swipe, someone has grasped her shoulders, saying curtly, "Come," and Mr. Dossett, with a yelp, drops the knife to the ground—an arrow has wounded his arm.

He screams, his eyes bulging. "You bitch . . ."

He reaches for her but she is tugged away, and suddenly she is fleeing through the undergrowth with Phyrnai and Ïada on either side. Branches slap her shoulders, twigs snap beneath her feet, and above them, the rustle of startled wings. It seems they will run forever, and in the gathering dark there is no sense of direction. All the world is a forest.

Eventually, they start slowing; Evie is finding it difficult to keep up. Sharp stabs run down the length of her arm, up her shoulder, in her head, and there is blood on her dress, her sleeve, down to her elbow, and flowing still, gushing from the wound.

They stop at a small clearing with a silver pool.

Her companions scoop up water for her, and she drinks gratefully. Ïada disappears and returns in a few minutes with a handful of leaves—tobacco, she thinks, and wild garlic—but first, says Phyrnai, they need to stem the blood. She grasps Evie's hand in both of hers, presses a leaf over the wound, and speaks a string of words into it, over and over.

"I cannot do what my grandfather does with this mantra," she says apologetically, "he is an experienced healer, but it should help for now."

They wash and bind her hand with the leaves, and a strip of cloth that Evie tears from her dress. In her hurry, she has left her bag of belongings behind.

"Do not worry," says Phyrnai, "now you can travel lightly."

Evie gazes down at her hand. It looks like someone else's—alien to her in its raw, swollen redness. It throbs painfully, but the greater hurt lies elsewhere.

"I didn't know they were following . . ."

"We believe you," says Phyrnai. In this light, it is hard to make out the look on her face, but Evie thinks she glimpses some softness.

"I am sorry about the Diengiei . . ."

The siblings glance at each other.

"That was not the Diengiei."

Evie looks up in disbelief. "What do you mean?" she manages to stutter.

Phyrnai sits beside her. "There are a few things we need to explain . . ."

✧ ✧ ✧

Every evening, Agnes stepped out to water her garden.

"It is so tiny," Evie would tease. "One day, I wish for you a garden the size of Kew."

Agnes, as practical as ever, would then remind her that she would need to employ a hundred gardeners and be as wealthy as the king. Later, after a quick supper, and coffee with Edward, they would set up for an evening of work. Miss Sargant had been unwell lately, and had asked Agnes to continue some of the experiments she had been conducting on monocotyledons. Evie's favourite time, though, was when they sat at the kitchen table, drawing. Agnes had a skilled hand—her father was an artist, after all—while Evie fumbled along, always the one to attempt conversation and ask questions.

One evening, she glanced up, at a sparganium plant standing in a bucket between them, while Agnes was absorbed in capturing a tangled root.

"Why do we do what we do?" she asked.

Usually, Agnes would not stop, offering a reply while continuing to work, but this time she looked up.

"Why do we do what we do?" she repeated.

"Yes," said Evie.

"Well, I do what I do because I am trying to find, not the right answers, but the right questions. It is much harder, I think, because we must look beyond our so-called area of specialization, and try to draw from the history of simply everything that might be involved in framing the question. To ask the right question is to look beyond the borders of botany and philosophy and art and mysticism. Suddenly, they all matter, because they always have."

Evie was silent, absorbing all of this.

"And you?" asked Agnes, smiling.

"I can't say anything half as articulate," she protested, but Agnes would have none of it.

So she stayed quiet for a while, and then began. On her visits to see

Grandma Grace, as a child, they would collect leaves to press between the pages of a book—a palmate chestnut, an egg-shaped alder with serrated edges, a sharper, more pointed silver birch, and her favourite, a deep-lobed hawthorn with its distinct teeth on the tip. Grandma Grace once told her that these trees were under the protection of fairies, and if the tree was cut down, they might seek revenge.

"And they did," said Evie. "When Grandma's neighbour cut down his hawthorn to build a conservatory, he died in his sleep. At least that's what she told me. But . . . that is not the point of the story." Evie picked up a book from the table. "I guess what I am trying to say is, where does knowledge really lie? In the book? In the leaves? For Grandma Grace, it was always the living over the dead, the organic over the inanimate. For me . . . well . . ." She looked up at her friend. "I am still trying to find out."

✧ ✧ ✧

At first the siblings say they will explain everything to her tomorrow. She is wounded, and exhausted, and she must rest. In the morning, she will feel better, they will reapply the herbal paste and bind it with a new strip of cloth. "For now," says Phyrnai, "you sleep." Only when Evie insists, no, please, no, do they light a small fire, and set her down close to it, handing her a cup of warm water with crushed turmeric and honey.

"How are you feeling?" asks Phyrnai.

Far from well. "Better, yes."

They watch her as though at any moment she might swoon.

"I'm all right," she says. "Please tell me . . . what you said you needed to explain."

Phyrnai glances at her brother. "You know, when we met first, we told you we could not help you, but this was not true . . ."

"What do you mean?"

"We cannot say no to anyone who wishes to see the Diengiei. The Nongïaid are its keepers, but we are . . . we are also bound by this agreement . . ."

"But why?"

Phyrnai hesitates. "Because it does not belong to us. It does not belong to anyone. We are only its caretakers."

Evie blinks. "So you must agree to everyone who asks?"

"There are not many . . . But still, because we cannot say no, our people have made up some . . . tests. If anyone asks us to take them to the Diengiei, we say first we will not, to see how they react . . . If they insist, we show them something like what we showed you, a beautiful orchid."

Evie's heart is once again racing. "And what do you test?"

Phyrnai looks down, unable to meet her eye. "What the person wants to do, what their intentions are, why they want to find it. Many fail at this point. Usually, they see the orchid, and like that man today, they want to take it . . ."

"And those who do not?"

She pauses. "Very few do not, but they will be taken to the Diengiei . . ."

Evie shakes her head. "I don't understand. Even if there are very few, as you say, surely word about the Diengiei would spread? When they return after having seen it . . . it doesn't make sense . . ."

"There is something else." Phyrnai looks at her, her eyes soft and sorrowful.

"Which is?"

"They must join the Nongïaid."

The forest by then is filled with night, and night life. The steady chorus of the crickets, the swoop of invisible wings, the rustle of something small and secret.

"I'm sorry . . . what?"

Phyrnai repeats herself. Evie's breath feels short, her head takes a little spin, and then she wants to laugh, like Kong Bathsheba, like the cousins at the remembering stones, loud and incredulous. *I hear such strange things.*

Phyrnai is undeterred, and goes on to explain: "They can say no, and we take them home safely, but if they wish to know the secrets of the Diengiei . . . this is what they must do."

Evie has no words. In her head hums a light blankness.

She finally manages to say, "It can't be true."

Phyrnai places a hand on her arm. "It is. You must decide." She stands up, and adds gently, "I am sorry, it cannot be any other way."

Evie shakes her head, it is impossible to believe. "No . . . but they can leave, can't they? I mean, what are these rules?" She suddenly feels enraged. "How are they binding? Are they written somewhere? Who decides? How can this be?"

Phyrnai looks at her a little sadly now. "I have told you. We give people our word, and they give us theirs. It is enough. They become keepers, too. It is no small thing. To hold knowledge is to hold responsibility, and to know truly is to know deeply, to give of yourself so that the knowing means something more than mere words. True knowing changes you; we believe you cannot go back to how you were in the world before. It has always been this way . . ."

There is a long silence. A bat swoops low overhead. Something in the fire hisses.

"But what happens . . ." begins Evie. *What happens to those who leave?*

She cannot bring herself to say this out loud; she is missing something—about a community to whom, over the centuries, everything binding lay in the spoken. What had Phyrnai called it? Ka ktien.

Eventually, she asks, "When you say join the Nongïaid, what do you mean?"

"It is as it sounds," says Phyrnai quietly. "They learn our language, they move around as we do. You become one of us. You do not have to. You have a choice. But you must decide." And with that, she joins Ïada on the other side of the bonfire, and spreads out her jaiñ kup for the night.

Evie lies here now looking up at the dark outlines of the forest, the sky that shimmers between cloud and branch and leaf, still finding it all hard to believe. *It is a dream, it is a dream.* Dare she scoff at the whole thing? Was it an elaborate ruse? But Phyrnai has been so clear, so definite—it would make little sense for her to be untruthful. And why would she? It does not feel like she or her brother mean Evie any harm. They have tended to her wound, and looked after her, and been nothing but kind.

And so . . . what if it were true? Evie allows the thought to linger, to sink in, to settle.

Above her, an owl hoots. From the undergrowth comes a quick rustle. But she is lost in thought and these noises do not distract her. Almost from nowhere, something comes to her—how in Goethe's last moments, when he was eighty-four, he turned to the window, saying, "More light, more light." Lulu and the others were convinced he was talking about the curtains, but Evie thought to herself that he was not. That he wanted his journey to go on and on, to be learning after learning, taking him towards one illumination and then another. *Is this also what she desires?*

As the night deepens her mind drifts. She is tired, *so tired*, but sleep will not come. How did this day begin? This journey? She cannot recall. Everything before this moment in the forest is a haze. Everything before is here. Is this the journey's beginning or the journey's end? *Always both*, she thinks, *and always neither.*

She turns onto her side; the fire is little more than a pile of glowing embers. It is so dark now that she cannot see her companions. She might be the only one in the forest. She, and the gods who are out to play, and the ones she imagines with her.

Her mother and father, with their quiet ways; Florence, and her new life; Agnes, steadfast and steady.

And Mr. Finlay, dear Mr. Finlay, his fingers on her palm. *You will travel the world.*

She will not fall asleep. This night will last and last, so she must never need to decide, to go, to stay. Dawn will not break over the mountains and pour into the sky, the roosters will stay quiet, the crickets unwavering, the sun will not shine.

And then it will.

The day will brighten, and the hour will come when she must rise, and tread upon the earth, and make her way through the forest.

SHAI

Fuck!"

"Guess you weren't expecting us?" Dajied asks, jokingly I think at first, but then I realize not. "Kima told me where you were," he adds, "and I tried to reach you. But I guess my texts didn't go through."

"Network," I mumble vaguely.

The young woman next to him narrows her eyes. "Have we met?"

"Yes, briefly."

"Was it at . . ."

"The Ever-Living Museum."

"Raphael's house . . . ?"

She doesn't remember.

"At the museum," I repeat, feeling foolish.

"Are you sure? I thought at Raff's place . . ." She waves her hand airily. "No matter. I'm Daphisha." She flashes me a wide, disarming smile. "Nice to meet you."

I nod. "And you, too."

Dajied is here on assignment—UCIL's contentious offer to build a road, connecting these villages to Wahkaji and Nongstoiñ and Shillong, regardless of being allowed to mine or not, has created a stir of interest in the decade-old uranium story. Magazines, newspapers, in Delhi and elsewhere, along with a foreign anti-nuclear organization, have commissioned him to take photographs, video clips, interviews—to capture anything of significance.

He tells me this now, but doesn't mention why Daphisha is accompanying him, and I don't ask. What I notice is the casual intimacy with which he calls her Daphi. They're here looking for Bah Albert; Dajied's contact at Wahkaji has fixed them up with him for accommodation. It makes sense: Bah Albert is possibly the only person in the village with an extra room.

They have come here together. The thought drums endlessly through my head. As does: *I shouldn't care, I shouldn't care.*

✧ ✧ ✧

Through the year, there are times when a depression in the Bay of Bengal causes heavy rain along the edge of the Shillong Plateau—in the East Khasi Hills, and here, where we are, the South West Khasi Hills. It will pour as though it will never stop, as though an ocean has exploded in the sky. In a day, Shillong will receive six inches of rain; Sohra fifteen, sometimes twenty-five. Rivers will swell, the slopes of hills will slide away, and sometimes lives will be lost. This is 'lap mynsaw, people will whisper, rain that's fraught with danger. It is sudden and strong and comes at you from nowhere.

We are in winter here in Mawmalang, in deep and dry December, but I find myself wishing for rain like this. A mad thunderous downpour that echoes the whirl inside me.

But nothing of the sort happens.

The day after the newcomers arrive is as peaceful as before, sunny yet mild, and biting cold at night. The rhythms of the village also continue as always. Early rising, long hours at the field, evening around the fire, deep, solid sleep.

Everything is the same, and yet not.

How is it permitted, the great and wholly unexpected?

Somewhere on our planet is an instrument called an interferometer that measures gravitational waves created by merging black holes. It recently detected a signal that lasted one tenth of a second, more than a billion light years away—which means one such merger took place when the universe was about half its present age. And yet here we are, victims of surprise and the unforeseen, with not a single instrument to tell us who will turn up on our doorstep, in our life, unconsidered, unannounced, out of the blue. We can look so very far into the past, and not a day into the future. All this we must reckon with by ourselves, alone.

After we tucked Oiñ back into bed that morning, after our mad barefoot capering outside, the household, too, slid back into normalcy. Bah Kit busy at his workshop, carving ladles and spoons, the twins to their play, the sisters Kong Thei and Mem back to cooking and cleaning, Banri and me to tending the livestock and the kper. We are harvesting baskets of oranges now—Khasi mandarin, glowing golden on the trees.

"Who are those people who've come?" she has asked me, and I pretend to be too busy collecting fruit to hear her.

Sadly, I'm unable to employ the same tactic over the phone with Mei.

In our conversations, she's beginning to sound exasperated: "I don't understand, Shai. What are you doing there?"

"Not much."

Sometimes she'll slip in a "So, when are you coming back?"

What for? I want to ask.

"There are people looking after Oiñ, no?" she'll say. "You told me so."

But at this, my obstinacy rises. "Yes, and I'd like to be one of those people."

She'll sigh. "Well, what news otherwise?"

No news. Unless she's interested in the height of the pea shoots.

She is not.

My father I've been calling more often. I didn't think I'd ever say this, but I find him easier to talk to these days. To begin with, he is deeply interested in the height of the pea shoots. He quizzes me on what's growing, what's doing well, and I'm happy to comply. The last time we spoke, he had a message for me from his friend Bah Kyn.

Bah Kyn was terribly excited to know of my whereabouts deep in rural Meghalaya. Where was I staying? With whom? What did the family keep in their kitchen and store in their khrum? Anything he could collect for his Ever-Living Museum? I'd laughed, saying I'd seen lots of ancient mohkhiew, and some old pliang. Now he wanted to know what kind of garden hoe exactly, what kind of plates, and, above all, how many I'd be willing to cart back to Shillong for him.

I don't tell him that at the moment Shillong feels far, far away.

✧ ✧ ✧

This afternoon, as usual, Banri and I are at Bah Kit's workshop.

He has recently managed to collect some birch, from a cluster near the stream. I don't ask how he has come upon it, because I've learned over my conversations with him that all the land here is nongkynti—property that does not belong to an individual. "That's how it always was," he explained to me, "village land belonged to everyone in the village . . . to everyone in the clan. If you tended a field, it was yours, and if you left it fallow for more than three years, it reverted back to the commons." This kind of shifting, fluid ownership didn't sit well with the British. He chuckled. "My grandfather was a rangbah shnong, a village chief, and bilati officers came to him asking if he would sell them land. 'Sell?' he said. 'I have no power to do that . . .' 'What do you mean? What powers *do* you have?'" Bak Kit's grandfather had pointed to a stone on the ground, saying, as much as that. Now, of course, it's different, Bah Kit went on to tell me. Private ownership has created a landed elite, corrupt politicians, contractors, and businessmen, ravaging these hills, doing what they will. I hadn't imagined Bah Kit to feel so strongly about this—or about anything else, to be honest—but he'd spoken about it with quiet outrage.

Now, though, he is in a good mood.

He's telling us how, whenever he fells a tree, he makes sure to leave something behind. Some fruit, a handful of rice, a vegetable or two. Today, some kwai.

"Nga don tang shi kyntein"—he had only one quarter of a betel nut on him, he says, but at least it was something. "It's simple. When you take," he adds, "you must give back."

Banri is incredulous. "A bit of kwai for a whole tree? Papa, it hardly seems enough."

"I've wondered about this," he admits, "but I think it's not about what you leave . . . which may be a small thing . . . but to acknowledge that you are taking."

"You've always said so . . . but why?" his daughter presses.

He looks up at us before saying, “It makes you take less. It makes you grateful.”

Something comes back to me, a faint memory of family picnics, and my father insisting I leave something behind, sweets, a ribbon, for the stones I’d gathered to carry home from the river. “It means,” I say, “that when you take, you also go without.”

Bah Kit looks pleased. “See, she understands. Bym shim kylliang,” he adds. Reciprocity. Ban leh markylliang—to balance on all sides. When you give something back, what you have been given becomes a gift, and gifts, he says, create continuing relationships. It’s not like going to a shop—where you take, pay, leave, forget.

Banri and I eat our soh khleh, chopped oranges drizzled with salt, chilli flakes, and mustard oil, and watch him work. He is making a new duli for our kitchen—the old one is too small, says Mem, too old, and since nothing is ever thrown away here, I will inherit it as an almirah for my clothes. The twins are playing near us, rolling around in the grass with a litter of plump puppies.

It’s a sunny afternoon, though already glimmering around the edges with winter chill. We have gathered a pile of tyrso today, and our syrwa will be pungent and wholesome this evening. I am thinking about this, enjoying the sun on my back, when Banri nudges me.

“What?” I mutter.

In the distance, the newcomers, walking out of someone’s house.

“What are they doing here?” asks Banri.

It’s too much effort to explain, so I just say work.

“What kind of work? Like a journalist?”

And though this isn’t entirely true, I say yes.

The sun doesn’t seem to have had a soporific effect on her. “Who are they?” she asks brightly. “You know them, no?”

“Only him.” I grunt.

She eyes me questioningly, but my face is as impassive as stone.

"And her?"

"I don't know her."

"But she told you her name that day when they arrived?"

"Yes. Daphisha." *Though he calls her Daphi.*

Banri is quiet a moment. "She is very pretty."

I say with no little irritation, "Go be her friend, then, go."

She takes this seriously. "Em phi . . . why would she want to talk to me?"

"Because," I say, though I'm not certain Banri's catching the sarcasm, "I'm sure that's what she's here to do, make friends with people."

Later, at the hillock behind the house, I'm on my own, or almost. The girl with the cat is hovering around, as she sometimes does, warily staring out from behind the hibiscus bushes.

I've tried to speak with her a few times: Kumno? Phi kyrteng aiu? But ever since I saw her on my first day at Mawmalang, she's stayed resolutely silent. Whose daughter is she? Nobody knows. People have tried to take her in, but she refuses to live with anyone. So she is fed at many homes, and sleeps God knows where. She seems to turn up and disappear, wilfully like a dragonfly.

Up here, my phone's alive with a slim bar of network. There is only one person I'd like to speak to, really, but when I try Kima's number, there's no answer. Almost immediately though, he calls back.

"What the fuck!" I yell. "Why didn't you tell me about them coming here?"

"I tried," he protests, "but we got cut off."

"Who is *she*?"

Daphisha, he tells me, is from the Mawlong family. As though that will explain everything. He forgets my years away from Shillong have rendered me sadly out of touch with all the local gossip.

"Who?"

Kima sighs. "Remember that rooftop bar we went to that evening? She owns it. That, and half a dozen other 'high-end' commercial properties in town, a nature resort in Sohra, an artisanal tea shop in Upper Shillong. And that 'Shillong from the Air' festival you've seen advertised on hoardings? Guess who the organizers are?"

I see. I hesitate before asking, but a memory has stirred, of conversations between Dajied and me while we were together.

"Is her mother a politician?" I ask.

"Yes, Dorothy Mawlong, East Shillong Constituency."

"Wasn't she involved in . . . ?"

"Shillong's scam of the century? Selling low-quality roofing material to the rural poor so when the rains came they were left with no shelter? The very same."

Hypocrite. Dajied had condemned the mother, the family, Shillong's corrupt elite, and here he is . . . dating the daughter. For shame!

Daphi's the third sister, Kima continues, second-youngest. The eldest is an airline stewardess, married to some Polish bloke and now living in Warsaw. The second sister, a single mum who oversees a swanky shopping mall in Laitumkhrah. "The youngest is still in school, I think."

"Is there anything you don't know, Kima?"

"Very little."

"And Daphisha? What does she do?"

"Actually, *that* I don't know. She's been away from Shillong for a few years . . . and now she's back . . ."

"And she's here?"

Kima and I fall silent, the same question running through our heads: What is Daphisha Mawlong doing in Mawmalang?

By the time I head back down to the house, evening is beginning to settle.

It's past the hour we usually begin watering the vegetables, and I see Banri is at it already. I hurry to join her, and we work side by side in silence, neatly wetting row upon row of earth, the smell of mud rising. The beans have been planted with the corn, the ginger with the pineapples, and they are growing well together.

I also spy another stout pumpkin, green for now and plumping, my favourite winter vegetable, sweet and creamy on its own, delectable when cooked, as a special treat, with slivers of smoked meat.

When we finish, I step inside. Dinner is being readied, Bah Kit is playing with the twins, and Oiñ, though frail as ever, is in a rare clear mood. We chat today about old Bollywood films we'd watched together—we don't remember any names—and I remind her of one of her favourite scenes that we'd rewind and watch over and again, involving a dashing hero in an open jeep, serenading a doe-eyed heroine in a train.

"Itynnad mo?" she says.

I agree. Yes, very lovely.

Later, Banri and I follow where the nong kñia goes, a warm hearth in someone's home. We meet more often in the winter, she tells me, and I can see why. The days splice swiftly with the nights, darkness settles before you know it, and then there's little to do in our village.

We follow the nong kñia because, as Banri says, he's stuffed with stories.

What will it be tonight? How the peacock won his colourful feathers? How lightning came to live in the sky? Or how Ren, the handsome fisherman, stole the heart of a fairy queen?

To ïa ap, to ïa sngap. Let us wait, let us listen.

In a room lit only by the fire, the smell of charcoal and wood in the air. All of us here, children, young lovers, the elderly, me—and the new ones. The young woman, with hair like 'tiew doh maw, a plant that grows so close to the ground it kisses stone, and the young man I once loved.

We sit around the fire, listening, listening.

Tonight, says the nong kñia, he will tell us an old favourite, the tale of our guardian, the rooster, custodian of day and night, intercessor with the gods, redeemer of wrongs. He strums the duitara, the strings twanging under his fingers.

Long, long ago, when the world was young, a great feast was thrown by all the earth's living creatures—everyone was invited, men, animals, birds, and also the sun and her brother, the moon.

On the day of the festival, there was much rejoicing, but the siblings arrived late, towards the end, and since the others were otherwise engaged, they danced together. "Look at those two clowns," hooted the owl. "Dancing alone on the empty grounds!" "Why come at all," taunted the mole. "You're too early for the next festival," teased the frog.

But what hurt the siblings most was the monkey's indictment. "Are you two brother and sister or husband and wife, dancing so close!"

This so angered the sun that she fled, vowing to never show her face again. She hid in Krem Lamet Latang, the Cave of the Holy Leaf, and the whole world was plunged into darkness.

Everyone was stricken, the nong kñia continues, overcome by remorse, and there was much fear and shedding of tears among the earthlings. They called after the sun, praying for her return, to light up their days again, but in vain. *All in darkness, all in darkness.* The duitara hummed.

Soon a council was called. They pleaded with the mighty elephant for his help, but he refused, quaking at the thought of confronting the heavenly being. He was also afraid to make the long, treacherous journey to the cave, across rivers and seas, bogs and mountains. "You're sending me to my doom!"

Who would go if the elephant, strongest and largest of all, would not?

The proud, handsome hornbill came forward—"I will go, my friends! How will she be able to resist me?" And so off he went, but when he presented himself to her, presumptuous and vain, treating this as a courtship, the sun flew into a rage. "You shameless creature! I curse you. You will fly sideways, trying to avoid my golden rays, for all the days of your life!"

Once more there was wailing and crying throughout the land. "Who will bring back the sun?" This time, in fear, no one volunteered. What would happen now, the nong kñia crooned, and we listened and we waited.

The council realized that at their gathering one creature was missing—the rooster, a wretched featherless bird, who wasn't even considered important enough to summon. "Call him!" they declared, and he appeared. "You who disobeyed and did not even attend the dance festival, you must be punished. Go to the Cave of the Holy Leaf and bring back the sun or be held responsible for all the wrongs in the world."

The rooster bowed his head. "My fellow beings, I am prepared to go and place myself in danger for your sake. Yet who am I to stand before such royalty as the sun? I am a lowly desperate wretch. Look at me!" Clothe me, he requested, in the resplendent tail of the skylark, in warm, bright feathers and finery, and all sorts of brilliant colours, and I promise to do the deed.

The council granted him all he asked—every bird in the world offering to the rooster a feather. And for his quest, he was endowed with a purple crest to mark him as an emissary to the gods.

Will he succeed, will he succeed? the nong kñia sang.

After he had travelled for many days, across rivers and seas, bogs and mountains, and undergone much hardship along the way, the rooster finally arrived at the retreat of the sun. Seeing his modesty, she welcomed him gladly, offering him royal food and a royal bed. But in his humility, he asked only for leftovers of winnowed rice to eat in the courtyard in front of her door—a creature such as him did not deserve more. Impressed, the sun asked, "Why did you come here?" And he told her—"O Mother, the whole world is in darkness, and all creatures live in dread. Unless you return, there will be no peace, no joy." He offered to stand accountable for all the injustices and transgressions of his fellow beings. "From now on, I will be answerable for all their wrongdoings, and I promise to see that no other outrage shall befall you."

In this way, he vowed to sound his bugle thrice every morning as a sign that the world was fit for her blessings. Listen, says the nong kñia, how he crows through the ages for her still.

After the story, we draw away and step outside, pulling our woolen shawls closer. Along the way there is chatter, our daily winding down, our laying out of the next day's plans, small hopes, gossip from the market, from the fields.

Then we scatter to our houses, each to each, calling out to say we've reached, we've reached. Thiah suk, thiah suk, sleep peaceful beloved, sleep.

✧ ✧ ✧

On the rare occasion that my parents and I travelled together, we stayed at a resort about two hours away from Shillong, close to the plains. All of us fretted and fussed about it in our own way and for our own reasons, though a nice-enough time was had by everyone.

What I remember vividly from that trip was a peepul tree that towered over all the others, its roots massively and magnificently coiling from trunk to ground, and deep, deeper below. I was younger, in my mid twenties, but even then, I stood there, thinking about roots. And when we returned to Shillong, and I met Dajied, I asked him: Where did mine lie?

"Right here."

We were in his room, on his bed, on a quiet humid afternoon, while his parents were away at work. He was lying next to me, bare-chested, cleanly hairless, the light turning his skin into molten gold—which is what distracted me, I think, for I don't remember continuing the conversation, but I think about that moment often. *Right here*. He'd always had a conviction about his place in the world that I envied and longed for. An orientation. North and south. Roots, steady and deep.

He was a sturdy old tree, and I a drifting leaf. If I'd told him this, he'd have laughed and called me sentimental. But it was true.

He was Khasi, born, brought up here, with no intention of ever leaving. "Too much to be done," he'd always say, and he meant it. He documented faithfully the streets of Shillong, its people, its hawkers, its beggars, with an eye that was sharp and tender. I knew, I'd seen his work—his videos and photographs, shiny black-and-whites, portraits, buildings, parking lots. The town bustling and at rest. Most of all, I heard him talk, late into the night over the phone, on long lazy afternoons, on our day-trip drives on his bike to Sohra and Smit. "I want to do something, Shai," he'd say. "I really want to make a difference." And I would beat back all my cynicism, my mother's voice saying this is a dead-end place, and nod, and ask, "What? What would you like to do?" He'd pause. "Tell these stories."

He was open, too, sharing his love for Shillong with me, not because he wished me to feel the same, I think, but because he took it for granted that I already did.

How could I not? Impossible not to love our labyrinth of a market, Ïew Duh, where we wandered around looking for cheap, delicious meals. Or the small tea shops we'd visit for sha saw and jingbam every afternoon. Or the tall pine trees towering over us on our walks, the narrow secret winding alleys, the busy streets, the friends he'd stop and speak to, the acquaintances he'd meet.

What I enjoyed most were the festivals he took me to—Shad Suk Mynsiem to celebrate spring and fertility, Nongkrem to invoke a good end-of-year harvest, Chad Sukra to give thanks to Ka Mei Ramew.

He understood why, though, while growing up, I didn't attend any of these. Not surprising, really, what with convent school, and my family's conversion to Christianity two generations ago. All this, to me, was lost. Like Khasi, the language I first learned to speak . . . forbidden within our school walls, while at home my mother insisted on English.

"This is why," Dajied had mused, "your mum doesn't like me."

"What," I'd exclaimed, "no!"

"It's true," he'd said ruefully. "I mean, the white people might be gone, but not much has changed. Like them, your mother also thinks I'm an unconverted savage, and all that's within me is darkness."

"But you're with me," I'd teased. "And I am the light." I plucked his sunglasses from his pocket and slid them up his nose.

Despite himself he'd laughed, and said yes, I'd saved him.

Though, truly, I think he'd saved me—from being wholly untethered, from living a life in Shillong narrowly confined to my parents' world. With him, a deepening, an enlargement, a frame of reference for all I could see around me.

And yet, and yet, even then I'd often ask myself—and I still do—what do I know of these hills? And their histories?

✧ ✧ ✧

This morning, I must head to Bah Albert's shop to pick up a few things, and I hope not to run into the newcomers—as everyone in the village calls them. They aren't too unsettled by Dajied's presence; they tell me that because of the mining, they're used to journalists coming and going, asking questions, disappearing, people from various religious youth groups dropping by to "do good" in a day, a politician or two making a promise-filled appearance, never to be seen again after the elections.

And Mawmalang is one of the few more welcoming villages in the area. Some of the others refuse to engage with any visitors. In fact, one couldn't just land up there without getting in touch with the rangbah shnong, and asking permission, and being given an appointment.

"They're fed up," they tell me. "People from the cities—Shillong, Delhi, elsewhere—showing up and expecting their inquiries to be entertained. As though they're doing us a favour." What they'd prefer is some sort of a deeper, more meaningful commitment. "Get us a hospital, a medical clinic, even, a school. And then we'll talk."

About Daphisha, the village is admittedly confused. Strutting about in her quilted jacket, her expensive knee-high leather boots, her dark glasses. "There is absolutely nothing for someone like her here." I silently agree. Rich people from the sor—the city—we have no interest in them, they tell me, or them in us. Unless, of course, they can make a quick and easy buck. Especially the ones in Shillong who declare "Let's mine the uranium ourselves!" Their idea of exploitation is only when someone other than themselves is doing it. "But let's see," they add with a wry smile, "what tidings this young woman will bring."

I'm at the shop counter and the newcomers are nowhere in sight. Good. I've managed to avoid them since they arrived—not that they've come seeking me out—and, I tell myself, it is better to keep it that way.

Bah Albert is reading a two-day-old Khasi newspaper.

"What news?" I ask.

"Not good," he says grimly.

The people in a nearby village, Mawthabah, or at least a large majority of them, are willing to give permission for the road to run through their land.

"Oh, but doesn't it have to be a collective decision?"

He sniffs. "There is no such thing."

I get a feeling it's best not to pursue this conversation at the moment. I ask for flour, and dish soap, and a packet of salt, and then casually inquire after his guests.

"Where are they?"

"Out?" he replies, shrugging. "Don't know."

I stand there as Bah Albert gathers the items for me, and places them in my shopping bag. *Well,* I think, hoisting it off the counter, *if they're keeping themselves busy, so will I.*

Usually, my day revolves around Oiñ anyway.

When she wakes, or goes to sleep, when it's time for her meals or tea. I like to make her treats, scrambled eggs, steamed fish, or flat rice cooked thick with milk and honey. On some days she eats with relish, on others not at all, and I must coax her—*just a little bit more.* I notice her clear, bright days seem to be receding, they are fewer now and far between. She has stopped asking me question after nosy question. We rarely browse through her photo album, pointing at pictures, giggling. "Look at your funny face!" More and more, she speaks about the past, but her memories are like the mist, soft and hazy.

"Do you remember," she asks me, "do you remember, the mulberry tree that grew in the garden?" I don't, in fact I don't think there ever was one, but I refrain from saying so. "Remember how in summer the fruit would ripen?" She closes her eyes. "How I long for a taste of that sweetness."

Sometimes I try to cajole her into recollection—our trips to Ward's Lake to feed the fish, her dropping me off to school and picking me up, our orange-juice-and-biscuits picnics at the bottom of the garden, catching butterflies and letting them go, her go-to-sleep stories, all the marvellous folk tales. But they return, I realize, only to me.

When I'm back from the shop, I step into the kitchen to find Kong Thei seated at the table, speaking to her sister. She sounds hassled. "She doesn't want to take them anymore," she's saying, "I don't know what to do."

"What's happened?" I ask.

The sisters exchange a glance before Mem replies, "Kong Thei was going to go to Mawkyrwat to fetch more medicines for Oiñ . . ."

"Maybe," I interrupt, "we should get her diagnosed properly first."

"Yes," says Mem, "we've done our best to explain her symptoms to the doctor. What can we do if she refuses to get checked? Not around here, not in Shillong." She throws up her hands. "And you've seen the condition of the road . . ."

I nod, my cheeks flaming. "Of course, I understand. What is Oiñ saying?"

"She's being stubborn. No more medicines, she just told Kong Thei. She says she has had enough."

Oiñ's room glows with bright midday light. The curtains, as always, stay undrawn.

She's looking outside, and doesn't notice at first that I've entered. I perch at the edge of her bed. I don't ask how she's feeling. *Do I look any better?* she'd barked the last time I'd inquired. Frail as she is, Oiñ can still be sharp as a wasp.

I decide to begin now with a gentle untruth. "I spoke to Mei," I say. "She was asking about you, how you are, what medicines you're taking . . ."

Oiñ grunts and continues to stare outside.

This is not going well. She's in a sullen mood. In the quiet, somewhere a chicken clucks, piglets squeal, and a sharp, wintry wind blows through the trees. I'm undecided—Should I leave?

"You know," she begins suddenly, "I had a husband once."

"Yes?" I knew this, though I don't remember her speaking much about him.

She nods. "He wasn't . . . he didn't treat me well."

My heart constricts. I want to say I'm sorry, Oiñ, but I'm also a little bewildered. Why is she bringing this up now?

"One night," she continues, "when he'd had so much to drink he collapsed on the bed, I thought, I thought . . ." She looks at me, her eyes filled with something I can't quite name. "I brought a large pot of water to boil, and I thought I would pour it on him . . . Get it over and done with." She looks back outside. "I didn't do it. I just left. The next day, I took the children and I left."

She's silent a long while after this, and so am I—I find I have no words. I don't know what to say. "Oiñ . . ." I begin and stop. Is it true? Does it matter? She hasn't seemed this lucid in days. It doesn't matter. *You are not a bad person.*

She looks at me, and something in her has shifted. "Don't make that long face," she chides. "I thought it," she adds. "That's all I wanted to say."

Later that day, I'm driven outside filled with some sort of sorrow, heavy as the yellow pomelo ripening on the trees.

I walk, almost run, to stretch my legs, to sweat, to set my heart racing. Granted, the sky is overcast, but the air is crisp and fresh, the hills washed in deep blues and greens, and everything around me, at this year's end, seems touched by a sense of passing, the new into the old and into the new again. I reach the edge of the forest, through which I'd trudged with Bah Karmel—it seems so long ago now—and then walk back up the road littered with mud and stone.

I'm almost at the bridge when I see Dajied and Daphisha. They've spotted me, too, so I cannot scamper down the slope, as I'd prefer to, and hide by the stream until they pass.

"Hello, how's it going?" Dajied is the first to ask.

"All right," I say. Perhaps we'll chat a bit about the weather and then I can be on my way. "So dull this sky," I begin helpfully.

"I like it," says Daphisha.

I should've known, she's a contrarian and enjoys it.

"I think it's quite lovely . . . this shade of silver."

"Silver?" I'm pleased to hear Dajied sound incredulous.

"You haven't seen grey until you've lived in London." If I'm expected to ask follow-up questions, I don't. She continues undeterred. "I was there two years," she tells me. "I did my masters, stayed on to work for a bit, and now"—she smiles mysteriously—"we'll see." She's back in Shillong, to do something—*shouldn't be too difficult,* I think, *with all the money your mum's filched from the poor*—and here, accompanying Dajied to see if they can work on a project together.

"What kind of project?" I inquire.

"We're trying to figure that out," she says, placing a hand lightly on his shoulder. "I've been involved in organizing a few festivals in and around Shillong . . . you know, music, traditional culture, food, that kind of stuff. Recently, Shillong from the Air."

Oh, I say, I've never heard of it.

She's also interested in initiatives where produce is sourced from local farmers to sell around the country. "You know, turmeric from Lakadong, cashew nuts from the Garo Hills, that sort of thing." She smiles at Dajied. "So we'll see. This place is so untapped, don't you think?"

Ripe and ready for you to pluck and reap for your own benefit. I look down at the stream; it's darkening now, and the water is so clear it's invisible. I can see the stones, and our reflections, and the reflections of the sky, and the trees.

"So what do you do?" she asks.

"Nothing."

She laughs, not quite sure what to make of this. "What do you mean, *nothing?*"

I shrug. "Exactly that. I spent a whole lot of time doing nothing in Delhi, and now I'm doing a whole lot of nothing here. Except this doesn't feel like a waste."

Daphisha widens her eyes. "I don't get it."

"It's like this, a small matter of perspective." Suddenly, I'm beginning to enjoy myself. "Take Jupiter, for instance . . . what everyone, for the longest time, called a failed star. Why? Because it's made of the same elements as the sun, hydrogen and helium, and it's massive, but not massive enough to generate the internal pressure and temperature necessary to turn it into a star. But what if"—and here I pause—"Jupiter's just really successful at being a planet?"

Daphisha blinks. Dajied, I'm pleased to see, looks quietly amused. "How long have you been here, Shai?" he asks.

I tell him I've lost count of weeks and days . . .

"Well, that's a change," he says smiling.

"It is," and I smile back.

Daphisha is watching us. She's a shrewd one, and misses little, I imagine. I wonder how much Dajied has told her—about us.

"So what's around here?" she asks suddenly, briskly.

"There are many walks, and trails, down to the river, and to other nearby villages." I also tell them about the abandoned village, once peopled by the Nongïaid. "Banri and I have been meaning to visit." I don't mention anything else—how it's said to be haunted, some say cursed, and that all this while, no matter how much I've tried to persuade her, Banri has refused to take me there on our own.

"Abandoned?" She makes a face. "Well, that's no good."

"You know," muses Dajied, "I read about an event in Italy called the Festival of Abandoned Places . . . where people gather to present papers, share their writing, read poetry, in villages that have long been left empty. It's evocative, I think."

Daphisha quickly switches stance—"Well, that does sound cool, actually. Why don't we go see this place? Maybe it will inspire us." She laughs, light and delicate. Her ears are studded with a row of small gold rings and they glisten.

Dajied says something vaguely affirmative.

"Let's!" she presses. "Let's go see this mysterious village soon."

I have no wish to accompany them, or to be in her company—but Dajied says okay, and looks at me, and I nod—*fool*—and agree.

✧ ✧ ✧

I haven't always been this compliant when it comes to Dajied.

When we were together, we sometimes visited his filmmaker friend Tarun, who lived in Motinagar, a hill away from my parents' house in Lum Kynjai. He was a dkhar, an outsider, married to a Khasi woman—*for a decade,* he'd say, *and still we never hear the end of it.*

I liked him, he was unpretentious, interested, and never condescending with us the way some adults could be with young people.

What are you two gurujis up to? he'd ask, and we'd tell him. Walks, talks, a visit to a local dance. Books we were reading, movies we'd watched, and documentaries.

Wah, so cultured, he'd tease.

We spent time downstairs, in his study, clustered around his iMac, where he was working on a film on Kashmir, or blues musicians in India. His wife, a lawyer for rural communities, was often away, busy at court, their four children upstairs, at piano lessons, playing video games, or teasing the cats. Their grandmother listening to the radio at a volume audible all the way downstairs. It was a full, noisy household.

In other words, a household very unlike mine.

If we wanted to smoke, we headed to the terrace. An open space where the washing was hung and the chillies were dried. One evening, just after the sun had set, Dajied and I stood there, puffing away, watching the smoke curl against a backdrop of hills and low tin roofs, darkening trees, and a magically lit sky.

"Have you ever found yourself thinking," Dajied began, "in moments like this, for instance . . . that this is it."

"This is it?"

"This is what I want in life."

What did he mean? A wife? Kids? A hard-of-hearing grandmother? A career as a filmmaker? A house and a domestic life like this? When I didn't reply, he gave me a curious look, or perhaps it was a falling shadow, I don't know, and perhaps because I felt I must say something, I rushed headlong in a panic and said no, not really . . . I didn't think so.

Something fell, his face, the cigarette, the evening light.

I often wonder if things would be different if I'd agreed. If I'd smiled at him and said, yes, this is it, I feel the same. Then I tell myself—perhaps as consolation—that it wasn't that simple, if not for him, for me. I wasn't meant to be there, those stints in Shillong were escapes from "real life" back in Delhi: the dusty commute, the haggling with auto drivers, the grocery runs and the paying of bills, the fending off of catcalls, the heat, always the heat, the attempt at building—laughable thought, really—what Mei called a successful career.

"Move back," he'd tell me, "just move back to Shillong."

And I'd refuse. Or I'd say I'd think about it. And I would try. But I don't know if I was even tempted to return, because at the time it seemed unthinkable to me. Where to begin? To tell my mother, "I don't think I'm happy here, Mei." I'd imagine her smiling, pity in her eyes. "Happiness isn't simply handed to us, child . . . It must be earned." The problem was no one wanted to work hard in our hometown, she often lamented. "See how the youth are so quick to join all these social organizations . . . when elections come along, agitate, get paid off, agitate again . . . at some point join politics, and then it's all quick and easy money." No one here wanted to *do* anything with their life. I don't remember Mei ever saying it to me directly, but what I grasped was this: that to return was to fail.

How to explain all this to Dajied?

He who knew where he wanted to spend all his days.

Eventually, he told me there was no point, really, in carrying on. "I give up. Me here, you there, and then what?"

He'd never spoken this way before, and it was like cold water being thrown over me. You can't mean that, I wanted to say. You can't.

"You're too scared to burst it, can't you see?" he'd said bitterly. "The little bubble your family offers you, extending to wherever you are. Boarding school, university, Delhi."

"But I'm living on my own now," I'd protested. "Almost."

"Didn't you tell me everything would be taken care of for you, someone sent across to be your live-in maid, to cook and clean."

"I didn't allow that," I stuttered.

"Not because you wanted to be fully independent, I'm sure. Maybe you were embarrassed. What would my flatmates think, or some such thing . . ."

To this, I had no retort. Because it was both unkind and not untrue.

He glanced at me and then quickly looked away. He was frowning, squinting at something far and invisible in the distance. "We can't be together, Shai."

I heard the words, and I didn't. My hands and heart cold and clammy. I managed only a feeble "Why?"

"Because being together would mean doing only what suits you—or rather your mother. Don't you see? Only that would keep your precious bubble intact and safe."

✧ ✧ ✧

Early in the new year, the Khasi Students' Union pays a visit, and we all gather around them as usual. They've called a meeting; no one will miss it. People drop whatever it is they're doing, working, snoozing, and come to listen. I can see the newcomers, too, at the edge of the crowd, Dajied with his camera, Daphisha next to him. There's little reason to take notice of them, I tell myself, when there are important announcements to listen to—the KSU informs us that a public hearing on the road will take place a few days from now, organized by the Community and Rural Development Department.

This is all good . . . except it will be held in Nongbah Jynrin.

A buzz of confusion arises.

"Yes, to us also it is surprising," they say. "We think they chose such an out-of-the-way place in the hope that no one would attend . . . But we urge you to go there and make your voices heard."

"Will the people from Mawthabah also be there?" someone asks. "And more important, who else will say yes to the road?"

The KSU members glance at one another and say hesitantly, "We don't know. To be honest, we've seen quite a mixed reaction so far . . ."

Bah Albert, next to me, clicks his tongue. "It's true, it is hard to tell," he says. "It's trickier because the debate is not directly about whether to mine yellowcake or not . . . it's about a road. And who doesn't want a road?"

Later, as I water the kper, I'm thinking about land, what goes and what stays, what this means for some and not for others, about Bah Karmel and so many like him, here in the villages around Mawmalang. How some things promise health, hope, light, but at such a cost.

"Banri," I ask, "what do you think? Road or no road?"

She looks up from harvesting the purple radish. "Doesn't matter what I think. Sooner or later, they'll do what they want, the people from the centre."

✧ ✧ ✧

After our strange conversation that afternoon, Oiñ keeps more to herself than ever. She sleeps all day—or at least this is what it looks like, turned away from us, her face to the wall. "Come," I try to coax her, "the twins want to sing you a song." Or "Look! A crop of tomatoes we saved from the birds." She barely responds, and even when she does, her attention is fleeting, fractured.

Soon she begins to dip low, quite suddenly, quite fast. She refuses her medicine, and then begins to refuse food. We cook rice and plain dal, and strain them into a warm soup—but even this she will not touch. She lies in bed, swaddled in a quilt, a woolen scarf over her head, which I realize, with a stab to my heart, is one of mine that I once used as a teenager and discarded. She breathes like a bird now, so faint it is merely a flutter, and I watch her, waiting for the slightest rise and fall of the blanket.

You must recover.

For a few days, our household hangs in the balance. Oiñ's nieces and I take turns, watching, waiting. People from the village drop by, offering to help, young men bring us firewood and water, women send hot meals, their husbands bring us vegetables from their fields. When one of us is unwell, all of us are unwell, they say in worry. Kong Thei still does all the heavy lifting—the changing and wiping, the cleaning and washing—and for the tenderness she shows Oiñ while she does all this, she has my heart, even if she doesn't think much of me. Why? I've never quite figured out. Perhaps to her I've always been the unwelcome outsider, a city slicker who walked into their lives uninvited, and disrupted, or worse, claimed—as she would see it—a place here.

And there is an intimate internal rhythm that the household falls into in times like these, like some sort of clockwork. The sisters are extraordinarily calm, Bah Kit keeps the twins out of the way, saying they ought not to see Meirad like this, Banri is a silent shadow, flitting in and out of the house, managing everything that we take care of together quite easily on her own. Everyone has their place. And even if, after all these weeks, I sometimes fit in a little awkwardly, I tell myself I'm here for Oiñ.

Nothing or no one else is as important. Which is why when Mem says, quietly, casually even, one morning, "I think she wants to go," I catch my breath, alarmed by the rage I suddenly feel towards her. *How can you say that?*

"Are you all right?" Banri asks, as I step out into the backyard for some fresh air, some sun, some calm, some quiet.

I think so, I say. I'm not sure.

She comes to stand next to me, but stays silent.

"Have you," I begin hesitantly, "have you seen . . . sick people before?" I cannot bring myself to say *dying*.

She nods. "Paieid, Meieid." Her maternal grandparents. "We looked after them here in the house only." She waits a moment before asking, "You?"

No, I tell her. My grandparents died when I was in boarding school, at university, at work. I returned home to place flowers and candles at their graves. I was sad, but it seems so sanitized now, so convenient to be able to do whatever I did after it was all over.

She nods again, and says in wisdom, "Most of the time all we can do is make them comfortable."

When I'm heading up the hillock later, the rarest thing happens. My phone rings.

It's Grace. "Hey," she says, and suddenly I want to weep, hearing her voice, bright, clear, and clean. "What's going on?" she asks. "I've been trying to reach you."

She's calling to ask if she can rent out my room to a friend who's in Delhi for work.

"Of course," I say distractedly, "that's fine."

"You okay? What's happened?"

She listens without interruption as I tell her about Oiñ.

"You're there," she says kindly. "She'll pull through."

I tell her I don't think she wants to.

At this, she pauses before saying, "You know, Shai, the other day, I was speaking to my mum, who told me she'd attended a funeral in Dimapur of a woman who'd been diagnosed with cancer last year . . . But the thing is, she refused all treatment, right from the beginning . . . that's what her children said . . . that their mother just wanted to pass from this life in peace . . ."

Something catches in my throat. "Oh, God, I hope they didn't . . ."

"Shai," she says, and then pauses again. "They let her go."

At this, I am silent.

"What I'm trying to say is," she continues, "sometimes we have to ask ourselves . . . Do we have the right?"

We do, we do. We must.

For a long while, I sit up at the hillock in silence. Around me, and beyond, stands the quietness of hibiscus and pine, bamboo and oak, and simul trees, their leaves green and motionless.

But this is an untruth, an illusion, I know. From the many videos that my father has sent me, I watched one about how, at all times, day and night, tiny stomata present in the leaves of plants open and close and regulate the loss of moisture, the absorption of air—I saw them, too, in the video, under a microscope, vivid green cells, dancing, moving according to how much sunlight was falling on the leaf. I was mesmerized.

The world is never at rest. Even now, looking around me, when it seems so still, with not the slightest breath of wind or life, the world is dancing.

Everything is moving, adjusting. Making space for living and dying.

✧ ✧ ✧

It must be a dream, for Oiñ is walking beside me, young and strong and steady.

We are on a path, somewhere in the wilderness, curving up a mountain. We walk until we come to a cave, and I know somehow that it is ancient. When we step inside, it towers above us, a place with high ceilings, large enough to house the sun. And even though there is only us, it doesn't feel empty. On the walls are markings—elephants and hornbills, owls and roosters, while stalagmites rise as towering white pillars from the ground. At the back, the cave narrows into a tunnel; it slopes not up, not level, but down, and we stumble on, deeper, soon losing all light, but then around us something glitters, glowing green and silver, falling like snow.

"Where are we?" I wonder.

And Oiñ lifts her finger to her mouth. "There is a forest," she says, "at the centre of the earth, and that is where we all must go."

✧ ✧ ✧

"You went where?" exclaims Mem.

We are sitting on the steps outside her house. She's splicing kwai, and smearing lime liberally with a knife on the tobacco leaf. She shudders. "The place gives me the creeps."

"It gave us the creeps, too," I say.

Earlier that day, we walked to the abandoned village, Dajied, Daphisha, Banri—who reluctantly agreed to take us—and me. We gathered at Bah Albert's shop, manned by his son Mayan, a sparsely moustached youth of about seventeen. He'd been there, too, he said, with his friends, but a while ago.

"My grandmother says the village is haunted," he told us.

"So I've heard." I was quite thrilled by all this; Banri less so.

Mayan laughed. "Old women's tales. It was given by the government of India to the Nongïaid."

Banri frowned. "But they were nomads . . ."

"Yes," he replied. "Maybe that's why the government built them a village. They're always giving people what they don't need."

It took us an hour to get there.

We followed the trail by the stream, then walked down a dusty track towards a sparse forest, at the edge of which stood the settlement. All the way, we marched in formation, first Banri and I, and the newcomers followed.

The village appeared more deserted than I had imagined—and less exciting, too. Most of the huts were reduced to stubby wooden points, the walls flapping in, the roofs missing, and the paths between them wildly overgrown. Everything reusable—wire, metal—had been pried out, stolen away.

Worse, in the air hung the smell of something dead and decaying.

Daphisha wasn't impressed—"Can we go?"—and for once I was likely to agree with her, but Dajied wished to take some pictures, so we waited. What I noticed was that the lots were evenly distributed—each an equal square, no more no less. It reminded me of the abandoned housing complex on the way to Wahkaji. If what Mayan said was true, that this was built by the government, it would explain the obsessive, orderly neatness.

I could see why stories had sprung up about this place. It was quite wretched. The birds were strangely silent, and even though it was early afternoon, and the sun was out, the trees cast long shadows, and the air felt oppressive and cold.

Were the Nongïaid really forced to live here? How awful. I do not understand the bigness of things, the workings of nations—but I have known a little the cruelty of being told, over and again, that one shouldn't live the life one wished to live.

"Who were the Nongïaid?" I ask Mem. "And why aren't they there anymore?"

She shrugs. "I don't know much about them, I've heard they didn't really mix with people from the other villages, that they kept to themselves . . ."

She offers me a kyntein of kwai, I refuse; she shoves it, with relish, into her mouth. "Why don't you speak to our nong kñia? He knows about all these things."

"You think he was around then?" I ask in surprise.

Mem laughs. "Don't you know? He was around when the world was born."

✧ ✧ ✧

The nong kñia lives at the edge of the village, near the forest. In a tin-and-wood shack, with a string of drying corn strung up under the rafters. A tumble of toddlers play out front, singing a little rhyme—*khynnah rit ba smat ba sting bam shana kulai*—a dog gambols happily with them, and in the middle of all this, the nong kñia perches serenely on his mula.

These must be his great-great-grandchildren, I think, as I carefully wend my way towards him. He waves me to a seat.

"It's you, Shailin," he says, even though I don't remember having told him my name. His hands rest gently on his lap; I'm unused to seeing him without a duitara. "Tea?" he asks, but somehow it doesn't sound like a question.

"Yes, please."

We sit there in not awkward silence, though I'm wondering whether I ought to explain why I'm here. The squealing children have tumbled off a little farther away. One of the older kids brings us tea, and biskit khlur, star-shaped cookies that taste of cinnamon. "These are my favourite," he says happily, "all the way from Smit."

Unlike most people I speak to these days, Mei, Kima, even Dajied, the nong kñia's first question isn't "When are you leaving?" Instead he asks, "So have you come for a story?"

He has a directness to his speech that I hadn't expected—different from when he's at the hearth, singing a story for us in marvellously convoluted ways.

I say yes, I'm curious about the Nongïaid.

His eyes shine with humour, and something else. "I know a song or two about them," he says. "Old songs that tell of how they passed through our villages like mad March winds and sudden April showers . . ."

"I'd love to hear them."

"One of these days, I'll sing them for you."

I thank him, saying that would be delightful, and then add, "But what happened? Do you know? Why don't they live in that village anymore?"

"They were people with many homes right up until Indian independence, and even for some time after," he begins. "Then to claim citizenship, they were told they had to settle down . . . A nation is such a fixed thing, don't you think? Its borders, arbitrary at best, suddenly imagined as having been in existence for all time . . . It was even more complicated to impose such a thing in this region, the northeast, with its numerous independent chiefs, of whom few, if anyone at all, wanted to join India . . . Add a nomadic tribe to the mix, and it was too much for the government. They couldn't handle it . . . So the Nongïaid were given this land, these houses . . . and told to stay! There was resistance, they fought, they perished—and now they exist only in song."

I say that's really sad, to be gone like that.

He shakes his head. "Not gone. The time something truly dies is when all stories about it are forgotten. It's this way with people, too . . ." In the distance, children laugh, squeal, the dog yaps happily. I'm still thinking about what he has said when he asks, "How is Kong Stian?"

Now, too, I decide to be honest. "Oiñ is not dying, but she's not really . . . living either."

I can feel his eyes on my face, old but clear and somehow all-perceiving. Maybe he knows already, how she lingers, how we watch for her breath, that we're not certain how she holds on, what it is that she's isn't letting go of, and why.

"There is someone you could consult, you know," he says. I look at him, there it is again, that look I sometimes catch but cannot decipher. "She's the best in our hills, some say. Kong Batimai . . . a medicine woman in Domiasiat."

Oh? This is strange—why haven't the sisters spoken about her? "Is it far?"

"From here, a little less than two hours." And he adds, "She might be able to help." He says it as though he knows something else about it all, but will not reveal it to me yet. *Because it is not time* or something similarly mysterious. Or maybe I'm only imagining this because he's the nong kñia and I expect him to be an oracle.

"How long have you lived here, Bah Sumar?"

He sips his tea long and leisurely. "Since men could turn into tigers, and fish would fly from the river into the kitchen, and chillies from their stalks onto your plate, since wounds could be healed by words, and we could bring rain with a song, and stop fire with a mantra, and the tree that was all trees grew quietly in the shade." He looks at me and smiles. "Every day of my waking life."

I make my way back through the village—past the old men dozing in the sun, the old women peeling oranges. Then someone calls out.

It's Dajied. He's sitting on someone's front steps, fiddling with his camera. Daphisha is, thankfully, nowhere to be seen.

"How's it going?" I ask as he rises and walks alongside me.

"Slow, as these things always are," he says.

We pass Bah Albert's shop; Mayan waves at us from behind the counter.

"Did you catch the KSU meeting the other day?" I ask to make conversation, and add, "I didn't see Shemphang." He was the leader who had addressed the village the last time.

Dajied looks surprised. "You know him?"

I nod. "He visited some weeks ago, because of suspicions that the UCIL and AMD might be involved in stealth illegal mining operations here. Did you hear about the packet discovered on the border of Manipur? And how it mysteriously disappeared?"

He looks at me, curiously. "You seem to know a lot about this . . ."

"And you seem surprised!"

He laughs. "Only because you were never interested in . . . this stuff before."

This is true; I can say nothing to dispute that.

I feel him glance at me, quickly. "I think being here . . . you're different."

Maybe because I moved out of my bubble.

Dajied is quiet for a moment. "Tell me," he says, "how has it been, living here?"

I look at him, those eyes, that mouth, the tilt of chin, the high stubbly cheeks. "Do you remember, once at Tarun's house you asked me: Sometimes in life don't you feel this is it? That this is all you want?"

"Did I?" His eyes crinkle at the edges, as they do when he's a little embarrassed.

"You did," I say, certain he remembers. "If you ask me now, I'd say yes, it is."

✧ ✧ ✧

"I don't understand," says the man in the striped shirt and black muffler. "Because this Atomic Minerals Directorate, or whoever, they are always telling us one thing and then another, for good or for bad I don't know, but first they told us they would dig only a little, but they dug a lot. Then they told us that where they were digging, there we should not drink the water. Then later they said the water was perfectly safe. I don't understand."

He stands at the centre of the makeshift tent—bamboo and tarpaulin to shelter us from the rain. There are so many people in attendance that we spill out onto the slopes, holding umbrellas or large yam leaves over our heads, chewing kwai, kneading tobacco, listening intently.

"Now they say they will build a road for free, as a goodwill gesture, but does this mean later they will do something else?"

The crowd jeers and cheers.

The man in the striped shirt continues, clutching the mic to his chest. "I am a villager," he says. "I don't know how to read or write, but I feel that earlier there were fish and fishlings in our rivers, but now I don't know, I don't see them anymore, do you?"

The crowd shouts in support. *Em em em.*

"Let me tell you . . ." he continues. "I come from the hills just across from here, and all I have is a bit of land, and I've vowed to make sure it cannot be dug or used to make this road . . . because there's something that I feel, it's more like a dream, that something is not right . . . and with that I give you my thanks, for coming and listening to me."

At this, the crowd erupts. *Kiw kiw kiw*, the young men shout, a word that's a summoning to war.

We have been here all day, after setting out early from Mawmalang.

"Go," Mem had urged, "it will do you good." And when I got here, I was glad I'd come. The event had a festive air about it. Families picnicking. Hawkers selling tea and snacks. People trickled in from all over the South

West Khasi Hills, walking through mud and rain. And there is, I realized, something nourishing about being amid people who cared about their land as family.

There have been a few other speakers, too—someone from Mawthabah, who spoke in support of the road, and was mostly booed. Bah Syiem, who gave a short, effective speech, making it clear where his village stood on the issue—not all agree to say no to the road, he said—and I remembered Bah Karmel, and looked for him in the crowd but couldn't see him. "But most of us feel," Bah Syiem continued, "we deserve a road built by the state government, for the sake of a road, and not with the hand of the UCIL behind it."

This received thunderous applause.

Now a woman is speaking. She, too, is condemning the move.

"The resistance continues," Bah Albert tells us, "but there are more subdued faces here than last time." Also, rumours abound that dissenting voices, those who wished to speak up in support of the road, had been threatened. "It's happened before," he adds. "A journalist who supported the mining was beaten up. Many people in the resistance would say this was not a bad thing."

"What do you think?" asks Dajied.

He doesn't look entirely comfortable. "I don't know . . . the journalist lives in Shillong, how can he know our ground realities here?" Then suddenly, Bah Albert glances at us—"I don't mean to say you don't understand what we go through . . ."

"We don't," says Dajied firmly. "Not in the way people living here would. And it's important not to pretend we do. How could we possibly understand?"

Afterwards, Dajied wanders off to take photographs, and I join the crowd, squeezing in between strangers, but they smile and make room, and one of them hands me a spare yam leaf to hold over my head. "Khublei," I say, touched by the gesture.

It's true, me, Dajied, Daphisha—sitting across from where I am, earphones plugged in, trying not to look deathly bored—we're all townspeople, whom everyone here sees as one and the same. And much as I would like to deny it, it's true, that I am as complicit in this exploitation as anyone else from Shillong, even if it's through my long-held ignorance, or worse, not taking the trouble to know better. Daphisha—ten years younger, prettier, richer—and I have this and possibly only this in common. As well as, I suppose, Dajied.

It's clear she is in love with him, though of the reverse, I'm not so sure. He's always careful around her when I'm there—but perhaps that's because he feels awkward, or thinks I would feel awkward.

And me? How do I feel about this? I don't know. Why dig up what's buried? It was all so long ago. In all honesty, I'm confused. And unwilling to reconcile myself to that old cliché: that we only ever want someone when we've let them get away.

The public hearing is meant to wind up after teatime, but I'd like to leave earlier and return before dark. Banri would like to leave, too—she's met a few friends, eaten a lot of shana, and she's done, she says, with her day out.

I tell Dajied we're off, and he says, "Oh, could Daphi walk back with you? I'm going to be here quite late."

"Sure." *What else to say?*

To be fair, she doesn't look pleased either. "Can't I come back with you?"

"Better not wait," he says firmly. "I don't know how long I'm going to be."

She's sensible enough to know that pleading will not work, so she shrugs, says fine, to convey that it isn't, and we head off. It will, I expect, be a largely silent walk back home. Banri will retreat into herself in shyness. I don't feel in the mood for conversation, and Daphi, well, for her we aren't the most glamorous of companions.

She is, however, keen to talk about Dajied. She tells me how they met. At a shoot last year, a modern-day retelling of the Nohkalikai story—you know the one in which the woman, maddened by grief, throws herself off a cliff and turns into a waterfall?

"Yes," I say, "I know the story."

"So I'd adapted it into a short film, as a final project for my master's, and I was searching for a cameraperson . . . Then this friend put me in touch with Dajied. We were camping out in Cherra, there near Kut Madan, at our resort . . ." She adds casually, "Have you been? You must come. We give all our friends a discount."

Well, that excludes me, then. I do not say this out loud, of course, and I must admit it isn't the easiest, being hostile to her. She has an open, even—I say this grudgingly—generous air, as though nothing in the world is too much trouble, probably because it hasn't ever been. Also, she is painfully, annoyingly pretty, especially now, in the soft, tender glow of dusk. I am aware I haven't glanced at a mirror in months. That my clothes are crushed and worn, and unlike hers, haven't been in fashion, if ever, for years.

"How long have you known him?"

"Sorry, who?"

She looks bemused. Dajied.

"Oh, ages," I mutter. "Since college."

"How long ago was that?"

"Too long."

But she's persistent. "Which year?"

I tell her.

Oh, her mouth rounds, and her eyes widen.

"And how did you meet?"

I tell her that, too. At a wedding, behind the tent, I was looking for a smoke.

"I'm glad he doesn't smoke anymore," she says. "Though I would've made him stop."

"Yeah, we both smoked a lot when we dated."

She slips on a mossy stone but manages to recover. "What?"

"We smoked a lot . . ."

She laughs, a little nervously. "No, not that. You guys dated?"

"Yes . . . did he not say . . . ?"

She furrows her brow. Despite the chill, sweat beads her face. "No, he didn't." The path we're on is particularly muddy, especially after the rain, so we fall into single file for a while. I don't know what made me say that—but I must admit I'm walking on without the slightest burden of regret. When we're back on a grassy track, she catches up with me. "How long were you guys together . . . if I may ask?"

I admit I exaggerate a little. Okay, maybe a lot.

"And so . . . then what happened?"

"We didn't really break up." *Why am I saying this?* "Just that he was in Shillong, and I was in Delhi . . . and it was difficult you know, being apart from each other. He came to see me in Delhi, and I would visit Shillong as often as I could . . . but long-distance relationships are hard." *Now*, I want to add, *I'm back*, but I don't. She must be thinking it, though; if it wasn't for the daylight fading, I would say she's turned a little pale. "It's the hardest thing, don't you think? When relationships have to end this way? Not for any major incompatibility, but just a matter of . . . timing."

This is enough, something tells me. I may even be feeling a twinge of guilt. Should I say something nice about them now? No, that would be inappropriate. And too little, too late.

Best I shut up and walk on.

Soon, though not soon enough, we're back in Mawmalang.

✧ ✧ ✧

It's true. Dajied visited me in Delhi. Once. And it was a disaster.

He arrived at the end of a bitterly cold January, as a birthday surprise, and I was much too shocked to even express gladness. I was living with my mum's cousin then, Nah Nah Pat, and there was no way he could come over—not because she'd mind my friends dropping in, but because it was him, of whom my mother disapproved.

"Where is it you stay again?" he'd asked.

"Vasant Vihar," I'd replied. "I think it's best we meet where you are."

But he, his parents, and his sister were at a hotel in Lajpat Nagar, on a family holiday, and sharing a large family room. Impossibly awkward for me to go over.

I think it unsettled us both, being in the same place but not being able to be together.

In Shillong, we had all the town to ourselves. Now we were reduced to sitting across from each other at a noisy, brightly lit Café Coffee Day.

"It's nice to see you," I attempted.

He stirred his coffee and stayed silent.

"What do you want to do? Humayun's Tomb? Dilli Haat? We could go watch a movie."

"I wanted to see *you*, Shai."

"I'm here," I said.

"Not like this." He gestured at the table and accidentally knocked my cup over.

When I saw him again, a few months later, in Shillong, it was as though none of that had ever happened. We were safe again, comfortable in our familiar surroundings. Nothing existed beyond the low hills that hemmed our town. It was easy to forget and keep the wider world at bay.

I remember thinking how for certain, *we*, him and me, could exist nowhere else.

✧ ✧ ✧

Who knew foraging could be this enjoyable?

For one, I had little idea that our forests were so benevolent. During the rains, there grew an abundance of edible wild mushrooms of every variety imaginable. "Some," Banri tells me, "even glow in the dark." At other times of the year, there are plenty of forest greens. Ja ut, jamyrdoh, jalynshir, jalem jatira, wild weeds to toss with lemon or grind with dried fish.

"Never pluck the first one you come across," Banri instructs.

"Why?"

"Because it may be the last in the area. And," she adds matter-of-factly, "you want it to speak well of you to the others. That you were not greedy, and have taken just enough."

This, I agreed, was important, and I said it not just to please her, for I have felt it—the sting of taking too much. Wild chestnuts, which I was so overjoyed to spy on the forest floor that I gathered and gathered until I filled my pockets, and dark brown nuts were spilling out of my hands. *Too much*, something told me, though it was more a sense, a sharp tug of a feeling, which I didn't heed, but as soon as I arrived home with my bounty, my phone dropped, suddenly, out of nowhere—the screen cracked neatly, and it felt as though gentle retribution had been meted out.

"Did you leave something behind?" asks Banri.

I shake my head, guiltily. She hmmms, displeased.

In the forests, also plentiful medicinal herbs. Jajew, with its metallic dark green leaves and pink flowers, used to treat the twins' diarrhoea. Jaraiñ for Kong Thei's high blood pressure. Khliang syiar, for when Bah Kit suffered a little acidity. And once, when I was blinded by a headache, Mem crushed the leaves of la thynriat into a thick, dark concoction, bitter and effective.

"You know," I tell everyone at the dinner table. "The nong kñia suggested I go see a medicine woman about Oiñ . . ."

Did he? they ask. Who?

"Kong Batimai in Domiasiat."

For a moment there is silence. Then Bah Kit speaks up. "You should go," he says. "The nong kñia must have had a reason to tell you so." Kong Thei looks annoyed.

"What good will come of it? Meirad is refusing the medicines I get for her anyway."

"But that's the thing," I say, "we have to try everything. She can't not get better, and just . . . exist like this."

"Maybe she doesn't want to get better," Kong Thei snaps back.

"How can you say that?" I sound as aghast as I am.

She draws herself up, saying coldly, "I would prefer we respect her wishes, but then, what do I know? I'm a villager. You've come from the big city to save us, to tell us how to live, and how to die."

Once, when I was a child, I accidentally trampled into a clump of stinging nettles, and broke out in sore red welts. This is like that all over again. Kong Thei pushes herself away from the table, picks up her plate, and strides out. I am frozen.

Mem has a worried look in her eyes. "She didn't mean that . . . she didn't mean that," she keeps repeating.

"No," I say, the rice under my hands cold like stone. "Maybe I have no right . . ."

"No right to what?" she asks.

To have a say in the matter. That it's best they all—family—decide, I tell her.

Mem snorts, and I'm chided, don't be silly, if I'm not also family then who is? Her sister, she adds, is a strange one. Always like this. Closed and possessive, not comfortable with change of any kind. "Why, we had a cousin from Mawkyrwat stay with us once, and Kong Thei drove the poor thing crazy. Nothing she did was ever right." It's the same with you, but just don't pay her any attention. "The thing is . . ." she continues, "Kong Batimai doesn't have a good reputation. I mean, she's a renowned doctor, people say, but not a good person."

"What do you mean?" I ask quietly.

"She charges people . . . but she doesn't ask only for money."

"Why?"

"She asks for favours, things in return. She's not a good person . . ." she repeats.

That night, I find it difficult to sleep.

I lie on my thin bedding, which has never felt uncomfortable until now. The night is long, and as the hours pass darkness folds upon darkness. At some point I fall into a fitful dream—then I wake.

Through the skylight glows a slit of milky white; it's almost six. The household will soon be up. I slip out the back door, past the pigs, the chickens, the kper, and I walk.

I need air, I need light. I don't head up the hillock. Instead, I take the path leading out of the village, past the fields and bridge, towards the forest. I don't make it that far, though. Sitting by the stream, pinned to a rock, is Dajied. He looks like he hasn't slept either. Should I greet him? I do. He looks a bit dazed.

I sit on a clump of grass not far from him. The stream trickles on, the quiet punctured by the sound of water and birdsong.

"Bad night?" he asks, without turning to look at me.

"Sort of. You?"

"Same."

Back to stream and birdsong.

"This isn't a refreshing morning walk, then?"

He shakes his head. "So . . ." He glances at me. "Apparently you told Daphi we were seeing each other . . . for ages."

Oh dear. I'd forgotten about that. "I might have."

"Well, she definitely made it clear that you did."

"I didn't know you hadn't told her . . . *anything*." I can't see his face, but I'm guessing he's angry. "I'm sorry," I add, "I shouldn't have."

"No, you're right. I ought to have said something . . . especially since we were going to meet here, of all places."

My voice is almost a whisper. "Why didn't you?"

"Stupidity." He sighs. "Also, she's never been wholly convinced I want to be with her, and I thought telling her this would somehow feed that fear . . ."

I stare at a grassy spot before me.

"Worse, I think she was right," he continues. "It hasn't felt real to me . . . So I didn't say anything, and now," he laughs hollowly, "she thinks I came here to find you."

"What?"

"Yup."

"Let me speak to her and explain . . ."

"You can do that," he nods, "whenever you're back . . . *if* you're back . . . in Shillong."

"What do you mean?"

"She's gone."

"How? Alone? That's crazy . . ."

Bah Albert was leaving for Wahkaji to pick up some supplies at dawn today, so she left with him, and asked for her car to pick her up from there.

No buses for Daphisha Mawlong, I'm thinking.

I tell him I feel terrible. I edge closer, squatting inelegantly on a stone beside the stream. "Why don't you give me her number? I can talk to her . . ."

He waves away my suggestion. "She hates you. She hates me."

"She's twenty, she hates everybody," I say.

After a moment's silence—just stream and birdsong—he laughs. "Twenty-*three*."

Again, I apologize, and add, though it sticks in my throat, that she seems sweet.

"Yes. And insecure. And I guess justifiably so, now." Even this morning, he continues, she wanted to leave, she didn't want to leave . . . "I think she wanted me to come with her . . . but I didn't say I would and then that upset her even more . . . What a mess." He says that helplessly, and I feel quite wretched. But . . . *Why didn't you leave?*

"Anyway, she didn't like it here . . . I mean she only tagged along because she—"

"Wanted to be with you?"

"Well . . . I think . . ." He's blushing. "She wanted to see if there was, you know, potential to develop her business ideas."

Right.

In the distance, a peacock-pheasant calls, stirring the quiet air.

"Aren't you mad at me?"

He shrugs. "You know, if it wasn't you, it would be someone else, if it wasn't this, it would be something else. I think we were damned anyway. But yes, it didn't help that you gave her the impression we were still in love . . . and separated only because of distance."

I make a face. "I think it annoyed me . . . that she was Dorothy Mawlong's daughter . . ."

"Yes, but if we're going to be judged by our parents' actions, we're all doomed."

It would be easy for me to agree, but I stay quiet.

"I know," he says, "black money begets more black money . . ."

"I was going to say it begets another godawful *nature* resort in Sohra . . . but yes, that, too."

Across the stream, two green pigeons flutter above the water.

"What about you? Are you usually up this early?"

Actually, yes, I lie. I was—and I fabricate as I go along—I was thinking of heading to Domiasiat.

"You were? Now?"

"Later today," I fumble.

He rises, dusting off his jeans. "I need to go, too. I mean I need to speak to people there, especially Kong Spelity. The woman who's been leading the mining resistance here all these years." I wait with bated breath and then he asks, "Maybe we could go together?"

I'm about to agree but stop. "What about . . ."

"Daphi? Bit too late to be considerate for her sake now."

I nod. True.

"Do you have someone to go with you? A translator? The dialect might be difficult to understand, for us I mean."

I confess I haven't yet made many . . . arrangements.

"Well, maybe Banri can take us?"

"No," I say quickly. "She's needed . . . at home."

He frowns. "Okay, then maybe I could request Mayan."

As we head back towards the village, he asks, "Why are you going there, by the way? Just like that?"

Not really, I tell him. I'd like to try to save a life.

✧ ✧ ✧

Before the sun is highest in the sky, we are on our way.

Mayan has happily delegated shopkeeping duties to his younger sister and mother and agreed to be our guide. Of the three of us, he's the most energized and, I think, thrilled at this unexpected opportunity for a change of scene. He tells us he doesn't usually get to go anywhere now that his friends have left the village for the big towns—with no plans to return.

"What do they do there?" asks Dajied.

"Construction," he replies. "Many of them drive taxis. Some find coolie work at Ïew Duh. It's hard to get any other kind of job. My father," he adds, "won't let me leave, he says we have a shop here and it's a better life, but . . ."

He falls silent although I can complete this for him—*Who is he to decide?*

For most of the way, Mayan chatters. Dajied and I are quiet, mainly because we're sleep-deprived. Sunlight blurs my vision, and a headache throbs at my temples. Dajied looks similarly troubled. But apart from this, we—or at least I am deeply aware of his presence next to mine.

We head out of the village, down the road to Wahkaji, but somewhere along the way we turn off and follow another path winding along the higher slopes. Mayan seems to know the scenic route, and we end up at viewpoint after viewpoint, where the hills undulate before us—there is no other way to describe it—like an endlessly rolling sea.

"You should come here at sunset," says Mayan proudly.

We stop once, for a quick, early lunch, and the mawbynna—sudden monuments, rising to the sky.

It's true, they are striking.

"Have you been to Nartiang?" asks Dajied.

"No," we chorus.

There, in the Jaintia Hills, stands a collection of two hundred or more stone monoliths, some more than twenty feet tall, towering next to paddy fields and a quiet road. But smaller clusters are found far and wide, all across these hills, Dajied tells us. "And for so many reasons, too."

In their various sizes and arrangements, the stones serve as containers of ash and bone, or resting points for weary travellers, as commemoration for ancestors, or markers for funeral processions—usually placed along the route to a clan's mawbah, the final resting place of all its family members. Here a group of three, one monolith rising tallest in the centre tapering at the top, two smaller ones—"mawpyrsa," says Dajied—on either side. Before them, the mawkynthei laid flat and low on four small stones. This is the iawbei tynrai, he explains, the root ancestress, the root of roots.

We sit to the side—me as reverently as I can—and unpack lunch. Mayan's mother, Kong Trill, has packed us rice and fried potato and minced meat cutlets, all wrapped in banana leaf.

"This is the female stone," Dajied continues, patting the mawkynthei. "And the standing ones . . ."

"Are male, I'm sure," I complete.

"We still have very little idea how they set them up, you know . . ."

I sense one of his mini lectures coming on, but I'm too hungry to interrupt.

"Some say the stones were lifted not with physical strength alone, but through words, that you needed to utter a prayer, a plea, to seek permission, and only then would they move."

I'm taken back to the Ever-Living Museum, to Bah Kyn speaking about the circular stone. I look up at the monoliths knifing the sky. "Wonder who put these up?"

"Difficult to know," says Dajied. "Probably people from a nearby village."

"And why?"

"If I'm not mistaken . . . this particular arrangement commemorates the death of the father."

When I'm done with my meal, I sit there quietly.

"I like that we compute our history like this . . ." Dajied nods, saying, "Who needs script when there's song and stone."

Domiasiat is a small village, no more than a cluster of huts, tin and wood and sometimes limewashed, although they are spread farther apart than at Mawmalang.

The people here mostly still practise jhum, Mayan tells us, when I notice that there aren't many kpers around the houses.

"Jhum?" I repeat. "As in shifting cultivation?" A vague and distant memory stirs of geography classes in school.

"Yes," he replies, "they burn and plant and move from place to place every few years. My father says we used to do it, too, you know, at least his grandparents and parents did . . . but it was stopped by the British or something, and then the Indian government also . . . I don't know why."

"Because they thought it ecologically destructive," says Dajied. "Which isn't entirely true. It can actually be good for the soil, replenishing and renewing it to a far greater degree than settled agriculture."

I give him a curious look.

He shrugs. "Some documentary I edited for an NGO; I didn't get paid much but I learned a lot."

The village seems quite desolate. People are probably in their fields. The houses lie quiet and still in the winter sunshine. A calico cat watches us from atop a crumbling stone wall. She appears friendly and butts her head against Dajied's hand as he strokes her.

"Will you tell us? Where's everyone?"

She purrs deep and loud, and then leaps off, running along a grassy track that leads sharply up the hill.

So we follow.

Up to the top, to a small tin house, guarded by a lone old woman.

"Phi leit shano? Where did you go? Running around like a mad creature . . ." She's sitting on her haunches, talking to the cat, and she holds a splicing knife, her hands gnarled but still deft enough to swiftly quarter the kwai. On the ground next to her lies a khukri for which Bah Kyn would probably sell his soul.

When we reach the top, she spots us, and if she feels any surprise or antagonism, she doesn't let on. We allow Mayan to address her first, to greet her and explain who we are. Dajied stands there smiling; I cannot take my eyes off her face. She has high, sharp cheekbones, with hollows underneath like pools, wild white hair tied in an unruly bun, a long nose, and eyes sunken with age and all the things she has seen.

"She is Kong Spelity," Mayan says, introducing us. This is her. The lady of rare and ferocious fire, spoken of around here with love and awe. Here she is, stroking a cat she calls Poi Ei, and offering us kwai.

Dajied is pleased; she's the one he is most keen to meet. She offers us water, and we accept gratefully. The food we'd packed at Mawmalang has sufficed for lunch, but our water has run out, and it was best not to drink from the streams.

I am grateful also to sit and rest. My feet, my head, are aching. I'm offered oranges, and peel one with delight, enjoying the feeling of stillness and warmth, and listening to their conversation. I don't follow everything, but I come to understand that she owns this hill and the next one, it's a lot of land, and of course it will pass on to her children—her youngest daughter, who lives with her. Her husband has passed away, and so has her son, at fifty-four, of throat cancer. Suddenly, so fast.

"Since they started digging," she says, "we've lost many members of our clan, to mysterious illnesses, and even now we suffer. There are some who can tell you of skin diseases, epilepsy, and ulcers, and other illnesses that have no name. Many women are barren, unable to conceive." Her voice quietens but her eyes flash silver.

For a moment, we are silent. Somewhere, in the distance, someone calls, and someone replies. Poi Ei has curled up near Kong Spelity's feet.

Around us stretches an expanse of hills and forest, and it feels as though we are at the very edge of the world.

I know I ought to head out to look for Kong Batimai, but I find I cannot rise. I am tired and held there also by Kong Spelity's voice.

"I'm not well-to-do," she insists, and insists again. "I'm not rich. At first . . ." She stops. "I admit I was tempted to sell the land; I was considering it . . . but one of the labourers employed by UCIL, who'd also worked in Jadugoda, told me, I thought you hill people were clever, do you not know how much you and your family will suffer? That's when I decided . . . I don't want that money."

UCIL had offered to pay her a sum so large for a thirty-year lease of her land that for the rest of her life, and the rest of her children's lives, and their children, for as long as her family continued, they would have been more than well off.

"It was a lot of money to turn down," Dajied says.

She sits there without uttering a word, splicing the last of the betel nut. She gently nudges Poi Ei out of the way as she rises, and gestures for us to follow.

She walks towards a clump of trees on the next hill, behind her house. Down the slope, and up, and through the scraggly pines. This is not the time to ask where she is taking us, and we say not a word as we walk behind her. In the air, only birdsong and the crunch of our footsteps on the dry winter undergrowth.

Then the trees open up to reveal a small waterfall, and a pool that's as clear as starlight. She stops, standing there lit by dappled afternoon sun—and I catch myself thinking, *What Eden is this?*

She begins speaking, slowly at first, and softly, then stronger, faster, more resilient. She's speaking so volubly now that Mayan has trouble keeping up with his translation, but this is not necessary, for somehow, I know distinctly she's saying something about freedom, how it is a thing in her hands, as real as mud and root and stone. It is family, and mother, and parent, and if this is so, would you sell your own blood? Would you?

This is what she is saying, how selling this land would be like selling her freedom, and when it is gone, and converted into numbers, and notes, and cheques and balances, then what can it buy, really?

Can it buy back her freedom?

Can the money buy this flowing stream, this grass, the seasons, this waterfall, these trees?

✧ ✧ ✧

We are to stay in Bah Freeman's house for the night.

Earlier, we arrived at Kong Batimai's house to find she wasn't there. "She's gone to gather bay leaves and pepper for the weekly market," a neighbour told us.

Do you know when she'll be back?

She looked at us as though we'd asked the silliest question. "No, of course not. People come and go here as they please."

So we decided to take a chance, try again tomorrow, and besides, we were tired.

Bah Freeman is the village headman, Kong Spelity's son-in-law, married to her eldest daughter. He's a soft-spoken gentleman who assures us it's not a problem for his young sons to vacate their room for us. They're teenagers, he says, they'll sleep anywhere. Meaning they'll drag their bedding to the front room and rough it out.

When the spare bedding, borrowed from a neighbour, is brought in for us, only two beds are placed in the room—Mayan insists on sleeping outside with the boys.

"Okay, we'll see how it goes," says Dajied, and I make no remark.

We eat an early meal—rice and dal, and fish that's been boiled and mashed with ginger and chillies. It's light and delicious, and I hadn't realized how hungry I was. Afterwards, we sit out on the steps. Dajied has suddenly taken to smoking a pipe—I think how Daphisha wouldn't be pleased.

Bah Freeman sits with us for a while, as does his wife, Kong Bernadethe. A less regal version of Kong Spelity, perhaps, but with a wide, friendly smile. She hands out kwai to us and a few neighbours who've joined in, and this time, out of politeness, I do not refuse.

We talk quietly as the light fades—many of the people here were at the public hearing, I discover, and on the same side as Mawmalang.

We will be punished, though, they say, and when we ask by whom, and what they mean, they look at one another, hesitating.

"It has happened before," Bah Freeman tells us. "The only school we had has ceased to function, and not a brick has been laid of the health clinic we were promised."

"We are so small, and so few," says another gentleman, also smoking a pipe, "that our votes count for little." He shrugs. "So the government doesn't care."

"Yes," speaks up a woman wrapped snugly in a shawl, "the only thing that gave us importance was the one thing we refused to part with . . . uranium. What will they take from us now? We have little or nothing anyway. They can't cut off our water, we get it from the stream . . . our electricity comes from the sun."

We learn that the KSU boys have set up a few solar panels in the village.

Kong Bernadethe speaks now. "It's not for us so much as for our children. We have to send them so far away to school . . ."

"Yes," say the others, "we are saving the land for our children, but at this rate they will inherit nothing else . . ."

Soon, one by one, people rise to leave, saying thiah suk, thiah suk as they go. Eventually, Bah Freeman also bids us goodnight, and then it's only Dajied and me.

He refills his pipe and relights it. The smoke is sweet and pungent and floats out into the late evening–it isn't brutally beautiful here, like pictures you see that render a place unreal, but it's quiet and tended and loved, and I think of this and, all of a sudden, I feel terribly sad.

"Do you think it will continue?" I ask. "What Kong Spelity has begun . . ."

For a long while, Dajied doesn't answer, and I think this is it. In his silence, he's confirming his uncertainty.

Then he begins: "You know, a few years ago . . . Tarun and I, we somehow managed to con our way into an exposure trip to Jadugoda that UCIL was organizing with some local Khasi notables . . . politicians, contractors, youth leaders, you get the idea. This was to counter the so-called false narrative that the anti-uranium movement was spreading with screenings of *Buddha Weeps in Jadugoda* . . ."

Yes, I say, I know about that.

"It so happened that this senior Bengali technocrat from UCIL took a liking to us . . . rather, to Tarun." He laughs, adding, "I haven't heard him talk so much Tagore before. Anyway, one day we asked him about uranium mining displacing people. He looked at us amazed—what displacement? We will rehabilitate them—it's so easy. How many have to be rehabilitated? Maximum thousand? We will pay them, make houses for them, give them salaried employment, they will become rich, and anyway they are such unproductive people, they may have land, but they don't know the value of that land, people work hard but don't get remunerated for it."

We look across the hills, a light winter mist now hangs over the grass, the ñiang-kongwieng wails long and sharp into the late evening.

"The thing is," Dajied continues, "what we realized was that for this Bengali man *this* was freedom. Freedom that comes out of monetizing ownership versus freedom that comes from belonging."

I think of the man in the striped shirt speaking at the public hearing, of Kong Spelity and the two hills she deemed not wealth but priceless.

"You know, I tease Tarun a lot about giving gyan, but that day he told me something I haven't forgotten."

I look at him curiously. "What?"

"Most people in this country, coming from feudal landlessness and exploitation, have no idea how to deal with others who think of land not merely as a factor of production but as imagination, an Eden to live in. The conflict of interpretation that a Marwari, Bengali, or Bihari has with a Munda, a Khasi, or a Naga is this mismatch of history. People who have lived with land being privatized, expropriated, labour being turned into commodity, and hierarchy being sacralized, find it difficult to understand Kong Spelity. It's a conflict between those who think a bigha of land makes you finally free and those who think many hills don't make you rich. It's the world of productivity against the dream of commons lived and kept alive."

We are both silent for a long moment before I say, "I've missed your lectures."

"Shut up," he says, but with a smile.

I laugh, and then add, yes, I see what he means—the question is not how long the resistance can be sustained, but whether this mismatch of history can be redressed, realigned.

It is cold already, but at this moment a small insistent sadness passes into the texture of things. Into the dusk, the trees, the silhouette of hills. Something lonely and lovely and out of reach.

Only when Dajied asks, shall we head inside, am I present again, in the cold, on the steps of the house. He takes my pause to mean something else.

"If you prefer, I can sleep with the boys . . . in the front room."

No, I say, it's all right.

We wash up at the back, from buckets of water set out for us by the kitchen door. There are no toilets. I must head into the bushes.

"You'll be okay?" asks Dajied awkwardly.

Yes, I reply as awkwardly.

It is not easy, and I'm hoping the plant I stepped on isn't a stinging variety. I can barely see in the late light. Somehow, I make it back. And stumble into the small room. Dajied is fiddling with his camera.

I take off my jacket, but it's too cold, so I put it back on, and lie down under a quilt that smells of straw.

In the darkness I am acutely aware that Dajied is lying not far from me. That this is the first night we're "spending together" since the last time he slipped into my room, or I into his—I can't remember which. Foolish, foolish me. He's probably asleep, dreaming of Daphisha, and here I am, awake, nervous as a teenager, wondering what it might be like to kiss him again, and whether he might want to kiss me.

I turn away from him and tell myself to sleep. Suddenly, in the silence, his voice rises. "Do you think . . ." he begins to ask, and then stops.

"What?"

"Nothing."

I half sit up. In the dark, I can make out only his sleeping silhouette. "Tell me."

"Do you think that . . . whenever you go back to Shillong this time, you'll stay?"

In that moment, I know I should say yes, even if it's just for now, to make something right, but I cannot. I begin to say something about not knowing when I'll be leaving Mawmalang, and something about Grace and Delhi, even though I haven't thought about them in a while. "I don't know many things," I finally say.

"Okay," he says, and falls quiet.

And the moment is lost.

We lie there turned away from each other, in silence.

✧ ✧ ✧

The morning is cold against my skin, and I'm glad to turn my face to the sun.

The mist has dissipated, the air is green and clear, the hills outlined sharply against the sky. I'm glad, too, for last night, and the things that did not happen. It is better this way.

I awoke earlier than Dajied and slipped quietly out of the room. After a cup of tea and plain putharo drizzled with honey, I made to set off.

"Should I come with you?" Mayan had asked.

"It's all right. Wait for Dajied."

"But won't you need someone to translate?"

"I'll manage."

I probably wouldn't, but I strongly wished to go alone.

I greet the neighbours who had visited us last evening, they're off to their fields, and Poi Ei bounds alongside as I make my way towards the hut by the forest. It doesn't look like anyone is around even now—except that clothes flutter on the clothes line that weren't there yesterday.

"Don mano mano?" I call, but there's no answer.

I walk around the front, past the laundry, and there towards the back sits a woman on her haunches, clumps of fresh pepper pods and bunches of bay leaves before her. She's spreading them out in sheaves on a wide flat basket on the ground.

"Kumno?" I call out. "Kong Batimai?"

"Hooid," she says. She's tied a cloth around her head and knotted it at the back. Beneath the fabric, I meet a pair of sharp dark eyes, a snub nose, freckles, a strong chin. "What can I do for you?" she says in Khasi, and not in dialect.

I tell her I've come to see her on the recommendation of Bah Sumar, the nong kñia at Mawmalang.

She smiles. "Ah, how is the old man? And what are you doing in Mawmalang? Aren't you from Shillong?" I wish it wasn't that obvious. She finishes with the bay leaves, and starts on the pepper pods; they're small and green, and shine like round jewels in the morning light. "You've come on your own?"

I hesitate. "With a friend, who's here on some work."

"Let me finish here and then we'll see if I can help you."

We don't drink tea; we drink warm water infused with lemon leaves. It's like holding summer to my lips.

We are sitting inside her house. It's a one-room place, and spacious in its bareness. I'd expected . . . well, something like an untidy apothecary, bottles and herbs and powders everywhere, but it's very neat, and the only hint that she's a medicine woman lies in the bunches of dried plants strung up in a row from the rafters.

She sees me looking around, and says, "I like keeping it light. Once every five years or so, I move from place to place." I was in Shillong, too, she adds, which explains her Khasi. "In Demthring."

I know the area, on the outskirts of town, a large working-class neighbourhood filled with car workshops and coal dust from the trucks that travel through it day and night. Once, my father told me, white storks migrated to the paddy fields there in winter.

"Did you like it? In Shillong."

"Shu biang hi . . . but I spent the least amount of time there."

"Why?" I ask, even though I feel maybe I oughtn't to.

"I don't like towns," she says simply. "And I like to move."

"Like the Nongïaid," I say before I can help it.

She looks bemused, but says, "They were people with many homes. I've had only one home at a time."

After this, Kong Batimai gets down to business. She asks me about Oiñ's ailments, and I tell her, in as much detail as I can. She listens without interrupting, until I finish, breathless, ending with what I've been saying to the others all along, that this wasn't death, but it was no life.

Kong Batimai stays quiet, lights herself a bidi, and leans against the wall. Even with her legs outstretched, she's small, yet something about her is formidable. I briefly wish I'd asked Dajied or Mayan to come along.

"What you ask of me is almost impossible . . ."

Heart in mouth, I wait.

She blows out a generous plume of smoke.

"See, your Oiñ is old, but not that old, well enough but not well enough, alive but not quite. Some people are like that. Uncertain, unable to make up their minds. It's like being on a journey that you don't wish to turn back from or complete."

"Yes." I hesitate. "I see what you mean . . . but I haven't really known Oiñ to be a confused kind of person. If she wanted to leave, she left . . ."

Kong Batimai narrows her eyes. "Then perhaps it's not her at all." She watches my face keenly. "Have you been having unusual dreams?"

"Not really." I hesitate. "Maybe once recently." I tell her about the forest, the cave.

Kong Batimai finishes her bidi and throws it into the hearth, where a dull fire glows. "It sounds to me like one of two things: she doesn't wish to leave you, and you don't wish to let her go." She raises an eyebrow. "Or both."

Of course I don't wish to let her go. I flare up a little. Is she insinuating that somehow this is my fault? Look, I want to say, will you be able to help me or not? But I'm sure she won't take kindly to that, and I don't wish to anger her, so I keep quiet.

Kong Batimai rises, patters to the back of the room, and brings out a kwai basket. I'm thinking I will refuse politely if she offers me some, but when she places it down, I see it contains banana leaves, folded into pouches.

"You know that I usually ask for something in return for my treatments . . . sometimes money, sometimes other things."

I nod. I've stuffed all the cash I had with me in my bag, just in case that's what she wants. I hope it's enough.

"But this time it's neither."

I frown, and ask her what she means.

"Because what needs to be done must be done not by me, but by you."

I say I don't understand.

Kong Batimai smiles. "It's very simple . . . you must collect a few leaves and put them in here." She hands me a pouch.

All right, I can do that. "Which leaves?"

Bay, tulsi, pepper, cardamom, cinnamon, orange, and tea.

I'll write this down, I say, so I don't forget.

"But . . . there is one thing."

The way she says it makes me look up sharply.

"All these leaves must be collected from the same plant."

"What?" I laugh, and shake my head, and wonder whether I've heard wrong. "That's impossible."

"No," she says cheerfully. "You collect them, and you wait . . ."

I'm hardly able to ask, "Wait? Where . . . ?"

"There, in the cave, in your dreams."

Where else?

"That is all," she says in finality, while I sit, unmoving, bewildered beyond belief.

"But Kong Batimai," I stutter, "what do you mean?"—but she will not listen.

"I have made clear to you all that is required."

"But this plant . . . with these leaves . . . I mean, where can I even find it? And this cave? It doesn't make any sense . . ."

She stands by the door, waiting for me to leave.

✧ ✧ ✧

By the time we approach Mawmalang later that day, the greens have deepened on the hills as the sun sinks lower, the blues darkened, and the shadows grown picturesquely long across the slopes.

"See," says Mayan, "what did I tell you? It's best at sunset."

And it is, undeniably so, there's something about the quality of light here, sharp and clear, yet softened by some temper of rare gold. I wish I were in a better mood to enjoy it all, though—our walk back home, our lunch that Kong Bernadethe had so generously packed, the bag of freshly plucked oranges. This day, which insists on being so beautiful. I can't say it doesn't irritate me a little that Dajied has had a productive time—he's managed to speak to many people at Domiasiat, filmed some decent footage, taken photographs.

"What about you?" he asks. "How did it go with Kong Batimai?"

"Fine."

He looks a little surprised at my reticence, but I'm in no mood to explain. I'm wishing I'd stopped at her door and asked for greater clarity. That's what I should've done. Not just shuffled out meekly like a lamb. I trample down the path, through leaves and stones and mud, quickly, not really in the mood to linger. Dajied leaves me alone, walking behind with Mayan, and they call out to me only when I miss a turning and take the wrong trail.

"You'll reach Dhaka that way," chuckles Mayan.

I turn around, climb back, carry on. We're not far from Mawmalang. I want to be back, and take a bath, and wash this incident off me, but also it niggles, how I left, the squabble with Kong Thei, and my chest contracts—walking to Bangladesh might not be such a bad idea after all.

Soon after we arrive at the village, we pass Bah Albert's house first and I bid them both goodbye, thanking Mayan for his help and time, and I walk on.

"Shai," calls Dajied, "wait." He looks embarrassed standing before me. "I wanted to apologize . . . for last night. I didn't mean to ask you something that made you uncomfortable."

Stupidly, I want to cry. "It's . . . it's fine, really."

"Are you sure?"

It looks like he wants to say something else, but he doesn't. He wishes me goodnight. Thiah suk, thiah suk, I wish him the same.

I head back to the house, where I expect to meet with some disapproval—but Mem looks ecstatic to see me, hugging me as I enter. "I was so worried," she says, "and then Kong Trill told us you'd left for Domiasiat with Mayan." She holds me by the shoulders, looks into my face. "Are you okay?"

I nod. "I am."

"I have told Kong Thei to . . ."

"She was right," I interrupt. "There was no need for me to visit Kong Batimai. I would like to apologize to her."

Mem pauses. "That's a different matter. The point is she should not have spoken to you like that . . . not in my house."

It's the first time I've heard her lay claim, as the youngest daughter, the khun khadduh, to her inheritance of this place.

"It's all right," I say, "really, it's unnecessary . . ."

"You must be so tired. Go see Meirad, I'll tell Banri to quickly put up some hot water for you."

Oiñ, I'm disheartened to see, doesn't show much improvement. In fact, I think she's the same as before I left. She stares outside, stares at me, stares back out the window, saying nothing, possibly registering nothing, too.

She's on a journey that she doesn't wish to turn back from or complete.

I try to shake off Kong Batimai's words though I've been carrying them around all day. They mean nothing. She was playing with me, having a laugh. A joke at my expense. But it really does feel now that there's nothing more I can do to help.

At our evening meal, I greet Kong Thei politely, "Kumno?" I feel wretched and am willing to endure whatever it is she throws at me.

But she is equally polite. "Kumne."

And this is as far as our reconciliation extends. We go back to doing what we do best: ignoring each other.

I head to my room early and lie down. In the darkness, I desperately hope to be taken back to my dream, to Oiñ and me walking, to the cave, to the promise of the deep, light-filled forest—perhaps I'll find something in there I hadn't noticed before, some sort of clue, some hope.

But tonight I do not dream that dream. Instead, only blank upon blank of tired oblivion, until I wake to hear the rooster crow. All is well in the world, he is saying to the sun, we are ready to receive your blessings.

✧ ✧ ✧

For a few days, I don't venture out.

I spend time with Oiñ, stroking her hair, massaging her hands, all the while speaking to her as though she were there. "Please recover," I whisper at one point. "Stay and I'll stay." And perhaps this is the only thing she hears, for she tightens her grip around my fingers. Is she agreeing? Or saying it is okay?

I stay in the house, tend to the garden as usual, and also learn to darn my T-shirts. Banri is shocked to hear I have never mended anything in my life. "Do you know how to thread a needle?" she asks. "Yes," I reply, and proceed to do so. "And then?" I look at her helplessly. "What now?" She teaches me to sew, to knot, and to patch.

"There," she says after we're done, "no need to throw things away."

No, and perhaps I'm learning this only now.

I don't see Dajied, though the news is he's travelled to Mawthabah, the "enemy" village, to speak to people there, and on his return receives a less than warm welcome. This is what I hear. I don't seek him out, and I assume he won't come see me either—until he does.

"Hey," he says, when I step out to find him waiting at the steps. "Walk?"

"Sure." We set off. "How was Mawthabah?" I ask.

"Oh, they are as convinced about the road as the people here—just about why they *should* get it."

"It's a tricky one, isn't it? Both sides believe they're fighting for the good of their community."

He looks at me. "Yes, that's exactly it."

When he does the polite thing and asks about my parents, and how they are, I tell him they're all right. That, funnily enough, we've fallen into a pattern, much as we did when I was in Delhi—calls over the weekend, and maybe a quick chat once or twice a week.

"I was going to ask," says Dajied, grinning. "What on earth does your mum make of you being here?"

I laugh. She isn't thrilled. "But she's given up asking when I might return."

"Maybe it's a new strategy on her part?"

I shrug. "Actually letting me be? Maybe."

We've reached the edge of the village, the sun is setting over the fields, and the air around us is stirred by the quick flit of dragonflies.

"At some point in our lives," says Dajied quietly, "we *will* do something or the other that our parents don't approve of, that they think we ought not to do. And guess what? It's okay."

I stand there with sudden clarity, clear as the breeze blowing through the white potato flowers, and wish someone had told me this earlier.

Quicker than breath, this becomes routine. I finish my chores for the day, and instead of heading up the hillock on my own, Dajied fetches me, and we wander, down to the stream, the forest, the fields.

We talk, a lot, as though to make up for lost days and years—and suddenly we are young again, as young as we were when we first met in Shillong, and nothing was too complicated, and everything could somehow be worked out because youth gave you that simple belief in more than ample measure. It isn't the same now, I know, but it is nice to pretend so under Mawmalang's clear skies and mild sunshine. That some things change only so they can become what they once were. Through all this, he doesn't make a move—to kiss me, or grab my hand—and neither do I, and I find it strange, this little platonic dance, which we keep up until one day we are lost in the sacred forest.

That afternoon, we decide on some new exploring. It rained the previous night, the vegetables need no watering, so I'm free earlier, and we have a few extra hours before we lose light. The sacred grove is a quiet place, though wild and unruly—and, we agree, also a little eerie. Is it possible that the trees are taller later in the day? They seem to reach higher, and crowd closer around us.

We also stumble over the cement reservoirs, dotting the ground, still discernible beneath the undergrowth. "Mining waste," Dajied tells me. "Hopefully all sealed up."

We've just reached the end of a sloping path, when I see the girl—the cat girl—up ahead. "There." I point her out to him. A little way farther. Was it her or a trick of light? We keep walking, briskly, but when we get to the spot, she's nowhere in sight. Instead, almost lost behind the tall ferns, stands the entrance to a small hollow.

Is this where she went? Possibly not, the foliage seems undisturbed. We part the leaves and look inside. It's rocky and moss-lined, and stones the size of fists lie scattered on the ground. Up ahead, a sinkhole has newly caved through, letting in a slant of light. Dust motes rise in the air. We step inside. It's dry but around us hangs the peculiar smell of earth—of mud and root and rock. We stop at the circle of sunshine falling to the floor.

I dig my foot into the soft, warm soil. "What will grow here now?"

Dajied smiles, and pulls me close. "New life."

On these cold January days, we also spend many evenings together around the hearth, huddling close, trying to capture whatever little warmth escapes the fire. Banri sits close to me, her arm entwined through mine, Dajied close behind.

I can hardly bring myself to say it, but I have never been happier.

On most evenings, it's the nong kñia strumming his duitara, but tonight the musicians are here to entertain us, and they bring raucous merriment to the air.

Tell us about the rooster! No, no, they say, about this bird we've recently heard . . . Young Ren and his fairy lover, then? They shake their heads. Not *again*, not again . . . Tell us about the Nongïaid! They raise their brows, nodding, saying it's time, it's time, to rhyme about these lost and ancient walkers . . .

What do they know, what do they know, where do they go, where do they go?

The ones who walk come like April showers and mad March flowers,
fleet of foot and light as leaves, tripping tripping with the breeze,
the oldest of our tribes, some say, around since the earliest days,
when man and animal would praise the young moon and the sun,
when the Diengiei, the tree that carries all trees, was no more than a sapling,
the walkers our oldest tribe, no hill too high for their grappling.

Shadow people who come and go like the wind, like the wind.

The ones who walk are the old ones, unbound by forest or land,
moving through the ages still, through all the days of man,
as villages rose and villages fell. The Nongïaid washed by rain,
darkened by the sun, except one, except one, a woman white
as frost, they say, a woman white as frost on a cold clear winter's day,
they say, with eyes the colour of winter skies, from far away,
from far away—oh, did she, did she walk along, beside the ancient walkers?

What do we know, what do we know? How many come, how many go?

The walkers cannot tell us now, they're long locked up in cages,
the forests emptied, the hills untrodden, their endless winter rages,
they wept to be enclosed by walls, and refused to sleep inside them,
for fear that they would die if upon waking they did not see the sky.

Usually, we step out afterwards, pull our shawls closer, and head home, walking with the others until we begin to scatter to our own houses. And Dajied and I will say, with all the promise that these three words hold—see you tomorrow.

Tonight, though, he asks if we can go for a walk.

It's late, it's freezing, but I look at his face and say, "Why not?"

For a moment, we stand unmoving. Where shall we go? Towards the stream? The edge of the forest? There's half a moon out so it isn't entirely dark, but still there isn't enough light to venture to either of those places. So I suggest the hillock behind Mem's house, and we set off.

From up there, the lamps of the village prick the darkness like small stars.

"I haven't come up here before," says Dajied, sitting himself down, drawing out his pipe. I sit next to him, close enough to smell the tobacco when he pulls out the pouch. It's pungent and strong, and from nowhere I feel the old desire to take a drag rising. He lights the pipe, releasing the smoke in a slow stream.

"Shai," he begins, "I have to leave soon."

"When?" I try to sound casual.

"Soon," he repeats. He glances at me, then looks away. "I extended my stay here as long as I could . . . but I have to get back to Shillong now . . . There's all this material to file, and work to get back to . . ."

And real life. And maybe even Daphisha.

"Of course," I say. "I mean, you must . . ."

"And you?"

Not far from us, the crickets chirrup. A series of short, sharp taps. The 'niang kynjah, the insect that's always lonely.

"Well?"

"Why can't we just stay here?" I ask, only half in jest.

He laughs, though not in mirth. "There you go, Shai, moving from one bubble to another."

This stings me more than the cold winter air. I say that isn't fair.

He turns to me, places an arm on mine. "Sorry. I only mean that you will have to decide, no? At some point . . . What it is that you want to do? Where you want to stay? And what you want to make of your life . . . ?"

I can barely see his face in this low light, but his voice is piercing and insistent. In my chest, a small flutter of panic. I want to say he's right; I need to figure it all out, but something stops me, and suddenly I laugh.

"What's so funny?" Rather than annoyed, he sounds bewildered.

"That there's more in common between you and my mother than you would think . . ."

"I don't know what you mean," he says stiffly.

"Look," I say, gently, "maybe later I'll come back to Shillong and stay . . . but for now . . ."

"For now?"

"I came here for Oiñ, and I want . . ."

"To be here until she's gone?"

"Or until she recovers."

The smoke from the pipe curls slowly between us.

"Is it only that?"

"It is only that."

If I try to explain to him how it isn't, it will only be less. It will fall short. Something will be lost. The lights down at the village are almost out; the sound of people talking, laughing, making their way home drift up to us.

"But you will be back?" I can hear it in his voice, the pressing need for certainty. I stay silent, and when I turn to him, I see his eyes glisten. "I can't believe this," he says, "that it has happened again." That he has allowed this to happen again.

"But it's different this time," I hear myself insisting. *I am different this time.*

He shakes his head. "It is the same. Me there, you here . . . sometimes even when we're in the same place."

✧ ✧ ✧

We are at the beginning of Rymphang, the second month of the year.

The days are noticeably warmer, though the evenings and nights still cold, and I still fill a bottle with hot water to take to bed to warm my toes. I go about my chores, feed the chickens, our family of squealing pigs, water and weed and sow—and nothing has changed except I carry a little lighter the remembrance of Dajied.

The days are quiet. Oiñ looks out the window. Kong Thei feeds her tenderly. Banri sits and studies and dreams. These days her mother and father are busy with the twins, who are both down with a sudden cold and fever.

Meanwhile, with the shift in season, our tyrso crop is thinning, but the beans and tomatoes are plentiful, as are the peas. The pumpkins are finished, but already in blossom so hopefully there will be more ripening soon. In the front of the house, I'm trying to plant a few flowers. Some sweet peas I begged Bah Albert to bring from Mawkyrwat market, and a few lady's slipper orchids I've stacked with bunches of moss up a tree. I remember Bah Kyn's garden, how little interested I was in its abundance. At one point, how little interested I was in abundance of all kinds.

I still head to the hillock every afternoon, though on occasion I don't even bother taking my phone—screen still neatly cracked. Yet this hasn't felt like a retreat from life so much as an immersion, with all that I've been learning.

How it begins with mud and seed and leaf, and how even if you think you need more, this is enough for you to begin to see widely, deeply. For eyes to open not just in your head but in your hands, and skin, and feet. And from here to know, little by little, how to read the signs of the world. When ants carry their food and eggs up a slope or into a gap in a rock, or fish leap in the pools of a river, or the sun is ringed by a brilliant rainbow circle—all these mean heavy rain will soon fall. When the 'tiew kheiñpor closes its petals it's a signal that work is done in the fields, and rice must be cooked for the evening meal. Now, around me, the leaves of the simul tree blaze green, but when they fall, and the ñiang kali chirps, these will herald summer. And if I spy the walnut trees and the cherry blossom flowering early, the year's harvest will be plentiful.

What does all this mean? That the world is story after story, living, breathing, coming to birth, to life, to death, to retreat—and great joy lies only in knowing deeply.

In the time I've spent in Mawmalang, Khasi too falls easier from my tongue. This is because I speak it every day, of course—rather than being thlun, like a blunt knife, it begins a little to sharpen—but I don't think this is the only reason. It is also because the world reveals itself through these words. I didn't have anyone to speak Khasi with in Delhi, and somehow, I can't quite imagine it there, amid the loud, aggressive bustle of the city in the north. Far from these hills where the words have been formed. *Language*, I think, *sounds like the place it comes from, it carries its own landscapes, thrives where the wind and the rain echo its rhythms.*

For so long I have wondered, but perhaps now I can begin to know—that to name the seasons in a language that matches them—ka Pyrem, ka Lyiur, ka Synrai, ka Tlang—to know the months by what they bring, black winds in Ïaïong, mustiness in Naitung, rain to form deep, clear pools in Jylliew—*this*, I think, *is what it means to be home.*

Sometimes I check in with the others. Messages from Grace, and Kima, filling me in on their news, though nothing from Dajied, and I suppose I cannot blame him. Calls to Mei and Papa, and they seem happily busy. My mother with a visiting cousin and her new baby, a baking class recently offered in Shillong, an education fair she's been roped in to help organize.

She rarely inquires anymore when it is I plan to return, though once she says, "I forgot to give it to you this time, didn't I?" What, Mei? "Khaw." Grains of rice, in a small pouch, pressed into my palm before a trip. A charm for safe travels, the Khasi believe, powered by home, the place in which the rice is grown. And I want to tell her that often it is the "unsafe" journeys, unplanned, on a whim, that lead you to where you need to be.

My father is still saving trees. Most recently, after the pines in our colony, a patch of towering, century-old cedars in the middle of town, slated to be felled to make way for a petrol station. He sat all day, all night for weeks, joined by a group of young climate change activists from neighbouring colleges and schools. It was all over the news, and social media. My father is a star.

He hasn't asked me yet, because he believes plants and people have to find their own roots, but if he ever were to ask if I was all right, I'd remind him how he once told me that houseplants thrive only when placed in a spot where they have a view of the sky.

And from where I am, the sky is blue and vast and undiminished.

On this mild, early spring afternoon, I allow myself to think of one of the last day trips Dajied and I made together out of Shillong.

We visited Laitlum, near Smit. We raced out of town, through open countryside, parked the bike near an opening in the hedge, and walked in, past a solitary hut, across grassy openness right to the edge of the slope.

We squatted, lit a joint.

Before us spread a deep, forested valley, with mountains rising endlessly on either side beyond the horizon—Laitlum, where the hills are set free.

I told him that all of this was once underwater. "Some fifty million years ago, a shallow sea extended across the Indian peninsula, all the way from here to Rajasthan."

"Some of our monsoons could pretty much fill it right back up," he joked.

I laughed. Truly, they could. "Can you imagine, though, the highest points on earth were once the lowest, deserts were oceans, and continents have been drifting apart and crashing together again since the world began."

Our joint was strong and smelly and tasted acrid in my mouth.

"What I find most incredible, though, is that all life started with one common ancestor . . ."

"Really?" This, he said, he hadn't known, or hadn't really thought about much.

I nodded, passing the joint. "A universal common ancestor that probably lived in high-temperature waters in the deep seas . . . Paths between plants and animals split only a billion and a half years ago." By this time a pleasant lightness hummed in my head. "All animals trace back to a bilaterian worm, all plants to one green cell." I gestured around us. "Pine and birch and bamboo, single-celled diatoms, they owe their existence to a tiny alga, eons ago, that swallowed a cyanobacterium and turned into a mini solar-power plant."

Dajied looked amused. "I love that you're . . . you're so . . . cosmic."

"Cosmic?" I thought I was the one who was stoned.

"It's true," he continued. "I'm local, provincial, small even, all about the here and now, and this place. And you . . ."

And me?

"You're something much larger," he said simply, and fondly, too, I'm sure. But I'm certain that he's also told himself that this is what pries us and keeps us apart.

Thinking about it now, I don't know if he is right. Could we not look at it another way? That here contains everywhere, and now, this moment, all time. This place, all places. This leaf—I look at the grass at my feet—is all leaves. Me, at this spot, carrying all my ancestors. Where are my borders? Where the boundary between me and the world? If we look for separation, we will always find it, I want to tell Dajied. It is the easiest thing to do, to split, to splinter, to divide. How much harder to see things in continuity, in extension, in expansion, as uninterruptedness—from the moment, the very second, the universe was born. That is in us, too. *We are stardust* isn't just a catchy line in some poem or hippy song—we truly do hold supernovas in our blood and bones. This is where they come from, the elements in our bodies. Iron and oxygen, carbon and calcium. From a star, over the course of billions of years and multiple galactic lifetimes. We are not born now—we are passed on from the first stars to the next, as they burn and die, their elements sweeping out into space, again and yet again, until here we are. We carry stardust. And each speck of this minute grain—invisible to the human eye, as old as our universe—within it carries us.

Behind me the birds are calling, the wind rises, soft and sweet, rustling the shrubs, the trees. I look down at the village. Mem's house. I think of Oiñ. Of a hut by the forest in Domiasiat. Of the medicine woman's instructions. *Bring me all these leaves.*

Something strikes me, and I rise and walk down the hillock. I go looking for the musicians, and when I find them, they're smoking their pipes, chatting; it's not every afternoon they play music, on these waiting-for-the-harvest days.

"Kumno?" I greet them.

"Kumne," they reply in chorus.

"I wanted ask you something," I begin.

How can we, the ñiang-kongwieng of the world, help you?

"In your songs, you sing about a tree . . ."

Tree? Which tree?

"Diengiei," I say patiently.

How does it go? When the world was young . . . kumno kumto? The lyrics keep changing, they tell me, they keep slipping out of our heads . . . Let's see, what do we know about the Diengiei? That it covered the world in darkness.

"In the song," I remind them, "you call it the tree that carries all trees . . ."

Yes, yes, we might have indeed.

"What does that mean?"

They glance at one another. That it's very big? And then they burst out laughing.

They're tricksters, happy crickets. So I thank them politely, and leave.

I head to where the nong kñia lives. He has gone for a walk to the stream, I'm told by one of his many grandchildren, and so I follow the route back. But instead of heading into the village, I walk towards the fields, the bridge, the stream, beyond where I found Dajied sitting on a rock early one morning.

Soon enough, I see him. His long, sinewy silhouette wrapped in a chequered shawl. He is standing there, looking out, at the distant hills.

When I approach him, he smiles.

"You were expecting me?" I ask.

His smile grows wider.

We both look out, the sky deepening above us, the hills beyond falling into silhouette.

"I did what you suggested, you know," I begin. "I went to see Kong Batimai . . ."

"Kong Batimai," he echoes.

"And she told me I can help Oiñ only if I do something for her."

"That is her way, yes."

"But what she's asked of me is impossible."

"This, too, has been known to happen."

I shrug. "What's the point? I mean . . . it didn't sound like she wanted to help."

He hesitates. "There are, fortunately or not, many ways to help someone."

"Maybe, or maybe she was just playing a trick on me . . . because it's impossible to collect seven kinds of leaves from the same tree . . ." I steal a glance at him. He remains impassive. "Unless you know of a tree that is all trees, like the Diengiei."

He stays silent a long while, then turns to me, and asks if I can hear it.

"Hear what?"

"The doh thli . . . in the stream. They've just spawned."

I peer into the water that's lilting over stone and mud, and cannot see any silver fishlings. Then I turn back to him, take a breath. "What do you know of the Diengiei?"

"What do I know?" His eyes still gaze into the water. "The ones who did are gone now. All I know are descriptions from fragments of songs, many lost, though some remain for those who want to listen, and those who want to sing . . . They exist in many variations . . . Some say it was magnificent, each leaf a different leaf, and in this way, it carried all the trees in the world. Other songs say that a tree that carries all trees could only be a seed, which can grow into anything. The site of all potential." He looks at me kindly, and repeats, "It varies."

A dragonfly dances before us, flitting from tip to tip, leaf to leaf. Farther away, a white egret watches and waits.

I remain quiet for a moment, before asking, "But what does it mean to us? The people with the stories about the Diengiei . . . this tree that carries all trees?"

He pulls his shawl closer. "What do any of our stories *mean*? Every time you tell them, they are different, their meanings as multiple as the versions they exist in. Such a tricky thing, don't you think? Hard to grasp. But is this bad? When meaning is direct, like an arrow through the heart, it can kill things."

I can see his eyes following the dance of the dragonfly.

"See?" He points. "How it moves? Darting above the water, from stone to leaf." He looks at me, he smiles, and says, "I prefer things to be alive."

By the time I return, the household is at rest.

I haven't been talking to the nong kñia all this time; I left him by the stream and walked through the village, from edge to edge to edge, as though to make a map I could fold and keep with me for always. I've been thinking about journeys. Across rivers and seas, and swamps and mountains. The ones that take us where we never thought we'd reach, caves and underworld forests, to a river's bend. And journeys that lead us to someone else's journey's end.

I move through the house quietly. I have come to know it well. Its walls and floor and low ceilings, the smell of ash and wood rising from the kitchen.

Everyone is at rest. The twins, still weak from the fever, are sleeping; Mem and Bah Kit talk quietly in their room; Kong Thei has also retired, and Banri is probably with her, chatting, mending clothes, reading.

I have missed dinner, and although Mem has left out food for me, I put it away. This is not the time to eat.

Instead, I sneak into Oiñ's room and sit by her bed.

She is asleep, but she's been unaware of anyone's presence for many weeks now. She is here but not here, perched on the edge of coming back and going. It cannot be long ago, all of us outside, dancing clumsily on the grass, barefoot, moving, stamping on the ground. To do that, skin on soil, blood on mud, allowed for something from Ka Mei Ramew to run through us, Mem had said, a life-giving force we have long dismissed or forgotten, that connects us to the earth, and the earth to us. I wish it could have sustained Oiñ a little longer, held her stronger and upright. But maybe sometimes it calls us instead, knowing it is time.

I look down at her face, the colour of bark, lined as leaves, hair wild as the moon.

This is the point at which I say, *Go in peace, Oiñ, go in peace. You go, I stay, and someday in the earth of our earth, we meet.*

Through the window, a breeze blows fresh and sweet, and somewhere, beyond the hillock, in a hollow in the forest, newly touched by sun and rain—something stirs, reaching towards the light.

Let us wait, let us listen.

When we gather, we gather as though for the last time.

Who knows when the hearth will glow with welcoming fire, and when it might expire? We gather as we always have. We gather safe, we gather warm.

What will it be tonight?

Tonight, it will be our story.

The one with a tree, the one with a tiger, and the small bird who knows.

The rest is smoke—but where's the fire?

Here, here, gather close.

Here is the song and here is the story, we cannot pry each from each.

Take both, we offer them lightly.

Tonight, what will it be?

This story that holds all stories, this song that carries all songs.

How abundant are we, shifting, unfurling, gathering every future that could be?

How do we grow but slowly?

Where do we turn to if not towards the light?

Here the darkness, here the light—bound together, like song and story.

How to live but lightly?

How to learn but gently?

All the while journeying through life after life after life.

Gather, gather, around the fire, listen, listen.

Breathe.

IN GRATITUDE

For this novel I have needed, and received in staggering abundance, so much help. The people at Pontas, particularly Anna Soler-Pont and Maria Cardona, fellow marvellers of the world, sensitive readers, ace agents. My editors in the USA and UK, Rakesh Satyal and Ore Agbaje-Williams, for unflinching faith every step of the way. Rahul Soni—my editor in India, though infinitely so much more—side by side, helping me plant the forest. Star publishers Udayan Mitra and Ananth Padmanabhan.

Ashoka University, for steady support, covering travel, time, space, and conversations with colleagues. Professors Upinder Singh, Malabika Sarkar, Mandakini Dubey, Bittu, Shivani Krishna, Saikat Majumdar, Devapriya Roy, Sumana Roy, Arunava Sinha, Amit Chaudhuri, Jonathan Gil Harris, and Madhavi Menon—for help and understanding at just the right moments.

Luigi Russi, for introducing me to Goethean science on a walk, long ago, by the sea.

Robert Macfarlane, for his excitement, for the immense generosity of his words.

Amitav Ghosh, for support, for synchronicity between place and reading.

Pranay Lal, for inspiration, introductions, and always, wonder.

Henry Noltie, caster of the sharpest eye over botanical references and much beyond.

Jim Reed, for day-long conversations, for his gift of Goethe's *Flight to Italy* in translation.

LeAnne Broadhead, for marvellous resonance across the seas.

Staffan Müller-Wille, for exciting new material on Linnaeus in Lapland.

Bengt G. Karlsson, for generosity and new eyes.

Andre Hahn, who so unhesitatingly answered questions and shared his expertise.

Ankita Anand and Anupam Chakravartty, for their patience, and their reportage on the uranium mining issue in Meghalaya.

Andrew May, for excitement over nineteenth-century botanists in the Khasi Hills.

The Toji Residency in South Korea, for a month of walks, tea, and nourishment.

The hospitality at Mimosa Ridge, Shillong—Anjali Nath, your home is a writer's dream.

Yogita Chandolia, for ushering me into Professor M. V. Rajam's laboratory at the Department of Genetics, University of Delhi, South Campus—and to all the scientists there for putting up with my amateur questions so patiently.

The librarians at the Kew Reading Room, especially Craig Brough, and at the Linnean Society Library. Anne Thomson, the archivist at Newnham College, Cambridge.

Nevin Gill, for wandering around Cambridge looking for Balfour Place with me until we found it!

Sam Miller. Before the beginning to beyond the end. All rounds at the Botanist on me.

Jeet Thayil, early listener, plier of endless martinis.

Shubhangi Swarup, who read this manuscript with such thrill and pleasure, despite the world burning outside.

Malvika Maheshwari, dear reader, dear friend, in whom I always find home.

Durba Chattaraj, for joy and bolstering and wicked, wicked humour.

Tishani Doshi and Akanksha Sharma, my stars.

Holly Ainley, for long chats and beautiful botanical-garden days.

Nandini Gopinadh, for books and conversations and the best wine.

Jini Reddy, fellow wanderer and seeker of secret trails.

Tarun Bhartiya, Angela Rangad, for words, actions, courage.

Sonal Shah and Soumojoy Dutta, for keeping 'em coming.

Anurag Banerjee, for conversations, and walks, and whisky sours, without end.

Reeju Ray, for conversations about everything and fathomless love.

Olivia Dalrymple, for friendship, and a heart full of love.

Willie Dalrymple, for all your enthusiasm always.

Samit Basu, for plotting patience and mischief.

Mukund Padmanabhan, for always asking, "How's the book going?"

The Carlings, Jane and Paul, for open doors, open arms.

Gaurav Deka. For learning and alignment, for bringing ancestors to peace and life.

Suraj Singh, for loving the world and everything in it as much as I do.

Samuel T. Sawian, for new trails, new stories, for helping me understand song and stone.

Suneet Singh Puri, fellow wide-eyed wonderer.

Katie Waldegrave, for always saving me a room.

Justine Del Corte. There is no one else I would like to be stuck with in Rome during a pandemic.

Deepthi Talwar, for forgiveness over forgotten birthdays, and long friendship.

Malati Shah, for leaves, and poetry, and dusty old books that served so well.

Mum and Papa, and Dina. Aunty Lorraine, Aunty Melanie. The three Cs. All of you, cousins, aunts, uncles, best family.

Pankaj Khanna, so much storm and shelter. For being my most patient reader, and listener of book rants.

And finally, Kitty, whose loving indifference helps keep everything in perspective.

A NOTE FROM THE AUTHOR

This novel brims with texts—books, academic articles, diary entries, social media posts—to which I am indebted for having opened doors to the plant world, the lives of colonial plant hunters, Goethean scientific ideas, Linnaeus's worldview, the Edwardian age, and the complicated politics of the hills I call home.

In the Linnaeus section I use *Tour in Lapland* (1811) as a source text, a translation of the original *Lachesis Lapponica* by James Edward Smith. The poems "How to Be a True Botanist" and "Baptism," however, are inspired by the lists in Linnaeus's *Philosophia Botanica*.

The details of Goethe's journey were sourced from the indispensable *Flight to Italy: Diary and Selected Letters*, translated by T. J. Reed, an authentic, unedited, day-to-day record of the first eight weeks of the poet's travels. Many of Goethe's "quotes" in the novel are taken directly from here. For the rest of Goethe's time in Italy I referred to an 1881 translation by the Reverend A. J. W. Morrison, *Letters from Switzerland and Travels in Italy*, as well as *Italian Journey: 1786–1788*, famously translated by W. H. Auden and Elizabeth Mayer. Henri Bertoft's excellent and accessible *Goethe's Scientific Consciousness* allowed me an early glimpse into Goethe's way of seeing, as did his *The Wholeness of Nature: Goethe's Way of Science*. I learned much also from Dana Pauly's thesis excerpt "Goethean Science: A Phenomenological Study of Plant Metamorphosis" and Agnes Arber's *The Natural Philosophy of Plant Form*. The wall lettuce experiment that Goethe conducts with his friends in Rome, and his life-cycle-of-a-poppy conversation with Moritz are taken from Craig Holdrege's outstanding *Thinking Like a Plant: A Living Science for Life*. Holdrege's article "Doing Goethean Science" was imperative to my understanding of the actual experiential practise of Goethean Science in daily life.

My insights into Edwardian England, British women in India, and travel during the time were gained largely thanks to Anne de Courcy's *The Fishing Fleet: Husband-Hunting in the Raj.* Evie's experience of journeying by ship to India and her time in Calcutta were brought to life by the wealth of details in this book. Equally fascinating and especially useful was Jessica Douglas-Home's *A Glimpse of Empire*, a recounting of her grandmother Lilah Wingfield's travels through India in 1911. The description of travelling through the Suez Canal was inspired by her words. While most of the travel memoirs Evie reads actually exist, these three—William Griffith's *Journals of Travels in Assam, Burma, Bootan, Affghanistan and the Neighbouring Countries*; *A Memoir of Some of the Natural Productions of the Angami Naga Hills, and Other Parts of Upper Assam* by J. W. Masters Esq.; and Joseph Dalton Hooker's *Himalayan Journals*—are said to mention the Diengiei. Do note this is a fabrication on my part. They contain many magical details but, alas, not this particular one!

Many details of Mr. Finlay's life are taken from Francis Kingdon-Ward's *In the Land of the Blue Poppies*, a collection of essays on his plant-hunting experiences across Asia.

I learned about the method or "stages" of conducting Goethean science from the very useful "Goethean Science as a Way to Read Landscape" by Isis Brook.

The conversation between Shai and Dajied about whether the resistance to uranium mining will continue in the West Khasi Hills quotes a Facebook post (December 30, 2019) by Tarun Bhartiya on land and belonging. The scene where they meet Kong Spelity Lyngdoh earlier in the day is also inspired by the same. The details about the mysterious package apprehended in Moreh and the suspicions that the UCIL and AMD were involved in stealth mining operations in the South West Khasi Hills were taken from a wealth of news articles—"Mystery Deepens over Recovery of Suspected Uranium in Moreh" by the *Northeast Live Web Desk* (May 19, 2019), "Manipur Recovery Proof of Uranium Mining: KSU" in *The Shillong Times* (May 20, 2019), "KSU Suspects Uranium Packets Seized from Manipur Are from Meghalaya" by *The Northeast Today* (May 19, 2019), "PDF Minister Demands Inquiry into Illegal Supply of Uranium" in *Syllad: The Rising Meghalaya* (May 20, 2019). To understand the uranium mining issue in greater detail, I turned to reportage by Dilnaz Boga for *The Caravan* and Ankita Anand for various publications including *Beyond Headlines* and the Mines and Communities website.

Shai's fascination with the natural world, and geology and geological time, is inspired by my reading of Pranay Lal's superb *Indica: A Deep Natural History of the Indian Subcontinent*, and watching, along with my father, a TV programme on Discovery Science called, rather unpoetically, "Strip the Cosmos."

Infused through the novel is the spirit of Robin Wall Kimmerer's *Braiding Sweetgrass: Indigenous Wisdom, Scientific Knowledge, and the Teachings of Plants*, a book that serves as a wise and wonderful guide to life.

ABOUT THE AUTHOR

Janice Pariat is the author of *Boats on Land: A Collection of Short Stories*, *Seahorse: A Novel* and the international bestseller *The Nine-Chambered Heart*. She was the recipient of the Young Writer Award from the Sahitya Akademi and the Crossword Book Award for Fiction in 2013. In 2023, she won the JK Paper–Times of India AutHer Award for Best Fiction, the Atta Galatta–Bangalore Literature Festival Book Prize for Fiction and the Sushila Devi Book Award. Janice's work has been translated into ten languages. She teaches at Ashoka University, and lives between New Delhi and Shillong with a cat of many names.

प्रभात
सूक्ति-कोश

प्रभात सूक्ति-कोश

सं. महेश दत्त शर्मा

प्रभात
पेपरबैक्स
www.prabhatbooks.com

प्रकाशक

प्रभात पेपरबैक्स

4/19 आसफ अली रोड, नई दिल्ली–110002

फोन : 23289777 • हेल्पलाइन नं. : 7827007777

इ–मेल : prabhatbooks@gmail.com ❖ वेब ठिकाना : www.prabhatbooks.com

संस्करण

प्रथम, 2020

मूल्य

तीन सौ रुपए

अ.मा.पु.स. 978-93-89982-08-4

मुद्रक

आर–टेक ऑफसेट प्रिंटर्स, दिल्ली

★

PRABHAT SUKTI KOSH *(Dictionary of Quotations)*
Ed. Shri Mahesh Dutt Sharma

Published by **PRABHAT PAPERBACKS**
4/19 Asaf Ali Road, New Delhi-110002

ISBN 978-93-89982-08-4

₹300.00

"मनुष्य अपनी क्षमताओं की कभी कद्र नहीं करता, वह हमेशा उस चीज की आस लगाए रहता है, जो उसके पास नहीं है।"

—हेलेन केलर

दो शब्द

सूक्तियाँ गागर में सागर भरे वे शब्द समूह हैं, जो सीधे मर्म पर चोट करते हैं। इन शब्दों में ऐसी शक्ति होती है कि ये इनसान को सोचने के लिए मजबूर कर देते हैं और कई बार वह क्षण जीवन का महत्त्वपूर्ण मोड़ साबित होता है, जो जीवन की दशा और दिशा को बदलकर रख देता है, यह व्यक्ति का मानो नया जन्म होता है; उसका चीजों को देखने का दृष्टिकोण पूरी तरह बदल जाता है। महात्मा बुद्ध के कुछ सूक्ति वाक्य ज्यों अंगुलिमाल का हृदय परिवर्तित कर देते हैं और वह डाकू से संत बन जाता है; सूक्तियाँ कुछ यों ही मन पर गहरा प्रभाव छोड़ती हैं।

प्रस्तुत पुस्तक में दुनिया भर के महान् विचारकों की सूक्तियों का संकलन किया गया है, जो प्रबुद्ध पाठकों के लिए निश्चित ही उपयोगी सिद्ध होगा।

—**महेश दत्त शर्मा**

अनुक्रम

सूक्तियाँ

सूक्तियाँ

अंत

- मार्ग का अंत नहीं है, परंतु चलने का अंत है। **—रवींद्रनाथ टैगोर**

अंतःकरण

- आदमी का अंत:करण दो हिस्सों में बँटा है, एक हिस्सा अचेतन, वृहत्, गुप्त और निश्चेष्ट होता है और दूसरा सचेतन, सक्रिय, चंचल और परिवर्तनशील होता है। **—रवींद्रनाथ टैगोर**
- अंत:करण की जड़ता से जो क्षति होती है, उसे पूरा करना संभव नहीं होता, जब हम क्षतिपूर्ति करना चाहते हैं तो मोह का सहारा लेते हैं। **—रवींद्रनाथ टैगोर**

अंतर

- गहन रात में पहली नींद से जागने पर मनुष्य अपनी संपूर्ण शक्ति का अनुभव नहीं कर पाता, इसलिए उसके दिन के चरित्र और रात के चरित्र में बड़ा अंतर पाया जाता है। **—रवींद्रनाथ टैगोर**

अज्ञान

- अज्ञान जैसा शत्रु दूसरा नहीं। **—चाणक्य**
- अपने शत्रु से प्रेम करो, जो तुम्हें सताए, उसके लिए प्रार्थना करो। **—ईसा**

- अज्ञानी होना मनुष्य का असाधारण अधिकार नहीं है, बल्कि स्वयं को अज्ञानी जानना ही उसका विशेषाधिकार है। **—राधाकृष्णन**
- अज्ञानी के लिए खामोशी से बढ़कर कोई चीज नहीं और यदि उसमें यह समझाने की बुद्धि हो तो वह अज्ञानी नहीं रहेगा। **—शेख सादी**

अज्ञात

- आपकी बुद्धि ही आपका गुरु है। **—अज्ञात**

अति

- अति से अमृत भी विष बन जाता है। **—लोकोक्ति**
- सभी वस्तुओं की अति दोष उत्पन्न करती है। **—भवभूति**
- अधिक खाने से मनुष्य श्मशान जाता है। **—लोकोक्ति**

अतिथि

- अतिथि जिसका अन्न खाता है, उसके पाप धुल जाते हैं। **—अथर्ववेद**
- यदि किसी को भी भूख-प्यास नहीं लगती तो अतिथि सत्कारका अवसर कैसे मिलता। **—विनोबा**
- आवत ही हरषे नहीं, नयनन नहीं सनेह। तुलसी वहाँ न जाइए, चाहे कंचन बरसे मेह॥ **—तुलसीदास**
- अतिथि का आतिथ्य करना श्रेष्ठ धर्म है। **—अश्वघोष**
- अतिथि सबके आदर का पात्र होता है। **—अज्ञात**
- दरिद्रों में दरिद्र वह है, जो अतिथि का सत्कार न करे। **—तिरुवल्लुवर**

अत्याचार

- अत्याचारी से बढ़कर अभागा कोई दूसरा नहीं, क्योंकि विपत्ति के समय उसका कोई मित्र नहीं होता। **—शेख सादी**
- अत्याचार सदा ही दुर्बलता है। **—जेम्स रसेल लावेल**

• गुलामों की अपेक्षा उन पर अत्याचार करनेवाले की हालत ज्यादा खराब होती है। **—महात्मा गांधी**

• अत्याचार करनेवाला उतना ही दोषी होता है, जितना उसे सहन करनेवाला। **—तिलक**

अधिक

• अधिक का अधिक फल होता है। **—अज्ञात**

अधिकार

• ईश्वर द्वारा निर्मित जल और वायु की तरह सभी चीजों पर सबका समान अधिकार होना चाहिए। **—महात्मा गांधी**

• अधिकार जताने से अधिकार सिद्ध नहीं होता। **—रवींद्रनाथ टैगोर**

• संसार में सबसे बड़ा अधिकार सेवा और त्याग से प्राप्त होता है। **—प्रेमचंद**

• अधिकार केवल एक है और वह है, सेवा का अधिकार, कर्तव्य-पालन का अधिकार। **—संपूर्णानंद**

• अधिकार पाने की जो मर्यादा है, उसे बचाना हो तो अधिकार के प्रयोग को संयत होना चाहिए। जितना मिलता है, उतने के लिए छीना-झपटी करना कँगले को शोभा देता है। **—रवींद्रनाथ टैगोर**

• मनुष्य को अधिकार माँगने नहीं होते, अधिकार की सृष्टि करनी होती है। **—रवींद्रनाथ टैगोर**

• अधिकार पाना और अधिकार होना, एक ही बात नहीं। **—रवींद्रनाथ टैगोर**

• अधिकार छोड़कर, अधिकार जमाए जाने जैसी विडंबना दूसरी नहीं। **—रवींद्रनाथ टैगोर**

अध्ययन

• अध्ययन उल्लास और योग्यता का कारण बनता है। **—बेकन**

- अध्ययन आनंद, अलंकार तथा योग्यता के लिए उपयोगी है। **—बेकन**
- सद्ग्रंथ इस लोक की चिंतामणि नहीं, उनके अध्ययन से सारी कुचिंताएँ मिट जाती हैं। संशय पिशाच भाग जाते हैं और मन में सद्भाव जाग्रत् होकर परम शांति प्राप्त होती है। **—अज्ञात**
- दिमाग के लिए अध्ययन की उतनी ही जरूरत है, जितनी शरीर को व्यायाम की। **—जोसफ एडिसन**
- इतिहास के अध्ययन से मनुष्य बुद्धिमान बनता है। **—बेकन**
- चरित्रहीन शिक्षा, मानवताविहीन विज्ञान और नैतिकताविहीन व्यापार खतरनाक होते हैं। **—सत्य साईंबाबा**
- अध्ययन से सरल कोई मनोरंजन नहीं, न कोई आनंद इतना चिरस्थायी है। **—लेडी मॉण्टेग्यू**
- सरस्वती से बढ़कर कोई वैद्य नहीं और उसकी साधना से बढ़कर कोई औषध नहीं। **—अज्ञात**
- जितना अध्ययन करते हैं, उतना ही हमें अपने अज्ञान का आभास होता जाता है। **—स्वामी विवेकानंद**
- प्रति की अपेक्षा अध्ययन के द्वारा अधिक मनुष्य महान् बने हैं। **—सिसरो**
- भविष्य का अनुमान लगाने के लिए अतीत का अध्ययन करो। **—कन्फ्यूशियस**
- हम जितना अध्ययन करते हैं, उतना हमें अज्ञान का आभास होता है। **—अज्ञात**

अनंत जीवन

- अनंत जीवन का एक मात्र पाथेय है धर्म। **—रवींद्रनाथ ठाकुर**

अनुभव

- बिना अनुभव कोरा शाब्दिक ज्ञान अंधा है। **—अज्ञात**
- अनुभव को खरीदने की तुलना में उसे दूसरों से माँग लेना अधिक अच्छा है। **—चार्ल्स कैलब काल्टन**
- बिना अनुभव के कोरा शाब्दिक ज्ञान अंधा है। **—स्वामी विवेकानंद**
- दूसरों के अनुभव से जान लेना भी मनुष्य के लिए एक अनुभव है। **—अज्ञात**
- यदि कोई केवल अनुभव से ही बुद्धिमान हो जाता तो लंदन के अजायबघर में रखे लोग इतने समय के बाद संसार के बड़े-से-बड़े बुद्धिमान से अधिक बुद्धिमान होते। **—बर्नार्ड**
- अच्छा निर्णय अनुभव से प्राप्त होता है, लेकिन दुर्भाग्यवश अनुभव का जन्म अकसर खराब निर्णयों से होता है। **—बिल गेट्स**
- दूसरों के अनुभव से जान लेना भी मनुष्य के लिए एक अनुभव है। बहादुर बनो, जोखिम उठाओ, अनुभव का कोई विकल्प नहीं है। **—बिल गेट्स**
- अनुभव की पाठशाला में जो पाठ सीखे जाते हैं, वे पुस्तकों और विश्वविद्यालयों में नहीं मिलते। **—बिल गेट्स**
- अनुभव महज एक नाम है, जो हम अपनी गलतियों को देते हैं। **—बिल गेट्स**
- अनुभव-प्राप्ति के लिए काफी मूल्य चुकाना पड़ सकता है, पर उससे जो शिक्षा मिलती है, वह और कहीं नहीं मिलती। **—बिल गेट्स**

अनुशासन

- अनुशासन परिष्कार की अग्नि है, जिससे प्रतिभा योग्यता बन जाती है। **—अज्ञात**

- अनुशासन के बिना न तो परिवार चल सकता है, न संस्था या राष्ट्र। वास्तव में अनुशासन ही संगठन की कुंजी और प्रगति की सीढ़ी है।

  —महात्मा गांधी

- अनुशासन का पालन तभी संभव है, जब मनुष्य का उस काम में अनुराग हो, जिसमें वह लगा हुआ है, इसके बिना तो अनुशासन अनुकरण मात्र होगा।

  —महात्मा गांधी

- किसी भी राष्ट्र का परिचय उसके अनुशासनबद्ध नागरिकों से मिल जाता है।

  —महात्मा गांधी

- सारे अनुशासनों की जड़ व्यक्तिगत अनुशासन है। जब तक कोई भी व्यक्ति अपने आप अनुशासन और नियम-पालन में बँध नहीं जाता, तब तक उसे दूसरे से वैसा कराने की आशा करना व्यर्थ है। **—महात्मा गांधी**

अन्यमनस्कता

- जो अभी-अभी चाहिए, उस पर जो ध्यान केंद्रित नहीं कर पाते, जो किसी और काल की बाँसुरी सुनते रहते हैं, वे विरहिणी शकुंतला की तरह हैं, वे अपने पास खड़े अतिथि की आवाज नहीं सुन पाते और उसी के शाप से दूर से जिन अतिथि पर वे मुग्ध रहते हैं, उसे भी खो देते हैं।

  —रवींद्रनाथ टैगोर

अन्याय

- अन्याय सहने से अन्याय करना अच्छा है, कोई भी इस सिद्धांत को स्वीकार नहीं करेगा। **—अरस्तू**

- अन्याय का राज्य बालू की भीत है। **—जयशंकर प्रसाद**

- अधर्म पर स्थापित राज्य कभी नहीं टिकता। **—सेनेका**

- अन्याय सहनेवाला भी उतना ही अपराधी होता है, जितना करनेवाला; क्योंकि अगर अन्याय न सहा जाए तो कोई भी अन्याय करने का साहस नहीं करेगा।

  —रवींद्रनाथ टैगोर

• अन्याय को मिटाओ, लेकिन अपने आप को मिटाकर नहीं। —**प्रेमचंद**

अपमान

• धूल स्वयं अपमान सह लेती है और बदले में फूलों का उपहार देती है। —**रवींद्रनाथ टैगोर**

• अपमान का डर कानून के डर से किसी तरह कम क्रियाशील नहीं होता। —**प्रेमचंद**

• अपमानपूर्ण जीवन से मृत्यु अच्छी है। —**कहावत**

• तलवार का घाव भर जाता है, पर अपमान का नहीं। —**एक कहावत**

• धूल भी पैरों से रौंदी जाने पर ऊपर उठती है, तब जो मनुष्य अपमान को सहकर भी स्वस्थ रहे, उससे तो वह पैरों की धूल ही अच्छी। —**माघकाव्य**

• इतिहास इस बात का साक्षी है कि किसी भी व्यक्ति को केवल उसकी उपलब्धियों के लिए सम्मानित नहीं किया जाता। समाज तो उसी का सम्मान करता है, जिससे उसे कुछ प्राप्त होता है। —**कल्विन कूलिज**

• अपमानपूर्वक अमृत पीने से तो अच्छा है सम्मानपूर्वक विषपान। —**रहीम**

अपराध

• दूसरों के प्रति किए गए छोटे अपराध अपने प्रति किए गए बड़े अपराध हैं, जिनका फल हमें भुगतना ही होता है। —**अज्ञात**

• अपराध मनुष्य के मुख पर लिखा होता है। —**महात्मा गांधी**

• अपराधी–मन संदेह का अड्डा है। —**शेक्सपियर**

अभय

• अभय ही ब्रह्म है। —**बृहदारण्यक उपनिषद्**

अभाव

• अभावों में अभाव है—बुद्धि का अभाव। दूसरे अभावों को संसार अभाव नहीं मानता। —**तिरुवल्लुवर**

अभिमान

- जरा रूप को, आशा धैर्य को, मृत्यु प्राण को, क्रोध श्री को, काम लज्जा को हरता है, पर अभिमान सबको हरता है। **—विदुर नीति**
- अभिमान नरक का मूल है। **—महाभारत**
- कोयल दिव्य आमरस पीकर भी अभिमान नहीं करती, लेकिन मेढक कीचड़ का पानी पीकर भी टर्राने लगता है।

  —प्रसंग रत्नावली
- कबिरा गरब न कीजिए कबहूँ न हसिए कोए। अबहूँ नाव समुद्र में का जाने का होए॥ **—कबीर**
- समस्त महान् गलतियों की तह में अभिमान ही होता है। **—रस्किन**
- किसी भी हालत में अपनी शक्ति पर अभिमान मत कर, यह बहुरूपिया आसमान हर घड़ी हजारों रंग बदलता है। **—हाफिज**
- जिसे होश है, वह कभी घमंड नहीं करता। **—शेख सादी**
- अभिमान को जीतने से नम्रता जाग्रत् होती है। **—महावीर स्वामी**
- शुभार्थियों को अभिमान नहीं होता। **—कल्हण**
- अभिमान करना अज्ञानी का लक्षण है। **—सूत्रतांग**

अभिमानी

- बिना जाने हठपूर्वक कार्य करनेवाला अभिमानी विनाश को प्राप्त होता है।

  —सोमदेव

अभिलाषा

- हमारी अभिलाषा जीवनरूपी भाप को इंद्रधनुष के रंग देती है।

  —रवींद्रनाथ टैगोर
- अभिलाषा सब दुःखों का मूल है। **—महात्मा बुद्ध**

- अभिलाषाओं से ऊपर उठ जाओ, वे पूरी हो जाएँगी, माँगोगे तो उनकी पूर्ति तुमसे और दूर जा पड़ेगी। **—रामतीर्थ**
- कोई अभिलाषा यहाँ अपूर्ण नहीं रहती। **—खलील जिब्रान**
- अभिलाषा ही घोड़ा बन सकती तो प्रत्येक मनुष्य घुड़सवार हो जाता। **—शेक्सपियर**

अभ्यास

- कोई ऐसी वस्तु नहीं है, जो अभ्यास करने पर भी दुष्कर हो। **—बोधिचर्यावतार**

अमृत

- अमृत की सार्थकता उसके अंतर्निहित सामंजस्य में है। **—रवींद्रनाथ टैगोर**

अरण्य

- धराशायी अट्टालिका पर धीरे-धीरे अरण्य जन्म लेता है। **—रवींद्रनाथ टैगोर**

अर्थशास्त्र

- सच्चा अर्थशास्त्र तो न्यायबुद्धि पर आधारित अर्थशास्त्र है। **—महात्मा गांधी**

अलगाव

- अलगाव तो बाहर की चीज है, केवल आँखों से दिखाई पड़नेवाला अलगाव। अंदर के प्राणों के तो टुकड़े नहीं होते। **—रवींद्रनाथ टैगोर**

अवगुण

- अवगुण नाव की पेंदी के छेद के समान है, जो चाहे छोटा हो या बड़ा, एक दिन उसे डुबो देगा। **—कालिदास**

- पराये धन का अपहरण, परस्त्री के साथ संसर्ग, सुहृदों पर अति शंका—ये तीन दोष विनाशकारी हैं।

—वाल्मीकि

अवतार

- शास्त्र के मत से अवतार बदलते भी हैं। कच्छप अचानक वराह हो जाते हैं और हड्डी की मोटी खोल की जगह दाँत निकल आते हैं, सबर की जगह गुर्राहट पैदा हो जाती है। **—रवींद्रनाथ टैगोर**

अवतारी पुरुष

- जो अवतारी पुरुष स्वर्ग से उतरकर यहाँ भी वहाँ की भाषा बोलते हैं, उनकी बातें यथार्थ नहीं होतीं। **—रवींद्रनाथ टैगोर**

अवसर

- जो अवसर को समय पर पकड़ ले, वही सफल होता है। **—गेटे**
- अवसर उनकी मदद कभी नहीं करता, जो अपनी मदद स्वयं नहीं करते।

—कहावत

- अवसर तुम्हारा दरवाजा एक ही बार खटखटाता है। **—कहावत**
- मनुष्य के लिए जीवन में सफलता का रहस्य आनेवाले अवसर के लिए तैयार रहना है। **—डिजरैली**
- जो प्रमादी है, वह सुयोग गँवा देगा। **—श्रीराम शर्मा आचार्य**
- धरती पर कोई निश्चितता नहीं है, बस अवसर हैं। **—डगलस मैंकआर्थर**
- आशावादी को हर खतरे में अवसर दिखता है और निराशावादी को हर अवसर में खतरा। **—विंस्टन चर्चिल**
- अवसर के रहने की जगह कठिनाइयों के बीच है। **—अल्बर्ट आइंस्टीन**
- हमारा सामना हरदम बड़े-बड़े अवसरों से होता रहता है, जो चालाकीपूर्वक असाध्य समस्याओं के वेश में छिपे रहते हैं। **—ली लोकोक्का**

- अवसर पर दुश्मन को न लगाया हुआ थप्पड़ अपने मुँह पर लगता है।

—फारसी कहावत

- विद्वत्ता, परिश्रम और योग्यता दुनिया के सभी समुदायों में समान रूप से बँटी है, किंतु निवेश व अवसर नहीं। **—बिल क्लिंटन**

- जो हानि हो चुकी है, उसके लिए शोक करना अधिक हानि को आमंत्रित करना है।

- समय और सागर की लहर किसी की प्रतीक्षा नहीं करतीं।

—रिचर्ड ब्रेथकेट

- मनुष्य के लिए जीवन में सफलता पाने का रहस्य है, हर आनेवाले अवसर के लिए तैयार रहना। **—डीजराइली**

- ऐसा न सोचो कि अवसर तुम्हारा दरवाजा दोबारा खटखटाएगा। **—शैंफोर्ट**

- कोई महान् व्यक्ति अवसर की कमी की शिकायत कभी नहीं करता। मुझे रास्ता मिलेगा नहीं, तो मैं बना लूँगा। **—सर फिलिप सिडनी**

- यदि मनुष्य प्यास से मर जाए तो मर जाने के बाद उसे अमृत के सरोवर का भी क्या लाभ? यदि कोई मनुष्य अवसर पर चूक जाए, तो उसका पछताना निष्फल है। **—सफोक्लिज**

- अवसर बुद्धिमान के पक्ष में लड़ता है। **—युरिपिडीज**

- बुद्धिमान व्यक्ति को जितने अवसर मिलते हैं, उनसे अधिक वह पैदा करता है। **—बेकन**

- अपना काम दूसरों पर छोड़ना भी एक तरह से दूसरे दिन काम टालने के समान ही है। ऐसे व्यक्ति का अवसर भी निकल जाता है और उसका काम भी पूरा नहीं होता। **—बिल गेट्स**

- अवसर उनकी सहायता कभी नहीं करता, जो अपनी सहायता नहीं करते।

—बिल गेट्स

- अवसर की प्रतीक्षा में मत बैठो। आज का अवसर ही सर्वोत्तम है।

—बिल गेट्स

- अवसर तुम्हारा दरवाजा एक ही बार खटखटाता है। **—बिल गेट्स**
- उतावला आदमी सफलता के अवसरों को बहुधा हाथ से गँवा देता है।

—बिल गेट्स

- अवसर सूर्योदय की तरह होते हैं, यदि आप ज्यादा देर तक प्रतीक्षा करते हैं तो आप उन्हें गँवा बैठते हैं। **—बिल गेट्स**
- आदर्श परिस्थितियों या सर्वश्रेष्ठ अवसरों की प्रतीक्षा न करें, वे कभी नहीं आनेवाले हैं। **—बिल गेट्स**
- उन्नति के किसी भी अवसर को खोना नहीं चाहिए। **—बिल गेट्स**

अविद्या

- अविद्या द्वारा मृत्यु को पार कर विद्या द्वारा अमृत प्राप्त करना चाहिए, यह चंचल संसार ही मृत्यु-निकेतन है, यही अविद्या है, इसको पार करने के लिए ही इसके भीतर से ही जाना पड़ता है। **—रवींद्रनाथ टैगोर**

असफलता

- असफलता यह बताती है कि सफलता का प्रयत्न पूरे मन से नहीं किया गया। **—श्रीराम शर्मा आचार्य**
- असफलता का मतलब यह नहीं कि आप असफल हैं, इसका मतलब सिर्फ इतना है कि आप अब तक सफल नहीं हो पाए हैं।

—बिल गेट्स

- जीवन के आरंभ में ही कुछ असफलताएँ मिल जाने का बहुत अधिक व्यावहारिक महत्त्व है। **—हक्स्ले**
- जो कभी भी कहीं असफल नहीं हुआ, वह आदमी महान् नहीं हो सकता।

—हर्मन मैलविल

- असफलता आपको महान् कार्यों के लिए तैयार करने की योजना है।
—नैपोलियन हिल

- असफलता का मौसम सफलता के बीज बोने के लिए सर्वश्रेष्ठ समय होता है। **—बिल गेट्स**

- असफलता केवल यह सिद्ध करती है कि सफलता का प्रयास पूरे मन से नहीं हुआ। **—बिल गेट्स**

- असफलता फिर से अधिक सूझ-बूझ के साथ कार्य आरंभ करने का एक मौका मात्र है। **—हेनरी फोर्ड**

- दो ही प्रकार के व्यक्ति वस्तुत: जीवन में असफल होते हैं—एक तो वे, जो सोचते हैं, पर उसे कार्य का रूप नहीं देते और दूसरे वे, जो कार्य-रूप में परिणित तो कर देते हैं, पर सोचते कभी नहीं। **—थामस इलियट**

- कल की असफलता वह बीज है, जिसे आज बोने पर आनेवाले कल में सफलता का फल मिलता है। **—बिल गेट्स**

- असफलता मुझे स्वीकार्य है, किंतु प्रयास न करना स्वीकार्य नहीं है।
—बिल गेट्स

- दूसरों को असफल करने के प्रयत्न ही हमें असफल बनाते हैं। **—एमर्सन**

- असफलता सफलता प्राप्त करने का एक महत्त्वपूर्ण हिस्सा है।
—बिल गेट्स

- असफलता से सफलता की शिक्षा मिलती है। **—बिल गेट्स**

- जीवन में दो ही व्यक्ति असफल होते हैं। पहले वे जो सोचते हैं, पर करते नहीं, दूसरे वे जो करते हैं, पर सोचते नहीं।
—श्रीराम शर्मा आचार्य

- प्रत्येक व्यक्ति को सफलता प्रिय है, लेकिन सफल व्यक्तियों से सभी लोग घृणा करते हैं। **—जॉन मैंकनरो**

• असफल होने पर आप को निराशा का सामना करना पड़ सकता है, परंतु प्रयास छोड़ देने पर आप की असफलता सुनिश्चित है।

—बेवेरली सिल्स

असंभव

• 'असंभव' एक शब्द है, जो मूर्खों के शब्दकोश में पाया जाता है।

—नेपोलियन

असमय

• असमय किया हुआ कार्य न किया हुआ जैसा ही है। **—अज्ञात**

असहयोग

• असहयोग अनुशासन और उत्सर्ग का कार्य है और उसमें विरोधी विचारों के प्रति धैर्य एवं आदर रखने की आवश्यकता पड़ती है। **—महात्मा गांधी**

• मैं काम करने के तरीकों, पद्धतियों और प्रणालियों से असहयोग करता हूँ, मनुष्यों से कदापि नहीं। **—महात्मा गांधी**

• असहयोग के हथियार से व्यक्तिगत, घरेलू, सामाजिक और राष्ट्रगत समस्याएँ अचूक रूप से हल हो सकती हैं, किंतु शर्त यह है कि उसका प्रयोग करने में गलती न हो। **—महात्मा गांधी**

• असहयोग में तो इतनी शक्ति है कि वह छोटी-से-छोटी इकाई परिवार को भंग कर देती है, फिर बड़ी इकाइयाँ, जिनमें असंख्य छोटी इकाइयाँ अंतर्भुक्त होती हैं, उसके सामने कैसे कायम रह सकती हैं। **—महात्मा गांधी**

अस्पृश्यता

• अस्पृश्यता हमारे राष्ट्र का अभिशाप है। **—महात्मा गांधी**

• अस्पृश्यता हिंदुत्व का कलंक है। **—महात्मा गांधी**

• अगर आत्मा एक है और ईश्वर एक है, तो फिर अछूत और अस्पृश्य कोई हो ही नहीं सकता। **—महात्मा गांधी**

- मेरी समझ में नहीं आता कि इनसान और इनसान के बीच अस्पृश्यता की भावना विवेक के सामने क्योंकर टिकी रह सकती है?

—महात्मा गांधी

- जहाँ अस्पृश्यता की भावना आ गई, मानवता वहाँ से विदा हो जाती है। कोई व्यक्ति मानवता का दंभ भरे और अस्पृश्यता भी कायम रखना चाहे तो वह ढोंगी है। **—महात्मा गांधी**

अहंकार

- वीर का असली दुश्मन उसका अहंकार है। **—अज्ञात**
- आदमी का सबसे बड़ा दुश्मन गरूर है। **—प्रेमचंद**
- जिसने गर्व किया, उसका पतन अवश्य हुआ है।

—स्वामी दयानंद सरस्वती

- मनुष्य जितना छोटा होता है, उसका अहंकार उतना ही बड़ा होता है।

—वाल्टेयर

- ज्यों-ज्यों अभिमान कम होता है, कीर्ति बढ़ती है। **—यंग**
- जो अहंकारपूर्वक प्रातः जलपान करता है, उसको सायंकाल का भोजन तिरस्कार से मिलता है। **—फ्रेंकलिन**
- अहंकार छोड़े बिना सच्चा प्रेम नहीं किया जा सकता।

—स्वामी विवेकानंद

- तलवार मारे एक बार, एहसान मारे बार-बार। **—लोकोक्ति**

अहिंसा

- अहिंसा परम श्रेष्ठ मानव-धर्म है, पशुबल से वह अनंत गुना महान् और उच्च है। **—महात्मा गांधी**
- उस जीवन को नष्ट करने का हमें कोई अधिकार नहीं, जिसके बनाने की शक्ति हममें न हो। **—महात्मा गांधी**

- जहाँ अहिंसा है, वहाँ अपार धीरज, भीतरी शांति, भले-बुरे का ज्ञान, आत्मत्याग और जानकारी भी है। **—महात्मा गांधी**
- अपने शत्रु से प्रेम करो, जो तुम्हें सताए, उसके लिए प्रार्थना करो। **—ईसा मसीह**
- संपूर्ण अहिंसा उच्चतम वीरता है। **—महात्मा गांधी**
- जब कोई व्यक्ति अहिंसा की कसौटी पर पूरा उतर जाता है तो अन्य व्यक्ति स्वयं ही उसके पास आकर बैरभाव भूल जाता है। **—पतंजलि**
- अहिंसा में इतनी ताकत है कि वह विरोधियों को मित्र बना लेती है, उनका प्रेम प्राप्त कर लेती है। **—महात्मा गांधी**
- जहाँ दया नहीं, वहाँ अहिंसा नहीं। जिसमें जितनी दया है, उतनी ही अहिंसा है। **—महात्मा गांधी**
- बिना अहिंसा के सत्य की खोज नामुमकिन है। **—महात्मा गांधी**
- सत्य के बाद असल में अहिंसा ही संसार में बड़ी-से-बड़ी सक्रिय शक्ति है। **—महात्मा गांधी**
- जो अहिंसा पर अंत तक डटा रहेगा, वह विजयी होकर रहेगा। **—महात्मा गांधी**
- अहिंसा का परिणाम देर से निकलता है, हिंसा का शीघ्र निकल आता है। **—महात्मा गांधी**
- हिंसा के मुकाबले में लाचारी का भाव आना अहिंसा नहीं कायरता है। अहिंसा को कायरता के साथ नहीं मिलाना चाहिए। **—महात्मा गांधी**

आँख

- अकेली आँख ही बता सकती है कि हृदय में प्रेम है अथवा घृणा। **—तिरुवल्लुवर**

आँसू

- जो औरों के लिए रोते हैं, उनके आँसू भी हीरों की चमक को हरा देते हैं।

—रांगेय राघव

- स्त्री! तूने अपने अथाह आँसुओं से संसार के हृदय को ऐसे घेर रखा है, जैसे समुद्र पृथ्वी को घेरे हुए है।

—रवींद्रनाथ टैगोर

- नारी के आँसू अपनी एक-एक बूँद में एक-एक बाढ़ लिये होते हैं।

—जयशंकर प्रसाद

- मेरी एक प्रबल कामना है कि मैं कम-से-कम एक आँख का आँसू पोंछ दूँ। **—महात्मा गांधी**

- सात सागरों में जल की अपेक्षा मानव के नेत्रों से कहीं अधिक आँसू बह चुके हैं। **—महात्मा बुद्ध**

आग्रह

- स्वयं पर आग्रह करो, अनुकरण मत करो। **—एमर्सन**

आचरण

- छोटी नदियाँ शोर करती हैं और बड़ी नदियाँ शांत, चुपचाप बहती हैं।

—सुत्तनिपात

- आचरण दर्पण के समान है, जिसमें हर मनुष्य अपना प्रतिबिंब दिखाता है।

—गेटे

- जैसा देश, वैसा भेष। **—कहावत**

- माता, पिता, गुरु, स्वामी, भ्राता, पुत्र और मित्र का कभी क्षण भर के लिए विरोध या अपकार नहीं करना चाहिए। **—शुक्रनीति**

- मनुष्य जिस समय पशु तुल्य आचरण करता है, उस समय वह पशुओं से भी नीचे गिर जाता है। **—रवींद्रनाथ टैगोर**

- शास्त्र पढ़कर भी लोग मूर्ख होते हैं, किंतु जो उसके अनुसार आचरण करता है, वह ही वस्तुतः विद्वान् है। **—अज्ञात**
- रोगियों के लिए भलीभाँति सोचकर निश्चित की गई औषधि नाम उच्चारण करने मात्र से किसी को निरोगी नहीं कर सकती। **—हितोपदेश**

आडंबर

- चिड़ियों की तरह हवा में उड़ना और मछलियों की तरह पानी में तैरना सीखने के बाद अब हमें इनसानों की तरह जमीन पर चलना सीखना है। **—सर्वपल्ली राधाकृष्णन**
- हिंदुस्तान का आदमी बैल तो पाना चाहता है, लेकिन गाय की सेवा करना नहीं चाहता। वह धार्मिक दृष्टि से पूजन का स्वाँग रचता है; लेकिन दूध के लिए तो भैंस की ही कद्र करता है। हिंदुस्तान के लोग चाहते हैं कि उनकी माता तो रहे भैंस और पिता हो बैल। योजना तो ठीक है, लेकिन वह भगवान् को मंजूर नहीं है। **—विनोबा**
- भारतीय संस्कृति और धर्म के नाम पर लोगों को जो परोसा जा रहा है, वह हमें धर्म के अपराधीकरण की ओर ले जा रहा है, इसके लिए पंडे, पुजारी, पादरी, महंत, मौलवी, राजनेता आदि सभी जिम्मेदार हैं। ये लोग धर्म के नाम पर नफरत की दुकानें चलाकर समाज को बाँटने का काम कर रहे हैं। **—स्वामी रामदेव**
- बकरियों की लड़ाई, मुनि के श्राद्ध, प्रातःकाल की घनघटा तथा पति-पत्नी के बीच कलह में प्रदर्शन अधिक और वास्तविकता कम होती है। **—नीतिशास्त्र**
- भूलना प्रायः प्रातिक है, जबकि याद रखना प्रायः कृत्रिम है। **—रत्वान रोमैन खिमैनेस**
- जो व्यक्ति सोने का बहाना कर रहा है, उसे आप उठा नहीं सकते। **—नवाजोजब**

- तुम्हारे खुद के दरवाजे की सीढ़ियाँ गंदी हैं तो पड़ोसी की छत पर पड़ी गंदगी का उलाहना मत दीजिए। **—कन्फ्यूशियस**

आत्मनिर्भरता

- आत्मनिर्भरता सद् व्यवहार की आधारशिला है। **—एमर्सन**

आत्मविश्वास

- आत्मविश्वास सफलता का मुख्य रहस्य है। **—एमर्सन**
- आत्मविश्वास किसी भी कार्य के लिए आवश्यक तत्त्व है, क्योंकि एक बड़ी खाई को दो छोटी छलाँगों में पार नहीं किया जा सकता। **—बिल गेट्स**
- आत्मविश्वास वीरता का सार है। **—एमर्सन**
- यह आत्मविश्वास रखो कि तुम पृथ्वी के सबसे आवश्यक मनुष्य हो। **—गोर्की**
- आत्मविश्वास के साथ आप गगन चूम सकते हैं और आत्मविश्वास के बिना मामूली सी उपलिब्धयाँ भी पकड़ से परे हैं। **—बिल गेट्स**
- जिसमें आत्मविश्वास नहीं, उसमें अन्य चीजों के प्रति विश्वास कैसे उत्पन्न हो सकता है। **—स्वामी विवेकानंद**
- आत्मविश्वास, आत्मज्ञान और आत्मसंयम केवल यही तीन जीवन को परम शांति संपन्न बना देते हैं। **—टेनीसन**
- आत्मविश्वास के साथ आप गगन चूम सकते हैं और आत्मविश्वास के बिना मामूली सी उपलब्धियाँ भी आपकी पकड़ से परे हैं। **—बिल गेट्स**
- आत्मविश्वास किसी भी कार्य के लिए आवश्यक तत्त्व है, क्योंकि एक बड़ी खाई को दो छोटी छलाँगों में पार नहीं किया जा सकता। **—अज्ञात**
- आत्मविश्वास के साथ आप गगन चूम सकते हैं और आत्मविश्वास के बिना मामूली सी उपलिब्धयाँ भी पकड़ से परे हैं। **—जिम लोहर**

- पेड़ की शाखा पर बैठा पंछी कभी भी इसलिए नहीं डरता कि डाल हिल रही है, क्योंकि पंछी डाली पर नहीं, अपने पँखों पर भरोसा करता है। **—अज्ञात**
- आत्मविश्वास वह संबल है, जो रास्ते की हर बाधा को धराशायी कर सकता है।

  —बिल गेट्स
- आत्मविश्वासी कभी हारता नहीं, कभी थकता नहीं, कभी गिरता नहीं और कभी मरता नहीं। **—बिल गेट्स**
- अनुभूतियों के सरोवर में आत्मविश्वास के कमल खिलते हैं।

  —अमृतलाल नागर
- आत्मविश्वासी व्यक्ति अपने कार्य को पूरा करके ही छोड़ता है।

  —स्वेट मार्डेन
- महान् वह है, जो दृढ़तम निश्चय के साथ सत्य का अनुसरण करता है।

  —सेनेका

आत्मसम्मान

- आत्मसम्मान रखना सफलता की सीढ़ी पर पग रखना है। **—अज्ञात**

आत्मा

- यह आत्मा ब्रह्म है। **—बृहदारण्यकोपनिषद्**
- मनुष्य की आत्मा उसके भाग्य से अधिक बड़ी होती है।

  —श्री अरविंद
- आत्मा को न शास्त्र काट सकता है, न आग जला सकती है, न जल भिगो सकता है और न हवा सुखा सकती है।

  —भगवद्गीता
- क्या तुम नहीं जानते, तुम ही ईश्वर का मंदिर हो और ईश्वर की आत्मा तुममें रहती है। **—इंजील**

- सबकी आत्मा एक जैसी है, सबकी आत्मा की शक्ति एक सामान है। कुछ की शक्ति प्रकट हो गई है और दूसरों की प्रकट होनी बाकी है।

—महात्मा गांधी

- आत्मा ही अपना स्वर्ग और नरक है। **—उमर खैयाम**

- आत्मा एक चेतन का तत्त्व है, जो अपने रहने के लिए उपयुक्त शक्ति का आश्रय लेता है और एक शरीर से दूसरे शरीर में जाता है। भौतिक शरीर इस आत्मा को धारण करने के लिए विवश होता है। **—गेटे**

- अहं की मृत्यु द्वारा आत्मा का वर्जन करते-करते अपने रूपांतरित स्वरूप को आत्मा प्रकाशित करती है। **—रवींद्रनाथ टैगोर**

- सबसे खतरनाक वह दिशा होती है, जिसमें आत्मा का सूरज डूब जाए।

—अवतार सिंह पाश

- अंतरात्मा हमें न्यायाधीश के समान दंड देने से पूर्व मित्र की भाँति चेतावनी देती है। **—अज्ञात**

- आवेश कोई भावनात्मक ऊर्जा नहीं, बल्कि आत्मा और बाहरी दुनिया का टकराव है। **—आंद्रेई तारकोव्स्की**

- हमेशा अपनी आत्मा की आवाज सुनो। शरीर के मामले में, जो स्थान साबुन का है, वही आत्मा के संदर्भ में आँसू का है।

—यहूदी कहावत

- जो अवगुण तुम्हें दूसरों में दृष्टिगत होते हैं, उन्हें अपने भीतर न रहने दो।

—स्प्रैट

- कोई अभियोक्ता इतना शक्तिशाली नहीं है, जितना कि अपना अंत:करण।

—सोफोक्लीज

- अंत:करण आत्मा की वाणी है। **—जे.जे. रूसो**

- सबसे उत्तम तीर्थ निश्चल मन है। —**शंकराचार्य**

- हमें लोहे के पुट्ठे और इस्पात के स्नायु चाहिए, जिनमें वज्र सा मन निवास करे। —**स्वामी विवेकानंद**

आत्मिक शक्ति

- आत्मिक शक्ति ही वास्तविक शक्ति है। —**स्वामी शिवानंद**

आदत

- मन की आदत है अपने साथ लड़ना। —**रवींद्रनाथ टैगोर**

- अच्छी आदतों से शक्ति की बचत होती है, अवगुण से बरबादी। —**बिल गेट्स**

आदमी

- आदमी में जो सबसे बड़ी चीज है, जो तपस्वी भाव है, जो सुंदरता है, उसे ही लोग रुला मारना चाहते हैं। —**रवींद्रनाथ टैगोर**

- आदमी का मन भी कितना अजीब होता है। एक पल में ही उसके पालों में उल्टी हवा भर जाती है। —**रवींद्रनाथ टैगोर**

आदमीयत

- भले आदमी की भी एक सीमा होती है, उसे पार करने से जाने कैसा आघात लगता है पौरुष पर। —**रवींद्रनाथ टैगोर**

आदर्श

- आदर्श कभी नहीं मरते। —**भगिनी निवेदिता**

- गुस्सा कहो, डर कहो, लज्जा कहो या नफरत कहो, ये सब जलानेवाली लकड़ी की तरह उनके दिल की आग को और बढ़ाकर खुद जलकर राख हो जाते हैं, जो चीज इन्हें काबू में रख सकती है, वह है आदर्श। —**रवींद्रनाथ टैगोर**

- बाहुबल और धनबल में तत्काल संतुष्टि के अवसर रहते हैं, परंतु आदर्श के बल को तो अनंत धैर्य रखना ही चाहिए। **—रवींद्रनाथ टैगोर**
- बहुत दिनों तक प्रयत्न करते-करते मनुष्य अपने मन की शक्ति से अपने आदर्श का गठन करता है, प्राण-शक्ति का अंधापन उसे तोड़ता है। **—रवींद्रनाथ टैगोर**
- आदर्श की रक्षा यथार्थ भाव से करना राष्ट्रीय कर्तव्य की अपेक्षा कठिन और अधिक महत्त्वपूर्ण है। **—रवींद्रनाथ टैगोर**
- जो आदर्श दूसरे आदर्श के प्रति विद्वेष का भाव रखता है, वह आदर्श ही नहीं है। **—रवींद्रनाथ टैगोर**

आनंद

- आनंद किस रूप में अपने को प्रकाशित करता है—प्राचुर्य में, ऐश्वर्य में, सौंदर्य में? **—रवींद्रनाथ टैगोर**
- जगत् में हमारा आनंद और हमारा प्रेम ही सत्य के प्रकाश की उपलब्धि है। **—रवींद्रनाथ टैगोर**
- आनंद वह खुशी है, जिसके भोगने पर पछतावा नहीं होता। **—सुकरात**
- पढ़कर आनंद के अतिरेक से आँखें यदि नीली न हो जाएँ तो वह कहानी कैसी? **—शरतचंद्र**
- मनुष्य का स्थायी आनंद किसी वस्तु के ग्रहण में नहीं, वरन् अपने को उसके प्रति समर्पित करने में है, जो अपनी अपेक्षा अधिक महान् है तथा अपने को उन विचारों के प्रति समर्पित करने में है, जो वैयक्तिक आत्मा की अपेक्षा अधिक विशाल है, जैसे अपने देश का विचार, मानवता का विचार, परमात्मा का विचार। **—रवींद्रनाथ टैगोर**
- आनंद की लहर में बाहर की अपेक्षा भीतर का आयोजन ही अधिक बड़ा है। **—रवींद्रनाथ टैगोर**

- आनंद अपने आप में बंदी होकर संपूर्ण नहीं होता, अपने त्याग से ही संपूर्ण होता है। **—रवींद्रनाथ टैगोर**
- आनंद का मूल है—संतोष। **—मनुस्मृति**
- आनंद वह खुशी है, जिसके भोगने पर पछताना नहीं पड़ता। **—सुकरात**
- केवल आत्मज्ञान ही आत्मा–हृदय को सच्चा आनंद प्रदान करता है। **—स्वामी रामतीर्थ**
- क्षण भर भी काम के बिना रहना ईश्वर की चोरी समझो, दूसरा कोई रास्ता भीतरी या बाहरी आनंद का नहीं जानता। **—महात्मा गांधी**
- हम स्वयं आनंद की अनुभूति लेने की बजाय दूसरों को यह विश्वास दिलाने की कोशिश करते हैं कि हम आनंद में हैं। **—कन्फ्यूशियस**
- जो वस्तु आनंद प्रदान नहीं कर सकती, वह सुंदर हो ही नहीं सकती। **—प्रेमचंद**
- आयु में आनंद है, समग्र शरीर के मंगल में, स्वास्थ्य में आनंद है। इसी आनंद का भाग करने पर दो वस्तुएँ प्राप्त होती हैं—एक ज्ञान और दूसरा प्रेम। **—रवींद्रनाथ टैगोर**

आपत्ति

- ईश्वर आपत्तियों का भला करे, क्योंकि इन्हीं से मित्र और शत्रु की पहचान होती है। **—अज्ञात**
- मनुष्य को आपत्ति का सामना करने में सहायता देने के लिए मुसकान से बड़ी कोई चीज नहीं है। **—तिरुवल्लुवर**
- आपत्ति मनुष्य बनाती है और संपत्ति राक्षस। **—विक्टर ह्यूगो**
- धीरज, धर्म, मित्र अरु नारी। आपत् काल परखिए चारी॥ **—तुलसीदास**

- आपत्ति काल में हमारी अजीब-अजीब लोगों से पहचान हो जाती है, जो अन्यथा संभव नहीं। **—शेक्सपियर**
- रंज से खूगर (अभ्यस्त) हुआ इनसान तो मिट जाता है रंज! **—अज्ञात**

आपदा

- आपदा एक ऐसी वस्तु है, जो हमें अपने जीवन की गहराइयों में अंतर्दृष्टि प्रदान करती है। **—विवेकानंद**

आभूषण

- नारी का आभूषण शील और लज्जा है। बाह्य आभूषण उसकी शोभा नहीं बढ़ा सकते हैं। **—बृहत्कल्पभाष्य**

आय

- विद्वत्ता, चतुराई और बुद्धिमानी की बात यही है कि मनुष्य अपनी आय से कम व्यय करे। **—अज्ञात**

आयु

- बुढ़ापा मेरी तुलना में 15 साल बड़ा है। **—ओलिवर वेंडेल होम्स**
- बुढ़ापा तूफान में उड़ रहे एक विमान की तरह है। एक बार आप बैठ गए तो फिर कुछ नहीं कर सकते। **—गोल्डा मीर**
- बुढ़ापा बाकी सभी चीजों की तरह ही है। इसे सफल बनाने के लिए जवानी में ही शुरुआत करनी पड़ती है। **—थिओडोर रूजवेल्ट**
- जब तक किसी को खुद का और अपने काम का साथ मिल रहा है, वह बूढ़ा नहीं महसूस कर सकता, चाहे उसकी उम्र कितनी भी हो। **—एमोस ब्रोंसन एल्कोट**
- झुर्रियों से बस यह संकेत मिलना चाहिए कि मुसकराहटें कहाँ-कहाँ थीं। **—मार्क ट्वैन**

- आप उम्र का बढ़ना नहीं रोक सकते, पर आपको बूढ़ा नहीं होना है।
—जॉर्ज बर्न्स

- जब आपकी काली पुस्तक में हर एक नाम के बाद एमडी लगा होता है, तब आप जान जाते हैं कि आप बूढ़े हो रहे हैं। **—हैरिसन फोर्ड**

- किसी स्त्री के लिए एक पुरातत्त्वविद् ही सबसे अच्छा पति हो सकता है। जितनी उसकी उम्र बढ़ेगी, उतनी उसके पति की उसमें जिज्ञासा।
—अगाथा क्रिस्टी

- जो सीखना छोड़ देता है, वह बूढ़ा है, चाहे बीस का हो या अस्सी का। जो सीखता रहता है, वह जवान रहता है। जिंदगी की सबसे बड़ी चीज है अपने दिमाग को जवान रखना। **—हेनरी फोर्ड**

- मध्य वय वह होता है, जब आपकी उम्र आपके बीच के हिस्से में दिखाई देने लगती है। **—बॉब होप**

- जैसे-जैसे आदमी की उम्र बढ़ती है, खिलौने और महँगे होते जाते हैं।
—मार्विन डेविस

- लज्जा युवाओं के लिए एक आभूषण, लेकिन बुढ़ापे के लिए एक तिरस्कार है। **—अरस्तू**

- चालीस के ऊपर के सभी व्यक्ति बदमाश हैं। **—जॉर्ज बर्नार्ड शा**

- चालीस जवानी का बुढ़ापा है, पचास बुढ़ापे की जवानी है।**—विक्टर ह्यूगो**

- मेरा सोचना है कि आपकी पूरी जिंदगी आपके चेहरे में दिखाई देती है और आपको उसपर गर्व होना चाहिए। **—लौरेल बैकाल**

- मैं कभी बुड्ढ़ा नहीं होऊँगा। मेरे लिए बुढ़ापा हमेशा मुझसे 15 साल बड़ा है। **—फ्रांसिस बेकन**

- जवानी में हम मुसीबतों के पीछे भागते हैं, बुढ़ापे में मुसीबतें हमारे पीछे।
—बेवेरली सिल्स

• बूढ़ा होना दु:ख की बात है, पर परिपक्व होना अच्छा है।

—ब्रिगिटते बैर्दोट

• जवान होने में बहुत वक्त लगता है। **—पाब्लो पिकासो**

• मध्य वय बिना छिछोरापन के जवानी है और बिना बीमारी के बुढ़ापा।

—डोरिस डे

• कभी किसी की उम्र इतनी नहीं होती कि वह और बेहतर न जान सके।

—होल्ब्रुक जैक्सन

• कोई उम्र का बढ़ना नहीं रोक सकता, पर अपनी उत्पादकता बढ़ाते हुए उम्रदराज होना कुछ और ही है। **—कैथेरीन ग्रेहम**

• जिनका उत्साह खत्म हो चुका है, उनसे वृद्ध कोई नहीं है।

—हेनरी डेविड थोरीओ

• बुढ़ापा अचानक ही आ जाता है, न कि धीरे-धीरे, जैसा कि सोचा जाता है।

—एमिली डिकिंसन

• जवानी धनवान होने के लिए सबसे अच्छा समय है और गरीब होने के लिए भी। **—युरिपाइड्स**

• जवानी प्रकृति का उपहार है, पर उम्र कला का एक काम है।

—स्तैंसला लेस

• युवावस्था वह है, जब आपको नए साल पर देर रात तक जागने की अनुमति दी जाती है। प्रौढ़ावस्था वह है, जब आपको जागने के लिए मजबूर किया जाता है। **—बिल वौगेन**

• बुढ़ापे में कायरता के लिए कोई जगह नहीं है। **—बेट्टे डेविस**

• जो कुछ भी इनसान को हो सकता है, उसमें बुढ़ापा सबसे अचानक होनेवाली चीज है। **—जेम्स थर्बर**

- बुढ़ापे की तैयारी किशोरावस्था से ही शुरू हो जानी चाहिए। ऐसी जिंदगी, जिसका 65 साल तक कोई उद्देश्य न रहा हो, वह अचानक सेवानिवृत्ति के समय सार्थक नहीं हो जाएगी।

—ड्वाइट एल. मूडी

- उम्र न बढ़ने की एक संभावना है, लेकिन वह आपके अंदर से आनी होगी।

—सुजैन एंटन

- बुढ़ापे जैसी कोई चीज नहीं है, है तो बस दुःख है। **—फेवेल्डन**
- जवानी में की गई ज्यादतियों को हम बुढ़ापे में भोगते हैं। **—जे.बी. प्रिस्तले**
- भले ही कवि, वक्ता या ज्ञानी कुछ भी कहें, बुढ़ापा तो बुढ़ापा ही है।

—सिंक्लेयर लुईस

आरोग्य

- आरोग्य परम लाभ है, संतोष परम धन है, विश्वास परम बंधु है, निर्वाण परम सुख है। **—धम्मपद**
- धर्म, अर्थ, काम और मोक्ष का प्रधान कारण आरोग्य है।

—चरक संहिता

आराम

- फोड़ा चीरने से पहले रोगी के डर और घबराहट की कोई सीमा नहीं होती, लेकिन नश्तर लगने पर रोगी देखता है कि दर्द तो है, पर आराम भी है और मामला कल्पना में जितना सांघातिक जान पड़ता था, वास्तव में उतना नहीं है। **—रवींद्रनाथ टैगोर**
- आदमी की जिंदगी में बहुत कम आराम लिखा है और कुछ नहीं तो पेट की चिंता ही उसे हमेशा सताया करती है। **—रवींद्रनाथ टैगोर**

आलस्य

- आलस्य जीवित मनुष्य की कब्र है। **—कूपर**

• आलस्य दरिद्रता की कुंजी और सारे अवगुणों की जड़ है।

—कार्लाइल

• जो बार-बार की ठोकरों से नहीं चेतता, वह अनिष्ट को आमंत्रण देता है।

• आलस्य में जीवन बिताना आत्महत्या के समान है। **—सुकरात**

• आलस्य मनुष्यों के शरीर में रहनेवाला घोर शत्रु है। **—भर्तृहरि**

• आलस्य दरिद्रता का मूल है। **—यजुर्वेद**

आलोचना

• समाज की आलोचना का अधिक मूल्य नहीं है, आज जिसे लेकर इतनी हलचल है, दो दिन बाद वह किसी को याद भी न रहेगा।

—रवींद्रनाथ टैगोर

• एक दूसरा नशा है भर्त्सना! शिष्ट भाषा में उसे आलोचना कह सकते हैं।

—रवींद्रनाथ टैगोर

• पराए के दोषों की आलोचना करने से मन छोटा हो जाता है, स्वभाव संदिग्ध हो जाता है और हृदय में सरलता नहीं रह जाती।

—रवींद्रनाथ टैगोर

आवश्यकता

• ज्ञानवृक्ष का फल खाने के बाद से जब तक कि उस फल को पूरी तरह हज्म नहीं कर लेता, मनुष्य की साज-सज्जा की आवशकताएँ बढ़ती ही जा रही हैं।

—रवींद्रनाथ टैगोर

• आवश्यकता आविष्कार की जननी है। **—लोकोक्ति**

• आवश्यकता से अधिक बोलना व्यर्थ है। **—तुकाराम**

• असीम आवश्यकता नहीं, तृष्णा होती है। **—जैनेंद्र**

• आवश्यकता अत्याचारी होती है। **—रवींद्रनाथ टैगोर**

आवेग

- जिसे थ्रिल-सनसनी कहते हैं या जिसे आवेग कहते हैं, वह है पहले नंबर की चीज, जो बड़े भाग्य से कदाचित् ही नसीब होती है। **—रवींद्रनाथ टैगोर**

आविष्कार

- आविष्कार से आविष्कार का जन्म होता है। **—एमर्सन**

आशा

- आशा और आत्मविश्वास ही वे वस्तुएँ हैं, जो हमारी शक्तियों को जाग्रत् करती हैं। **—स्वेट मार्डेन**
- प्रयत्नशील मनुष्य के लिए सदा आशा है। **—गेटे**

आशा

- फल मिलना निश्चित होता तो देरी भी सही जाती। भोग की आशा अनिश्चित है। **—रवींद्रनाथ टैगोर**
- आशा के साथ तैयार की गई सड़क पर यात्रा करना, उस सड़क पर यात्रा करने से कहीं अधिक आनंददायक होता है, जिसे निराशा के साथ तैयार किया जाता है, चाहे आशा एक नदी है, उसमें इच्छा रूपी जल है, तृष्णा उस नदी की तरंगें हैं, आसक्ति उसके मगर हैं; तर्क-वितर्क उसके पक्षी हैं, उन दोनों की मंजिल एक ही क्यों न हो। **—बिल गेट्स**
- मोह रूपी भँवरों के कारण वह सुकुमार तथा गहरी है। चिंता ही उसके ऊँचे-नीचे किनारे हैं, जो धैर्य के वृक्षों को नष्ट करते हैं।
- जो शुचित्त उसके पास चले जाते हैं, वे बड़ा आनंद पाते हैं। **—कहावत**
- आशा प्रयत्नशील मनुष्य का साथ कभी नहीं छोड़ती। **—बिल गेट्स**
- आशा अमर है, उसकी आराधना कभी निष्फल नहीं होती। **—महात्मा गांधी**
- आशा प्रयत्नशील मनुष्य का साथ कभी नहीं छोड़ती। **—गेटे**

• आशा कभी आपको छोड़कर नहीं जाती है, आप इसे छोड़ते हैं।
—बिल गेट्स

• जितनी अधिक आशा रखोगे, उतनी अधिक निराशा होगी। **—कहावत**

• स्मृति पीछे दृष्टि डालती है और आशा आगे। **—रामचंद्र टंडन**

• मेरी मानो अपनी नाक से आगे न देखा करो। तुम्हें हमेशा मालूम होता रहेगा, उसके आगे भी कुछ है, और यह ज्ञान तुम्हें आशा और आनंद से मस्त रखेगा। **—बर्नार्ड शा**

• आशाएँ जितनी बड़ी होती हैं, भीतर-बाहर उतनी ही बड़ी बाधाएँ ले आती हैं। **—रवींद्रनाथ टैगोर**

आश्रय

• संसार में ज्यादा साधनहीन व्यक्ति को आश्रय देना ही सबसे कठिन है। उसे आश्रय की आवश्यकता जितनी अधिक होती है, आश्रय की बाधाएँ भी उसके लिए उतनी ही विषम होती हैं। **—रवींद्रनाथ टैगोर**

• विपत्ति स्वयं आकर आश्रय माँगे तो उसे लौटाया नहीं जा सकता।
—रवींद्रनाथ टैगोर

• पेड़ की अपनी डाल टूटकर पराई हो जाए तो पेड़ उसे किसी तरह से अपनी नहीं बना सकता, लेकिन बाहर से जो लता बढ़ आती है, उसे आश्रय दे सकता है, यहाँ तक कि ऊँचे में उसके गिराने पर भी उसे फिर उठा देने में कोई दिक्कत नहीं होती। **—रवींद्रनाथ टैगोर**

आसक्ति

• विषयों के प्रति आसक्ति मोह उत्पन्न करती है। **—भारवि**

• वह (आसक्ति) शुभ नहीं है, शांत नहीं है, वह मन की तरह लाल है, मद की तरह तीव्र है, वह बुद्धि को स्थिर नहीं रहने देती, वह एक वस्तु को दूसरी ही वस्तु करके दिखाती है। **—रवींद्रनाथ टैगोर**

आह्वान

- अपनी सृष्टि-शक्ति से देश को अपना बनाने का आह्वान बहुत बड़ा है।
—रवींद्रनाथ टैगोर

आहार

- आहार शरीर के लिए है, न कि शरीर आहार के लिए। **—महात्मा गांधी**
- संसार में भूख से पीड़ित होकर उतने व्यक्ति नहीं मरते, जितने अधिक भोजन करने के कुपरिणाम से मरते हैं। **—महात्मा गांधी**
- हम लोग अधिक भोजन करने के थोड़े-बहुत अपराधी हैं, इसलिए धार्मिक दृष्टि से कभी-कभी व्रत रखने के नियम बनाए हैं। सचमुच स्वास्थ्य की दृष्टि से पक्ष में एक दिन व्रत-उपवास करना जरूरी है। **—महात्मा गांधी**
- आहार मानव-जीवन की दैनिक आवश्यकताओं में से है, पर उसका नियंत्रण अनिवार्य है। **—महात्मा गांधी**
- आहार संतुलित और विवेकपूर्ण हो, तो शरीर में कोई रोग हो ही नहीं सकता। **—महात्मा गांधी**
- जब तक आहार में स्वाद की प्रधानता है, तब तक उसमें सात्त्विकता आ ही नहीं सकती। **—महात्मा गांधी**

इंटरनेट

- इंटरनेट के उपयोक्ता वांछित डाटा को शीघ्रता से और तेजी से प्राप्त करना चाहते हैं। उन्हें आकर्षक डिजाइनों तथा सुंदर साइटों से बहुधा कोई मतलब नहीं होता है।
—टिम बर्नर्स ली
- शाम वर्ल्ड वाइड वेब पर बिताना ऐसा ही है, जैसा कि आप दो घंटे से कुरकुरे खा रहे हों और आपकी उँगली मसाले से पीली पड़ गई हो, आपकी भूख खत्म हो गई हो, परंतु आपको पोषण तो मिला ही नहीं।
—क्लिफोर्ड स्टॉल

इंद्रियाँ

- जिसने इंद्रियों को अपने वश में कर लिया है, उसे स्त्री तिनके के समान जान पड़ती है।

—चाणक्य

- अविवेकी और चंचल आदमी की इंद्रियाँ बेखबर सारथी के दुष्ट घोड़ों की तरह बेकाबू हो जाती हैं।

—कठोपनिषद्

- जब मनुष्य अपनी इंद्रियों को विषयों से खींच लेता है, तभी उसकी बुद्धि स्थिर होती है।

—महाभारत

- सब इंद्रियों को वश में रखकर सर्वत्र समत्व का पालन करके, जो दृढ़, अचल और अचिंत्य, सर्वव्यापी, स्वर्णीय, अविनाशी स्वरूप की उपसना करते हैं, वे सब प्राणियों के हित में लगे हुए मुझे ही पाते हैं।

—भगवान् कृष्ण

इच्छा

- इच्छा मन की एक मात्र चाल (गति) है और उसी के अनुसार चलने को मूर्ख लोग आजादी कहते हैं, किंतु हमारे देश में विद्वान् लोग समझते हैं कि इच्छा ही हमारे सभी कामों और गतिविधि का एक नामकरण है, वही सारे बंधनों की जड़ है। अतः मुक्ति पाने के लिए वे लोग सलाह देते हैं कि इच्छा को जड़ से काट दो।

—रवींद्रनाथ टैगोर

- इच्छा ही सृष्टि का मूल है और इच्छा के पीछे शक्ति-ऐश्वर्य रहता है, जो अदमनीय है, जो उदारता से अपने आपको व्यक्त करना चाहता है।

—रवींद्रनाथ टैगोर

- कार्य, विशेषतः अच्छा कार्य, तभी सरल हो पाता है, जब इच्छा आत्मानुशासन सीख लेती है।

इच्छाशक्ति

- इच्छाशक्ति न रहने पर भी छोटे-मोटे काम तो जैसे-तैसे उधार पर चलाए जा सकते हैं, लेकिन असली जरूरत के समय दूसरे का हवाला देकर काम नहीं चलाया जा सकता। **—रवींद्रनाथ टैगोर**

इज्जत

- मन की इज्जत चली गई तो आदमी जिंदा रहते हुए भी मरे के समान है। **—रवींद्रनाथ टैगोर**

इतिहास

- पूरे यत्न से इतिहास की रक्षा करनी चाहिए। इतिहास और अपना प्राचीन गौरव नष्ट कर देने से विनाश निश्चित है। **—महाभारत**
- इतिहास के तजुर्बों से हम सबक नहीं लेते, इसीलिए इतिहास अपने आपको दोहराता है। **—विनोबा**
- इतिहास का कोई वाहन नहीं होता, पुष्पक विमान की तरह वह स्वयंचालित होता है। कम-से-कम उसके चालक को कोई वेतन नहीं देना होता। **—रवींद्रनाथ टैगोर**
- इतिहास सदा विजेता द्वारा ही लिखा जाता है। **—बिल गेट्स**
- इतिहास से हम सीखते हैं कि हमने उससे कुछ नहीं सीखा। **—बिल गेट्स**
- उचित रूप से देखें तो कुछ भी इतिहास नहीं है, सबकुछ मात्र आत्मकथा है। **—एमर्सन**
- इतिहास असत्यों पर एकत्र की गई सहमति है। **—नेपोलियन बोनापार्ट**
- इंजीनियर इतिहास का निर्माता रहा है और आज भी है। **—जेम्स के. फिंक**

- ज्ञानी लोगों का कहना है कि जो भी भविष्य को देखने की इच्छा रखता हो, भूत (इतिहास) से सीख ले। **—मैक्यावेली द प्रिंस**
- इतिहास स्वयं को दोहराता है, इतिहास के बारे में यही एक बुरी बात है। **—सी डैरो**
- शक्तिशाली लोगों द्वारा उनके धन और बल की रक्षा के लिए लिखा जाता है। **—अज्ञात**
- संक्षेप में, मानव इतिहास सुविचारों का इतिहास है। **—एच.जी. वेल्स**
- जो इतिहास को याद नहीं रखते, उनको इतिहास को दुहराने का दंड मिलता है। **—जॉर्ज संतायन**
- सभ्यता की कहानी सार रूप में इंजीनियरिंग की कहानी है—वह लंबा और विकट संघर्ष, जो प्रकृति की शक्तियों को मनुष्य के भले के लिए काम कराने के लिए किया गया। **—एस डीकैंप**

इनसान

- इनसान को उसके काम से आँका जाता है। **—बिल गेट्स**
- इनसान जितनी सहजता से सलाह देता है, उतनी सहजता से और कुछ नहीं देता। **—बिल गेट्स**

इनसाफ

- इनसाफ के लिए डटकर खड़े हो जाने से ही अन्याय का प्रतिकार होता है। **—रवींद्रनाथ टैगोर**
- राजा के सामने इनसाफ के लिए दौड़ने पर चाहे वादी हो, चाहे प्रतिवादी, चाहे दोषी हो, चाहे निर्दोष, प्रजा को रोना ही पड़ता है।

ईर्ष्या

- मनुष्य की जितनी ईर्ष्या मनुष्य पर होती है, उतनी यम पर नहीं। **—रवींद्रनाथ टैगोर**

- ईर्ष्या करनेवालों का सबसे बड़ा शत्रु उसकी ईर्ष्या ही है। **—तिरुवल्लुवर**
- ईर्ष्यालु को मृत्यु के समान दुःख भोगना पड़ता है। **—वेदव्यास**

ईमानदारी

- मनुष्य की प्रतिष्ठा ईमानदारी पर ही निर्भर है। **—अज्ञात**
- ईमानदार मनुष्य ईश्वर की सर्वोत्कृष्ट कृति है। **—अज्ञात**
- ईमानदारी किसी कायदे-कानून की मोहताज नहीं होती। **—आल्बेर काम**

ईश्वर

- मैं ईश्वर से डरता हूँ और ईश्वर के बाद उससे डरता हूँ, जो ईश्वर से नहीं डरता। **—शेख सादी**
- ईश्वर सभी अच्छी-बुरी बातों का हिसाब रखता है। दुनिया में इससे बड़ा हिसाबी दूसरा कोई नहीं है। **—महात्मा गांधी**
- पैसे में परमेश्वर को देखना परमेश्वर को भूलने जैसा है। **—महात्मा गांधी**
- ईश्वर अपनी सृष्टि को किसी अवस्था में साँकल से बाँधकर नहीं रखते, उसे नए-नए परिवर्तनों के बीच निरंतर नवीन करते हुए सजग रखते हैं। **—रवींद्रनाथ टैगोर**
- ईश्वर एक है और वह एकता को पसंद करता है। **—हजरत मोहम्मद**
- जबान से ईश्वर, खुदा, सत्श्री अकाल, कुछ भी नाम लो, वह झूठा है, अगर दिल में यह नाम नहीं है। **—महात्मा गांधी**
- जो ईश्वर के न्याय के बारे में शंका करते हैं, उनका हृदय कभी प्रफुल्लित नहीं रहता। **—महात्मा गांधी**
- हे प्रभु! तुम्हारी वाणी सरल है, परंतु उनकी नहीं, जो तुम्हारे विषय में बताते हैं। **—रवींद्रनाथ टैगोर**

- ईश्वर के अस्तित्व के लिए बुद्धि से प्रमाण नहीं मिल सकता, क्योंकि ईश्वर सिद्ध से परे है। **—महात्मा गांधी**
- यदि ईश्वर नहीं है तो उसका आविष्कार कर लेना जरूरी है। **—वाल्टेयर**
- जो ईश्वर को अपने पास समझता है, वह कभी नहीं हारता। **—महात्मा गांधी**
- पूजा की विधि या शब्दों की तरफ ईश्वर नहीं देखता, वह तो हमारे हठित और वाणी के आर-पार भी देख सकता है। **—महात्मा गांधी**
- अशुद्ध मस्तिष्क और अशुद्ध शरीर से हम प्रभु का आशीर्वाद नहीं पा सकते। **—महात्मा गांधी**
- ईश्वर एक शाश्वत बालक है, जो शाश्वत बाग में शाश्वत खेल खेल रहा है। **—श्री अरविंद**
- तैयार न हों और जब हम तैयार हों, तो वह न आए। **—रवींद्रनाथ टैगोर**
- ईश्वर की महाशक्ति मंद झोंके में है, तूफान में नहीं। **—रवींद्रनाथ टैगोर**
- ईश्वर बड़े साम्राज्यों से विमुख हो सकता है, पर छोटे-छोटे फूलों से कभी खिन्न नहीं होता। **—रवींद्रनाथ टैगोर**
- ईश्वर को देखा नहीं जा सकता, इसीलिए तो वह हर जगह मौजूद है। **—यासुनारी कावाबाता**
- यदि ईश्वर का अस्तित्व न होता, तो उसके आविष्कार की आवश्यकता पड़ती। **—वाल्टेयर**
- ईश्वर यदि है, तो मेरी बुद्धि उन्हीं की देन है। वही बुद्धि कहती है कि ईश्वर नहीं है, अतएव ईश्वर कहता है कि ईश्वर नहीं है। **—रवींद्रनाथ टैगोर**

• तुम्हें जान लेने पर कोई पराया नहीं रहेगा। न कोई टोकेगा और न ही किसी का भय रहेगा। —**रवींद्रनाथ टैगोर**

उत्तेजना

• निषिद्ध कर्म में उत्तेजना अधिक रहती है। —**रवींद्रनाथ टैगोर**

उत्थान-पतन

• कभी किसी शत्रु की आँधी से जिनका अकस्मात् पतन होता है, वे किसी दूसरे हृदयावेग से फिर उठ सकते हैं। —**रवींद्रनाथ टैगोर**

उद्दंडता

• जो लोग बुद्धि-विचार को तिलांजलि देकर समाज के कर्णधारों के मतानुसार स्वधर्म का पालन करते हैं, उनकी उद्दंडता अतिशय दुस्सह, साथ ही निरर्थक होती है।

—**रवींद्रनाथ टैगोर**

उत्साह

• उत्साह मनुष्य के भाग्य का पैमाना है। —**तिरुवल्लुवर**

• उत्साह से बढ़कर कोई दूसरा बल नहीं है, उत्साही मनुष्य के लिए संसार में कोई भी वस्तु दुर्लभ नहीं है।

—**वाल्मीकि**

• विश्व इतिहास में प्रत्येक महान् और महत्त्वपूर्ण आंदोलन उत्साह द्वारा ही सफल हो पाया है। —**एमर्सन**

उदारता

• यह मेरा है, यह तेरा है, ऐसा संकीर्ण हृदयवाले मानते हैं। उदार चित्तवाले तो सारे संसार को एक कुटुंब समझते हैं।

—**हितोपदेश**

• उदार व्यक्ति दे-देकर अमीर बनता है, लोभी जोड़-जोड़कर गरीब होता है।

—**जर्मन कहावत**

- चार तरह के लोग होते हैं, मक्खीचूस—जो न आप खाए, न दूसरों को खाने दे। कंजूस—जो आप खाए, पर दूसरों को न दे। उदार—जो आप भी खाए और दूसरों को भी दें। दाता—जो आप न खाए, पर दूसरों को दे।
- सब लोग दाता नहीं तो कम-से-कम उदार तो बन ही सकते हैं।

—अफलातून

उधार

- न उधार दो, न लो; क्योंकि उधार देने से अकसर पैसा और मित्र दोनों ही खो जाते हैं।

—शेक्सपियर

- उधार माँगना भीख माँगने जैसा है। **—अज्ञात**
- उधार वह मेहमान है, जो एक बार आने के बाद जाने का नाम नहीं लेता।

—प्रेमचंद

उन्नति

- हृदय की विशालता ही उन्नति की नींव है। **—जवाहरलाल नेहरू**
- यदि एक मनुष्य की उन्नति होती है तो सारे संसार की उन्नति होती है और अगर एक व्यक्ति का पतन होता है तो सारे संसार का पतन होता है।

—महात्मा गांधी

- मनुष्य स्वभाव के भीतर विश्वास, ज्ञान और काम में विचित्रता का होना उन्नति की अत्यंत निम्न सीढ़ी है। तीनों का अटूट संबंध मनुष्य की चरम उन्नति है, परंतु जिस जगह विश्वास, ज्ञान और काम में विचित्रता एवं विभिन्नता नहीं होती, वहाँ अविलंब मेल हो जाता है।

—रवींद्रनाथ टैगोर

- हम परोपकार करेंगे, यह सोच लेने से ही उपकार नहीं कर सकते। उपकार करने का अधिकार रहना चाहिए।

—रवींद्रनाथ टैगोर

• मनुष्य के भीतर सारे उपद्रवकारी पदार्थ रहते हैं। ऐसी दुर्दांत दुरंत शक्तियाँ सारा हिसाब और श्रृंखला-सामंजस्य नष्ट-भ्रष्ट कर देती हैं।

—रवींद्रनाथ टैगोर

• वही उन्नति कर सकता है, जो अपने आप को उपदेश देता है।

—रामतीर्थ

• त्रुटियों के संशोधन का नाम ही उन्नति है। **—लाला लाजपत राय**

उपकार

• वृक्ष खुद गरमी सहन कर शरण में आए राहगीर को गरमी से बचाता है।

—कालिदास

• जो दूसरों पर उपकार जताने का इच्छुक है, वह द्वार खटखटाता है। जिसके हृदय में प्रेम है, उसके लिए द्वार खुले हैं। **—रवींद्रनाथ टैगोर**

• उपकार के लिए अगर कुछ जाल भी करना पड़े तो उससे आत्मा की हत्या नहीं होती। **—प्रेमचंद**

• उपकार करके जताना इस बात का प्रतीक है कि किया गया समर्थन या कार्य उपकार नहीं है। **—अज्ञात**

उपदेश

• बिना माँगे किसी को उपदेश न दो। **—जर्मन कहावत**

• जो नसीहत नहीं सुनता, उसे लानत-मलामत सुनने का शौक है।

—शेख सादी

• पेट भरे पर उपवास का उपदेश देना सरल है। **—कहावत**

• जिसने स्वयं को समझ लिया हो, वह दूसरों सो समझाने नहीं जाएगा।

—धम्मपद

• लोगों की समझ-शक्ति के मुताबिक उपदेश देना चाहिए। **—हदीस**

• उपदेश देना सरल है, उपाय बताना कठिन है। **—रवींद्रनाथ टैगोर**

उपयुक्त आसन

• अपने घर में बैठकर हम अपने लिए चाहे जितना बड़ा आसन बनाएँ, दूसरों के बीच आते ही अपने आप हमारे लिए उपयुक्त आसन मिल जाता है।

—रवींद्रनाथ टैगोर

उपहार

• जिन उपहारों की बड़ी आस लगी रहती है, वे भेंट नहीं किए जाते, अदा किए जाते हैं। **—फ्रेंकलिन**

• शत्रु को क्षमा, विरोधी को सहनशीलता, मित्र को अपना हृदय, बालक को उत्तम, पिता को आदर, माता को ऐसा आचरण, जिससे वह तुम पर गर्व कर सके, अपने को प्रतिष्ठा और सबको उपहार।

—बालफोर

उपाय

• उपाय चीज ही हीन है। सीढ़ी हो या रास्ता हो, वह पैरों के नीचे ही रहता है। उपाय अगर उच्च श्रेणी का हो तो उसे काम में लाते भी बहुत सोचना पड़ता है। **—रवींद्रनाथ टैगोर**

उपेक्षा

• प्रेम सबकुछ सह लेता है, लेकिन उपेक्षा नहीं सह सकता। **—अज्ञात**

• रोग, सर्प, आग और शत्रु को तुच्छ समझकर कभी उसकी उपेक्षा नहीं करनी चाहिए। **—सुभाषित**

एक

• एक को आँख मूँदकर आसानी से निगलकर ही एक दो बनता है, वरना एक तो एक सरल रेखा की तरह सपाट होकर चलता रहता है, कभी दो नहीं बन पाता। **—रवींद्रनाथ टैगोर**

एकता

• सभी देशों के सभी समाजों में दोष और अपूर्णता है, किंतु देश के लोग जब

तक जाति-प्रेम के बंधन से एकता में बँधे रहते हैं, तब तक उनका कोई कुछ बिगाड़ नहीं सकता है। **—रवींद्रनाथ टैगोर**

- एकता चापलूसी से कायम नहीं की जा सकती। **—महात्मा गांधी**
- यदि चिड़ियाँ एकता कर लें तो शेर की खाल खींच सकती हैं। **—शेख सादी**
- मनुष्य के स्वभाव के विभिन्न अंशों के अंदर एक अटूट एकता का होना ही मनुष्यता का असली लक्ष्य है। **—रवींद्रनाथ टैगोर**

एकांत

- जो एकांत में खुश रहता है, वह या तो पशु है या देवता। **—अज्ञात**
- एकांत मूर्ख के लिए कैदखाना है और ज्ञानी के लिए स्वर्ग। **—अज्ञात**
- मुझे एकांत से बढ़कर योग्य साथी कभी नहीं मिला। **—थोरो**

एकांतवास

- समाज से बहुत दिनों तक दूर और अकेले रहना आदमी के मन को दुर्बल बना डालता है तथा आदिम संस्कार प्रकृति के प्रभाव से गहन हो उठते हैं। **—रवींद्रनाथ टैगोर**
- एकांतवास शोकवाले के लिए समीर के समान है। **—प्रेमचंद**

एकाग्रचित्त

- चाहे आप में कितनी भी योग्यता क्यों न हो, केवल एकाग्रचित्त होकर ही आप महान् कार्य कर सकते हैं। **—बिल गेट्स**

एकाग्रता

- जब तक आशा लगी है, तब तक एकाग्रता नहीं हो सकती। **—रामतीर्थ**
- झूठ, कपट, चोरी, व्यभिचार आदि दुराचारों की वृत्तियों के नष्ट हुए बिना

एकाग्र होना कठिन है और एकाग्र हुए बिना ध्यान और समाधि नहीं हो सकती। —**मनु**

- मन की एकाग्रता मनुष्य की विजय शक्ति है, यह मनुष्य जीवन की समस्त शक्तियों को समेटकर मानसिक क्रांति उत्पन्न करती है। —**अज्ञात**
- ज्ञान–प्राप्ति का एक ही मार्ग है, जिसका नाम है एकाग्रता। शिक्षा का सार है, मन को एकाग्र करना, तथ्यों का संग्रह करना नहीं। —**श्रीमाँ**
- एकाग्रता ही सभी नश्वर सिद्धियों का शाश्वत रहस्य है। —**स्टीफन जेविग**

ऐश्वर्य

- भोग के दमन में ही ऐश्वर्य का गर्व है। —**रवींद्रनाथ टैगोर**
- कदम पीछे न हटानेवाला ही ऐश्वर्य को जीतता है। —**ऋग्वेद**
- स्वयं को हीन माननेवाले को उत्तम प्रकार के ऐश्वर्य प्राप्त नहीं होते। —**महाभारत**
- धन न भी हो तो आरोग्य, विद्वत्ता सज्जन–मैत्री तथा स्वाधीनता मनुष्य के महान् ऐश्वर्य हैं। —**अज्ञात**
- ऐश्वर्य उपाधि में नहीं, बल्कि इस चेतना मैं है कि हम उसके योग्य हैं। —**अरस्तू**
- दुनिया में जो शासक लोग हैं, उनका सबसे बड़ा हथियार है ऐश्वर्य का सम्मोहन। गरीबी को स्वीकार करना, उनके लिए दुःख को स्वीकार करना नहीं, बल्कि आत्महत्या है। —**रवींद्रनाथ टैगोर**

कंजूस

- अकसर हम विचारहीनता को ही उदारता कहते हैं और जो आदमी दृढ़ संकल्प के साथ युक्ति का दीया लेकर टेढ़े–मेढ़े रास्ते को छोड़कर नियम की पगडंडी पर चलता है, उसे दुनिया कंजूस आदि नाम से पुकारती है। —**रवींद्रनाथ टैगोर**

कंजूसी

- जब मन हर चीज को नितांत दुर्लभ मानकर ग्रहण करता है, तभी वह अपनी कंजूसी को अलग करके पूरा मूल्य देता है।

—रवींद्रनाथ टैगोर

- कंजूसी मैं तुझे जानता हूँ! तू विनाश करनेवाली और व्यथा देनेवाली है।

—अथर्ववेद

- संसार में सबसे दयनीय कौन है ? जो धनवान होकर भी कंजूस है।

—विद्यापति

कर्तव्य

- मेरे दाएँ हाथ में कर्म है और बाएँ हाथ में जय। **—अथर्ववेद**
- कर्तव्य एक चुंबक है, जिसकी ओर आकर्षित हुआ अधिकार दौड़ा आता है। **—बिल गेट्स**
- कर्तव्य-पालन ही जीवन का सच्चा मूल्य है। **—बिल गेट्स**
- कर्तव्यों के विषय में आनेवाले कल की कल्पना एक अंधविश्वास है।

—बिल गेट्स

- फल की इच्छा छोड़कर निरंतर कर्तव्य करो। जो फल की अभिलाषा छोड़कर कर्तव्य करते हैं, उन्हें अवश्य मोक्ष प्राप्त होता है। **—अज्ञात**
- सौभाग्य उन्हीं को प्राप्त होता है, जो अपने कर्तव्य-पथ पर अविचल रहते हैं। **—प्रेमचंद**
- कर्तव्य कभी आग और पानी की परवाह नहीं करता। कर्तव्य-पालन में ही चित्त की शांति है। **—प्रेमचंद**
- तज्ञता एक कर्तव्य है, जिसे पूरा करना चाहिए। **—रूसो**
- विदेश में विद्या, घर में पत्नी, रोगी के लिए औषधि और मृतक का मित्र धर्म है। **—अज्ञात**

- कर्तव्य एक चुंबक है, जिसकी ओर आकर्षित हुआ अधिकार दौड़ा आता है। **—अज्ञात**

कर्म

- कर्मों की आवाज शब्दों से ऊँची होती है। **—कहावत**
- कर्म वह आईना है, जो हमारा स्वरूप हमें दिखा देता है, इसलिए हमें कर्म का एहसानमंद होना चाहिए। **—विनोबा**
- मनुष्य का कर्तव्य है कि वह उदार बनने से पहले त्यागी बने। **—डिकेंस**
- मैंने कर्म से ही अपने को बहुगुणित किया है। **—नेपोलियन**
- हमारी आनंदपूर्ण बदकारियाँ ही हमारी उत्पीड़क चाबुक बन जाती हैं। **—शेक्सपियर**
- अपनी करनी कभी-कभी निष्फल नहीं जाती। **—कबीर**
- समस्त कर्म का लक्ष्य आनंद की ओर है। **—रवींद्रनाथ टैगोर**

कला

- जो कला आत्मा को आत्मदर्शन करने की शिक्षा नहीं देती, वह कला नहीं है। **—महात्मा गांधी**
- कला ईश्वर की परपौत्री है। **—दान्ते**
- प्रकृति ईश्वर का प्रकट रूप है, कला मानुष का। **—लॉन्गफेलो**
- कला का अंतिम और सर्वोच्च ध्येय सौंदर्य है। **—गेटे**
- मानव की बहुमुखी भावनाओं का प्रबल प्रवाह जब रोके नहीं रुकता, तभी वह कला के रूप में फूट पड़ता है। **—रस्किन**
- कलाकार प्रकृति का प्रेमी होता है, अर्थात् वह उसका दास भी है और स्वामी भी। **—अज्ञात**

- कला-सृष्टि में रस-सत्य के प्रकाश की जो समस्या है, वह है रूप द्वारा ही अरूप को आच्छन्न करके देखना।

—रवींद्रनाथ टैगोर

- रचनात्मक अभिव्यक्तियाँ नियंत्रित मनोवेगों के द्वारा अपना परिपूर्ण स्वरूप प्राप्त करती हैं। **—रवींद्रनाथ टैगोर**

कल्पना

- अपनी याददाश्त के सहारे जीने की बजाय अपनी कल्पना के सहारे जिओ।

—लेस ब्राउन

- व्यावहारिक जीवन की उलझनों का समाधान किन्हीं नई कल्पनाओं में मिलेगा, उन्हें ढूँढ़ो। **—श्रीराम शर्मा आचार्य**

- शिल्प में, साहित्य में, यहाँ तक कि विज्ञान और इतिहास में भी मनुष्य की कल्पना-वृत्ति की जगह है, एक अकेले धर्म में ही उसका कोई स्थान नहीं है?

—रवींद्रनाथ टैगोर

- कल्पना ही इस संसार पर शासन करती है। **—नेपोलियन**

- मन जिस रूप की कल्पना करता है, वैसा हो जाता है, आज जैसा वह है, वैसी उसने कल कल्पना की थी। **—योगवसिष्ठ**

- कल्पना विश्व पर शासन करती है। **—नेपोलियन**

- पागल, प्रेमी और कवि की कल्पनाएँ एक सी होती हैं। **—शेक्सपियर**

- कल्पना ज्ञान से अधिक महत्त्वपूर्ण है। ज्ञान तो सीमित है, कल्पना संसार को घेर लेती है। **—अल्बर्ट आइंस्टीन**

- तर्क आपको किसी एक बिंदु से दूसरे बिंदु तक पहुँचा सकते हैं, लेकिन कल्पना आप को सर्वत्र ले जा सकती है।

—अल्बर्ट आइंस्टीन

कवि

- कवि लिखने के लिए तब तक तैयार नहीं होता, जब तक उसकी स्याही प्रेम की आहों से सराबोर नहीं हो जाती। —**शेक्सपियर**
- कवि की कीर्ति स्तंभ की तरह नहीं, नौका की तरह होती है। भँवरों को पार करते हुए काल-स्रोत की सभी परीक्षाओं और संकटों से यदि वह नौका उत्तीर्ण हो सके और अंत में यदि उसे लंगर डालने के लिए अच्छा सा घाट मिल जाए, तभी साहित्य के स्थायी इतिहास ग्रंथ के किसी पृष्ठ पर उसका नाम अंकित होता है। —**रवींद्रनाथ टैगोर**
- जो कवि भाव-स्वातंत्र्य और भाषा-स्वातंत्र्य के अनिवार्य द्वंद्व को दबाकर सौंदर्य की रक्षा कर सकते हैं, वे ही धन्य हैं। —**रवींद्रनाथ टैगोर**
- इतिहास की अपेक्षा कविता सत्य के अधिक निकट होती है। —**प्लेटो**
- कवि वह सपेरा है, जिसकी पिटारी में साँपों के स्थान पर हृदय बंद होते हैं। —**प्रेमचंद**

कष्ट

- आज के कष्ट का सामना करनेवाले के पास आगामी कल के कष्ट आने से घबराते हैं। —**अज्ञात**

काम-1

- अगर कोई कर सकता है, तुम भी कर सकते हो, अगर कोई नहीं कर सकता तो तुम्हें जरूर करना है। —**बिल गेट्स**
- अगर कोई भी काम कोई व्यक्ति अच्छे से कर सकता है, तो मैं कहूँगा, उसे करने दीजिए, उसे एक मौका दीजिए। —**बिल गेट्स**
- काम के आदमी के साथ आपकी बात संक्षिप्त और व्यापक होनी चाहिए। —**बिल गेट्स**

- काम छोटा हो या बड़ा, उसकी उत्कृष्टता ही करनेवाले का गौरव है।

—बिल गेट्स

- काम से ज्यादा काम के पीछे निहित भावना का महत्त्व होता है।

—बिल गेट्स

- किसी काम को करने का अधिकार आपको है, पर इस बात का मतलब यह नहीं होता कि वह करना सही भी है। **—बिल गेट्स**

- यदि हम अपने काम में लगे रहें तो हम जो चाहें, कर सकते हैं।

—बिल गेट्स

- किसी काम को करने से पहले इसे करने की दृढ़ इच्छा अपने मन में कर लें और सारी मानसिक शक्तियों को उस ओर झुका दें। इससे आपको अधिक सफलता प्राप्त होगी। **—बिल गेट्स**

- अगर आप काम खराब करते हैं, तो आपको कारोबार से बाहर जाना होगा।

—बिल गेट्स

काम-2

- काम से शोक उत्पन्न होता है। **—धम्मपद**

- काम, क्रोध और लोभ, ये तीनों नरक के द्वार हैं। **—गीता**

कारोबार

- एक कारोबार का मुख्य उद्देश्य लाभ को बढ़ाते रहना होता है।

—बिल गेट्स

- कारोबार का प्रबंधन तय करता है कि कैसे ग्राहक संतुष्टि को सुधारा जाए या नए उत्पाद की क्षमताओं को सुधारा जाए—इस तरह से लाभ बढ़ेगा और यह एक ऐसी व्यवस्था को विकसित करेगा, जो कि नियमित आधार पर पूर्वोक्त बातों का मापन करे। **—बिल गेट्स**

कार्य

- दौड़ना काफी नहीं है, समय पर चल पड़ना चाहिए। **—फ्रांसीसी कहावत**
- जिसने निश्चय कर लिया, उसके लिए बस करना बाकी रह जाता है। **—इटैलियन कहावत**
- अपने कार्यों में व्यवस्था, नियमितता, सुंदरता, मनोयोग तथा जिम्मेदारी का ध्यान रखें। **—बिल गेट्स**
- कार्य उद्यम से सिद्ध होते हैं, मनोरथों से नहीं। **—हितोपदेश**
- वही काम करना ठीक है, जिसके लिए बाद में पछताना न पड़े और जिसके फल को प्रसन्न मन से भोग सकें। **—महात्मा बुद्ध**
- यदि कोई काम नहीं करता तो उसे खाना भी नहीं चाहिए। **—बाइबिल**
- किसी भी काम को खूबसूरती से करने के लिए उसे मन से करना चाहिए। **—नेपोलियन**
- बिना काम के सिद्धांत दिमागी अय्याशी है, बिना सिद्धांत के कार्य अंधे की टटोल है। **—जवाहरलाल नेहरू**
- सोच-विचार करने में समय लगाएँ, लेकिन जब काम का समय आए, तो सोचना बंद करें और आगे बढ़ें। **—नेपोलियन बोनापार्ट**
- कार्य उसी का सिद्ध होता है, जो समय को विचार कर कार्य करता है, वह खिलाड़ी कभी नहीं हारता, जो दाँव पर विचार कर खेलता है। **—बिल गेट्स**
- कार्य ही सफलता की बुनियाद है। **—बिल गेट्स**
- अच्छी शुरुआत से आधा काम हो जाता है। **—अरस्तू**
- कर्म के बिना दूरदर्शिता एक दिवास्वप्न है। दूरदर्शिता के बिना कर्म दुःस्वप्न है। **—जापानी कहावत**

• किसी काम को करने के बारे में जरूरत से ज्यादा सोचना अकसर उसके बिगड़ जाने का कारण बनता है। **—ईवा यंग**

• किसी कार्य के लिए कला एवं विज्ञान ही पर्याप्त नहीं हैं, उसमें धैर्य की भी आवश्यकता पड़ती है। **—बिल गेट्स**

• कार्य कुशल व्यक्ति की सभी जगह जरूरत पड़ती है। **—बिल गेट्स**

• परिश्रम वह चाबी है, जो किस्मत का दरवाजा खोल देती है।

—चाणक्य

• किसी कार्य को खूबसूरती से करने के लिए मनुष्य को उसे स्वयं करना चाहिए। **—नेपोलियन**

• ईमानदारी और बुद्धिमानी के साथ किया हुआ काम कभी व्यर्थ नहीं जाता।

—हजारी प्रसाद द्विवेदी

• मनुष्य जन्म से नहीं, बल्कि कर्म से शूद्र या ब्राह्मण होता है। **—गौतम बुद्ध**

• जो श्रम से लजाता है, वह सदैव परतंत्र रहता है। **—शरण**

• कार्य की अधिकता से उकताने वाला व्यक्ति कभी कोई बड़ा कार्य नहीं कर सकता। **—अब्राहम लिंकन**

• कोई भी कार्य करने से पहले सोचो, समझो, फिर करो। **—बिल गेट्स**

• कोई भी कार्य सही या गलत नहीं होता, हमारी सोच उसे सही या गलत बनाती है। **—बिल गेट्स**

• अपने से हो सके, वह काम दूसरे से न कराओ। **—महात्मा गांधी**

• सच्चा काम अहंकार और स्वार्थ को छोड़े बिना नहीं होता।

—स्वामी रामतीर्थ

• काम की अधिकता नहीं, अनियमितता आदमी को मार डालती है।

—महात्मा गांधी

- महान् कार्य शक्ति से नहीं, अपितु उद्यम से संपन्न होते हैं। —**जॉनसन**
- पहले कहना और बाद में करना, इसकी अपेक्षा पहले करना और फिर कहना अधिक श्रेयस्कर है। —**अज्ञात**
- कमजोर आदमी हर काम को असंभव समझता है, जबकि वीर साधारण। —**मदनमोहन मालवीय**
- अच्छे कार्य करने के लिए कभी शुभ मुहूर्त मत पूछो। —**अज्ञात**
- बड़े कार्य, छोटे कार्यों से आरंभ करने चाहिए। —**शेक्सपियर**
- स्वतंत्र वही है, जो अपना काम स्वयं कर लेता है। —**विनोबा भावे**
- योग्यता से बिताए हुए जीवन को, हमें वर्षों से नहीं, बल्कि कर्मों के पैमाने से तौलना चाहिए। —**शेरिडेन**
- जो काम आ पड़े, साधना समझकर पूरा करो। —**स्वामी रामदास**
- कहने की प्रकृति छोड़ो, करने का अभ्यास करो। —**अज्ञात**
- प्रत्येक अच्छा कार्य पहले असंभव नजर आता है। —**अज्ञात**
- जो अपने योग्य कर्म में जी-जान से लगा रहता है, वही संसार में प्रशंसा का पात्र होता है। —**ब्राह्मण ग्रंथ**
- गलत काम करने का कोई सही तरीका नहीं है। —**अज्ञात**
- जीवन में सबसे ज्यादा आनंद उसी काम को करने में है, जिसके बारे में लोग कहते हैं कि तुम नहीं कर सकते हो। —**अज्ञात**
- कीर्ति वीरोचित कार्यों की सुगंध है। —**अज्ञात**
- जीवन में ऐसा काम करो कि परिवार, गुरु और परमात्मा तीनों तुमसे खुश रहें। —**स्वामी ज्योतिनंद**
- कर्म करने में ही अधिकार है, फल में नहीं। —**अज्ञात**
- कर्म सरल है, विचार कठिन। —**अज्ञात**

• अपने काम में सुंदरता तलाशो। उससे सुंदर और कुछ हो ही नहीं सकता।

—रूमी

• हमारे लिए चींटी से बढ़कर और कोई उपदेशक नहीं है, वह काम करती है और खामोश रहती है।

• अगर कुछ महत्त्व रखता है तो वह है कर्म और प्रेम। **—सिगमंड फ्रायड**

कायर

कायर तभी धमकी देता है, जब सुरक्षित होता है। **—गेटे**

जो दूसरों की स्वाधीनता छीनते हैं, वास्तव में कायर हैं। **—अब्राहम लिंकन**

कायरता से कहीं ज्यादा अच्छा है, लड़ते-लड़ते मर जाना। **—महात्मा गांधी**

• कुरीति के अधीन होना कायरता है, उसका विरोध करना पुरुषार्थ है।

—महात्मा गांधी

• कायर अपने जीवन काल में ही अनेक बार मरते हैं, परंतु वीर पुरुष केवल एक ही बार मरते हैं। **—अज्ञात**

कायरता

• अत्याचार और भय दोनों कायरता के दो पहलू हैं। **—अज्ञात**

• घर का मोह कायरता का दूसरा नाम है। **—अज्ञात**

• मैं कायरता तो किसी हाल में सहन नहीं कर सकता। आप कायरता से मरें, इसकी बजाय बहादुरी से प्रहार करते हुए और प्रहार सहते हुए मरना कहीं बेहतर समझूँगा। **—महात्मा गांधी**

काव्य

• इन गीतों ने मुझे अनेक शिक्षाएँ दी हैं, कई गुप्त मार्ग दिखाए हैं तथा हृदय-गगन में अनेक नक्षत्रों से परिचित कराया है। **—रवींद्रनाथ टैगोर**

• काव्य मात्र भावना या अभिव्यक्ति नहीं है, यह तो रूप की रचना है। कवि के

अंदर छिपे सूक्ष्म क्रियात्मक कौशल के कारण विचार आकार ग्रहण करते हैं, यह सर्जनात्मक शक्ति काव्य का उद्गम है। इंद्रियानुभूति, भावनाएँ और भाषा तो इसके केवल उपादान के रूप हैं। **—रवींद्रनाथ टैगोर**

- काव्य का एक गुण यह है कि कवि की रचना-शक्ति पाठकों की रचना-शक्ति को उद्विग्न कर देती है, तब अपनी प्रतिभा के अनुसार कोई सुंदरता की, कोई नीति की और कोई तत्त्व की सृष्टि करने लगता है और ऐसा प्रतीत होता है, मानो यह आतिशबाजी का तमाशा हो। काव्य वही अग्नि शिखा है। **—रवींद्रनाथ टैगोर**

कुरूपता

- मेरे दोस्त किसी चीज को कुरूप न कहो, सिवाय उस भय के, जिसकी मारी कोई आत्मा स्वयं अपनी स्मृतियों से डरने लगे। **—खलील जिब्रान**
- कुरूपता मनुष्य की सौंदर्य विद्या है। **—चाणक्य**

कौशल

- नैतिक बल के द्वारा ही मनुष्य दूसरों पर अधिकार कर सकता है। **—स्वामी रामदास**
- मनुष्य धन अथवा कुल से नहीं, दिव्य स्वभाव और भव्य आचरण से महान् बनता है। **—आविद**
- ज्ञानी वह है, जो वर्तमान को ठीक प्रकार समझे और परिस्थिति के अनुसार आचरण करे। **—विनोबा भावे**
- केवल बुद्धि के द्वारा ही मानव का मनुष्यत्व प्रकट होता है। **—प्रेमचंद**
- कार्यकुशल व्यक्ति की सभी जगह जरूरत पड़ती है। **—प्रेमचंद**
- गुण छोटे लोगों में द्वेष और महान् व्यक्तियों में स्पर्धा पैदा करता है। **—फील्डिंग**
- कार्य कुशल व्यक्ति के लिए यश और धन की कमी नहीं है। **—अज्ञात**

- यदि तुम अपने आपको योग्य बना लो, तो सहायता स्वयमेव तुम्हें आ मिलेगी। **—स्वामी रामतीर्थ**

क्रांति

- क्रांति का उदय सदा पीड़ितों के हृदय एवं त्रस्त व्यक्तियों के अंत:करण में हुआ करता है। **—अज्ञात**
- क्रांति का अर्थ होता है अतीत और भविष्य के बीच एक जबरदस्त संघर्ष। **—फिदेल कास्त्रो**
- कुशासन के प्रति विद्रोह करना, ईश्वर की आज्ञा मानना है। **—फ्रेंकलिन**
- जहाँ कहीं अन्याय के चरण पड़ते हैं, वहाँ अंततः विद्रोह का ज्वालामुखी फूटता है। **—अज्ञात**

क्रोध

- क्रोध से मूढ़ता उत्पन्न होती है, मूढ़ता से स्मृति भ्रांत हो जाती है, स्मृति भ्रांत हो जाने से बुद्धि का नाश हो जाता है और बुद्धि नष्ट होने पर प्राणी स्वयं नष्ट हो जाता है। **—श्रीकृष्ण**
- क्रोध से बदले की भावना बढ़ती है और उसके भयंकर परिणाम होते हैं। **—महात्मा गांधी**
- क्रोध यमराज है। **—चाणक्य**
- क्रोध एक प्रकार का क्षणिक पागलपन है। **—महात्मा गांधी**
- क्रोध में की गई बातें अकसर अंत में उल्टी निकलती हैं। **—मीनेंदर**
- जो मनुष्य क्रोधी पर क्रोध नहीं करता और क्षमा करता है, वह अपनी और क्रोध करनेवाले की महासंकट से रक्षा करता है। **—वेदव्यास**
- क्रोध ऐसा दावानल है, जो उस व्यक्ति को ही जलाता है, जिसमें वह उत्पन्न होता है। **—महात्मा गांधी**

- क्रोध खुद को तो जलाता है, आस-पास के और संबद्ध लोगों को भी पीड़ित कर डालता है। **—महात्मा गांधी**
- सुबह से शाम तक काम करके आदमी उतना नहीं थकता, जितना क्रोध या चिंता से पल भर में थक जाता है। **—जेम्स एलन**
- क्रोध में हो तो बोलने से पहले दस तक गिनो, अगर ज्यादा क्रोध में हो तो सौ तक। **—जेफरसन**
- ईर्ष्या और क्रोध से जीवन क्षय होता है। **—बाइबिल**
- क्रोध को जीतने में मौन सबसे अधिक सहायक है। **—महात्मा गांधी**
- मूर्ख मनुष्य क्रोध को जोर-शोर से प्रकट करता है, किंतु बुद्धिमान शांति से उसे वश में करता है। **—बाइबिल**
- क्रोध करने का मतलब है, दूसरों की गलतियों की सजा स्वयं को देना।
- जब क्रोध आए तो उसके परिणाम पर विचार करो। **—कन्फ्यूशियस**
- क्रोध से धनी व्यक्ति घृणा और निर्धन तिरस्कार का पात्र होता है। **—कहावत**
- क्रोध मूर्खता से प्रारंभ और पश्चात्ताप पर खत्म होता है। **—पाइथागोरस**

क्रोध के सिंहासनासीन होने पर बुद्धि वहाँ से खिसक जाती है। **—एम हेनरी**

- क्रोध से मनुष्य उसकी ही बेइज्जती नहीं करता, जिस पर क्रोध करता है, स्वयं अपनी प्रतिष्ठा भी गँवाता है। **—महात्मा गांधी**
- क्रोधहीन मनुष्य देवता है। **—महात्मा गांधी**
- क्रोध एक तरह का रोग है, जिसे क्षणिक पागलपन भी कह सकते हैं। **—महात्मा गांधी**
- जो मन की पीड़ा को स्पष्ट रूप में नहीं कह सकता, उसी को क्रोध अधिक आता है। **—रवींद्रनाथ ठाकुर**

- क्रोध मस्तिष्क के दीपक को बुझा देता है। अत: हमें सदैव शांत व स्थिरचित्त रहना चाहिए। —**इंगरसोल**

खुशी

- खुशी ही जीवन का अर्थ और उद्देश्य है और मानव अस्तित्व का लक्ष्य और मनोरथ। —**अरस्तू**
- हँसी के क्षणों के बिना बीता दिन सबसे खराब दिन है। —**ई.ई. कमिंग्स**
- इनसान जितना अपने मन को मना सके, उतना खुश रह सकता है। —**अब्राहम लिंकन**
- जो व्यक्ति सभी को खुश रखना चाहेगा, वह किसी को खुश नहीं रख सकता।

ख्याति

- ख्याति की अभिलाषा वह पोशाक है, जिसे ज्ञानी भी सबसे अंत में उतारते हैं। —**कहावत**
- ख्याति वह प्यास है, जो कभी नहीं बुझती। अगस्त्य ऋषि की तरह वह सागर को पीकर भी शांत नहीं होती। —**प्रेमचंद**

गणतंत्र

- किसी गणतंत्र में इस नियम का ध्यान रखना चाहिए कि बहुमत के पास प्रबल शक्ति न हो। —**मार्कस टूलियस सिसेरो**
- दुनिया सामान्यता का एक गणराज्य है और हमेशा थी। —**थॉमस कार्लाइल**
- सहिष्णुता और स्वतंत्रता एक महान् गणतंत्र की नींव हैं। —**फ्रैंक लॉयड राइट**
- सोसाइटी एक रिपब्लिक है। जब कोई खुद को औरों से ऊपर उठाना चाहता है तो उन्हें उपहास या बदनामी के द्वारा लोग नीचे खींच लेते हैं। —**विक्टर ह्यूगो**

• बाइबिल वह चट्टान है, जिस पर यह गणतंत्र टिका है। **—एंड्रू जैक्सन**

• गणतंत्र का भाग्य बदलने की शक्ति भावी पीढ़ी के पत्रकारों के हाथों में होगी। **—जोसेफ पुलित्जर**

• हमारा गणतंत्र और उसकी प्रेस एक साथ उठेंगे या गिर जाएँगे। **—जोसेफ पुलित्जर**

• नया गणतंत्र विविधता, सम्मान और सभी के लिए समान अधिकार पर आधारित होना चाहिए। **—एवो मोरालेस**

• कानून और व्यवस्था राजनीतिक शरीर की दवा है और जब राजनीतिक शरीर बीमार पड़े तो दवा जरूर दी जानी चाहिए। **—बी.आर. आंबेडकर**

• एक बात स्पष्ट है, हमारे संस्थापक कभी ऐसा देश नहीं चाहते थे, जहाँ नागरिकों को लगभग अपनी पूरी कमाई का आधा हिस्सा सरकार को देना पड़े। **—रॉन पॉल**

• मैं अपने देश से प्रेम करता हूँ, अपनी सरकार से नहीं। **—जेसी वेंचुरा**

• मृत को जीवित पर शासन नहीं करना चाहिए। **—थॉमस जेफरसन**

• सामान्यता के गणराज्य में प्रतिभा खतरनाक है। **—रॉबर्ट ग्रीन इंगरसोल**

• मैंने हमेशा यह माना है कि किसी आदमी के गुण को उसे धोखा देने का साधन बनाना मानव प्रति के महान् गणतंत्र के खिलाफ राजद्रोह के सामान है। **—सैमुअल जानसन**

• सच्चा गणराज्य आदमी, उनके अधिकार और कुछ नहीं, औरत, उनके अधिकार और उससे कम कुछ नहीं। **—फ्रेंकलिन पी. एडम्स**

• गणतंत्र की उम्मीद किस पर टिकी हुई है—एक देश, एक भाषा, एक झंडा ? **—अलेक्जेंडर हेनरी**

• हमारा संविधान काम करता है। हमारा महान् गणतंत्र कानूनों की सरकार है, पुरुषों की नहीं। **—गेराल्ड आर फोर्ड**

गणित

• ज्यामिति की रेखाओं और चित्रों में हम वे अक्षर सीखते हैं, जिनसे यह संसार रूपी महान् पुस्तक लिखी गई है। **—गैलीलियो**

• गणित एक ऐसा उपकरण है, जिसकी शक्ति अतुल्य है और जिसका उपयोग सर्वत्र है, यह एक ऐसी भाषा, जिसकी ध्वनि अवश्य सुनेगी और जिसका सदा वह उत्तर देगी। **—प्रो. हाल**

• गणित एक भाषा है। **—जे.डब्ल्यू. गिब्स**

गरीब

• गरीब वह है, जिसकी अभिलाषाएँ बढ़ी हुई हैं। **—डेनियल**

• गरीबों के बहुत से बच्चे होते हैं, अमीरों के संबंधी। **—एनॉन**

गरीबी

• गरीबी लज्जा नहीं है, लेकिन गरीबी से लज्जित होना लज्जा की बात है। **—कहावत**

• गरीबी मेरा अभिमान है। **—हजरत मोहम्मद**

• जो गरीबों पर दया करता है, वह अपने कार्य से ईश्वर को ऋणी बनाता है। **—बाइबिल**

• गरीबी दैवीय अभिशाप नहीं, मानवीय सृष्टि है। **—महात्मा गांधी**

• उस मनुष्य से गरीब कोई नहीं, जिसके पास केवल धन है। **—कहावत**

• कुबेर भी यदि आय से अधिक व्यय करे तो निर्धन हो जाता है। **—चाणक्य**

• गरीबों की सेवा ही ईश्वर की सेवा है। **—सरदार वल्लभभाई पटेल**

• गरीबी दैवी अभिशाप नहीं, बल्कि मानवरचित षड्यंत्र है।

—महात्मा गांधी

• निर्धनता से मनुष्य में लज्जा आती है। लज्जा से आदमी तेजहीन हो जाता है। निस्तेज मनुष्य का समाज तिरस्कार करता है। तिरस्कृत मनुष्य में वैराग्य भाव उत्पन्न हो जाते हैं और तब मनुष्य को शोक होने लगता है। जब मनुष्य शोकातुर होता है तो उसकी बुद्धि क्षीण होने लगती है और बुद्धिहीन मनुष्य का सर्वनाश हो जाता है। **—मृच्छकटिकम्**

गलती

• गलती करना मनुष्य का स्वभाव है। की हुई गलती को मान लेना और इस प्रकार आचरण करना कि फिर गलती न हो, मर्दानगी है। **—महात्मा गांधी**

• जो मान गया कि उससे गलती हुई और उसे ठीक नहीं करता, वह एक और गलती कर रहा है। **—कन्फ्यूशियस**

• बहुत सी तथा बड़ी गलती किए बिना कोई व्यक्ति बड़ा और महान् नहीं बनता। **—ग्लेडस्टोन**

• गलती मान लेना झाड़ू लगाने का सा काम है। यह गंदगी को बुहारकर सतह को साफ कर देता है। **—महात्मा गांधी**

• अगर तुम गलतियों को रोकने के लिए दरवाजे बंद कर दोगे तो सत्य भी बाहर आ जाएगा। **—रवींद्रनाथ टैगोर**

• हम यह सोचने की गलती न करें कि हम कभी भूल कर ही नहीं सकते।

—महात्मा गांधी

• गलती करने से डरना सबसे बड़ी गलती है। **—एल्बर्ट हब्बार्ड**

• मैं इसलिए आगे निकल पाया कि मैंने उन लोगों से ज्यादा गलतियाँ कीं, जिनका मानना था कि गलती करना बुरा है, या गलती करने का मतलब था कि वे मूर्ख थे। **—राबर्ट कियोसाकी**

• गलती मान लेने से हमको बहुत लाभ होता है, उसमें शुद्ध व्यवहार है।

—महात्मा गांधी

• गलती हर इनसान से होती है, लेकिन जब इनसान अपनी गलती को छिपाता है या उस पर मुलम्मा चढ़ाने के लिए और झूठ बोलता है, तो यह खतरनाक बन जाती है। **—महात्मा गांधी**

• सीधे तौर पर अपनी गलतियों को ही हम अनुभव का नाम दे देते हैं।

—आस्कर वाइल्ड

• गलती तो हर मनुष्य कर सकता है, पर केवल मूर्ख ही उस पर बने रहते हैं।

—सिसरो

• अपनी गलती स्वीकार कर लेने में लज्जा की कोई बात नहीं है। इससे दूसरे शब्दों में यही प्रमाणित होता है कि कल की अपेक्षा आज आप अधिक समझदार हैं। **—अलेक्जेंडर पोप**

• भूल करके आदमी सीखता तो है, पर इसका यह मतलब नहीं कि जीवन भर भूल ही करता जाए और कहे कि हम सीख रहे हैं। **—महात्मा गांधी**

• सच्चा मनुष्य वही है, जो अपनी गलती को मान ले और फिर उसे त्यागकर अपने-आप में सुधार कर ले। **—महात्मा गांधी**

• दोष निकालना सुगम है, उसे ठीक करना कठिन। **—प्लूटार्क**

• त्रुटियों के बीच में से ही संपूर्ण सत्य को ढूँढ़ा जा सकता है।

—सिगमंड फ्रायड

गुण

• गुणों से ही मनुष्य महान् होता है, ऊँचे आसन पर बैठने से नहीं। महल के ऊँचे शिखर पर बैठने मात्र से कौवा गरुड़ नहीं हो सकता। **—चाणक्य**

• सद्‌गुणशील, मुंसिफ मिजाज और अक्लमंद आदमी तब तक नहीं बोलता, जब तक खामोशी नहीं हो जाती। **—शेख सादी**

- कस्तूरी को अपनी मौजूदगी कसम खाकर सिद्ध नहीं करनी पड़ती, गुण स्वयं ही सामने आ जाते हैं। **—अज्ञात**

- रूप की पहुँच आँखों तक है, गुण आत्मा को जीतते हैं। **—पोप**

- बड़े बड़ाई न करें, बड़े न बोलें बोल।
  रहिमन हीरा कब कहै, लाख टका मेरो मोल॥ **—रहीम**

- मनुष्य अपने गुणों से आगे बढ़ता है, न कि दूसरों की कृपा से। **—लाला लाजपतराय**

गुरु

- शिष्य के ज्ञान पर सही करना यही गुरु का काम है, बाकी के लिए शिष्य स्वावलंबी है। **—विनोबा**

- अगर शुद्ध गुरुभक्ति न हो, तो चरित्र-गठन नहीं हो सकता। **—महात्मा गांधी**

- गुरु ऐसा होना चाहिए, जो शिष्य को सद्ज्ञान दे, उसका आध्यात्मिक कल्याण चाहे और उससे धन ऐंठने की वृत्ति न रखे। **—महात्मा गांधी**

- गुरु के बिना किसी भी क्षेत्र का समुचित ज्ञान प्राप्त करना कठिन होता है। **—महात्मा गांधी**

- सच्चा गुरु अनुभव है। **—स्वामी विवेकानंद**

- गुरु से ज्ञान तभी मिल सकता है, जब शिष्य में गुरु के प्रति श्रद्धा हो और उसकी सेवा करने की भावना। **—महात्मा गांधी**

- मैं गुरु-परंपरा को माननेवाला हूँ, किंतु प्रत्येक शिक्षक गुरु नहीं होता, गुरु शिष्य का संबंध आध्यात्मिक और स्वयं स्फुरित है। **—महात्मा गांधी**

- बुद्धिमान लोग गुरु का गुण बहुत बड़ा मानते हैं, क्योंकि और गुण तो आसानी

से लौटाए जा सकते हैं, ज्ञान दान का गुण सबके लिए लौटाना संभव ही नहीं है। —**महात्मा गांधी**

- कबिरा ते नर अंध हैं, गुरु को मानत और।
हरि रूठै गुरु ठौर है, गुरु रूठै नहिं ठौर॥ —**कबीर**

ज्ञान

- जो आपके अंदर है, उसे अपने दिल में बनाए रखिए, क्योंकि केवल वह ही वास्तविक और शाश्वत ज्ञान का स्रोत है। —**उपनिषद्**
- सुख मानव जीवन का उद्देश्य नहीं है, बल्कि यह तो अपने सच्चे स्वरूप का ज्ञान है। —**आदि शंकराचार्य**
- सच्चा ज्ञान अपनी अज्ञानता की सीमा को जानने मैं है। आप क्या जानते हैं और क्या नहीं जानते हैं, इसे जानने में ही सच्चा ज्ञान निहित है। —**कन्फ्यूशियस**
- ज्ञान प्राप्ति की इच्छा धन पाने की चाहत की तरह हमेशा इसे पाने के साथ बढ़ती है। —**लॉरेंस स्टर्न**
- जानना यह जानना है कि आप कुछ भी नहीं जानते हैं, यह ही सच्चे ज्ञान का तात्पर्य है। —**सुकरात**
- सच्चे ज्ञान के प्रकाश में सारे संदेह मिट जाते हैं। —**गौतम बुद्ध**
- संसार के विरुद्ध एक मात्र बचाव इसका संपूर्ण ज्ञान ही है। —**जॉन लॉक**
- ज्ञान का आरंभ किसी ऐसी वस्तु की खोज है, जिसे हम नहीं समझते हैं। —**फ्रैंक हर्बर्ट**
- चाहे बादल हमें पद और अधिकार दे दें, चाहे समृद्धि हमें खोजती फिरे, लेकिन आखिर में हमें ही ज्ञान को खोजना पड़ेगा। —**अर्नहेम यॉन्ग**
- विवशता में जो ज्ञान हासिल किया जाता है, वह मन पर कोई संस्कार नहीं डाल पाता। —**प्लेटो**

- इस बारे में सचेत होना कि आप अज्ञानी हैं, ज्ञान की ओर बढ़ाया गया एक बड़ा कदम है। **—बेंजामिन डिजरायली**

- ज्ञान को प्राप्त करने के लिए साहसी बनिए। सत्य और कारण का अनुसरण करने में कभी भी मत डरिए, फिर चाहे वे कैसा भी परिणाम प्रस्तुत करें। **—थॉमस जेफरसन**

- सभी पुरुष स्वभाववश ज्ञान चाहते हैं। **—अरस्तू**

- ज्ञान एक दौलत है, लेकिन अभ्यास ही इसकी कुंजी है। **—लाओत्जू**

- ज्ञान के समान कोई दौलत नहीं है और अज्ञान के समान कोई गरीबी नहीं। **—महात्मा बुद्ध**

- ज्ञान पर अधिकार आश्चर्य और रहस्य की समझ को समाप्त नहीं कर देता है। यहाँ सदैव और ज्यादा रहस्य हैं। **—अनीस निन**

- मैं किसी को कुछ भी नहीं सिखा सकता हूँ। मैं केवल उन्हें सोचने को तैयार कर सकता हूँ। **—सुकरात**

- अपने ज्ञान को बाँटना अमरता को हासिल करने का एक रास्ता है। **—दलाई लामा**

- अगर आप पैसे से आजादी की उम्मीद करते हैं तो आप इसे कभी हासिल नहीं कर सकेंगे। इस दुनिया में सच्ची सुरक्षा केवल ज्ञान, अनुभव और योग्यता की उपलब्धि में है। **—हेनरी फोर्ड**

- मैं उस तथ्य से बिल्कुल चिंतित नहीं होता, जिससे मैं अनजान हूँ। मैं तब चिंतित होता हूँ, जब मैं दूसरों को नहीं जानता। **—कन्फ्यूशियस**

- यदि ज्ञान मुसीबतें पैदा कर सकता है तो यह अज्ञान नहीं है, जिसके जरिए हम उन्हें सुलझा सकते हैं। **—इसाक असिमोव**

- निरर्थक ज्ञान से भी बहुत खुशी हासिल होती है। **—बर्ट्रेंड रसेल**

- आपने ज्ञान व्यर्थ ही हासिल किया है, अगर आप इसे दूसरों को नहीं बाँटते हैं। **—पुरानी कहावत**
- कोई भी व्यक्ति आपके लिए उसे छोड़कर कुछ भी प्रकट नहीं कर सकता, जो पहले से ही आपके ज्ञान के उषाकाल के अंदर अर्ध-निद्रित पड़ा हुआ है। **—खलील जिब्रान**
- पंडित होना एक बात है और उस ज्ञान के अनुसार होना दूसरी बात। **—महात्मा गांधी**
- ज्ञान ही सच्चा मत है। ज्ञान आत्मा का भोजन है। **—प्लेटो**
- अज्ञानता ईश्वर का शाप है, ज्ञान वह पंख है, जिससे हम स्वर्ग तक उड़ सकते हैं। **—विलियम शेक्सपियर**
- ज्ञान तब तक केवल जानकारी है, जब तक इसे सही आचरण में न परिवर्तित कर दिया जाए। **—पंडित श्रीराम शर्मा आचार्य**
- लोग इस बात को महत्त्व नहीं देते कि आप कितना जानते हैं, जब तक कि वे यह नहीं जान जाते कि आप कितना ध्यान रखते हैं। **—जॉन सी मैक्सवेल**
- किसी भी व्यक्ति का ज्ञान उसके अनुभव से बढ़कर नहीं हो सकता। **—जॉन लॉक**
- ज्ञान प्रेम, प्रकाश और दृष्टि है। **—हेलेन केलर**
- स्वयं का ज्ञान प्राप्त किए बिना, अपनी मशीन की कार्यविधि और उसके कार्यों की समझ के बिना, मनुष्य स्वतंत्र नहीं हो सकता, वह खुद पर शासन नहीं कर सकता और हमेशा एक गुलाम ही बना रहेगा। **—जॉर्ज गुरजिएफ**
- जानिए या फिर उन्हें सुनिए, जो जानते हैं। **—बलस्टर ग्रेसियन**
- विश्वास के लिए जगह बनाने के लिए आपको अपना अधूरा ज्ञान हटाना पड़ेगा। **—इम्मानुएल कांट**
- विश्वव्यापी मन समस्त ज्ञान को समाहित किए हुए है, यह सभी चीजों की

संभावित अंतिम अवस्था है, इसके लिए सब चीजें संभव हैं।

—अर्नेस्ट होम्स

घटना

- सच्ची घटना के गवाहों की संख्या सीमित होती है, कभी-कभी तो कोई गवाह नहीं होता, पर अगर आदमी जुगाड़ू हो तो जो घटना घटी ही नहीं, उसके गवाहों की कोई कमी नहीं होती। **—रवींद्रनाथ टैगोर**
- दुनिया में कुछ भी हमारी सुविधा के अनुसार आराम से नहीं होता। घटनाएँ भी पहले शिकारी बाघ की तरह दबे पाँव बढ़ती रहती हैं और फिर हठात् एक ही छलाँग में गला धर दबाती हैं। फिर उनकी खबर भी आग की तरह पहले दबी-ही-दबी सुलगती है और फिर सहसा धधककर जल उठती है, तब उसे सँभालना मुश्किल हो जाता है।

  —रवींद्रनाथ टैगोर

घर

- घर के समान कोई स्कूल नहीं, न ईमानदारी व सदाचारी माता-पिता के समान कोई अध्यापक है। **—अज्ञात**
- जब घर में अतिथि हो, तब चाहे अमृत ही क्यों न हो, अकेले नहीं पीना चाहिए।

  —तिरुवल्लुवर
- दृश्य की दृष्टि से टूटे पुराने घर का भी अपना एक सौंदर्य है, लेकिन उस घर को केवल चित्र की दृष्टि से देखने से नहीं चलता, उसमें रहना पड़ता है। इसलिए उसकी मरम्मत की आवश्यकता होती है। **—रवींद्रनाथ टैगोर**

घिनौनापन

- चोरी-चुपके में एक घिनौनापन होता है। **—रवींद्रनाथ टैगोर**

घुन

- कच्ची लकड़ी के तख्ते में बहुत जल्दी घुन लगता है।

  —रवींद्रनाथ टैगोर

घृणा

- घृणा पाप से करो, पापी से नहीं। —**महात्मा गांधी**
- गुस्सा सह लिया जा सकता है, लेकिन घृणा सहना व्यक्ति के लिए बड़ा कठिन होता है। —**रवींद्रनाथ टैगोर**
- घृणा द्वारा मनुष्य को केवल दूर हटाकर ही नहीं रखा जाता, बल्कि जिसके साथ घृणा की जाती है, उसका मन भी छोटा हो जाता है। वह भी अपनी हीनता के संकोच से समाज में कुंठित होकर रहता है, जहाँ रहता है, वहाँ कोई अधिकार नहीं जताता।

  —**रवींद्रनाथ टैगोर**
- घृणा की अंधता अज्ञान की अंधता से अधिक बुरी है, क्योंकि अज्ञान जिस प्रकाश को जगाए बिना छोड़ देता है, घृणा उसे बुझा देती है।
- जिनके भीतर नफरत होती है, वे दरअसल हारे हुए लोग होते हैं, जो अपने जीते हुए होने का स्वाँग कर रहे होते हैं। —**पॉलो कोएल्हो**
- जो सच्चाई पर निर्भर है, वह किसी से घृणा नहीं करता। —**नेपोलियन**
- घृणा और प्रेम दोनों अंधे हैं। —**कहावत**
- घृणा हृदय का पागलपन है। —**बायरन**
- घृणा घृणा से कभी कम नहीं होती, प्रेम से ही होती है। —**महात्मा बुद्ध**

चतुराई

- चतुराई दरबारियों के लिए गुण है, साधुओं के लिए दोष। —**शेख सादी**
- सबसे बड़ी चतुराई यह है कि कोई चतुराई न की जाए।

  —**फ्रांसीसी कहावत**

चरित्र

- चरित्र वृक्ष है और प्रतिष्ठा उसकी छाया। —**अब्राहम लिंकन**
- चरित्र के बिना ज्ञान बुराई की ताकत बन जाता है, जैसे कि दुनिया के कितने

ही चालाक चोरों और भले मानुष बदमाशों के उदाहरण से स्पष्ट है।

—महात्मा गांधी

- दुर्बल चरित्र का व्यक्ति उस सरकंडे जैसा है, जो हवा के हर झोंके पर झुक जाता है। **—माघ**
- चरित्र मनुष्य के अंदर रहता है, यश उसके बाहर। **—अज्ञात**
- श्वास की क्रिया के सामन हमारे चरित्र में एक ऐसी सहज क्षमता होनी चाहिए, जिसके बल पर जो कुछ प्राप्य है, वह अनायास ग्रहण कर लें और जो त्याज्य है, वह बिना क्षोभ के त्याग सकें।

—रवींद्रनाथ टैगोर

- समाज के प्रचलित विधि-विधानों का उल्लंघन केवल चरित्र-बल पर ही सहन किया जा सकता है। **—शरतचंद्र**
- कठिनाइयों को जीतने, वासनाओं का दमन करने और दु:खों को सहन करने से चरित्र उच्च, सुदृढ़ और निर्मल होता है। **—अज्ञात**
- विचार से कर्म की उत्पत्ति होती है, कर्म से आदत की उत्पत्ति होती है, आदत से चरित्र की उत्पत्ति होती है और चरित्र से आपके प्रारब्ध की उत्पत्ति होती है। **—बौद्ध कहावत**
- बुद्धिमान व्यक्तियों की प्रशंसा की जाती है, धनवान व्यक्तियों से ईर्ष्या की जाती है, बलशाली व्यक्तियों से डरा जाता है, लेकिन विश्वास केवल चरित्रवान व्यक्तियों पर ही किया जाता है। **—अल्फ्रेड एडलर**
- तुम बर्फ के समान विशुद्ध रहो और हिम के समान स्थिर तो भी लोकनिंदा से नहीं बच पाओगे।
- अच्छी आदतों से शक्ति की बचत होती है, अवगुण से बरबादी।

—जेम्स एलन

- हमारी दुनिया को सबसे ज्यादा एक नए नैतिक ढाँचे की दरकार है।

—ह्यूगो शावेज

- चरित्र एक वृक्ष है, मान एक छाया। हम हमेशा छाया की सोचते हैं, लेकिन असलियत तो वृक्ष ही है। **—अब्राहम लिंकन**
- किसी व्यक्ति के चरित्र को उसके द्वारा प्रयुक्त विशेषणों से जाना जा सकता है। **—मार्क ट्वेन**
- बुद्धि के साथ सरलता, नम्रता तथा विनय के योग से ही सच्चा चरित्र बनता है। **—अज्ञात**
- आचरण अच्छा हो तो मन में अच्छे विचार ही आते हैं। **—अज्ञात**
- सुंदर आचरण, सुंदर देह से अच्छा है। **—एमर्सन**
- जैसे आचरण की तुम दूसरों से अपेक्षा रखते हो, वैसा ही आचरण तुम दूसरों के प्रति करो। **—ल्यूक**
- अपकीर्ति दंड में नहीं, अपितु अपराध में है। **—एलफिरी**
- दूसरों को क्षति पहुँचाकर अपनी भलाई की आशा नहीं करनी चाहिए। **—अज्ञात**
- चरित्रवान व्यक्ति अपने पद और शक्ति का अनुचित लाभ नहीं उठाते। **—अज्ञात**
- चरित्र आत्म-सम्मान की नींव है। **—अज्ञात**
- अपने चारित्रिक सुधार का आर्किटेक्ट खुद को बनना होगा। **—अज्ञात**
- जैसा अन्न, वैसा मन। **—अज्ञात**
- अपकीर्ति अमर है, जब कोई उसे मृतक समझता है, तब भी वह जीवित रहती है। **—प्ल्यूटस**
- जो मानव अपने अवगुण और दूसरों के गुण देखता है, वही महान् व्यक्ति बन सकता है। **—सुकरात**
- बहता पानी और रमता जोगी ही शुद्ध रहते हैं। **—स्वामी विवेकानंद**

• वृक्ष, सरोवर, सज्जन और मेघ, ये चारों परमार्थ हेतु देह धारण करते हैं।

—महात्मा कबीर

• चरित्र की शुद्धि ही सारे ज्ञान का ध्येय होनी चाहिए। **—महात्मा गांधी**

• संयम और श्रम मानव के दो सर्वोत्तम चिकित्सक हैं। **—रूसो**

• अच्छा स्वभाव, सौंदर्य के अभाव को पूरा कर देता है। **—एडीसन**

• व्यवहार वह दर्पण है, जिसमें प्रत्येक का प्रतिबिंब देखा जा सकता है।

—गेटे

• चरित्र वृक्ष है और प्रतिष्ठा उसकी छाया। **—अब्राहम लिंकन**

• समाज के प्रचलित विधि-विधानों का उल्लंघन केवल चरित्र-बल पर ही सहन किया जा सकता है। शरतचंद्र चरित्र मनुष्य के अंदर रहता है, यश उसके बाहर। **—अज्ञात**

• चरित्र के बिना ज्ञान बुराई की ताकत बन जाता है, जैसे कि दुनिया के कितने ही 'चालाक चोरों' और 'भले मानुष बदमाशों' के उदाहरण से स्पष्ट है।

—महात्मा गांधी

• कठिनाइयों को जीतने, वासनाओं का दमन करने और दुःखों को सहन करने से चरित्र उच्च, सुदृढ़ और निर्मल होता है। **—अज्ञात**

• दुर्बल चरित्र का व्यक्ति उस सरकंडे जैसा है, जो हवा के हर झोंके पर झुक जाता है। **—माघ**

चरित्र-निर्माण

• व्यक्ति के चरित्र से ही राष्ट्र का अंदाजा लगाया जाता है।

—महात्मा गांधी

• चरित्र-निर्माण का काम कुछ कम महत्त्वपूर्ण नहीं, इसके बिना आजादी पाकर भी भारतीय मनुष्य का मूल्य नहीं बढ़ सकता। **—महात्मा गांधी**

- चरित्र की संपत्ति दुनिया की तमाम दौलतों से बढ़कर है।

—महात्मा गांधी

- चरित्र की रक्षा किसी भी मूल्य पर होनी चाहिए। **—महात्मा गांधी**
- शिक्षा का उद्‌देश्य चरित्र-निर्माण होना चाहिए। शिक्षा वही है, जिसके द्वारा साहस का विकास हो, गुणों में वृद्धि हो और ऊँचे उद्‌देश्यों के प्रति लगन जागे। **—महात्मा गांधी**
- यदि चरित्र-निर्माण न हुआ, तो सारे रचनात्मक कार्यक्रम व्यर्थ हैं।

—महात्मा गांधी

चापलूसी

- चापलूस आपको हानि पहुँचाकर अपना स्वार्थ सिद्ध करना चाहता है।

—हरिऔध

- चापलूसी तीन घृणित दुर्गुणों से भरी है—असत्य, दासत्व और विश्वासघात।

—अज्ञात

- चापलूस आपकी चापलूसी इसीलिए करता है, क्योंकि वह खुद को अयोग्य समझता है, लेकिन आप उसके मुँह से अपनी प्रशंसा सुनकर फूले नहीं समाते। **—टलस्टॉय**

चिंता

- चिंता चिता समान है। **—अज्ञात**
- चिंता एक प्रकार की कायरता है और वह जीवन को विषमय बना देती है।

—चैनिंग

- निश्चिंत मन भरी थैली से अच्छा है। **—अरबी कहावत**
- अगर इनसान सुख-दुःख की चिंताओं से ऊपर उठ जाए तो आसमान की ऊँचाई भी उसके पैरों तले आ जाए। **—शेख सादी**

• कुटुंब की चिंता से परेशान व्यक्ति की कुलीनता, शील और गुण कच्चे घड़े में रखे पानी की तरह हैं। **—संस्कृत सूक्ति**

• चिंता वहाँ तक तो वांछनीय है, जहाँ तक वह रचनात्मक ध्येय की पूर्ति के लिए विविध उपायों का मनन करने तक सीमित हो, परंतु जब चिंता इतनी बढ़ जाए कि वह शरीर को खाने लगे तो वह अवांछनीय हो जाती है, क्योंकि फिर तो वह अपने ध्येय को ही हरा बैठती है। **—महात्मा गांधी**

• चिंता के समान शरीर का क्षय और कुछ नहीं करता और जिसे ईश्वर में जरा भी विश्वास है, उसे किसी भी विषय में चिंता करने में ग्लानि होनी चाहिए।

—महात्मा गांधी

• कार्य की अधिकता मनुष्य को नहीं मारती, बल्कि चिंता मारती है।

—स्वेट मार्डेन

• अगर इनसान सुख-दुःख की चिंता से ऊपर उठ जाए, तो आसमान की ऊँचाई भी उसके पैरों तले आ जाए। **—शेख सादी**

• चिंताएँ, परेशानियाँ, दुःख और तकलीफें परिस्थितियों से लड़ने से नहीं दूर हो सकतीं, वे दूर होंगी अपनी अंदरूनी कमजोरी दूर करने से, जिसके कारण ही वे सचमुच पैदा हुई हैं। **—स्वामी रामतीर्थ**

• प्राणियों के लिए चिंता ही ज्वर है। **—शंकराचार्य**

• बिस्तर पर चिंताओं को ले जाना पीठ पर गट्ठर बाँधकर सोना है।

—हैली बर्टन

• चिंता रोग का मूल है। **—प्रेमचंद**

• चिंता करता हूँ मैं जितनी उस अतीत की, उस सुख की, उतनी ही अनंत में बनती जाती रेखाएँ दुःख कीं। **—जयशंकर प्रसाद**

• चिंता एक काली दीवार की भाँति चारों ओर से घेर लेती है, जिसमें से निकलने की फिर कोई गली नहीं सूझती। **—प्रेमचंद**

चुनौतियाँ

- चुनौतियाँ जीवन को अधिक रुचिकर बनाती हैं और उन्हें दूर करना जीवन को अर्थपूर्ण बनाता है। **—बिल गेट्स**
- चुनौतियों को स्वीकार करनेवाले ही असली बहादुर होते हैं। **—बिल गेट्स**
- चुनौतियों को स्वीकार करें, ताकि आप विजय के हर्ष का आनंद महसूस कर सकें। **—बिल गेट्स**
- चुनौतियों से घबराइए मत, सामना कीजिए। आग तो हर व्यक्ति के भीतर छिपी है, बस उसे जगाने की जरूरत है। **—बिल गेट्स**
- जो चुनौतियों का सामना करने से डरता है, उसका असफल होना तय है। **—बिल गेट्स**

चेहरा

- चेहरा मस्तिष्क का प्रतिबिंब है और आँखें बिना कहे दिल के राज खोल देती हैं। **—सैंट जेरोम**
- भोली-भाली सूरतवाले होते हैं जल्लाद भी। **—उर्दू कहावत**
- सुंदर चेहरा सबसे अच्छा प्रशंसा पात्र है। **—रानी एलिजाबेथ**

चिकित्सा

- संयम और परिश्रम मनुष्य के दो सर्वोत्तम चिकित्सक हैं। परिश्रम की भूख तेज होती है और संयम अतिभोग से रोकता है। **—रूसो**
- समय सबसे बड़ा चिकित्सक है। **—अज्ञात**
- वक्त हर घाव का मरहम है। **—कहावत**
- मन की प्रसन्नता से समस्त मानसिक और शारीरिक रोग दूर हो जाते हैं। **—रामदास**

चोर

- आवश्यकता से अधिक एकत्र करनेवाला प्रत्येक व्यक्ति चोर है। **—भगवद् गीता**

- ईश्वर ने आदमी को मेहनत करके खाने के लिए बनाया है और कहा है कि जो मेहनत किए बगैर खाते हैं, वे चोर हैं।

—महात्मा गांधी

- जो मेरा धन चुराता है, वह मेरी सबसे तुच्छ वस्तु ले जाता है।

—शेक्सपियर

छटपटाना

- जब मरने का वक्त होगा, तब हम भी बड़े हो लेंगे, पर जब जलने की उम्र हो तो छटपटाना ही शोभा देता है। **—रवींद्रनाथ टैगोर**

छल

- छल करने में कोई कम कौशल नहीं लगाता, लड़ाई के कला-कौशल के समान ही है, बात इतनी ही है कि उसमें कुछ मधु भी खर्च करना पड़ता है।

—रवींद्रनाथ टैगोर

छाहर

- छाहर जब मन में फैलता है तो मौत की पीड़ा तो होती है, किंतु मौत नहीं होती। **—रवींद्रनाथ टैगोर**

जगत्

- जगत् यंत्र का कल-कारखाना अत्यंत जटिल और लौह-कठिन दुःख-सुख, विपद-संपद, संकट-संशय और नैराश्य-परिताप से मिश्रित है।

—रवींद्रनाथ टैगोर

जड़-चेतन

- जड़ और चेतन के संबंध में ही संसार का असली संबंध है। अतः वस्तु-विज्ञान की जानकारी चाहे कितनी ही हासिल क्यों न करो, वह लोक-व्यवहार की शिक्षा में जरा भी मदद नहीं कर सकती, परंतु जो जीवन का आभूषण है, जिनमें सौंदर्य, काव्य और मिठास की उत्पत्ति है, वे वास्तव में मनुष्य के बीच ठीक संबंध जोड़ते हैं, एक-दूसरे की राह का काँटा दूर कर, स्पर्धा को

समाप्त कर उसके ज्ञानचक्षु खोल देते हैं और जीवन को मर्त्य से स्वर्ग तक प्रसारित कर देते हैं।

—रवींद्रनाथ टैगोर

जनता

- जनता की आवाज ईश्वर की आवाज है। **—कहावत**
- राजमहलों की चालबाजियाँ, सभा भवनों की राजनीति, समझौते और लेन-देन का जमाना उसी दिन खत्म हो जाता है, जब जनता राजनीति में प्रवेश करती है। **—जवाहरलाल नेहरू**

जननी

- जननी और जन्मभूमि स्वर्ग से बढ़कर है। **—वाल्मीकि रामायण**
- माता का हृदय शिशु की पाठशाला है। **—बीचर**

जन्म और मृत्यु

- जन्म और मृत्यु दो स्थितियाँ नहीं हैं, अपितु वे एक ही स्थिति के दो पहलू हैं। **—महात्मा गांधी**

जरूरत

- सारी जरूरतें जब घेरती हैं तो परिणाम को कुएँ में डाल आना होता है।

  —रवींद्रनाथ टैगोर
- जरूरत नाम की चीज का कोई अंत है ? खाने की जरूरत नहीं है, पेट भरने पर उसका अंत मिल जाता है, नशे की जरूरत नहीं है, इस कारण उसका अंत भी नहीं है। **—रवींद्रनाथ टैगोर**

जहाज

- जहाज जब डूबता है तो उसके चारों तरफ जो लोग अपने प्राण बचाने के लिए तैयार रहे होते हैं, उन्हें भी पानी के अंदर खींच ले जाता है।

  —रवींद्रनाथ टैगोर

जागरण

- जागरण का अर्थ है कर्म में अवतीर्ण करना। **—जयशंकर प्रसाद**

जाति

- मनुष्य जब मर जाता है, तब उसकी जात-पाँत कहाँ रहती है? भगवान् का बनाया हुआ आदमी जब आदमी का चेहरा चाहता है, तब जाति का सवाल कहाँ उठता है? **—रवींद्रनाथ टैगोर**
- प्रत्येक जाति का, जिस तरह एक जाति-धर्म है, उसी प्रकार जाति-धर्म के अतीत एक श्रेष्ठ धर्म है, जो सर्वसाधारण मानव मात्र के लिए है। **—रवींद्रनाथ टैगोर**
- साधारण आदमी के साथ आदमी जैसा व्यवहार कर सकता है, उसके हजार तरीके हैं, पर आग की जात अलग है, वह एक पल में आँखों को बाँध लेती है, प्रलय को सुंदर बना देती है। **—रवींद्रनाथ टैगोर**

जाति-भेद

- एक प्रकार का जाति भेद ऐसा भी होता है, जो समाज का नहीं, रक्त का होता है। किसी तरह उस जाति को वहीं तोड़ा जा सकता, यह जो रक्तगत जाति का असामंजस्य है, उसकी मार स्त्री पर जैसे मार्मिक रूप में पड़ती है, वैसी पुरुष पर नहीं। **—रवींद्रनाथ टैगोर**
- जिस जाति-भेद से मनुष्य के प्रति मनुष्य में ऐसा अपमान और घृणा का भाव पैदा हो, उसे अधीन न कहा जाए तो क्या कहा जाए? **—रवींद्रनाथ टैगोर**

जिंदगी

- जिंदगी एक उबाऊ कहानी की तरह है, जिसे दो बार सुना गया हो, लेकिन एक ऊँघते हुए इनसान के कानों की सफाई कर देने के लिए यह बेहतरीन साधन है। **—बिल गेट्स**
- जिंदगी का हर पल कुछ-न-कुछ सिखाता है। **—बिल गेट्स**
- जिंदगी में खुश रहना है तो हँसने का बहाना तलाशें। **—बिल गेट्स**

जिम्मेदारी

- हालाँकि मुझे दूसरों को क्या करना चाहिए, के बारे में बात करने का कोई अधिकार नहीं है, मुझे लगता है कि मैं बहुत भाग्यशाली रहा हूँ और एक बहुत ही महत्त्वपूर्ण जिम्मेदारी जब तक हाथों में नहीं आती, तब तक उसे निभाने की योग्यता भी पैदा नहीं होती।

  —रवींद्रनाथ टैगोर

- मनुष्य को एक जोड़ा हाथ मिले हैं। इसी से वह मनुष्य है। अगर एक जोड़ा खुर भी मिला होता हो, इनके साथ ऐंठने लायक एक पूँछ भी अपने आप ही उठ आती।

  —रवींद्रनाथ टैगोर

- तरीके से समाज को वापस देने के लिए एक जिम्मेदारी महसूस की है।

  —बिल गेट्स

जीव

- जीव स्वर्ग से इस संसार में आया है, वह यहाँ सुख-दुःख के सबक सीखता है।

  —रवींद्रनाथ टैगोर

जीवन

- मनुष्य के जीवन की गति एक महान्दी सी है, वह अपने वेग से अकल्पनीय ढंग से ऐसी नई-नई दिशाओं में रास्ता बना लेती है, जिधर को पहले उसका प्रवाह नहीं था।

  —रवींद्रनाथ टैगोर

- कहानी जहाँ खत्म होती है, जीवन वहीं से शुरू होता है।

  —बिल गेट्स

- आप अपने जीवनकाल के लिए कुछ नहीं कर सकते हैं, लेकिन आप इसे मूल्यवान बनाने के लिए कुछ अवश्य ही कर सकते हैं।

  —बिल गेट्स

- अपने आदर्शों के साथ जीवन बिताओ। जब भी दुनिया को आभास होगा कि आप क्या हैं, आप नजरों में आएँगे और इन्हीं मूल्यों के कारण लोग आपकी ओर आकर्षित हो सकेंगे।

  —बिल गेट्स

- जीवन की गति संभवतः रहस्यपूर्ण है, उसमें आत्म-खंडन और पूर्वापर के असामंजस्य रहते हैं। **—रवींद्रनाथ टैगोर**
- जीवन-शक्ति का धर्म यह है कि वह अपना प्रयोग वहीं करती है, जहाँ जीवन का आभास मिले।
- जीवन को गतिशील रखने के लिए कुछ इच्छाएँ आवश्यक हैं। **—समुएल जोहंसन**
- जीने के लिए तो एक पल ही काफी है, बशर्ते आपने उसे किस तरह जिया। **—बिल गेट्स**
- जीवन एक नाटक है, यदि हम इसके कथानक को समझ लें तो सदैव प्रसन्न रह सकते हैं। **—बिल गेट्स**
- जीवन एक पाठशाला है, जिसमें अनुभवों के आधार पर हम शिक्षा प्राप्त करते हैं। **—बिल गेट्स**
- जीवन का हर क्षण उज्ज्वल भविष्य की संभावना लेकर आता है। **—बिल गेट्स**
- जीवन की त्रासदी इस बात में नहीं है कि आप अपने लक्ष्य तक नहीं पहुँचते हैं, त्रासदी तो इस बात की है कि आपके पास प्राप्त करने के लिए कोई लक्ष्य नहीं है। **—बिल गेट्स**
- जीवन-निर्वाह के लिए कमाने में इतने व्यस्त न हो जाएँ कि जीवन जीना भूल जाएँ। **—बिल गेट्स**
- जीवन में महत्त्वपूर्ण चीज विजय नहीं, संघर्ष है। मुख्य बात जीतना नहीं, बल्कि अच्छी तरह जूझना है। **—बिल गेट्स**
- जीवन में सफलता इतना अधिक प्रतिभा अथवा अवसर का विषय नहीं है, जितना वह लक्ष्य के प्रति प्रतिबद्धता और डटे रहने का है। **—बिल गेट्स**
- जीवन विकास का सिद्धांत है, स्थिर रहने का नहीं। **—बिल गेट्स**

- जिंदगी वैसी नहीं है, जैसी आप इसके लिए कामना करते हैं, यह तो वैसी बन जाती है, जैसा आप इसे बनाते हैं। **—एंथनी रयान**

- मेरी समझ में मनुष्य का व्यक्तिगत अस्तित्व एक नदी की तरह का होना चाहिए। नदी प्रारंभ में बहुत पतली होती है। पत्थरों, चट्टानों, झरनों को पार करके मैदान में आती है, एक क्रम से उसका विस्तार होता है, फिर भी बड़ी मंथर गति से बहती है और बिना क्रम भंग किए अंत में समुद्र में विलीन हो जाती है। समुद्र में अपने अस्तित्व को समाप्त करते समय वह किसी भी प्रकार की पीड़ा का अनुभव नहीं करती, जो वृद्ध पुरुष जीवन को इस रूप में देखता है, मृत्यु के भय से मुक्त रहता है।

  —बर्टेंड रसेल

- जीवन की दुर्घटनाओं में अकसर बड़े महत्त्व के नैतिक पहलू छिपे हुए होते हैं।

  —बिल गेट्स

- जीवन के आरंभ में ही कुछ असफलताएँ मिल जाने का बहुत अधिक व्यावहारिक महत्त्व है। **—बिल गेट्स**

- जीवन के प्रति आपका रुख निश्चित करता है, जीवन का आपके प्रति रुख।

  —बिल गेट्स

- यह जीवन न दीर्घता के हिसाब से बड़ा है, न गुण के हिसाब से, तो भी इसका एक विशेष मूल्य है, यह उस फूल के समान है, जिसके वक्ष पर भ्रमर आ बैठा हो और उसी पटाक्षेप के इतिहास ने उसके जीवन के फल में गुठली का सा रूप धारण कर लिया है। **—रवींद्रनाथ टैगोर**

- सृष्टिकर्ता आग में तपाकर हथौड़ी से ठोंककर जीवन की प्रतिमा तैयार करते हैं। **—रवींद्रनाथ टैगोर**

- जीवन की कहानी सुख-दु:ख के बीच से विलंबित गति से आगे बढ़ती चलती है। अंतिम अध्याय में अचानक टक्कर होती है, तब सबकुछ नष्ट-भ्रष्ट

होकर स्तब्ध हो जाता है। विधाता अपनी कहानी को बड़े धीरे-धीरे ही गढ़ते हैं, मगर तोड़ते एक ही चोट में हैं। **—रवींद्रनाथ टैगोर**

- जीवन छोटा ही क्यों न हो, समय की बरबादी से वह और भी छोटा हो जाता है। **—बिल गेट्स**
- जीवन न्याययुक्त नहीं है, इसकी आदत डाल लीजिए। **—बिल गेट्स**
- जीवन छोटा है, पर सुंदर है। **—बिल गेट्स**
- जीवन दिन काटने के लिए नहीं, कुछ महान् कार्य करने के लिए है। **—बिल गेट्स**
- जैसे नदी बह जाती है और लौटकर नहीं आती, उसी तरह रात-दिन मनुष्य की आयु लेकर चले जाते हैं, फिर नहीं आते। **—महाभारत**
- बीस वर्ष की आयु में व्यक्ति का जो चेहरा रहता है, वह प्रकृति की देन है, तीस वर्ष की आयु का चेहरा जिंदगी के उतार-चढ़ाव की देन है; लेकिन पचास वर्ष की आयु का चेहरा व्यक्ति की अपनी कमाई है। **—अष्टावक्र**
- जीवन को रोकर बहा देने से अच्छा है, हँसकर उड़ा देना। **—रवींद्रनाथ टैगोर**
- जीवन कोई पानी की सतह पर तैरता केले का खंभा नहीं है कि जहाँ-तहाँ ठोकर खाता, अटकता चले। **—रवींद्रनाथ टैगोर**
- आदर्श के साँचे में जब भी जीवन को फिट करना चाहता हूँ, जीवन उसे तोड़कर निकल जाता है। **—रवींद्रनाथ टैगोर**
- यह जीवन तो एक जाल की तरह है, पर उसमें बीच-बीच में सुराख रह गया है। **—रवींद्रनाथ टैगोर**
- जोर लगाकर बंधन तोड़ने की कोशिश में देह लहूलुहान हो जाती है। **—रवींद्रनाथ टैगोर**

• जीवन किसी चारदीवारी या दल की सीमा में बँधा नहीं है।

—रवींद्रनाथ टैगोर

• दिखावा, आक्रामकता सिर्फ एक मुखौटा है, जिसके पीछे मनुष्य अपनी कमजोरियों को, अपने से और संसार से छिपाकर चलता है। असली और स्थायी शक्ति सहनशीलता में है। त्वरित और कठोर प्रतिक्रिया सिर्फ कमजोर लोग करते हैं और इसमें वे अपनी मनुष्यता को खो देते हैं।

—फ्रांत्स काफ्का

• जीवन भर ज्ञानार्जन के बाद में केवल इतना ही जान पाया हूँ कि मैं कुछ भी नहीं जान पाया हूँ। **—सुकरात**

• लंबी जिंदगी सब चाहते हैं, बूढ़ा होना कोई नहीं चाहता।

• किसी भी व्यक्ति के पास स्वयं को अभिव्यक्त करने का केवल एक ही माध्यम होता है, उसका जीवन। **—एमरे कर्तेश**

• आदर्श, अनुशासन, मर्यादा, परिश्रम, ईमानदारी तथा उच्च मानवीय मूल्यों के बिना किसी का जीवन महान् नहीं बन सकता है। **—स्वामी विवेकानंद**

• हम जीवन से वही सीखते हैं, जो उससे वास्तव में सीखना चाहते हैं।

—जैक्सन ब्राउन

• आत्मज्ञान, आत्मसम्मान, आत्मसंयम, ये तीनों ही जीवन को परम संपन्न बनाते हैं। **—टेनीसन**

• साझा की गई खुशी दुगनी होती है, साझा किया गया दुःख आधा होता है।

—स्वीडन की कहावत

• जिंदगी जीने के दो तरीके होते हैं—पहला, जो पसंद है, उसे हासिल करना सीख लो। दूसरा, जो हासिल है, उसे पसंद करना सीख लो।

• जिंदगी की जड़ें, जब स्पष्ट जीवन-मूल्यों, उद्देश्य और समर्पण में होती हैं, वे दृढ़ और अडिग होती हैं।

• जब से मैंने जाना कि जीवन क्षणभंगुर है, मैं करुणा में डूब गया।

—जेरेक्स

• मरते तो सभी हैं, लेकिन महत्त्वपूर्ण यह है कि आपने अपनी जिंदगी किस प्रकार गुजारी है। **—अज्ञात**

• जीवन में आनंद को कर्तव्य बनाने की अपेक्षा कर्तव्य को आनंद बनाना अधिक महत्त्वपूर्ण है। **—अज्ञात**

• जीवन में कभी समझौता करना पड़े तो कोई बड़ी बात नहीं है, क्योंकि झुकता वही है, जिसमें जान होती है, अकड़ तो मुरदे की पहचान होती है।

—अज्ञात

• जीवन का सबसे बड़ा उपयोग इसे किसी ऐसी चीज में लगाने में है, जो इसके बाद भी रहे। **—विलियम जेम्स**

• जीवन एक आग है, जो खुद को भी झुलसा देती है, लेकिन जब एक शिशु जन्म लेता है, यह आग फिर भड़क उठती है। **—जॉर्ज बर्नार्ड शॉ**

• किसी चीज की कीमत यह है कि आप उसके बदले में अपनी कितनी जिंदगी लगा देते हैं। **—हेनरी डेविड थोर**

• जिंदगी लोगों से प्रेम करने, उनकी सेवा करने, उन्हें सशक्त बनाने और उन्हें प्रोत्साहित करने का नाम है।

• सार्थक जीवन में समस्याएँ हो सकती हैं, परंतु उसमें कोई पश्चात्ताप नहीं होना चाहिए।

• जीवन छोटा है, पर सुंदर है। **—सोफोक्लेस**

• जिंदगी एक उबाऊ कहानी की तरह है, जिसे दो बार सुना गया हो, लेकिन एक ऊँघते हुए इनसान के कानों की सफाई कर देने के लिए यह बेहतरीन साधन है। **—विलियम शेक्सपियर**

• जीवन विकास का सिद्धांत है, स्थिर रहने का नहीं।

—जवाहरलाल नेहरू

- जिंदगी में खुश रहना है तो हँसने का बहाना तलाशें। **—अज्ञात**
- जिंदगी का हर पल कुछ-न-कुछ सिखाता है। **—अज्ञात**
- जीवन एक नाटक है, यदि हम इसके कथानक को समझ लें तो सदैव प्रसन्न रह सकते हैं। **—अज्ञात**
- जीने के लिए तो एक पल ही काफी है, बशर्ते आपने उसे किस तरह जिया। **—अज्ञात**
- जिस जीवन की समीक्षा व परख न की गई हो, वह जीने योग्य ही नहीं है। **—अज्ञात**
- जिसने जीवन में संघर्ष नहीं किया, उसका जीवन व्यर्थ है। **—अज्ञात**
- जीवन का एक क्षण करोड़ स्वर्ण मुद्राएँ देने पर भी नहीं मिलता। **—चाणक्य**
- मूर्ति के समान मनुष्य का जीवन सभी ओर से सुंदर होना चाहिए। **—सुकरात**
- यदि तुम्हारे पास दो पैसे हों तो एक से रोटी और दूसरे से फूल लो, रोटी तुम्हें जीवन देगी और फूल तुम्हें जीवन जीने की कला सिखाएगा। **—चीनी कहावत**
- जियो और जीने दो। **—स्काच कहावत**
- जो अच्छी तरह जीता है, वह दो बार जीता है। **—लैटिन कहावत**
- मैं ही आग हूँ, मैं ही कूड़ा-करकट। अगर मेरी आग कूड़ा-करकट जलाकर भस्म कर दे तो मैं अच्छा जीवन पाऊँगा। **—खलील जिब्रान**
- अपना जीवन लेने के लिए नहीं, देने के लिए है। **—स्वामी विवेकानंद**

- जीवन किसी को स्थायी संपत्ति के रूप में नहीं मिला है, वह तो केवल प्रयोग के लिए है। **—लुक्रीटस**

- मनुष्य जीवन अनुभव का शास्त्र है। **—विनोबा**

- जीवन एक फूल है और प्रेम उसका मधु। **—ह्यूगो**

जीवन का सत्य

- जीवन के सत्य का देर से ही आविष्कार किया है, किंतु इसीलिए उसे अस्वीकार तो नहीं कर सकते। **—रवींद्रनाथ टैगोर**

जीवन-नाट्य

- संसार में अधिकांश बड़े-बड़े जीवन-नाट्य परदे के पीछे ही जमा होते रहते हैं, पंचमांक के अंत में वह परदा अचानक ही उठ जाता है। **—रवींद्रनाथ टैगोर**

जीवन-प्रवाह

- जीवन-प्रवाह की जो गंभीरतम तलहटी बहुत दिनों की गति बन गई है, वह इच्छा की आँधी कहीं तो तोड़ती है, पर कहीं जाकर ठिठक जाती है।

  —रवींद्रनाथ टैगोर

जीवन-मरण

- जीवन बसंत के पुष्पों की तरह सुंदर हो और मृत्यु पतझर में पत्तों जैसी।

  —रवींद्रनाथ टैगोर

- मृत्यु में अनेक एक हो जाता है और जीवन में एक अनेक हो जाता है।

  —रवींद्रनाथ टैगोर

- मृत्यु की मोहर जीवन के सिक्के को मूल्य प्रदान करती है, जिससे जीवन के द्वारा वस्तुतः बहुमूल्य वस्तु का क्रय संभव हो जाता है।

  —रवींद्रनाथ टैगोर

जीवात्मा-परमात्मा

- है दूर से दूर और समीप से समीप! जहाँ तुम निकट हो, वहाँ तुम मेरे हो और जहाँ तुम सुदूर हो, वहाँ मैं तुम्हारा हूँ। **—रवींद्रनाथ टैगोर**

जीवित और मृत

- जिसका रोग अच्छा होने की कोई संभावना नहीं है, उसका मरना ही भला है; क्योंकि जीवित रहने से स्वयं भी सुख नहीं मिलता और दूसरों को भी दुःख होता है। **—रवींद्रनाथ टैगोर**

जीविका

- व्यवसाय समय का यंत्र है। **—नेपोलियन**
- व्यस्त मनुष्य को आँसू बहाने का अवकाश नहीं। **—बायरन**
- वह जीविका श्रेष्ठ है, जिसमें अपने धर्म की नहीं, जिससे कुटुंब का पालन हो। **—शुक्रनीति**

जोखिम

- यदि आपके जीवन में असफलताएँ नहीं हैं, तो आप पर्याप्त जोखिम नहीं उठा रहे हैं। **—बिल गेट्स**
- यह संकल्प कर लें कि यह जोखिम लेने योग्य है, तो आपको तत्काल कर्म करने का साहस जुटा लेना चाहिए। **—बिल गेट्स**
- जोखिम उठाइए! पूरी जिंदगी एक जोखिम है। सबसे आगे निकलनेवाला व्यक्ति सामान्यतया वह होता है, जो कर्म और दुस्साहस के लिए इच्छुक रहता है। **—बिल गेट्स**
- जोखिम उठाएँ, यदि आप जीत जाते हैं तो आप प्रसन्न होंगे, यदि आप हार जाते हैं, तो आप समझदार बन जाएँगे। **—बिल गेट्स**

ज्वार-भाटा

- सहसा किसी पूर्णिमा को जीवन में जब ज्वार आता है, तब दोनों किनारे प्लावित कर मनुष्य सोचता है, मेरी कहीं सीमा नहीं। उस समय जो एक

विराट् प्रतिज्ञा कर बैठता है, जीवन के सुदीर्घ भाटे के समय, उस प्रतिज्ञा की रक्षा के लिए उसके संपूर्ण प्राणों में खिंचाव पड़ता है। **—रवींद्रनाथ टैगोर**

- जिस चाँद के आकर्षण से ज्वार आता है, उसी के आकर्षण से भाटा भी आता है। **—रवींद्रनाथ टैगोर**

झगड़ा

- लोग फल के बजाय छिलके पर अधिक झगड़ते हैं। **—अज्ञात**
- झगड़े में शामिल दोनों पक्ष गलत होते हैं। **—अज्ञात**

झूठ

- थोड़ा सा झूठ भी मनुष्य का नाश कर सकता है। **—महात्मा गांधी**
- झूठ की सजा यह नहीं कि उसका विश्वास नहीं किया जाता, बल्कि वह किसी का विश्वास नहीं कर सकता। **—शेक्सपियर**
- एक झूठ को झूठ के रूप में पहचान गया हूँ, इसीलिए जीवन के सभी सच आज उजाड़ हो गए हैं। **—रवींद्रनाथ टैगोर**
- जहाँ झूठ सच के समान हो, वहाँ झूठ ही सच हो जाता है। **—रवींद्रनाथ टैगोर**
- स्पष्ट शब्दों में बोले गए झूठ से कही बुरा है। **—रस्किन**
- एक झूठ को छिपाने के लिए अनेक झूठ बोलने पड़ते हैं। **—कहावत**
- यदि झूठ बोलने से किसी की जान बचती है तो वह झूठ पाप नहीं, पुण्य है। **—प्रेमचंद**

टीस

- संबंध का बंधन जब प्रकट हो जाता है, तब उसकी टीस बहुत लोगों के भीतर होने लगती है, बहुत जगह से तनाव-खिंचाव पड़ने लगता है, भला किसको दोष देंगे? **—रवींद्रनाथ टैगोर**

ठगी

- दुनिया के साढ़े-पंद्रह आना लोग आदमी को झूठ द्वारा ठगते हैं।

—रवींद्रनाथ टैगोर

ठोकर

- ठोकर लगे और दर्द हो, तभी मैं सीख पाता हूँ। **—महात्मा गांधी**
- दूसरों के अनुभव से होशियारी सीखने की मनुष्य को इच्छा नहीं होती, उसको स्वतंत्र ठोकर चाहिए। **—विनोबा**
- ठोकरें केवल धूल ही उड़ाती हैं, फसलें नहीं उगातीं।

—रवींद्रनाथ टैगोर

डर

- अपने मन में डर हो, तभी इस अगर-मगर और किंतु-परंतु का बल और बढ़ जाता है। **—रवींद्रनाथ टैगोर**
- अज्ञानी के लिए झूठ ही सच होता है। अगर वह इस मिथ्या से हट जाए तो वह सत्य से हट जाने जैसा ही होगा। **—रवींद्रनाथ टैगोर**
- कल्पना मूर्ति से डरने का कोई कारण नहीं है, केवल वास्तविक चीजों से ही डरने का कारण हो सकता है। **—रवींद्रनाथ टैगोर**
- देश की हवा में जैसे मलेरिया होता है, वैसे ही डर भी होता है, उससे ऊपर नहीं उठा जा सकता। **—रवींद्रनाथ टैगोर**

डरावना अनुभव

- जो चिर-परिचित है, वह जब एक पल में अपरिचित हो जाता है तो वह एक डरावना अनुभव बन जाता है। **—रवींद्रनाथ टैगोर**

डॉक्टरी

- डॉक्टरी विद्या सिर्फ पुस्तकों की ही नहीं होती, किसी-किसी में उसका दुर्लभ दैव संस्कार होता है। **—रवींद्रनाथ टैगोर**

डायरी

- डायरी एक बनावटी जीवन है, लेकिन जब हम उसे लिखते हैं, तब वह हमारे प्राकृतिक जीवन पर अपना आधिपत्य जमा लेती है। **—रवींद्रनाथ टैगोर**

डायरी लेखन

- डायरी लिखने से जीवन-गठन का बोझ दो मनुष्यों पर डाल देना पड़ता है। बहुत अंशों में डायरी के अनुसार जीवन होता है और कितने ही अंशों में तो डायरी जीवन के अनुसार। **—रवींद्रनाथ टैगोर**

ढोंग

- धर्म के नाम पर जो लोग ढोंग करते हैं, ऐसे धर्मव्यय साथियों के समान संकीर्ण चित्त और विश्व निंदक संसार में और कोई नहीं है।

  —रवींद्रनाथ टैगोर

तत्त्व

- तत्त्व पर बिगड़ना फिजूल है, वह अच्छा भी नहीं होता, बुरा भी नहीं होता, जो होता है, सो होता है, उसके विरुद्ध जाओ तो होने के ही विरुद्ध जाओगे।

  —रवींद्रनाथ टैगोर

तपस्या

- नवयौवन के नवजाग्रत् प्रेम में एक-एकांत तपस्या होती है।

  —रवींद्रनाथ टैगोर

- तपस्या की सिद्धि आसान नहीं होती, उसका रास्ता बहुत लंबा है, उसकी गति बड़ी धीमी है। **—रवींद्रनाथ टैगोर**

- तपस्या आनंद का ही एक अंग है। **—रवींद्रनाथ टैगोर**

तर्क

- जो तर्क नहीं सुने, वह कट्टर है, जो तर्क न कर सके, वह मूर्ख है और जो तर्क करने का प्रयत्न न करे, वह गुलाम है।

  —ड्रमंड

- तर्क केवल बुद्धि का विषय है, हृदय की सिद्धि तक बुद्धि नहीं पहुँच सकती। जिसे बुद्धि माने, मगर हृदय न माने, वह तजने योग्य है।

—महात्मा गांधी

तलवार

- निपुण शस्त्रकार ऐसी तेज तलवार का निर्माण कर सकता है कि उससे आदमी के दो टुकड़े करने पर भी उसे पता न चले, अंत में हिलाने पर ही आधे-आधे भाग अलग हो जाते हैं। विधाता की तलवार ऐसी ही है।

—रवींद्रनाथ टैगोर

ताकत

- जिसके पास ताकत है, अगर सेंध भी लगा रहा हो तो बहादुरी दिखाकर उसे पकड़वाए जाने पर वह झेंपकर सिर नहीं झुकाता, बल्कि उल्टे चिमटा उठाकर परम साधु की भाँति हुंकार कर मारने आता है। **—रवींद्रनाथ टैगोर**

तुच्छ

- इस संसार में जो सबसे अधिक तुच्छ है, वही सबसे अधिक कठिन क्यों है ?

—रवींद्रनाथ टैगोर

- आदमी किसी चीज को अपनी जिंदगी का चरम लक्ष्य मानकर उसको हासिल करने के लिए लगातार कठिन परिश्रम करता है और आखिर में सफल हो, उन चीजों को हाथ में लेकर देखता है तो उसे तुच्छ मायाजाल पाता है।

—रवींद्रनाथ टैगोर

तीन बातें

- तीन बातें कभी न भूलें—प्रतिज्ञा करके, कर्ज लेकर और विश्वास देकर।

—महावीर

- तीन बातें करो—उत्तम के साथ संगीत, विद्वान् के साथ वार्त्तालाप और सहृदय के साथ मैत्री। **—विनोबा**

- तीन अनमोल वचन—धन गया तो कुछ नहीं गया, स्वास्थ्य गया तो कुछ गया और चरित्र गया तो सब गया। **—अंग्रेजी कहावत**

- तीन से घृणा न करो—रोगी से, दुःखी से और निम्न जाति से। **—मुहम्मद साहब**

- तीन के आँसू पवित्र होते हैं—प्रेम के, करुणा के और सहानुभूति के। **—बुद्ध**

- तीन बातें सुखी जीवन के लिए—अतीत की चिंता मत करो, भविष्य का विश्वास न करो और वर्तमान को व्यर्थ मत जाने दो।

- तीन चीजें किसी का इंतजार नहीं करतीं—समय, मौत, ग्राहक।

- तीन चीजें जीवन में एक बार मिलती हैं—माँ, बाप और जवानी।

- तीन चीजें परदे योग्य हैं—धन, स्त्री और भोजन।

- तीन चीजों से सदा सावधान रहिए—बुरी संगत, परस्त्री और निंदा।

- तीन चीजों में मन लगाने से उन्नति होती है—ईश्वर, परिश्रम और विद्या।

- तीन चीजों को कभी छोटी न समझें—बीमारी, कर्जा, शत्रु।

- तीनों चीजों को हमेशा वश में रखो—मन, काम और लोभ।

- तीन चीजें निकलने पर वापस नहीं आतीं—तीर कमान से, बात जुबान से और प्राण शरीर से।

- तीन चीजें कमजोर बना देती है—बदचलनी, क्रोध और लालच।

- तीन चीजें असल उद्देश्य से रोकती हैं—बदचलनी, क्रोध और लालच।

- तीन चीजें कोई चुरा नहीं सकता—अकल, चरित्र, हुनर।

- तीन व्यक्ति वक्त पर पहचाने जाते हैं—स्त्री, भाई, दोस्त।

- तीनों व्यक्ति का सम्मान करो—माता, पिता और गुरु।

- तीनों व्यक्ति पर सदा दया करो—बालक, भूखे और पागल।

- तीन चीजें कभी नहीं भूलनी चाहिए—कर्ज, मर्ज और फर्ज।
- तीन बातें कभी मत भूलें—उपकार, उपदेश और उदारता।
- तीन चीजें याद रखना जरूरी हैं—सच्चाई, कर्तव्य और मृत्यु।
- तीन बातें चरित्र को गिरा देती हैं—चोरी, निंदा और झूठ।
- तीन चीजें हमेशा दिल में रखनी चाहिए—नम्रता, दया और माफी।
- तीन चीजों पर कब्जा करो—जबान, आदत और गुस्सा।
- तीन चीजों से दूर भागो—आलस्य, खुशामद और बकवास।
- तीन चीजों के लिए मर मिटो—धैर्य, देश और मित्र।
- तीन चीजें इनसान की अपनी होती हैं—रूप, भाग्य और स्वभाव।
- तीन चीजों पर अभिमान मत करो—ताकत, सुंदरता, यौवन।
- तीन चीजें अगर चली गईं तो कभी वापस नहीं आतीं—समय, शब्द और अवसर।
- तीन चीजें इनसान कभी नहीं खो सकता—शांति, आशा और ईमानदारी।
- तीन चीजें, जो सबसे अमूल्य हैं—प्यार, आत्मविश्वास और सच्चा मित्र।
- तीन चीजें, जो कभी निश्चित नहीं होतीं—सपने, सफलता और भाग्य।
- तीन चीजें, जो जीवन को सँवारती है—कड़ी मेहनत, निष्ठा और त्याग।
- तीन चीजें किसी भी इनसान को बरबाद कर सकती हैं—शराब, घमंड और क्रोध।
- तीन चीजों से बचने की कोशिश करनी चाहिए—बुरी संगत, स्वार्थ और निंदा।
- कोई भी कार्य करने से पहले सोचो, समझो, फिर करो। **—अज्ञात**

त्याग

- संसार में रहकर भी तो संसार को त्यागा जा सकता है।

—रवींद्रनाथ टैगोर

- जो हमारे हाथ में आता है, उसे हम पूरी तरह से प्राप्त नहीं करते। जब त्याग द्वारा उसे पाते हैं, यथार्थ में वह हमारे हृदय का धन बन जाता है।

—रवींद्रनाथ टैगोर

- त्याग के द्वारा, दान, तपस्या दुःख के द्वारा ही गंभीर अवबोधन संभव है सुख या आराम के द्वारा नहीं। **—रवींद्रनाथ टैगोर**
- जन्म का आधार वेदना है, त्याग के मार्ग से ही लक्ष्य तक पहुँचा जा सकता है। **—रवींद्रनाथ टैगोर**
- प्राणी कर्म का त्याग नहीं कर सकता, कर्मफल का त्याग ही त्याग है।

—भगवान् कृष्ण

- प्राणों का मोह त्याग करना वीरता का रहस्य है। **—जयशंकर प्रसाद**
- महान् त्याग से ही महान् कार्य संभव है। **—स्वामी विवेकानंद**
- यश त्याग से मिलता है, धोखाधड़ी से नहीं। **—प्रेमचंद**
- अच्छे व्यवहार छोटे-छोटे त्याग से बनते हैं। **—एमर्सन**
- त्याग से पाप का मूलधन चुकता है और दान से ब्याज। **—विनोबा**
- पर-स्त्री, पर-धन, पर-निंदा, परिहास और बड़ों के सामने चंचलता का त्याग करना चाहिए। **—संस्कृत सूक्ति**
- त्याग यह नहीं कि मोटे और खुरदरे वस्त्र पहन लिये जाएँ और सूखी रोटी खाई जाए, त्याग तो यह है कि अपनी इच्छा, अभिलाषा और तृष्णा को जीता जाए। **—सुफियान सौरी**

त्रुटियाँ

- दोष और त्रुटियाँ तो उन बड़े-बड़े वीर पुरुषों में भी रही हैं, जो अपने माहात्म्य से उन्नत मस्तक हैं। उन त्रुटियों को आत्मसात् करके ही वे बड़े हुए हैं। **—रवींद्रनाथ टैगोर**

दंड

- दंड अन्यायी के लिए न्याय है। **—अगस्तियन**
- अपराधी को दंड से नहीं रोका जा सकता। **—रस्किन**
- अपराधी के दंड में उपयोगिता होनी चाहिए। **—वाल्टेयर**

दया

- दया धर्म का मूल है, पाप मूल अभिमान।
  तुलसी दया न छोड़िए, जब लग घट में प्राण॥ **—तुलसीदास**
- जिसमें दया नहीं, उसमें कोई सद्गुण नहीं। **—हजरत मोहम्मद**
- दया और सत्यता परस्पर मिलते हैं, धर्म और शांति एक-दूसरे का साथ देते हैं। **—बाइबिल**
- हम सभी ईश्वर से दया की प्रार्थना करते हैं और वही प्रार्थना हमें दूसरों पर दया करना सिखाती है। **—शेक्सपियर**
- जो निर्बलों पर दया नहीं करता, उसे बलवानों के अत्याचार सहने पड़ेंगे। **—शेख सादी**
- दया चरित्र को सुंदर बनाती है। **—जेम्स एलन**
- आत्मा के आनंदरूपी सामंजस्य का बाहरी रूप दया है। **—विलियम हैजलित**
- सब पर दया करनी चाहिए, क्योंकि ऐसा कोई नहीं है, जिसने कभी अपराध नहीं किया हो। **—रामायण**
- कितने देव, कितने धर्म, कितने पंथ चल पड़े, पर इस शोकग्रस्त संसार को केवल दयावानों की आवश्यकता है। **—विलकास्य**
- हम सभी ईश्वर से दया की प्रार्थना करते हैं और वही प्रार्थना हमें दया करना भी सिखाती है। **—शेक्सपियर**

- दयालु चेहरा सदैव सुंदर होता है। **—बेली**
- प्रेम के बाद सहानुभूति मानव हृदय की पवित्रतम भावना है। **—बर्क**
- जो सचमुच दयालु है, वही सचमुच बुद्धिमान है और जो दूसरों से प्रेम नहीं करता, उस पर ईश्वर की कृपा नहीं होती। **—होम**
- दया के छोटे-छोटे से कार्य, प्रेम के जरा-जरा से शब्द हमारी पृथ्वी को स्वर्गोपम बना देते हैं।
  —जूलिया कार्नी
- न्याय करना ईश्वर का काम है, आदमी का काम तो दया करना है।
  —फ्रांसिस
- दयालुता हमें ईश्वर तुल्य बनाती है। **—क्लाडियन**
- दया मनुष्य का स्वाभाविक गुण है। **—प्रेमचंद**
- दया सबसे बड़ा धर्म है। **—महाभारत**
- दया दो-तरफा कृपा है। इसकी कृपा दाता पर भी होती है और पात्र पर भी।
  —शेक्सपियर
- दयालुता दयालुता को जन्म देती है।
  —सोफोक्लीज
- परोपकारियों का मार्ग न समुद्र रोक सकता है और न पर्वत। **—अज्ञात**
- कितने देव, कितने धर्म, कितने पंथ चल पड़े, पर इस शोकग्रस्त संसार को केवल दयावानों की आवश्यकता है।
  —विलकास्य
- हम सभी ईश्वर से दया की प्रार्थना करते हैं और वही प्रार्थना हमें दूसरों पर दया करना सिखाती है। **—शेक्सपियर**
- जहाँ तुम्हारा अपना थोड़ा भी लगाव हो, वहीं पर तुम्हारी सारी दया उमड़ती है। **—रवींद्रनाथ टैगोर**

- दया वृत्ति ही अच्छे-बुरे की ठीक-ठीक पहचान करने पर क्षमता को भी तो विकृत कर देती है। **—रवींद्रनाथ टैगोर**
- दया करने की झोंक में आकर हम सत्य को निर्विकार भाव से देखने की शक्ति खो बैठते हैं। **—रवींद्रनाथ टैगोर**
- सब पर दया करनी चाहिए, क्योंकि ऐसा कोई नहीं है, जिसने कभी अपराध नहीं किया हो। **—रामायण दया**
- स्त्री पर स्त्री को दया नहीं आती। **—रवींद्रनाथ टैगोर**
- हम जिसे दया कहते हैं, वह दरअसल अपने ऊपर ही दया होती है। हम दूसरों को सिर्फ इसलिए चोट नहीं पहुँचाते कि कहीं बाद में खुद को कष्ट न हो। **—रवींद्रनाथ टैगोर**

दरिद्र

- दरिद्र की आकांक्षा भी दरिद्र ही होती है। **—रवींद्रनाथ टैगोर**
- लोग जब दरिद्र हो जाते हैं, तब बाहर की ओर गौरव ढूँढ़ते फिरते हैं। **—रवींद्रनाथ टैगोर**

दरिद्रता

- त्याग का दारिद्र्य भूषण है, अभाव का दारिद्र्य भूषण नहीं। **—रवींद्रनाथ टैगोर**
- दया और सत्यता परस्पर मिलते हैं, धर्म और शांति एक-दूसरे का साथ देते हैं। **—बाइबिल**

दर्शन

- दर्शन का उद्‌देश्य जीवन की व्याख्या करना नहीं, उसे बदलना है। **—सर्वपल्ली राधाकृष्णन**
- जब जिंदगी को अपने दिल के गीत सुनाने का मौका नहीं मिलता, तब वह अपने मन के विचार सुनाने के लिए दार्शनिक पैदा कर देती है। **—खलील जिब्रान**

- दार्शनिक होने का अर्थ केवल सूक्ष्म विचारक होना या केवल किसी दर्शन प्रणाली को चला देना नहीं है, बल्कि यह है कि हम ज्ञान के ऐसे प्रेमी बन जाएँ कि उसके इशारों पर चलते हुए विश्वास, सादगी, स्वतंत्रता और उदारता का जीवन व्यतीत करने लगें। **—थोरो**

दान

- सैकड़ों हाथों से इकट्ठा करो और हजारों हाथों से बाँटो। **—अथर्ववेद**
- दान से वस्तु घटती नहीं, बल्कि बढ़ती है। **—अज्ञात**
- जो दान अपनी कीर्ति-गाथा गाने को उतावला हो उठता है, वह अहंकार एवं आडंबर मात्र रह जाता है। **—हुट्टन**
- जब घर में धन और नाव में पानी आने लगे, तो उसे दोनों हाथों से निकालें ऐसा करने में बुद्धिमानी है। **—अज्ञात**
- हमें धन की अधिकता सुखी नहीं बनाती। **—संत कबीर**
- सज्जनों की रीति यह है कि कोई अगर उनसे कुछ माँगे तो वे मुख से कुछ न कहकर, काम पूरा करके ही उत्तर देते हैं। **—कालिदास**
- जो जल बाढ़े नाव में, घर में बाढ़े दाम।
दोउ हाथ उलीचिए, यहि सज्जन का काम॥ **—कबीर**
- तुम्हारा बायाँ हाथ जो देता है, उसे दायाँ हाथ न जानने पाए। **—बाइबिल**
- सबसे उत्तम दान यह है कि आदमी को इतना योग्य बना दो कि वह बिना दान के काम चला सके। **—तालमुद**

दिमाग

- दिमाग जब बड़े-बड़े विचार सोचने के अनुरूप बड़ा हो जाता है, तो पुनः अपने मूल आकार में नहीं लौटता। **—बिल गेट्स**

- दिमाग पैराशूट के समान है, वह तभी कार्य करता है, जब खुला हो।

—बिल गेट्स

- मुझे यकीन है कि हर व्यक्ति प्रतिभा के साथ पैदा होता है।

—बिल गेट्स

दिल

- एक टूटा हुआ दिल, टूटे हुए शीशे के समान होता है, इसको टूटा हुआ छोड़ देना ज्यादा बेहतर होता, क्योंकि दोनों को जोड़ने में खुद को ज्यादा दुःख पहुँचता है। **—अज्ञात**
- चेहरा हृदय का प्रतिबिंब है। **—कहावत**
- सुंदर हृदय का मूल्य सोने से भी बढ़कर है। **—शेक्सपियर**
- भरे दिल में सबके लिए जगह होती है, पर खाली दिल में किसी के लिए नहीं। **—अज्ञात**

दुःख

- दुःख की उपेक्षा करो, वह कम हो जाएगा। **—सद्गुरु श्रीब्रह्मचैतन्य**
- अन्याय सहनेवाले से ज्यादा दुःखी अन्याय करनेवाला होता है। **—प्लेटो**
- किसी दुःखी व्यक्ति के लिए थोड़ी सहायता ढेरों उपदेशों से कहीं ज्यादा अच्छी है। **—बुलवर**
- संसार के दुखियों में पहला दुःखी निर्धन है। उससे दुःखी वह है, जिसे किसी का ऋण चुकाना हो। इन दोनों से अधिक दुःखी वह है, जो सदा रोगी रहता हो और सबसे दुःखी वह है, जिसकी पत्नी दुष्टा हो।

—विदुर नीति

- विचित्र बात है कि सुख की अभिलाषा मेरे दुःख का एक अंश है।

—खलील जिब्रान

- एक बात, जो मैं दिन की तरह स्पष्ट देखता हूँ, यह है कि दुःख का कारण अज्ञान है और कुछ नहीं। **—स्वामी विवेकानंद**

• पाप का संचय ही दुःखों का मूल है। **—महात्मा बुद्ध**

दुनिया

• दुनिया को बदल डालो या घर पर बैठो। दुनिया को और बेहतर बनाने के लिए काम करो। भले ही वह एक वर्जन, प्लेटफॉर्म, सिस्टम, आइडिया, रीजन या इनोवेशन हो, इसे करना ही चाहिए। **—बिल गेट्स**

दुर्बलता

• स्वयं को भेड़ बना लोगे तो भेड़िए आकर तुम्हें खा जाएँगे।

—जर्मन कहावत

• मन की दुर्बलता से भयंकर और कोई पाप नहीं।

—स्वामी विवेकानंद

• दुर्बल को न सताइए, जाकी मोटी हाय। मुई खाल की साँस सों, सार भसम हो जाय॥ **—कबीर**

दुर्भावना

• दुर्भावना को मैं मनुष्य का कलंक समझता हूँ। **—महात्मा गांधी**

• दुर्भावना अपने विष का आधा भाग स्वयं पीती है। **—सैनेका**

• आदमी की दुर्भावना उसके दुश्मन की बजाय, उसे ही अधिक दुःख देती है। **—चार्ल बक्सटन**

दुर्वचन

• दुर्वचन पशुओं तक को अप्रिय होते हैं। **—महात्मा बुद्ध**

• दुर्वचन कहनेवाला तिरस्कृत नहीं करता, बल्कि दुर्वचन के प्रति हृदय में उठी हुई भावना तिरस्कार करती है, इसीलिए जब कोई तुम्हें उत्तेजित करता है तो यह तुम्हारे अंदर की भावना ही है, जो तुम्हें उत्तेजित करती है।

—एपिक्टेटस

• दुर्वचन का सामना हमें सहनशीलता से करना चाहिए।

—महात्मा गांधी

दुश्मन

• अपने दुश्मनों को माफ कर दें, लेकिन उनके नाम कभी न भूले।

—जॉन एफ. कैनेडी

• अहिंसा अच्छी चीज है, लेकिन शत्रुहीन होना अच्छी बात है।

—विमल मित्र

• दुश्मन का लोहा गरम भले ही हो, पर हथौड़ा तो ठंडा ही काम दे सकता है।

—सरदार पटेल

• अपने विरोधियों से मित्रता कर लेना क्या विरोधियों को नष्ट करने के समान नहीं है ?

—अब्राहम लिंकन

देवनागरी

• हिंदुस्तान की एकता के लिए हिंदी भाषा जितना काम देगी, उससे बहुत अधिक काम देवनागरी लिपि दे सकती है।

—आचार्य विनोबा भावे

• देवनागरी किसी भी लिपि की तुलना में अधिक वैज्ञानिक एवं व्यवस्थित लिपि है।

—सर विलियम जोंस

• मानव मस्तिष्क से निकली हुई वर्णमालाओं में नागरी सबसे अधिक पूर्ण वर्णमाला है।

—जॉन क्राइस्ट

• उर्दू लिखने के लिए देवनागरी अपनाने से उर्दू उत्कर्ष को प्राप्त होगी।

—खुशवंत सिंह

देशभक्ति

• दुरात्मा के लिए देशभक्ति अंतिम शरण है।

—जॉनसन

• यदि देशभक्ति का मतलब व्यापक मानव मात्र का हित चिंतन नहीं है तो उसका कोई अर्थ ही नहीं है।

—महात्मा गांधी

• आपको देशभक्ति में इतना अंधा नहीं हो जाना चाहिए कि आप सच्चाई का सामना न कर सकें। जो गलत है, वह गलत है, फिर चाहे, जो इसे कहे।

—मैलकम एक्स

• देशभक्ति मूल रूप से एक धारणा है कि कोई देश इसलिए दुनिया में सबसे अच्छा है, क्योंकि आप वहाँ पैदा हुए थे। **—जॉर्ज बर्नार्ड शा**

• सच्ची देशभक्ति कहीं और से अधिक अपने ही देश में हो रहे अन्याय से घृणा करती है। **—क्लेरेंस डैरो**

• हर देश खुद को और देशों से बेहतर समझता है। इसी से देशभक्ति आती है और युद्ध भी। **—डेल कार्नेगी**

• क्या कुछ इससे भी अधिक मूर्खतापूर्ण हो सकता है कि किसी व्यक्ति को मुझे मारने का अधिकार सिर्फ इसलिए है, क्योंकि वह नदी के उस पार रहता है और उसके शासक का मेरे शासक से झगड़ा हो गया है, जबकि मैंने उसके साथ कोई झगड़ा नहीं किया है।

—ब्लेज पास्कल

• देशप्रेम आमतौर पर किसी खास वर्ग के प्रति घृणा से मजबूत होता है और अंतरराष्ट्रीयता से हमेशा ही मजबूत होता है।

—जॉर्ज ऑरवेल

• देश के प्रति वफादारी हमेशा सरकार के प्रति वफादारी, जब वह इसकी हकदार हो। **—मार्क ट्वेन**

• कोई भी झंडा इतना बड़ा नहीं है कि वह निर्दोषों की हत्या की शर्मिंदगी को ढक सके। **—हॉवर्ड जिन**

• पहले वे लिखा करते थे कि अपने देश के लिए मरना अच्छा और सही है,

लेकिन आजकल के युद्ध में आपके मरने में न कुछ अच्छा है, न सही है। आप बिना किसी खास वजह के कुत्ते की तरह मारे जाएँगे।

—अर्नेस्ट हेमिंग्वे

- कभी-कभार आजादी के पेड़ को देशभक्तों और तानाशाहों के खून से सींचा जाना चाहिए। **—थॉमस जेफर्सन**
- देशभक्त का कर्तव्य है कि वह अपने देश की रक्षा उसकी सरकार से करे। **—थॉमस पेन**
- अच्छा आदमी और अच्छा नागरिक होना हमेशा एक जैसा नहीं होता। **—अरस्तू**
- सबसे बड़ी देशभक्ति अपने देश को यह बताना है कि कब वह नीचतापूर्ण, मूर्खतापूर्ण और दोषपूर्ण व्यवहार कर रहा है। **—जूलियन बार्न्स**
- देशभक्ति भ्रष्टाचारियों का गुण है। **—ऑस्कर वाइल्ड**
- देशप्रेमी हमेशा अपने देश के लिए मरने की बात करते हैं, पर कभी अपने देश के लिए मारने की बात नहीं करते। **—बरट्रैंड रस्सेल**
- सभी युद्ध गृहयुद्ध हैं, क्योंकि सभी इनसान आपस में भाई-बंधु हैं, हर एक व्यक्ति अपनी मातृभूमि से कहीं ज्यादा मानवजाति का कर्जदार है। **—फ्रांकोइस फेनेलॉन**
- देशभक्ति किसी दुष्ट व्यक्ति की आखिरी शरण है। **—सैमुएल जॉनसन**
- अगर हम कभी यह भूल जाते हैं कि हम ईश्वर के अधीन एक देश हैं, तब हम एक बरबाद देश बन जाएँगे। **—रोनाल्ड रीगन**
- राष्ट्रवाद एक बचकानी बीमारी है, यह मानवजाति का खसरा है। **—अल्बर्ट आइंस्टीन**

- देशभक्ति मामूली कारणों से मरने–मारने की इच्छा रखना है।

—बरट्रैंड रस्सेल

- जितना बड़ा देश, उतनी ही गलत और क्रूर उसकी देशभक्ति और उतनी ही बड़ी यातना, जिस पर उसकी सत्ता का निर्माण हुआ है।

—लियो टालस्टॉय

- देशभक्ति तब है, जब अपने लोगों के प्रति प्रेम पहले आए या राष्ट्रवाद तब जब अपने लोगों के अलावा और लोगों के प्रति नफरत पहले आए।

—चार्ल्स डी गौले

- असंतोष देशभक्ति का उच्चतम रूप है। **—हॉवर्ड जिन**

- लड़ने के लिए मेरे पास कोई देश नहीं है, यहाँ क्योंकि पृथ्वी ही मेरा देश है और मैं इस दुनिया का नागरिक हूँ। **—यूजीन वी. डब्स**

- मेरी नजर में आत्मा को भूगोल द्वारा नियंत्रित करना घोर अपमान की तरह है। **—जॉर्ज संतयाना**

- देशभक्ति एक तरह का धर्म है, यह वह अंडा है, जिससे युद्ध निकलता है।

—गाए डी मौपाइसेंट

- बुद्धि से मैं जानता हूँ कि अमेरिका किसी और देश से बेहतर नहीं है, यहाँ भावनात्मक रूप से मैं जानता हूँ कि वह हर एक देश से बेहतर है।

—सिंक्लेयर लूइस

- अपने देश के लिए झूठ बोलना हर एक व्यक्ति का देशभक्तिपूर्ण कर्तव्य है।

—अल्फ्रेड एडलर

- देशभक्ति एक तात्कालिक प्रतिक्रिया है, जो युद्ध शुरू होने पर खत्म हो जाती है। **—मिक जैगर**

- मेरा देश मेरे लिए बहुत अच्छा रहा है, मुझे भी अपने देश के लिए अच्छा होना चाहिए। **—वाल्टर ऐनेनबर्ग**

- सभी महान् चीजें बड़ी सरल होती हैं और कइयों को हम बस एक शब्द में

व्यक्त कर सकते हैं—स्वतंत्रता, न्याय, सम्मान, कर्तव्य, दया, आशा।

—विंस्टन चर्चिल

- जो लोग दूसरों को आजादी नहीं देते उन्हें खुद भी इसका हक नहीं होता।

—अब्राहम लिंकन

- किसी भी कीमत पर स्वतंत्रता का मोल नहीं किया जा सकता, वह जीवन है। भला जीने के लिए कोई क्या मोल नहीं चुकाएगा?

—महात्मा गांधी

- जब तक गलती करने की स्वतंत्रता न हो, तब तक स्वतंत्रता का कोई अर्थ नहीं है। **—महात्मा गांधी**

- हिंसक तरीकों से हिंसक स्वतंत्रता मिलेगी, यह दुनिया के लिए और खुद भारत के लिए एक गंभीर खतरा होगा। **—महात्मा गांधी**

- आततायी कभी स्वेच्छा से आजादी नहीं देता, पीड़ितों द्वारा इसकी माँग की जानी चाहिए। **—मार्टिन लूथर किंग जूनियर**

- स्वतंत्रता की कीमत हमेशा अधिक होती है, लेकिन अमरीकियों ने हमेशा यह कीमत चुकाई है और हमें एक मार्ग कभी नहीं चुनना चाहिए और वह मार्ग है समर्पण एवं हार मानने का। **—जॉन एफ. केनेडी**

- विकास के लिए सबसे अच्छा मार्ग आजादी का मार्ग है।

—जॉन एफ. केनेडी

- हीरो वह होता है, जो स्वतंत्रता के साथ आई जिम्मेदारियों को समझता है।

—बॉब डाइलेन

- मैंने वियतनाम युद्ध और उसे रोकने, दोनों के संघर्ष में साहस देखा है। मैंने सीखा कि देशभक्ति में विरोध भी शामिल है, सिर्फ मिलिट्री सर्विस ही नहीं।

—जॉन एफ. केरी

- भगवान् के प्रति प्रेम के बाद देशप्रेम सबसे अच्छा अपराध निवारक है।

—जॉर्ज बार्रो

- राष्ट्रवाद मूर्ख मुरगे का अपनी ही गंदगी के ढेर पर खुश होना है।

—रिचर्ड अल्डिंग्टन

- दिखावटी देशभक्ति के नाटक से बचो। **—जॉर्ज वाशिंगटन**

- दुनिया तब तक शांत नहीं होगी, जब तक हम देशभक्ति को मानवजाति से निकाल नहीं फेंकते। **—जॉर्ज बर्नार्ड शॉ**

- ये शहीद नायक उस देश के चरित्र को दरशाते हैं, जिसका देशभक्ति और सम्मान का लंबा इतिहास है और जिस देश ने आतंक से मुक्त रहने के लिए बहुत सी लड़ाइयाँ लड़ी हैं।

—माइकल एन. कैसल

- देशभक्ति झंडा लहराने में नहीं है, बल्कि इस प्रयास में है कि देश सही भी हो और मजबूत भी।

—जेम्स ब्रायस

- मैंने बहुत पहले से माना है कि बलिदान देशभक्ति का शिखर है।

—बॉब रिले

- युद्ध के समय नफरत काफी सम्मानजनक हो जाती है, तब भी, जबकि अकसर इसे देशभक्ति के वेश में छिपाना पड़ता है। **—हॉवर्ड थुरमैन**

- अपने देश के लिए देशभक्ति कुछ ऐसा है, जो दिल से आता है। यह आपको आपके अभिभावकों द्वारा सिखाया जाना चाहिए। **—जेसी वेंचुरा**

- मैं मिलिट्री को गिरते हुए नहीं देखना चाहती। मैं मिलिट्री को पेशेवर और सच्ची देशभक्ति की सम्मानजनक ऊँचाई तक उठते हुए देखना चाहती हूँ।

—औंग सान सू की

- एक लेखक के लिए केवल एक तरह की देशभक्ति मायने रखती है, भाषा के प्रति उसका नजरिया। **—जोसफ ब्रॉडस्की**

- मैं देशभक्ति के प्रकाश को प्रकाशित करना चाहता हूँ। **—लेकवालेसा**

- जब कुत्ता चाँद पर भौंकता है तो यह धर्म है, पर जब वह अनजाने लोगों पर भौंकता है तो यह देशभक्ति है।

  —डेविड स्टार जॉर्डन

- देशभक्ति नरक का धर्म है। **—जेम्स ब्रांच केबल**

- देशभक्ति बर्बरता से सभ्यताओं की रक्षा करने का अनिवार्य हथियार है।

  —बिल क्रिस्टल

- दुर्भाग्यवश धर्म का देशभक्ति की तरह राजनीतिक मकसद से गलत उपयोग किया जा सकता है। **—क्जेल मैग्ने बोंडेविक**

- देशभक्ति शर्मिंदा होने की उतनी ही काबिलीयत माँगती है, जितना कि गर्व महसूस करने की। **—ऐनी मारिए स्लॉटर**

- नामुमकिन मुसीबतों के वक्त जो लोग इस वतन से मोहब्बत करते हैं, वे इसे बदल सकते हैं। **—बराक ओबामा**

देह

- देह आत्मा के रहने की जगह होने के कारण तीर्थ जैसी पवित्र है।

  —महात्मा गांधी

- देह एक रथ है, इंद्रियाँ उसमें घोड़े, बुद्धि सारथी और मन लगाम है। केवल देह पोषण करना आत्मघात है। **—ज्ञानेश्वरी**

दैत्य

- व्यक्ति तो मात्र एक है, किंतु उसके गोलमाल करने के यंत्र अनेक हैं। यही है दैत्य का लक्षण, यह उसके अपने लिए अशांतिकर नहीं भी हो सकते हैं।

  —रवींद्रनाथ टैगोर

दोष

- दोष पराए देखकर चालत हँसत-हँसत।
  अपने याद न आवई, जिनका आदि न अंत॥ **—कबीर**

- यदि शांति चाहते हो तो दूसरों के दोष मत देखो, बल्कि अपने ही दोष देखो।
—अज्ञात

- जब हम अपनी भूल पर लज्जित होते हैं, तो यथार्थ बात अपने आप ही मुँह से निकल पड़ती है। **—प्रेमचंद**

- अपराध स्वीकार कर लेने से, वह आधा हो जाता है।
—पुर्तगाली कहावत

- ज्ञानी मनुष्य दूसरों की भूलों से अपनी भूलें सुधारता है।
—पबलिस साइरस

- अपनी गलती स्वीकार करने में लज्जा की कोई बात नहीं है। **—अज्ञात**

- अपनी भूल अपने ही हाथ सुधर जाए, तो यह उससे कहीं अच्छा है कि दूसरा उसे सुधारे। **—प्रेमचंद**

- विवेकशील पुरुष दूसरे की गलतियों से अपनी गलती सुधारते हैं।
—साइरस

- गलतियों के लिए दूसरों को दोष देने की अपेक्षा उनसे सबक लो।
—स्पेनिश कहावत

- स्वार्थवश मनुष्य दोषों को नहीं देखता। **—चाणक्य**

- त्रुटियाँ उसी से नहीं होंगी, जो कोई काम करे ही नहीं। **—लेनिन**

- गलतियाँ किए बिना कोई व्यक्ति बड़ा और महान् नहीं बनता है।
—ग्लेडस्टन

- दूसरों की गलतियों से सीखिए, क्योंकि आपको गलती करने का मौका नहीं मिलेगा।

- स्वयं के दोषों का निरीक्षण और दूसरों के गुणों का पर्यावलोकन करना उज्ज्वल व्यक्तित्व की पहचान है।
—अज्ञात

- एक गुण समस्त दोषों को ढक लेता है। **—अज्ञात**
- अपने आपको दोष देना सबसे बड़ा पाप है। **—अज्ञात**
- तू दूसरे की आँख का तिनका क्यों देखता है, अपनी आँख का शहतीर तो निकाल। **—बाइबिल**
- साधारण लोग अपनी हर बुराई का दोषी किसी और को ठहराते हैं, अल्पज्ञानी स्वयं को, पर ज्ञानी किसी को नहीं। **—इपिक्टेतस**
- मूर्ख आदमी अपने बड़े-से-बड़े दोष अनदेखे करता है, किंतु दूसरे के छोटे-से-छोटे दोष को देखता है।

  —संस्कृत सूक्ति

दोस्ती

- जीवन में अनेक परिवर्तन होते हैं, बहुत सी चीजें छोड़ देनी पड़ती हैं, लेकिन इससे दोस्ती का नाता थोड़े ही टूट जाता है।

  —रवींद्रनाथ टैगोर

दौलत

दौलत जैसी चीज को नाचीज समझकर नफरत की निगाह से तभी देखा जा सकता है, जब उससे सिर्फ कुछ दिन काटे जाते हैं, पर जब उसकी चोटी को पहाड़ की चोटी की तरह ऊँचा कर दिया जाता है, तब आम लोग उसकी इज्जत करने लगते हैं। उससे अपना कोई उपकार या फायदा न होने से उसके बड़प्पन को देखकर लोग और भी ज्यादा खुश होते हैं, उसकी तारीफ करने में ही साधारण लोगों के मन को स्फूर्ति मिलती है। **—रवींद्रनाथ टैगोर**

धन

- धन तो सभी अर्जित कर लेते है, पर नाम अर्जित केवल वही व्यक्ति करता है, जो दूसरों के हृदय में विराजते हैं। **—अज्ञात**
- दौलत की संतति—अहंकार, दिखावा, आडंबर, अभिमान, निर्दयता।

  —मार्क ट्वेन

- पैसा और शाबाशी लेना तो सभी चाहते हैं, देना कोई नहीं चाहता।

—अज्ञात

- संपत्ति उस व्यक्ति की होती है, जो इसका आनंद लेता है, न कि उस व्यक्ति की, जो इसे अपने पास रखता है।

—अफगानी कहावत

- एक बार सिकंदर से पूछा गया कि तुम धन क्यों एकत्र नहीं करते? तब उसका जवाब था कि इस डर से कि उसका रक्षक बनकर कहीं भ्रष्ट न हो जाऊँ। **—अज्ञात**

- दान, भोग और नाश, ये धन की तीन गतियाँ हैं। जो न देता है और न ही भोगता है, उसके धन की तृतीय गति (नाश) होती है। **—भर्तृहरि**

- संसार के व्यवहारों के लिए धन ही सार-वस्तु है। अतः मनुष्य को उसकी प्राप्ति के लिए युक्ति एवं साहस के साथ यत्न करना चाहिए।

—शुक्राचार्य

- मनुष्य मनुष्य का दास नहीं होता। हे राजा, वह तो धन का दास होता है।

—पंचतंत्र

- रुपए ने कहा, मेरी फिक्र न कर, पैसे की चिंता कर। **—चेस्टरफील्ड**

- धन अपना-पराया नहीं देखता। **—चाणक्य**

- धन अच्छा सेवक है, परंतु खराब स्वामी भी है। **—चाणक्य**

- कुबेर भी अगर आय से ज्यादा व्यय करे, तो कंगाल हो जाता है।

—चाणक्य

धरती

- याद रखो कि धरती तुम्हारे पैरों का स्पर्श करना चाहती है और हवा तुम्हारे बालों को सहलाना चाहती है।

—खलील जिब्रान

- खिले हुए फूल और कुछ नहीं, बल्कि धरती की मुसकराहट हैं।

—ई.ई. कमिंग्स

- हम इस धरती को माँ कहकर संबोधित करते हैं, पत्थर पूजते हैं, पीपल और बरगद के छायादार पेड़ को बाबा मानते हैं, पर आत्मा के भीतर उसकी आध्यात्मिकता का अनुभव नहीं करते। **—रवींद्रनाथ टैगोर**

- प्रति की गहराई में देखें और आप हर चीज को बेहतर समझा पाएँगे।

—अल्बर्ट आइंस्टीन

- धूल स्वयं अपमान सह लेती है और बदले में फूलों का उपहार देती है।

—रवींद्रनाथ टैगोर

धर्म

- जितने भी धर्म या मजहब हैं, सबके सब ऊँचे हैं। धर्म में कसर नहीं है, कसर है तो उनके आदमियों में। **—महात्मा गांधी**

- शांति से बढ़कर कोई ताप नहीं, संतोष से बढ़कर कोई सुख नहीं, तृष्णा से बढ़कर कोई व्याधि नहीं और दया के समान कोई धर्म नहीं।

—चाणक्य

- वह धर्म, जो व्यावहारिक मामलों पर ध्यान नहीं देता और उन्हें सुलझाने में सहायक नहीं, धर्म नहीं। **—महात्मा गांधी**

- हर अवसर और हर अवस्था में जो अपना कर्तव्य दिखाई दे, उसी को धर्म समझकर पूरा करना चाहिए। **—गीता**

- कौन किस धर्म में रहे, यह निश्चय करना तो हर एक व्यक्ति का अपना ही काम है। धर्म को किसी रूप में खरीदा नहीं जा सकता और आध्यात्मिक बातों के लिए अगर इस तरह की कोई बात कही जा सकती हो, तो हम यही कह सकते हैं कि धर्म का सौदा तो अपने रक्त से किया जा सकता है।

—महात्मा गांधी

• धर्म का उद्‍देश्य मानव को पथभ्रष्ट होने से बचाना है।

—श्रीराम शर्मा आचार्य

• जैसे अनेक नाम होने पर भी ईश्वर एक ही है, वैसे ही अनेक नाम होते हुए धर्म एक ही है, क्योंकि सारे धर्म ईश्वर से आए हैं। अगर वे ईश्वर से नहीं आए हैं तो वे निकम्मे हैं। जो धर्म ईश्वर का नहीं है, वह शैतान का है और वह किसी का नहीं हो सकता।

—महात्मा गांधी

• धर्म जब स्वयं दरवाजे पर दुहाई दे रहा हो तो उसकी अवहेलना नहीं करनी चाहिए।

—रवींद्रनाथ टैगोर

• मैं धर्म से भिन्न राजनीति की कल्पना नहीं कर सकता। वास्तव में धर्म तो हमारे हर एक काम में व्यापक होना चाहिए। यहाँ धर्म का अर्थ कट्टरपंथ से नहीं है, उसका अर्थ है, विश्व की एक नैतिक सुव्यवस्था।

—महात्मा गांधी

• हम अपने धर्म का पालन कर सकते हैं। दूसरे के धर्म पर हमारा कोई हस्तक्षेप नहीं हो सकता।

—रवींद्रनाथ टैगोर

• मनुष्य का इतिहास सारे देशों, सारी जातियों को लेकर बना है, इसलिए राजनीति में भी धर्म को बेचकर देश को आगे करने से काम नहीं चलेगा।

—रवींद्रनाथ टैगोर

• जिसका जो कर्म-फल है, जो निर्दिष्ट धर्म है, उसे एक दिन घूम-फिरकर उसी धर्म के पथ पर आना ही होगा···कोई उसे रोक नहीं सकेगा। भगवान् की जैसी इच्छा है···हम लोग क्या कर सकते हैं···हम तो निमित्त भर हैं।

—रवींद्रनाथ टैगोर

• व्यक्ति और समाज दोनों के ऊपर धर्म है, उसी पर नजर रखकर चलना होगा।

—रवींद्रनाथ टैगोर

• समाज से धर्म को निकालकर फेंक देने का प्रयत्न बाँझ के घर पुत्र पैदा करने जितना ही निष्फल है और अगर यह कहीं सफल हो जाए, तो समाज का उसमें नाश है। **—महात्मा गांधी**

• एक धर्म की विशेषता दूसरे धर्म की विशेषता के प्रतिकूल नहीं हो सकती, जगत् के सर्वमान्य सिद्धांतों की विरोधी नहीं हो सकती।

—महात्मा गांधी

• जब धर्म की ओर सच्चा आकर्षण न हो, तब धर्म भी वंश, मान, रुपए-पैसे की तरह अहंकार करने की सामग्री बन जाता है। **—रवींद्रनाथ टैगोर**

• मनुष्य की सभी वृत्तियों का चरम-प्रकाश धर्म में होता है।

—रवींद्रनाथ टैगोर

• धर्म के भी तो दो पक्ष होते हैं, एक नित्य पक्ष और लौकिक पक्ष। जहाँ धर्म समाज के नियम में प्रकाशित होता है, वहाँ उसकी अवहेलना नहीं की जा सकती, करने से समाज बिखर जाता है। **—रवींद्रनाथ टैगोर**

• जिनमें बचपन से धार्मिक संस्कार डाले जाते हैं, उनमें श्रद्धा, विश्वास आदि सद्गुणों का विकास होता है। **—महात्मा गांधी**

• हमारा सबसे बड़ा धर्म है, आत्मा का ज्ञान प्राप्त करना। चाहे धन, मान, कुटुंब और प्राणों तक का त्याग करना पड़े, पर धर्म को कदापि न छोड़ा जाए।

—महात्मा गांधी

• कथनी-करनी भिन्न जहाँ हैं, धर्म नहीं, पाखंड वहाँ है।

—श्रीराम शर्मा आचार्य

• उसी धर्म का अब उत्थान, जिसका सहयोगी विज्ञान।

—श्रीराम शर्मा आचार्य

• धर्म, व्यक्ति एवं समाज, दोनों के लिए आवश्यक है।

—डॉ. सर्वपल्ली राधाकृष्णन

- धर्म की उपलब्धि की जा सकती है, किंतु प्रश्न यह है कि क्या तुम उसके अधिकारी हो, क्या तुम्हें धर्म की आवश्यकता वास्तव में है? यदि तुम ठीक-ठीक प्रयत्न करो, तभी तुम्हें प्रत्यक्ष उपलब्धि होगी और तभी तुम वास्तव में धार्मिक होगे।

—स्वामी विवेकानंद

- धर्म एक भ्रमात्मक सूर्य है, जो मनुष्य के गिर्द घूमता रहता है, जब तक मनुष्य मनुष्यता के गिर्द नहीं घूमता। **—कार्ल मार्क्स**

- दो धर्मों का कभी झगड़ा नहीं होता, सब धर्मों का अधर्म से ही झगड़ा होता है। **—विनोबा**

- देश में केवल वंशानुक्रम से सामाजिक धर्म जीवित रहता है और जीवन-धर्म का ह्रास होता है।

—रवींद्रनाथ टैगोर

- धर्म सत्य है, मन की आस्तिकता है, उसके अल्पमात्र प्रभाव से प्रकांड विद्वान् की पराजय होती है। **—रवींद्रनाथ टैगोर**

- भारत का धर्म समस्त समाज का ही धर्म है, उसका मूल मिट्टी की तह में है और मस्तक आकाश में है। **—रवींद्रनाथ टैगोर**

- धर्म की सीमा का अतिक्रमण करने लगे तो उस अवस्था में विनाश का छिद्र दिखाई देगा। **—रवींद्रनाथ टैगोर**

- हमारे देश में धर्म का जो आदर्श है, वह आंतरिक सामग्री है, वह बाहरी सीमा के भीतर प्रतिष्ठित करने के लिए नहीं है। **—रवींद्रनाथ टैगोर**

- हमारे देश में यह कहा जाता है कि युद्ध में भी धर्म की रक्षा करनी चाहिए। **—रवींद्रनाथ टैगोर**

- स्वार्थ के प्रातिक नियम ने हमारे धर्म को तैयार नहीं किया है, धर्म के नियम ने ही हमारे स्वार्थ को संयत बनाने की चेष्टा की है।

—रवींद्रनाथ टैगोर

- धर्म हमको एक में मिला नहीं सका है, वरन् उसने हजारों घेरे डालकर उन बाधाओं को इतिहास का अतीत शाश्वत मानकर सुदृढ़ बना दिया है।

—रवींद्रनाथ टैगोर

- एक-एक जाति का एक-एक काम उसके धर्म का ही अंग है।

—रवींद्रनाथ टैगोर

- धर्म परमेश्वर की कल्पना कर मनुष्य को दुर्बल बना देता है, उसमें आत्मविश्वास उत्पन्न नहीं होने देता और उसकी स्वतंत्रता का अपरहण करता है।

—नरेंद्र देव

- दूसरे धर्मों की निंदा करना गलत है। सच्चा व्यक्ति वह है, जो दूसरे धर्मों की भी हर उस बात का सम्मान करता है, जो सम्मान के लायक है।

—सम्राट् अशोक

- हम भारतीय सभी धर्मों के प्रति केवल सहिष्णुता में ही विश्वास नहीं करते, वरन् सभी धर्मों को सच्चा मानकर स्वीकार भी करते हैं।

—स्वामी विवेकानंद

- जो उपकार करे, उसका प्रत्युपकार करना चाहिए, यही सनातन धर्म है।

—वाल्मीकि

- प्रलोभन और भय का मार्ग बच्चों के लिए उपयोगी हो सकता है, लेकिन सच्चे धार्मिक व्यक्ति के दृष्टिकोण में कभी लाभ-हानिवाली संकीर्णता नहीं होती। **—आचार्य तुलसी**

- मनुष्य की धार्मिक वृत्ति ही उसकी सुरक्षा करती है। **—आचार्य तुलसी**

- धार्मिक व्यक्ति दुःख को सुख में बदलना जानता है। **—आचार्य तुलसी**

- धार्मिक वृत्ति बनाए रखनेवाला व्यक्ति कभी दुःखी नहीं हो सकता और धार्मिक वृत्ति को खोनेवाला कभी सुखी नहीं हो सकता।

—आचार्य तुलसी

- अहिंसा ही धर्म है, वही जिंदगी का एक रास्ता है। **—महात्मा गांधी**

- अभागा वह है, जो संसार के सबसे पवित्र धर्म कृतज्ञता को भूल जाता है। **—जयशंकर प्रसाद**

- धर्म द्वारा समाज की जैसी महान् क्षति हुई है, वैसी अन्य किसी सांसारिक उद्योग से नहीं। **—रवींद्रनाथ टैगोर**

धीरज

- कबीरा धीरज के धरे, हाथी मन भर खाय।
  टूक एक के कारने, स्वान घरे घर जाय॥ **—कबीर**

- शोक में, आर्थिक संकट में या प्राणोत्कारी भय उत्पन्न होने पर जो अपनी बुद्धि से दु:ख निवारण के उपाय का विचार करते हुए धीरज धारण करता है, उसे कष्ट नहीं उठाना पड़ता। **—वाल्मीकि**

- जितनी जल्दी करोगे, उतनी देर लगेगी। **—चर्चिल**

- सब्र जिंदगी के मकसद का दरवाजा खोलता है, क्योंकि सिवाय सब्र के उस दरवाजे की कोई और चाबी नहीं है। **—शेख सादी**

धैर्य

- धैर्य प्रतिभा का आवश्यक अंग है। **—डिजराइली**

- जिसके पास धैर्य है, उसको उसका फल अवश्य मिलता है। **—फ्रैंकलिन**

- धैर्य सफलता का एक प्रमुख तत्त्व है। **—बिल गेट्स**

- धीर-गंभीर कभी उबाल नहीं खाते। **—चाणक्य**

- नीति निपुण निंदा करें या प्रशंसा करें, लक्ष्मी आए, चाहे चली जाए, मृत्यु चाहे आज ही हो या एक युग के बाद, परंतु धीर मनुष्य न्यायमार्ग से एक पग भी विचलित नहीं होते। **—भर्तृहरि**

- वास्तव में वे ही मनुष्य धीर हैं, जिनका मन विकार उत्पन्न करनेवाली परिस्थितियों में भी विचलित नहीं होता। **—कालिदास**

- धीरज सारे आनंदों और शक्तियों का मूल है।

—जॉन रस्किन

- सुख में गर्व न करें, दु:ख में धैर्य न छोड़ें।

—श्रीराम शर्मा आचार्य

- वह व्यक्ति महान् है, जो शांतचित्त होकर धैर्यपूर्वक कार्य करता है। **—डॉ. सर्वपल्ली राधाकृष्णन**

- धैर्य और परिश्रम से हम वह प्राप्त कर सकते हैं, जो शक्ति और शीघ्रता से कभी नहीं कर सकते। **—ला फांटेन**

धोखा

- अगर कोई व्यक्ति मुझे धोखा देता है तो धिक्कार है उस पर, और अगर कोई दूसरी बार मुझे धोखा देता है तो लानत है मुझ पर। **—कहावत**

- धूर्त को धोखा देना धूर्तता नहीं है। **—कहावत**

- हेत प्रति से जो मिले, ताको मिलिए धाय।
अंतर राखे जो मिले तासौं मिल। बलाय॥ **—कबीर**

- सब धोखों में प्रथम और खराब अपने आप को धोखा देना है। **—बेली**

- स्पष्टभाषी धोखेबाज नहीं होता। **—चाणक्य**

- मुँह में राम बगल में छुरी। **—कहावत**

- मुझे जितनी जहन्नुम से, फाटकों से घृणा है, उतनी ही उस व्यक्ति से घृणा है, जो दिल में एक बात छुपाकर दूसरी कहता है। **—होमर**

- ज्यादा मधुर बानी धोखेबाजी की निशानी। **—कहावत**

ध्यान

- केवल ध्यान के माध्यम से आप विश्वस्तरीय काम कर सकते हैं।

—बिल गेट्स

ध्येय

- ध्येय जितना महान् होता है, उसका रास्ता उतना ही लंबा और बीहड़ होता है। **—अज्ञात**
- यदि परिस्थितियाँ अनुकूल हों तो सीधे अपने ध्येय की ओर चलो, लेकिन परिस्तिथियाँ अनुकूल न हों तो उस राह पर चलो, जिसमें सबसे कम बाधा आने की संभावना हो। **—तिरुवल्लुवर**
- अपने लक्ष्य को न भूलो, अन्यथा जो कुछ मिलेगा, उसमें संतोष मानने लगोगे। **—बर्नार्ड शा**
- लक्ष्य रखना काफी नहीं है, उसे प्राप्त करना चाहिए। **—इतालियन कहावत**
- अपने जीवन का लक्ष्य बनाओ और अपनी सारी शारीरिक और मानसिक शक्ति उसे पाने में लगा दो। **—कार्लाइल**

नकल

- किसी को अपना व्यक्तित्व छोड़कर दूसरे का व्यक्तित्व नहीं अपनाना चाहिए। **—चैनिंग**
- नकल के लिए भी कुछ अक्ल चाहिए। **—फारसी कहावत**
- मानव नकल करनेवाला प्राणी है और जो सबसे आगे रहता है, वह नेतृत्व करता है। **—शिलर**
- उपदेश के बजाय कहीं ज्यादा हम करके सीखते हैं। **—बर्क**
- जहाँ नकल है, वहाँ खाली दिखावट होगी, जहाँ खाली दिखावट है, वहाँ मूर्खता होगी। **—जॉनसन**

नम्रता

- बड़े को छोटा बनकर रहना चाहिए, क्योंकि जो अपने आपको बड़ा मानता है, वह छोटा बन जाता है और जो छोटा बनता है, वह बड़ा पद पाता है। **—ईसा**

- नमस्कार करनेवाला व्यक्ति विनम्रता को ग्रहण करता है और समाज में सभी के प्रेम का पात्र बन जाता है। —**प्रेमचंद**
- महान् मनुष्य की पहली पहचान उसकी नम्रता है। —**अज्ञात**
- नम्रता के संसर्ग से ऐश्वर्य की शोभा बढ़ती है। —**कालिदास**
- नम्रता और खुदा के खौफ से इज्जत और जिंदगी मिलती है। —**सुलेमान**
- संसार के विरुद्ध खड़े रहने के लिए शक्ति प्राप्त करने की जरूरत नहीं है। —**अज्ञात**
- ईसा दुनिया के खिलाफ खड़े रहे, महात्मा बुद्ध भी अपने जमाने के खिलाफ गए, प्रह्लाद ने भी वैसा ही किया। ये सब नम्रता के धनी थे। अकेले खड़े रहने की शक्ति नम्रता के बिना असंभव है। —**महात्मा गांधी**
- मेरा विश्वास है कि वास्तविक महान् पुरुष की पहचान उसकी नम्रता है। —**रस्किन**
- नम्रता तन की शक्ति, जीतने की कला और शौर्य की पराकाष्ठा है। —**विनोबा**
- ऊँचे पाने न टिके, नीचे ही ठहराए।
  नीचे हो सो भरी पिबैं, ऊँचा प्यासा जाए॥ —**कबीर**

नया साल

- नव वर्ष सुख-समृद्धि से भरपूर हो।
- नव वर्ष में आप फलें-फूलें।
- नया साल आपके लिए नई खुशियाँ लाए।
- नव वर्ष शुभ हो।
- नया साल आपको नया उत्साह प्रदान करे।
- नया साल आपको नया अनुभव दे।

- नया साल आपको नया उत्साह प्रदान करे।
- नव वर्ष में आपकी सभी मनोकामनाएँ पूरी हों।
- नव वर्ष में हर कदम पर आपको सफलता मिले।
- नव वर्ष में भाग्य सदैव आपका साथ दे।
- नव वर्ष आपके जीवन में उमंग लाए।
- नव वर्ष के आगमन पर हार्दिक बधाई।
- नव वर्ष में आपकी दिन दोगुनी, रात चौगुनी तरक्की हो।
- नया साल आपके लिए लाभदायक हो।
- नव वर्ष आपके लिए हितकारी हो।

नरक

- संसार में छल, प्रवंचना और हत्याओं को देखकर कभी-कभी मान लेना पड़ता है की यह जगत् ही नरक है। **—जयशंकर प्रसाद**
- काम, क्रोध, मद, लोभ सब, नाथ नरक के पंथ। **—तुलसीदास**
- अति क्रोध, कटु वाणी, दरिद्रता, स्वजनों से बैर, नीचों का संग और अकुलीन की सेवा, यह नरक में रहनेवालों के लक्षण हैं। **—चाणक्य नीति**

नशा

- जो आदमी नशे में मदहोश हो, उसकी सूरत उसकी माँ को भी बुरी लगती है। **—तिरुवल्लुवर**
- नशे की हालत में क्रोध की भाँति, ग्लानि का वेग भी सहज ही बढ़ जाता है। **—प्रेमचंद**
- नशा करनेवाले मित्र से भले कोई कितना ही प्रेम क्यों न करता हो, पर जब निर्भर करने का अवसर आता है तो वह भरोसा उस पर करता है, जो नशा न करता हो। **—शरतचंद्र**

नागरिकता

- नागरिकता देश की सेवा में निहित है। **—जवाहरलाल नेहरू**

नाम

- नाम में क्या रखा है, जिसे हम गुलाब कहते हैं, वह किसी और नाम से भी सुगंध ही देगा। **—शेक्सपियर**
- अपना नाम सदा कायम रखने के लिए मनुष्य बड़े से बड़ा जोखिम उठाने, धन खर्च करने, हर तरह के कष्ट सहने, यहाँ तक कि मरने के लिए भी तैयार हो जाता है। **—सुकरात**
- अपने नाम को कमल की तरह निष्कलंक बनाओ। **—लाँफैलो**
- आदि नाम परस अहै, मन है मैला लोह।
परसत ही कंचन भया, छूटा बंधन मोह॥ **—कबीर**

नारी

- सुंदर नारी या तो मूर्ख होती है या अभिमानी। **—स्पेनी कहावत**
- पुरुष का नारी के समान कोई बंधु नहीं। **—महाभारत**
- यह लौकिक पुरुष के अत्याचार का बहुत निर्बल बहाना है कि नारी का सद्गुण सच्चरित्रता और आज्ञाकारिता है। **—राधाकृष्णन**
- नारी की उन्नति पर ही राष्ट्र की उन्नति या अवनति निर्धारित है। **—अरस्तू**
- बदला लेने और प्रेम करने में नारी पुरुष से आगे होती है। **—नीत्शे**
- सौंदर्य से नारी अभिमानी बनती है, उत्तम गुणों से उसकी प्रशंसा होती है और लज्जाशील होकर वह देवी बन जाती है। **—शेक्सपियर**
- नारी को अबला कहना उसका अपमान है। **—महात्मा गांधी**
- औरतें कभी भूल नहीं करतीं, यदि करें भी तो किसी बुद्धिमान पुरुष के लिए उसका उल्लेख करना उचित नहीं है, उसे अपने ही सिर पर ले लेना बुद्धिमानी है। **—रवींद्रनाथ टैगोर**

- तपस्वियों के लिए औरतों में एक विशेष आकर्षण होता है। —**रवींद्रनाथ टैगोर**
- नारी दासी अवश्य है, किंतु साथ-ही-साथ नारी रानी भी है। —**रवींद्रनाथ टैगोर**
- प्रखरता को छिपाकर रख सकतीं, स्पष्ट बातों की धार को कुछ कम कर सकतीं और पुरुष मंडली के साथ यथोचित संकोच की रक्षा करती हुई चलतीं, ऐसा नारी जनोचित संयोग उन्हें नहीं मिला। —**रवींद्रनाथ टैगोर**
- नारी सबकुछ सह सकती है, पर अपनी इच्छा के विरुद्ध प्रेम नहीं कर सकती। —**सुदर्शन**
- नारी सबकुछ सह सकती है, दारुण से दारुण दुःख, बड़े-से-बड़ा संकट। नहीं सह सकती तो अपनी उमंगों का कुचला जाना। —**प्रेमचंद**

नास्तिक

- नास्तिक के लिए लोगों की भलाई करने में एकदम निजी नुकसान के अतिरिक्त और कुछ नहीं है, उसमें पुण्य है, न पुरस्कार है, न किसी देवता, शास्त्र की पा का विज्ञापन अथवा नाराजगी है। —**रवींद्रनाथ टैगोर**
- हम लोग नास्तिक हैं, यह गर्व ही हमारे लिए एकदम निष्कलंक, निर्मल होना चाहिए। हम लोग किसी को नहीं मानते, इसी कारण हमें स्वयं को अधिक मानने की विशेष आवश्यकता होती है। —**रवींद्रनाथ टैगोर**
- हम नास्तिकों के धर्म-शास्त्र में अच्छे काम के लिए निंदारूपी नरक-भोग करने का ही विधान है। —**रवींद्रनाथ टैगोर**

निंदक

- कुछ भी करो, निंदक की जुबान बंद नहीं होती।

निंदा

- यदि तुम्हारी कोई निंदा करे तो भीतर-ही-भीतर प्रसन्न हों, क्योंकि तुम्हारी निंदा करके वह तुम्हारे पाप अपने ऊपर ले रहा है। —**ब्रह्मानंद सरस्वती**

- ऐ ईमानवालो, दूसरे पर शक मत करो। दूसरों पर शक करना कभी-कभी गुनाह हो जाता है। **—कुरान**
- निंदक नियरे रखिए, आँगन कुटी छवाय।
बिन पानी बिन साबुन, निर्मल करे सुभाय॥ **—कबीर**
- हर किसी की निंदा सुन लो, लेकिन अपना निर्णय गुप्त रखो। **—शेक्सपियर**
- जो तेरे सामने और की निंदा करे, वह और के सामने तेरी निंदा करेगा। **—कहावत**

निद्रा

- निद्रावस्था जाग्रतावस्था की स्थिति का आईना है। **—महात्मा गांधी**
- निद्रा रोगी की माता, भोगी की प्रियतमा और आलसी की बेटी है। **—अज्ञात**
- निद्रा एक ऐसा अथाह सागर है, जिसमें हम सब अपने दुःखों को डुबो देते हैं। **—प्रेमचंद**
- सोता साथ जगाइए, करै नाम का जाप।
यह तीनों सोते भले, साकत, सिंह और साँप॥ **—कबीर**

नियम

- अपवाद के बिना कोई भी नियम लाभकर नहीं होता। **—थॉमस फुलर**
- थोड़ा-बहुत अन्याय किए बिना कोई भी महान् कार्य नहीं किया जा सकता। **—लुइस दी उलोआ**
- सभी वास्तविक राज्य भ्रष्ट होते हैं। अच्छे लोगों को चाहिए कि नियमों का पालन बहुत कड़ाई से न करें। **—एमर्सन**
- कानून चाहे कितना ही आदरणीय क्यों न हो, वह गोलाई को चौकोर नहीं कह सकता। **—फिदेल कास्त्रो**

निराशा

- निराशा दुर्बलता का चिह्न है। **—रामतीर्थ**
- निराशा में प्रतीक्षा अंधे की लाठी है। **—प्रेमचंद**
- निराशा स्वर्ग की सीलन है, जैसे प्रसन्नता स्वर्ग की शांति। **—डाने**

नियम

- नियम यदि एक क्षण के लिए टूट जाए तो सारा सूर्यमंडल अस्त-व्यस्त हो जाए। **—महात्मा गांधी**
- जो अपने लिए नियम नहीं बनाता, उसे दूसरों के नियमों पर चलना पड़ता है। **—हरिभाऊ उपाध्याय**
- प्रकृति का यह साधारण नियम है, जो कभी नहीं बदलेगा, कि योग्य अयोग्यों पर शासन करते रहेंगे। **—दायोनीसियस**

निश्चय

- अनुभव बताता है कि आवश्यकता काल में दृढ़ निश्चय पूरी सहायता करता है। **—शेक्सपियर**
- जिसका निश्चय दृढ़ और अटल है, वह दुनिया को अपने सोच में ढाल सकता है। **—गेटे**
- जिसने निश्चय कर लिया, उसके लिए केवल करना शेष रह जाता है। **—बिल गेट्स**
- हम अपने अच्छे-से-अच्छे कर्मों पर भी लज्जित हो सकते हैं, यदि लोग केवल उस निश्चय को देख सकें, जिसकी प्रेरणा से वे किए गए हैं। **—रोची**
- सच्ची-से-सच्ची और अच्छी-से-अच्छी चतुराई निश्चय है। **—नेपोलियन**
- जो व्यक्ति निश्चय कर सकता है, उसके लिए कुछ असंभव नहीं है। **—बिल गेट्स**

- साहस और दृढ़ निश्चय जादुई तावीज हैं, जिनके आगे कठिनाइयाँ दूर हो जाती हैं और बाधाएँ उड़न-छू हो जाती हैं।

—बिल गेट्स

- जो व्यक्ति निश्चय कर सकता है, उसके लिए कुछ असंभव नहीं है।

—एमर्सन

नीचता

- स्वभाव की नीचता वर्षों में भी मालूम नहीं होती। **—शेख सादी**

- कुछ कहीं नीच न छेड़िए, भलो न बाको संग।
  पाथर दारे कीच में, उछारे बिगारे अंग॥ **—वृंद**

- नीच मनुष्य के साथ मैत्री और प्रेम कुछ भी नहीं करना चाहिए। कोयला अगर जल रहा है, तो छूने से जला देता है और अगर ठंडा है, तो हाथ काले कर देता है। **—हितोपदेश**

- दाग जो काला नील का सा मन साबुन धोय।
  कोटि जतन पर बोधिये, कागा हँस न होय॥ **—कबीर**

- जो उपकार करनेवाले को नीच मनाता है, उससे अधिक नीच कोई दूसरा नहीं। **—विनोबा**

- शक्तियों का एक नियम है, जिसके कारण चीजें समुद्र में एक खास गहराई से नीचे नहीं जा सकतीं; लेकिन नीचता के समुद्र में हम जितने गहरे जाएँ, डूबना उतना ही आसान होता है। **—लाबैल**

- नीच को देखने और उसकी बातें सुनने से ही हमारी नीचता का आरंभ होता है। **—कन्फ्यूशियस**

नीति

- जातियाँ न पैसे के बल पर टिकती हैं और न सेना के बल पर, वे केवल नीति के आधार पर ही टिकती हैं, यह विचार सदा मन में रखकर, परमार्थ-रूपी परम नीति का आचरण करना मनुष्य मात्र का कर्तव्य है। **—महात्मा गांधी**

- नीति का वास हमारे हृदय में है। —**महात्मा गांधी**
- नीति के नियम अचल हैं। मत बदलते रहते हैं, परंतु नीति नहीं बदलती। हमारी आँख खुली होने पर हमें सूर्य दिखाई देता है और बंद रहने पर नहीं, यह परिवर्तन हमारी दृष्टि में हुआ, न कि सूर्य के अस्तित्व में। यही बात नीति के नियमों के संबंध में भी समझनी चाहिए। संभव है, अज्ञान की दशा में हम नीति को न समझ पाएँ, पर ज्ञानचक्षु खुलने पर उसे समझने में हमें कठिनाई नहीं होती। —**महात्मा गांधी**
- नीति के बिना धर्म टिक नहीं सकता। सच्ची नीति में धर्म का बहुत कुछ समावेश हो जाता है। जो लोग अपने स्वार्थ के लिए नहीं, बल्कि नीति के लिए ही नीति-नियमों का पालन करते हैं, उन्हें धार्मिक कहा जा सकता है। —**महात्मा गांधी**
- नीति के समस्त नियमों का दोहन किया जाए, तो हम देखेंगे कि मानव-जाति के कल्याण के लिए प्रयास करना ही उत्कृष्ट नीति है। इस कुंजी से नीति रूपी मंजूषा को खोलकर देखने पर, नैतिकता के अन्य नियम हमें उसमें मिल जाएँगे। —**महात्मा गांधी**

नेकी

- नेकी कर दरिया में डाल। —**कहावत**
- मधुमक्खियाँ केवल अँधेरे में काम करती हैं, विचार केवल मौन में काम आते हैं। नेक कार्य भी गुप्त रहकर ही कारगर होते हैं। —**कार्लाइल**
- नेकी का इरादा बदी की ख्वाहिश को दबा देता है। —**हजरत अली**
- जितने दिन जिंदा हो, उसे गनीमत समझो और इससे पहले कि लोग तुम्हें मुर्दा कहें, नेकी कर जाओ। —**शेख सादी**

नुकसान

- नुकसान तो ऐसे भी हो सकते हैं, जिनकी भरपाई इस लोक-परलोक में भी नहीं हो पाती। —**रवींद्रनाथ टैगोर**

• चूहा जब जहाज की पेंदी में बिल खोदने लगता है, तब अपनी सुविधा और प्रवृत्ति की ही सोचता है, वह यह नहीं देखता कि इतने बड़े आश्रय में छेद करने से उसे जितनी सुविधा होगी, उसकी तुलना में और सबका कितना बड़ा नुकसान होगा। **—रवींद्रनाथ टैगोर**

नेतृत्व

• प्रभावी नेतृत्व महत्त्वपूर्ण चीजों को पहले रखना होता है।

• बिना पहल के लीडर महज एक श्रमिक है, जो लीडर बनकर बैठा हुआ है।

• नेतृत्व का रहस्य है, आगे-आगे सोचने की कला। **—मैरी पार्कर फोलेट**

• नेताओं का मुख्य काम अपने आस-पास नेता तैयार करना है।

—मैक्सवेल

• अपने अंदर योग्यता का होना अच्छी बात है, लेकिन दूसरों में योग्यता खोज पाना असली परीक्षा है।

—एल्बर्ट हब्बार्ड

• मैं सिर्फ उतने ही दिमाग का इस्तेमाल नहीं करता, जितना मेरे पास है, बल्कि वह सब भी, जो मैं उधार ले सकता हूँ। **—वुडरो विलसन**

• उपहार और विरोध तो सुधारक के पुरस्कार हैं। **—प्रेमचंद**

• अगर अंधा अंधे का नेतृत्व करे तो दोनों खाई में गिरेंगे।

• नेतृत्व का महत्त्वपूर्ण नियम है, सीखने के आनंद की फिर से खोज करना, ताकि हम अपनी क्षमताओं और उत्पादकता को बढ़ा सकें।

• वास्तविक नेता सर्वसम्मति की तलाश नहीं करता, उसे निर्मित करता है।

—मार्टिन लूथर किंग

• तर्क और निर्णय नेता के गुण हैं। **—टेसीटस**

• निर्णय करने के लिए तीन तत्त्वों की आवश्यकता होती है—अनुभव, ज्ञान और व्यक्त करने की क्षमता। **—अज्ञात**

नेत्रहीन

- नेत्रहीन में अनुभव करने की शक्ति अधिक होती है। **—रवींद्रनाथ टैगोर**

नैराश्य

- नैराश्य मृत्यु की विच्छेद-वेदना को काल-क्रम में सुन्न कर देता है। **—रवींद्रनाथ टैगोर**

नैवेद्य

- नैवेद्य देवता पर चढ़ाए जाते हैं, किंतु देवता को उससे कोई प्रयोजन नहीं रहता। **—रवींद्रनाथ टैगोर**

न्याय

- बुराई तो बाहर से की जा सकती है, लेकिन न्याय करने के लिए भीतर पैठना होता है। केवल घटना के कारण किसी को दोषी न ठहरा दें। **—रवींद्रनाथ टैगोर**

- व्यक्ति और समाज की भीति पर धर्म नहीं खड़ा है, धर्म की भीति पर ही व्यक्ति और समाज है। जिसे समाज चाहता है, उसी को धर्म कहकर मानना पड़े तो समाज की ही मुसीबत हो जाए। **—रवींद्रनाथ टैगोर**

- धर्म मनुष्य की व्यक्तिगत साधना की चीज है, उसे किसी समाज के साथ बाँधना उचित नहीं है। **—रवींद्रनाथ टैगोर**

- न्याय का मोती दया के हृदय में मिलता है। **—जर्मन कहावत**

- मनुष्य का कर्तव्य है कि वह उदास बनने से पूर्व त्यागी बने। **—डिकेंस**

- जबसे मुझे पता चला है कि मखमल के गद्दों पर सोनेवालों के सपने जमीन पर सोनेवालों के सपने से मधुर नहीं होते, तब से मुझे न्याय प्रभु के न्याय में श्रद्धा हो गई है। **—खलील जिब्रान**

- न्याय की बात कहने के लिए हर समय ठीक है। **—सोफोक्लिज**

- न्याय में देर करना न्याय को अस्वीकार करना है। ईश्वर की चक्की धीरे चलती है, पर बारीक पीसती है। **—कहावत**

पछतावा

- अब पछताए होत क्या, जब चिड़ियाँ चुग गईं खेत। **—कहावत**
- करता सा सो क्यों किया, अब करि क्यों पछताए।
बोवे पेड़ बबूल का, आम कहाँ से खाए॥ **—कबीर**
- पछतावा हृदय की वेदना है और निर्मल जीवन का उदय। **—शेक्सपियर**
- सुधार के बिना पश्चात्ताप ऐसा है, जैसे सुराख बंद किए बिना जहाज में से पानी निकलना। **—पामर**
- मुझे कोई पछतावा नहीं, क्योंकि मैंने किसी का बुरा नहीं किया। **—महात्मा गांधी**

पड़ोसी

- कोई भी इतना धनी नहीं कि पड़ोसी के बिना काम चला सके। **—डेनिस कहावत**
- जब तुम्हारे पड़ोसी के घर में आग लगी तो तुम्हारी संपत्ति पर भी खतरा है। **—होरेस**
- सच्चा पड़ोसी वह नहीं, जो तुम्हारे साथ उसी गली में रहता है, बल्कि वह है, जो तुम्हारे विचार स्तर पर रहता है। **—रामतीर्थ**

पतन

- दूसरों का अस्त्र छीन लेने से अपना अस्त्र निर्भयता से उच्छृंखल हो उठता है, यही है मनुष्य का पतन। **—रवींद्रनाथ टैगोर**

पतवार

- हमारी समस्या यह नहीं है कि स्रोत को किस तरह से अलग करें, समस्या यही

है कि नाव किस तरह से डूबेगी नहीं, चलती रहेगी। उसी के लिए पतवार की आवश्यकता है। **—रवींद्रनाथ टैगोर**

पति-पत्नी

- योग्य पति अपनी पत्नी को सम्मान की अधिकारिणी बना देता है। **—मनु**
- जिसे पति बनना है, उसके लिए पुरुष बनना जरूरी है।
—रवींद्रनाथ टैगोर
- पति को कभी-कभी अंधा और कभी-कभी बहरा होना चाहिए।
—कहावत
- पति के किए पत्नी कार्य में मंत्री के समान सलाह देनेवाली, सेवा में दासी के समान काम करनेवाली, माता के सामान सुंदर भोजन करानेवाली, शयन के समय रंभा के समान सुख देनेवाली, धर्म के अनुकूल और क्षमादि गुण धारण करने में पृथ्वी के समान स्थिर रहनेवाली होती है।
—संस्कृत सूक्ति

पदाघात

- भृगु के पदाघात का चिह्न विष्णु सदा वक्ष पर धारण किए रहे, दुनिया में अत्याचारी लोग जहाँ जितना अन्याय करते हैं, उससे भगवान् की छाती का यह चिह्न और गहरा होता जाता है।
—रवींद्रनाथ टैगोर

परजीवी

- परजीवी मनुष्य केवल वह नहीं है, जो जड़भाव से दूसरों पर निर्भर रहे। जो व्यक्ति परंपरागत वस्तुओं से जकड़ा रहता है, जो बहती हुई धारा में निष्क्रिय भाव से आत्म-समर्पण करता है, वह भी परजीवी है।
—रवींद्रनाथ टैगोर

परदा

- जब परदा रहता है, तब अनंतकाल का व्यवधान रहता है, जब परदा हट जाता

है, तब वह एक पल का फासला रह जाता है। **—रवींद्रनाथ टैगोर**

परनिंदा

- विषयी लोग परनिंदा और नुक्ताचीनी करते रहते हैं, लेकिन जो लोग धार्मिकता की भाषा में यह काम करते हैं, उनकी इस निंदा के साथ एक आध्यात्मिक अहंकार भी मिला रहता है, जो संसार में बहुत बड़ा उपद्रव खड़ा कर देता है। **—रवींद्रनाथ टैगोर**

परम शक्ति

- परम शक्ति किसी मनुष्य-विशेष के सामने किसी विशेष मनुष्य के रूप में ही प्रकट होती है। **—रवींद्रनाथ टैगोर**

पराधीनता

- पराधीन को जिंदा कहें तो मुरदा कौन है। **—हितोपदेश**
- कोई ईमानदार आदमी हड्डी की खातिर अपने को कुत्ता नहीं बना सकता और अगर वह ऐसा करता है तो वह ईमानदार नहीं है।

  —डेनिस कहावत
- नौकर रखना बुरा है, लेकिन मालिक रखना और भी बुरा है।

  —पुर्तगाली कहावत
- पराधीनता समाज के समस्त मौलिक निमयों के विरुद्ध है। **—मान्तेस्क्यू**
- जिन्हें हम हीन या नीच बनाए रखते हैं, वे भी क्रमश: हमें हेय और दीन बना देता है।

  —रवींद्रनाथ टैगोर
- गुलामी में रखना इनसान की शान के खिलाफ है। जिस गुलाम को अपनी दशा का मान है और फिर भी जंजीरों को तोड़ने का प्रयास नहीं करता, वह पशु से हीन है। अंत:करण से प्रार्थना करनेवाला कभी गुलामी को बरदाश्त नहीं कर सकता। **—महात्मा गांधी**

परिचय

- परिचय का अर्थ ही यही है कि जो छोड़ने योग्य है, उसे छोड़कर जो ग्रहण करने योग्य है, उसे ग्रहण करना।

  —रवींद्रनाथ टैगोर

- नंगे का कोई परिचय नहीं होता, बना-सँवारकर तैयार किए हुए कपड़ों से ही कोई राजा होता है, कोई भिखारी होता है। **—रवींद्रनाथ टैगोर**

परिवर्तन

- हर चीज बदलती है, नष्ट कोई चीज नहीं होती। **—अरविंद घोष**
- लोग हमेशा परिवर्तन से डरते हैं। बिजली के आविष्कार के वक्त भी लोग डर गए थे? **—बिल गेट्स**
- परिवर्तन ही सृष्टि है, जीवन है और स्थिर होना मृत्यु।

  —जयशंकर प्रसाद

- स्वयं को बदल दो, भाग्य बदल जाएगा। **—कहावत**
- मैं अपने भविष्य के बारे में बहुत आशावादी हूँ, लेकिन यह परिवर्तन और आश्चर्य से भरा एक भविष्य है। **—बिल गेट्स**
- कभी-कभी बहुत छोटे-छोटे निर्णय ही हमारे जीवन को हमेशा के लिए बदल देते हैं। **—केरी रसैल**
- बहुधा वातावरण में परिवर्तन से कहीं अधिक व्यक्ति के भीतर ही बदलाव की जरूरत होती है। **—ए.सी. बेंसन**
- दुनिया परिवर्तन से नफरत करती है, लेकिन यही एक मात्र वस्तु है, जिससे प्रगति का जन्म हुआ है। **—बिल गेट्स**
- परिवर्तन के बीच व्यवस्था और व्यवस्था के बीच परिवर्तन को बनाए रखना ही प्रगति की कला है। **—बिल गेट्स**
- परिवर्तन नए अवसर लाता है। **—बिल गेट्स**

- परिवर्तन विज्ञानसम्मत है। परिवर्तन को अस्वीकार नहीं किया जा सकता, जबकि प्रगति राय और विवाद का विषय है। **—बर्नार्ड रसेल**

- हमें वह परिवर्तन खुद में करना चाहिए, जिसे हम संसार में देखना चाहते हैं। **—महात्मा गांधी**

- परिवर्तन का मानव के मस्तिष्क पर अच्छा-खासा मानसिक प्रभाव पड़ता है। डरपोक लोगों के लिए यह धमकी भरा होता है, क्योंकि उनको लगता है कि स्थिति और बिगड़ सकती है या आशावान लोगों के लिए यह उत्साहपूर्ण होता है, क्योंकि स्थिति और बेहतर हो सकती है या और विश्वास-संपन्न लोगों के लिए यह प्रेरणादायक होता है, क्योंकि स्थिति को बेहतर बनाने की चुनौती विद्यमान होती है। **—राजा ह्विटनी जूनियर**

- नई व्यवस्था लागू करने के लिए नेतृत्व करने से अधिक कठिन कार्य नहीं है। **—मैक्यावेली**

- यदि किसी चीज को अच्छी तरह समझना चाहते हो तो इसे बदलने की कोशिश करो। **—कुर्त लेविन**

- आप परिवर्तन का प्रबंध नहीं कर सकते, केवल उसके आगे रह सकते हैं। **—पीटर ड्रकर**

- जिस सभ्यता में बड़ी तादाद में असंतुष्ट और आक्रोशित लोग हैं, वह लंबे समय तक नहीं टिक सकती। **—सिगमंड फ्रायड**

- दुनिया बदलने की शुरुआत हमें उस चेहरे से करनी चाहिए, जो हमें आईने में नजर आता है। **—माइकल जैक्सन**

- बदलाव से पूरी मुक्ति, मतलब गलतियों से पूरी मुक्ति है, लेकिन यह तो अकेली सर्वज्ञता का विशेषाधिकार है। **—सी.सी. काल्टन**

- परिवर्तन ही सृष्टि है, जीवन होना मृत्यु है। **—अज्ञात**

- सिर्फ अतीत की जुगाली करने से कोई लाभ नहीं है।
स्वयं को बदल दो, भाग्य बदल जाएगा। **—कहावत**

परिश्रम

- परिश्रम करने से ही कार्य सिद्ध होते हैं, केवल इच्छा करने से नहीं।

—हितोपदेश

- कठिन परिश्रम से भविष्य सुधरता है, आलस्य से वर्तमान।

—स्टीवन राइट

- चींटी से परिश्रम करना सीखें। **—अज्ञात**
- मरते दम तक तू अपने पसीने की रोटी खाना। **—बाइबिल**
- मनुष्य की सबसे अच्छी मित्र उसकी दस उँगलियाँ हैं। **—राबर्ट कोलियर**
- मानव सुख जीवन में है और जीवन परिश्रम में है। **—अज्ञात**

परिस्थिति

- जिसे परिस्थिति कहा जाता है, वह अचानक ही आ पहुँचती है और आती है तो सदल-बल। **—रवींद्रनाथ टैगोर**

पसंद

- जिस व्यक्ति के पास हृदय है, वह क्या केवल दहेज के रुपयों और आँख-नाक की लंबाई-चौड़ाई पसंद कर लेने योग्य है। **—रवींद्रनाथ टैगोर**

पहचानना

- मनुष्य को पहचानना कितना कठिन है। कौन जानता था (है) कि जो व्यक्ति इतना लिख सकता है, उसके पास हृदय है ही नहीं।

—रवींद्रनाथ टैगोर

पागलपन

- पागल हो जाने पर बहुत सी कठिन बातें बड़ी सरलता से कह जाने की शक्ति पैदा हो जाती है। पागलपन वह जूता है, जिसे पाँव में डालकर संसार की हजार-हजार तुच्छ बातों को एकदम लाँघा जा सकता है।

—रवींद्रनाथ टैगोर

पाना

- लकड़हारा केवल पेड़ ही काटना जानता है, वह पेड़ को नहीं पाता, केवल लकड़ी ही पाता है। माली पेड़ को रखना जानता है, इसलिए पाता है फूल और फल।

—रवींद्रनाथ टैगोर

पाना और खोना

- पूरा पाना ही सबसे बड़ी चीज है, अगर ऐसा एकदम संभव न हो तो पूरा खो देना ही ठीक है।

—रवींद्रनाथ टैगोर

पानी

- कुएँ का पानी कुएँ में ही रहता है। पोखर गड्ढे का पानी पोखर गड्ढे में ही शांत रहता है, परंतु पहाड़ की चोटी का पानी पहाड़ की चोटी पर नहीं रहता, मेघ का पानी मेघ का बंधन नहीं मानता।

—रवींद्रनाथ टैगोर

पाप

- जो पाप में पड़ता है, वह मनुष्य है, जो उसमें पड़ने पर दुःखी होता है, वह साधु है और जो उस पर अभिमान करता है, वह शैतान होता है।

—फुलर

- मनुष्य के लिए निराशा के समान दूसरा पाप नहीं है। इसलिए मनुष्य को पापरूपिणी निराशा को समूल हटाकर आशावादी बनना चाहिए।

—हितोपदेश

पाप और क्षमा

- हे प्रभु! यदि मैं कभी भी अपराध करूँ तो मुझे माफ नहीं करना, मेरे ऊपर जरा भी दया मत करना। मुझे मेरे पाप के लिए दंड दो। पाप का दंड भोगा जा सकता है, किंतु क्षमा का भार नहीं वहन किया जा सकता।

—रवींद्रनाथ टैगोर

पाप-पुण्य

- वास्तव में पाप-पुण्य कुछ भी नहीं, कौन किसका पिता है, कौन किसका भाई है, किसी का कोई नहीं। हत्या यदि पाप है, तब सब प्रकार की हत्या समान है, किंतु हत्या को पाप कौन कहता है ? हत्या तो प्रतिदिन होती रहती है। सिर पर पत्थर के टुकड़े के गिर जाने से किसी की हत्या होती है तो कोई बाढ़ के पानी में डूबकर मर जाता है। किसी को मगर निगल जाता है तो किसी आदमी की छुरी किसी का काम तमाम कर देती है। न मालूम कितनी चींटियाँ पैरों के नीचे दबकर मर जाती हैं। यही न कि उनकी अपेक्षा हम कुछ बड़े हैं, यह सब क्षुद्र प्रणालियों के जीवन-मरण का खेल नहीं तो और क्या है ?

—रवींद्रनाथ टैगोर

- दोषी होने पर भी भाई को निर्वासित करना पाप है, उसके फल से छुटकारा नहीं मिल सकता। कौरवों के दुराचारी होने पर भी पांडव उनका वध कर प्रसन्नचित्त से राज्य का सुख-भोग नहीं कर सके थे।

—रवींद्रनाथ टैगोर

पीड़ा

- नारी के भीतर की विचित्र रसमय प्राणों की प्रवर्तना यदि पुरुष के उद्यम में संचारित होते समय बँध पाती है तो उसी सृष्टि से यंत्र का प्राधान्य घट जाता है, उस समय मनुष्य स्व-निर्मित यंत्र के आघात से केवल पीड़ा ही पहुँचाता है और स्वयं भी पीड़ित होता है।

—रवींद्रनाथ टैगोर

पुण्य

- पुण्य का पुरस्कार पुण्य ही है। **—रवींद्रनाथ टैगोर**

पुरुष

- जो सही अर्थ में आदमी है, वह आदमी होकर देवता जैसी पूजा लेने में शरमाता है और अगर पूजा पाता है तो अपने आपको उनके लायक बनाने की चेष्टा करता है, पर हिंदुस्तान में तो उल्टी गंगा बहती है। यहाँ तो आदमी ढोंग

रचकर अपना उल्लू सीधा करने में फूले नहीं समाता। अयोग्य आदमी अपने ढोंग से योग्य होने की कोशिश करता है। **—रवींद्रनाथ टैगोर**

- मोर के सुंदर पंख लगाकर मोर बनने की नाकामयाब कोशिश करनेवाला कौवा जिस तरह शरम नहीं करता, उसी तरह शिक्षित मर्द अपने असली रूप को बनावटी बनाकर ऐंठने में शरम नहीं करता। **—रवींद्रनाथ टैगोर**

पुरुष की वीरता

- पुरुष की वीरता केवल स्त्री के सामने ही प्रकट होती है।

—रवींद्रनाथ टैगोर

पुरुषार्थ

- बड़ी कोई चीज गढ़ डालने में ही पुरुष का पुरुषार्थ है।

—रवींद्रनाथ टैगोर

पुस्तक

- सभी अच्छी पुस्तकों को पढ़ना पिछली शताब्दियों के बेहतरीन व्यक्तियों के साथ संवाद करने जैसा है। **—रेने डकार्टेस**

- जो पुस्तकें हमें सोचने के लिए विवश करती हैं, वे हमारी सबसे अधिक सहायक हैं। **—जवाहरलाल नेहरू**

- मेरे लिए तुलसी-रामायण (रामचरितमानस) भक्तिरस का सर्वोत्तम ग्रंथ है।

—महात्मा गांधी

- पुस्तकों में इतना खजाना छुपा है, जितना कोई लुटेरा कभी लूट नहीं सकता।

—वाल्ट डिजनी

- सही पुस्तक वह नहीं है, जिसे हम पढ़ते हैं, सही पुस्तक वह है, जो हमें पढ़ती है। **—डबल्यू एच ऑडेन**

- पुस्तकों को नहीं पढ़ना, पुस्तकों को जलाने से बढ़कर अपराध है।

—रे ब्रेडबरी

- पुस्तकों का मूल्य रत्नों से भी अधिक है, क्योंकि रत्न बाहरी चमक-दमक दिखाते हैं, जबकि पुस्तकें अंतःकरण को उज्ज्वल करती हैं।

  —महात्मा गांधी

- लोगों को मारा जा सकता है। लेखकों को भी, लेकिन पुस्तकों को मारना संभव नहीं। **—अमोस ओज**

- किसी मूर्ख व्यक्ति के लिए पुस्तकें उतनी ही उपयोगी हैं, जितना कि एक अंधे व्यक्ति के लिए आईना। **—चाणक्य**

- बिना ग्रंथों का कक्ष, बिना आत्मा की देह है। **—शरण**

- पुस्तकों का मूल्य रत्नों से भी अधिक है, क्योंकि पुस्तकें अंतःकरण को उज्ज्वल करती हैं। **—महात्मा गांधी**

- पुस्तकों की उपमा विचारों के रत्नकण से दी जा सकती है।

  —महात्मा गांधी

- पुस्तकें ज्ञान-प्रसार के लिए अमूल्य और सुगम साधन हैं। कोई गाँव बिना पुस्तकालय के नहीं होना चाहिए।

  —महात्मा गांधी

- विचारों के युद्ध में, पुस्तकें ही अस्त्र हैं। **—जॉर्ज बर्नार्ड शॉ**

- आज के लिए और सदा के लिए सबसे बड़ा मित्र है अच्छी पुस्तक।

  —टसर

- अच्छा ग्रंथ एक महान् आत्मा का अमूल्य जीवन-रक्त है। **—मिल्टन**

पूजनीय

- संसार में जिन लोगों को अत्यधिक श्रद्धा की दृष्टि से देखा गया है, वे दुःख के अवतार रहे हैं, सुख-चैन में जीवन बितानेवाले लक्ष्मी के दास कभी पूजनीय नहीं हुए है।

  —रवींद्रनाथ टैगोर

पूजा

- हमारे देश में पूजा का पथ पड़ा प्रशस्त है। इसी रास्ते से भक्ति की धारा को देश की ओर मोड़ देना होगा। **—रवींद्रनाथ टैगोर**

पूर्णता

- स्त्री द्वारा पुरुष अपनी पूर्णता प्राप्त करता है। **—रवींद्रनाथ टैगोर**
- मुक्ति शून्यता में नहीं, पूर्णता में है। पूर्णता सृष्टि करती है, ध्वंस नहीं करता। **—रवींद्रनाथ टैगोर**

पृथ्वी

- पुराण के वासुकि जिस पौराणिक पृथ्वी को थामे हुए हैं, वह पृथ्वी स्थिर है, किंतु संसार में जिस कन्या को वेदना की पृथ्वी वहन करनी होती है, उसकी वह पृथ्वी पल-पल में नए आघातों से तैयार होती जा रही है।

  —रवींद्रनाथ टैगोर
- पुरुष की माँग की पूर्ति करना ही धरती के लिए आनंद का विषय है। इस अनंत माँग को पूरा करते-करते ही पृथ्वी उबरी हुई है, सुंदर हुई है, सार्थक हुई है, वरना जंगलों से ढकी रहकर वह खुद अपने लिए भी अपरिचित रह जाती। **—रवींद्रनाथ टैगोर**

प्यार

- प्यार बुद्धिमत्ता के ऊपर कल्पना की विजय है। **—एच.एल. मैंकिन**
- अपने आप से प्यार करना जीवन भर चलनेवाली प्रेमलीला की शुरुआत है। **—ऑस्कर वाइल्ड**
- मैं मानता हूँ कि कल्पना ज्ञान से ज्यादा शक्तिशाली है, कि मिथक इतिहास से ज्यादा ताकतवर है, कि सपने तथ्यों से ज्यादा शक्तिशाली हैं कि आशा हमेशा अनुभव पर विजय हासिल करती है, कि हँसी दुःख की एक मात्र औषधि है और मैं यह मानता हूँ कि प्यार मौत से ज्यादा शक्तिशाली है।

  —राबर्ट फल्घुम

- हम जिंदगी से प्यार करते हैं, इसलिए नहीं कि हम जीने के अभ्यस्त हैं, बल्कि इसलिए, क्योंकि हम प्यार के आदी हैं। **—फ्रेडरिक नीत्से**

- यह जान पाना मुश्किल है कि किस क्षण प्यार शुरू होता है, लेकिन यह जान पाना कम मुश्किल है कि यह शुरू हो चुका है।

—हेनरी वड्सवर्थ लोंग्फेलो

- प्यार एक सुंदर फूल की तरह है, जिसे मैं शायद छू न सकूँ, लेकिन जिसकी खुशबू बगीचे को उसकी तरह एक आनंददायक स्थान बना देती है।

—हेलेन केलर

- जब तक प्यार पागलपन नहीं है, यह प्यार नहीं है।

—पेड्रो काल्डेरों बरका

- प्यार एक ऐसा खेल है, जिसे दो खेल सकते हैं और दोनों ही जीत भी सकते हैं। **—ईवा गबर**

- जितने भी जुनून हैं, उनमें प्यार सबसे उग्र और सबसे ज्यादा ताकतवर है, क्योंकि यह एक ही समय में दिल, दिमाग और इंद्रियों पर हमला करता है।

—लाओत्जू

- बिना प्यार के एक जिंदगी एक बिना फल के पेड़ के जैसी है।

—खलील जिब्रान

- मित्रता अकसर प्यार में बदल जाती है, लेकिन प्यार दोस्ती में कभी नहीं।

—अल्बर्ट कैमस

- आप जानते हैं कि आप प्यार में हैं, जब आप सो नहीं सकते; क्योंकि वास्तविकता आखिरकार आपके सपनों से ज्यादा बेहतर है। **—डॉ. सूस**

- अँधेरा अंधकार को दूर नहीं कर सकता, केवल रोशनी ही यह कर सकती है। नफरत घृणा को दूर नहीं कर सकती, केवल प्यार ही यह कर सकता है।

—मार्टिन लुथर किंग

- उस व्यक्ति को मत चुनिए, जो संसार के लिए अच्छा है। किसी ऐसे व्यक्ति को चुनिए, जो आपकी दुनिया को सुंदर बनाए। **—अज्ञात**
- प्यार एक-दूसरे की ओर एकटक देखते रहने में नहीं है, बल्कि साथ-साथ एक ही दिशा में देखते रहने में है।

  —एंटोनी डी एक्सुपेरी
- प्यार ही एकमात्र वास्तविकता है और यह केवल एक भावना मात्र नहीं है, यह परम सत्य है, जो सृष्टि के हृदय में स्थित है।

  —रवींद्रनाथ टैगोर
- गुरुत्वाकर्षण लोगों के प्यार में पड़ जाने के लिए उत्तरदायी नहीं है।

  —अल्बर्ट आइंस्टीन
- जिंदगी का सबसे बड़ा सुख यह दृढ़ विश्वास है कि हमें प्यार मिला, खुद के लिए प्यार मिला। **—विक्टर ह्यूगो**
- प्यार आँखों से नहीं देखता, बल्कि मन से देखता है और इसीलिए पंखयुक्त कामदेव है, जो अंधा चित्रित किया गया है।

  —विलियम शेक्सपियर
- अपनी सारी जिंदगी, मेरा दिल एक ऐसी चीज के लिए तरसा है, जिसे मैं नाम नहीं दे सकता। **—आंद्रे ब्रेटन**
- बहुत प्यार करने का अर्थ है, बहुत जीना और हमेशा प्यार करने का मतलब है सदा के लिए जीना। **—हेनरी ड्रमंड**
- श्रद्धा सब चीजें संभव कर देती है। प्यार सब चीजें सरल बना देता है।

  —डी.एल. मूडी
- प्यार किए जाने के लिए प्यार करना मानवीय है, लेकिन प्रेम करने के लिए ही प्यार करना दैवीय है। **—अलफोंस लमर्तिन**
- प्यार से डरने का मतलब है जीवन से डरना और जो जिंदगी से डरते हैं, पहले ही तीन हिस्से मर चुके हैं। **—बरट्रेंड रसेल**

- एक व्यक्ति दूसरे के मन की बात जान सकता है, तो केवल सहानुभूति और प्यार से, उम्र और बुद्धि से नहीं।

  —अज्ञात

- इस संसार में प्यार करने लायक दो वस्तुएँ हैं—एक दुःख और दूसरा श्रम। दुःख के बिना हृदय निर्मल नहीं होता और श्रम के बिना मनुष्य का विकास नहीं होता। **—अज्ञात**

- हम जब तक स्वयं माता-पिता नहीं बन जाएँ, माता-पिता का प्यार कभी नहीं जान पाते।

  —हेनरी वार्ड बीचर

- अपने स्नेह का पूर्ण प्रदर्शन किए बिना आप अपना स्नेहभाव दूसरों तक नहीं पहुँचा सकते। **—स्वेट मार्डन**

प्रटत भाव

- मैं मानव समाज में किसी नई नीति का प्रचार करने नहीं बैठा हूँ, न समाज भंग करने आया हूँ, बंधन तोड़ना भी नहीं चाहता। मैं तो बस अपने मन का प्रकट भाव व्यक्त कर रहा हूँ। हमारे मन में जो भाव उदित होते हैं, वे क्या सब-के-सब तर्कसंगत होते हैं। **—रवींद्रनाथ टैगोर**

प्रकाश

- प्रकाश—अंधकार की निःशब्द आवर्तन-ध्वनि है। **—रवींद्रनाथ टैगोर**

प्रकृति

- प्रकृति आत्मसमर्पण करती है, मगर लुटेरों के हाथों! क्योंकि चाहने की, लेने की और पाने की ताकत का उपभोग करना उसे अच्छा लगता है।

  —रवींद्रनाथ टैगोर

- प्रकृति अकेली, अखंड और निश्चिंत है, उसके समीप नीले ललाट पर बुद्धि की लकीर तक नहीं है। सिर्फ प्रतिभा की चमक हमेशा जगमगा रही है।

  —रवींद्रनाथ टैगोर

• मनुष्य की प्रकृति बहुमुखी होती है, उसकी आवश्यकताएँ अनेक प्रकार की होती हैं और इसीलिए उसे तरह-तरह की वस्तुओं की खोज करनी पड़ती है।

—रवींद्रनाथ टैगोर

प्रगति

• प्रगति का वर्णन, लक्ष्यों को निर्धारित करना और उनके लिए प्रगति का मूल्यांकन करना है।

—बिल गेट्स

• प्रगति करना दुर्लभ और अनिश्चित होने की नियति नहीं है, हम वस्तुतः इसे सामान्य बना सकते हैं। **—बिल गेट्स**

• गति और प्रगति में संदेह न करें, कोल्हू के बैल दिनभर चलते हैं, लेकिन कोई प्रगति नहीं करते हैं। **—बिल गेट्स**

• यदि संघर्ष नहीं है तो प्रगति नहीं है। **—बिल गेट्स**

प्रतिकार

• जो कुछ भी हमारे देश को चोट पहुँचाता है, उसका प्रतिकार जरूरी है, वह चाहे कितना ही प्रबल क्यों न हो और वह प्रतिकार एक मात्र हमारे ही साथ में है।

—रवींद्रनाथ टैगोर

• तंग किनारों के बीच नई वर्षा की जलराशि सहसा आ जाने से बड़ी खलबली मचती है। उसका एक मात्र प्रतिकार यही है कि उसे खुले क्षेत्र की ओर बह जाने दिया जाए।

—रवींद्रनाथ टैगोर

प्रतिभा

• प्रतिभा धैर्य की महान् क्षमता मात्र है। **—बिल गेट्स**

• यदि आप प्रतिभा के साथ उत्कृष्टता प्राप्त नहीं कर सकते हैं, तो प्रयास से विजयी बनें। **—बिल गेट्स**

- हर व्यक्ति में प्रतिभा होती है। दरअसल उस प्रतिभा को निखारने के लिए गहरे अँधेरे रास्ते में जाने का साहस कम लोगों में ही होता है।

—बिल गेट्स

- अक्ल की बजाय प्रतिभा को हम ऊँचा समझते हैं। अक्ल हर रोज, हर पल हमारे सैकड़ों कामों में अन्याय करती है, उसके बिना हमें जीवन धारण करना मुश्किल हो जाता है और प्रतिभा कभी–कभी हमारे काम आती है और ज्यादा समय उससे हमें कोई लाभ ही नहीं होता, परंतु अक्ल का संबंध मन से है और प्रतिभा मन के नियमानुसार न चलकर हवा की तरह आती है और चली जाती है, किसी की पुकार की उपेक्षा नहीं करती।

—रवींद्रनाथ टैगोर

- प्रतिभा अपना मार्ग स्वयं निर्धारित कर लेती है और अपना दीपक स्वयं लिये चलती है। **—बिल गेट्स**

- अन्य के भीतर प्रवेश करने की शक्ति और अन्य को संपूर्ण रूप से अपना बना लेने का जादू ही प्रतिभा का सर्वस्व, प्रतिभा का वैशिष्ट्य है। **—रवींद्रनाथ टैगोर**

- प्रतिभा एक प्रतिशत प्रेरणा और निन्यानबे प्रतिशत श्रम है। **—एडीसन**

प्रतिरोध

- जीवन में जब बाहर से कोई बाधा आती है, तब उससे लड़ने का साहस सहज ही प्राप्त हो जाता है, स्वयं देवता उसके लिए सहायक हो जाते हैं, किंतु जब बाहर का विरोध सहसा एकदम परास्त हो जाता है, तब लड़ाई तो थम जाती है, पर संधि नहीं हो पाती। तब बाहर निकल आता है अपने भीतर का प्रतिरोध।

—रवींद्रनाथ टैगोर

प्रतिष्ठा

- मनुष्य सामाजिक महत्त्व से भी प्रतिष्ठा प्राप्त कर सकता है, राष्ट्रनीतिक महत्त्व से भी। **—रवींद्रनाथ टैगोर**

प्रपंच

• आकाश के तारे जैसे हृदय के मध्य आकर फुसफुसाकर बोलें, ऐसा ही है, हम तो हजार-हजार सालों से देखते आ रहे हैं, संसार-व्यापी यह सारा आयोजन इतना ही बड़ा प्रपंच है। **—रवींद्रनाथ टैगोर**

प्रतिस्पर्धा

• अपने प्रतिस्पर्धियों से अलग दिखने और कुछ अलग करने के लिए सबसे सार्थक तरीके खोजें।

—बिल गेट्स

• निंदा करने की जरूरत होने पर जैसे भी हो, एक प्रतिपक्षी तो खड़ा करना ही पड़ता है। **—रवींद्रनाथ टैगोर**

प्रभुत्व

• अनेक बार दुर्बल व्यक्ति प्रभुत्व पाकर प्रचंड और स्वेच्छाचारी बन जाते हैं। **—रवींद्रनाथ टैगोर**

प्रलय

• प्रलय का बीज जब तक मिट्टी के नीचे रहता है, तब तक डर की कोई बात नहीं होती, पर ज्यों ही वह मिट्टी के ऊपर अँकुराता है, वह बहुत तेजी से बढ़ता है और तब आँचल से, सोने से, यहाँ तक कि प्राणों से भी उसे ढका नहीं जा सकता। **—रवींद्रनाथ टैगोर**

प्रवृत्ति

• प्रवृत्ति ही तो प्रवृत्ति का वह लैंपपोस्ट है, जिसकी रोशनी में हमें सब रास्तों का पता चलता है। प्रवृत्ति को जो लोग गलत बताते हैं, वे अपनी आँखें फाड़कर दिव्य दृष्टि पाने की दुराशा करते हैं। **—रवींद्रनाथ टैगोर**

• जो लोग सारी चीजों को प्रवृत्ति के साथ ही जोड़कर देखने के आदी हैं, वे प्रवृत्ति को तो विकृत करते ही हैं, सत्य को भी नहीं देख पाते।

—रवींद्रनाथ टैगोर

प्रशंसा

- मानव में जो कुछ सर्वोत्तम है, उसका विकास प्रशंसा तथा प्रोत्साहन से किया जा सकता है। **—चार्ल्स श्वेव**

- आप हर इनसान का चरित्र बता सकते हैं, यदि आप देखें कि वह प्रशंसा से कैसे प्रभावित होता है। **—सेनेका**

- मानव प्रकृति में सबसे गहरा नियम प्रशंसा प्राप्त करने की लालसा है। **—विलियम जेम्स**

- अगर किसी युवती के दोष जानने हों तो उसकी सखियों में उसकी प्रशंसा करो। **—फ्रेंकलिन**

- मेरी चापलूसी करो और मैं आप पर भरोसा नहीं करूँगा। मेरी आलोचना करो और मैं आपको पसंद नहीं करूँगा। मेरी उपेक्षा करो और मैं आपको माफ नहीं करूँगा, मुझे प्रोत्साहित करो और मैं कभी आपको नहीं भूलूँगा। **—विलियम ऑर्थर वार्ड**

- हमारे साथ प्राय: समस्या यही होती है कि हम झूठी प्रशंसा के द्वारा बरबाद हो जाना तो पसंद करते हैं, परंतु वास्तविक आलोचना के द्वारा सँभल जाना नहीं। **—नॉर्मन विंसेंट पील**

प्रसन्नता

- आप अपनी आँख बंद करके ध्यान लगाएँ और खुद से पूछें कि कौन सा काम करते समय आपको आनंद आता है, ऐसी कौन सी दुनिया है, जो आपको बुलाती है। तभी तुम सही फैसला कर पाओगे।

- प्रसन्नता आत्मा को शांति देती है। **—सैम्युअल स्माइल्स**

- आनंद ही ब्रह्म है, आनंद से ही सब प्राणी उत्पन्न होते हैं। उत्पन्न होने पर आनंद से ही जीवित रहते हैं और मृत्यु से आनंद में समा जाते हैं। **—उपनिषद्**

- प्रसन्नता स्वास्थ्य देती है, विषाद रोग देता है। **—अज्ञात**

- मनुष्य अपने आनंद का निर्माता स्वयं है। —**थोरो**
- प्रसन्नचित्त मनुष्य अधिक जीते हैं। —**शेक्सपियर**
- प्रसन्न करने का उपाय है, स्वयं प्रसन्न रहना।
- हर्ष के साथ शोक और भय इस प्रकार लगे हैं, जैसे प्रकाश के संग छाया, सच्चा सुखी वही है, जिसकी दृष्टि में दोनों समान हैं।

  —**धम्मपद**
- प्रसन्नता बसंत की तरह, हृदय की सब कलियाँ खिला देती है।

  —**जीनपॉल**

प्रश्न

- भाषा की खोज प्रश्न पूछने के लिए की गई थी। उत्तर तो संकेत और हाव-भाव से भी दिए जा सकते हैं, पर प्रश्न करने के लिए बोलना जरूरी है। जब आदमी ने सबसे पहले प्रश्न पूछा तो मानवता परिपक्व हो गई। प्रश्न पूछने के आवेग के अभाव से सामाजिक स्थिरता जन्म लेती है।

  —**एरिक हाफर**
- मूर्खतापूर्ण प्रश्न कोई भी नहीं होते और कोई भी तभी मूर्ख बनता है, जब वह प्रश्न पूछना बंद कर दे। —**स्टीनमेंज**
- मैं छह ईमानदार सेवक अपने पास रखता हूँ, इन्होंने मुझे वह हर चीज सिखाई है, जो मैं जानता हूँ, इनके नाम हैं—क्या, क्यों, कब, कैसे, कहाँ और कौन।

  —**रुडयार्ड किपलिंग**

प्रांजलता

- प्रांजलता की यह खास खूबी है कि वह मन के साथ अत्यंत समीप का नाता जोड़ लेती है।

  —**रवींद्रनाथ टैगोर**

प्राण

- मनुष्य के प्राण अपने ही अंदर नाना चिंताओं से घुल-घुलाकर मैले हो गए हैं।

इसलिए प्राणों का विशुद्ध रूप देखना हो तो देखना चाहिए घास की ओर, पेड़ की ओर।

—रवींद्रनाथ टैगोर

- जो प्राण सीमाबद्ध नहीं है, उसमें हिस्सा बँटाने के लिए किसी के साथ किसी के झगड़े की कोई जरूरत ही नहीं है। **—रवींद्रनाथ टैगोर**

प्रार्थना

- प्रार्थना अपनी योग्यता और दुर्बलता को स्वीकार करना है।

  —महात्मा गांधी
- प्रार्थना ही आत्मा की खुराक है। **—महात्मा गांधी**
- ईश्वर को पत्र लिखने में न कागज चाहिए, न कलम-दवात, न शब्द। उस पत्र का नाम है प्रार्थना, पूजा। **—महात्मा गांधी**
- प्रार्थना या भजन जीभ से नहीं, हृदय से होता है। इसी से गूँगे, तोतले और मूढ़ भी प्रार्थना कर सकते हैं। **—महात्मा गांधी**
- प्रार्थना तभी प्रार्थना है, जब वह अपने-आप से निकलती है।

  —महात्मा गांधी
- प्रार्थना का आमंत्रण निश्चय ही आत्मा की व्याकुलता का द्योतक है।

  —महात्मा गांधी
- प्रार्थना वाणी से नहीं, हृदय से करने की चीज है। **—महात्मा गांधी**
- प्रार्थना धर्म का प्राण और सार है। **—महात्मा गांधी**
- प्रार्थना के लिए कोई जटिल या कठोर नियम नहीं बनाया जा सकता, न समय नियत किया जा सकता है यह तो अपने-अपने स्वभाव पर निर्भर है।

  —महात्मा गांधी
- प्रार्थना द्वारा ईश्वर की कृपा और सहायता से हम अपनी कमजोरियों पर विजय प्राप्त कर सकते हैं। **—महात्मा गांधी**

प्रायश्चित्त

- प्रायश्चित्त से पिछले पाप के प्रति विरक्ति उत्पन्न होती है और आगे के लिए सावधानी।
  —महात्मा गांधी
- जो व्यक्ति हृदय से प्रायश्चित्त कर लेता है, वह सहानुभूति का अधिकारी होता है।
  —महात्मा गांधी
- प्रायश्चित्त वहीं होना चाहिए, जहाँ जानबूझकर कोई भारी पाप हो गया हो।
  —महात्मा गांधी

प्रीति

- भलाई करने का एक मात्र ईश्वरप्रदत्त अधिकार है, वह है प्रीति।
  —रवींद्रनाथ टैगोर

प्रेम

- हम लोग शायद किसी वस्तु को नहीं, बल्कि उसकी प्रतिध्वनि को प्यार करते हैं, क्योंकि एक समय हम जिस चीज की तरफ ताकते भी नहीं, दूसरे समय वही चीज हमारे समस्त तन को बेसुध कर देती है।
  —अज्ञात
- प्रेम जैसी पवित्र वस्तु संसार में और कोई नहीं है। **—महात्मा गांधी**
- मन में जब एक प्रबल आनंद या बृहत् प्रेम का संचार होता है, तब मनुष्य सोचता है, मैं कुछ कर सकता हूँ। तब अचानक आत्मविसर्जन की एक इच्छा बलवती हो उठती है। स्रोत का उच्छ्‌वास जैसे कठिन तट पर अपने वेग से मूर्च्छित करता है, वैसे ही प्रेम का आवेग, आनंद का उच्छ्‌वास, एक महत् त्याग, एक बृहत् दुःख के ऊपर अपने को जैसे निक्षेप करना चाहता है।
  —रवींद्रनाथ टैगोर
- हमें तो इतना देखना चाहिए कि जो बो रहे हैं, वह प्रेम है या और कुछ।
  —महात्मा गांधी
- यदि दो प्रेमियों में से एक वफादार है और दूसरा ईर्ष्यालु और झूठा, तो कैसे

उनकी मित्रता टिकी रह सकती है, क्योंकि प्यार मर चुका होता है।

—मेरी डी फ्रांस

- जिससे प्यार किया जाता है, उसके निकटवर्ती परिजनों का संग भी मधुर लगता है। **—रवींद्रनाथ टैगोर**
- सामान्य का असामान्य रूप में आविष्कार करता है प्रेम। **—रवींद्रनाथ टैगोर**
- जहाँ प्रेम है, वहाँ डर को स्थान कहाँ? **—महात्मा गांधी**
- प्रेम सत्य से खुश रहता है, सब सहन करता है, सब मान लेता है, आशामय है, कभी निष्फल नहीं होता। **—महात्मा गांधी**
- अहंकार छोड़े बिना सच्चा प्रेम नहीं किया जा सकता। **—अज्ञात**
- सारे दुःख-दुर्लक्षणों में प्रेम ही बड़ा है। **—रवींद्रनाथ टैगोर**
- प्रेम खुशी-खुशी ठगा जाता है। **—रवींद्रनाथ टैगोर**
- दूसरों से प्रेम करना अपने आप से प्रेम करना है। **—अज्ञात**
- जहाँ प्रेम है, वहाँ परमात्मा है। **—महात्मा गांधी**
- प्रेम का दर्शन हम पिता-पुत्र, भाई-बहन और मित्र-मित्र के बीच करते हैं, किंतु इसका उपयोग सभी जीवित प्राणियों के बीच होना चाहिए। **—महात्मा गांधी**
- सबसे कीमती चीज है प्रेम, सो उसे क्या लुटा-बिखेर सकते हैं। **—रवींद्रनाथ टैगोर**
- प्रेम एक ऐसा फल है, जो हर मौसम में मिलता है और जिसे सभी पा सकते हैं। **—मदर टेरेसा**
- हमें प्रेम का क्षेत्र घर से गाँव भर में, गाँव से जिले भर में, जिले से प्रांत और प्रांत से देश भर में फैलाकर तब उसे सारे विश्व के लिए विस्तृत बना देना चाहिए। **—महात्मा गांधी**

- नारी की संपत्ति हृदय है। भले ही वह सबकुछ खो दे, जो कुछ बाहरी है, जिसे देखा जा सकता है, स्पर्श किया जा सकता है, भोग किया जा सकता है, फिर भी बचा रहता है प्रेम का आदर्श, जो अव्यक्तिगत नहीं है।

—रवींद्रनाथ टैगोर

- दांपत्य में गुस्सा न मिलने से मोहब्बत में स्वाद नहीं मिलता जैसे सब्जी में नमक-मिर्च के बिना। **—रवींद्रनाथ टैगोर**

- हर सच्चा क्रांतिकारी वास्तव में गहन प्रेम की भावना से संचालित होता है।

—चे ग्वेरा

- मोहब्बत त्याग की माँ है, जहाँ जाती है, बेटे को साथ ले जाती है।

—सुदर्शन

- जो प्यार करता है, उसे कैसे खुश करना चाहिए, हृदय अपने-आप ही यह बता देता है। **—रवींद्रनाथ टैगोर**

- प्रेम की वेदना में सारे जल-थल-आकाश के केंद्र-कुहर से ऐसी धुन में, बाँसुरी बजती है। **—रवींद्रनाथ टैगोर**

- प्रेम स्वभाव से ही बैरागी होता है, वह खुद ही पथ के किनारे मिट्टी में हजार-हजार फूल खिला देता है। **—रवींद्रनाथ टैगोर**

- हमारे प्रेम का प्रदीप जब जलता है तो उसकी शिखा ऊपर ही उठती है, दीपक का जला हुआ तेल ही नीचे की तरफ जाता है। **—रवींद्रनाथ टैगोर**

- प्रेम की शक्ति दंड की शक्ति से हजार गुनी प्रभावशाली और स्थायी होती है। **—महात्मा गांधी**

- वही समाज सदैव सुखी रहकर तरक्की कर सकता है, जिसमें लोगों ने आपसी प्रेम को आत्मसात् कर लिया। **—अज्ञात**

- प्यार के माध्यम से मनुष्य अपने परम मूल्य की उपलब्धि प्राप्त करता है।

—रवींद्रनाथ टैगोर

- अहंकार और अवज्ञा छोड़कर, नम्र होकर, प्रेम देकर पहले अपने को सच्चे दिल से सबके साथ मिलाइए, उस प्रेम के आगे हजारों त्रुटियाँ और कमजोरियाँ सहज ही हार मान लेंगी। **—रवींद्रनाथ टैगोर**
- विच्छेद के समय प्रेम और प्रबल हो उठता है। **—रवींद्रनाथ टैगोर**
- मनुष्य की समूची प्रकृति को पल भर में जगा देने का उपाय प्रेम ही है। **—रवींद्रनाथ टैगोर**
- जब आप अपने जीवन में पीछे लौटते हैं तो आप पाएँगे कि वे क्षण जब आप वास्तव में जिए थे, वे क्षण हैं, जब आपने चीजें प्रेम की उद्यत भावना में की थी। **—हेनरी ड्रमंड**
- जब कोई प्रेम हमें एकदम विचलित कर देता है, तब वह भी हम लोगों को संसार के क्षुद्र बंधन से छुड़ाकर अनंत की ओर मिला देता है, वह एक महान् तपस्या का रूप बना लेता है और देश-काल के शिलामुख को चीरकर झरने की तरह अतुल की ओर बह जाता है। इसी प्रकार प्रबल स्पंदन हमें विश्वस्पंदन में मिला देता है। **—रवींद्रनाथ टैगोर**
- सच्चा प्रेम भूत की तरह है—चर्चा उसकी सब करते हैं, देखा किसी ने नहीं। **—अज्ञात**
- प्रेम के बिना जीवन एक ऐसे वृक्ष के समान है, जिस पर न कोई फूल हो, न फल। **—खलील जिब्रान**
- इस दुनिया में सर्वप्रधान प्रेम है। जिंदगी का सर्वप्रधान प्रेम, जैसे सबकी अपेक्षा प्रबल हुआ करता है, वैसे ही दुनिया का सर्वप्रथम प्रेम भी सरल और मुश्किल होता है। **—रवींद्रनाथ टैगोर**
- देह का प्यार दुनिया में सबसे पहले प्रकट हुआ था। **—रवींद्रनाथ टैगोर**
- हमें प्रेम करना ही पड़ता है और प्रेम को तोड़ना भी पड़ता है। दुनिया का यही सबसे बड़ा विशादमय नियम है और इस नियम के अनुसार ही हमें चलना पड़ेगा। **—रवींद्रनाथ टैगोर**

- उपयुक्त अवसर पर स्त्री-पुरुष के हृदय में परस्पर प्रेम का संचार होना कोई असंभव ही नहीं। **—रवींद्रनाथ टैगोर**
- प्रेम का फल एक दिन का नहीं होता, कुछ दिनों का भी नहीं होता, प्रेम के फल की सार्थकता प्रेम के बीच होती है। **—रवींद्रनाथ टैगोर**
- एक सच्ची, प्रिय मानवीय आत्मा का दूसरी पर होनेवाला प्रभाव सौभाग्यदायक है। दो मानवीय आत्माओं के लिए इससे ज्यादा महान् बात और क्या हो सकती है कि वे यह महसूस करें कि वे जुड़े हुए हैं, एक-दूसरे को मजबूत करने के लिए। खामोश, कही न जा सकनेवाली यादों में एक-दूसरे के साथ एक होने के लिए। **—जॉर्ज इलियट**
- प्रेम और स्नेह का रहस्य अति प्राचीन है, दुर्गम है, वह अपनी सार्थकता के लिए तर्क पर निर्भर नहीं होता। **—रवींद्रनाथ टैगोर**
- प्रेम में भय न होने से उसका रस फीका हो जाता है। **—रवींद्रनाथ टैगोर**

प्रेरणादायक

- मैं शुक्रगुजार हूँ उन तमाम लोगों का, जिन्होंने बुरे वक्त मैं मेरा साथ छोड़ दिया; क्योंकि उन्हें भरोसा था कि मैं मुसीबतों से अकेले ही निपट सकता हूँ। **—अज्ञात**
- जब दूसरे व्यक्ति सोए हों, तो उस समय अध्ययन करें, उस समय कार्य करें, जब दूसरे व्यक्ति अपने समय को नष्ट करते हैं, उस समय तैयारी करें, जब दूसरे खेल रहे हों, और उस समय सपने देखें, जब दूसरे केवल कामना ही कर रहे हों। **—विलियम आर्थर वार्ड**
- जब बिल्कुल अंधकार होता है, तब इनसान सितारे देख पाता है। **—राल्फवाल्डो एमर्सन**
- स्वतंत्रता और नियति एक साथ नहीं हो सकते। ये दोनों एक-दूसरे के विपरीत हैं। **—इमरे कर्तेश**

• इच्छा हमेशा योग्यता को हरा देती है।
सच्चा प्रयास कभी निष्फल नहीं होता। **—विल्सन एडवर्ड**

• जब सपने और इच्छाएँ पर्याप्त बड़े होते हैं, परिस्थितियों से कोई फर्क नहीं पड़ता।

• रत्न मिट्टी से ही निकलते हैं, स्वर्ण मंजूषाओं ने तो कभी एक भी रत्न उत्पन्न नहीं किया। **—जयशंकर प्रसाद**

• असंभव शब्द मूर्खों के शब्दकोश में पाया जाता है।

—नेपोलियन

• निराशावादी व्यक्ति को हर अवसर में कठिनाइयाँ ही नजर आती हैं, जबकि एक आशावादी व्यक्ति हर कठिनाई में भी अवसरों की तलाश कर लेता है।

—विंस्टन चर्चिल

• उन्नति की क्षमता रखनेवालों पर ही समय-समय पर आपत्ति आती है।
—वेदव्यास

• आपकी मरजी के बिना कोई भी आपको तुच्छ होने का एहसास नहीं करा सकता है। **—एलिएनॉर रूजवेल्ट**

• प्यार कभी निष्फल नहीं होता, चरित्र कभी नहीं हारता, धैर्य और दृढ़ता से सपने अवश्य सच हो जाते हैं। **—पीट मेराविच**

• मानव जीवन की दिशा बदलने में, एक छोटी सी बात भी अद्‌भुत प्रभाव रखती है। **—स्वेट मार्डेन**

• किनारे पर खड़ा जहाज सबसे सुरक्षित होता है, लेकिन क्या जहाज इसलिए बनाए जाते हैं। जीवन में चुनौतियाँ लेने की ताकत ही आपकी क्षमताओं को तय करती है। **—अज्ञात**

• आप कुछ भी कर पाने में सक्षम हैं, चाहे वह आपकी सोच हो, आपका जीवन हो या आपके सपने हों, सब सच हो सकते हैं। आप जो चाहें, वह कर सकते

हैं। आप इस अनंत ब्रह्मांड की तरह ही अनंत संभावनाओं से परिपूर्ण हैं।

—शेड हेल्मस्टेटर

- अगर हम अपनी क्षमता के अनुसार कर्म करें तो हम अपने आपको ही अचंभित कर डालेंगे। **—थॉमस एडीसन**
- संकल्प ही मनुष्य का बल है। **—अज्ञात**
- संपूर्ण लेखन जैसी कोई चीज नहीं होती। ठीक वैसे ही, जैसे संपूर्ण निराशा नहीं होती। **—हारुकि मुराकामी**
- अपने शक्तियों पर भरोसा करनेवाला कभी असफल नहीं होता। **—अज्ञात**
- वह सच्चा साहसी है, जो कभी भी निराश नहीं होता। **—अज्ञात**
- मंजिल तो मिल ही जाएगी, भटककर ही सही, गुमराह तो वे हैं, जो घर से निकला ही नहीं करते। **—अज्ञात**
- वही सबसे तेज चलता है, जो अकेला चलता है। **—अज्ञात**
- जिसने निश्चय कर लिया, उसके लिए केवल करना शेष रह जाता है। **—इटालियन कहावत**
- प्रचंड वायु में भी पहाड़ विचलित नहीं होते। **—अज्ञात**
- हर परिस्थिति एक सौगात है और हर अनुभव खजाना। **—अज्ञात**
- मेहनत, हिम्मत और लगन से कल्पना साकार होती है। **—अज्ञात**
- विवेक बहादुरी का उत्तम अंश है। **—अज्ञात**
- कोई भी पूर्ण नहीं होता और कोई भी हर समय नहीं जीतता। **—अज्ञात**
- बिना उत्साह के कभी किसी उच्च लक्ष्य की प्राप्ति नहीं होती। **—एमर्सन**
- सतह की 'चमक' कभी उतनी महत्त्वपूर्ण नहीं होती है, जितनी कि इसके नीचे की नींव होती है। **—अज्ञात**
- ऊँची जगहों पर जाने का एक मात्र मार्ग घुमावदार सीढ़ियाँ हैं। **—अज्ञात**

- अगर आप इस बात की परवाह नहीं करें कि श्रेय किसे मिलेगा, तो आप बहुत कुछ कर सकते हैं। **—अज्ञात**
- ऐसे असंख्य लोग हैं, जो बार-बार असफल हुए, तब कहीं जाकर वे 'अचानक सामने' आए। **—अज्ञात**
- अग्नि से सोना परखा जाता है और विपत्ति से वीर पुरुष। **—सेनेका**
- गुण स्वयं ही सामने आ जाते हैं, क्योंकि कस्तूरी को अपनी उपस्थिति प्रमाणित नहीं करनी पड़ती। **—शेस्टन**
- संभव की सीमाओं को जानने का एक ही तरीका है, उनसे थोड़ा आगे असंभव के दायरे में निकल जाइए। **—आर्थर सी क्लार्क**
- खुश रहिए, रचनात्मक बनिए। इनसान अपने अस्तित्व का अर्थ जानकर ही विश्वास से भर उठता है और यही विचार उसकी मजबूती बढ़ाता है। **—स्टीफन ज्विग**
- अगर हम गिरते हैं, तो अधिक अच्छी तरह चलने का रहस्य सीख जाते हैं। **—महर्षि अरविंद घोष**
- जो यह सोचते हैं कि वे किसी प्रकार की सेवा करने योग्य नहीं हैं, वे शायद पशुओं और वृक्षों को भूल जाते हैं।
- लगन को काँटों की परवाह नहीं होती। **—प्रेमचंद**

फूल

- ईश्वर हमसे उन पुष्पों के लिए उत्तर की अपेक्षा करता है, जिन्हें वह हमारे पास भेजता है, न कि सूर्य और पृथ्वी के लिए। **—रवींद्रनाथ टैगोर**

फूलदान

- केवल फूलदान में सजाकर रखने से फूल का आदर नहीं होता। **—रवींद्रनाथ टैगोर**

बंधन

- शास्त्रों में पढ़ा है, इच्छा ही बंधन है। वह व्यक्ति को भी बाँधती है और दूसरों को भी। **—रवींद्रनाथ टैगोर**

- हम जिसे पिंजरे में बाँधते हैं, वह हमें हमारी इच्छा से बाँधता है। इच्छा का वह बंधन जंजीर के बंधन से ज्यादा सख्त होता है। **—अज्ञात**

- गले की फाँसी को निकालकर फेंकने का प्रयत्न करने पर बंधन और भी कठोर हो जाता है। **—रवींद्रनाथ टैगोर**

- जो बंधन कारागृह में मनुष्य को जकड़कर रखता है, वही बंधन दुर्गम पर्वत-पथ पर आगे बढ़ने में उसकी मदद करता है। **—रवींद्रनाथ टैगोर**

- किसी-किसी प्राणी का बचपन जल्दी समाप्त हो जाता है, किसी-किसी का बहुत दिन तक रहता है। **—रवींद्रनाथ टैगोर**

बड़ा परिवर्तन

- साधारणत: बड़ा परिवर्तन हर एक के लिए संभव नहीं है। बड़े परिवर्तन के लिए बड़ी शक्ति आवश्यक होती है। **—रवींद्रनाथ टैगोर**

बनाना-बिगाड़ना

- जो बना नहीं सकता, उसे बिगाड़ने का कोई अधिकार नहीं। **—रवींद्रनाथ टैगोर**

बर्बर

- बर्बर जातीय मनुष्य का प्रधान लक्षण है कि उसका आत्मबोध संकीर्ण और सीमाबद्ध रहता है। **—अज्ञात**

बर्बरता

- लड़कियों की पसंदगी की परवाह न करके माँ-बाप की पसंद से विवाह करना बर्बरता है। **—रवींद्रनाथ टैगोर**

बात

- जो भी हो, बात में विष रहता है, बातें एकदम व्यर्थ नहीं होतीं।

—रवींद्रनाथ टैगोर

- बातें आती हैं और चली जाती हैं, उन्हें थामकर नहीं रखा जा सकता।

—रवींद्रनाथ टैगोर

- सिद्धांत के रूप में कोई बात जैसे मानी जाती है, मनुष्यों पर प्रयोग करके उसे सदैव उसी निश्चित भाव से नहीं माना जा सकता।

—रवींद्रनाथ टैगोर

बाधाएँ

- बाधाओं को मानकर चलना जिसका काम है, वह यदि बुद्धि को मानकर चलना चाहे तो ठोकर खा-खाकर उसका सिर ही फूटेगा।

—रवींद्रनाथ टैगोर

बुद्धि

- जिसके पास बुद्धि है, बल उसी के पास है। **—पंचतंत्र**
- जिसमें बुद्धि नहीं, उसमें बल नहीं। **—महात्मा गांधी**
- सत्य की सारी समझ एक उपमा की खोज में निहित है। **—थोरो**
- प्रत्येक व्यक्ति के लिए उसके विचार ही सारे तालों की चाबी हैं।

—एमर्सन

- बुद्धि की कुछ-न-कुछ मात्र प्राणि-मात्र में होती है, पर जब तक उसका विकास न किया जाए, तब तक मानवता नहीं प्राप्त होती।

—महात्मा गांधी

- बुद्धि के बिना मनुष्य अपंग के समान है। **—महात्मा गांधी**
- खाली दिमाग को खुला दिमाग बना देना ही शिक्षा का उद्देश्य है।

—फोर्ब्स

- अठारह वर्ष की उम्र तक इकट्ठा किए गए पूर्वग्रहों का नाम ही सामान्य बुद्धि है। **—आइंस्टीन**

- गिने-चुने लोग ही वर्ष में दो या तीन से अधिक बार सोचते हैं या मैंने हफ्ते में एक या दो बार सोचकर अंतरराष्ट्रीय छवि बना ली है। **—जॉर्ज बर्नार्ड शॉ**

- बुद्धि का दुरुपयोग हुआ तो वह संसार में बड़े से बड़ा अनर्थ करने का कारण बन जाती है। **—महात्मा गांधी**

- संसार में बुद्धि-बल बहुत बड़ा बल है। **—महात्मा गांधी**

- दिन-रात बुद्धिमानों के बीच रहते-रहते बुद्धि कुंठित हो जाती है। **—रवींद्रनाथ टैगोर**

- जब सब लोग एक समान सोच रहे हों तो समझो कि कोई भी नहीं सोच रहा। **—जॉन वुडेन**

- पठन तो मस्तिष्क को केवल ज्ञान की सामग्री उपलब्ध कराता है या यह तो चिंतन है, जो पठित चीज को अपना बना देता है। **—जॉन लॉक**

- एकाग्र-चिंतन वांछित फल देता है। **—जिग जिग्लर**

- दिमाग पैराशूट के समान है, वह तभी कार्य करता है, जब खुला हो। **—जेम्स देवर**

- अगर हमारी सभ्यता को जीवित रखना है तो हमें महान् लोगों के विचारों के आगे झुकने की आदत छोड़नी पड़ेगी। बड़े लोग बड़ी गलतियाँ करते हैं। **—कार्ल पापर**

- बुद्धि का एक लक्षण यह भी है कि वह सरल वस्तु को भी जटिल बना देती है। पृथ्वी पर बड़े-बड़े विद्वानों के नहीं रहने से पृथ्वी के अनेक काम सरलता से संपादित होते हैं। **—रवींद्रनाथ टैगोर**

- सारी चीजों के बारे मैं कुछ-कुछ और कुछेक के बारे मैं सबकुछ सीखने की कोशिश करनी चाहिए। **—थॉमस हक्स्ले**

- शिक्षा प्राप्त करने के तीन आधार-स्तंभ हैं—अधिक निरीक्षण करना, अधिक अनुभव करना और अधिक अध्ययन करना। **—केथराल**
- शिक्षा राष्ट्र की सस्ती सुरक्षा है। **—बर्क**
- अपनी अज्ञानता का एहसास होना ज्ञान की दिशा में एक बहुत बड़ा कदम है। **—डिजरायली**
- बुद्धि एक खजाना है, लेकिन अभ्यास इसकी चाभी है। **—थामस फुलर**

बोझ

- चारों ओर फैली हुई उत्साहहीन जीवनहीन जड़ता के समान भारी बोझ दूसरा नहीं है। **—रवींद्रनाथ टैगोर**

ब्रह्मचर्य

- ब्रह्मचर्य-व्रत पालन के चार उपाय हैं—पहला है, उसकी आवश्यकता को अच्छी तरह समझना, दूसरा है इंद्रियों को धीरे-धीरे वश में करना, तीसरा है शुद्ध साथी, शुद्ध मित्र और शुद्ध पुस्तकें रखना और चौथा है नित्य नियमपूर्वक रामनाम दिल से लेना और ईश्वर की कृपा की याचना। **—महात्मा गांधी**
- ब्रह्मचर्य भी अन्य व्रतों के समान ही सत्य से निकलता है और उसी के वास्ते है। **—महात्मा गांधी**
- ब्रह्मचर्य का पालन मन, वचन और कर्म से करना चाहिए। **—महात्मा गांधी**
- ब्रह्मचारी को जीने के लिए ही खाना चाहिए। **—महात्मा गांधी**
- ब्रह्मचारी आँखों का उपयोग देव-दर्शन के लिए करता है और कानों का हरिकथा-श्रवण के लिए, जबकि अब्रह्मचारी भोग-विलास और अश्लीलता देखने और श्रृंगार-रस के गीत सुनने का प्रेमी होता है। **—महात्मा गांधी**
- ब्रह्मचर्य जीवन की पहली सीढ़ी है। बिना इसको नियमपूर्वक्र चढ़े आदमी ऊपर नहीं पहुँच सकता। **—महात्मा गांधी**

ब्राह्मण

- ब्राह्मण को भी बहुतों का मंगल साधना है, इसीलिए वह भी समूह के संसर्ग से वंचित है। **—रवींद्रनाथ टैगोर**
- एक ओर देवता और दूसरी ओर भक्त, दोनों के बीच सेतु-रूप ब्राह्मण दोनों को मिलता है।

  —रवींद्रनाथ टैगोर
- भक्ति-विफलता ब्राह्मण के उपयोग की चीज नहीं है, ब्राह्मण-ज्ञान के शिखर पर बैठकर इस भक्ति के रस को सर्वसाधारण के उपभोग के लिए, कुछ रखने के लिए तपस्या करता है। **—अज्ञात**
- संसार में ब्राह्मण के लिए आराम का योग नहीं है, वैसे ही देवार्चना में भी ब्राह्मण के लिए भक्ति का योग नहीं है। इसी में ब्राह्मण का गौरव है।

  —रवींद्रनाथ टैगोर
- संसार में ब्राह्मण के लिए नियम-संयम है, धर्म-साधना में ब्राह्मण के लिए ज्ञान है। **—रवींद्रनाथ टैगोर**

भक्ति

- भक्ति कोई तेल भीगी बत्ती नहीं, यह तो आग है। **—अज्ञात**
- भक्ति में आदमी के समान होने पर कोई बाधा नहीं आती। भक्ति में पूज्य, पुजारी को ऊपर खींचकर अपने समान करना चाहता है, इसीलिए समान होने का आनंद उसमें बराबर मिलता है। **—रवींद्रनाथ टैगोर**

भगवान्

- भगवान् केवल रसना से ही नहीं, एक-एक अंग से बोलते हैं।

  —रवींद्रनाथ टैगोर

भद्रता

- स्त्रियों से स्वभावतः कुछ दूरी रखकर चलना ही पुरुष के लिए भद्रता है।

  —चाणक्य

भय

- भय है मन की नास्तिकता। उसे नकारात्मक रूप से परास्त नहीं किया जा सकता। उसका एक कारण समाप्त होते ही दूसरा उत्पन्न होता है और वह जटिल रहता है। **—रवींद्रनाथ टैगोर**

- जिसे भविष्य का भय नहीं रहता, वही वर्तमान का आनंद उठा सकता है। **—अज्ञात**

- भय ही पतन और पाप का निश्चित कारण है। **—स्वामी विवेकानंद**

- जैसे ही भय आपकी ओर बढ़े, उस पर आक्रमण करते हुए उसे नष्ट कर दो। **—चाणक्य**

- जो चुनौतियों का सामना करने से डरता है, उसका असफल होना तय है। **—अज्ञात**

- भय से तब तक ही डरना चाहिए, जब तक भय पास न आया हो। आए हुए भय को देखकर बिना शंका के उस पर प्रहार करना चाहिए। **—पंचतंत्र**

- जो लोग भय का हेतु अथवा हर्ष का कारण उपस्थित होने पर भी विचार-विमर्श से काम लेते हैं तथा कार्य को जल्दी से नहीं कर डालते, वे कभी भी संताप को प्राप्त नहीं होते। **—पंचतंत्र**

- 'भय' और 'घृणा', ये दोनों भाई-बहन लाख बुरे हों, पर अपनी माँ बर्बरता के प्रति बहुत ही भक्ति रखते हैं। जो कोई इनका सहारा लेना चाहता है, उसे ये सबसे पहले अपनी माँ के चरणों में डाल जाते हैं। **—बर्ट्रेंड रसेल**

- मित्र से, अमित्र से, ज्ञात से, अज्ञात से हम सबके लिए अभय हो। रात्रि के समय हम सब निर्भय हों और सब दिशाओं में रहनेवाले हमारे मित्र बनकर रहें। **—अथर्ववेद**

- 'हिंसा' को आप सर्वाधिक शक्ति संपन्न मानते हैं तो मानें, पर एक बात निश्चित है कि हिंसा का आश्रय लेने पर बलवान व्यक्ति भी सदा 'भय' से प्रताड़ित रहता है। दूसरी ओर हमें तीन वस्तुओं की आवश्यकता है—अनुभव

करने के लिए हृदय की, कल्पना करने के लिए मस्तिष्क की और काम करने के लिए हाथ की। **—स्वामी विवेकानंद**

- आदमी सिर्फ दो लीवर के द्वारा चलता रहता है—डर तथा स्वार्थ।

—नेपोलियन

- डर सदैव अज्ञानता से पैदा होता है। **—एमर्सन**

भरोसा

- बहुत अधिक भरोसा करने पर हो सकता है आप धोखा खा जाएँ, लेकिन यदि आप पर्याप्त भरोसा नहीं करेंगे तो आप पीड़ा में जिएँगे। **—फ्रैंक क्रेन**
- जब मैं तार्किक होती हूँ और अपने सहज ज्ञान पर भरोसा नहीं करती, तभी मैं मुसीबत में पड़ जाती हूँ। **—एंजेलिना जोली**
- जिस काम को चाहते हो, उसमें अपना विश्वास रखो, उसे करना जारी रखो और वह तुम्हें वहाँ ले जाएगा, जहाँ तुम्हें जाने की जरूरत है।

—नताली गोल्डबर्ग

- सबसे जरूरी बात, जो मैंने इस लंबे जीवन में सीखी है, वह यह कि किसी व्यक्ति को विश्वसनीय बनाने का एक ही तरीका है, उस पर विश्वास करना या और किसी को अविश्वसनीय बनाने का पक्का तरीका है, उस पर विश्वास न करना। **—हेनरी एल स्टिम्सन**
- बहुत दूर रह रहे पति पर कभी भरोसा मत करो और न ही बहुत करीब रह रहे कुँवारे पर। **—हेलेन रोलैंड**
- दिखावे पर बहुत अधिक भरोसा मत करो। **—वरजिल**
- किसी पर पूरी तरह से भरोसा करना आनंदित करनेवाला है।

—जेफ गोडब्लम

- अपनी याददाश्त पर भरोसा मत करो, यह छिद्रों से भरा जाल है, सबसे खूबसूरत उपहार इससे निकल जाते हैं। **—जॉर्ज डुहामेल**

- क्या तुम किसी ऐसे व्यक्ति के साथ व्यापार करना चाहोगे, जो 99 प्रतिशत ईमानदार हो। **—सिडनी मैडवेड**

- आपको किसी-न-किसी चीज में विश्वास करना ही होगा अपने गट्स में, अपनी डेस्टिनी में, अपनी जिंदगी या फिर अपने कर्म में। **—स्टीव जॉब्स**

- प्रेम का सबसे अच्छा प्रमाण विश्वास है। **—जोयस ब्रदर्स**

- किसी पर भरोसा किया जा सकता है कि नहीं, यह जानने का सबसे अच्छा तरीका है, उस पर भरोसा करना है। **—अर्नेस्ट हेमिंग्वे**

- विश्वास करो, लेकिन जाँच कर लो। **—रोनाल्ड रीगन**

- वह जो अधिक भरोसा नहीं करता, उस पर भरोसा नहीं किया जाएगा। **—लाओत्जू**

- मैं, मैं बेईमान हूँ और आप एक बेईमान का हमेशा बेईमान होने पर भरोसा कर सकते हैं। ईमानदारी से कहूँ तो ये ईमानदार लोग होते हैं, जिनको देखना पड़ता है। **—जॉनी डेप्प**

- किसी को उस औरत पर कभी भी भरोसा नहीं करना चाहिए, जो अपनी सही उम्र बता दे। जो औरत यह बता सकती है, वह कुछ भी बता सकती है। **—ऑस्कर वाइल्ड**

- सभी से प्रेम करो, कुछ पर भरोसा करो, किसी के साथ गलत मत करो। **—विलियम शेक्सपियर**

- मैं इसलिए परेशान नहीं हूँ कि तुमने मुझसे झूठ कहा, मैं परेशान हूँ कि मैं अब से तुम पर भरोसा नहीं कर सकूँगा। **—फ्रीडरिच नैतजस्चे**

- मैं उन लोगों पर भरोसा नहीं करती, जो खुद से प्यार नहीं करते और फिर भी मुझसे कहते हैं, मैं तुमसे प्यार करता हूँ। एक अफ्रीकी कहावत है—जब कोई नंगा आदमी अपनी शर्ट दे तो उससे सावधान रहिए। **—माया एंगेलो**

- क्या आप में इतना साहस है कि प्यार पर एक और बार भरोसा करें तथा हमेशा एक और बार भरोसा करें। **—माया एंगेलो**
- हममें से कोई नहीं जानता कि अगले क्षण क्या होगा, फिर भी हम आगे बढ़ते हैं। क्योंकि हम भरोसा करते हैं, क्योंकि हमारे अंदर आस्था है। **—पाउलो कोएलो**
- हम सभी से कभी-न-कभी गलतियाँ होती हैं, कभी-कभी हम गलत चीजें करते हैं, ऐसी चीजें, जिनके परिणाम बुरे होते हैं, पर इसका यह मतलब नहीं है कि हम बुरे हैं या इसके बाद हम पर कभी भी विश्वास नहीं किया जा सकता। **—एलिसन क्रोगन**
- झूठ बोलने के हर एक अच्छे कारण के बदले में सच कहने का उससे भी अच्छा कारण होता है। **—बो बेनेट**
- सीधे व्यक्ति का विश्वास ही झूठे व्यक्ति का सबसे उपयोगी साधन है। **—स्टीफेन किंग**
- विश्वासघात होने से पहले विश्वास को होना होगा। **—सुजेन कोलिंस**
- विश्वास किया जाना प्रेम किए जाने से बेहतर प्रशंसा है। **—जॉर्ज मैकडोनाल्ड**
- भरोसा करना सीखना जीवन के सबसे कठिन कार्यों में से एक है। **—आइजैक वाट्स**
- ईश्वर पर प्रश्न उठाना छोड़ो और उस पर भरोसा करना शुरू करो। **—जोएल ऑस्टीन**
- जब तक सच जूते पहन रहा हो, तब तक एक झूठ आधी दुनिया की सैर कर सकता है। **—चार्ल्स स्परजन**
- कभी ऐसे व्यक्ति पर विश्वास मत करिए, जिसे वह चाहिए, जो आपके पास है। दोस्त हो या नहीं, जलन एक सशक्त भावना है। **—यूबी ब्लेक**

- सबसे जरूरी चीज, जो मैंने सीखी है, वह है हर परिस्थिति में ईश्वर पर भरोसा करना। **—ऐलिसन फेलिक्स**
- जो श्रद्धा धर्म के लिए है, वही विश्वास मानवीय संबंधों के लिए है, यह शुरुआती बिंदु है, ऐसी नींव जिस पर और अधिक निर्माण किया जा सकता है। जहाँ विश्वास है, वहाँ प्रेम फल-फूल सकता है। **—बारबरा स्मिथ**
- अपनी इंट्यूशन पर भरोसा करो। आमतौर पर वे उन तथ्यों पर आधारित होती हैं, जो जागरूकता के स्तर से नीचे मौजूद होती हैं। **—जॉयस ब्रदर्स**
- खुद पर भरोसा करो, तब तुम जान पाओगे कि कैसे जिया जाए। **—जॉन वोल्फगैंग वोन गोएथे**
- यकीन रखो, तुम जितना सोचते हो, उससे अधिक जानते हो। **—बेंजामिन स्पोक**
- जो आदमी किसी पर भरोसा नहीं करता, वह किसी के द्वारा भरोसा न किए जाने के उपयुक्त है। **—हैरोल्ड मैकमिलन**
- आप पानी पर भरोसा नहीं कर सकते, यहाँ तक कि एक सीधी छड़ी भी इसमें तिरछी नजर आती है। **—डब्ल्यू सी फील्ड्स**
- उम्र चार चीजों में सबसे अच्छी प्रतीत होती है, जलाने के लिए पुरानी लकड़ी, पीने के लिए पुरानी शराब, भरोसा करने के लिए पुराने दोस्त और पढ़ने के लिए पुराने लेखक। **—फ्रांसिस बेकन**
- जब ट्रेन किसी सुरंग से निकलती है और अँधेरा हो जाता है, तब आप अपना टिकट फेंककर ट्रेन से कूद नहीं जाते। आप बैठे रहते हैं और इंजीनियर पर भरोसा रखते हैं। **—कौरी टेन बूम**
- एक शादी की सालगिरह प्यार, विश्वास, साझेदारी, सहिष्णुता और तप का उत्सव है। हर साल के लिए बस क्रम भिन्न होता है। **—पॉल स्वीनी**
- केवल एक गोरा व्यक्ति, जिस पर आप यकीन कर सकते हैं, वह है मरा हुआ गोरा व्यक्ति। **—रॉबर्ट मुगाबे**

- बुद्धि समय-समय पर धोखा देती है और यह समझदारी है कि जिसने तुम्हें एक बार भी धोखा दिया हो, उस पर कभी पूरी तरह से भरोसा मत करो।

—रीन डेसकार्टेस

- विश्वास जीवन का गोंद है, यह प्रभावी संचार का सबसे अनिवार्य अंग है, यह सभी रिश्तों को जोड़नेवाला मूलभूत सिद्धांत है। **—स्टीफेन कोवी**

- मैं किसी पर भरोसा नहीं करता, खुद पर भी नहीं।

—जोसफ स्टालिन

- दूसरों पर भरोसा करना अच्छा है, लेकिन ऐसा न करना कहीं ज्यादा अच्छा है। **—बेनिटो मुसोलिनी**

- विश्वास अर्जित करना होता है और यह केवल समय बीतने के साथ आना चाहिए। **—आर्थर ऐश**

- हर एक तानाशाह के हृदय में अंत में एक छाहर रह जाता है कि वह किसी दोस्त पर भरोसा नहीं कर सकता। **—ऐस्किलस**

- अगर तुम्हें पायलट पर भरोसा नहीं है तो मत जाओ। **—डेंजेल वाशिंगटन**

- यकीन आस्था के जैसा नहीं है। एक दोस्त कोई ऐसा होता है, जिस पर आप भरोसा कर सकते हैं। किसी में आस्था रखना एक गलती है।

—क्रिस्टोफर हिचेंस

- कभी मुसीबत में पड़े व्यक्ति की सलाह पर यकीन मत करो। **—एसोप**

- जिम्मेदारी उसे दी जाती है, जिस पर भरोसा होता है। जिम्मेदारी हमेशा भरोसे का संकेत होती है। **—जेम्स कैश पेन्नी**

- भरोसा करना मुश्किल है, यह जानना कि किस पर भरोसा किया जाए और भी मुश्किल है। **—मारिया वी सिंडर**

- भरोसा सच के साथ शुरू होता है और सच के साथ खत्म।

—संतोष कलवार

• शांति और विश्वास बनने में सालों लगते हैं और टूटने में कुछ पल।

—महोगनी सिल्वरराइन

• जो कोई भी कहता है कि उसे पता है, उनसे सावधान रहिए। मुझ पर भरोसा करिए यह उन्हें नहीं पता, यह नहीं तो उन्हें कहना नहीं पड़ता कि उन्हें पता है। **—हार्वे फैरस्टीन**

• एक बगीचा बहुत बड़ा शिक्षक होता है। वह हमें धैर्य और सावधानीपूर्वक देखना सिखाता है या वह हमें मेहनत और किफायत सिखाता है और सबसे बढ़कर वह हमें विश्वास करना सिखाता है।

—गरट्रूड जेकिल

• लोग आपकी जिंदगी में आते हैं और चले जाते हैं। बस आपको भरोसा करना होता है कि जिंदगी ने आपके लिए एक रोड बना रखी है।

—ऑर्लेंडो ब्लूम

• आपको लोगों पर विश्वास और भरोसा करना पड़ता है, नहीं तो जिंदगी असंभव हो जाती है। **—ऐंटन चेखोव**

• अपने अंदर की उस हल्की सी आवाज, जो कहती है, क्या वह रोचक नहीं होता अगर…, पर भरोसा करिए और फिर उसे कर डालिए।

—डुआने मिचलस

• विश्वास मर जाता है, लेकिन अविश्वास फलता-फूलता रहता है।

—सोफोकल्स

• केवल खुद पर भरोसा करो और कोई तुम्हें धोखा नहीं दे पाएगा।

—विलियम पेन्न

• विश्वास स्थिरता के साथ बनता है। **—लिंकन चेफी**

• जहाँ बहुत बड़ी रकम की बात हो, वहाँ किसी पर भरोसा न करना उचित है। **—अगाथा क्रिस्टी**

• अपना ट्रस्ट मनी में मत रखो, बल्कि अपनी मनी ट्रस्ट में रखो।

—ओलिवर वेंडेल होम्स

• जीवन एक उपहार है, बस भरोसा करो, एक बच्चे की तरह।

—ऐनी मोरो लिंडबर्ग

• जीवन में जो कुछ भी होता है, अच्छा है, बस उसमें विश्वास रखो।

—ऑर्लेंडो ब्लूम

भलाई

• भलाई में आनंद है, क्योंकि वह तुम्हारे स्वास्थ्य और सुख में वृद्धि करती है। **—जरथ्रुष्ट**

• भलाई करना मानवता है, भला होना दिव्यता है। **—ला मार्टिन**

• भलाई अमरत्व की ओर ले जाती है, बुराई विनाश की ओर। **—ह्विमैन**

भविष्य

• भविष्य के बारे में पूर्वकथन का सबसे अच्छा तरीका भविष्य का निर्माण करना है। **—डॉ. शाकली**

• अपने भविष्य का निर्माण स्वयं कीजिए। **—बिल गेट्स**

• अपने भाग्य के निर्माता स्वयं बनिए। **—बिल गेट्स**

• रात में देर तक कठिन परिश्रम कीजिए। सदैव अपने परिवेश के बारे में चैतन्य रहिए। आप जो कुछ देखते हैं, वही संसार है। वर्तमान के रूप में ही भविष्य आपके सामने आएगा। **—बिल गेट्स**

• किसी भी व्यक्ति का अतीत जैसा भी हो, भविष्य सदैव बेदाग होता है।

—जॉन राइस

भाग्य

• सारा उत्तरदायित्व अपने कंधों पर लो। याद रखो कि तुम स्वयं अपने भाग्य के निर्माता हो। तुम जो कुछ बल या सहायता चाहो, सब तुम्हारे ही भीतर विद्यमान है।

- भाग्य के ऊपर किसका वश चल सकता है? —**अज्ञात**
- अप्रसन्न भाग्य पर क्रोध करके उसको दोगुना घातक बना देना चोर के ऊपर क्रोध करके जमीन पर भात खाने के समान है। —**रवींद्रनाथ टैगोर**
- उत्साह आदमी की भाग्यशीलता का पैमाना है। —**तिरुवल्लुवर**
- भाग्य साहसी का साथ देता है। —**अज्ञात**
- मनुष्य स्वयं अपने भाग्य का निर्माता है। —**अज्ञात**
- भाग्य साहसी का मित्र है। —**अज्ञात**
- मानव अपने भाग्य का स्वयं निर्माता है। —**स्वामी रामतीर्थ**
- भाग्य भी निडर का ही साथ देता है। —**वर्जल**
- हम स्वयं अपने भविष्य का निर्माण करते हैं, फिर इसे भाग्य का नाम दे देते हैं। —**अज्ञात**

भारत

- भारत हमारी संपूर्ण (मानव) जाति की जननी है तथा संस्कृत यूरोप की सभी भाषाओं की जननी है—भारतमाता हमारे दर्शनशास्त्र की जननी है, अरबों के रास्ते हमारे अधिकांश गणित के जनक हैं, महात्मा बुद्ध के रास्ते ईसाइयत में निहित आदर्शों के जनक हैं, ग्रामीण समाज के रास्ते स्व-शासन और लोकतंत्र के जनक हैं। अनेक प्रकार से भारत माता हम सबकी माता है। —**विल्ल डुरांट**
- हम भारतीयों के बहुत ऋणी हैं, जिन्होंने हमें गिनना सिखाया, जिसके बिना कोई भी मूल्यवान वैज्ञानिक खोज संभव नहीं होती। —**अल्बर्ट आइंस्टीन**
- भारत मानव जाति का पलना है, मानव-भाषा की जन्मस्थली है, इतिहास की जननी है, पौराणिक कथाओं की दादी है और प्रथाओं की परदादी है। मानव

इतिहास की हमारी सबसे कीमती और सबसे ज्ञान-गर्भित सामग्री केवल भारत में ही संचित है।

—मार्क ट्वेन

- यदि इस धरातल पर कोई स्थान है, जहाँ पर जीवित मानव के सभी स्वप्नों को तब से घर मिला हुआ है, जब मानव ने अस्तित्व के सपने देखना आरंभ किया था, तो वह भारत ही है।

—रोम्याँ रोलाँ

- भारत ने अपनी सीमा के पार एक भी सैनिक भेजे बिना चीन को जीत लिया और लगभग बीस शताब्दियों तक उस पर सांस्कृतिक रूप से राज किया।

—हू शिह

- यूनान, मिस्र, रोमां, सब मिट गए जहाँ से। अब तक मगर है बाकी, नाम-ओ-निशाँ हमारा। कुछ बात है कि हस्ती, मिटती नहीं हमारी। सदियों रहा है दुश्मन, दौर-ए-जहाँ हमारा।

—मुहम्मद इकबाल

- अगर कोई देश है, जो मानवता के लिए पूर्ण और आदर्श है, तो एशिया की ओर उँगली उठाऊँगा, जहाँ भारत है।

—मैक्समूलर

- भारत मानवता का पलना है, इसके ऊँचे हिमालय से ज्ञान-विज्ञान की सरिताएँ निकली हैं। सृष्टि की उषा में इसका आँगन ज्ञान से आलोकित हुआ था। मैं भगवान् से प्रार्थना करता हूँ कि भारत का अतीत मेरी मातृभूमि के भविष्य में बदल जाए।

—जैको लाइट

- जब तुम भारत के सान्निध्य में आओगे तो तुम्हें अनश्वर शांति का दिव्य मार्ग मिलेगा।

—विल डूरंट

- देवता गीत गाते हैं कि स्वर्ग और अपवर्ग की मार्गभूत भारत भूमि के भाग में जनमे लोग देवताओं की अपेक्षा भी अधिक धन्य हैं, अर्थात् स्वर्ग और अपवर्ग (मोक्ष-कैवल्य) के मार्ग स्वरूप भारत-भूमि को धन्य-धन्य कहते हुए देवगण इसका शौर्य-गान गाते हैं। यहाँ पर मनुष्य जन्म पाना देवत्व पद प्राप्त करने से भी बढ़कर है।

—विष्णु पुराण

- भारत वस्तुतः विश्व पुरुष की कुंडलिनी शक्ति है। जब भारत जाग्रत् होगा तो

विश्व पुरुष का देवता में रूपांतरण हो जाएगा। अगर भारत सो गया, न जागा तो विश्व-मानवता ही समाप्त हो जाएगी।

—श्रीअरविंद

- मैं भौगोलिक मूर्तिपूजा में विश्वास नहीं करता हूँ। मेरा भारत जड़ भारत नहीं है, अपितु वह ज्ञानालोक है, जिसका आविर्भाव ऋषियों की आत्मा में हुआ है। **—रवींद्रनाथ टैगोर**
- जब यूरोप के लोग भारतीय दर्शन के संपर्क में आएँगे तो उनके विचार और आस्थाएँ बदलेंगी। वे बदले हुए लोग यूरोप के विचारों और विश्वास को प्रभावित करेंगे। आगे चलकर यूरोप में ही ईसाई-धर्म के लिए संकट उत्पन्न हो जाएगा। **—शापेन हावर**
- अब तक भारतवर्ष अपनी अभ्यंतर व्यवस्था के बल पर ही बचा रहा है। **—रवींद्रनाथ टैगोर**
- भारतवर्ष ने जिस साधना को ग्रहण किया है, वह है विश्व-ब्रह्मांड के साथ चित्त का योग, आत्मा का योग अर्थात् संपूर्ण योग, केवल ज्ञान का नहीं, बोध का योग। **—रवींद्रनाथ टैगोर**
- पश्चिम निरंतर ऐसी यांत्रिक शक्ति उत्पन्न कर रहा है, जो उसके आत्मिक निमंत्रण से बढ़कर है तथा भारत ने यांत्रिक नियंत्रण की ऐसी पद्धति रची है, जो उसकी जीवन-शक्ति से बढ़कर है। **—रवींद्रनाथ टैगोर**

भारतीय

- हम भारतीय हैं, पहले और आखिर में। **—बी.आर. आंबेडकर**

भाव

- जिसका जो सत्य भाव है, उसी पर डटे रहना अच्छा है। अनेक बार खोटे काम के अंदर ऊँचा भाव भरकर हम ऊँचे भाव का भी महत्त्व फीका कर देते हैं।

—तिरुवल्लुवर

- भाव का सौंदर्य जब तक कृत्रिम भूषण और तरह-तरह के अलंकारों से

लदकर नहीं आता, तब तक हम उसका आदर ही नहीं करते।

—रवींद्रनाथ टैगोर

- भाव की बात को बार-बार अनुभव करके भी थकावट का बोध नहीं होता।

—अज्ञात

भाषा

- भाषा एक नगर है, जिसके निर्माण के लिए प्रत्येक व्यक्ति एक-एक पत्थर लाया है। **—एमर्सन**

- भाषा हमारे सोचने के तरीके को स्वरूप प्रदान करती है और निर्धारित करती है कि हम क्या-क्या सोच सकते हैं। **—बेंजामिन होर्फ**

- आर्थिक युद्ध का एक सूत्र है कि किसी राष्ट्र को नष्ट करने का सुनिश्चित तरीका है, उसकी मुद्रा को खोटा कर देना और यह भी उतना ही सत्य है कि किसी राष्ट्र की संस्कृति और पहचान को नष्ट करने का सुनिश्चित तरीका है, उसकी भाषा को हीन बना देना, लेकिन यदि विचार भाषा को भ्रष्ट करते हैं तो भाषा भी विचारों को भ्रष्ट कर सकती है। **—जॉर्ज ओर्वेल**

- जो एक विदेशी भाषा नहीं जानता, वह अपनी भाषा के बारे में कुछ नहीं जानता। **—गोथे**

- शिकायत करने की अपनी गहरी आवश्यकता को संतुष्ट करने के लिए ही मनुष्य ने भाषा ईजाद की है। **—लिली टॉमलिन**

भीड़

- भीड़ की मानसिकता एक अंधी शक्ति होती है। **—रवींद्रनाथ टैगोर**

- जनता की भीड़ ही मेरे लिए युद्ध का घोड़ा है। मेरा आसन उसकी पीठ है, उसकी रास मेरे हाथों में है, वह अपना कर्तव्य नहीं जानती। सिर्फ मैं जानता हूँ, उसे कहाँ पहुँचना है। काँटों से उसके पाँव लहूलुहान हो जाएँगे, कीचड़ से उसकी देह सन जाएगी, फिर भी मैं उसे दौड़ाता जाऊँगा।

—रवींद्रनाथ टैगोर

भूल

- जो भूल देह-मन को दु:ख पहुँचाती है, वह अधर्म है···भूल चाहे जैसी भी हो, उससे दु:ख तो मिलेगा ही। **—अज्ञात**

भ्रम

- आदमी अपने को जो समझता है, वह दरअसल होता नहीं है। इसलिए अघटनीय घटनाएँ घटती हैं। **—रवींद्रनाथ टैगोर**

मंदिर

- मंदिरों में मेरा विश्वास है—यह सिद्ध करने के लिए कोई जरूरी नहीं कि मैं मंदिरों में जाऊँ ही। इतना काफी है कि ईश्वर में मेरा विश्वास है और मैं प्रतिदिन उसकी पूजा करता हूँ और यह पूजा मात्र एक आडंबर नहीं होती, बल्कि मेरे आध्यात्मिक आहार का एक अनिवार्य अंग होती है। हाँ, मैं प्रतिदिन खुले मैदान में होनेवाली प्रार्थना में शामिल होने के लिए हरिजनों को खास तौर से जरूर आमंत्रित करता हूँ, लेकिन ऐसा उन्हें सनातनी-मंदिरों में जाने की इच्छा से विमुख करने के लिए नहीं करता। **—महात्मा गांधी**
- मानव हृदय ही सच्चा मंदिर है। उसी के भीतर तलवार पर शान चढ़ाई जाती है और एक हजार नरबलि दी जाती है। देवमंदिर में तो मात्र इसका सामान्य अभिनय होता है। **—रवींद्रनाथ टैगोर**

मजदूर

- यह बात सच नहीं है कि सिर्फ काम ही मानव जीवन का आदि-अंत है। आदमी सिर्फ मजदूर नहीं है, भले ही वह सत्य की मजदूरी हो या फिर धर्म की मजदूरी हो। **—भर्तृहरि**
- पैसा जगत् में बहुत-कुछ कर सकता है, किंतु मजदूर का यह मानना घोर अंधविश्वास है कि वह पैसेवालों का दास है, यह अज्ञान का लक्षण है। **—महात्मा गांधी**
- मिल-मालिकों के साथ हमें लड़ना पड़े, तो भी उनसे द्वेष नहीं करना है,

उनके साथ लड़ना ही हो तो इस तरह लड़ें, जैसे कि आप माँ या अपनी स्त्री या बच्चों के साथ लड़ते-झगड़ते हैं। एक ही रक्त-मांस के मनुष्यों के साथ जिस तरह और जैसे प्रसंग के लिए, जितने प्रेम और वेदना से तथा आदर और विनय से हम लड़ते हैं, उसी तरह मिल-मालिकों के साथ लड़ें।

—महात्मा गांधी

- यदि मजदूर स्वाधीन रहना चाहते हों, स्वाभिमान की रक्षा करना चाहते हों और आजीविका के बारे में निर्भय रहना चाहते हों, तो उन्हें आजीविका के अनेक साधन अपनाने चाहिए। मेरी राय में विविध धंधों को कर सकने की शक्ति मजदूर वर्ग के लिए वैसी ही वस्तु है, जैसी पूँजीपति के लिए उसकी पूँजी, जैसे पूँजीपति अपनी पूँजी को मजदूर के सहयोग के बिना सफल नहीं बना सकता, वैसे ही मजदूर अपने श्रम को पूँजी के सहयोग के बिना सफल नहीं बना सकता। यदि मजदूर और पूँजीपति दोनों में बुद्धि हो और दोनों को सामान्यतया एक-दूसरे की शक्ति के सहयोग का भरोसा रहे, तो वे एक-दूसरे के प्रति सम्मानपूर्ण व्यवहार की आवश्यकता को समझने लगें।

—महात्मा गांधी

मत

- भगवान् ने तुम्हें जिस जगह भेज दिया है, वह चाहे जैसी भी हो; लेकिन यदि तुम्हारा मत तुम्हें वहाँ से खींचकर हटा ले जाएगा तो उससे कभी तुम्हारे मत की जय नहीं होगी।

—रवींद्रनाथ टैगोर

मन

- अभावनीय परिहास से मनोविज्ञान को धोखा देने के लिए मन की सृष्टि हुई है।

—श्रीराम शर्मा आचार्य

- मनुष्य का मन कभी ठीक रहता है, कभी नहीं रहता···सब दिन एक समान थोड़े ही होते हैं?

—रवींद्रनाथ टैगोर

- जिस समय मन व्यक्तिगत कारणों से उत्तेजित हो, उस समय क्या ठीक से विचार हो सकता है।

—रवींद्रनाथ टैगोर

• मन हमारी बहुत ही भलाई करता है, परंतु उसकी आदत ही ऐसी है कि वह हमारे साथ कभी भी अच्छी तरह हिल-मिल नहीं सकता।

—रवींद्रनाथ टैगोर

• मन के साथ हमारी शत्रुता इतनी है कि जिस काम में उसका जितना ही कम हाथ होगा, हम उसका उतना ही आदर करेंगे। **—रवींद्रनाथ टैगोर**

• पूँछ के साथ मन का इतना ही फर्क है कि मन आगे दौड़ता है और पूँछ पीछे पड़ी रहती है। इसीलिए दुनिया में पूँछ हेय दृष्टि से देखी जाती है और मन आदर की दृष्टि से। **—रवींद्रनाथ टैगोर**

• हमारा मन नियमों की परिधि से बाहर है, उस पर किसी का अंकुश नहीं है।

—अज्ञात

• समाज जैसा विचित्र होता है, मन भी वैसा ही विचित्र होता है।

—रवींद्रनाथ टैगोर

• मन का चलाचल जितना अधिक होता है, मनुष्य उतना ही बड़ा होता है। मनुष्य को शक्ति देने के लिए मन को विस्तृत करना चाहिए।

—रवींद्रनाथ टैगोर

मनुष्य

• आचार-संचालित मनुष्य कठपुतली की तरह है। **—रवींद्रनाथ टैगोर**

• मनुष्य का मूल्यांकन इस आधार पर किया जाना चाहिए कि उसने कितने दोस्त या दुश्मन बनाए हैं। **—फ्रेंकलिन रूजवेल्ट**

• मनुष्य का परिवर्तन मनुष्यत्व की राह पर ही होगा—बच्चा क्रम से बूढ़ा हो जाता है, लेकिन मनुष्य सहसा कुत्ता-बिल्ली तो नहीं हो जाता।

—रवींद्रनाथ टैगोर

• किसी राष्ट्र की संस्कृति उसके लोगों के दिलों और आत्माओं में बसती है।

—महात्मा गांधी

- आदमी में, यदि भाव से अभाव को ढककर रखने की शक्ति न होती तो अब तक मनुष्य, मनुष्य न रह जाता, बल्कि पशुतुल्य हो गया होता।

—रवींद्रनाथ टैगोर

- किसी भी देश की संस्कृति उसके लोगों के हृदय और आत्मा में बसती है।

—महात्मा गांधी

- ईश्वर ने मनुष्य को विचित्र ही बनाया है और विचित्र ही रखना चाहता है।

—रवींद्रनाथ टैगोर

- अकृतज्ञता मनुष्यत्व का विष है। **—सर पी. सिडनी**

- मानव द्वारा अपनाया जानेवाला विवेक व माधुर्य समाज को प्रसन्नता प्रदान करता है। **—अज्ञात**

- मनुष्य भूल करता है, असफल भी होता है, दुःख भी पाता है, लेकिन बैठा नहीं रहता, जो उचित समझता है, उसके लिए आत्म-समर्पण करता है।

—रवींद्रनाथ टैगोर

- जिन पापों को मनुष्य करना पसंद करते हैं, उन्हें सुनना पसंद नहीं करते।

—अज्ञात

- बेचारे मनुष्य को ऐसा ही बनाया गया है कि वह जितना आसान तरीका अपनाना चाहता है, उतना ही वह जटिल बंधन में जकड़ा जाता है।

—रवींद्रनाथ टैगोर

- मनुष्य बड़ा आश्चर्यनक, बड़ा रहस्यमय प्राणी है। उसके द्वारा और भी कितने गहरे रहस्यों का निर्माण हो रहा है, यह तो भगवान् रुद्र ही जानते हैं।

—रवींद्रनाथ टैगोर

मर्यादा

- हर कोई अपनी मर्यादा की रक्षा स्वयं न करता रहे तो वह न केवल जाने-अनजाने अपना अनिष्ट कर बैठता है, बल्कि दूसरे का हित करने की अपनी

शक्ति भी खो बैठता है। हिल-मिल जाने से कई प्रवृत्तियाँ प्रबल हो उठती हैं और ज्ञान को, निष्ठा को और शक्ति को धुँधला कर देती हैं।

—रवींद्रनाथ टैगोर

महान्

- महान् कार्य शक्ति से नहीं, अपितु उद्यम से संपन्न होते हैं।

  —बिल गेट्स

- महान् कार्यों को पूरा करने के लिए न केवल हमें कार्य करना चाहिए, बल्कि स्वप्न भी देखने चाहिए। न केवल योजना बनानी चाहिए, अपितु विश्वास भी करना चाहिए। **—बिल गेट्स**

- महान् विचार ही कार्य रूप में परिणत होकर महान् कार्य बनते हैं।

  —बिल गेट्स

- महान् सपने देखनेवालों के महान् सपने हमेशा पूरे होते हैं। **—बिल गेट्स**

- मैं महान् उसको मानता हूँ, जो स्वत: अपना मार्ग बनाते हैं, परंतु कहीं मिथ्या मार्ग पर चल पड़ें तो लौट आने का साहस और बुद्धि भी रखते हैं।

  —बिल गेट्स

- महान् व्यक्ति न किसी का अपमान करता है और न उसको सहता है।

  —होम

महापुरुष

- सभी जमाने में और सभी देशों में कुछ ऐसे महापुरुष होते हैं, जो समाज के अंदर रहकर भी समाज से विरक्त रहते हैं, कोई रीति-रस्म नहीं मानते।

  —अज्ञात

- जो वास्तव में महापुरुष होते हैं, वे जन्म लेते ही महान् युग में स्थान ग्रहण करते हैं। अतीत में भी वे वर्तमान होते हैं और सुविस्तीर्ण भविष्य में भी विराजते हैं। **—रवींद्रनाथ टैगोर**

- श्रेष्ठ महापुरुष वही होते हैं, जो सारे धर्म, इतिहास और नीति से पृथ्वी के श्रेष्ठ दान को ग्र हण करते हैं। **—अज्ञात**

माँ

- बच्चा जब चलना आरंभ करता है, तब बार-बार भूल से इधर-उधर पैर फेंकता है, किंतु माता का स्नेह उतने से ही उछल पड़ता है। **—शेक्सपियर**
- यह पृथ्वी वास्तव में पशु-पक्षियों का ही भरण-पोषण करनेवाली यथार्थ माँ है, जो स्वयं अपने हाथ से उनके मुँह में आहार डाल देती है। मनुष्य तो इस पृथ्वी के मानो सौतेले लड़के हैं। **—अज्ञात**
- रूपहीन, ज्ञानातीत, भीषण शक्ति ने ही मेरे लिए यह मातृस्वरूप धारण किया है। **—रवींद्रनाथ टैगोर**
- गृहस्थी में बँधी रहने पर भी माँ विश्व भर की माँ होती है। **—फ्रेंकलिन**

माता-पिता

- माता-पिता की सेवा पुत्र का प्रथम कर्तव्य है। **—महात्मा गांधी**
- माता के समान पूजनीय विभूति संसार में दूसरी नहीं होती। **—महात्मा गांधी**
- माता-पिता का ऋण संतान जन्म-भर नहीं चुका सकती। **—महात्मा गांधी**
- माता-पिता को अपनी संतान को योग्य बनाने के लिए अपनी पूरी शक्ति लगा देनी चाहिए। **—महात्मा गांधी**
- संतान के लिए तो माता-पिता ही प्रथम गुरु और सर्वथा पूज्य हैं। **—महात्मा गांधी**

मानव-जीवन

- जिसके पास न विद्या है, न तप है, न दान है, न ज्ञान है, न शील है, न गुण है और न धर्म है या वे मृत्युलोक पृथ्वी पर भार होते हैं और मनुष्य रूप तो हैं, पर पशु की तरह चरते हैं। **—भर्तृहरि**
- मनुष्य कुछ और नहीं, भटका हुआ देवता है। **—श्रीराम शर्मा आचार्य**

- हर दिन नया जन्म समझें, उसका सदुपयोग करें।
  —श्रीराम शर्मा आचार्य

- मानव तभी तक श्रेष्ठ है, जब तक उसे मनुष्यत्व का दरजा प्राप्त है। बतौर पशु, मानव किसी भी पशु से अधिक हीन है। **—रवींद्रनाथ टैगोर**

- आदर्श के दीपक को पीछे रखनेवाले अपनी ही छाया के कारण अपने पथ को अंधकारमय बना लेते हैं। **—रवींद्रनाथ टैगोर**

- क्लोज-अप में जीवन एक त्रासदी है, तो लंबे शॉट में प्रहसन।
  —चार्ली चैपलिन

- आपके जीवन की खुशी आपके विचारों की गुणवत्ता पर निर्भर करती है।
  —मार्क ऑरेलियस अंतोनियस

- हमेशा बत्तक की तरह व्यवहार रखो। सतह पर एकदम शांत, परंतु सतह के नीचे दीवानों की तरह पैडल मारते हुए। **—जेकब एम ब्रॉदे**

- जैसे-जैसे हम बूढ़े होते जाते हैं, सुंदरता भीतर घुसती जाती है।
  —रॉल्फ वाल्डो एमर्सन

- अव्यवस्था से जीवन का प्रादुर्भाव होता है, तो अनुक्रम और व्यवस्थाओं से आदत का। **—हेनरी एडम्स**

- हम जानते हैं कि हम क्या हैं, पर यह नहीं जानते कि हम क्या बन सकते हैं।
  —शेक्सपियर

मानवता

- मानवता का आदर्श चाहे कितना ही ऊँचा क्यों न हो, उसे भी दोनों जून मुट्ठी भर अन्न की जरूरत पड़ती है। **—रवींद्रनाथ टैगोर**

- मानवता एक ओर तो अपने को अमिट समझती है, तो दूसरी ओर अदना सी चीज के लिए माथा पीटकर मर जाती है। चाहे जो हो, उसे प्रतिदिन सांसारिक बातों के लिए संघर्ष करना ही पड़ता है। **—रवींद्रनाथ टैगोर**

मानव सभ्यता

- संसार में भाव और ज्ञान के बड़े-बड़े कुलाल-चक्र घूम रहे हैं, जिसमें मानव सभ्यता थोड़ी कुछ तैयार होकर आग में तपकर पक्की हो उठी है।

—रवींद्रनाथ टैगोर

माया

- माया अंधकार की तरह है। बाह्य शक्ति से उसका अतिक्रमण नहीं किया जा सकता। **—रवींद्रनाथ टैगोर**

मित्र

- मित्र वह है, जो आपके अतीत को समझता हो, आपके भविष्य में विश्वास रखता हो और आप जैसे हैं, वैसे ही आपको स्वीकार करता हो।

—अज्ञात

- मित्र का सम्मान करो, पीठ पीछे उसकी प्रशंसा करो और आवश्यकता पड़ने पर उसकी सहायता करो। **—अरस्तू**

- दोस्त वह है, जो आपको अपनी तरह जीने की पूरी आजादी दे।

—जिम मॉरिसन

- सच्चा प्रेम दुर्लभ है, सच्ची मित्रता और भी दुर्लभ है। **—अज्ञात**

- ज्ञानी दोस्त जिंदगी का सबसे बड़ा वरदान है। **—यूरीपिडीज**

- कृतज्ञता मित्रता को चिरस्थायी रखती है और नए मित्र बनाती है।

—फ्रेंकलिन

- झूठे मित्र साये की तरह होते हैं। धूप में साथ चलते हैं और अँधेरे में साथ छोड़ देते हैं। **—अज्ञात**

- सच्चे मित्र के तीन लक्षण हैं—अहित को रोकना, हित की रक्षा करना और विपत्ति में साथ नहीं छोड़ना। **—अज्ञात**

- सच्चे मित्र के सामने दुःख आधा और हर्ष दुगुना प्रतीत होता है।

—जॉनसन

मित्रता

उनसे कभी मित्रता न करो, जो तुमसे बेहतर नहीं। **—बिल गेट्स**

उनसे दूर रहो, जो भविष्य को निराशाजनक बताते हैं। **—बिल गेट्स**

मीठी बोली

- ऐसी बानी बोलिए, मन का आपा खोय।
  औरन को शीतल करे, आपहुँ शीतल होय॥ **—कबीरदास**

- नम्रता और मीठे वचन ही मनुष्य के सच्चे आभूषण होते हैं। **—तिरुवल्लुवर**

मुकुट

- मुकुट पहनना तो कठिन है ही, किंतु उसे उतारना उससे भी कठिन है। **—रवींद्रनाथ टैगोर**

मुक्ति

- मनुष्य के लिए सबसे बड़ी चीज मुक्ति ही है, उसके बराबर और कुछ भी नहीं है, कुछ भी नहीं। **—रवींद्रनाथ टैगोर**

- दुःख के भीतर से मुक्ति आती है और वह मुक्ति उस दुःख से बड़ी होती है। **—रवींद्रनाथ टैगोर**

- कर्म–मात्र का त्याग करके बिल्कुल जड़ होकर बैठने में भी इनसान की मुक्ति है। **—रवींद्रनाथ टैगोर**

मुसकान

- मुसकान प्रेम की भाषा है। **—हेवर**

- मुसकान एक शक्तिशाली हथियार है, आप इससे फौलाद भी तोड़ सकते हैं।

- हँसी प्रकृति की सबसे बड़ी नियामत है। **—डॉ. लक्ष्मणपति वार्ष्णेय**

- हँसी मन की गाँठें बड़ी आसानी से खोल देती है। **—महात्मा गांधी**

- शांति की शुरुआत एक मुसकान के साथ होती है। —मदर टेरेसा

- कभी-कभी आपकी खुशी आपकी मुसकान का कारण होती है, लेकिन कभी-कभी आपकी मुसकान आपकी खुशी का स्रोत हो सकती है।

  —थिक ऐट ऐन

- आप अपनी मुसकान बस कुछ ही देर तक बनाए रह सकते हैं, उसके बाद बस दाँत रह जाते हैं। —चक पलहनीयक

- अगर आपके अंदर बस एक मुसकान बची है तो उसे उन्हें दीजिए, जिनसे आप प्रेम करते हैं। —माया एंजिलो

- अगर मैं तुम्हारी आँखों में दर्द देख सकूँ तो मेरे साथ अपने आँसू बाँटो। अगर मैं तुम्हारी आँखों में खुशियाँ देख सकूँ तो मेरे साथ अपनी मुसकान बाँटो।

  —संतोष कलवार

- इसलिए मत रो कि सब खत्म हो गया, मुसकराओ कि ऐसा हुआ।

  —डॉ. सेयस

- यदि आप यह पढ़ रहे हैं तो बधाई हो, आप जीवित हैं। अगर मुसकराने के लिए यह एक कारण नहीं है तो मुझे पता नहीं क्या है।

  —चौड सग

- मैं कल मुसकरा रहा था, मैं आज मुसकरा रहा हूँ और मैं कल भी मुसकराऊँगा। महज इसलिए, क्योंकि यह जिंदगी किसी भी चीज के लिए रोने के लिए बहुत छोटी है। —संतोष कलवार

- तुम पाओगे कि जीवन तब भी सार्थक है, अगर तुम सिर्फ मुसकरा सको।

  —चार्ली चैपलिन

- चलिए एक काम करते हैं, जब मुसकराना मुश्किल हो, तब हम एक-दूसरे से मुसकराते हुए मिलें। एक-दूसरे पर मुसकराओ, अपने परिवार में एक-दूसरे के लिए समय निकालो। —मदर टेरेसा

- अगर आप तब मुसकराते हैं, जब आप अकेले हैं, तब आप वास्तव में मुसकरा रहे होते हैं। **—एंडी रूनी**
- दुनिया एक दर्पण की तरह है, आप इस पर क्रोधित होइए और यह आप पर क्रोधित होगी। आप मुसकराइए और यह भी मुसकराएगी। **—हर्बर्ट सैमुअल्स**
- महिलाओं के शस्त्रागार में मुसकान से बढ़कर कोई हथियार नहीं है, जिसके आगे पुरुष इतना असहाय पड़ जाए। **—डोरोथी डिक्स**
- आप मुसकान के साथ बहुत आगे तक जा सकते हैं। आप मुसकान और बंदूक के साथ कहीं आगे तक जा सकते हैं। **—अलकैपोन**
- हर उस व्यक्ति के लिए मुसकान रखो, जिससे तुम मिलने और मारने की योजना रखते हो। **—ब्रैड थॉर**
- एक पल के लिए ही सही, किसी और के चेहरे की मुसकान बनो। **—डेजन स्टोजनोविक**
- मुसकान को तभी रोको, जब वह किसी को चोट पहुँचा सकती हो। नहीं तो खिलखिलाकर हँसो। **—वेरा नजरिअन**
- विज्ञान सोचना सिखाता है, लेकिन प्रेम मुसकराना सिखाता है। **—संतोष कलवार**
- चलिए हम हमेशा एक–दूसरे से मुसकान के साथ मिलें, क्योंकि मुसकान प्रेम की शुरुआत है। **—मदर टेरेसा**
- जिस किसी के चेहरे पर निरंतर मुसकान रहती है, वह एक ऐसी कठोरता छुपाए रहता है, जो लगभग भयावह होती है। **—ग्रेटा गार्बो**
- मैं तुम्हारे चेहरे पर मुसकान और आँखों में दुःख से मोहित हो गया हूँ। **—जेरेमी एल्डना**

- मुसकराने और भूल जाने में बस एक क्षण लगता है, फिर भी जिसे इसकी जरूरत हो, उसके लिए यह जीवन भर बनी रहती है।

  —स्टीव मरबोली

- एक मुसकान मुसीबत से निकलने का सबसे अच्छा तरीका है, तब भी, जब यह बनावटी हो। **—मासशी किशिमोटो**

मृत्यु

- मृत्यु एक महान् विजेता है, लेकिन इसके बावूजद वह केवल तभी जीत सकती है, जब हम सुस्ता रहे हों। **—फेदरीको लोर्का**
- भय ही पतन और पाप का निश्चित कारण है। **—स्वामी विवेकानंद**
- मनुष्य की मृत्यु है, भूत की तो मृत्यु नहीं है। **—रवींद्रनाथ टैगोर**
- मृत्यु और विनाश बिना बुलाए ही आया करते हैं, क्योंकि ये हमारे मित्र के रूप में नहीं, शत्रु के रूप में आते हैं। **—भगवतीचरण वर्मा**
- अंतिम चोट होती है मृत्यु। **—रवींद्रनाथ टैगोर**
- जिधर मृत्यु है, उधर संसार की असीमता है। **—रवींद्रनाथ टैगोर**
- जिसे भविष्य का भय नहीं रहता, वही वर्तमान का आनंद उठा सकता है।

  —अज्ञात

- हमारे सर्वोच्च मंगल का आदर्श मृत्यु के मुख में है। **—रवींद्रनाथ टैगोर**
- जो चुनौतियों का सामना करने से डरता है, उसका असफल होना तय है।

  —अज्ञात

- मृत्यु को जीता नहीं जा सकता, अमृत प्राप्त करने का लक्ष्य ही भ्रष्ट हो जाता है। **—रवींद्रनाथ टैगोर**

मोह

- जिस काम को सत्य मानकर हम सम्मान देते हैं, उसे साधन बनाने के लिए

मोह को अपने दल में शामिल करना ठीक न होगा। **—रवींद्रनाथ टैगोर**

- मोह के बिना छोटे लोगों का काम ही नहीं चलता। **—रवींद्रनाथ टैगोर**
- मोह को जिंदा रखने के लिए सभी देशों में देवता की कल्पना की गई है। **—रवींद्रनाथ टैगोर**
- लोभ और मोह हो तो कामना मिट्टी में मिल जाती है। मोह अतीत और भविष्य को जोड़कर उत्पन्न होता है। **—रवींद्रनाथ टैगोर**
- इस दुनिया में ऐसे लोगों की एक बड़ी संख्या है, जो पैरों तले रहने के आदी हैं। अगर उन्हें पाँवों की धूल नियमित रूप से न मिले तो वे कोई काम नहीं कर पाते। इनसे काम लेने के लिए मोह एक बहुत बड़ी ताकत है। **—रवींद्रनाथ टैगोर**

मौन

- प्रत्येक स्थान और समय बोलने के योग्य नहीं होते, कभी-कभी मौन रह जाना बुरी बात नहीं। **—अज्ञात**
- वाणी का वर्चस्व रजत है, किंतु मौन का मूल्य स्वर्ण के समान है। **—अज्ञात**
- मौन निद्रा के सदृश है, यह ज्ञान में नई स्फूर्ति पैदा करता है। **—बेकन**
- मौन सारे काम बना देता है। **—पंचतंत्र**
- आओ हम मौन रहें, ताकि फरिश्तों की कानाफूसियाँ सुन सकें। **—एमर्सन**
- मौन में शब्दों की अपेक्षा अधिक वाक्-शक्ति होती है। **—कार्लाइल**
- कभी-कभी मौन रह जाना, सबसे तीखी आलोचना होती है। **—अज्ञात**
- धनुष से छूटा हुआ तीर ओर मुख से निकला हुआ शब्द कभी वापस नहीं लौटता। **—अज्ञात**
- इसका खेद अनेक बार हुआ कि मैं बोल क्यों पड़ा। **—पाइथोगोरस**

- बोलने में समझदारी से काम लेना, वाक्पटुता से अच्छा है। **—बेकन**
- थोड़ा पढ़ना और अधिक सोचना, कम बोलना और अधिक सुनना, यही बुद्धिमान बनने का उपाय है। **—अज्ञात**
- जो झुकना जानता है, दुनिया उसे उठाती है, जो केवल अकड़ना जानता है, दुनिया उसे उखाड़ फेंकती है। **—अज्ञात**
- खामोश रहो या ऐसी बात कहो, जो खामोशी से बेहतर हो। **—पाइथोगोरस**
- मौन बातचीत की एक महान् कला है। **—हैजलिट**
- तुम्हें प्रत्येक का उपदेश सुनना चाहिए, जबकि अपना उपदेश कुछ ही व्यक्तियों को दो।
- जितना दिखाते हो, उससे ज्यादा तुम्हारे पास होना चाहिए, जितना जानते हो, उससे कम तुम्हें बोलना चाहिए।
- मौन शक्ति का उत्कृष्ट स्रोत है। **—लाओत्जू**
- मौन घृणा की उत्तम अभिव्यक्ति है। **—जॉर्ज बर्नार्ड शॉ**

मौनव्रत

- मौनव्रत विपत्ति की एकमात्र अमोघ औषधि नहीं है। **—रवींद्रनाथ टैगोर**

यथार्थ

- मनुष्य का यथार्थ स्वरूप उसकी आत्म-शुद्धि-संपन्न अंत:प्रकृति में है। **—रवींद्रनाथ टैगोर**
- शक्ति के साथ शक्ति का समझौता हो जाने से ही वह यथार्थ कार्य होता है। यथार्थ कार्य से दोनों ही पक्षों का मंगल होता है। **—रवींद्रनाथ टैगोर**
- नीचे के लोगों का विस्तार किए बिना तुम्हारा यथार्थ विस्तार कभी नहीं होगा। नाव के तले में छेद हो तो नाव का मस्तूल कभी अकड़कर नहीं चल सकता, चाहे वह कितना ही ऊँचा क्यों न हो। **—रवींद्रनाथ टैगोर**

यात्रा

- हजार मील का सफर भी एक कदम से ही आरंभ होता है। —**लाओत्जू**
- न जल्दी करो, न परेशान हो, क्योंकि आप यहाँ एक छोटी सी यात्रा पर हैं; इसलिए आराम से रुकिए और फूलों की खुशबू का आनंद उठाइए। —**वाल्टर हेगन**
- सही मार्ग पर चलना 'यात्रा' है और बिना लक्ष्य के गलत राह पर चलना 'भटकना' है। —**अज्ञात**

युक्ति

- युक्ति के बदले, उक्ति से काम कभी नहीं चलेगा। —**रवींद्रनाथ टैगोर**

युद्ध

- युद्ध समाज का अत्यंत आवश्यक कर्म है। एक संप्रदाय यदि उस कठिन कर्तव्य को अपना धर्म समझकर ही ग्रहण करता है, तो कर्म के साथ धर्म की रक्षा होती है। —**रवींद्रनाथ टैगोर**

युवा

- युवा होने का सबसे बड़ा प्रमाण यही है कि भावनाओं का पुंज और उत्साह का स्रोत हो। —**गणेश शंकर**

युवावस्था

- युवावस्था में डाली गई अच्छी आदतें सारा अंतर ला देती हैं। —**अरस्तू**
- दुनिया की सबसे बड़ी शक्ति नौजवानी और औरत की सुंदरता है। —**चाणक्य**
- युवा आसानी से धोखा खा जाता है, क्योंकि वह उम्मीद करने में बहुत तेज होता है। —**अरस्तू**
- लज्जा युवाओं के लिए एक आभूषण, लेकिन बुढ़ापे के लिए एक तिरस्कार है। —**अरस्तू**

- मैं भविष्य जानने के लिए युवाओं को पढ़ाने जाता हूँ। **—रॉबर्ट फ्रॉस्ट**
- चालीस यौवन का बुढ़ापा है, पचास बुढ़ापे का यौवन है। **—विक्टर ह्यूगो**
- युवाओं का कर्तव्य है भ्रष्टाचार को ललकारना। **—कर्ट कोबैन**
- युवावस्था एक अधूत चीज है। इसे बच्चों पर बरबाद करना कितना बड़ा अपराध है। **—जॉर्ज बर्नार्ड शॉ**
- अपने जवानी के सपनों के साथ सच्चे बने रहें। **—फ्रेडरिक स्किलर**
- जवानी वह है, जब आपको नव वर्ष के मौके पर आधी रात तक जागने दिया जाता है। अधेड़ावस्था वह है, जब आपको इसके लिए मजबूर किया जाता है। **—बिल वोन**
- अकसर परिपक्वता जवानी से अधिक बेतुकी होती है और बहुत बार युवाओं के साथ सबसे अधिक अन्यायपूर्ण भी। **—थॉमस एल्वा एडिसन**
- आयु सोचती है, जवानी करती है। **—रवींद्रनाथ टैगोर**
- एक आरामदायक बुढ़ापा अच्छी तरह से बिताई गई जवानी का इनाम होता है। **—मौरिस चेवालिए**
- जवानी की कोई उम्र नहीं होती। **—पाब्लो पिकासो**
- वरिष्ठ व्यक्ति जंग का ऐलान करते हैं, लेकिन वे तो नौजवान हैं, जिन्हें लड़ना और मरना होता है। **—हर्बर्ट हुवर**
- यौवन खुशहाल है, क्योंकि उसके अंदर खूबसूरती देखने की क्षमता है। जो कोई भी खूबसूरती देखने की क्षमता रखता है, वह कभी बूढ़ा नहीं होता। **—फ्रेंज काफ्का**
- यौवन युवाओं पर बरबाद हो जाता है। **—ऑस्कर वाइल्ड**
- खुशहाल बचपन जीने के लिए कभी बहुत देर नहीं हुई होती है। **—टॉम रॉबिंस**

• जवान होने में बहुत समय लगता है। **—पाब्लो पिकासो**

• एक फिट, स्वस्थ्य शरीर, यही सबसे अच्छा फैशन स्टेटमेंट है। **—जेस सी. स्कॉट**

• यौवन एक सपना है, एक तरह का रासायनिक पागलपन। **—एफ. स्कॉट फिह्जगेरॉल्ड**

• आप केवल एक बार युवा होते हैं, पर आप अनिश्चित काल के लिए अपरिपक्व रह सकते हैं। **—ओगडेन नैश**

• सच कहना बहुत कठिन होता है और युवा बहुत कम ही इसकी क्षमता रखते हैं। **—लियो टालस्टॉय**

• अपनी जवानी का आनंद लो। तुम इस क्षण जितने युवा हो, उतने फिर कभी नहीं होगे। **—चौड सग**

• युवा रहने का राज है, कभी अनुपयुक्त भावना मत रखो। **—ऑस्कर वाइल्ड**

• मैं उस एकांत में रहता हूँ, जो युवावस्था में तकलीफदेह है, लेकिन परिपक्वता के दिनों में स्वादिष्ट। **—एल्बर्ट आइंस्टीन**

• किसी युवा को भ्रष्ट करने का पक्का तरीका है कि उसे यह सिखाओ कि वह अपने से अलग सोचनेवालों की तुलना में खुद उसके जैसी सोच रखनेवालों का अधिक सम्मान करे। **—फ्रेडरिक नित्जे**

• जॉर्ज वाशिंगटन एक लड़के के रूप में युवाओं की आम उपलब्धियों से अनभिज्ञ थे। वे झूठ भी नहीं बोल सकते थे। **—मार्क ट्वेन**

• शिक्षा सबसे अच्छी मित्र है। एक शिक्षित व्यक्ति हर जगह सम्मान पता है। शिक्षा सौंदर्य और यौवन को परास्त कर देती है। **—चाणक्य**

- एक लेखक को अपनी पीढ़ी के युवाओं के लिए, अगली पीढ़ी के आलोचकों के लिए और उससे भी बाद की पीढ़ी के अध्यापकों के लिए लिखना चाहिए। **—एफ. स्कॉट फिट्जगेराल्ड**

- जो कोई भी अपनी जवानी में सीखने पर ध्यान नहीं देता, अपना अतीत खो देता है और भविष्य के लिए मर चुका होता है। **—यूरीपाईड्स**

- जवानी खुशियों का वादा करती है, लेकिन जिंदगी गमों की असलियत सामने ला देती है। **—निकोलस स्पार्क्स**

- युवा हमारे भविष्य की आशा हैं। **—जोस रिजाल**

- लगभग हर एक चीज जो महान् है, युवाओं द्वारा की गई है। **—बेंजामिन डिजरेली**

- शोहरत जवानी की प्यास है। **—लॉर्ड बायरन**

- यौवन और सुंदरता में ज्ञान होता है, पर बहुत कम ही! **—होमर**

- जवानी आती है, लेकिन जिंदगी में एक बार। **—हेनरी वड्र्सवर्थ लाँगफेलो**

- मौत हमें नीद, कभी न खत्म होनेवाला यौवन और अमरता देती है। **—जीन पॉल**

- बाल रँगने से जवानी वापस नहीं आ जाती। **—अबु बकर**

- आप पैसों के बिना जवान हो सकते हैं, लेकिन आप इसके बिना बूढ़े नहीं हो सकते। **—अरस्तू**

- युवाओं को नौकरी खोजनेवाला की जगह नौकरी पैदा करनेवाला बनाने की आवश्यकता है। **—अब्दुल कलाम**

- हम जवानी में सीखते हैं, हम बुढ़ापे में समझते हैं। **—मारी वोन एबनर-एस्चेंबैक**

• बढ़ती उम्र के साथ जवानी का नशा हमेशा हल्का नहीं पड़ता, कभी-कभी यह और गाढ़ा हो जाता है। **—कार्ल जंग**

• जवानी एक भूल है, मर्दानगी एक संघर्ष है, बुढ़ापा एक अफसोस है। **—बेंजामिन डिजरेली**

• यौवन प्रकृति का उपहार है, लेकिन उम्र कला की एक कृति है। **—स्तानिस्लाव लेस**

• युवा समृद्धि के संरक्षक हैं। **—बेंजामिन डिजरेली**

• बूढ़ा होना जवानी का खोना नहीं, बल्कि नए अवसर और ताकत का मंच है। **—बेट्टी फ्रीडैन**

• आतुरता युवाओं की है, बुद्धिमानी वृद्धों की। **—मार्क्स टुलीयस सिसरो**

• युवावस्था अमीर होने के लिए सबसे अच्छा समय है और गरीब होने के लिए भी। **—यूरीपाइड्स**

योग्यता

• केवल बुद्धि के द्वारा ही मानव का मनुष्यत्व प्रकट होता है। **—प्रेमचंद**

• कार्यकुशल व्यक्ति की सभी जगह जरूरत पड़ती है। **—प्रेमचंद**

• गुण छोटे लोगों में द्वेष और महान् व्यक्तियों में स्पर्धा पैदा करता है। **—फील्डिंग**

• कार्यकुशल व्यक्ति के लिए यश और धन की कमी नहीं है। **—अज्ञात**

• मनुष्य अपने गुणों से आगे बढ़ता है, न कि दूसरों कि कृपा से। **—लाला लाजपतराय**

• यदि तुम अपने आपको योग्य बना लो, तो सहायता स्वयं तुम्हें आ मिलेगी। **—स्वामी रामतीर्थ**

- महान् व्यक्ति न किसी का अपमान करता है और न उसको सहता है।

—होम

- नैतिक बल के द्वारा ही मनुष्य दूसरों पर अधिकार कर सकता है।

—स्वामी रामदास

- मनुष्य धन अथवा कुल से नहीं, दिव्य स्वभाव और भव्य आचरण से महान् बनता है। —आविद

- ज्ञानी वह है, जो वर्तमान को ठीक प्रकार समझे और परिस्थिति के अनुसार आचरण करे। —विनोबा भावे

योजना

- अच्छी योजना बनाना बुद्धिमानी का काम है, पर उसको ठीक से पूरा करना धैर्य और परिश्रम का।

—बिल गेट्स

यौवन

- यौवन के उतार का समय ही सबसे अधिक खतरे का होता है।

—रवींद्रनाथ टैगोर

रणनीति

- एक बुरी रणनीति अच्छी-से-अच्छी जानकारी को अनुपयोगी बना सकती है। —बिल गेट्स

राजनीति

- निश्चित ही राज्य तीन शक्तियों के अधीन है। शक्तियाँ मंत्र, प्रभाव और उत्साह हैं, जो एक-दूसरे से लाभान्वित होकर कर्तव्यों के क्षेत्र में प्रगति करती हैं। मंत्र (योजना, परामर्श) से कार्य का ठीक निर्धारण होता है, प्रभाव (राजोचित शक्ति, तेज) से कार्य का आरंभ होता है और उत्साह (उद्यम) से कार्य सिद्ध होता है। —दशकुमारचरित

• यथार्थ को स्वीकार न करने में ही व्यावहारिक राजनीति निहित है।

—हेनरी एडम

• विपत्तियों को खोजने, उन्हें सर्वत्र प्राप्त करने, गलत निदान करने और अनुपयुक्त चिकित्सा करने की कला ही राजनीति है।

—सर अर्नेस्ट वेम

• मानव स्वभाव का ज्ञान ही राजनीतिक-शिक्षा का आदि और अंत है।

—हेनरी एडम

• राजनीति में किसी भी बात का तब तक विश्वास मत कीजिए, जब तक कि उसका खंडन आधिकारिक रूप से न कर दिया गया हो।

—ओटो वान बिस्मार्क

• सफल क्रांतिकारी राजनीतिज्ञ होता है, असफल अपराधी।

—एरिक फ्रॉम

• राजनीति में एक पक्ष अन्य पक्षों की सर्वदा निंदा ही करता है।

—रवींद्रनाथ टैगोर

राजनीतिज्ञ

• राजनीतिज्ञ लोगों की एक अलग जाति होती है, उनका आदर्श मानव के महान् आदर्श से मेल नहीं खाता। **—रवींद्रनाथ टैगोर**

राजा

• राजा को मारने से ही राजत्व नहीं मिलता···पृथ्वी को वश में करके ही राजा बना जाता है। **—रवींद्रनाथ टैगोर**

• साधारण लोगों के लिए असली या नकली एक राजा तो होना ही चाहिए, नहीं तो बड़ा अनिष्ट होता है। **—रवींद्रनाथ टैगोर**

राष्ट्र

• राष्ट्र का पुनर्निर्माण उसके आदर्शों के पुनर्निर्माण के बिना नहीं हो सकता है।

—भगिनी निवेदिता

• राष्ट्र की सृष्टि देश के समग्र लोगों के सम्मिलित प्रयास से होती है, इस सृष्टि में सारे देश की हृदय-वृत्ति, बुद्धि तथा इच्छा-शक्ति व्यक्त होती है, यह योगलब्ध धन है।
—रवींद्रनाथ टैगोर

• राष्ट्र ही सभ्यता की अभिव्यक्ति है। **—रवींद्रनाथ टैगोर**

• वर्तमान के जोश में भविष्य के बीज तक को निर्जीव बना देना राष्ट्र को नष्ट करना है।
—रवींद्रनाथ टैगोर

राष्ट्रभाषा हिंदी

• राष्ट्रभाषा की जगह एक हिंदी ही ले सकती है, कोई दूसरी भाषा नहीं।
—महात्मा गांधी

• यदि हम भारत की राष्ट्रभाषा बनाना चाहते हैं तो हिंदी ही हमारी राष्ट्रभाषा हो सकती है।
—महात्मा गांधी

• अगर हिंदुस्तान को हमें एक राष्ट्र बनाना है तो राष्ट्रभाषा हिंदी ही हो सकती है।
—महात्मा गांधी

• राष्ट्रीय व्यवहार में हिंदी को काम में लाना देश की एकता और उन्नति के लिए आवश्यक है।
—महात्मा गांधी

• आज की अंग्रेजी शिक्षा ने हमें निकम्मा और नकलची बना दिया।
—महात्मा गांधी

• दुनिया से कह दो, गांधी अंग्रेजी नहीं जानता। **—महात्मा गांधी**

• यदि हमारा विश्वास हमारी भाषाओं पर से उठ गया हो तो वह इस बात की निशानी है कि हमारा अपने आप पर विश्वास नहीं रहा। यह हमारी गिरी हुई हालत की निशानी है और जो भाषाएँ हमारी माताएँ बोलती हैं, उनके लिए हमें जरा भी मान न हो, तो किसी तरह की स्वराज्य की योजना, भले ही वह कितनी भी परोपकारी वृत्ति या उदारता से हमें दी जाए, हमारे लिए कभी स्वराज्य भोगनेवाली पूजा नहीं बना सकेगी।
—महात्मा गांधी

- कोई भी देश सच्चे अर्थों में तब तक स्वतंत्र नहीं है, जब तक वह अपनी भाषा में नहीं बोलता। **—महात्मा गांधी**

- विदेशी भाषा के माध्यम से शिक्षा की हिमायत करनेवाले जनता के दुश्मन हैं। **—महात्मा गांधी**

रास्ता

- रास्ता बनाते चलो। हमेशा आपके लिए कोई रास्ता तैयार नहीं रहेगा। आपको कुछ तो करना ही होगा। कभी लोगों को यह भी लगेगा कि आप सनकी हैं। कई बार आप कदम मंजिल के पास हो सकते हैं। **—बिल गेट्स**

- अपने आपको अधिक समझने व मानने से स्वयं अपना रास्ता बनानेवाली बात है। **—बिल गेट्स**

रुपया

- रुपया अच्छी चीज नहीं है। उससे मन दब जाता है। जब मन शासन करता है, तब वह अपना सुख स्वयं तैयार कर सकता है, किंतु धन जब सुख-संचय का भार लेता है, तब मन का कोई प्रयोजन नहीं रह जाता। तब पहले, जहाँ मन का सुख था, उस जगह को माल-असबाब का घटाटोप घेर लेता है। **—रवींद्रनाथ टैगोर**

- सरलतापूर्वक लेन-देन चलाने के लिए ही रुपए की सृष्टि हुई है। **—रवींद्रनाथ टैगोर**

लक्ष्मी

- लक्ष्मी का अमृत भंडार कभी चुकता नहीं, इसीलिए कभी-कभी वह हमारे पात्र तोड़कर, हमें रुलाकर खुद हँसती है। **—रवींद्रनाथ टैगोर**

- अवसादग्रस्त निरुत्साह को लक्ष्मी छोड़ जाती है। **—रवींद्रनाथ टैगोर**

लक्ष्य

- लक्ष्य-प्राप्ति के लिए सहज प्रवृत्तियों को होम कर देना होता है। **—संपूर्णानंद**

• अगर मैं पहले से कोई अंतिम लक्ष्य बनाकर चलता तो क्या आपको नहीं लगता है कि मैं उसे सालों पहले पूरा कर चुका होता। **—बिल गेट्स**

• हमारे लक्ष्य निर्धारित करते हैं कि हम क्या बनने जा रहे हैं। **—बिल गेट्स**

• सब मनुष्यों के कर्मों का लक्ष्य उन्नति की चरम सीमा को प्राप्त करना है।

—सत्य साईं बाबा

• अपने लक्ष्यों को पूरा होते देखने का सिद्धांत जीवन के सभी क्षेत्रों में काम करता है। अगर कुछ करना व बनना चाहते हो तो सर्वप्रथम लक्ष्य को निर्धारित करें, वरना जीवन में उचित उपलब्धि नहीं कर पाएँगे।

—बिल गेट्स

• स्पष्ट लक्ष्य निर्धारित करने और ऐसे उपाय ढूँढ़ने होंगे, जो मानवीय स्थिति को सुधार सकनेवाली प्रगति की ओर संकेत करते हों।

—बिल गेट्स

• विश्व के सबसे गरीब लोगों के जीवन को सुधारने पर लक्षित आठ लक्ष्यों ने स्वास्थ्य और विकास में सर्वोच्च प्राथमिकता को नया फोकस प्रदान किया है।

—बिल गेट्स

• सभी का न हो, किंतु किसी-किसी मनुष्य का जीवन में कोई एक लक्ष्य रहता है।

—रवींद्रनाथ टैगोर

• सार्थकता हासिल करने के लिए स्पष्ट तसवीर बिल्कुल अनिवार्य है।

—अज्ञात

• अपने लक्ष्यों को पूरा होते देखने का सिद्धांत जीवन के सभी क्षेत्रों में काम करता है।

—बिल गेट्स

• लक्ष्य के बारे में सबसे जरूरी चीज है कि वह होना चाहिए।

—बिल गेट्स

• किसी अन्य व्यक्ति की तुलना में अपने लक्ष्य की प्राप्ति के लिए कार्यरत रहने

की आपकी इच्छा आपकी सर्वाधिक मूल्यवान संपत्ति हो सकती है।

—बिल गेट्स

• जहाँ संकल्प बड़ा होता है, वहाँ विपदा और संकट बड़े नहीं हो सकते।

—मैकियावेली

• बाहरी चीजों के अंबार लगाना ही आदमी के जीवन का अंतिम लक्ष्य हो रहा है। **—रवींद्रनाथ टैगोर**

• आपने चाहे कितने ही लक्ष्य क्यों न पूरे कर लिये हों, अपनी निगाह अगले लक्ष्य पर टिका लें। **—बिल गेट्स**

• एक बार लक्ष्य निर्धारित करने के बाद बाधाओं और व्यवधानों के भय से उसे छोड़ देना कायरता है। **—बिल गेट्स**

• लक्ष्य जितना बड़ा होता है, उसका रास्ता भी उतना ही लंबा और बीहड़ होता है। **—साने गुरुजी**

• सबकी सुनने और माननेवाला किसी नतीजे पर नहीं पहुँचता। **—अज्ञात**

• सत्य आदमी का लक्ष्य नहीं है, आदमी का लक्ष्य है फल पाना।

—रवींद्रनाथ टैगोर

• जब भी लक्ष्य तय करो, उसके लिए जुनूनी होना होगा। नाकामियों का आप पर नकारात्मक असर नहीं होना चाहिए। लक्ष्य को हासिल करने में कितना समय लग रहा है, उससे विचलित होने की जरूरत नहीं है।

—बिल गेट्स

• अपने जीवन का कोई लक्ष्य बनाइए, क्योंकि लक्ष्यविहीन जीवन बिना पतवार की नाव के समान इधर-उधर भटकता रहता है। **—अज्ञात**

• हमारा जीवन पक्षी है, केवल थोड़ी ही दूर तक उड़ सकता है, इसने पंख फैला दिए हैं, देखो, जल्दी से इसकी दिशा सोच लो। **—अज्ञात**

लज्जा

- लज्जा के कारण जो लेने लायक चीज को नहीं लेते, वे ही न लेने का दुःख ढकने के लिए लज्जा को बड़ी चीज मानते हैं। **—रवींद्रनाथ टैगोर**
- जो समूचे को देखते हैं, उनके पास सत्य को ढकने की जरूरत नहीं पड़ती। अर्धसत्य ही लज्जा का विषय है। **—रवींद्रनाथ टैगोर**

लीडर

- जब हम अगली सदी की तरफ देखते हैं, लीडर वही होंगे, जो दूसरों को सशक्त बना सकेंगे। **—बिल गेट्स**

लोकतंत्र

- लोकतंत्र का मूल उदारता में है। **—अरस्तू**
- लोकतंत्र जनता की, जनता द्वारा, जनता के लिए सरकार होती है। **—अब्राहम लिंकन**
- लोकतंत्र इस धारणा पर आधारित है कि साधारण लोगों में असाधारण संभावनाएँ होती हैं। **—हेनरी एमर्शन फास्डिक**
- शांतिपूर्वक सरकार बदल देने की शक्ति प्रजातंत्र की आवश्यक शर्त है। प्रजातंत्र और तानाशाही में अंतर नेताओं के अभाव में नहीं है, बल्कि नेताओं को बिना उनकी हत्या किए बदल देने में है। **—लॉर्ड बिवरेज**
- बहुमत का शासन जब जोर-जबरदस्ती का शासन हो जाए तो वह उतना ही असहनीय हो जाता है, जितना कि नौकरशाही का शासन। **—महात्मा गांधी**
- जैसी जनता, वैसा राजा। प्रजातंत्र का यही तकाजा। **—श्रीराम शर्मा आचार्य**
- अगर हम लोकतंत्र की सच्ची भावना का विकास करना चाहते हैं तो हम असहिष्णु नहीं हो सकते। असहिष्णुता से पता चलता है कि हमें अपने

उद्‌देश्य की पवित्रता में पूरा विश्वास नहीं है। बहुमत का शासन जब जोर-जबरदस्ती का शासन हो जाए तो वह उतना ही असहनीय हो जाता है, जितना कि नौकरशाही का शासन। **—महात्मा गांधी**

लोग

- अन्य लोगों के अंतिम संस्कार में अवश्य शरीक हों, अन्यथा लोग आपके में शरीक नहीं होंगे। **—योगी बेरा**
- महान् लोग हमेशा अपने समय से आगे होते हैं, जबकि चतुर सुजान लोग केवल अपने समय का दोहन ही कर पाते हैं। **—ज्यां बोद्रिला**
- महान् आदमी वे होते हैं, जो पहले कभी न सोचे गए और न किए गए काम को अंजाम देते हैं। **—जावेद अख्तर**
- कुछ लोग नकल करने के इतने अभ्यस्त हो जाते हैं कि वे धीरे-धीरे दूसरों की गलतियों की भी नकल करने लग जाते हैं। **—अज्ञात**
- शिष्ट लोग भी अनेक कष्ट सहते हैं, लेकिन अपनी भद्रता के कारण वे उसका प्रदर्शन नहीं करते। **—अज्ञात**

लोभ

- लोभ करने का स्वाभाविक अधिकार होता है, इसीलिए तो लोभ करना स्वाभाविक है। **—रवींद्रनाथ टैगोर**
- लोभ में पड़कर प्रकृति के प्रति व्यभिचार करने से हमें बचना चाहिए।

  —रवींद्रनाथ टैगोर

वक्त

- घंटा सबको यह बतलाता है कि वक्त बैठा नहीं रहता। वक्त चलता जा रहा है। **—रवींद्रनाथ टैगोर**
- केवल खास बातों के लिए वक्त है। बेकार में वक्त बरबाद करने का वक्त नहीं है। **—रवींद्रनाथ टैगोर**

वफादार

- छोटी-छोटी चीजों के प्रति वफादार रहें, क्योंकि आपकी बड़ी ताकत इन्हीं छोटी चीजों में बसती है। **—मदर टेरेसा**

विकास

- बीज आधारभूत कारण है, पेड़ उसका प्रगति परिणाम, विचारों की प्रगतिशीलता और उमंग भरी साहसिकता उस बीज के समान है। **—श्रीराम शर्मा आचार्य**
- विकास की कोई सीमा नहीं होती, क्योंकि मनुष्य की मेधा, कल्पनाशीलता और कौतूहल की भी कोई सीमा नहीं है। **—रोनाल्ड रीगन**

विज्ञान

- विज्ञान हमें ज्ञानवान बनाता है, लेकिन दर्शन (फिलॉसफी) हमें बुद्धिमान बनाता है। **—विल्ल डुरांट**
- विज्ञान की तीन विधियाँ हैं—सिद्धांत, प्रयोग और सिमुलेशन। **—अज्ञात**
- विज्ञान की बहुत सारी परिकल्पनाएँ गलत हैं, यह पूरी तरह ठीक है, ये गलत परिकल्पनाएँ ही सत्य-प्राप्ति के झरोखे हैं। **—अज्ञात**
- हम किसी भी चीज को पूर्णत: ठीक तरीके से परिभाषित नहीं कर सकते। अगर ऐसा करने की कोशिश करें तो हम भी उसी वैचारिक पक्षाघात के शिकार हो जाएँगे, जिसके शिकार दार्शनिक होते हैं। **—रिचर्ड फेनिमैन**

विज्ञापन

- मैंने कोई विज्ञापन ऐसा नहीं देखा, जिसमें पुरुष स्त्री से कह रहा हो कि यह साड़ी या स्नो खरीद लो। अपनी चीज वह खुद पसंद करती है, मगर पुरुष की सिगरेट से लेकर टायर तक में वह दखल देती हैं। **—हरिशंकर परसाई**

विचार

- मन में बुरे विचार आने से ही नहीं, बल्कि असंगत, अव्यवस्थित और अवांछित विचार आने से भी इस जीवनीशक्ति का न केवल सतत क्षय होता

रहता है, बल्कि इस रीति से क्षय होता रहता है कि हमें उसका पता भी नहीं चलता और चूँकि विचार सारे वचनों और कार्यों के प्रेरणा-स्रोत हैं, इसलिए जैसा विचार होगा, वैसा ही वचन और कार्य भी होगा। इसलिए पूर्ण मनोनिग्रहपूर्वक किया गया विचार, अपने आप में अधिक-से-अधिक समर्थ शक्ति है और यह भी हो सकता है कि बिना किसी बाहरी साधन-उपक्रम के यह विचार ही वांछित कार्य भी करने लग जाए।

—महात्मा गांधी

- मनुष्य की वास्तविक पूँजी धन नहीं, विचार हैं।

—श्रीराम शर्मा आचार्य

- मन:स्थिति बदले, तब परिस्थिति बदले। **—श्रीराम शर्मा आचार्य**
- विकारी विचार भी बीमारी की निशानी है। इसलिए हम सब विकार से बचते रहें। **—महात्मा गांधी**
- विचारों की शक्ति अकूत है। विचार ही संसार पर शासन करते है, मनुष्य नहीं।

—सर फिलिप सिडनी

- विचार संसार में सबसे घातक हथियार हैं। **—डब्ल्यू.ओ. डगलस**
- किस तरह विचार संसार को बदलते हैं, यही इतिहास है। **—अज्ञात**
- विचारों की गति ही सौंदर्य है। **—जे.बी. कृष्णमूर्ति**
- गलतियाँ मत ढूँढ़ो, उपाय ढूँढ़ो। **—हेनरी फोर्ड**
- शुद्ध विचारों में बहुत बड़ी शक्ति है, ऐसा आज के वैज्ञानिक स्वीकार करते हैं और इसी से यह कहा जाता है कि मनुष्य जैसे विचार करता है, वैसा हो जाता है। हत्या का नित्य चिंतन करनेवाला हत्यारा हो जाएगा। व्यभिचार का चिंतन करनेवाला व्यभिचारी हो जाएगा, सत्य का चिंतन करनेवाला सत्यमय, अहिंसा का चिंतन करनेवाला अहिंसामय, और भगवान् का चिंतन करनेवाला भगवानस्वरूप हो जाएगा।

—महात्मा गांधी

- जब तक आप ढूँढ़ते रहेंगे, समाधान मिलते रहेंगे। **—जॉन बेज**
- उस विचार को रोक पाना नामुमकिन है, जिसका वक्त आ गया हो। **—विक्टर ह्यूगो**
- संसार में न कोई तुम्हारा मित्र है, न शत्रु। तुम्हारा अपना विचार ही इसके लिए उत्तरदायी है। **—चाणक्य**
- व्यक्ति के पास जितने अधिक विचार होते हैं, उतने ही कम शब्दों में वह उनको अभिव्यक्त कर देता है। **—अज्ञात**
- अच्छे विचार रखना भीतरी सुंदरता है। **—स्वामी रामतीर्थ**
- हम बात को समझते ही नहीं कि कर्म या वचन के मुकाबले विचार कहीं अधिक शक्तिशाली होता है। जब विचार, वचन और कर्म इन तीनों में सामंजस्य होता है, तब विचार को वचन और कर्म, दोनों मर्यादित करते हैं; इतना ही नहीं, स्वयं वचन को कर्म मर्यादित करता है। कहने की जरूरत नहीं कि विचार से मेरा आशय उस जीवंत विचार से ही है, जिसका वचन और कर्म में रूपांतरण संभव है। सामर्थ्य से रहित विचार, हवाई किले से अधिक अर्थ नहीं रखते और वे हवा में ही विलीन हो जाते हैं। **—महात्मा गांधी**
- मनुष्य अपने हृदय में जैसा विचारता है, वैसा ही बन जाता है। **—बाइबिल**
- महान् विचार कार्यरूप में परिणत होकर, महान् कृतियाँ बन जाते हैं। **—हेजलिट**
- जिसके साथ श्रेष्ठ विचार रहते हैं, वह कभी भी अकेला नहीं रह सकता। **—स्वामी विवेकानंद**
- हम दुनिया को नहीं बदल सकते, मगर दुनिया के प्रति अपना दृष्टिकोण तो बदल सकते हैं। **—स्वामी रामदास**

विद्या

- विद्या जाहिर करने के लिए नहीं और दूसरे का उपकार करने के लिए भी

नहीं, वह है बातें कर-करके चिंतन करना, ज्ञान हजम करने की एक व्यायाम प्रणाली। **—रवींद्रनाथ टैगोर**

- विद्या अमूल्य और अनश्वर धन है। **—ग्लेडस्टन**
- विद्या-लाभ विद्यालय के ऊपर नहीं, बल्कि मुख्यत: छात्र के ऊपर निर्भर करता है। **—रवींद्रनाथ टैगोर**
- निर्लिप्त भाव से बाहर से विद्या सीखी जा सकती है, परंतु जब तक हम उसमें लिप्त होकर व्यावहारिक शिक्षा ग्रहण नहीं करते, तक तक उसका प्रयोग नहीं कर सकते। **—रवींद्रनाथ टैगोर**

विद्यार्थी

- विद्यार्थियों को दलबंदीवाली राजनीति में कभी भाग नहीं लेना चाहिए। **—महात्मा गांधी**
- विद्यार्थी राजनीतिक हड़तालें न करें। **—महात्मा गांधी**
- विद्यार्थी कोई काम लुक-छिपकर न करें। **—महात्मा गांधी**
- विद्यार्थी अपने साथ पढ़नेवाली बहनों के साथ सभ्यता, शिष्टाचार और शालीनता का व्यवहार करें। **—महात्मा गांधी**
- विद्यार्थी यदि अपनी छुट्टी के दिनों में देहातों में जाकर लोकसेवा करें, तो उनके लिए इससे अच्छी और कोई बात नहीं होगी। **—महात्मा गांधी**
- मौज-शौक से पैसे बहाते हुए विद्यार्थी अपने माँ-बाप का भी नुकसान करते हैं और अपना भी। **—महात्मा गांधी**
- विद्यार्थी भोग-विलास में पड़े कि उनका विद्यार्थी-जीवन समाप्त हुआ। **—महात्मा गांधी**
- विद्यार्थी-जीवन में पान, सिगरेट या शराब की आदत डालना आत्मघात के समान है। **—महात्मा गांधी**

- विद्यार्थी अपने किसी भी पड़ोसी की निस्संकोच सेवा करने के लिए तैयार रहें। **—महात्मा गांधी**
- विद्यार्थी को तो आलस्य छू ही नहीं जाना चाहिए। **—महात्मा गांधी**

विनम्रता

- विनम्रता ही मनुष्य का मूलधन होती है। उसे जितना ही खर्च करोगे, उतना ही ऐश्वर्य बढ़ेगा। **—रवींद्रनाथ टैगोर**

विफलता

- प्रयोग-योग्य विफलता को पुरस्कृत करें। **—बिल गेट्स**
- अपनी शक्तियों पर भरोसा करनेवाला कभी असफल नहीं होता। **—बिल गेट्स**
- ऐसे असंख्य लोग हैं, जो बार-बार असफल हुए, तब कहीं जाकर वे अचानक सामने आए। **—बिल गेट्स**

विलासिता

- अति विलासिता से मनुष्यत्व धीरे-धीरे अकर्मण्य और बाँझ हो जाता है। **—रवींद्रनाथ टैगोर**

विवाद

- मत का उत्तर मत से, युक्ति का उत्तर युक्ति से दिया जा सकता है, परंतु बुद्धि के विषय में क्रोध करके दंड देना बर्बरता है। **—रवींद्रनाथ टैगोर**

विवाह

- मनुष्य की एक अवस्था होती है, जब वह चिंता किए बिना ही विवाह कर सकता है, वह अवस्था पार हो जाने पर विवाह करने में दु:साहस की आवश्यकता होती है। **—रवींद्रनाथ टैगोर**
- हमारे देश में विवाह मुख्यतया व्यक्तिगत संबंध नहीं, बल्कि पारिवारिक संबंध है। **—रवींद्रनाथ टैगोर**

विविध

- घाव पर कपड़ा भी छुरी बनकर लगता है। दु:खे हुए अंग को हवा भी दु:खा देती है। **—सुदर्शन**

- काँच का कटोरा, नेत्रों का जल, मोती और मन; ये एक बार टूटने पर पहले जैसी स्थिति को प्राप्त नहीं कर सकते।

  —लोकोक्ति

- बच्चों का हृदय कोमल थाला है, चाहे इसमें कटीली झाड़ी लगा दो, चाहे फूलों के पौधे। **—जयशंकर प्रसाद**

- ज्यों-ज्यों लाभ होता है, त्यों-त्यों लोभ होता है। इस प्रकार लाभ से लोभ निरंतर बढ़ता जाता है। **—उत्तराध्ययन**

- मनुष्य अपनी क्षमताओं की कभी कदर नहीं करता, वह हमेशा उस चीज की आस लगाए रहता है, जो उसके पास नहीं है। **—हेलेन केलर**

- कष्ट और विपत्ति मनुष्य को शिक्षा देनेवाले श्रेष्ठ गुण हैं।

  —बालगंगाधर तिलक

- जिसने अपने को वश में कर लिया है, उसकी जीत को देवता भी हार में नहीं बदल सकते। **— महात्मा बुद्ध**

- मन की दुर्बलता से अधिक भयंकर और कोई पाप नहीं है।

  —स्वामी विवेकानंद

- हम हमेशा खुद को खोजते हुए दूसरों की कहानियों में प्रवेश कर जाते हैं।

  —एमरे करतेश

- सिद्धांत न त्यागें, चाहे ऐसा करनेवाले आप अकेले क्यों न हों।

  —जॉन एडम्स

- कष्ट सहने के फलस्वरूप ही हमें बुद्धि-विवेक की प्राप्ति होती है।

  —राधाकृष्णन्

- चुनाव जनता को राजनीतिक शिक्षा देने का विश्वविद्यालय है।

—जवाहरलाल नेहरू

- जब जादू के पास छिपाने के लिए कुछ नहीं होता तो वह कला बन जाता है। **—बेन ओकरी**

- ऐश्वर्य उपाधि में नहीं, वरन् इस चेतना में है कि हम उसके योग्य हैं।

—अरस्तू

- उपदेश देना सरल है, पर उपाय बताना कठिन। **—रवींद्रनाथ टैगोर**

- दूसरों के अनुभवों से लाभ उठानेवाला बुद्धिमान होता है।

—जवाहरलाल नेहरू

- प्रतिष्ठा बनाने में कई वर्ष लग जाते हैं, कलंक एक क्षण में लग जाता है।

—अज्ञात

- गुस्सा आपको छोटा बनाता है, क्षमा आपको विस्तार देती है। **—अज्ञात**

- परामर्श तो अनेक प्राप्त करते हैं, किंतु उससे लाभ उठाना बुद्धिमानों को ही आता है। **—साइरस**

- सावधानी बुद्धिमानी की सबसे बड़ी संतान है। **—विक्टर ह्यूगो**

- निंदा से बचने का अचूक एवं शीघ्र उपचार स्वयं को सुधार लेना ही है।

—डिमास्थनीज

- किसी मित्र को अपना ऐसा भेद मत बताओ, जिसके जाहिर हो जाने पर बदनामी हो। **—थेल्स**

- नीतिसम्मत है कि स्वार्थवश भी दुर्जन व्यक्ति को साथ नहीं लेना चाहिए।

—अज्ञात

- चतुर मनुष्य अपना ज्ञान छिपाकर रखता है, पर मूर्ख अपनी मूर्खता का प्रदर्शन करता है। **—बाइबिल**

- न तो इतने कड़वे बनो कि कोई थूक दे और न ही इतने मीठे बनो कि कोई निगल जाए। **—टालस्टॉय**

- जब घर में अतिथि हो, तब चाहे अमृत ही क्यों न हो, अकेले नहीं पीना चाहिए। **—तिरुवल्लुवर**

- अगर तुम पढ़ना जानते हो, तो हर व्यक्ति स्वयं में एक पुस्तक है। **—चैनिंग**

- बहुमत की आवाज न्याय का द्योतक नहीं है। **—अज्ञात**

- जीवन का एक क्षण करोड़ स्वर्ण मुद्राएँ देने पर भी नहीं मिलता। **—चाणक्य**

- मुसकान एक शक्तिशाली हथियार है, आप इससे फौलाद भी तोड़ सकते हैं। **—अज्ञात**

- मनुष्य अपने सबसे अच्छे रूप में सभी जीवों में सबसे उदार होता है, लेकिन यदि कानून और न्याय न हों तो वह सबसे खराब बन जाता है। **—अरस्तू**

- तुम्हारे वस्त्र तुम्हारे बहुत से सुंदर अंश को छिपा लेते हैं, लेकिन असुंदर को नहीं, हालाँकि तुम वस्त्रों में अपनी गुप्तता की आजादी खोजते हो, लेकिन तुमको प्राप्त होते हैं—बंधन और बाधा। **—खलील जिब्रान**

- काश धूप और वायु से तुम्हारा मिलन तुम्हारी त्वचा द्वारा अधिक होता और वस्त्रों द्वारा कम, क्योंकि जीवन के प्राण सूर्य के प्रकाश में हैं और जीवन के हाथ हवा के झोंकों में हैं। **—खलील जिब्रान**

- भूलो मत कि मलिन मन की आँखों के सम्मुख लज्जा ढाल के सामान है और जब मलिन मन ही न होंगे, तब लज्जा केवल एक बेड़ी और विकृत करनेवाली वस्तु के सिवा क्या होगी? **—खलील जिब्रान**

- और भूलो मत कि धरती तुम्हारी नंगी पग-तलियों का स्पर्श पाकर प्रसन्न होती है और पवन तुम्हारे केशों से अठखेलियाँ करना चाहता है। **—खलील जिब्रान**

- खूबसूरती चेहरे पर नहीं होती, यह तो दिल की रोशनी है, बहुत ध्यान से देखनी पड़ती है। —**खलील जिब्रान**

- मनुष्य के सभी कार्य इन सातों में से किसी एक या अधिक वजहों से होते हैं—मौका, प्रकृति, मजबूरी, आदत, कारण, जुनून, इच्छा। —**अरस्तू**

- तुम्हारा घर जहाज का लंगर न बने, बल्कि मस्तूल बने, तुम दरवाजे में से गुजर सको, इसके लिए तुम अपने पंख समेटो मत और कहीं छत से टकरा न जाएँ, इसलिए सिरों को झुकाओ मत, कहीं दीवारें दरककर गिर न पड़ें, इसलिए साँस लेने से डरो मत। —**खलील जिब्रान**

- तुम उन मकबरों में मत रहो, जो मुर्दों ने जीवितों के लिए बनाए हैं, भले ही तुम्हारा घर भव्य और सुंदर न हो, लेकिन तुम्हारा घर न तो तुम्हारे राजों को छुपाए और न तुम्हारी तृष्णाओं का आश्रय हो। —**खलील जिब्रान**

- क्योंकि वह जो तुममें अनंत है, आकाश के महल में रहता है, जिसका फाटक प्रभात का कोहरा है और जिसकी खिड़कियाँ रात की रागनियाँ और खामोशियाँ हैं। —**खलील जिब्रान**

- तुम्हारा दोस्त तुम्हारी जरूरतों का जवाब है, वह तुम्हारी फसल है, जिसे तुम बड़े प्रेम से बोते हो और बड़े प्रेम से काटते हो, वह तुम्हारे भोजन का थाल है और तुम्हारा अपना घर है, क्योंकि तुम अपनी भूख लेकर उसके पास पहुँचते हो और अपने आराम के लिए उसी को तलाशते रहे हो।

  —**खलील जिब्रान**

- कोई भी उस व्यक्ति से प्रेम नहीं करता, जिससे वह डरता है। —**अरस्तू**

- अच्छा व्यवहार सभी गुणों का सार है। —**अरस्तू**

- बुरे व्यक्ति पश्चात्ताप से भरे होते हैं। —**अरस्तू**

- कोई भी क्रोधित हो सकता है, यह आसान है, लेकिन सही व्यक्ति से सही सीमा में सही समय पर और सही उद्‍देश्य के साथ सही तरीके से क्रोधित होना सभी के वश की बात नहीं है और यह आसान नहीं है। —**अरस्तू**

• जो हर झाड़ी की जाँच करता है, वह वन में क्या घुस पाएगा।

—जर्मन कहावत

• सैकड़ों हाथों से इकट्ठा करो और हजारों हाथों से बाँटो। **—अथर्ववेद**

• मेरे दाएँ हाथ में कर्म है और बाएँ हाथ में जय! **—अथर्ववेद**

• जहाँ दोस्ती है, वहाँ शब्दों का इस्तेमाल किए बिना ही सारे विचार, सारी कामनाएँ और सारी आशाएँ जन्म लेती हैं तथा खुशी-खुशी बाँट ली जाती हैं, एक-दूसरे की वाह-वाही किए बिना ही। **—खलील जिब्रान**

• अगर कभी अपने दोस्त से बिछड़ना पड़े तो शोक मत करो, क्योंकि उसकी जिन बातों को तुम सबसे ज्यादा पसंद करते हो, वे उसके न होने पर स्पष्ट हो जाएँगी, स्नेह को बढ़ाने के अलावा अपनी दोस्ती का और कोई उद्देश्य मत होने दो। **—खलील जिब्रान**

• वह दोस्त किस काम का हुआ, जिसे तुम सिर्फ वक्त काटने के लिए तलाश करो, उसे हमेशा अपने पूरे वक्त को जीने के लिए तलाश करो, क्योंकि दोस्ती तुम्हारी जरूरत को पूरा करने के लिए है, तुम्हारे खालीपन को भरने के लिए नहीं। **—खलील जिब्रान**

• दोस्ती की मिठास में अपनी मुसकराहटों को बाँटो और अपनी खुशियों को शामिल होने दो, क्योंकि इन्हीं छोटी-छोटी खुशियों में दिल को अपनी सुबह मिल जाती है और वह ताजगी महसूस करने लगता है। **—खलील जिब्रान**

• दर्द उस खोल का टूटना है, जो तुम्हारी समझ को घेरे रहता है; अपने दर्द के काफी अंश को तुम खुद चुनते हो। **—खलील जिब्रान**

• तुम्हारी संतान तुम्हारे माध्यम से उत्पन्न हुई है, परंतु तुमसे नहीं, तुम उसे अपना प्यार तो दे सकते हो, किंतु विचार नहीं; क्योंकि ये अपने ही विचार रखते हैं, तुम उनके समान बनने की कोशिश तो कर सकते हो, परंतु उन्हें अपने समान बनाने की लालसा मत रखो। **—खलील जिब्रान**

• यदि तुम एक बादल पर बैठ जाओ और नीचे देखो तो तुम पाओगे कि दो

देशों को विभाजित करनेवाली किसी सीमा का अस्तित्व ही नहीं है और न ही एक खेत को दूसरे खेत से अलग करने का निर्देशक पत्थर ही है। दयनीय तो यह है कि तुम बादल पर बैठ ही नहीं सकते।

—खलील जिब्रान

- मूर्खों से बहस करके कोई भी व्यक्ति बुद्धिमान नहीं कहला सकता, मूर्ख पर विजय पाने का एकमात्र उपाय यही है कि उसकी ओर ध्यान नहीं दिया जाए। **—संत ज्ञानेश्वर**
- मनुष्य प्राकृतिक रूप से ज्ञान की इच्छा रखता है। **—अरस्तू**
- सभी भुगतानयुक्त नौकरियाँ दिमाग को अवशोषित और अयोग्य बनाती हैं। **—अरस्तू**
- डर बुराई की अपेक्षा से उत्पन्न होनेवाला दर्द है। **—अरस्तू**
- क्रोध को जीतने में मौन सबसे अधिक सहायक है। **—महात्मा गांधी**
- मूर्ख मनुष्य क्रोध को जोर-शोर से प्रकट करता है, किंतु बुद्धिमान शांति से उसे वश में करता है। **—बाइबिल**
- क्रोध करने का मतलब है, दूसरों की गलतियों की सजा स्वयं को देना।
- घर के समान कोई स्कूल नहीं, न ईमानदारी व सदाचारी माता-पिता के समान कोई अध्यापक है।
- संकोच युवाओं के लिए एक आभूषण है, लेकिन बड़ी उम्र के लोगों के लिए धिक्कार। **—अरस्तू**
- आवेश कोई भावनात्मक ऊर्जा नहीं, बल्कि आत्मा और बाहरी दुनिया का टकराव है। **—आंद्रेई तारकोव्स्की**
- हमेशा अपनी आत्मा की आवाज सुनो।
- शरीर के मामले में जो स्थान साबुन का है, वही आत्मा के संदर्भ में आँसू का है। **—यहूदी कहावत**

- दुर्भाग्य घोड़े पर सवार होकर आता है और पैदल वापस जाता है।

—फ्रांसीसी लोकोक्ति

- बुद्धिमान व्यक्तियों को सलाह की आवश्यकता नहीं होती है, मूर्ख लोग इसे स्वीकार नहीं करते हैं। **—बेंजामिन फ्रेंकलिन**

- प्रत्येक कलाकार एक दिन नौसिखिया ही होता है।

—राल्फ वाल्डो एमर्सन

- चरित्र को हम अपनी बात मनवाने का सबसे प्रभावी माध्यम कह सकते हैं। **—अरस्तू**

- लोकतंत्र तब होगा, जब गरीब, न कि धनाढ्य शासक हों। **—अरस्तू**

- शिक्षा बुढ़ापे के लिए सबसे अच्छा प्रावधान है। **—अरस्तू**

- क्रोध एक तेजाब है, जो उस बरतन का अधिक अनिष्ट कर सकता है, जिसमें वह भरा होता है, न कि उसका, जिस पर वह डाला जाता है।

—मार्क ट्वेन

- जो व्यक्ति दूसरों की भलाई चाहता है, वह अपनी भलाई को सुनिश्चित कर लेता है। **—कन्फ्यूशियस**

- लोभी को पूरा संसार मिल जाए तो भी वह भूखा रहता है, लेकिन संतोषी का पेट एक रोटी से ही भर जाता है। **—शेख सादी**

- धन से अच्छे गुण नहीं मिलते, धन अच्छे गुणों से मिलता है। **—सुकरात**

- कठिन परिश्रम से भविष्य सुधरता है, आलस्य से वर्तमान। **—अज्ञात**

- आपको सबकुछ नहीं मिल सकता, आप इसे रखेंगे कहाँ? **—अज्ञात**

- आकार का इतना अधिक महत्त्व नहीं होता है, ह्वेल मछली का अस्तित्व खतरे में है, जबकि चींटी एक सहज जीवन जी रही है। **—बिल वाघन**

- यदि आप बार-बार शिकायत नहीं करते हैं तो आप किसी भी कठिनाई को दूर कर सकते हैं। **—अज्ञात**

• मैंने सीखा है कि लोग भूल जाते हैं कि आपने क्या कहा था, लोग भूल जाते हैं कि आपने क्या किया था, लेकिन लोग कभी नहीं भूलते कि आपने उनके साथ कैसा बरताव किया था।

—माया एंजेलो

• मेरी सलाह यह है कि तुम अपने मिनटों का ध्यान रखो, घंटे अपनी परवाह खुद कर लेंगे। **—अर्ल ऑफ चेस्टरफील्ड**

• जिस आदमी के पास सिर्फ हथौड़ा होता है, उसे अपने सामने आनेवाली हर चीज कील ही दिखती है। **—अब्राहम मासलो**

• जब मैं किसी नारी के सामने खड़ा होता हूँ तो ऐसा प्रतीत होता है कि ईश्वर के सामने खड़ा हूँ। **—एलेक्जेंडर स्मिथ**

• यदि कोई व्यक्ति आपको गुस्सा दिलाने में सफल होता है, तो ऐसा मान लें कि आप उसके हाथ की कठपुतली हैं। **—एलिजाबेथ कैन्नी**

• पिता एक प्रकाश-स्तंभ की तरह होते हैं, जब धुंध होती है तो बच्चे प्रकाश के लिए हमेशा उन पर निर्भर रह सकते हैं। **—क्रिस्टी बोरजेल्ड**

• मजबूरी की स्थिति आने से पहले ही परिवर्तन कर लें। **—जैक वेल्च**

• समस्त संसार के लिए हो सकता है कि आप केवल एक इनसान हों, लेकिन संभव है कि किसी एक इनसान के लिए आप समस्त संसार हों।

—जोसेफीन बिलिंग्स

• जो शत्रु तुम पर आक्रमण करता है, उससे मत डरो, उन मित्रों से डरो, जो तुम्हारी चापलूसी करते हैं। **—जनरल ओवगोन**

• प्रकृति का तमाशा भी खूब है, सृजन में समय लगता है, जबकि विनाश कुछ ही पलों में हो जाता है।

• डाक टिकट की तरह बनिए, मंजिल पर जब तक न पहुँच जाएँ, उसी चीज पर जमे रहिए। **—जोश बिलिंग्स** (1818-1885)

- कुछ लोग चाहे जितने बूढ़े हो जाएँ, उनकी सुंदरता नहीं मिटती, यह बस उनके चेहरों से उतरकर उनके दिलों में आ बसती है।

—मार्टिन बक्सबाम

- सूर्य की तरफ मुँह करो और तुम्हारी छाया तुम्हारे पीछे होगी।

—माओरी

- हम दूसरों का अहंकार इसलिए सहन नहीं कर पाते, क्योंकि उससे हमारा अपना अहंकार आहत होता है। **—ला रोशफूको**

- भूलना प्राय: प्राकृतिक है, जबकि याद रखना प्राय: कृत्रिम है।

—रत्वान रोमेन खिमेनेस

- इनसान से यह उम्मीद कैसे मुमकिन है कि वह सलाह ले लेगा, जबकि वह चेतावनी तक से सावधान नहीं होता। **—स्विफ्ट**

- वह लेखक सबसे अच्छा लिखता है, जो अपने पाठकों का सबसे कम समय लेकर उन्हें सबसे अधिक ज्ञान देता है। **—सिडनी स्मिथ**

- आंदोलन से विद्रोह नहीं पनपता, बल्कि शांति कायम रहती है।

—वेडेल फिलिप्स

- कोई आज छाया में इसलिए बैठा हुआ है, क्योंकि किसी ने काफी समय पहले एक पौधा लगाया था। **—वारेन बफेट**

- पीड़ा तो अवश्यंभावी है, लेकिन निर्धनता वैकल्पिक होती है।

—टिम हैंसेंल

- हम वस्तुओं को जैसी हैं, वैसे नहीं देखते हैं, हम उन्हें वैसे देखते हैं, जैसे हम हैं। **—टालमड**

- बुद्धिमान व्यक्ति बोलते हैं, क्योंकि उनके पास बोलने के लिए कुछ होता है, मूर्ख व्यक्ति बोलते हैं; क्योंकि उन्हें कुछ कहना होता है। **—प्लेटो**

- हमें कुछ भी ऐसा नहीं करना चाहिए, जिसे हम अपने बच्चों को करते हुए देखने के इच्छुक नहीं हैं। **—ब्रिघम यंग**
- दो व्यक्तियों ने एक ही सलाखों से बाहर झाँका, एक को कीचड़ दिखाई देता है, दूसरे को तारे दिखाई देते हैं (आशावादी बनें)। **—फ्रेडरिक लैंगब्रिज**
- सज्जन लोग स्वभाव से ही स्वार्थ सिद्धि में आलसी और परोपकार में दक्ष होते हैं। **—भास**
- दुनिया में सिर्फ दो संपूर्ण व्यक्ति हैं, एक मर चुका है, दूसरा अभी पैदा नहीं हुआ है।
- इतने मधुर न हों कि लोग आपको निगल लें, इतने कटु भी नहीं कि वे आपको उगल दें। **—पश्तो की कहावत**
- हमारी पहचान हमेशा हमारे द्वारा छोड़ी गई उपलब्धियों से होती है। **—अमेरिकी कहावत**
- अगर आप काँटे फैलाते हैं तो नंगे पैर न चलें। **—इटली की कहावत**
- सभी जो चर्च जाते हैं, संत नहीं होते। **—इटली की कहावत**
- जो धीरे चलते हैं, वे दूर तक जाते हैं। **—इटली की कहावत**
- आप ज्वाला से आग नहीं बुझा सकते। **—तुर्की की कहावत**
- एक छटाँक खून किलो भर दोस्ती से ज्यादा कीमती होता है। **—स्पेनी कहावत**
- माल कैसा भी हो, हाँक हमेशा ऊँची लगानी चाहिए। **—स्पेनी कहावत**
- जो वस्तु हमें पसंद होती है, जरूरी नहीं कि वह हमें मिल ही जाए, इसलिए जो मिलता है, उसे ही पसंद कर लिया जाना चाहिए। **—स्पेनी कहावत**
- विचार से कर्म की उत्पत्ति होती है, कर्म से आदत की उत्पत्ति होती है, आदत से चरित्र की उत्पत्ति होती है और चरित्र से आपके प्रारब्ध की उत्पत्ति होती है। **—बौद्ध कहावत**

- एक झूठ हजार सच्चाइयों का नाश कर देता है। **—घाना की कहावत**
- मित्रता आनंद को दुगुना और दुःख को आधा कर देती है। **—मिस्र की कहावत**
- शरीर के मामले में जो स्थान साबुन का है, वही आत्मा के संदर्भ में आँसू का। **—यहूदी कहावत**
- शिक्षक द्वार खोलते हैं, लेकिन प्रवेश आपको स्वयं ही करना होता है। **—चीनी कहावत**
- अध्यापक मार्गदर्शक का काम करते हैं, चलना आपको स्वयं पड़ता है। **—चीनी कहावत**
- जो हाथ फूल बाँटता है, उस हाथ में भी सुगंध आ जाती है। **—चीनी कहावत**
- गुलाब के फूल देनेवाले हाथों से खुशबू चिपकी रहती है। **—चीनी कहावत**
- रईस जहाँ मौजूद होते हैं, वहाँ की हवा की खुशबू बदल जाती है। **—चीनी कहावत**
- यदि आप गुस्से के एक क्षण में धैर्य रखते हैं, तो आप दुःख के सौ दिन से बच जाएँगे। **—चीनी कहावत**
- आप अपने पास दुःखों को आने से नहीं रोक सकते हैं, लेकिन आप उन दुःखों से घबराएँ नहीं, ऐसा तो आप कर सकते हैं। **—चीनी कहावत**
- गज में कब्जा करने से बेहतर है, इंच में कब्जा करना। **—चीनी कहावत**
- यदि आपको एक दिन की खुशी चाहिए, तो एक घंटा ज्यादा सोएँ। यदि एक

हफ्ते की खुशी चाहिए, तो एक दिन पिकनिक पर अवश्य जाएँ। यदि एक माह की खुशी चाहिए, तो अपने लोगों से मिलें। यदि एक साल के लिए खुशियाँ चाहिए, तो शादी कर लें और जिंदगी भर की खुशियाँ चाहिए तो किसी अनजान व्यक्ति की सहायता करें।

—चीनी कहावत

- खाली गिलास को ही भरा जा सकता है, भरे हुए गिलास में कुछ भी डालो, छलक ही पड़ेगा। **—चीनी कहावत**
- अगर आप किसी को एक दिन का खाना देते हो तो उसका पेट एक दिन के लिए ही भरता है, परंतु अगर आप उसे कमाना सिखा देते हो तो फिर उसे किसी से खाना माँगना नहीं पड़ता। **—चीनी कहावत**
- जिंदगी तो कुल एक पीढ़ी भर की होती है, पर नेक काम पीढ़ी-दर-पीढ़ी चलता है। **—जापानी कहावत**
- खुशबू को इत्र बेचनेवाले की सिफारिश की जरूरत नहीं होती। **—फारसी कहावत**
- जो जानता नहीं कि वह जानता नहीं, वह मूर्ख है, उसे दूर भगाओ। जो जानता है कि वह जानता नहीं, वह सीधा है, उसे सिखाओ। जो जानता नहीं कि वह जानता है, वह सोया है, उसे जगाओ। जो जानता है कि वह जानता है, वह सयाना है, उसे गुरु बनाओ। **—अरबी कहावत**
- ईश्वर के सामने सिर झुकाने से क्या होगा, जब हृदय ही अशुद्ध हो। **—गुरुनानक**
- ईश्वर न तो काष्ठ में विद्यमान रहता है, न पाषाण में और न ही मिट्टी की मूर्ति में, वह तो भावों में निवास करता है। **—चाणक्य**

विवेक

- विवेक बुद्धि की पूर्णता है। जीवन के सभी कर्तव्यों में वह हमारा पथ-प्रदर्शक है। **—बरुचे**

• विवेक की सबसे प्रत्यक्ष पहचान सतत प्रसन्नता है। **—मांतेन**

विश्वास

• बुद्धिमान व्यक्तियों की प्रशंसा की जाती है, धनवान व्यक्तियों से ईर्ष्या की जाती है, बलशाली व्यक्तियों से डरा जाता है, लेकिन विश्वास केवल चरित्रवान व्यक्तियों पर ही किया जाता है।

—अल्फ्रेड एडलर

• विश्वास से आश्चर्यजनक प्रोत्साहन मिलता है।

• विश्वास करना एक गुण है, अविश्वास दुर्बलता की जननी है।

—महात्मा गांधी

• असंतोष अपने ऊपर अविश्वास का फल है, यह कमजोर इच्छा का रूप है।

—एमर्सन

• प्राय: संसार में देखा जाता है कि मनुष्य पर विश्वास करने से मनुष्य विश्वासी हो उठता है। ग्रहों के बारे में भी यही बात लागू होती है।

—रवींद्रनाथ टैगोर

• वह नास्तिक है, जो अपने आप में विश्वास नहीं रखता।

—स्वामी विवेकानंद

• वे ही विजयी हो सकते हैं, जिन्हें विश्वास है कि वे विजयी होंगे।

—वर्जिल

• विश्वास आदमी को ठगता भले हो, पर उससे मन पर एक तरह का लावण्य आ जाता है। **—रवींद्रनाथ टैगोर**

• विश्वास का अभाव अज्ञान है। **—स्वामी रामतीर्थ**

• अपने से अधिक किसी पर भी विश्वास किया जा सकता है ?

—रवींद्रनाथ टैगोर

• विश्वास जीवन की शक्ति है। **—टालस्टॉय**

वेदना

- वेदना की जहाँ गहराई हो, वहाँ गंभीर होना चाहिए, नहीं तो सत्य की मर्यादा नहीं रहती। **—रवींद्रनाथ टैगोर**

व्यवस्था

- समस्त विश्व की व्यवस्था में निःश्वास और उच्छ्वास, निमेष और उन्मेष, निद्रा और जागरण का क्रम बँधा हुआ है…रुकने और चलने के अविरत योग से ही विश्व की गतिक्रिया संपन्न होती है। **—रवींद्रनाथ टैगोर**

व्यापार

- राष्ट्रों का कल्याण जितना मुक्त व्यापार पर निर्भर है, उतना ही मैत्री, ईमानदारी और बराबरी पर। **—कार्डेल हल्ल**
- इससे कोई फर्क नहीं पड़ता कि कौन शासन करता है, क्योंकि सदा व्यापारी ही शासन चलाते हैं। **—थामस फुलर**

शक्ति

- जो मनुष्य अपनी शक्ति के अनुसार बोझ लेकर चलता है, वह किसी भी स्थान पर गिरता नहीं है और न दुर्गम रास्तों में विनष्ट ही होता है। **—मृच्छकटिकम्**
- आत्म-वृक्ष के फूल और फल शक्ति को ही समझना चाहिए। **—श्रीमद्भागवत**
- अधिकांश लोग अपनी दुर्बलताओं को नहीं जानते, यह सच है; लेकिन यह भी उतना ही सच है कि अधिकतर लोग अपनी शक्ति को भी नहीं जानते। **—जोनाथन स्विफ्ट**
- माता-पिता जीवन देते हैं, लेकिन जीने की कला तो शिक्षक ही सिखाते हैं। **—अरस्तू**
- गुरु की डाँट-डपट पिता के प्यार से अच्छी है। **—शेख सादी**
- अपने विवेक को अपना शिक्षक बनाओ। **—अज्ञात**

शराब

- अगर मद्य–निषेध का मतलब भारत में महान् नैतिक जागृति है, तब तो शराब की दुकानों के बंद होने का अर्थ उस महान् आंदोलन का अनिवार्य प्रारंभ मात्र होना चाहिए, जिसके अंत में उन तमाम गरीबों और कुछ अमीरों को भी, जिनके शरीर और आत्मा दोनों को इन नशीली चीजों की लत ने तबाह कर दिया है, इससे पूरी तरह विमुख कर देना है, यह कार्य केवल राज्य के प्रयत्न से संपन्न नहीं हो सकता।

  —महात्मा गांधी

- चाय–कॉफी और शराब की परस्पर कोई तुलना नहीं हो सकती। यदि चाय और कॉफी बहुत अधिक मात्रा में ली जाए, तो उससे स्वास्थ्य पर बुरा असर होता है, लेकिन शराब तो दवा के सिवा किसी के रूप में नपी–तुली मात्रा में भी नहीं ली जा सकती, वह शरीर, मन तथा आत्मा सबका नाश करती है।

  —महात्मा गांधी

- मद्यपान एक अत्यंत पतनकारी वस्तु है, जो मनुष्य को पशु बना देती है, यह शरीर और आत्मा दोनों को दूषित कर देती है, यह नैतिक और घरेलू जीवन, दोनों को नष्ट कर देती है।

  —महात्मा गांधी

- शराब पीना एक दुर्गुण नहीं, बल्कि रोग है। इसलिए एक रोगी को बचाने के लिए उस रोगी के विरुद्ध कार्य करना होगा। **—महात्मा गांधी**

शांति

- यदि शांति पाना चाहते हो तो लोकप्रियता से बचो। **—अब्राहम लिंकन**
- शांति प्रगति के लिए आवश्यक है। **—डॉ. राजेंद्र प्रसाद**
- क्षमा में ही शांति है। **—रवींद्रनाथ टैगोर**
- वायु का जो नित्य प्रवाह है, उसमें शांति है और इसीलिए उसमें आधी से अधिक शक्ति है। **—रवींद्रनाथ टैगोर**

शिक्षक

• जब शिक्षक ही शिक्षा की सबसे बड़ी बाधा हो तो निर्बल छात्र की क्या मजाल कि वह विद्या के वन में राह बनाकर चल सके। **—रवींद्रनाथ टैगोर**

शिक्षा

• शिक्षा एक योग है। **—महात्मा गांधी**

• जीवन में प्रत्येक वयक्ति से शिक्षा ग्रहण की जा सकती है। **—दत्तात्रेय**

• जिस शिक्षा से न राष्ट्र को लाभ हो और न व्यक्ति को, उसका खर्चा भरना अपराध है। मेरी राय में व्यक्तिगत लाभ नाम की वास्तव में ऐसी कोई चीज नहीं है, जो राष्ट्र के लिए भी लाभदायक सिद्ध न की जा सकती हो और मेरे अधिकांश आलोचक भी इस बात को स्वीकार करते ही हैं कि वर्तमान उच्चतर शिक्षा का और उच्चतर शिक्षा का ही क्यों, प्राथमिक और माध्यमिक शिक्षा का वास्तविकता से कोई संबंध नहीं है। अगर बात ऐसी है, तो स्पष्ट ही वह शिक्षा राज्य के लिए भी लाभदायक नहीं हो सकती।

—महात्मा गांधी

• शिक्षा का सबसे बड़ा अंग समझा देना नहीं है, मन पर चोट लगना है।

—रवींद्रनाथ टैगोर

• बालकों को जीवनपर्यंत स्वयं को शिक्षित करते रहने में सक्षम बनाना ही शिक्षा का ध्येय है। **—रोबर्ट एम. हचिंस**

• जिस शिक्षा या विद्या से त्रिविध—आर्थिक, सामाजिक और आध्यात्मिक मुक्ति मिलती है, वही वास्तविक शिक्षा या विद्या है। **—महात्मा गांधी**

• शिक्षा जीवन की परिस्थितियों का सामना करने की योग्यता का नाम है।

—जॉन जी. हिबन

• शिक्षा का उद्देश्य पैसा कमाना नहीं, बल्कि अच्छा बनना और देश-सेवा करना है। यदि यह उद्देश्य सफल न हो, तो शिक्षा पर किए गए खर्च को बेकार समझ सकते हैं। **—महात्मा गांधी**

• लिखना–पढ़ना ही शिक्षा है और यही शिक्षा वह रास्ता है।

—रवींद्रनाथ टैगोर

• बच्चों को शिक्षित करना तो जरूरी है ही, उन्हें अपने आपको शिक्षित करने के लिए छोड़ देना भी उतना ही जरूरी है। **—अर्नेस्ट डिमनेट**

• शिक्षा का विषय है चरित्र गढ़ना। **—महात्मा गांधी**

• संसार में जितने प्रकार की प्राप्तियाँ हैं, शिक्षा सबसे बढ़कर है।

—सूर्यकांत त्रिपाठी

• मातृभाषा में शिक्षा की धारा प्रशस्त न हो तो इस क्रियाहीन देश के मरुवासी मन का क्या होगा?

—रवींद्रनाथ टैगोर

• शिक्षा से मेरा मतलब है—बच्चे या मनुष्य की तमाम शारीरिक, मानसिक और आत्मिक शक्तियों का सर्वतोमुखी विकास। अक्षर–ज्ञान, शिक्षा का न तो प्रारंभ है और न अंत। वह तो उन अनेक उपायों में से एक है, जिनके द्वारा स्त्री–पुरुषों को शिक्षित किया जा सकता है। केवल अक्षर–ज्ञान को शिक्षा कहना गलत है। इसलिए बच्चे की शिक्षा का प्रारंभ मैं किसी दस्तकारी की तालीम से ही करूँगा और उसी क्षण से उसे कुछ निर्माण करना सिखा दूँगा। इस प्रकार हर पाठशाला स्वावलंबी बना सकती है।

—महात्मा गांधी

• शिक्षा जीवन की तैयारी का शिक्षण काल है। **—विल्मट**

• उच्चतम शिक्षा वह नहीं है, जो आपको मात्र सूचनाएँ प्रदान करती है।

—अज्ञात

• हमारा शिक्षित वर्ग सुसंस्कृत वर्ग नहीं है, अपितु उपाधिकारी उम्मीदवारों का वर्ग है। **—रवींद्रनाथ टैगोर**

• शिक्षा का उद्देश्य है विद्यार्थी को मनुष्य बनाना। **—महात्मा गांधी**

- उच्चतम शिक्षा वह है, जो आपको संपूर्ण अस्तित्व और उसके परे भी जो है, उसके साथ एक करती है। —अज्ञात
- सच्ची शिक्षा तो वह है, जिसके द्वारा हम अपने को, आत्मा को, ईश्वर को, सत्य को पहचान सकें। इसके लिए किसी को साहित्य के ज्ञान की जरूरत होती है, किसी को भौतिक-शास्त्र की, किसी को कला की, आदि-आदि, लेकिन शिक्षामात्र का उद्देश्य आत्मदर्शन होना चाहिए। —महात्मा गांधी
- हम लोग अधिकार प्राप्त करने के लिए कितनी ही लड़ाई लड़ते रहें, यदि शिक्षा में पिछड़े हुए रहे, तो किसी भी हालत में हमारी स्थिति, जैसी होनी चाहिए, वैसी नहीं हो पाएगी। —महात्मा गांधी
- श्रेष्ठ शिक्षा वह नहीं, जो केवल जानकारी दे, सच्ची शिक्षा वह है, जो हमारे जीवन और वातावरण में सामंजस्य स्थापित करे। —रवींद्रनाथ टैगोर
- शिक्षा के बिना मानव-मस्तिष्क का विकास हो ही नहीं सकता। —महात्मा गांधी
- शिक्षा ऊँचा गुण है, पर चरित्र से ऊँचा नहीं। —महात्मा गांधी
- युवकों की शिक्षा पर ही राज्य आधारित है। —अरस्तू

शिशु

- छोटे शिशु को छाती से लगाकर ही समझ में आता है कि दुनिया में जात लेकर कोई नहीं जन्मता। —रवींद्रनाथ टैगोर

श्रद्धा

यदि श्रद्धा और विश्वास न रहे तो क्षण भर में प्रलय हो जाए। —महात्मा गांधी

- जिनमें श्रद्धा होती है, उनके कंधों से सभी चिंताओं का भार उतर जाता है। —महात्मा गांधी

- श्रद्धा का अर्थ है आत्मविश्वास और आत्मविश्वास का अर्थ है ईश्वर पर विश्वास। **—महात्मा गांधी**
- जहाँ बड़े-बड़े बुद्धिमानों की बुद्धि काम नहीं करती, वहाँ एक श्रद्धा काम कर जाती है। **—महात्मा गांधी**
- श्रद्धा की कसौटी यह है कि अपना फर्ज अदा करने के बाद जो कुछ भी भला या बुरा नतीजा हो, इनसान उसे मान ले। **—महात्मा गांधी**

संकल्प

- अच्छे काम का संकल्प कर लेना भी कठिन है, उसके साधन जुटाने के मार्ग में भी इतनी बाधाएँ होंगी। **—रवींद्रनाथ टैगोर**

संगति

- हीन लोगों की संगति से अपनी भी बुद्धि हीन हो जाती है, समान लोगों के साथ रहने से समान बनी रहती है और विशिष्ट लोगों की संगति से विशिष्ट हो जाती है। **—महाभारत**
- एकता से कार्य सिद्ध होते हैं। **—पंचतंत्र**
- अच्छे मित्रों को पाना कठिन, वियोग कष्टकारी और भूलना असंभव होता है। **—रैनडाल्फ**

संतोष

- संतोष मनुष्य का महत् गुण है। **—रवींद्रनाथ टैगोर**

संदेह

- बड़ी चीज को छोटा करके देखने से ही संदेह उत्पन्न होता है। **—रवींद्रनाथ टैगोर**

संप्रदाय

- संप्रदाय ऐसी चीज है कि लोगों को यह जो सबसे सीधी बात है कि इनसान इनसान है, यही भुला देता है। **—रवींद्रनाथ टैगोर**

संयम

- संयम सौष्ठवता का एक मुख्य लक्षण है। **—रवींद्रनाथ टैगोर**
- सब संयमी बनकर सेवा-भाव से अपने-अपने काम करने लग जाएँ तो वर्णाश्रम का पुनरुद्धार अशक्य नहीं है। **—महात्मा गांधी**
- अधिक-से-अधिक कर्मशील मनुष्य ज्यादा-से-ज्यादा संयमी होगा। **—महात्मा गांधी**
- संयमहीन स्त्री या पुरुष को तो गया-बीता समझिए। इंद्रियों को निरंकुश छोड़ देनेवाले का जीवन कर्णधारहीन नाव के समान है, जो निश्चय ही पहली ही चट्टान से टकराकर चूर-चूर हो जाएगी। **—महात्मा गांधी**
- संयम की कोई मर्यादा नहीं, इसलिए अहिंसा की भी कोई मर्यादा नहीं। **—महात्मा गांधी**
- संयम जीवन का स्वर्णिम सूत्र है। **—महात्मा गांधी**
- संयमशील का जीवन सदा सुखी रहता है। **—महात्मा गांधी**

संसार

- हमारे भीतर संपूर्ण नियमों का जो एक व्यतिक्रम देखा जाता है, संसार में उसका कोई मूल आदर्श नहीं। **—रवींद्रनाथ टैगोर**
- बड़ा दुःख है, बड़ी व्यथा है, सामने यह कष्टों का संसार है। हाय, यहाँ तो बड़ी दरिद्रता है, शून्यता है, बड़ी क्षुद्रता है, बड़ा अंधकार है। **—रवींद्रनाथ टैगोर**

संस्कार

- ऐसे अनेक रीति-रिवाज और संस्कार हैं, जो देश को एक नहीं होने देते। **—रवींद्रनाथ टैगोर**
- असल बात संस्कार की होती है, दलील तो केवल उपलक्ष्य हो जाती है। **—रवींद्रनाथ टैगोर**

संस्कार पूरा न हो तो प्रेम विदा नहीं होता। **—रवींद्रनाथ टैगोर**

संस्कृत

- इसकी पुरातत्त्वता जो भी हो, संस्कृत भाषा एक आश्चर्यजनक संरचनावाली भाषा है, यह ग्रीक से अधिक परिपूर्ण है और लैटिन से अधिक शब्दबहुल है तथा दोनों से अधिक सूक्ष्मतापूर्वक दोषरहित की हुई है।

  —सर विलियम जोंस

- सभ्यता के इतिहास में पुनर्जागरण के बाद, अठारहवीं शताब्दी के उत्तरार्ध में संस्कृत साहित्य की खोज से बढ़कर कोई विश्वव्यापी महत्त्व की दूसरी घटना नहीं घटी है। **—आर्थर एंथोनी मैक्डोनेल**

- कंप्यूटर को प्रोग्राम करने के लिए संस्कृत सबसे सुविधाजनक भाषा है।

  —फोर्ब्स पत्रिका

- यह लेख प्रतिपादित करता है कि एक प्रांतिक भाषा (संस्कृत) एक कृत्रिम भाषा के रूप में भी कार्य कर सकती है और कृत्रिम बुद्धि के क्षेत्र में किया गया अधिकांश काम हजारों वर्ष पुराने पहिए (संस्कृत) को खोजने जैसा ही रहा है। **—रिक् ब्रिग्स**

संस्कृति

- आधुनिकता की सबसे बड़ी समस्या यह है कि हमारी संस्कृति विज्ञान जितनी प्रगति नहीं कर पाई है। **—अंतोनियोनी**

- आदमी या औरत की संस्कृति का पता इस बात से लगता है कि व्यक्ति झगड़े के समय कैसा आचरण करता है। **—जॉर्ज बर्नार्ड शॉ**

- आस्तिक भावना और ईश्वर में विश्वास भारतीय संस्कृति का मुख्य अंग है।

  —प्रकाशवीर शास्त्री

- हिंदू संस्कृति आध्यात्मिकता की अमर आधारशिला पर आधारित है।

  —स्वामी विवेकानंद

• भारत की एकता का मुख्य आधार है एक संस्कृति, जिसका उत्साह कभी नहीं टूटा। यही इसकी विशेषता है। भारतीय संस्कृति अक्षुण्ण है, क्योंकि भारतीय संस्कृति की धारा निरंतर बहती रही है और बहेगी।

—महामना मदनमोहन मालवीय

• कोई भी संस्कृति जीवित नहीं रह सकती, यदि वह अपने को अन्य से पृथक् रखने का प्रयास करे। **—महात्मा गांधी**

संस्था

• व्यक्तियों से राष्ट्र नहीं बनता, संस्थाओं से राष्ट्र बनता है। **—डिजरायली**

सच

• जैसे सोना बनाया नहीं जा सकता, वैसे ही सच बातें भी बनाई नहीं जा सकती। **—रवींद्रनाथ टैगोर**

सच्चाई

• जो सच्चाई है, उसमें सहज मित्रता की भी कोई बाधा उचित नहीं है।

—रवींद्रनाथ टैगोर

• समाज में मिथ्या आचरण के लिए जगह है और सच्चाई के लिए नहीं है ?

—रवींद्रनाथ टैगोर

• विरोध और बाधा के बिना तो सच्चाई की परीक्षा हो ही नहीं सकती··हर युग के सामने बाधाओं और विरोधों के बीच से सत्य को नया होकर प्रकट होना होगा। **—रवींद्रनाथ टैगोर**

सज्जन

• बुरे आदमी के साथ भी भलाई करनी चाहिए, कुत्ते को रोटी का एक टुकड़ा डालकर उसका मुँह बंद करना ही अच्छा है। **—शेख सादी**

सत्य

• आप इसे मोड़ और मरोड़ सकते हैं। आप इसका बुरा और गलत प्रयोग कर

सकते हैं, लेकिन ईश्वर भी सत्य को बदल नहीं सकते हैं।

—माइकल लेवी

- कठोर सत्य भले ही शिष्ट और विनम्र ढंग से कहा जाए, लेकिन उसे कहने के लिए प्रयुक्त शब्द, संबंधित व्यक्ति को कटु ही लगेंगे। अगर हम सत्यवादी बनना चाहते हैं, तो झूठे को झूठा कहना पड़ेगा। 'झूठ' शब्द शायद कठोर है, लेकिन उसका प्रयोग इस प्रसंग में अनिवार्य है। **—महात्मा गांधी**

- सत्य के आभास मात्र को जब देखता हूँ, तब भी मुक्ति की हवा देह को शीतल कर जाती है। **—रवींद्रनाथ टैगोर**

- सत्य के लिए मरकर मनुष्य अमर हो जाता है। कोई भी जाति, जो सत्य के लिए मरती है, मनुष्य के इतिहास में अमर हो जाती है।

  —रवींद्रनाथ टैगोर

- कर्तव्य का बोध सदा दीपक के प्रकाश की भाँति स्पष्ट नहीं होता। सत्य के पुजारी को बहुत बार गोते खाने पड़ते हैं। **—महात्मा गांधी**

- व्यक्ति जब सत्य को जीता है, तब उसकी बोलने की, शाब्दिक अभिव्यक्ति की इच्छा नहीं होती। सत्य कम-से-कम शब्दों की अपेक्षा रखता है। इसलिए जीवन में अधिक सच्चा या दूसरा कोई धर्म-प्रचार का रास्ता है ही नहीं।

  —महात्मा गांधी

- अनेक लोगों के निकट प्रमाणित हुए बिना सत्य की प्रतिष्ठा नहीं होती।

  —रवींद्रनाथ टैगोर

- सत्य की कठोर तपस्या की परीक्षा करने के लिए सत्य देवता का ही यह काम है। **—रवींद्रनाथ टैगोर**

- सत्य ईश्वर है। **—महात्मा गांधी**

- जो व्यक्ति पूर्ण सत्यमय होता है, उसके लिए निराशा जैसी कोई चीज नहीं।

  —महात्मा गांधी

- जो चिरकाल के सत्य हैं, वही अकेले चहुँ ओर छाए हुए हैं, दूसरा न कोई, दूसरा न कोई। **—रवींद्रनाथ टैगोर**
- सत्य का सबसे खतरनाक दुश्मन अंधा विश्वास होता है, झूठ या असत्य नहीं। **—फ्रेडरिक नीत्शे**
- देवताओं के नाम चाहे अलग-अलग हों, सत्य एक है। **—रवींद्रनाथ टैगोर**
- अगर हमारे जीवन में सच्चाई है, तो उसका असर अपने आप लोगों पर पड़ेगा। **—महात्मा गांधी**
- सत्य आलोक की तरह है, उसकी शिखा जलते ही हम देख पाते हैं कि माया का अस्तित्व वास्तविक नहीं है। **—रवींद्रनाथ टैगोर**
- सत्य सर्वांश में ही व्यक्ति निरपेक्ष है, शुभ्र निरंजन है। **—रवींद्रनाथ टैगोर**
- जो अपने भीतर सर्वभूत को और सर्वभूतों में अपने को जानते हैं, वे ही सत्य को जानते हैं। **—रवींद्रनाथ टैगोर**
- बहुमत या तलवार के जोर से मिली हुई ताकत सच्ची ताकत नहीं है। दरअसल सच्चाई ही सच्ची ताकत है। **—महात्मा गांधी**
- सत्य और अहिंसा के बीच चुनाव करना पड़े, तो मैं अहिंसा को छोड़कर सत्य रखने में आगा-पीछा नहीं करूँगा। **—महात्मा गांधी**
- हर युग के सामने बाधाओं और विरोधियों के बीच से सत्य को नया होकर प्रकट होना होगा। **—रवींद्रनाथ टैगोर**
- सत्य को सूचक ही नहीं, प्रेरक भी होना चाहिए। **—रवींद्रनाथ टैगोर**
- सत्य की सरिता अपनी भूलों की वाहिकाओं से होकर बहती है। **—रवींद्रनाथ टैगोर**
- दुनिया के तमाम सच मिलकर एक बड़े झूठ में इजाफा करते हैं। **—बॉब डिलन**
- पृथ्वी सत्य पर टिकी हुई है। **—महात्मा गांधी**

- सत्य एक विशाल वृक्ष है। उसकी ज्यों-ज्यों सेवा की जाती है, त्यों-त्यों उसमें अनेक फल आते हुए दिखाई देते हैं। **—महात्मा गांधी**
- अगर आप सच बोलते हैं, तो आपको ज्यादा कुछ याद रखने की जरूरत नहीं है। **—मार्क ट्वेन**
- सत्य की उपलब्धि हो जाए तो उसके आगे आत्म-समर्पण करना ही होगा। **—रवींद्रनाथ टैगोर**
- सत्य को कह देना ही मेरा मजाक करने का तरीका है। संसार में यह सबसे विचित्र मजाक है। **—जॉर्ज बर्नार्ड शॉ**
- जहाँ सत्य नहीं है, वहाँ शुद्ध ज्ञान नहीं हो सकता। **—महात्मा गांधी**
- सत्य बोलना श्रेष्ठ है, लेकिन सत्य क्या है, यही जानना कठिन है। जो प्राणिमात्र के लिए अत्यंत हितकर हो, मैं इसी को सत्य कहता हूँ। **—वेद व्यास**
- जिन्हें सत्य की शक्ति पर विश्वास है, वे अपनी जबरदस्ती को संयत रखते हैं। **—रवींद्रनाथ टैगोर**
- सत्य स्वयंसिद्ध नहीं है, उसे सिद्ध करना पड़ता है।
- वस्तुगत यथार्थ वास्तव में स्वप्न के भीतर एक और स्वप्न की तरह है। **—एडगर एलन पो**
- सत्य के सिवा और किसी चीज की हस्ती है ही नहीं। **—महात्मा गांधी**
- अपने आपको जान लेना सत्य को पहचानना है। **—महात्मा गांधी**
- सत्य के वाहकों के मन, वचन और कर्म में एक सहज, सरल शांति रहनी चाहिए। **—रवींद्रनाथ टैगोर**
- सत्य को यथार्थ सत्य मानकर ग्रहण कर रहा है या नहीं, इसकी परीक्षा तो मनुष्य को देनी ही होगी। **—रवींद्रनाथ टैगोर**

- सत्य का व्यापार ऐसा शौकिया व्यापार नहीं है कि रत्न भी मिल जाए और दाम भी न चुकाना पड़े।

—रवींद्रनाथ टैगोर

- जब तक सत्य से प्यार नहीं किया जाएगा, तब तक उसे ग्रहण ही नहीं किया जा सकता।

—रवींद्रनाथ टैगोर

- डरपोक प्राणियों में सत्य भी गूँगा हो जाता है। **—प्रेमचंद**

- असत् का अस्तित्व नहीं है और सत् का नाश नहीं है।

—योगीराज श्रीकृष्ण

सत्याग्रह

- आजकल हथियारबंद या दूसरी तरह के किसी भी विरोध को सत्याग्रह का नाम देना एक फैशन सा हो गया है। इससे समाज को नुकसान होता है। इसलिए अगर आप लोग सत्याग्रह के पूरे अर्थ को समझ लें और यह जान लें कि सत्य और प्रेम के रूप में जीता-जागता भगवान् सत्याग्रही के साथ रहता है, तो आपको यह मानने में कोई हिचकिचाहट नहीं होगी कि सत्याग्रह पर कोई विजय नहीं पा सकता।

—महात्मा गांधी

- सत्य का आग्रह रखने की कला हस्तगत होते ही अन्याय का सामना करने की शक्ति आ ही जाती है, किंतु सत्य का आग्रह तो प्रतिदिन निरालस भाव से कोई विशुद्ध पारमार्थिक कार्य—निस्स्वार्थ, मोहरहित सेवा अर्थात् विशुद्ध यज्ञ करने से ही उत्पन्न होता है।

—महात्मा गांधी

- सत्याग्रह का अर्थ है—सत्य का आग्रह। यह आग्रह रखनेवाले मनुष्य में अतुल बल आ जाता है। इस बल को हम सत्याग्रह के नाम से पहचानते हैं। अगर सत्य का आग्रह सच्चा हो, तो माता-पिता, स्त्री-पुरुष-पुत्रादि के विरुद्ध, राजा-प्रजा के विरुद्ध और आखिरकार सारे जगत् के विरुद्ध उसका प्रयोग किया जा सकता है।

—महात्मा गांधी

- सत्याग्रह का मतलब है सत्य पर आग्रह रखना। जब कोई आदमी सत्य पर

आग्रह करता है, तो उसे उससे बल मिलता है। अगर उसके सही बोध के बिना कोई उसका प्रयोग करता है, तो मानना चाहिए कि वह सत्याग्रह का नाम व्यर्थ ही ले रहा है। **—महात्मा गांधी**

- सत्याग्रह लोकमत को शिक्षा देने की एक ऐसी प्रक्रिया है, जो समाज के समस्त तत्त्वों को प्रभावित करके अंत में अजेय बन जाती है। हिंसा से उस प्रक्रिया में बाधा पड़ती है और सारे समाज की सच्ची क्रांति में विलंब होता है। **—महात्मा गांधी**

- एक सत्याग्रही डर नाम की वस्तु को भूल जाता है, इसलिए अपने विरोधी का विश्वास करने में वह कभी नहीं डरता, उसका विरोधी भले ही उसे बीस बार धोखा दे, सत्याग्रही इक्कीसवीं बार भी उस पर विश्वास करने में तत्पर रहेगा, क्योंकि मानव-प्रकृति पर चरम आस्था उसका अखंड विश्वास है! **—महात्मा गांधी**

- सत्याग्रही अपने हर कर्म में कृत्रिमता से दूर हो, हर कार्य स्वाभाविक रूप से करता है एवं स्वत: प्रेरित होकर करता है।

- सत्याग्रही का अविनयी होना तो दूध में छाहर पड़ने के समान समझना चाहिए। **—महात्मा गांधी**

सदाचार

- मेरे लिए तो सदाचार, नैतिक नियम और धर्म एक ही बात है। आदमी अगर पूरी तरह से सदाचारी हो, परंतु धार्मिक न हो, तो उसका जीवन बालू पर खड़ी की गई इमारत की तरह समझिए। इसी तरह सदाचारहीन धर्म भी दूसरों को दिखाने भर के लिए होता है और आपस में सिर-फुटौवल का कारण बनता है। **—महात्मा गांधी**

सर्वधर्म समभाव

- मुझे जितनी आस्था 'गीता' पर है, उतनी ही 'बाइबिल' पर है। मैं मानता हूँ कि दुनिया के सारे महान् धर्म उतने ही सच्चे हैं, जितना कि मेरा धर्म। **—महात्मा गांधी**

- सभी धर्म एक ही जगह पर ले जानेवाले अलग-अलग मार्गों की तरह हैं। अगर वे हमें अपने लक्ष्य पर पहुँचा देते हों, तो फिर उनके अलग-अलग होने से अंतर क्या पड़ता है ? वस्तुत: तो जितने व्यक्ति, उतने ही धर्म भी हैं···जब तक अलग-अलग धर्म विद्यमान हैं, तब तक प्रत्येक धर्म के लिए किसी विशेष बाह्य प्रतीक की आवश्यकता भले ही हो, परंतु जब वह बाह्य प्रतीक आडंबर मात्र रह जाए और दूसरों के धर्म से अपने धर्म को श्रेष्ठ बताने के लिए उसका प्रयोग किया जाने लगे तो वह त्याज्य हो जाता है।

- हम सब जाने या अनजाने, पृथ्वी पर शांति और मानव-जाति में परस्पर सद्भाव स्थापित करने को लालायित हैं और उसके लिए प्रयत्न करते हैं। मेरा दृढ़ विश्वास है कि हम विभिन्न धर्मों के अनुयायियों की कलह और वाद-विवाद द्वारा दुनिया में न शांति स्थापित कर सकते हैं, न सद्भाव। तुच्छ-से-तुच्छ मनुष्य के पास भी जब हम मन में प्रार्थना का भाव लेकर जाएँगे, तभी हमें सत्य, शांति और सद्भाव की प्राप्ति हो सकेगी। **—महात्मा गांधी**

सपने

- हमारे कई सपने शुरू में असंभव लगते हैं, फिर असंभाव्य और फिर जब हममें संकल्पशक्ति आती है तो ये सपने अवश्यंभावी हो जाते हैं।

—क्रिस्टोफर रीव

- सपने देखना बेहद जरूरी है, लेकिन केवल सपने देखकर ही मंजिल को हासिल नहीं किया जा सकता, सबसे ज्यादा जरूरी है जिंदगी में खुद के लिए कोई लक्ष्य तय करना। **—डॉ. अब्दुल कलाम**

- स्वप्नद्रष्टा और यथार्थ के सृष्टा बनिए। **—अज्ञात**

- अभिलाषा तभी फलदायक होती है, जब वह दृढ़ निश्चय में परिणत कर दी जाती है। **—स्वेट मार्डेन**

सफल

- सफल व्यक्ति बैठकर घटनाओं का इंतजार नहीं करते अपितु आगे बढ़ते हैं और कार्य को अंजाम देते हैं। **—बिल गेट्स**

- सफल व्यक्ति वही है, जो सुबह उठकर पहले यह तय करता है कि आज उसे क्या-क्या काम करने हैं और रात तक वह उन सारे कामों को कई परेशानियों के बाद भी पूरा कर लेता है।

—बिल गेट्स

- सफल होने के लिए आपको असफलता का स्वाद अवश्य चखना चाहिए, ताकि आपको यह पता चल सके कि अगली बार क्या नहीं करना है।

—बिल गेट्स

सफलता

- सफलता बहुत अच्छी होती है, लेकिन हमें ध्यान रखना चाहिए कि हम एक सफलता को बार-बार दोहराएँ नहीं।

—जैक निकलसन

- सफलता एक घटिया शिक्षक है, यह लोगों में यह सोच विकसित कर देती है कि वे असफल नहीं हो सकते। **—बिल गेट्स**
- अपने सकारात्मक विचारों को ईमानदारी और बिना थके हुए कार्यों में लगाएँ और आपको सफलता के लिए प्रयास नहीं करना पड़ेगा, अपितु अपरिमित सफलता आपके कदमों में होगी। **—बिल गेट्स**
- हमारी सफलता इस बात पर निर्भर करती है कि हम अपने जीवन का प्रतिक्षण, प्रतिघंटा और प्रतिदिन कैसे बिताते हैं। **—बिल गेट्स**
- मेरा मानना है कि सफलता का कोई नियम नहीं है, लेकिन आप असफलता से बहुत कुछ सीख सकते हैं। **—बिल गेट्स**
- सफलता की खुशी मानना अच्छा है, पर उससे जरूरी है, अपनी असफलता से सीख लेना। **—बिल गेट्स**
- अगर आप सफल होना चाहते हैं, तो आपको सफलता के घिसे-पिटे रास्तों पर चलने के बजाय नए रास्ते बनाने चाहिए। **—बिल गेट्स**

- समस्याओं में रहने से सफलता कठिन है। **—बिल गेट्स**

- सफलता एक ऐसा शिक्षक है, जो कुशाग्र बुद्धि संपन्न लोगों को यह सोचने के लिए प्रेरित करता है कि वे पराजित नहीं हो सकते।

  —बिल गेट्स

- हमें अधिकांश सफलताएँ तब मिलती हैं, जब हमारे प्रतिद्वंद्वी अपने कार्यों को सही तरीके से नहीं करते और यही मेरे लिए सौभाग्य बन जाता है, किंतु मैं विश्वास करता हूँ कि आपको किसी ऐसी नीति पर कार्य नहीं करना चाहिए, जो दूसरों की गलतियों पर आधारित हो, यद्यपि उन्होंने निश्चित रूप से अनेक त्रुटियाँ की होंगी। **—बिल गेट्स**

- समस्त सफलताएँ कर्म की नींव पर आधारित होती हैं। **—एंथनी रॉबिंस**

- सफलता पाने हेतु हर हाल में स्वयं के आसरे ही आगे बढ़ना होता है।

  —बिल गेट्स

- सफल हमें अपने बल पर होना होता है, भाग्य या भगवान् का आसरा नहीं खोजना चाहिए। **—बिल गेट्स**

- अपनी सफलता अथवा असफलता की, संभावनाओं के आकलन में समय नष्ट न करें, केवल अपना लक्ष्य, निर्धारित करें और काम शुरू कर दें।

  —बिल गेट्स

- प्रतिदिन की छोटी-छोटी उपलब्धियों से ही मिलकर सफलता बनती है।

  —बिल गेट्स

- सफलता अपने सामर्थ्य को साकार करना है। **—बिल गेट्स**

- जिसने अपने को वश में कर लिया है, उसकी जीत को देवता भी हार में नहीं बदल सकते। **—महात्मा बुद्ध**

- सफलता का कोई रहस्य नहीं है, वह केवल अत्यधिक परिश्रम चाहती है।

  —बिल गेट्स

- सफलता की कामना करनेवाले व्यक्ति को शीर्ष पर पहुँचने की प्रक्रिया के एक हिस्से के रूप में असफलता को एक अपरिहार्य हिस्सा मानना चाहिए। **—बिल गेट्स**

- सफलता की गिनती यह नहीं कि आप खुद कितने ऊँचे तक उठे हैं, बल्कि इसमें है कि आप अपने साथ कितने लोगों को लाए हैं। **—बिल गेट्स**

- सफलता की सभी कथाएँ बड़ी-बड़ी असफलताओं की कहानी हैं। **—बिल गेट्स**

- सफलता के मार्ग में कठिनाइयों का आंना स्वभाविक है। **—बिल गेट्स**

- सफलता के लिए किसी सफाई की जरूरत नहीं होती और असफलता की कोई सफाई नहीं होती। **—बिल गेट्स**

- जो अकले चलते हैं, वे शीघ्रता से बढ़ते हैं। **—नेपोलियन**

- सफलता के लिए कोई लिफ्ट नहीं जाती, इसलिए सीढ़ियों से ही जाना पड़ेगा। **—बिल गेट्स**

- सफलता सार्वजनिक उत्सव है, जबकि असफलता व्यक्तिगत शोक। **—बिल गेट्स**

- विफल होना मंजूर किया जा सकता है, लेकिन सफल होने के लिए प्रयास न करना मंजूर नहीं किया जा सकता। **—माइकल**

सभ्यता

- हमारी सभ्यता तो आध्यात्मिक सभ्यता है। **—रवींद्रनाथ टैगोर**

- मनुष्यत्व को प्राप्त करने के लिए बड़े झूठ की अपेक्षा छोटा सत्य अधिक मूल्यवान है। **—रवींद्रनाथ टैगोर**

- हिंदू सभ्यता के मूल में समाज है और यूरोपीय सभ्यता के मूल में राष्ट्रनीति है। **—रवींद्रनाथ टैगोर**

समझ

- ईश्वर ने समझ की कोई सीमा नहीं रखी है। **—बेकन**
- संघर्ष और उथल-पुथल के बिना जीवन बिल्कुल नीरस हो जाता है। इसलिए जीवन में आनेवाली विषमताओं को सह लेना ही समझदारी है। **—विनोबा भावे**
- समझ मस्तिष्क का प्रकाश है। **—विल्स**

समय

- समय पर कार्य नहीं करने से व्यक्ति लाभ और उन्नति से कोसों दूर हो जाता है। **—बाबा फरीद**
- भविष्य वर्तमान के द्वारा क्रय किया जाता है। **—जॉनसन**
- आपका समय एक बहुमूल्य संसाधन है। **—बिल गेट्स**
- अस्त-व्यस्त रीति से समय गँवाना अपने ही पैरों पर कुल्हाड़ी मारना है। **—बिल गेट्स**
- जो समय बचाते हैं, वे धन बचाते हैं और बचाया हुआ धन, कमाएँ हुए धन के बराबर है। **—महात्मा गांधी**
- जो समय का ज्यादा दुरुपयोग करते हैं, वे ही समय की कमी की सबसे ज्यादा शिकायत करते हैं। **—ब्रुयर**
- जिसके द्वारा समय व्यर्थ नष्ट किया जाता है, ऐसे नर-पशु को नमस्कार।
- समय को व्यर्थ नष्ट मत करो, क्योंकि यही वह चीज है, जिससे जीवन का निर्माण हुआ है। **—बेंजामिन फ्रैंकलिन**
- आप बच्चों के साथ कितना समय बिताते हैं, वह इतना महत्त्वपूर्ण नहीं है, जितना यह कि कैसे बिताते हैं। **—बिल गेट्स**
- आपके पास जितना समय अभी है, उससे अधिक समय कभी नहीं होगा। **—बिल गेट्स**

- काल्ह करै सो आज कर, आज करै सो अब।
  पल में परलय होएगी, बहुरि करेगो कब॥ **—कबीरदास**

- समयनिष्ठ होने पर समस्या यह हो जाती है कि इसका आनंद अकसर आपको अकेले लेना पड़ता है। **—एनॉन**

- समय पर किया हुआ थोड़ा सा भी कार्य उपकारी होता है। **—योगवसिष्ठ**

- बिता हुआ समय और मुख से निकले शब्द कदापि वापस नहीं आते। **—कहावत**

- आप समय को नष्ट करेंगे तो समय भी आपको नष्ट कर देगा। **—बिल गेट्स**

- कभी न लौटनेवाला समय जा रहा है। **—बिल गेट्स**

- आप अतीत को तो बदल नहीं सकते, लेकिन आप वर्तमान को भविष्य की चिंता में नष्ट जरूर कर सकते हैं। **—अज्ञात**

- हर दिन मेरा सर्वश्रेष्ठ दिन है, यह मेरी जिंदगी है। मेरे पास यह क्षण दोबारा नहीं होगा। **—बर्नी सीगल**

- दूरदर्शिता, जो दूसरे नहीं देख पाएँ, उसे देख पाने की कला है। **—जोनाथन स्विफ्ट**

- हम सीमित हैं, हमारी क्षमताओं से नहीं, लेकिन हमारी दूरदर्शिता से। **—अज्ञात**

- व्यस्त रहना काफी नहीं है, व्यस्त तो चींटियाँ भी रहती हैं। सवाल यह है कि हम किसलिए व्यस्त हैं। **—हेनरी डेविड थौरु**

- किसी भी काम के लिए आपको कभी भी समय नहीं मिलेगा। यदि आप समय पाना चाहते हैं तो आपको इसे बनाना पड़ेगा।

- सभी महान् उपलब्धियाँ समय माँगती हैं। —बिल गेट्स
- समय की रेत पर कदमों के निशान बैठकर नहीं बनाए जा सकते। —बिल गेट्स
- जो अपने समय का सबसे ज्यादा दुरुपयोग करते हैं, वे ही समय की कमी की सबसे ज्यादा शिकायत करते हैं। —ब्रुयर
- जीवन छोटा ही क्यों न हो, समय की बरबादी से वह और भी छोटा हो जाता है। —जॉनसन
- वर्तमान परिस्थिति में हम क्या करते, सोचते और विश्वास करते हैं, उसी से हमारा भविष्य तय होता है।
- समय पर कार्य नहीं करने से व्यक्ति लाभ और उन्नति से कोसों दूर हो जाता है। —बिल गेट्स
- समय सबसे कम पाया जानेवाला संसाधन है और जब तक इसका अच्छा प्रबंधन नहीं किया जाता है, तो बाकी किसी चीज का प्रबंधन नहीं किया जा सकता। —बिल गेट्स
- समय हमेशा कड़ी मेहनत करनेवालों का मित्र रहा है। —बिल गेट्स
- सिर्फ अतीत की जुगाली करने से कोई लाभ नहीं है। —अज्ञात
- सोने का प्रत्येक धागा मूल्यवान होता है, इसी प्रकार समय का प्रत्येक क्षण भी मूल्यवान होता है। —मैसन
- समय किसी की प्रतीक्षा नहीं करता। —अज्ञात
- बीता हुआ समय और कहे हुए शब्द कदापि वापस नहीं आ सकते। —कहावत
- प्रकृति के सब काम धीरे-धीरे होते हैं। —अज्ञात
- समय का उचित उपयोग करना समय को बचाना है। —बेकन

- समय महान् चिकित्सक है। **—अज्ञात**
- एक युग विशाल नगरों का निर्माण करता है, एक क्षण उसका ध्वंस कर देता है। **—सेनेका**
- हर दिन वर्ष का सर्वोत्तम दिन है।
- राजा—कुछ ऐसा लिखो, जिसे पढ़कर खुशी में गम हो और गम में पढ़ो तो खुशी हो। वजीर—यह समय बीत जाएगा। **—अज्ञात**
- दौड़ना काफी नहीं है, समय पर चल पड़ना चाहिए। **—फ्रांसीसी कहावत**
- समय पर थोड़ा सा प्रयत्न भी आगे की बहुत से परेशानियों को बचाता है। **—कहावत**
- बुद्धिमान लोग अतीत की घटनाओं पर नहीं पछताते, वे भविष्य की चिंता नहीं करते, केवल वर्तमान जगत् मैं पूर्णतया कर्म करते हैं। **—अज्ञात**
- सही काम करने के लिए समय हर वक्त ही ठीक होता है। **—मार्टिन लूथर किंग जूनियर**
- जैसे नदी बह जाती है और लौटकर नहीं आती, उसी प्रकार रात और दिन मनुष्य की आयु लेकर चले जाते हैं, फिर नहीं आते। **—महाभारत**
- मैंने समय को नष्ट किया है। अब समय मुझको नष्ट कर रहा है। **—शेक्सपियर**
- समय फिरने पर मित्र भी शत्रु हो जाते हैं। **—गोस्वामी तुलसीदास**
- हर संत का एक अतीत होता है और हर पापी का एक भविष्य। **—ऑस्कर वाइल्ड**
- सही टाइमिंग पर लगभग हर बात सकारात्मक तरीके से कही जा सकती है।
- हम आज अच्छे हैं, यह भी एक किस्म का पागलपन है। **—एडवर्ड यंग**
- वक्त को बरबाद न करो, क्योंकि जिंदगी इसी से बनी है। **—फ्रेंकलिन**

समस्या

- जिस प्रकार से श्रम करने से शरीर मजबूत होता है, उसी प्रकार से कठिनाइयों से मस्तिष्क सुदृढ़ होता है। **—सेनेका**
- दुनिया की बहुत सारी समस्याएँ खत्म हो जाएँ, अगर लोग दूसरों के बारे में बात करने की बजाय दूसरों से बात करना शुरू कर दें। **—अज्ञात**
- विपत्ति मनुष्य को विचित्र साथियों से मिलाती है। **—अज्ञात**
- मैं अति प्रतिभाशाली व्यक्ति नहीं हूँ, लेकिन मैं निश्चित तौर पर अधिक जिज्ञासु हूँ और किसी भी समस्या को सुलझाने में अधिक देर तक लगा रहता हूँ। **—अल्बर्ट आइंस्टीन**
- आपत्तियाँ हमें आत्म-ज्ञान कराती हैं, ये हमें दिखा देती हैं कि हम किस मिट्टी के बने हैं। **—जवाहरलाल नेहरू**
- आपदा ही एक ऐसी स्थिति है, जो हमारे जीवन की गहराइयों में अंतर्दृष्टि पैदा करती है। **—स्वामी विवेकानंद**
- हम अपनी समस्याओं को उसी सोच के साथ नहीं सुलझा सकते, जिस सोच के साथ हमने उनका निर्माण किया था। **—अल्बर्ट आइंस्टीन**
- हमारी अधिकतर बाधाएँ पिघल जाएँगी, अगर उनके सामने दुबकने की बजाय हम उनसे निडरतापूर्वक निपटने का मानस बनाएँ। **—ओरिसन स्वेट मार्डन**
- इस दुनिया की असली समस्या यह है कि मूर्ख और अड़ियल लोग तो अपने बारे में हमेशा पक्के होते हैं कि वे सही हैं, किंतु बुद्धिमान लोग हमेशा संदेह में रहते हैं कि मैं गलत तो नहीं हूँ। **—अज्ञात**
- विकट परिस्थितियाँ ही महापुरुषों का विद्यालय है। **—अरस्तू**
- आनंद विनोद के सामने कठिनाइयाँ पिघल जाती हैं। **—स्वेट मार्डेन**

- आपात स्थिति में, मन को डाँवाँडोल नहीं होने देना चाहिए।

—महावीर स्वामी

- मुसीबतों से दुःखी न हों, क्योंकि दुःखी होना मूर्खों का काम है।

—हजरत अली

- विपत्ति से बढ़कर अनुभव सिखानेवाला कोई विद्यालय आज तक नहीं खुला। **—मुंशी प्रेमचंद**

- जब सपने और इच्छाएँ पर्याप्त बड़े होते हैं, परिस्थितियों से कोई फर्क नहीं पड़ता है। **—अज्ञात**

- बेहतर विकल्प के लिए समस्याओं से मुकाबला करना चाहिए। तभी आप में 'स्किल' आती है। परेशानियों से डरकर किसी दूसरे का सहारा लेने की आदत न पालें तो बेहतर है। **—अज्ञात**

समाज

- हमारा समाज हमारे धर्म-विश्वास पर ही प्रतिष्ठित है। **—रवींद्रनाथ टैगोर**

- समाज के लिए मनुष्य को संकुचित होकर रहना पड़े, यह कभी ठीक नहीं हो सकता, समाज को ही मनुष्य के लिए अपने को बराबर प्रशस्त करते चलना होगा। **—रवींद्रनाथ टैगोर**

- समाज अगर समय की गति में बाधा दे तो उसे चोट सहनी ही होगी।

—रवींद्रनाथ टैगोर

- समाज को सुंदर, परिमार्जित श्रृंखलित बनाना हम सभी का फर्ज है।

—रवींद्रनाथ टैगोर

- समाज जितनी ही उन्नति करता जाता है, उसके दायित्व और कर्तव्य की जटिलता स्वभावतः उतनी ही बढ़ती जाती है। **—रवींद्रनाथ टैगोर**

समाजवाद

- समाजवाद सुंदर शब्द है, क्योंकि इसके अनुसार समाज के सभी सदस्य बराबर हैं, न कोई ऊँच है, न नीच। **—महात्मा गांधी**

- समाजवाद के सिद्धांतानुसार राजा और किसान, धनाढ्य और गरीब, मालिक और नौकर, सब समान स्तर के हैं। **—महात्मा गांधी**

- सच्चा समाजवाद वही हो, जिसमें वाद न हो।

  —महात्मा गांधी

- मैं तो अपने आपको समाजवादी ही कहता हूँ। मुझे यह शब्द ही पसंद है, पर मेरा समाजवाद वह नहीं है, जिसका समाजवादी उपदेश करते फिरते हैं।

  —महात्मा गांधी

- समाजवाद के बारे में मेरा यह विचार है कि हम सब बराबर या समान रूप में पैदा हुए हैं और हमें समान अवसर प्राप्त होने का अवसर मिलना चाहिए, परंतु मैं इतना तो कहूँगा कि सभी व्यक्तियों में समान क्षमता नहीं होती।

  —महात्मा गांधी

- समाजवाद राजनीतिक जगत् में एक प्रगतिपूर्ण सुधार का कदम है।

  —महात्मा गांधी

- यदि वाद के चक्कर में न पड़कर केवल समाज के हित के लिए काम किया जाए, तो वह सर्वोत्तम समाजवाद है। **—महात्मा गांधी**

सम्मान

- जब तुम खुद का सम्मान करोगे, तभी दूसरे भी तुम्हारा सम्मान करेंगे।

  —कन्फ्यूशियस

- आत्मसम्मान की रक्षा हमारा सबसे पहला धर्म है। **—प्रेमचंद**

- यदि सम्मान खोकर आय बढ़ती हो, तो उससे निर्धनता श्रेयस्कर है।

  —शेख सादी

- दूसरों का सम्मान करो, लोग तुम्हारा भी सम्मान करेंगे।

  —कन्फ्यूशियस

सलाह

- इनसान जितनी सहजता से सलाह देता है, उतनी सहजता से कुछ और नहीं देता। **—रोचेफोकोल्ड**
- बिना माँगे किसी को हरगिज नसीहत मत दो। **—जर्मन कहावत**
- जब हम किसी नई परियोजना पर विचार करते हैं तो बड़े गौर से उसका अध्ययन करते हैं, महज सतही तौर पर नहीं, बल्कि उसके हर एक पहलू का। **—वाल्ट डिज्नी**

संविधान

- मुझे लगता है संविधान व्यावहारिक है, यह शांतिकाल और युद्धकाल दोनों ही समय देश को बाँधे रखने के लिए लचीला है और मजबूत भी। वास्तव में मैं कह सकता हूँ कि यदि नए संविधान के अंतर्गत कुछ गलत होता है, तो उसका कारण यह नहीं होगा कि हमारा संविधान खराब है, हमें यह कहना होगा कि यह मनुष्य की नीचता थी। **—बी.आर. आंबेडकर**
- मुझे उन लोगों से समस्या है, जो संविधान को हल्के में लेते हैं और बाइबिल को हकीकत में। **—बिल मेहर**
- संविधान में किसी चीज के साथ हस्तक्षेप नहीं कीजिए, उसे बनाए रखा जाना चाहिए, क्योंकि हमारी स्वतंत्रता का यही एक रक्षक है। **—अब्राहम लिंकन**

साधना

- साधना हमें ईश्वर तक पहुँचाती है, तपस्या ब्रह्म तक। **—रवींद्रनाथ टैगोर**
- पाने की उत्कृष्ट प्रणाली साधना है, तपस्या है। **—रवींद्रनाथ टैगोर**
- महामानव की अभ्यर्थना तो वही मानव कर सकता है, जिसने मनुष्यत्व की साधना की है, पूर्णता की साधना की है। **—रवींद्रनाथ टैगोर**

- जो सबसे अधिक असाध्य है, उसकी साधना कौन करेगा, वह जब आता है, अपने आप सहज में ही चला आता है। **—रवींद्रनाथ टैगोर**

साहस

- बिना निराश हुए ही हार को सह लेना पृथ्वी पर साहस की सबसे बड़ी परीक्षा है। **—आर.जी. इंगरसोल**
- मुट्ठी भर संकल्पवान लोग, जिनकी अपने लक्ष्य में दृढ़ आस्था है, इतिहास की धारा को बदल सकते हैं। **—महात्मा गांधी**
- किसी की करुणा व पीड़ा को देखकर मोम की तरह दयार्द्र हो पिघलनेवाला हृदय तो रखो, परंतु विपत्ति की आँच आने पर कष्टो-प्रतिकूलताओं के थपेड़े खाते रहने की स्थिति में चट्टान की तरह दृढ़ व ठोस भी बने रहो। **—द्रोणाचार्य**
- यह सच है कि पानी में तैरनेवाले ही डूबते हैं, किनारे पर खड़े रहनेवाले नहीं, मगर ऐसे लोग कभी तैरना भी नहीं सीख पाते। **—वल्लभभाई पटेल**
- दिलेरी डर की गैर-मौजूदगी नहीं, बल्कि यह फैसला है कि डर से भी जरूरी कुछ है। **—मेग काबोट**
- डर से डरो नहीं। वह तुम्हें डराने के लिए नहीं हैं। वह तुम्हें ये बताने के लिए है कि कुछ ऐसा है, जो इस लायक है। **—सी. जॉयबेल सी**
- साहस आगे बढ़ने की शक्ति होना नहीं है, यह शक्ति न होने पर भी आगे बढ़ते जाना है। **—नेपोलियन बोनापार्ट**
- किसी के द्वारा प्रगाढ़ता से प्रेम किया जाना आपको शक्ति देता है और किसी से प्रगाढ़ता से प्रेम करना आपको साहस देता है। **—लाओत्से**
- सफलता कभी अंतिम नहीं होती, विफलता कभी घातक नहीं होती। जो मायने रखता है, वह है साहस। **—विंस्टन चर्चिल**

• जो आप सचमुच हैं, वह बनने के लिए साहस चाहिए होता है।

—ई.ई. कमिंग्स

• खड़े होकर बोलने के लिए साहस चाहिए होता है, बैठकर सुनने के लिए भी साहस चाहिए होता है। **—विंस्टन चर्चिल**

• हर चीज से बढ़कर अपने जीवन की नायिका बनिए, शिकार नहीं।

—नोरा एफ्रान

• साहस सभी गुणों में सबसे महत्त्वपूर्ण है, क्योंकि बिना साहस के आप किसी और गुण का निरंतरता के साथ अभ्यास नहीं कर सकते। **—माया एंजिलो**

• यकीन करो कि तुम कर सकते हो और तुमने आधा रास्ता तय कर लिया है।

—थियोडोर रूजवेल्ट

• बिना भय के साहस नहीं हो सकता। **—क्रिस्टोफर पाओलीनी**

• अपना सपना दूसरों को दिखाने के लिए बहुत साहस चाहिए होता है।

—एरमा बोंबेक

• सच स्वीकारने के लिए शक्ति और साहस चाहिए होता है।

—रिक रिओरडैन

• यदि हमारे अंदर कोई भी प्रयास करने का साहस नहीं होता तो जिंदगी कैसी होती? **—विन्सेंट वेन गोह**

• कुछ लोगों में दिमाग से अधिक साहस होता है। **—जॉन ग्रीशैम**

• जीवन किसी के साहस के अनुपात में सिमटता या विस्तृत होता है।

—एनेस निन

• स्वतंत्रता निर्भीक होने में निहित है। **—रॉबर्ट फ्रोस्ट**

• प्यार पर एक और बार और हमेशा एक और बार यकीन करने का साहस रखिए। **—माया एंजिलो**

- तुम जो भी करो, तुम्हें साहस की जरूरत पड़ेगी। तुम जो भी रास्ता चुनो, हमेशा कोई–न–कोई यह बतानेवाला मिल जाएगा कि तुम गलत हो।

—राल्फ वाल्डो एमर्सन

- जब हमें सबसे कम उम्मीद होती है, जिंदगी हमारे साहस और बदलने की इच्छा का परिक्षण करने के लिए एक चुनौती देती है, ऐसे समय में, ऐसा दिखावा करना कि कुछ नहीं हुआ या यह कहने में कि हम अभी तैयार नहीं हैं, का कोई मतलब नहीं है। चुनौती इंतजार नहीं करेगी। जिंदगी पीछे नहीं देखती। एक हफ्ते का समय आवश्यकता से अधिक समय है, यह तय करने के लिए कि हमें अपनी नियति स्वीकार है या नहीं। **—पाउलो कोएलो**

- आध्यात्मिक मार्ग पर दो सबसे कठिन परीक्षण हैं, सही समय की प्रतीक्षा करने का धैर्य और जो सामने आए, उससे निराश न होने का साहस।

—पाउलो कोएलो

- साहस दबाव में अनुग्रह है। **—अर्नेस्ट हेमिंग्वे**

- साहस ऐसी जगह पाया जाता है, जहाँ उसकी संभावना कम हो।

—जे.आर.आर. टोकन

- प्रसन्नता का राज स्वतंत्रता है, स्वतंत्रता का राज साहस है। **—कैरी जोंस**

- मैंने यह जाना है कि डर का न होना साहस नहीं है, बल्कि डर पर विजय पाना साहस है। बहादुर वह नहीं है, जो भयभीत नहीं होता, बल्कि वह है, जो इस भय को परास्त करता है। **—नेल्सन मंडेला**

- यह ध्यान रखिए कि बहुत से लोग अपनी धारणा के चलते जान दे चुके हैं, वास्तव में यह बहुत आम है। सच्चा साहस उस चीज के लिए जीने और कष्ट सहने में है, जिसमें आप यकीन करते हैं। **—क्रिस्टोफर पाओलीनी**

- वस्तुतः अच्छा समाज वह नहीं है, जिसके अधिकांश सदस्य अच्छे हैं, बल्कि वह है, जो अपने बुरे सदस्यों को प्रेम के साथ अच्छा बनाने में सतत प्रयत्नशील है। **—डब्ल्यू.एच. आडेन**

- शोक मनाने के लिए नैतिक साहस चाहिए और आनंद मनाने के लिए धार्मिक साहस। अनिष्ट की आशंका करना भी साहस का काम है, शुभ की आशा करना भी साहस का काम, परंतु दोनों में आकाश–पाताल का अंतर है। पहला गर्वीला साहस है, दूसरा विनीत साहस। **—किर्केगार्द**
- किसी दूसरे को अपना स्वप्न बताने के लिए लोहे का जिगर चाहिए होता है। **—एरमा बॉम्बेक**
- अपने प्रयोजन में दृढ़ विश्वास रखनेवाला एक कृशकाय शरीर भी इतिहास के रुख को बदल सकता है। **—महात्मा गांधी**
- निराश हुए बिना पराजय को सह लेना, पृथ्वी पर साहस की सबसे बड़ी मिसाल है। **—इंगरसोल**
- हमारी सुरक्षा, हमारी अर्थव्यवस्था और हमारे ग्रह के लिए बदलाव लाने का हममें साहस और प्रतिबद्धता होनी चाहिए। **—बराक ओबामा**
- मानव के सभी गुणों में साहस पहला गुण है, क्योंकि यह सभी गुणों की जिम्मेदारी लेता है। **—चर्चिल**
- प्रेरणा की हर अभिव्यक्ति में पुरुषार्थ और पराक्रम की आवश्यकता है। **—जैनेंद्र कुमार**
- यह संकल्प कर लें कि यह जोखिम लेने योग्य है, तो आपको तत्काल कर्म करने का साहस जुटा लेना चाहिए। **—अज्ञात**
- सच्चा साहसी वह है, जो बड़ी–से–बड़ी विपत्ति को बुद्धिमत्तापूर्वक सह सकता है। **—शेक्सपियर**
- हर परिस्थिति मैं शांत रहनेवाला निश्चित ही शिखर को छूता है। **—अज्ञात**
- साहस का अर्थ होता है, यह पता होना कि किस बात से डरना नहीं चाहिए। **—प्लेटो**

साहित्य

- साहित्य···परिवर्तनशील मानव-जगत् का चंचल प्रतिबिंब है।
—रवींद्रनाथ टैगोर

- साहित्य का विषय ही पुराना है, पर वह शक्ल धारण कर नया हो जाया करता है। **—रवींद्रनाथ टैगोर**

- साहित्य का विषय मानव-हृदय एवं मानव-चरित्र है। **—रवींद्रनाथ टैगोर**

- सच्चे साहित्य का निर्माण एकांत चिंतन और एकांत साधना में होता है।
—अनंत गोपाल शेवड़े

- साहित्य व्यक्ति विशेष का नहीं होता, वह रचयिता का नहीं होता, वह देववाणी है। **—रवींद्रनाथ टैगोर**

- साहित्य का प्रधान अवलंबन ज्ञान का विषय नहीं है, भाव का विषय है।
—रवींद्रनाथ टैगोर

- सर्व-साधारण की वस्तु को विशेष भाव से अपना बनाकर, उसी उपाय से उसे फिर विशेष भाव से सर्व साधारण का बना देना ही साहित्य का काम है।
—रवींद्रनाथ टैगोर

- साहित्य का कर्तव्य केवल ज्ञान देना नहीं है, परंतु एक नया वातावरण देना भी है। **—डॉ. सर्वपल्ली राधाकृष्णन**

- साहित्य में जो दिखता है, वह प्राकृतिक होने पर भी प्रत्यक्ष नहीं है।
—रवींद्रनाथ टैगोर

- मन जिसे बनाता है, वह अपनी आवश्यकता के लिए, साहित्य जिसे बनाता है, वह सबके आनंद के लिए है। **—रवींद्रनाथ टैगोर**

- साहित्य का आदिम सत्य होता है, प्रकाशमात्र, परंतु उसका परिणाम सत्य होता है, इंद्रिय, मन एवं आत्मा के समष्टिगत मनुष्य का प्रकाश।
—रवींद्रनाथ टैगोर

- यथार्थ साहित्य जिस तरह यथार्थ राष्ट्रीय एकता का फल है, उसी तरह राष्ट्रीय ऐक्य साधन का प्रधानतम उपाय साहित्य है।

—रवींद्रनाथ टैगोर

- साहित्य समाज का दर्पण होता है। **—अज्ञात**

- साहित्य की मूल नीति चिरंतन है अर्थात् रस-संभोग का जो नियम है, वह मनुष्य के नित्य स्वभाव के अंतर्गत है। **—रवींद्रनाथ टैगोर**

- साहित्य में विषय-वस्तु निश्चेष्ट हो जाती है, यदि उसकी सजीवता न रहे।

—रवींद्रनाथ टैगोर

- साहित्य में जहाँ पर सच्चा रूप जग उठता है, वहाँ भय नहीं है।

—रवींद्रनाथ टैगोर

- सृष्टि के साथ साहित्य की तुलना होती है, यह असीम सृष्टि-कार्य असीम अवसर के भीतर निमग्न है। **—रवींद्रनाथ टैगोर**

- साहित्य के बारे में यदि कोई बात हो तो संक्षेप में समाप्त करो और भी संक्षेप में पूरी करो। **—रवींद्रनाथ टैगोर**

- साहित्य का सार-संकलन नहीं किया जा सकता। इतिहास, दर्शन, विज्ञान का सार-संकलन किया जा सकता है।

—रवींद्रनाथ टैगोर

- जिन सब खबरों को सभी लोग जानते हैं, अधिकांश साहित्य उन्हीं को लेकर रचा जाता है। **—रवींद्रनाथ टैगोर**

- साहित्य जीवन का स्वाभाविक प्रकाश होता है, वह प्रयोजन का प्रकाश नहीं है। **—रवींद्रनाथ टैगोर**

- हृदय का जगत् स्वयं को व्यक्त करने के लिए व्याकुल रहता है। इसीलिए सदैव मनुष्य के भीतर साहित्य का आवेग रहता है।

—रवींद्रनाथ टैगोर

• चित्र एवं संगीत ही साहित्य के प्रधान उपकरण हैं। चित्र भाव को आकार देता है एवं संगीत भाव को गति प्रदान करता है। चित्र देह एवं संगीत प्राण हैं।

—रवींद्रनाथ टैगोर

• साहित्य व्यवसायी को अपने अंदर से तरह-तरह के भाव और पात्र बाहर निकालने पड़ते हैं। वह उन भावों को स्वतंत्र और संपूर्ण रूप में प्रकट करता है, वह ज्यों ही उन्हें साफ-साफ प्रकट करता है, वे अमर हो जाते हैं।

—रवींद्रनाथ टैगोर

• जो साहित्य चर्चा करते हैं, उनकी रसज्ञता की शक्ति केवल मस्तिष्क में ही नहीं, रसना में भी खूब प्रबल रहती है। **—रवींद्रनाथ टैगोर**

साहित्यकार

• जगत् के साथ मन का जो संबंध है, मन के साथ साहित्यकार की प्रतिभा का वही संबंध है। **—रवींद्रनाथ टैगोर**

• साहित्यकार की मानवता ही सृजनकर्ता है। **—रवींद्रनाथ टैगोर**

• साहित्य, संगीत और कला से हीन पुरुष साक्षात् पशु ही है, जिसकी पूँछ और सींग नहीं हैं। **—भर्तृहरि**

सीखना

• व्यथा और वेदना की पाठशाला में जो पाठ सीखे जाते हैं, वे पुस्तकों तथा विश्वविद्यालयों में नहीं मिलते। **—अज्ञात**

• विष से भी अमृत तथा बालक से भी सुभाषित ग्रहण करें। **—मनु**

• यदि मनुष्य सीखना चाहे, तो उसकी हर भूल उसे कुछ शिक्षा दे सकती है।

—महात्मा गांधी

• नई चीज सीखने की जिसने आशा छोड़ दी, वह बूढ़ा है। **—विनोबा भावे**

• मनुष्य सफलता से कुछ नहीं सीखता, विफलता से बहुत कुछ सीखता है।

—अरबी लोकोक्ति

सुख

- सुख की न तो कोई परिभाषा है और न कोई सीमा है।

—रवींद्रनाथ टैगोर

- किसी वस्तु में सुख नहीं है। हिंसा में सुख नहीं, आधिपत्य में सुख नहीं, तुमने जिस पथ का अवलंब किया है, एक मात्र उसी में सुख है।

—रवींद्रनाथ टैगोर

- सुख जब तुम्हारी मुट्ठी में हो तो उसे इस तरह से भोगो कि औरों को ईर्ष्या न हो। **—रवींद्रनाथ टैगोर**

- सहज सुख सहज नहीं है। जिसे मूल्य देकर खरीदना नहीं पड़ता, वह यदि अपने हाथ के पास न मिले तो उसे किसी प्रकार से कहीं भी खोजकर पाना संभव नहीं है। **—रवींद्रनाथ टैगोर**

- सुख सर्वत्र मौजूद है, उसका स्रोत हमारे हृदयों में है। **—रस्किन**

- सुख का रहस्य त्याग में है। **—एंड्रयू कारनेगी**

- सुख बाहर से मिलने की चीज नहीं, मगर अहंकार छोड़े बगैर इसकी प्राप्ति भी होनेवाली नहीं। **—महात्मा गांधी**

- जीवन का वास्तविक सुख, दूसरों को सुख देने में हैं, उनका सुख लूटने में नहीं। **—मुंशी प्रेमचंद**

- जीवन के प्रति जिस व्यक्ति की कम-से-कम शिकायतें हैं, वही इस जगत् में अधिक-से-अधिक सुखी है।

सुख-दुःख

- संसार में सबसे अधिक दुःखी प्राणी कौन है ? बेचारी मछलियाँ, क्योंकि दुःख के कारण उनकी आँखों में आनेवाले आँसू पानी में घुल जाते हैं, किसी को दिखते नहीं। अतः वे सारी सहानुभूति और स्नेह से वंचित रह जाती हैं। सहानुभूति के अभाव में तो कणमात्र दुःख भी पर्वत हो जाता है।

—खलील जिब्रान

• सुखी होना चाहते हैं, तो सब बातों को मन में मत रख। दूसरे को दोषी बनाने का जो सुख है, मन में दोष रखने का दु:ख उससे कहीं बड़ा है।

—रवींद्रनाथ टैगोर

• संसार में प्राय: सभी जन सुखी एवं धनशाली मनुष्यों के शुभेच्छु हुआ करते हैं। विपत्ति में पड़े मनुष्यों के प्रियकारी दुर्लभ होते हैं। **—मृच्छकटिकम्**

• व्याधि शत्रु से भी अधिक हानिकारक होती है। **—चाणक्य सूत्र**

• विपत्ति में पड़े हुए का साथ बिरला ही कोई देता है। **—रावणार्जुनीयम्**

• हम इन सब सुखों-दु:खों को संसार के साथ, शास्त्र के साथ मिलकर उसे भला-बुरा एक नाम देकर परे कर देते हैं।

—रवींद्रनाथ टैगोर

• मनुष्य के जीवन में दो तरह के दु:ख होते हैं—एक यह कि उसके जीवन की अभिलाषा पूरी नहीं हुई और दूसरा यह कि उसके जीवन की अभिलाषा पूरी हो गई।

—बर्नार्ड शॉ

• मेरी हार्दिक इच्छा है कि मेरे पास जो भी थोड़ा-बहुत धन शेष है, वह सार्वजनिक हित के कामों में यथाशीघ्र खर्च हो जाए। मेरे अंतिम समय में एक पाई भी न बचे, मेरे लिए सबसे बड़ा सुख यही होगा।

—पुरुषोत्तमदास टंडन

• मानव जीवन में दो और दो चार का नियम सदा लागू होता है। उसमें कभी दो और दो पाँच हो जाते हैं। कभी गण तीन भी और कई बार तो सवाल पूरे होने के पहले ही स्लेट गिरकर टूट जाती है।

—सर विंस्टन चर्चिल

• स्वयं के समीप सुख-दु:ख को प्रमाणित करने की आवश्यकता नहीं होती, दूसरों के समीप उसे प्रमाणित करना होता है। **—रवींद्रनाथ टैगोर**

• तपाया और जलाया जाता हुआ लौहपिंड दूसरे से जुड़ जाता है, वैसे ही दु:ख से तपते मन आपस में निकट आकर जुड़ जाते हैं। **—लहरीदशक**

- चाहे राजा हो या किसान, वह सबसे ज्यादा सुखी है, जिसको अपने घर में शांति प्राप्त होती है। **—गेटे**

सुधार

- अपना सुधार संसार की सबसे बड़ी सेवा है। **—बिल गेट्स**
- अपने आपको सुधार लेने पर संसार की हर बुराई सुधर सकती है। **—बिल गेट्स**

सुनना

- सुनना एक कला है। इस कला के लिए कान और ध्यान दोनों चाहिए। **—अज्ञात**
- व्यर्थ की बातों से खुद को बचाना भी एक कला है। **—अज्ञात**
- वाणी चाँदी है तो मौन सोना है। **—अज्ञात**
- बीती बातों को भूलने का सर्वोत्तम तरीका है, हमेशा नई और रचनात्मक बातें सुनना व उनको रमण करना। **—अज्ञात**
- मौन से मतलब वाणीविहीन बनना नहीं है। सही समय पर सही बात कहना है। **—अज्ञात**

सुंदर

- सुंदर को हम तब तक नहीं देख पाते, जब तक हम उसे छोड़ नहीं देते। **—रवींद्रनाथ टैगोर**
- सुंदर का जवाब सुंदर ही पाता है। असुंदर जब जवाब छीन लेना चाहता है तो वीणा के तार नहीं बजते, टूट जाते हैं। **—रवींद्रनाथ टैगोर**

सुंदरता

- सुंदरता बिना श्रृंगार के मन मोहती है। **—सादी**
- वास्तविक सौंदर्य हृदय की पवित्रता में है। **—महात्मा गांधी**

• सुंदर वही हो सकता है, जो कल्याणकारी हो।

—भगवतीचरण वर्मा

• सौंदर्य आकार और सममिति पर निर्भर होता है। चाहे कोई जीव छोटा हो या बेहद बड़ा, वह खूबसूरती को परिभाषित नहीं करता, क्योंकि उसको एक दृष्टि मात्र में देखने पर उसकी स्थिति स्पष्ट नहीं होती है, इसलिए वे परिपूर्ण की श्रेणी में नहीं आते। **—अरस्तू**

• मेरी नजर में मेरा करीबी दोस्त कभी भी वृद्ध नहीं हो सकता, वह वैसा ही रहेगा, जैसा मैंने उसे पहली बार देखा था, उसकी सुंदरता अनुभव करने के लिए सुंदर चीज की जरूरत नहीं होती। **—रवींद्रनाथ टैगोर**

• खूबसूरती वैसी ही दिखेगी, जैसी मैंने पहली नजर में देखी थी।

—विलियम शेक्सपियर

• अतिशय सुंदरता कभी-कभी हमें भयानक रूप से ठेस भी पहुँचा सकती है।

—एदुआर्दो गैलियानो

• खूबसूरती एक अनुभव है, इसके सिवा कुछ भी नहीं। इसे बयाँ करने के लिए स्थापित मानक नहीं है, न ही नाक-नक्श का वर्णन करना काफी है।

—डी.एच. लॉरेंस

• खूबसूरती चेहरे पर नहीं होती, यह तो दिल की रोशनी है, बहुत ध्यान से देखनी पड़ती है। **—खलील जिब्रान**

• जो सुंदरता आँखों द्वारा देखी जाती है, वह कुछ ही पल की होती है, यह जरूरी भी नहीं कि हमारे भीतर से भी वही खूबसूरती दिखाई दे।

—जॉर्ज सेंड

• दुनिया की सबसे अच्छी और खूबसूरत चीजें कभी देखी या छुई नहीं गईं, वे बस दिल के साथ घुल-मिल गईं। **—हेलेन कलर**

• सुंदर चीजों पर यकीन बनाए रखिए, याद रहे—सूरज डूब गया तो वसंत भी नहीं आएगा। **—गिल्सन**

• एक शख्स हर दिन संगीत सुने, थोड़ी सी कविता पढ़े और अपने जीवन की सुंदर तसवीर रोज देखे, उसे सुंदरता की परिभाषा तलाशने की जरूरत ही नहीं, क्योंकि भगवान् ने सासरे संसार का सौंदर्य उसकी झोली में डाल रखा है।

—गोयथे

• खूबसूरती में मानव खुद को पूर्णता के स्तर पर देखता है, कुछ परिस्थितियों में वह खुद की पूजा करता है, मनुष्य यह मान लेता है कि यह पूरा विश्व खूबसूरती से भरा हुआ है, यह भूल जाता है कि जो सुंदरता वह देख रहा है, वह उसके द्वारा बनाई हुई है। **—अज्ञात**

• मानव ने अकेले ही इस जहान को खूबसूरती अर्पित की है।

—फ्रेडरिक नीत्शे

• सुंदरता जब आपको आकर्षित कर रही होती है, व्यक्तित्व तब तक आपके दिल पर कब्जा कर चुका होता है। **—अज्ञात**

• हम सारी दुनिया घूमते और खूबसूरती तलाशते रहते हैं। कभी मुड़के भी नहीं देखते, अपने पास ही छुपी हुई खूबसूरती की ओर। **—एमर्सन**

• कभी भी कुछ सुंदर देखने का मौका मत छोड़ो, सच तो यह है कि खूबसूरती भगवान् की लिखावट है। हर चेहरे पर, धुले-धुले आसमान में, हर फूल में उसकी लिखावट नजर आएगी और हे भगवान्, इस सौंदर्य के लिए हम आपके आभारी हैं।

—राल्फ वाल्डो एमर्सन

• सुंदरता सबको चाहिए, इसके लिए आओ, बाहर आओ। पूजाघर में और खेल के मैदानों में सौंदर्य बिखरा पड़ा है। उससे अपना तन और मन भर लो। **—जॉन मुइर**

सेवा

• त्याग के लिए त्याग करना मुश्किल होता है, परंतु सेवा के निमित्त आसान हो जाता है। **—महात्मा गांधी**

- अपंग की सेवा एक धर्म है। भगवान् हमें अपंग के रूप में हमेशा दर्शन देते हैं। —**महात्मा गांधी**
- मानव-सेवा के काम में राजनीतिक मतभेदों और संघर्षों के बावजूद सबको एक होना चाहिए। —**महात्मा गांधी**
- शून्यवत् होकर रहने का मतलब है, सबकी सेवा करना और दुःख में दूसरों की टहल करना। —**महात्मा गांधी**
- सेवा का भी मोह हो सकता है। मोह भाव छोड़ने से ही सच्ची सेवा हो सकती है। —**महात्मा गांधी**
- सेवा मानव-वृत्तियों में सबसे ऊँची और महान् वृत्ति है। —**महात्मा गांधी**
- सेवा से बढ़कर व्यक्ति को द्रवित करनेवाली और कोई चीज संसार में नहीं है। —**महात्मा गांधी**
- सेवा तो मूक ही होनी चाहिए, जिसने अपनी सेवा का ढिंढोरा पीटा, वह मानो अपने आपको समाप्त कर चुका। —**महात्मा गांधी**

सौंदर्य

- बाहरी सौंदर्य न हो तो पुरुषों की आँखें देवी को देख नहीं पातीं। —**रवींद्रनाथ टैगोर**
- सौंदर्य आत्मा और जड़ के भीतर एक पुल के समान है। पदार्थ केवल पिंड है। —**रवींद्रनाथ टैगोर**
- भाषा मनुष्य की सृष्टि है, परंतु सौंदर्य को पैदा करनेवाला संपूर्ण संसार का सृष्टिकर्ता ही है। —**रवींद्रनाथ टैगोर**

सौभाग्य

- सौभाग्य, जो अचानक हमारे दरवाजे पर आकर हमें पुकार जाता है, वह केवल यह दिखाने के लिए कि उसे ग्रहण करने की शक्ति हममें नहीं है। —**रवींद्रनाथ टैगोर**

स्त्री

- यदि स्त्रियों में आत्मविश्वास आ जाए, उनकी श्रद्धा दृढ़ हो जाए, तो स्त्रियाँ खुद ही जान जाएँगी कि उनके मन में जो भय था, वैसा भय रखने का कोई कारण ही नहीं है। मनुष्य–मात्र में राम और रावण रहते हैं। यदि स्त्रियाँ अपने हृदय में निवास करनेवाले राम की सहायता से काम करें, तो मनुष्यों में रहनेवाला रावण सिर नहीं उठा सकता। स्त्रियों की अपेक्षा पुरुषों में राम देर से जागता है। जिसे राम राखे, उसे कौन चाखे और जिससे राम रूठे, उसे कौन राखे? **—महात्मा गांधी**
- जीवन की कला को अपने हाथों से साकार कर नारी ने सभ्यता और संस्कृति का रूप निखारा है, नारी का अस्तित्व ही सुंदर जीवन का आधार है।
- इसे भूलने से काम नहीं चलेगा कि स्त्रियाँ ही पुरुषों में प्रेरणा जुटाती हैं। **—रवींद्रनाथ टैगोर**
- स्त्री की उन्नति या अवनति पर ही राष्ट्र की उन्नति निर्भर है। **—अरस्तू**
- सुयोग्य स्त्री परिवार की शोभा तथा गृह की लक्ष्मी है। **—मनु**
- स्त्रियाँ तो त्याग, दया और अहिंसा की मूर्ति हैं। जहाँ अहिंसा–धर्म को केवल बुद्धि से ही समझते हैं, वहाँ स्त्रियों के लिए वह एक ऐसी वस्तु है, जिसे वे जन्म से ही जानती हैं। पुरुष तो बहुत थोड़ी जिम्मेदारी उठाकर ही अपने को कृतकार्य मान लेता है, किंतु बहनों को तो पति की, बालकों की तथा परिवार के अन्य सदस्यों की सेवा करनी पड़ती है। **—महात्मा गांधी**
- स्त्रियों की मान–हानि साक्षात् लक्ष्मी और सरस्वती की मानहानि है। **—सूर्यकांत त्रिपाठी 'निराला'**
- आप एक आदमी को शिक्षित करते हैं, तो आप एक आदमी को शिक्षित करते हैं, आप एक औरत को शिक्षित करते हैं, तो आप एक पीढ़ी को शिक्षित करते हैं। **—ब्रिघैम यंग**
- स्त्रियों को अबला जाति कहना उनका अपमान है, ऐसा कहकर पुरुष स्त्रियों

के प्रति अन्याय ही करते हैं। बल का अर्थ पशुबल किया जाए, तो सचमुच स्त्री पुरुष की अपेक्षा कम पशु है, परंतु बल का अर्थ नैतिक बल हो, तो उसमें पुरुष से स्त्री कहीं श्रेष्ठ है।

• स्त्रियों के हाथों ही जो पलते हैं, उनके दूध के दाँत कभी भी नहीं टूटते।

—रवींद्रनाथ टैगोर

• किसी स्त्री के सलाह लीजिए और जो कुछ भी वह कहे, उसका उल्टा कीजिए निश्चित रूप से आप बुद्धिमान बन जाएँगे।

—टॉमस मूर

• औरत के बाल आमतौर पर लंबे होते हैं, पर उसकी जुबान और भी ज्यादा लंबी होती है। **—शेक्सपियर**

• हर स्त्री का मन एक साँचे में ढला होता है। **—रवींद्रनाथ टैगोर**

• स्त्री में यदि विनाश की शक्ति है तो कल्याण की भी शक्ति उसके अंदर छिपी हुई है। मेरी यही कामना है कि वह अपनी उस कल्याणकारी शक्ति को पहचाने। यदि वह ऐसा सोचना बंद कर दे कि वह कमजोर और पुरुषों के खेलने की गुड़िया बनने के ही योग्य है, तो वह अपने लिए और पुरुष के लिए भी, चाहे पुरुष उसका पिता हो या पुत्र अथवा पति, संसार को अधिक सुखमय बना सकती है।

—महात्मा गांधी

• जब लड़की शरमाना बंद कर देती है तो वह अपनी सुंदरता का सबसे शक्तिशाली आकर्षण खो देती है। **—ग्रेगरी**

• एक आकर्षक स्त्री रत्नजड़ित आभूषण है एवं एक अच्छी स्त्री कोषाध्यक्ष।

—अज्ञात

• स्त्री एवं संगीत को कभी समय से संबंधित नहीं करना चाहिए। **—अज्ञात**

• मैं देखता हूँ, जब मर्द औरत से प्यार करता है, वह अपनी जिंदगी का बहुत

छोटा हिस्सा देता है, पर जब औरत प्यार करती है, वह सबकुछ दे देती है।

—आस्कर वाइल्ड

- स्त्रियाँ ही तो समाज की शोभा होती हैं। **—रवींद्रनाथ टैगोर**
- मेरा विचार है कि अच्छी औरतों का प्रभाव सभ्यता को मापने के लिए पर्याप्त है। **—राल्फ वाल्डो एमर्सन**
- महिलाएँ पुरुषों से अधिक बुद्धिमान होती हैं, क्योंकि वे जानती कम हैं और समझती ज्यादा हैं। **—जेम्स थर्बर**
- स्त्रियाँ तो देवी हैं। **—रवींद्रनाथ टैगोर**
- पारिवारिक बंधन का मूल्य स्त्रियों के लिए बहुत अधिक होता है। **—रवींद्रनाथ टैगोर**

स्त्री-पुरुष

- स्त्री और पुरुष का एक-दूसरे पर समान अधिकार होता है, इसीलिए उनके बीच समान प्रेम का संबंध होता है। **—रवींद्रनाथ टैगोर**
- स्त्रियों को ईश्वर ने अपने मानस से सिरजा और और पुरुषों को उन्होंने अपने हाथों से, हथौड़ी से पीट-पीटकर बनाया है। **—रवींद्रनाथ टैगोर**

स्पर्धा

स्पर्धा और प्रतिस्पर्धा से वातावरण दीप्त और उद्दीप्त रहता है।

—जैनेंद्र कुमार

स्मृति

- स्मृति एक अद्भुत उपकरण है, वह अमिट नहीं है, लेकिन वह क्षणभंगुर भी नहीं है। **—प्राइमो लेवी**

स्वतंत्र चिंतन

- कोई व्यक्ति कितना ही महान् क्यों न हो, आँखें मूँदकर उसके पीछे न चलिए।

यदि ईश्वर की ऐसी ही मंशा होती तो वह हर प्राणी को आँख, नाक, कान, मुँह, मस्तिष्क आदि क्यों देता?

—स्वामी विवेकानंद

- मानवी चेतना का परावलंबन, अंत:स्फुरणा का मूर्च्छाग्रस्त होना, आज की सबसे बड़ी समस्या है। लोग स्वतंत्र चिंतन करके परमार्थ का प्रकाशन नहीं करते, बल्कि दूसरों का ऊटपटाँग अनुकरण करके ही रुक जाते हैं।

—श्रीराम शर्मा आचार्य

- बिना वैचारिक-स्वतंत्रता के, बुद्धि जैसी कोई चीज हो ही नहीं सकती और बोलने की स्वतंत्रता के बिना जनता की स्वतंत्रता नहीं हो सकती।

—बेंजामिन फ्रेंकलिन

- प्रत्येक व्यक्ति के लिए उसके विचार ही सब तालों की चाबी हैं।

—एमर्सन

- शारीरिक गुलामी से बौद्धिक गुलामी अधिक भयंकर है।

—श्रीराम शर्मा आचार्य

- ग्रंथ, पंथ हो अथवा व्यक्ति, नहीं किसी की अंधी भक्ति।

—श्रीराम शर्मा आचार्य

- सर्वोत्तम मानव मस्तिष्क की पहचान है, किन्हीं दो पूर्णत: विपरीत विचारधाराओं को साथ-साथ ध्यान में रखते हुए भी स्वतंत्र रूप से कार्य करने की क्षमता का होना।

—स्कॉट फिट्जेराल्ड

- अपना दीपक स्वयं बनो। **—गौतम बुद्ध**

स्वतंत्रता

- किसी भी कीमत पर स्वतंत्रता का मोल नहीं किया जा सकता, वह जीवन है। भला जीने के लिए कोई क्या मोल नहीं चुकाएगा?

—महात्मा गांधी

• जब तक गलती करने की स्वतंत्रता न हो, तब तक स्वतंत्रता का कोई अर्थ नहीं है।

—महात्मा गांधी

• हिंसक तरीकों से हिंसक स्वतंत्रता मिलेगी, यह दुनिया के लिए और खुद भारत के लिए एक गंभीर खतरा होगा।

—महात्मा गांधी

• आततायी कभी स्वेच्छा से आजादी नहीं देता, पीड़ितों द्वारा इसकी माँग की जानी चाहिए।

—मार्टिन लूथर किंग जूनियर

• स्वतंत्रता की कीमत हमेशा अधिक होती है, लेकिन अमरीकियों ने हमेशा यह कीमत चुकाई है और हमें एक मार्ग कभी नहीं चुनना चाहिए और वह मार्ग है समर्पण और हार मानने का।

—जॉन एफ. केनेडी

• विकास के लिए सबसे अच्छा मार्ग आजादी का मार्ग है।

—जॉन एफ. केनेडी

• हीरो वह होता है, जो स्वतंत्रता के साथ आई जिम्मेदारियों को समझता है।

—बॉब डाइलेन

• तुम मुझे खून दो, मैं तुम्हें आजादी दूँगा।

—सुभाष चंद्र बोस

• ईश्वर की कृपा से हमारे देश में तीन बेहद कीमती चीजें उपलब्ध हैं, भाषण की स्वतंत्रता, अंतरात्मा की स्वतंत्रता और इनमें से किसी का भी प्रयोग न करने का विवेक।

—मार्क ट्वैन

• सभी महान् चीजें बड़ी सरल होती हैं और कइयों को हम बस एक शब्द में व्यक्त कर सकते हैं—स्वतंत्रता, न्याय, सम्मान, कर्तव्य, दया, आशा।

—विंस्टन चर्चिल

• जो लोग दूसरों को आजादी नहीं देते, उन्हें खुद भी इसका हक नहीं होता।

—अब्राहम लिंकन

स्वदेश

- वह हृदय नहीं है पत्थर है, जिसमें स्वदेश का प्यार नहीं।

—मैथिलीशरण गुप्त

स्वाधीन

- मनुष्य जहाँ स्वभाव से स्वाधीन है, धर्म से स्वाधीन है, वहाँ उसके खाने-सोने-बैठने को भी समाज ने बिल्कुल निरर्थक बंधनों में बाँध रखा है।

—रवींद्रनाथ टैगोर

- अगर समाज को लाँघना चाहते हो तो तुम्हें समाज से बड़ा बनना होगा।

—रवींद्रनाथ टैगोर

स्वाधीनता

- पराधीन सपनेहु सुख नाहीं। **—गोस्वामी तुलसीदास**

- आजादी मतलब जिम्मेदारी, तभी तो लोग उससे घबराते हैं।

—जॉर्ज बर्नार्ड शॉ

स्वामी

- जो मनुष्य सदा बाहरी आचार से ही चालित होता है, उसकी पंगुता वैसी ही होती है, जैसी कि प्रत्येक विषय में दास पर निर्भर रहनेवाले मालिक की। आंतरिक मनुष्य ही स्वामी है, जब वह बाह्य प्रथा पर पूर्णतया अवलंबित होता है तथा उसकी दुर्गति का कोई अंत नहीं होता। **—रवींद्रनाथ टैगोर**

स्वार्थ

- मनुष्य के स्वार्थ का कोई अंत नहीं। **—रवींद्रनाथ टैगोर**

- स्वार्थ-बुद्धि के कारण सहोदर भाइयों में भी झगड़े होने लगते हैं और आगे बढ़कर ये झगड़े मृत्यु तक के कारण बन जाते हैं। **—रवींद्रनाथ टैगोर**

स्वावलंबन

- स्वावलंबन सफलता की पहली सीढ़ी है। **—महात्मा गांधी**

• स्वावलंबन व्यक्ति के लिए भी उतना ही वांछनीय है, जितना समाज और राष्ट्र के लिए। **—महात्मा गांधी**

• देश के हर बालक को पहले स्वावलंबी बनने का पाठ पढ़ाना चाहिए। हमें यह गुण पाश्चात्य देशवासियों से सीखना चाहिए।

—महात्मा गांधी

• संसार के बहुतेरे महान् पुरुष स्वावलंबी और अध्यवसायी रहे हैं।

—महात्मा गांधी

स्वास्थ्य

• हमारा कर्तव्य है कि हम अपने शरीर को स्वस्थ रखें अन्यथा हम अपने मन को सक्षम और शुद्ध नहीं रख पाएँगे। **—गौतम बुद्ध**

• शरीर में ही सबकुछ है। जो इसमें नहीं है, वह जगत् में भी नहीं है।

—महात्मा गांधी

• शीघ्र सोने और प्रातःकाल जल्दी उठनेवाला मानव आरोग्यवान, भाग्यवान और ज्ञानवान होता है। **—जयशंकर प्रसाद**

• जहाँ तक हो सके निरंतर हँसते रहो, यह सस्ती दवा है। **—अज्ञात**

• केवल वही मनुष्य स्वस्थ है, जिसका स्वस्थ दिमाग तंदुरुस्त शरीर में है।

—महात्मा गांधी

• अच्छा स्वास्थ्य एवं अच्छी समझ जीवन के दो सर्वोत्तम वरदान हैं।

—साइरस

• स्वास्थ्य अच्छा रखने के लिए ब्रह्मचर्य का पालन बहुत ही जरूरी है।

—महात्मा गांधी

• स्वास्थ्य केवल शारीरिक या मानसिक दुरुस्ती को नहीं कहते, जब तक दोनों का संतुलन न हो, मनुष्य स्वस्थ नहीं कहा जा सकता।

—महात्मा गांधी

- शरीर और मन के बीच इतना घनिष्ठ संबंध है कि दो में से किसी को क्षति पहुँचे, तो सारे शरीर को कष्ट सहन करना पड़ता है। इससे यह सिद्ध होता है कि शुद्ध चरित्र ही स्वास्थ्य की कुंजी है और हम कह सकते हैं कि इससे भिन्न विचार और बुरी वासनाएँ तरह-तरह की बीमारियाँ हैं।

—महात्मा गांधी

- यदि तन और मन दोनों स्वस्थ हुए तभी मनुष्य स्वस्थ कहा जा सकता है।

—महात्मा गांधी

- प्रतिदिन एक सेब खाने से डॉक्टर की आवश्यकता नहीं होती।

—अंग्रेजी कहावत

- स्वास्थ्य परिश्रम में है और श्रम के अलावा वहाँ तक पहुँचने का कोई दूसरा राजमार्ग नहीं। **—वेंडेल फिलप्स**

- शरीर के स्वस्थ होने का यह भी मतलब है कि मनुष्य की इंद्रियाँ और मन भी स्वस्थ हैं। **—महात्मा गांधी**

- शरीर को हवा, पानी, खुराक नियमित रूप में मिलती रहे और वह बिना आलस्य के ठीक तौर से काम करता रहे, तो अस्वस्थ होने का कोई कारण नहीं हो सकता। **—महात्मा गांधी**

- अच्छा मजाक आत्मा का स्वास्थ्य है, चिंता उसका विष। **—स्टैनली**

हँसी

- जब मैं स्वयं पर हँसता हूँ तो मेरे मन का बोझ हल्का हो जाता है।

—रवींद्रनाथ टैगोर

- देवता की हँसी सूर्य का प्रकाश है, उससे बर्फ तो पिघल जाती है, किंतु पत्थर नहीं गलता। **—रवींद्रनाथ टैगोर**

हरिजन

- केवल जन्म के कारण कोई मनुष्य अछूत नहीं माना जा सकता।

—महात्मा गांधी

- अछूतपन को दूर किए बिना अस्पृश्यों में सुधार या प्रचार नहीं हो सकता।

—महात्मा गांधी

- मनुष्य के प्राथमिक हकों के बारे में कानून की नजरों में तो वही होना चाहिए, जिस तरह कि जात-पाँत और वर्ण का लिहाज रखे बिना हम लोगों में भूख-प्यास इत्यादि सर्वमान्य हैं।

—महात्मा गांधी

- इस सीधे-सादे सिद्धांत को मानने में कि जन्म के कारण कोई मनुष्य अछूत नहीं माना जा सकता, कोई उच्च दार्शनिक सिद्धांत बीच में नहीं आता।

—महात्मा गांधी

- मैं स्वेच्छा से हरिजन बन गया हूँ और मेरा विश्वास है कि यदि मैंने निस्स्वार्थ भाव से हरिजनों की सेवा की होगी, तो अंत में वे उसे स्वीकार करेंगे।

—महात्मा गांधी

- उन्नति-मार्ग में बाधक अस्पृश्यता का कृत्रिम अड़ंगा दूर होते ही उसी क्षण हरिजनों की आर्थिक, नैतिक, सामाजिक तथा राजनीतिक अवस्था उन्नत हो जाएगी।

—महात्मा गांधी

- मैं हरिजनों के लिए भीख माँगना अपना कर्तव्य समझता हूँ।

—महात्मा गांधी

हिंदी

- हिंदी हमारे राष्ट्र की अभिव्यक्ति का सरलतम स्रोत है। **—सुमित्रानंदन पंत**
- राष्ट्रीय व्यवहार में हिंदी को काम में लाना देश की उन्नति के लिए आवश्यक है। **—महात्मा गांधी**
- हिंदी ज्ञान मेरे लिए अमृतपान है, जितनी बार उसे पीता हूँ, उतनी बार लगता है पुनः जीता हूँ। **—डॉ. ओदेलेन स्मैकल**
- राष्ट्रभाषा के बिना आजादी बेकार है। **—अवनींद्रकुमार विद्यालंकार**

- हिंदी का काम देश का काम है, समूचे राष्ट्रनिर्माण का प्रश्न है।
—बाबूराम सक्सेना

- समस्त भारतीय भाषाओं के लिए यदि कोई एक लिपि आवश्यक हो तो वह देवनागरी ही हो सकती है। **—स्वामी अय्यर**

- हिंदी का पौधा दक्षिणवालों ने त्याग से सींचा है। **—शंकरराव कप्पीकेरी**

- अकबर से लेकर औरंगजेब तक मुगलों ने जिस देशभाषा का स्वागत किया, वह ब्रजभाषा थी, न कि उर्दू। **—रामचंद्र शुक्ल**

- राष्ट्रभाषा हिंदी का किसी क्षेत्रीय भाषा से कोई संघर्ष नहीं है।
—अनंत गोपाल शेवड़े

- दक्षिण की हिंदी विरोधी नीति वास्तव में दक्षिण की नहीं, बल्कि कुछ अंग्रेजी भक्तों की नीति है। **—के.सी. सारंगमठ**

- हिंदी ही भारत की राष्ट्रभाषा हो सकती है। **—वी. कृष्णस्वामी अय्यर**

- राष्ट्रीय एकता की कड़ी हिंदी ही जोड़ सकती है।
—बालकृष्ण शर्मा नवीन

- विदेशी भाषा का किसी स्वतंत्र राष्ट्र के राजकाज और शिक्षा की भाषा होना सांस्कृतिक दासता है। **—वाल्टर चेनिंग**

- हिंदी को तुरंत शिक्षा का माध्यम बनाइए। **—बेरिस कल्यएव**

- अंग्रेजी सिर पर ढोना डूब मरने के बराबर है। **—संपूर्णानंद**

- देश को एक सूत्र में बाँधे रखने के लिए एक भाषा की आवश्यकता है।
—सेठ गोविंददास

- इस विशाल प्रदेश के हर भाग में शिक्षित-अशिक्षित, नागरिक और ग्रामीण सभी हिंदी को समझते हैं। **—राहुल सांकृत्यायन**

- समस्त आर्यावर्त या ठेठ हिंदुस्तान की राष्ट्र तथा शिष्ट भाषा हिंदी या हिंदुस्तानी है। **—सर जॉर्ज ग्रियर्सन**

- भारत की परंपरागत राष्ट्रभाषा हिंदी है। **—नलिनविलोचन शर्मा**
- जबसे हमने अपनी भाषा का समादर करना छोड़ा, तभी से हमारा अपमान और अवनति होने लगी।

  —राधिकारमण प्रसाद सिंह
- यदि पक्षपात की दृष्टि से न देखा जाए तो उर्दू भी हिंदी का ही एक रूप है।

  —शिवनंदन सहाय
- प्रत्येक नगर प्रत्येक मोहल्ले में और प्रत्येक गाँव में एक पुस्तकालय होने की आवश्यकता है। **—कीर्तयानंद सिंह**
- अपनी सरलता के कारण हिंदी प्रवासी भाइयों की स्वतः राष्ट्रभाषा हो गई।

  —भवानीदयाल संन्यासी
- यह कैसे संभव हो सकता है कि अंग्रेजी भाषा समस्त भारत की मातृभाषा के समान हो जाए? **—चंद्रशेखर मिश्र**
- साहित्य की उन्नति के लिए सभाओं और पुस्तकालयों की अत्यंत आवश्यकता है। **—महामहो. पं. सकलनारायण शर्मा**
- जो साहित्य केवल स्वप्नलोक की ओर ले जाए, वास्तविक जीवन को उन्नत करने में असमर्थ हो, वह नितांत महत्त्वहीन है।

  —काशीप्रसाद जायसवाल
- भारतीय एकता के लक्ष्य का साधन हिंदी भाषा का प्रचार है।

  —टी. माधवराव
- हिंदी हिंद की, हिंदियों की भाषा है। **—र.रा. दिवाकर**
- यह संदेह निर्मूल है कि हिंदीवाले उर्दू का नाश चाहते हैं। **—राजेंद्र प्रसाद**
- समाज और राष्ट्र की भावनाओं को परिमार्जित करनेवाला साहित्य ही सच्चा साहित्य है।

  —जनार्दनप्रसाद झा द्विज

• मजहब को यह मौका न मिलना चाहिए कि वह हमारे साहित्यिक, सामाजिक, सभी क्षेत्रों में टाँग अड़ाए। **—राहुल सांकृत्यायन**

• शिक्षा के प्रसार के लिए नागरी लिपि का सर्वत्र प्रचार आवश्यक है।

—शिवप्रसाद सितारेहिंद

• हमारी हिंदी भाषा का साहित्य किसी भी दूसरी भारतीय भाषा से किसी अंश में कम नहीं है। **—रामरणविजय सिंह**

• वही भाषा जीवित और जाग्रत् रह सकती है, जो जनता का ठीक-ठीक प्रतिनिधित्व कर सके। **—पीर मुहम्मद मूनिस**

• भारतेंदु और द्विवेदीजी ने हिंदी की जड़ पाताल तक पहुँचा दी है, उसे उखाड़ने का जो दुस्साहस करेगा, वह निश्चय ही भूकंपध्वस्त होगा।

—शिवपूजन सहाय

• यह निर्विवाद है कि हिंदुओं को उर्दू भाषा से कभी द्वेष नहीं रहा।

—ब्रजनंदन दास

• देहात का विरला ही कोई मुसलमान प्रचलित उर्दू भाषा के दस प्रतिशत शब्दों को समझ पाता है। **—सांवलिया बिहारीलाल वर्मा**

• हिंदी भाषा अपनी अनेक धाराओं के साथ प्रशस्त क्षेत्र में प्रखर गति से प्रकाशित हो रही है। **—छविनाथ पांडेय**

• देवनागरी ध्वनिशास्त्र की दृष्टि से अत्यंत वैज्ञानिक लिपि है।

—रविशंकर शुक्ल

• हमारी नागरी दुनिया की सबसे अधिक वैज्ञानिक लिपि है।

—राहुल सांकृत्यायन

• नागरी प्रचार देश उन्नति का द्वार है। **—गोपाललाल खत्री**

• साहित्य का स्रोत जनता का जीवन है। **—गणेशशंकर विद्यार्थी**

• अंग्रेजी से भारत की रक्षा नहीं हो सकती। **—पं. पिल्लयार**

- उसी दिन मेरा जीवन सफल होगा, जिस दिन में सारे भारतवासियों के साथ शुद्ध हिंदी में वार्त्तालाप करूँगा। **—शारदाचरण मित्र**
- हिंदी के ऊपर आघात पहुँचाना हमारे प्राणधर्म पर आघात पहुँचाना है। **—जगन्नाथप्रसाद मिश्र**
- हिंदी जाननेवाला व्यक्ति देश के किसी कोने में जाकर अपना काम चला लेता है। **—देवव्रत शास्त्री**
- हिंदी और नागरी का प्रचार तथा विकास कोई भी रोक नहीं सकता। **—गोविंदवल्लभ पंत**
- भारत की सारी प्रांतीय भाषाओं का दर्जा समान है। **—रविशंकर शुक्ल**
- किसी साहित्य की नकल पर कोई साहित्य तैयार नहीं होता। **—सूर्यकांत त्रिपाठी 'निराला'**
- भाषा ही से हृदयभाव जाना जाता है। शून्य, किंतु प्रत्यक्ष हुआ सा दिखलाता है। **—माधव शुक्ल**
- संस्कृत माँ, हिंदी गृहिणी और अंग्रेजी नौकरानी है। **—डॉ. फादर कामिल बुल्के**
- भाषा विचार की पोशाक है। **—डॉ. जॉनसन**
- रामचरितमानस हिंदी साहित्य का कोहिनूर है। **—यशोदानंदन अखौरी**
- साहित्य के हर पथ पर हमारा कारवाँ तेजी से बढ़ता जा रहा है। **—रामवृक्ष बेनीपुरी**
- कवि सम्मेलन हिंदी प्रचार के बहुत उपयोगी साधन है। **—श्रीनारायण चतुर्वेदी**
- हिंदी चिरकाल से ऐसी भाषा रही है, जिसने मात्र विदेशी होने के कारण किसी शब्द का बहिष्कार नहीं किया। **—राजेंद्र प्रसाद**

- देवनागरी अक्षरों का कलात्मक सौंदर्य नष्ट करना कहाँ की बुद्धिमानी है ?

—शिवपूजन सहाय

- जिस देश को अपनी भाषा और अपने साहित्य के गौरव का अनुभव नहीं है, वह उन्नत नहीं हो सकता। **—डॉ. राजेंद्र प्रसाद**

- कविता कामिनि भाल में हिंदी बिंदी रूप, प्रकट अग्रवन में भई ब्रज के निकट अनूप। **—राधाचरण गोस्वामी**

- हिंदी समस्त आर्यावर्त की भाषा है। **—शारदाचरण मित्र**

- हिंदी भारतीय संस्कृति की आत्मा है। **—कमलापति त्रिपाठी**

- मैं उर्दू को हिंदी की एक शैली मात्र मानता हूँ। **—मनोरंजन प्रसाद**

- हिंदी भाषा को भारतीय जनता तथा संपूर्ण मानवता के लिए बहुत बड़ा उत्तरदायित्व सँभालना है। **—सुनीति कुमार चटर्जी**

- राष्ट्रभाषा हिंदी हो जाने पर भी हमारे व्यक्तिगत और सार्वजनिक जीवन पर विदेशी भाषा का प्रभुत्व अत्यंत गर्हित बात है।

—कमलापति त्रिपाठी

- सभ्य संसार के सारे विषय हमारे साहित्य में आ जाने की ओर हमारी सतत चेष्टा रहनी चाहिए। **—श्रीधर पाठक**

- भारतवर्ष के लिए हिंदी भाषा ही सर्वसाधारण की भाषा होने के उपयुक्त है।

—शारदाचरण मित्र

- हिंदी भाषा और साहित्य ने तो जन्म से ही अपने पैरों पर खड़ा होना सीखा है। **—धीरेंद्र वर्मा**

- जब हम अपना जीवन जननी हिंदी, मातृभाषा हिंदी के लिए समर्पण कर दे, तब हम किसी के प्रेमी कहे जा सकते हैं। **—सेठ गोविंददास**

- कविता सुखी और उत्तम मनुष्यों के उत्तम और सुखमय क्षणों का उद्गार है। **—शेली**

• भाषा की समस्या का समाधान सांप्रदायिक दृष्टि से करना गलत है।

—लक्ष्मीनारायण सुधांशु

• भारतीय साहित्य और संस्कृति को हिंदी की देन बड़ी महत्त्वपूर्ण है।

—संपूर्णानंद

• हिंदी के पुराने साहित्य का पुनरुद्धार प्रत्येक साहित्यिक का पुनीत कर्तव्य है।

—पीतांबरदत्त बड़थ्वाल

• परमात्मा से प्रार्थना है कि हिंदी का मार्ग निष्कंटक करें।

—हरगोविंद सिंह

• अहिंदी भाषा–भाषी प्रांतों के लोग भी सरलता से टूटी–फूटी हिंदी बोलकर अपना काम चला लेते हैं। **—अनंतशयनम् अयंगार**

• वह हृदय नहीं है पत्थर है, जिसमें स्वदेश का प्यार नहीं।

—मैथिलीशरण गुप्त

• दाहिनी हो पूर्ण करती है अभिलाषा, पूज्य हिंदी भाषा हंसवाहिनी का अवतार है। **—अज्ञात**

• हिंदुस्तान की भाषा हिंदी है और उसका दृश्यरूप या उसकी लिपि सर्वगुणकारी नागरी ही है। **—गोपाललाल खत्री**

• कविता मानवता की उच्चतम अनुभूति की अभिव्यक्ति है।

—हजारी प्रसाद द्विवेदी

• हिंदी ही के द्वारा अखिल भारत का राष्ट्रनैतिक ऐक्य सुदृढ़ हो सकता है।

—भूदेव मुखर्जी

• हिंदी का शिक्षण भारत में अनिवार्य ही होगा।

—सुनीति कुमार चटर्जी

• हिंदी, नागरी और राष्ट्रीयता अन्योन्याश्रित हैं। **—नंददुलारे वाजपेयी**

- देशभाषा की उन्नति से ही देशोन्नति होती है। **—सुधाकर द्विवेदी**
- हिंदी साहित्य धर्म-अर्थ-काम-मोक्ष इस चतु:पुरुषार्थ का साधक, अतएव जनोपयोगी। **—डॉ. भगवानदास**
- हिंदी उन सभी गुणों से अलंकृत है, जिनके बल पर वह विश्व की साहित्यिक भाषाओं की अगली श्रेणी में सभासीन हो सकती है।

  —मैथिलीशरण गुप्त
- वाणी, सभ्यता और देश की रक्षा करना सच्चा धर्म यज्ञ है।

  —ठाकुरदत्त शर्मा
- निष्काम कर्म ही सर्वोत्तम कार्य है, जो तृप्ति प्रदाता है और व्यक्ति और समाज की शक्ति बढ़ाता है। **—पंडित सुधाकर पांडेय**
- अब हिंदी ही माँ भारती हो गई है—वह सबकी आराध्या है, सबकी संपत्ति है। **—रविशंकर शुक्ल**
- बच्चों को विदेशी लिपि की शिक्षा देना उनको राष्ट्र के सच्चे प्रेम से वंचित करना है। **—भवानीदयाल संन्यासी**
- भाषा और राष्ट्र में बड़ा घनिष्ठ संबंध है।

  —(राजा) राधिकारमण प्रसाद सिंह
- अगर उर्दूवालों की नीति हिंदी के बहिष्कार की न होती तो आज लिपि के सिवा दोनों में कोई भेद न पाया जाता।

  —डॉ. राजेंद्र प्रसाद
- हिंदी भाषा की उन्नति का अर्थ है राष्ट्र और जाति की उन्नति।

  —रामवृक्ष बेनीपुरी
- बाजारवाली बोली विश्वविद्यालयों में काम नहीं दे सकती। **—संपूर्णानंद**
- भारतेंदु का साहित्य मातृमंदिर की अर्चना का साहित्य है।

  —बदरीनाथ शर्मा

• तलवार के बल से न कोई भाषा चलाई जा सकती है, न मिटाई।

—शिवपूजन सहाय

• अखिल भारत के परस्पर व्यवहार के लिए ऐसी भाषा की आवश्यकता है, जिसे जनता का अधिकतम भाग पहले से ही जानता-समझता है।

—महात्मा गांधी

• हिंदी को राजभाषा करने के बाद पूरे पंद्रह वर्ष तक अंग्रेजी का प्रयोग करना पीछे कदम हटाना है। **—राजर्षि पुरुषोत्तमदास टंडन**

• भाषा राष्ट्रीय शरीर की आत्मा है। **—स्वामी भवानीदयाल संन्यासी**

• हिंदी के राष्ट्रभाषा होने से जहाँ हमें हर्षोल्लास है, वहीं हमारा उत्तरदायित्व भी बहुत बढ़ गया है। **—मथुरा प्रसाद दीक्षित**

• भारतवर्ष में सभी विद्याएँ सम्मिलित परिवार के समान पारस्परिक सद्‌भाव लेकर रहती आई हैं। **—रवींद्रनाथ ठाकुर**

• इतिहास को देखते हुए किसी को यह कहने का अधिकारी नहीं कि हिंदी का साहित्य जायसी के पहले का नहीं मिलता।

—डॉ. काशीप्रसाद जायसवाल

• संप्रति जितनी भाषाएँ भारत में प्रचलित हैं, उनमें से हिंदी भाषा प्राय: सर्वत्र व्यवहृत होती है। **—केशवचंद्र सेन**

• हिंदी ने राष्ट्रभाषा के पद पर सिंहासनारूढ़ होने पर अपने ऊपर एक गौरवमय एवं गुरुतर उत्तरदायित्व लिया है। **—गोविंदवल्लभ पंत**

• हिंदी जिस दिन राजभाषा स्वीकृत की गई, उसी दिन से सारा राजकाज हिंदी में चल सकता था। **—सेठ गोविंददास**

• हिंदीभाषी प्रदेश की जनता से वोट लेना और उनकी भाषा तथा साहित्य को गालियाँ देना कुछ नेताओं का दैनिक व्यवसाय है।

—डॉ. रामविलास शर्मा

• जब एक बार यह निश्चय कर लिया गया कि सन् 1965 से सब काम हिंदी

में होगा, तब उसे अवश्य कार्यान्वित करना चाहिए। —**सेठ गोविंददास**

- जिसका मन चाहे, वह हिंदी भाषा से हमारा दूर का संबंध बताए, मगर हम बिहारी तो हिंदी को ही अपनी भाषा, मातृभाषा मानते आए हैं।

  —**शिवनंदन सहाय**

- उर्दू का ढाँचा हिंदी है, लेकिन सत्तर-पचहत्तर फीसदी उधार के शब्दों से उर्दू दाँ तक तंग आ गए हैं। —**राहुल सांकृत्यायन**

- मानस भवन में आर्यजन जिसकी उतारें आरती। भगवान् भारतवर्ष में गूँजे हमारी भारती। —**मैथिलीशरण गुप्त**

- गद्य जीवनसंग्राम की भाषा है। इसमें बहुत कार्य करना है, समय थोड़ा है।

  —**सूर्यकांत त्रिपाठी 'निराला'**

- अंग्रेजी हमें गूँगा और कूपमंडूक बना रही है। —**ब्रजभूषण पांडेय**

- लाखों की संख्या में छात्रों की उस पलटन से क्या लाभ, जिनमें अंग्रेजी में एक प्रार्थना-पत्र लिखने की भी क्षमता नहीं है। —**कंक**

- मैं राष्ट्र का प्रेम, राष्ट्र के भिन्न-भिन्न लोगों का प्रेम और राष्ट्रभाषा का प्रेम, इसमें कुछ भी फर्क नहीं देखता। —**र.रा. दिवाकर**

- देवनागरी लिपि की वैज्ञानिकता स्वयंसिद्ध है।

  —**महावीर प्रसाद द्विवेदी**

- हिमालय से सतपुड़ा और अंबाला से पूर्णिया तक फैला हुआ प्रदेश हिंदी का प्रांत है। —**राहुल सांकृत्यायन**

- किसी राष्ट्र की राजभाषा वही भाषा हो सकती है, जिसे उसके अधिकाधिक निवासी समझ सकें।

  —**आचार्य चतुरसेन शास्त्री**

- साहित्य के इतिहास में काल विभाजन के लिए तत्कालीन प्रवृत्तियों को ही मानना न्यायसंगत है। —**अंबाप्रसाद सुमन**

• हिंदी भाषा हमारे लिए किसने बनाई—प्रकृति ने, हमारे लिए हिंदी प्रतिसिद्ध है। **—पं. गिरिधर शर्मा**

• हिंदी भाषा उस समुद्र जलराशि की तरह है, जिसमें अनेक नदियाँ मिली हों। **—वासुदेवशरण अग्रवाल**

• भाषा देश की एकता का प्रधान साधन है। **—आचार्य चतुरसेन शास्त्री**

• क्रांतदर्शी होने के कारण ऋषि दयानंद ने देशोन्नति के लिए हिंदी भाषा को अपनाया था। **—विष्णुदेव पोद्दार**

• सच्चा राष्ट्रीय साहित्य राष्ट्रभाषा से उत्पन्न होता है। **—वाल्टर चेनिंग**

• हिंदी के पौधे को हिंदू-मुसलमान दोनों ने सींचकर बड़ा किया है। **—जहूरबख्श**

• अंग्रेजी का पद चिरस्थायी करना देश के लिए लज्जा की बात है। **—संपूर्णानंद**

• हिंदी राष्ट्रभाषा है, इसलिए प्रत्येक व्यक्ति को, प्रत्येक भारतवासी को इसे सीखना चाहिए। **—रविशंकर शुक्ल**

• हिंदी प्रांतीय भाषा नहीं, बल्कि वह अंत:प्रांतीय राष्ट्रीय भाषा है। **—छविनाथ पांडेय**

• विश्व की कोई भी लिपि अपने वर्तमान रूप में नागरी लिपि के समान नहीं। **—चंद्रबली पांडेय**

• भाषा की एकता जाति की एकता को कायम रखती है। **—राहुल सांकृत्यायन**

• जिस राष्ट्र की जो भाषा है, उसे हटाकर दूसरे देश की भाषा को सारी जनता पर नहीं थोपा जा सकता। **—वासुदेवशरण अग्रवाल**

• पराधीनता की विजय से स्वाधीनता की पराजय सहस्त्र गुना अच्छी है। **—अज्ञात**

- समाज के अभाव में आदमी की आदमीयत की कल्पना नहीं की जा सकती। **—पं. सुधाकर पांडेय**
- तुलसी, कबीर, नानक ने जो लिखा है, उसे मैं पढ़ता हूँ तो कोई मुश्किल नहीं आती। **—मौलाना मुहम्मद अली**
- भाषा का निर्माण सेक्रेटेरियट में नहीं होता, भाषा गढ़ी जाती है जनता की जिह्वा पर। **—रामवृक्ष बेनीपुरी**
- हिंदी भाषा ही एक ऐसी भाषा है, जो सभी प्रांतों की भाषा हो सकती है। **—रंगनाथ पिल्लयार**
- जब हम हिंदी की चर्चा करते हैं तो वह हिंदी संस्कृति का एक प्रतीक होती है। **—शांतानंद नाथ**
- भारतीय धर्म की है घोषणा घमंड भरी, हिंदी नहीं जाने, उसे हिंदू नहीं जानिए। **—नाथूराम शंकर शर्मा**
- राजनीति के चिंतापूर्ण आवेग में साहित्य की प्रेरणा शिथिल नहीं होनी चाहिए। **—राजकुमार वर्मा**
- हिंदी में जो गुण है, उनमें से एक यह है कि हिंदी मर्दानी जबान है। **—सुनीति कुमार चटर्जी**
- स्पर्धा ही जीवन है, उसमें पीछे रहना जीवन की प्रगति खोना है। **—निराला**
- कविता हमारे परिपूर्ण क्षणों की वाणी है। **—सुमित्रानंदन पंत**
- बिना मातृभाषा की उन्नति के देश का गौरव कदापि वृद्धि को प्राप्त नहीं हो सकता। **—गोविंद शास्त्री दुगवेकर**
- उर्दू लिपि की अनुपयोगिता, भ्रामकता और कठोरता प्रमाणित हो चुकी है। **—रामरणविजय सिंह**
- राष्ट्रभाषा राष्ट्रीयता का मुख्य अंश है। **—श्रीमती सौ.चि. रमणम्मा देव**

• बानी हिंदी भाषन की महरानी। चंद्र, सूर, तुलसी से जामैं भए सुकवि लासानी। **—पं. जगन्नाथ चतुर्वेदी**

• जय-जय राष्ट्रभाषा जननि। जयति जय-जय गुण उजागर राष्ट्रमंगलकरनि।

—देवी प्रसाद गुप्त

• हिंदी हमारी हिंदू संस्कृति की वाणी ही तो है। **—शांतानंद नाथ**

• आज का लेखक विचारों और भावों के इतिहास की वह कड़ी है, जिसके पीछे शताब्दियों की कड़ियाँ जुड़ी हैं।

—माखनलाल चतुर्वेदी

• विज्ञान के बहुत से अंगों का मूल हमारे पुरातन साहित्य में निहित है।

—सूर्यनारायण व्यास

• कोई कौम अपनी जबान के बगैर अच्छी तालीम नहीं हासिल कर सकती।

—सैयद अमीर अली मीर

• हिंदी और उर्दू में झगड़ने की बात ही नहीं है। **—ब्रजनंदन सहाय**

• कविता हृदय की मुक्त दशा का शाब्दिक विधान है। **—रामचंद्र शुक्ल**

• हमारी राष्ट्रभाषा का मुख्य उद्देश्य राष्ट्रीयता का दृढ़ निर्माण है।

—चंद्रबली पांडेय

• जिस शिक्षा से स्वाभिमान की वृत्ति जाग्रत् नहीं होती, वह शिक्षा किसी काम की नहीं। **—माधवराव सप्रे**

• कालोपयोगी कार्य न कर सकने पर महापुरुष बन सकना संभव नहीं है।

—सू.च. धर

• मैं दुनिया की सब भाषाओं की इज्जत करता हूँ, परंतु मेरे देश में हिंदी की इज्जत न हो, यह मैं नहीं सह सकता। **—विनोबा भावे**

• आज का आविष्कार कल का साहित्य है। **—माखनलाल चतुर्वेदी**

- भाषा के सवाल में मजहब को दखल देने का कोई हक नहीं।

—राहुल सांकृत्यायन

- जब तक संघ शक्ति उत्पन्न न होगी, तब तक प्रार्थना में कुछ जान नहीं हो सकती।

—माधव राव सप्रे

- हिंदी विश्व की महान् भाषा है। **—राहुल सांकृत्यायन**

- राष्ट्रीय एकता के लिए एक भाषा से कहीं बढ़कर आवश्यक एक लिपि का प्रचार होना है।

—ब्रजनंदन सहाय

- जो ज्ञान तुमने संपादित किया है, उसे वितरित करते रहो और सबको ज्ञानवान बनाकर छोड़ो।

—संत रामदास

- पाँच मत उधर और पाँच मत इधर रहने से श्रेष्ठता नहीं आती।

—माखनलाल चतुर्वेदी

- मैं मानती हूँ कि हिंदी प्रचार से राष्ट्र का ऐक्य जितना बढ़ सकता है, वैसा बहुत कम चीजों से बढ़ सकेगा।

—लीलावती मुंशी

- हिंदी-उर्दू के नाम को दूर कीजिए एक भाषा बनाइए। सबको इसके लिए तैयार कीजिए।

—देवी प्रसाद गुप्त

- साहित्यकार विश्वकर्मा की अपेक्षा कहीं अधिक सामर्थ्यशाली है।

—पं. वागीश्वरजी

- हिंदी भाषा और हिंदी साहित्य को सर्वांगसुंदर बनाना हमारा कर्तव्य है।

—डॉ. राजेंद्र प्रसाद

- हिंदी साहित्य की नकल पर कोई साहित्य तैयार नहीं होता।

—सूर्यकांत त्रिपाठी 'निराला'

- भाषा के उत्थान में एक भाषा का होना आवश्यक है। इसलिए हिंदी सबकी साझा भाषा है।

—रंगनाथ पिल्लयार

• हिंदी हमारे देश और भाषा की प्रभावशाली विरासत है।

—माखनलाल चतुर्वेदी

• यदि आप मुझे कुछ देना चाहती हों तो इस पाठशाला की शिक्षा का माध्यम हमारी मातृभाषा कर दें। **—एक फ्रांसीसी बालिका**

• निर्मल चरित्र ही मनुष्य का शृंगार है। **—पंडित सुधाकर पांडेय**

• हिंदुस्तान को छोड़कर दूसरे मध्य देशों में ऐसा कोई अन्य देश नहीं है, जहाँ कोई राष्ट्रभाषा नहीं हो। **—सैयद अमीर अली मीर**

• इतिहास में जो सत्य है, वही अच्छा है और जो असत्य है, वही बुरा है।

—जयचंद्र विद्यालंकार

• सरलता, बोधगम्यता और शैली की दृष्टि से विश्व की भाषाओं में हिंदी महान्तम स्थान रखती है।

—अमरनाथ झा

• हिंदी सरल भाषा है। इसे अनायास सीखकर लोग अपना काम निकाल लेते हैं। **—जगन्नाथ प्रसाद चतुर्वेदी**

• एक भाषा का प्रचार रहने पर केवल इसी के सहारे, यदि लिपिगत भिन्नता न हो तो अन्यान्य राष्ट्र गठन के उपकरण आ जाने संभव हो सकते हैं।

—अयोध्याप्रसाद वर्मा

• किसी भाषा की उन्नति का पता उसमें प्रकाशित हुई पुस्तकों की संख्या तथा उनके विषय के महत्त्व से जाना जा सकता है। **—गंगाप्रसाद अग्निहोत्री**

• जीवन के छोटे-से-छोटे क्षेत्र में हिंदी अपना दायित्व निभाने में समर्थ है।

—पुरुषोत्तमदास टंडन

• बिहार में ऐसा एक भी गाँव नहीं है, जहाँ केवल रामायण पढ़ने के लिए दस-बीस मनुष्यों ने हिंदी न सीखी हो।

—सकलनारायण पांडेय

• संस्कृत की इशाअत (प्रचार) का एक बड़ा फायदा यह होगा कि हमारी मुल्की जबान (देशभाषा) वसीअत (व्यापक) हो जाएगी।

—मौलवी महमूद अली

• संसार में देश के नाम से भाषा को नाम दिया जाता है और वही भाषा वहाँ की राष्ट्रभाषा कहलाती है। **—ताराचंद्र दुबे**

• सर्वसाधारण पर जितना पद्य का प्रभाव पड़ता है, उतना गद्य का नहीं।

—राजा कृत्यानंद सिंह

• जो गुण साहित्य की जीवनी-शक्ति के प्रधान सहायक होते हैं, उनमें लेखकों की विचारशीलता प्रधान है। **—नरोत्तम व्यास**

• भाषा और भाव का परिवर्तन समाज की अवस्था और आचार-विचार से अधिक संबंध रखता है। **—बदरीनाथ भट्ट**

• साहित्य पढ़ने से मुख्य दो बातें तो अवश्य प्राप्त होती हैं, अर्थात् मन की शक्तियों को विकास और ज्ञान पाने की लालसा। **—बिहारीलाल चौबे**

• देवनागरी और बँगला लिपियों को साथ मिलाकर देखना है।

—मन्नन द्विवेदी

• है भव्य भारत ही हमारी मातृभूमि हरी-भरी।
हिंदी हमारी राष्ट्रभाषा और लिपि है नागरी॥ **—मैथिलीशरण गुप्त**

• संस्कृत की विरासत हिंदी को तो जन्म से ही मिली है।

—राहुल सांकृत्यायन

• कैसे निज सोए भाग को कोई सकता है जगा,
जो निज भाषा-अनुराग का अंकुर नहिं उर में उगा॥ **—हरिऔध**

• हिंदी में हम लिखें-पढ़ें, हिंदी ही बोलें।

—पं. जगन्नाथप्रसाद चतुर्वेदी

• जिस वस्तु की उपज अधिक होती है, उसमें से बहुत सा भाग फेंक भी दिया

जाता है। ग्रंथों के लिए भी ऐसा ही हिसाब है। **—गिरजाकुमार घोष**

- यह जो है कुरबान खुदा का, हिंदी करे बयान सदा का। **—अज्ञात**
- क्या संसार में कहीं का भी आप एक दृष्टांत उद्धृत कर सकते हैं, जहाँ बालकों की शिक्षा विदेशी भाषाओं द्वारा होती हो। **—डॉ. श्यामसुंदर दास**
- बँगला वर्णमाला की जाँच से मालूम होता है कि देवनागरी लिपि से निकली है और इसी का सीधा-सादा रूप है। **—रमेशचंद्र दत्त**
- वास्तव में वेश, भाषा आदि के बदलने का परिणाम यह होता है कि आत्मगौरव नष्ट हो जाता है, जिससे देश का जातित्व गुण मिट जाता है। **—सैयद अमीर अली मीर**
- दूसरों की बोली की नकल करना भाषा के बदलने का एक कारण है। **—गिरींद्रमोहन मित्र**
- समालोचना ही साहित्य मार्ग की सुंदर सड़क है। **—गिरधर शर्मा चतुर्वेदी**
- नागरी वर्णमाला के समान सर्वांगपूर्ण और वैज्ञानिक कोई दूसरी वर्णमाला नहीं है। **—बाबू राव विष्णु पराड़कर**
- अन्य देश की भाषा ने हमारे देश के आचार-व्यवहार पर कैसा बुरा प्रभाव डाला है। **—अनादिधन बंद्योपाध्याय**
- व्याकरण चाहे जितना विशाल बने, परंतु भाषा का पूरा-पूरा समाधान उसमें नहीं हो सकता। **—अनंतराम त्रिपाठी**
- स्वदेशप्रेम, स्वधर्मभक्ति और स्वावलंबन आदि ऐसे गुण हैं, जो प्रत्येक मनुष्य में होने चाहिए। **—रामजी लाल शर्मा**
- गुणवान खानखाना सदृश्य प्रेमी हो गए, रसखान और रसलीन से हिंदीप्रेमी हो गए। **—राय देवीप्रसाद**

- वैज्ञानिक विचारों के पारिभाषिक शब्दों के लिए, किसी विषय के उच्च भावों के लिए, संस्कृत साहित्य की सहायता लेना कोई शर्म की बात नहीं है।

  —गणपति जानकीराम दुबे

- हिंदुस्तान के लिए देवनागरी लिपि का ही व्यवहार होना चाहिए, रोमन लिपि का व्यवहार यहाँ हो ही नहीं सकता। **—महात्मा गांधी**

- हिंदी किसी के मिटाने से मिट नहीं सकती। **—चंद्रबली पांडेय**

- भाषा की उन्नति का पता मुद्रणालयों से भी लग सकता है।

  —गंगाप्रसाद अग्निहोत्री

- हमारी भारत-भारती की शैशवावस्था का रूप ब्राह्मी या देववाणी है, उसकी किशोरावस्था वैदिक भाषा और संस्कृति उसकी यौवनावस्था की सुंदर मनोहर छटा है। **—बदरीनारायण चौधरी प्रेमघन**

- निज भाषा उन्नति अहै, सब उन्नति को मूल। **—भारतेंदु हरिश्चंद्र**

- आर्यों की सबसे प्राचीन भाषा हिंदी ही है और इसमें तद्भव शब्द सभी भाषाओं से अधिक हैं। **—वीम्स साहब**

- राष्ट्रभाषा के बिना राष्ट्र गूँगा है। **—महात्मा गांधी**

- भारतवर्ष के लिए देवनागरी साधारण लिपि हो सकती है और हिंदी भाषा ही सर्वसाधारण की भाषा होने के उपयुक्त है। **—शारदाचरण मित्र**

- भारत के एक सिरे से दूसरे सिरे तक हिंदी भाषा कुछ-न-कुछ सर्वत्र समझी जाती है। **—रंगनाथ पिल्लयार**

- जापानियों ने जिस ढंग से विदेशी भाषाएँ सीखकर अपनी मातृभाषा को उन्नति के शिखर पर पहुँचाया है, उसी प्रकार हमें भी मातृभाषा का भक्त होना चाहिए। **—श्यामसुंदर दास**

- विचारों का परिपक्व होना भी उसी समय संभव होता है, जब शिक्षा का माध्यम प्रकृतिसिद्ध मातृभाषा हो। **—पं. गिरधर शर्मा**

- यह महात्मा गांधी का प्रताप है, जिनकी मातृभाषा गुजराती है, पर हिंदी को राष्ट्रभाषा जानकर जो उसे अपने प्रेम से सींच रहे हैं।

—लक्ष्मण नारायण गर्दे

- हिंदी भाषा के लिए मेरा प्रेम सब हिंदी प्रेमी जानते हैं। **—महात्मा गांधी**
- किसी देश में ग्रंथ बनने तक वैदेशिक भाषा में शिक्षा नहीं होती थी। देश भाषाओं में शिक्षा होने के कारण स्वयं ग्रंथ बनते गए हैं।

—साहित्याचार्य रामावतार शर्मा

- जो भाषा सामयिक दूसरी भाषाओं से सहायता नहीं लेती, वह बहुत काल तक जीवित नहीं रह सकती। **—पांडेय रामवतार शर्मा**
- जितना और जैसा ज्ञान विद्यार्थियों को उनकी मातृभाषा में शिक्षा देने से अल्पकाल में हो सकता है, उतना और वैसा पराई भाषा में सुदीर्घ काल में भी होना संभव नहीं है। **—घनश्याम सिंह**
- विदेशी भाषा में शिक्षा होने के कारण हमारी बुद्धि भी विदेशी हो गई है।

—माधवराव सप्रे

- मैं महाराष्ट्री हूँ, परंतु हिंदी के विषय में मुझे उतना ही अभिमान है, जितना किसी हिंदीभाषी को हो सकता है। **—माधवराव सप्रे**
- मनुष्य सदा अपनी मातृभाषा में ही विचार करता है। इसलिए अपनी भाषा सीखने में जो सुगमता होती है, दूसरी भाषा में हमको वह सुगमता नहीं हो सकती। **—डॉ. मुकुंदस्वरूप वर्मा**
- हिंदी भाषा का प्रश्न स्वराज्य का प्रश्न है। **—महात्मा गांधी**
- राष्ट्रीयता का भाषा और साहित्य के साथ बहुत ही घनिष्ठ और गहरा संबंध है। **—डॉ. राजेंद्र प्रसाद**
- यदि हम अंग्रेजी दूसरी भाषा के समान पढ़ें तो हमारे ज्ञान की अधिक वृद्धि हो सकती है। **—जगन्नाथप्रसाद चतुर्वेदी**

- हिंदी पर न मारो ताना, सभा बतावे हिंदी माना। **—नूर मुहम्मद**
- आप जिस तरह बोलते हैं, बातचीत करते हैं, उसी तरह लिखा भी कीजिए। भाषा बनावटी न होनी चाहिए। **—महावीर प्रसाद द्विवेदी**
- हिंदी भाषा की उन्नति के बिना हमारी उन्नति असंभव है। **—गिरधर शर्मा**
- भाषा ही राष्ट्र का जीवन है। **—पुरुषोत्तमदास टंडन**
- देह प्राण का ज्यों घनिष्ठ संबंध अधिकतर है, उससे भी अधिक देशभाषा का गुरुतर। **—माधव शुक्ल**
- जब हम अपना जीवन जननी हिंदी, मातृभाषा हिंदी के लिए समर्पण कर दें, तब हम हिंदी के प्रेमी कहे जा सकते हैं। **—गोविंददास**
- नागरी प्रचार देश उन्नति का द्वार है। **—गोपाललाल खत्री**
- देश तथा जाति का उपकार उसके बालक तभी कर सकते हैं, जब उन्हें उनकी भाषा द्वारा शिक्षा मिली हो। **—पं. गिरधर शर्मा**
- राष्ट्रभाषा की साधना कोरी भावुकता नहीं है। **—जगन्नाथप्रसाद मिश्र**
- सिख-गुरुओं ने आपातकाल में हिंदी की रक्षा के लिए ही गुरुमुखी रची थी। **—संतराम शर्मा**
- हिंदी जैसी सरल भाषा दूसरी नहीं है। **—मौलाना हसरत मोहानी**
- ऐसे आदमी आज भी हमारे देश में मौजूद हैं, जो समझते हैं कि शिक्षा को मातृभाषा के आसन पर बिठा देने से उसकी कीमत ही घट जाएगी। **—रवींद्रनाथ ठाकुर**
- हमारे साहित्य को कामधेनु बनाना है। **—चंद्रबली पांडेय**
- भारत के विभिन्न प्रदेशों के बीच हिंदी प्रचार द्वारा एकता स्थापित करनेवाले सच्चे भारत बंधु हैं। **—अरविंद**

- मेरा आग्रहपूर्वक कथन है कि अपनी सारी मानसिक शक्ति हिंदी के अध्ययन में लगाएँ। **—विनोबा भावे**
- साहित्यिक इस बात को कभी न भूलें कि एक खयाल ही क्रिया का स्वामी है, उसे बढ़ाने, घटाने या ठुकरा देनेवाला।
- एशिया के कितने ही राष्ट्र आज यूरोपीय राष्ट्रों के चंगुल से छूट गए हैं, पर उनकी आर्थिक दासता आज भी टिकी हुई है। **—वी.सी. जोशी**
- हिंदी द्वारा सारे भारत को एक सूत्र में पिरोया जा सकता है। **—स्वामी दयानंद**
- जैसे-जैसे हमारे देश में राष्ट्रीयता का भाव बढ़ता जाएगा, वैसे-ही-वैसे हिंदी की राष्ट्रीय सत्ता भी बढ़ेगी। **—श्रीमती लोकसुंदरी रामन**
- राष्ट्रीय व्यवहार में हिंदी को काम में लाना देश की शीघ्र उन्नति के लिए आवश्यक है। **—महात्मा गांधी**
- शिक्षा का प्रचार और विद्या की उन्नति इसलिए अपेक्षित है कि जिससे हमारे स्वत्व का रक्षण हो। **—माधवराव सप्रे**
- जीवित भाषा बहती नदी है, जिसकी धारा नित्य एक ही मार्ग से प्रवाहित नहीं होती। **—बाबूराव विष्णु पराड़कर**
- हिंदी उन सभी गुणों से अलंकृत है, जिनके बल पर वह विश्व की साहित्यिक भाषाओं की अगली श्रेणी में सभासीन हो सकती है। **—मैथिलीशरण गुप्त**
- हिंदी भाषा और साहित्य ने तो जन्म से ही अपने पैरों पर खड़ा होना सीखा है। **—धीरेंद्र वर्मा**
- बिना मातृभाषा की उन्नति के देश का गौरव कदापि वृद्धि को प्राप्त नहीं हो सकता। **—गोविंद शास्त्री दुगवेकर**
- अंग्रेजी को भारतीय भाषा बनाने का यह अभिप्राय है कि हम अपने भारतीय अस्तित्व को बिल्कुल मिटा दें। **—रंगनाथ पिल्लयार**

- अंग्रेजी का मुखापेक्षी रहना भारतीयों को किसी प्रकार से शोभा नहीं देता है।

—भास्कर गोविंद धाणेकर

- यह हमारा दुर्भाग्य है कि हमारी शिक्षा विदेशी भाषा में होती है और मातृभाषा में नहीं होती। **—माधवराव सप्रे**

- भाषा ही राष्ट्र का जीवन है। **—पुरुषोत्तमदास टंडन**

- हिंदी स्वयं अपनी ताकत से बढ़ेगी। **—पं. नेहरू**

- भाषा विचार की पोशाक है। **—डॉ. जॉनसन**

- हमारी देवनागरी इस देश की ही नहीं, समस्त संसार की लिपियों में सबसे अधिक वैज्ञानिक है। **—सेठ गोविंददास**

- अंग्रेजी के माया-मोह से हमारा आत्मविश्वास ही नष्ट नहीं हुआ है, बल्कि हमारा राष्ट्रीय स्वाभिमान भी पददलित हुआ है।

—लक्ष्मीनारायण सिंह सुधांशु

- आइए हम-आप एकमत हो कोई ऐसा उपाय करें, जिससे राष्ट्रभाषा का प्रचार घर-घर हो जाए और राष्ट्र का कोई भी कोना अछूता न रहे।

—चंद्रबली पांडेय

- जैसे जन्मभूमि जगदंबा का स्वरूप है, वैसे ही मातृभाषा भी जगदंबा का स्वरूप है। **—गोविंद शास्त्री दुगवेकर**

- हिंदी और उर्दू की जड़ एक है, रूपरेखा एक है और दोनों को अगर हम चाहें तो एक बना सकते हैं। **—डॉ. राजेंद्र प्रसाद**

- हिंदी आज साहित्य के विचार से रूढ़ियों से बहुत आगे है। विश्वसाहित्य में ही जानेवाली रचनाएँ उसमें हैं। **—सूर्यकांत त्रिपाठी निराला**

- भारत की रक्षा तभी हो सकती है, जब इसके साहित्य, इसकी सभ्यता तथा इसके आदर्शों की रक्षा हो। **—रंगनाथ पिल्लयार**

- हिंदी संस्कृत की बेटियों में सबसे अच्छी और शिरोमणि है। **—ग्रियर्सन**
- मैं नहीं समझता, सात समुंदर पार की अंग्रेजी का इतना अधिकार यहाँ कैसे हो गया। **—महात्मा गांधी**
- मेरे लिए हिंदी का प्रश्न स्वराज्य का प्रश्न है। **—राजर्षि पुरुषोत्तमदास टंडन**
- संस्कृत को छोड़कर आज भी किसी भी भारतीय भाषा का वाङ्मय विस्तार या मौलिकता में हिंदी के आगे नहीं जाता। **—डॉ. संपूर्णानंद**
- उर्दू और हिंदी दोनों को मिला दो। अलग-अलग नाम नहीं होना चाहिए। **—मौलाना मुहम्मद अली**
- राष्ट्रभाषा के विषय में यह बात ध्यान में रखनी होगी कि यह राष्ट्र के सब प्रांतों की समान और स्वाभाविक राष्ट्रभाषा है। **—लक्ष्मण नारायण गर्दे**
- विदेशी भाषा के शब्द, उसके भाव तथा दृष्टांत हमारे हृदय पर वह प्रभाव नहीं डाल सकते, जो मातृभाषा के चिर-परिचित तथा हृदयग्राही वाक्य। **—मन्नन द्विवेदी**
- जातीय भाव हमारी अपनी भाषा की ओर झुकता है। **—शारदाचरण मित्र**
- हिंदी अपनी भूमि की अधिष्ठात्री है। **—राहुल सांकृत्यायन**
- सारा शरीर अपना, रोम-रोम अपने, रंग और रक्त अपना, अंग-प्रत्यंग अपने, किंतु जुबान दूसरे की, यह कहाँ की सभ्यता और कहाँ की मनुष्यता है। **—रणवीर सिंहजी**
- वाणी, सभ्यता और देश की रक्षा करना सच्चा यज्ञ है। **—ठाकुरदत्त शर्मा**
- हिंदी व्यापकता में अद्वितीय है। **—अंबिका प्रसाद वाजपेयी**
- हमारी राष्ट्रभाषा की पावन गंगा में देशी और विदेशी सभी प्रकार के शब्द मिल-जुलकर एक हो जाएँगे। **—डॉ. राजेंद्र प्रसाद**

- नागरी की वर्णमाला है विशुद्ध महान।
  सरल सुंदर सीखने में सुगम अति सुखदान॥ —**मिश्रबंधु**
- मनुष्य सदा अपनी भातृभाषा में ही विचार करता है। —**मुकुंदस्वरूप वर्मा**
- बिना भाषा की जाति नहीं शोभा पाती है और देश की मार्यादा भी घट जाती है। —**माधव शुक्ल**
- हिंदी और उर्दू एक ही भाषा के दो रूप हैं और दोनों रूपों में बहुत साहित्य है। —**अंबिका प्रसाद वाजपेयी**
- हम हिंदीवालों के ह्रदय में किसी संप्रदाय या किसी भाषा से रंचमात्र भी ईर्ष्या, द्वेष या घृणा नहीं है। —**शिवपूजन सहाय**
- भारत के विभिन्न प्रदेशों के बीच हिंदी प्रचार द्वारा एकता स्थापित करनेवाले सच्चे भारत बंधु हैं। —**अरविंद**
- राष्ट्रीय एकता के लिए हमें प्रांतीयता की भावना त्यागकर सभी प्रांतीय भाषाओं के लिए एक लिपि देवनागरी अपना लेनी चाहिए। —**शारदाचरण मित्र**
- समूचे राष्ट्र को एकताबद्ध और दृढ़ करने के लिए हिंद भाषी जाति की एकता आवश्यक है। —**रामविलास शर्मा**
- हिंदी को राष्ट्रभाषा बनने के हेतु हुए अनुष्ठान को मैं संस्कृति का राजसूय यज्ञ समझता हूँ। —**आचार्य क्षितिमोहन सेन**
- हिंदी का भविष्य उज्ज्वल है, इसमें कोई संदेह नहीं। —**अनंत गोपाल शेवड़े**
- अरबी लिपि भारतीय लिपि होने योग्य नहीं। —**सैयद अली बिलग्रामी**
- हिंदी को ही राजभाषा का आसन देना चाहिए। —**शचींद्रनाथ बख्शी**
- अंतरप्रांतीय व्यवहार में हमें हिंदी का प्रयोग तुरंत शुरू कर देना चाहिए। —**र.रा. दिवाकर**

- हिंदी का शासकीय प्रशासकीय क्षेत्रों से प्रचार न किया गया तो भविष्य अंधकारमय हो सकता है। **—विनयमोहन शर्मा**
- अंग्रेजी इस देश के लिए अभिशाप है, यह हर साल हमारे सामने प्रकट होता है, फिर भी उसे हम पूतना न मानकर चामुंडमर्दिनी दुर्गा मान रहे हैं।

  —अवनींद्र कुमार विद्यालंकार
- हिंदी को राष्ट्रभाषा बनाने में प्रांतीय भाषाओं को हानि नहीं वरन् लाभ होगा।

  —अनंतशयनम् आयंगार
- संस्कृत के अपरिमित कोश से हिंदी शब्दों की सब कठिनाइयाँ सरलता से हल कर लेगी। **—राजर्षि पुरुषोत्तम दास टंडन**
- हिंदी हमारे राष्ट्र की अभिव्यक्ति का सरलतम स्रोत है। **—सुमित्रानंदन पंत**
- कलकत्ता से लेकर लाहौर तक, कुमाऊँ के पहाड़ों से लेकर नर्मदा नदी तक, भारत (तब अविभाजित) के जिस हिस्से में भी मुझे काम करना पड़ा, मैंने उसी भाषा का आम व्यवहार देखा। मैं कन्याकुमारी से लेकर कश्मीर तक या जावा से सिंधु तक इस विश्वास के साथ यात्रा की हिम्मत कर सकता हूँ कि मुझे हर जगह ऐसे लोग मिल जाएँगे, जो हिंदुस्तानी बोल सकते होंगे।

  —सी.टी. मैटकाफ
- राष्ट्रीय व्यवहार में हिंदी को काम में लाना देश की उन्नति के लिए आवश्यक है। **—महात्मा गांधी**
- हिंदी उन सभी गुणों से अलंकृत हैं, जिनके बल पर वह विश्व की साहित्यिक भाषाओं की अगली श्रेणी में आसीन हो सकती है।

  —मैथिलीशरण गुप्त
- प्रांतीय ईर्ष्या-द्वेष को दूर करने में जितनी सहायता हिंदी के प्रचार-प्रसार से मिलेगी, उतनी दूसरी किसी चीज से नहीं मिल सकती। अपनी प्रांतीय भाषाओं की भरपूर उन्नति कीजिए, उसमें कोई बाधा नहीं डालना चाहता और न हम किसी की बाधा को सहन ही कर सकते हैं, पर सारे प्रांतों की सार्वजनिक

भाषा का पद हिंदी या हिंदुस्तानी को ही मिला है।

—सुभाषचंद्र बोस

हिंदुत्व

- मैं हिंदुत्व के प्रति वही भावना रखता हूँ, जो अपनी पत्नी के प्रति। उसके दोष जानकर भी मैं उससे अलग नहीं हो सकता।

—महात्मा गांधी

- हिंदुत्व एक विशाल वृक्ष के समान है, जिसने अपनी अगणित शाखाएँ फैला रखी हैं। **—महात्मा गांधी**
- मैं पूरा सुधारक हूँ, पर मैं हिंदुत्व की महत्त्वपूर्ण बातों को मानने से इनकार नहीं कर सकता। **—महात्मा गांधी**
- मैं हिंदू शब्द को, चाहे उसका कुछ भी अर्थ हो, बदलने के खिलाफ हूँ।

—महात्मा गांधी

हिंदू

- हिंदू तो एक जाति है, यह जाति इतनी बड़ी है कि इसका जातित्व किसमें है, यह किसी परिभाषा में बाँधा ही नहीं जा सकता।

—रवींद्रनाथ टैगोर

- हिंदू एकाएक नहीं हुआ जा सकता, उसके लिए जन्म-जन्मांतर का पुण्य चाहिए। **—रवींद्रनाथ टैगोर**

हिंदू धर्म

- जिस धर्म ने रामकृष्ण, चैतन्य, शंकर और विवेकानंद को पैदा किया है, वह धर्म केवल अंधविश्वासों का ढेर नहीं हो सकता। आप यह जानते होंगे और न जानते हों तो आपको मैं बता देना चाहता हूँ कि मेरी अपनी मान्यता तो ऐसी है कि संसार के सभी धर्म न केवल सच्चे हैं, बल्कि वे सब समान भी हैं।

—महात्मा गांधी

- हिंदू धर्म माँ की तरह अनेक मत-विश्वासों के लोगों को अपनी गोद में लेने का यत्न करता रहा है। **—रवींद्रनाथ टैगोर**

- बचपन से ही मैंने हिंदू धर्म का अभ्यास करने का प्रयत्न किया है। बचपन से मुझे जो शिक्षा मिली, उसके अनुसार आचरण करने की भी कोशिश की है और यथाशक्ति हिंदू शास्त्रों का अध्ययन किया है।

  —महात्मा गांधी

- दुनिया में केवल हिंदू धर्म ने मनुष्य को मनुष्य कहकर जाना है।

  —रवींद्रनाथ टैगोर

- सत्य से ही धर्म बढ़ता है और यह बात तो मैंने हिंदू धर्म से ही सीखी है—'सत्यान्नास्ति परो धर्म' और 'अहिंसा परमो धर्म' भी हिंदू धर्म ने सिखाया है। भगवान् पतंजलि हैं, जिन्होंने अहिंसा, अपरिग्रह, अस्तेय, ब्रह्मचर्य आदि पाँच व्रतों को हिंदू धर्म में विज्ञान का स्थान दिया और धर्मों में भी ये बातें हैं, लेकिन इनका विज्ञान हिंदू धर्म ने ही रचा है। **—महात्मा गांधी**

- हिंदू-धर्म में एक बड़ी बात यह है कि उसकी सच्ची आस्था है कि समस्त जीव (मनुष्य ही नहीं, समस्त जीवधारी प्राणी) एक ही हैं, अर्थात् सारे जीवों की उत्पत्ति एक ही स्रोत से हुई है, चाहे आप उसे अल्लाह कहिए या गॉड या परमेश्वर...जीव की यह एकता हिंदू-धर्म की अपनी विशेषता है, इसके अनुसार मुक्ति प्राप्त करना मानव तक ही सीमित नहीं है, बल्कि ईश्वर के रचे सभी प्राणियों के लिए संभव है। **—महात्मा गांधी**

- हिंदू धर्म मूढ़ को भी मानता है, ज्ञानी को भी मानता है और ज्ञान की भी केवल एक मूर्ति को नहीं मानता, उसके अनेक प्रकार के विकास को मानता है।

  —रवींद्रनाथ टैगोर

हिंदू-शास्त्र

- हिंदू-शास्त्र बड़ी गहरी चीज है। ऋषि लोग जो धर्म स्थापित कर गए हैं, उसकी गहराई को समझना, जिसका-तिसका काम नहीं है; बिना समझे-बूझे,

उसे लेकर न उलझना ही अच्छा है। —**रवींद्रनाथ टैगोर**

हिंसा

- दुनिया में जितनी तरह की हिंसा होती है, मनुष्य के प्रति मनुष्य का दुरात्म भाव उससे भी कितना अधिक भयानक है, उसके पीछे समाज की और राजा की शक्ति दलबद्ध खड़ी होकर उसे और भी चंड बना देती है।

—**रवींद्रनाथ टैगोर**

हीनता

- हीनता को हीनता कहकर तदनुरूप अनुभव करना ही अच्छा है, किंतु बुद्धिबल से निर्जीवता को साधुता और असमर्थता को सर्वश्रेष्ठता कहकर तद्वत प्रमाणित करने से सद्गति के मार्ग को चारों ओर से बंद ही कर देना होता है।

—**रवींद्रनाथ टैगोर**

हीरा

- हीरे की चमक हीरे में खुद प्रकाशित होती है, उसे जाहिर करने के लिए हीरे को तोड़कर उसमें से चमक बाहर नहीं निकालनी होती।

—**रवींद्रनाथ टैगोर**

क्षमता

- देवता नई सृष्टि तो कर सकते हैं, किंतु क्या उनमें भी इतनी क्षमता है कि किसी टूटे हुए हृदय को दोबारा जोड़ सकें? —**रवींद्रनाथ टैगोर**

- मानव की क्षमता बहुत स्वल्प है, फिर भी ईश्वर ने उसे भिखारी नहीं बनाया।

—**रवींद्रनाथ टैगोर**

- जिसमें क्षमता नहीं होती, वह सोचता है कि सुयोग के अभाव से ही अक्षम है, लेकिन जब अवसर मिलता है तो वह देखता है कि इच्छाशक्ति की कमजोरी ही उसकी अक्षमता का कारण है। —**रवींद्रनाथ टैगोर**

क्षमा

- क्षमा ब्रह्म है, क्षमा सत्य है, क्षमा भूत है, क्षमा भविष्य है, क्षमा तप है, क्षमा पवित्रता है, क्षमा ने ही संपूर्ण जगत् को धारण कर रखा है। —**वेदव्यास**
- वृक्ष अपने काटनेवाले को भी छाया देता है। —**चैतन्य**
- क्षमा कर देना दुश्मन पर विजय पा लेना है। —**हजरत अली**
- दूसरे का अपराध सहनकर अपराधी पर उपकार करना, यह क्षमा का गुण पृथ्वी से सीखना और पृथ्वी पर सदा परोपकाररत रहनेवाले पर्वत और वृक्षों से परोपकार की दक्षता लेना। —**कृष्ण**
- माँगने से पूर्व अपने आप गले पड़कर क्षमा करने का मतलब है मनुष्य का अपमान करना। —**शरतचंद्र**

□□□